Stern held the little yawl to her course, alone where uncounted
thousands of keels had once vexed the brine.

See page 175

DOOMSDAY CLASSICS

DARKNESS & DAWN

The Complete Dystopian Science Fiction Masterwork

George Allan England

Introduction by Jess Nevins

DOVER PUBLICATIONS, INC.
Mineola, New York

Bibliographical Note

Darkness and Dawn: The Complete Dystopian Science Fiction Masterwork,
first published by Dover Publications, Inc., in 2015, is an unabridged
republication of *Darkness and Dawn*, originally published in 1914 by Small,
Maynard and Company, Boston.

Library of Congress Cataloging-in-Publication Data

England, George Allan, 1877-1936.
 Darkness and Dawn: The Complete Dystopian Science Fiction Masterwork/
George Allan England; Introduction by Jess Nevins.
  pages cm.—(Dover doomsday classics)
  Summary: "A science-fiction classic in the H. G. Wells tradition, this gripping
trilogy of tales recounts the adventures of a young couple transported 1,500 years
into the future. In a post-apocalyptic wasteland inhabited by the debased
remnants of humanity, they must not only survive but also lay the foundations
for a new civilization. Includes a new introduction by Jess Nevins"—Provided
by publisher.
  ISBN-13: 978-0-486-79655-0
  ISBN-10: 0-486-79655-8
  1. Dystopias—Fiction. I. Nevins, Jess. II. Title.
 PS3509.N4D38 2015
 813'.52—DC23   2014044389

Manufactured in the United States by Courier Corporation
79655801   2015
www.doverpublications.com

INTRODUCTION TO THE DOVER EDITION

INFLUENTIAL and popular authors are all too often ignored or given scant credit and respect within a generation of their deaths. Posterity is cruel in this way; the ground-breakers of one generation become the also-rans of the next. George Allan England falls into this category of authors—a state of affairs which is particularly unfortunate, because not only was England, during his lifetime, a creative and popular author of fantastic and socialist literature, he was also a hugely influential author, not only on his contemporaries, but on successive generations of writers. The *Darkness and Dawn* trilogy is a good example of why England was so popular during his lifetime and why he has been so influential since the trilogy's publication.

England (1877-1936) was born in Nebraska, at what later became known as Fort McPherson, and grew up at a number of Army posts before his family moved to Boston. He worked his way through Harvard, earning a Master's degree in English literature and a Phi Beta Kappa key. After graduation he married and took a job with an insurance company in New York City, but two years later he developed tuberculosis and nephritis, forcing him to leave his job and go to the childhood home of his wife, in rural Maine. There, to supplement what little money he and his wife received from his in-laws, England began writing. In 1903 he sold his first story, and in 1905 he sold his first science fiction story, "The Time Reflector." By the end of 1906 England was successful and prolific enough as a writer to sign a contract with the Munsey magazine publishing company, and from there he wrote steadily until the end of his life, in a variety of genres, everything from science fiction to romance to travel to adventure, from newspaper articles to fifteen novels and short story collections. In addition, after recovering from his illnesses, he became physically active, hunting in the Arctic and going on deep sea diving expeditions looking for sunken treasure. Most prominently, he became an active socialist, writing for a number of socialist journals and even running for Congress in 1908 and for governor of Maine in 1912 as the candidate of the Socialist Party. (He did not succeed in either election, becoming instead, in his own words, "the most unpopular man in the country, politically.")

England is a good representative of men like Johnston McCulley, Victor Rousseau, Arthur O. Friel, and H. Bedford-Jones—professional writers during the pulp era who made their living by writing fiction. They wrote quickly and competently, they wrote for a large number of different magazines, both pulp and mainstream, and they wrote in a number of different genres. What sets England apart is that he wrote a significant amount of science fiction in the early years of the pulps, before they became specialized and balkanized. Although the pulps began in 1896, for a number of years the most popular pulps were general interest. The first romance pulp did not appear until 1913, the first mystery pulp until 1915, the first Westerns pulp until 1919, and the first science fiction pulp until 1926. Before—and indeed after—the advent of the single-subject pulps, most pulps would often publish issues with a variety of stories, everything from romance to sports to science fiction. Many writers wrote science fiction before the debut of *Amazing Stories* in 1926, but few made it the subject of most of their output. England was one of those who did.

Moreover, unlike most of his pulp writer colleagues, England had higher goals than to merely entertain and earn money. A committed socialist since his days at Harvard, England's goal in much of his science fiction was to incorporate socialist ideas in popular fiction, to entertain his socialist fans and politically educate his science fiction fans, to whet the reader's appetite for scientific material, and to draw in women readers with his work's romantic sub-plots.

Which brings us to *Darkness and Dawn*, the trilogy made up of the magazine serials "The Vacant World" (*Cavalier*, January 1912), "Beyond the Great Oblivion" (*Cavalier*, Jan-Feb. 1913), and "The Afterglow" (*Cavalier*, June-July 1913). *Darkness and Dawn*'s central story, of the struggle of a man and a woman to reconstruct society after the apocalypse, resulting in a new socialist civilization, is a prominent example of what scholar Walter Rideout called the "radical romance," the sub-genre of literature which combined the adventure-tropes and plots of popular fiction with visions of a future in which socialism has risen to dominance. The radical romance was a mixture of 19th century novels of end-of-civilization violent revolution (ala Ignatius Donnelly's *Caesar's Column* [1890]) and 19th century utopian novels like Edward Bellamy's *Looking Backward* (1888).

England was not the first to write a radical romance, of course. The subgenre dates into the 19th century, although its best known example is Jack London's *Iron Heel* (1907). But England's radical romance was the most popular of the sub-genre; the response to "The Vacant World" was exceptionally enthusiastic, leading to an outpouring of letters to *Cavalier* asking for a sequel. England, a professional writer at this point, had already moved on to other stories, but *Cavalier's* editor, Robert H. Davis, prevailed upon England to write two sequels, paying for them on delivery (rather than on publication, as was the practice at the time in the pulps). When demand did not slacken, Davis put the three novellas together as *Darkness and Dawn* in 1914, but could not persuade England to write any more in the series. (England said that he had exhausted the story).

The three *Darkness and Dawn* serials and novel publication appeared at the same time as Edgar Rice Burroughs' first two "Tarzan of the Apes" novels and his first three "John Carter of Mars" novels, also in Munsey magazines. Thanks to *Darkness and Dawn*, Tarzan, and John Carter of Mars, the Munsey publications became the premiere publisher of science fiction, and England and Burroughs became the most influential American science fiction writers of the time. While both authors' work has aged—inevitably, changes in audience taste and expectations have meant that England and Burroughs' work is viewed now as somewhat padded and stilted—both were influential, and both representative of a number of elements of American culture of the era. Like Burroughs, England used—and was largely responsible for—the trope, later common in the pulps, of degenerate "lost" white races and of heroic white men fighting dark-skinned savages. And like Jack London, England has the heroic, aggressive engineer, the prototypical pulp scientist, organizing society along scientific lines.

And *Darkness and Dawn*, as a radical romance, incorporates the common—for that era—socialist discourse on science and exemplifies it, so that not only was the trilogy the most popular radical romance, it is the best example of it. The socialist ideas of the 1910s were heavily influenced by the evolutionary ideas of the British philosopher Herbert Spencer and the anthropologist Lewis Morgan. Spencer's concept was that a social organism would become increasingly interdependent while moving from a "militant" to an "industrial" stage. Morgan's model of cultural evolution portrayed cultures as inevitably moving from savagery to barbarism to civilization. Additionally, socialist thinkers conceived of an advanced socialist culture as being dominated by scientists, engineers, and other technocratic elites. Socialism became scientific, in other words, rather than doctrinaire Marxism—and *Darkness and Dawn* is an exemplary fictional portrayal of this trend.

There's more to the trilogy than scientific socialism, of course; England was much too skilled an author to write a work which simply or programmatically espouses a political point of view. *Darkness and Dawn* is a classic of science fiction—and is widely regarded as such—for its thematic content, its plot, and its style. Naturally, England's prose style is of its era, which means it has—inevitably—dated somewhat, but his prose is certainly professional and competent, and it remains above all readable—no mean feat for a work over a century old. The imagination on display is notable, especially compared to contemporaneous science fiction, the great majority of which was much less daring and creative and much less competently told. The story retains its ability to excite, especially through its plot twists, and the character of Beatrice Kendrick is a creditable attempt at creating and describing a modern, 20th century heroine, free of Victorian attitudes and behavior.

More broadly, the trilogy was the most influential post-apocalyptic story to be published in the Munsey magazines—and by extension the pulps themselves—during the 1910s, and its effects can be seen in the imitations written in the pulps over the next three decades. Similarly, *Darkness and Dawn* was the prototype for the craze (most notable in the 1910s and 1920s) about stories reimagining contemporary urban life post-apocalypse, with race, class, and gender relations inverted. W.E.B. Dubois' famous short story "The Comet" (1920), in which a catastrophe that wipes out New York's population leads to the erasure of racial differences, would not have been written without the *Darkness and Dawn* trilogy. Even more recent works, like the spate of 21st century films and video games set in post-apocalyptic urban scenarios, owe much to England and his trilogy.

However, any discussion of the trilogy must take into account the racism of the work. Scientific socialists of the early 20th century believed that evolution applied both to living beings and to societies at the same time, and that evolution was a progressive movement away from (social and biological) self-serving barbarism toward (social and biological) harmony.

Scientific socialists' purpose was to cooperate with evolution, resulting in a social and biological organism which represented the triumph of humanity over our primitive impulses. In the *Darkness and Dawn* trilogy, these primitive impulses, the challenge to the evolution of human society, is black: the Horde. Scientific socialism, despite its futuristic focus, was after all a product of its time and place, and racism—in the form of seeing those of African descent as inferior—was as common among the scientific socialists as among anyone else in the United States in the early years of the 20th century. But the racism of the scientific socialists was given a theoretical and scientific apparatus to support it, the notion that there were definite borders between the races, borders that could be scientifically proven. The Horde violates these borders, being some kind of "degeneration from the man-standard," while still being black—but degenerative blacks, like those in Haiti and Liberia.

Because of this violation of the borders, as well as the symbolic threat that black masses pose to white civilization, the *Darkness and Dawn* trilogy offers only one solution to the problem of the presence of the Horde: complete extermination. The presence of the Horde is the main impediment to the scientific socialist utopia that Allan Stern plans for—and ultimately achieves. This was the era of lynchings in the South, the Springfield race riots of 1908, and D.W. Griffith's *The Birth of a Nation* (1915); the white imagination persistently turned to conflict between blacks and whites as inevitable and even welcome, and to genocide—both as a theoretical position and in popular fiction. In the *Darkness and Dawn* trilogy, the Horde are throwbacks, both evolutionarily and as proto-capitalists, and it is necessary both for the white race and for the new socialist society of the future that they be eliminated. Utopia can be achieved, but only once the troubling question of the presence of African-Americans is permanently resolved.

The *Darkness and Dawn* trilogy is hardly alone in either its racism or its genocidal conclusion, something which must be kept in mind while judging George Allan England and his fiction. As mentioned, this was a time of pronounced racism in America, and racism was common in popular fiction of all genres, while genocide was portrayed in fantastic fiction as one of a number of viable options for dealing with non-white races. While the pulps have been unfairly portrayed as being exceptional in this—racism was omnipresent in American culture during the 1910s,

1920s, and 1930s, within the pulps and without—the pulps were no better than the slicks, novelized fiction, movies, or radio, either. The racism became more visible as the pulps expanded in the 1920s, but it was neither more nor less common then than in the 1910s. In this respect *Darkness and Dawn* was not influential on contemporary and later pulp fiction; it was typical of it.

But that was all that the *Darkness and Dawn* trilogy was typical of. Creatively and imaginatively, there was nothing like it in the pulp magazines and novels of its time. Stylistically, the trilogy remains more readable than many of its contemporaries. Thematically, the trilogy has been influential where the vast majority of its contemporaries have been forgotten. And the trilogy's content remains enjoyable, even to the jaded modern reader. The *Darkness and Dawn* trilogy is a work of early science fiction that well deserves the title of "classic."

Jess Nevins
October, 2014

CONTENTS

BOOK I

THE VACANT WORLD

BOOK II

BEYOND THE GREAT OBLIVION

BOOK III

THE AFTERGLOW

ILLUSTRATIONS

BOOK I
THE VACANT WORLD

CHAPTER I

THE AWAKENING

DIMLY, like the daybreak glimmer of a sky long wrapped in fogs, a sign of consciousness began to dawn in the face of the tranced girl.

Once more the breath of life began to stir in that full bosom, to which again a vital warmth had on this day of days crept slowly back.

And as she lay there, prone upon the dusty floor, her beautiful face buried and shielded in the hollow of her arm, a sigh welled from her lips.

Life—life was flowing back again! The miracle of miracles was growing to reality.

Faintly now she breathed; vaguely her heart began to throb once more. She stirred. She moaned, still for the moment powerless to cast off wholly the enshrouding incubus of that tremendous, dreamless sleep.

Then her hands closed. The finely tapered fingers tangled themselves in the masses of thick, luxuriant hair which lay outspread all over and about her. The eyelids trembled.

And, a moment later, Beatrice Kendrick was sitting up, dazed and utterly uncomprehending, peering about her at the strangest vision which since the world began had ever been the lot of any human creature to behold—the vision of a place transformed beyond all power of the intellect to understand.

For of the room which she remembered, which had been her last sight when (so long, so very long, ago) her eyes had closed with that sudden and unconquerable drowsiness, of that room, I say, remained only walls, ceiling, floor of rust-red steel and crumbling cement.

Quite gone was all the plaster, as by magic. Here or there a heap of whitish dust betrayed where some of its detritus still lay.

Gone was every picture, chart, and map—which—but an hour since, it seemed to her—had decked this office of Allan Stern, consulting engineer, this aerie up in the forty-eighth story of the Metropolitan Tower.

Furniture, there now was none. Over the still-intact glass of the windows cobwebs were draped so thickly as almost to exclude the light of day—a strange, fly-infested curtain where once neat green shade-rollers had hung.

Even as the bewildered girl sat there, lips parted, eyes wide with amaze, a spider seized his buzzing prey and scampered back into a hole in the wall.

A huge, leathery bat, suspended upside down in the far corner, cheeped with dry, crepitant sounds of irritation.

Beatrice rubbed her eyes.

"What?" she said, quite slowly. "Dreaming? How singular! I only wish I could remember this when I wake up. Of all the dreams I've ever had, this one's certainly the strangest. So real, so vivid! Why, I could swear I was awake—and yet—"

All at once a sudden doubt flashed into her mind. An uneasy expression dawned across her face. Her eyes grew wild with a great fear; the fear of utter and absolute incomprehension.

Something about this room, this weird awakening, bore in upon her consciousness the dread tidings this was *not* a dream!

Something drove home to her the fact that it was real, objective, positive! And with a gasp of fright she struggled up amid the litter and the rubbish of that uncanny room.

"Oh!" she cried in terror, as a huge scorpion, malevolent, and with its tail raised to strike, scuttled away and vanished through a gaping void where once the corridor-door had swung. "Oh, oh! Where *am* I? What—*what has—happened?*"

Horrified beyond all words, pale and staring, both hands clutched to her breast, whereon her very clothing now had torn and crumbled, she faced about.

To her it seemed as though some monstrous, evil thing were lurking in the dim corner at her back. She tried to scream, but could utter no sound, save a choked gasp.

Then she started toward the doorway. Even as she took the first few steps her gown—a mere tattered mockery of raiment—fell away from her.

And, confronted by a new problem, she stopped short. About her she peered in vain for something to protect her disarray. There was nothing!

"Why—where's—where's my chair? My desk?" she exclaimed thickly, starting toward the place by the window where they should have been, and were not. Her shapely feet fell soundlessly in that strange and impalpable dust which thickly coated everything.

"My typewriter? Is—can *that* be my typewriter? Great Heavens! What's the matter here, with everything? Am I mad?"

There before her lay a somewhat larger pile of dust mixed with soft and punky splinters of rotten wood. Amid all this decay she saw some bits of rust, a corroded type-bar or two, even a few rubber key-caps, still recognizable, though with the letters quite obliterated.

All about her, veiling her completely in a mantle of wondrous gloss and beauty, her lustrous hair fell, as she stooped to see this strange, incomprehensible phenomenon. She tried to pick up one of the rubber caps. At her merest touch it crumbled to an impalpable white powder.

Back with a shuddering cry the girl sprang, terrified.

"Merciful Heavens!" she supplicated, "What—what does all this mean?"

For a moment she stood there, her every power of thought, of motion, numbed. Breathing not, she only stared in a wild kind of cringing amazement, as perhaps you might do if you should see a dead man move.

Then to the door she ran. Out into the hall she peered, this way and that, down the dismantled corridor, up the wreckage of the stairs all cumbered, like the office itself, with dust and webs and vermin.

Aloud she hailed: "Oh! Help, help, *help!*" No answer. Even the echoes flung back only dull, vacuous sounds that deepened her sense of awful and incredible isolation.

What? No noise of human life anywhere to be heard? None! No familiar hum of the metropolis now rose from what, when she had fallen asleep, had been swarming streets and miles on miles of habitations.

Instead, a blank, unbroken leaden silence, that seemed part of the musty, choking atmosphere—a silence that weighed down on Beatrice like funeral-palls.

Dumfounded by all this, and by the universal crumbling of every perishable thing, the girl ran, shuddering, back into the office. There in the dust her foot struck something hard.

She stooped; she caught it up and stared at it.

"My glass ink-well! What? Only such things remain?"

No dream, then, but reality! She knew at length that some catastrophe, incredibly vast, some disaster cosmic in the tragedy of its sweep, had desolated the world.

"Oh, my mother!" cried she. "My mother—*dead?* Dead, now, how long?"

She did not weep, but just stood cowering, a chill of anguished horror racking her. All at once her teeth began to chatter, her body to shake as with an ague.

Thus for a moment dazed and stunned she remained there, knowing not which way to turn nor what to do. Then her terror-stricken gaze fell on the doorway leading from her outer office to the inner one, the one where Stern had had his laboratory and his consultation-room.

This door now hung, a few worm-eaten planks and splintered bits of wood, barely supported by the rusty hinges.

Toward it she staggered. About her she drew the sheltering masses of her hair, like a Godiva of another age; and to her eyes, womanlike, the hot tears mounted. As she went, she cried in a voice of horror.

"Mr. Stern! Oh—Mr. Stern! Are—are *you* dead, too? You *can't* be—it's too frightful!"

She reached the door. The mere touch of her out-stretched hand disintegrated it. Down in a crumbling mass it fell. Thick dust bellied up in a cloud, through which a single sun-ray that entered the cobwebbed pane shot a radiant arrow.

Peering, hesitant, fearful of even greater terrors in that other room, Beatrice peered through this dust-haze. A sick foreboding of evil possessed her at thought of what she might find there—yet more afraid was she of what she knew lay behind her.

An instant she stood within the ruined doorway, her left hand resting on the moldy jam. Then, with a cry, she started forward—a cry in which terror had given place to joy, despair to hope.

Forgotten now the fact that, save for the shrouding of her massy hair, she stood naked. Forgotten the wreck, the desolation everywhere.

"Oh—thank Heaven!" gasped she.

There, in that inner office, half-rising from the wrack of many things that had been and were now no more, her startled eyes beheld the figure of a man—of Allan Stern!

He lived!

At her he peered with eyes that saw not, yet; toward her he groped a vague, unsteady hand.

He lived!

Not quite alone in this world-ruin, not all alone was she!

CHAPTER II

REALIZATION

THE joy in Beatrice's eyes gave way to poignant wonder as she gazed on him. Could this be *he?*

Yes, well she knew it was. She recognized him even through the grotesquery of his clinging rags, even behind the mask of a long, red, dusty beard and formidable mustache, even despite the wild and staring incoherence of his whole expression.

Yet how incredible the metamorphosis! To her flashed a memory of this man, her other-time employer—keen and smooth-shaven, alert, well-dressed, self-centered, dominant, the master of a hundred complex problems, the directing mind of engineering works innumerable.

Faltering and uncertain now he stood there. Then, at the sound of the girl's voice, he staggered toward her with outflung hands. He stopped, and for a moment stared at her.

For he had had no time as yet to correlate his thoughts, to pull himself together.

And while one's heart might throb ten times, Beatrice saw terror in his blinking, bloodshot eyes.

But almost at once the engineer mastered himself. Even as Beatrice watched him, breathlessly, from the door, she saw his fear die out, she saw his courage well up fresh and strong.

It was almost as though something tangible were limning the man's soul upon his face. She thrilled at sight of him.

And though for a long moment no word was spoken, while the man and woman stood looking at each other like two children in some dread and unfamiliar attic, an understanding leaped between them.

Then, womanlike, instinctively as she breathed, the girl ran to him. Forgetful of every convention and of her disarray, she seized his hand. And in a voice that trembled till it broke she cried:

"What is it? What does all this mean? Tell me!"

To him she clung.

"Tell me the truth—and save me! Is it *real?*"

Stern looked at her wonderingly. He smiled a strange, wan, mirthless smile.

All about him he looked. Then his lips moved, but for the moment no sound came.

He made another effort, this time successful.

"There, there," said he huskily, as though the dust and dryness of the innumerable years had got into his very voice. "There, now, don't be afraid!

"Something seems to have taken place here while—we've been asleep. What? What is it? I don't know yet. I'll find out. There's nothing to be alarmed about, at any rate."

"But—*look!*" She pointed at the hideous desolation.

"Yes, I see. But no matter. You're alive. I'm alive. That's two of us, anyhow. Maybe there are a lot more. We'll soon see. Whatever it may be, we'll win."

He turned and, trailing rags and streamers of rotten cloth that once had been a business suit, he waded through the confusion of wreckage on the floor to the window.

If you have seen a weather-beaten scarecrow flapping in the wind, you have some notion of his outward guise. No tramp you ever laid eyes on could have offered so preposterous an appearance.

Down over his shoulders fell the matted, dusty hair. His tangled beard reached far below his waist. Even his eyebrows, naturally rather light, had grown to a heavy thatch above his eyes.

Save that he was not gray or bent, and that he still seemed to have kept the resilient force of vigorous manhood, you might have thought him some incredibly ancient Rip Van Winkle come to life upon that singular stage, there in the tower.

But little time gave he to introspection or the matter of his own appearance. With one quick gesture he swept away the shrouding tangle of webs, spiders, and dead flies that obscured the window. Out he peered.

"Good Heavens!" cried he, and started back a pace.

She ran to him.

"What is it?" she breathlessly exclaimed.

"Why, I don't know—yet. But this is something *big!* Something universal! It's—it's—no, no, you'd better not look out—not just yet. "

"I must know everything. Let me see! "

Now she was at his side, and, like him, staring out into the clear sunshine, out over the vast expanses of the city.

A moment's utter silence fell. Quite clearly hummed the protest of an imprisoned fly in a web at the top of the window. The breathing of the man and woman sounded quick and loud.

"All *wrecked?*" cried Beatrice. "But—then—"

"Wrecked? It looks that way," the engineer made answer, with a strong effort holding his emotions in control. "Why not be frank about this? You'd better make up your mind at once to accept the very worst. I see no signs of anything else."

"The worst? You mean—"

"I mean just what we see out there. You can interpret it as well as I."

Again the silence while they looked, with emotions that could find no voicing in words. Instinctively the engineer passed an arm about the frightened girl and drew her close to him.

"And the last thing I remember," whispered she, "was just—just after you'd finished dictating those Taunton Bridge specifications. I suddenly felt—oh, so sleepy! Only for a minute I thought I'd close my eyes and rest, and then—then—"

"*This?*"

She nodded.

"Same here," said he. "What the deuce *can* have struck us? Us and everybody—and everything? Talk about your problems! Lucky I'm sane and sound, and—and—"

He did not finish, but fell once more to studying the incomprehensible prospect.

Their view was towards the east, but over the river and the reaches of what had once upon a time been Long Island City and Brooklyn, as familiar a scene in the other days as could be possibly imagined. But now how altered an aspect greeted them!

"It's surely all wiped out, all gone, gone into ruins," said Stern slowly and carefully, weighing each word. "No hallucination about *that*." He swept the sky-line with his eyes, that now peered keenly out from beneath those bushy brows. Instinctively he brought his hand up to his breast. He started with surprise.

"What's this?" he cried. "Why, I—I've got a full yard of whiskers. My good Lord! Whiskers on *me?* And I used to say—"

He burst out laughing. At his beard he plucked with merriment that jangled horribly on the girl's tense nerves. Suddenly he grew serious. For the first time he seemed to take clear notice of his companion's plight.

"Why, *what* a time it must have been!" cried he. "Here's some calculation all cut out for me, all right. But—you can't go that way, Miss Kendrick. It—it won't do, you know. Got to have something to put on. Great Heavens, what a situation!"

He tried to peel off his remnant of a coat, but at the merest touch it tore to shreds and fell away. The girl restrained him.

"Never mind," said she, with quiet, modest dignity. "My hair protects me very well for the present. If you and I are all that's left of the people in the world, this is no time for trifles."

A moment he studied her. Then he nodded, and grew very grave.

"Forgive me," he whispered, laying a hand on her shoulder. Once more he turned to the window and looked out.

"So then, it's all gone?" he queried, speaking as to himself. "Only a skyscraper standing here or there? And the bridges and the islands—all changed.

"Not a sign of life anywhere; not a sound; the forests growing thick among the ruins? A dead world if—if all the world is like this part of it! All dead, save *you* and *me!*"

In silence they stood there, striving to realize the full import of the catastrophe. And Stern, deep down in his heart, caught some glimmering insight of the future and was glad.

CHAPTER III

ON THE TOWER PLATFORM

SUDDENLY the girl started, rebelling against the evidence of her own senses, striving again to force upon herself the belief that, after all, it *could not* be so.

"No, no, no!" she cried. "This can't be true. It mustn't be. There's a mistake somewhere. This simply *must* be all an illusion, a dream!

"If the whole world's dead, how does it happen *we're* alive? How do we know it's dead? Can we see it all from here? Why, all we see is just a little segment of things. Perhaps if we could know the truth, look farther, and know—"

He shook his head.

"I guess you'll find it's real enough," he answered, "no matter how far you look. But, just the same, it won't do any harm to extend our radius of observation.

"Come, let's go on up to the top of the tower, up to the observation-platform. The quicker we know all the available facts the better. Now, if I only had a telescope—!"

He thought hard a moment, then turned and strode over to a heap of friable disintegration that lay where once his instrument case had stood, containing his surveying tools.

Down on his ragged knees he fell; his rotten shreds of clothing tore and ripped at every movement, like so much water-soaked paper.

A strange, hairy, dust-covered figure, he knelt there. Quickly he plunged his hands into the rubbish and began pawing it over and over with eager haste.

"Ah!" he cried with triumph. "Thank Heaven, brass and lenses haven't crumbled yet!"

Up he stood again. In his hand the girl saw a peculiar telescope.

"My 'level,' see?" he exclaimed, holding it up to view. "The wooden tripod's long since gone. The fixtures that held it on won't bother me much.

"Neither will the spirit-glass on top. The main thing is that the telescope itself seems to be still intact. *Now* we'll see."

Speaking, he dusted off the eye-piece and the objective with a bit of rag from his coat-sleeve.

Beatrice noted that the brass tubes were all eaten and pitted with verdigris, but they still held firmly. And the lenses, when Stern had finished cleaning them, showed as bright and clear as ever.

"Come, now; come with me," he bade.

Out through the doorway into the hall he made his way while the girl followed. As she went she gathered her wondrous veil of hair more closely about her.

In this universal disorganization, this wreck of all the world, how little the conventions counted!

Together, picking their way up the broken stairs, where now the rust-bitten steel showed through the corroded stone and cement in a thousand places, they cautiously climbed.

Here, spider-webs thickly shrouded the way, and had to be brushed down. There, still more bats hung and chippered in protest as the intruders passed.

A fluffy little white owl blinked at them from a dark niche; and, well toward the top of the climb, they flushed up a score of mud-swallows which had ensconced themselves comfortably along a broken balustrade.

At last, however, despite all unforeseen incidents of this sort, they reached the upper platform, nearly a thousand feet above the earth.

Out through the relics of the revolving door they crept, he leading, testing each foot of the way before the girl. They reached the narrow platform of red tiling that surrounded the tower.

Even here they saw with growing amazement that the hand of time and of this maddening mystery had laid its heavy imprint.

"Look!" he exclaimed, pointing. "What this all means we don't know yet. How long it's been we can't tell. But to judge by the appearance up here, it's even longer than I thought. See, the very tiles are cracked and crumbling.

"Tilework is usually considered highly recalcitrant—-but *this* is gone. There's grass growing in the dust that's settled between the tiles. And— why, here's a young oak that's taken root and forced a dozen slabs out of place."

"The winds and birds have carried seeds up here, and acorns," she answered in an awed voice. "Think of the time that must have passed. Years and years.

"But tell me," and her brow wrinkled with a sudden wonder, "tell me how we've ever lived so long? *I* can't understand it.

"Not only have we escaped starvation, but we haven't frozen to death in all these bitter winters. How can *that* have happened?"

"Let it all go as suspended animation till we learn the facts, if we ever do," he replied, glancing about with wonder.

"You know, of course, how toads have been known to live embedded in rock for centuries? How fish, hard-frozen, have been brought to life again? Well—"

"But *we* are human beings."

"I know. Certain unknown natural forces, however, might have made no more of us than of non-mammalian and less highly organized creatures.

"Don't bother your head about these problems yet a while. On my word, we've got enough to do for the present without much caring about how or why.

"All we definitely know is that some very long, undetermined period of time has passed, leaving us still alive. The rest can wait."

"How long a time do you judge it?" she anxiously inquired.

"Impossible to say at once. But it must have been something extraordinary—probably far longer than either of us suspect.

"See, for example, the attrition of everything up here exposed to the weather." He pointed at the heavy stone railing. "See how *that* is wrecked, for instance."

A whole segment, indeed, had fallen inward. Its débris lay in confusion, blocking all the southern side of the platform.

The bronze bars, which Stern well remembered—two at each corner, slanting downward and bracing a rail—had now wasted to mere pock-marked shells of metal.

Three had broken entirely and sagged wantonly awry with the displacement of the stone blocks, between which the vines and grasses had long been carrying on their destructive work.

"Look out!" Stern cautioned. "Don't lean against any of those stones." Firmly he held her back as she, eagerly inquisitive, started to advance toward the railing.

"Don't go anywhere near the edge. It may all be rotten and undermined, for anything we know. Keep back here, close to the wall."

Sharply he inspected it a moment.

"Facing stones are pretty well gone," said he, "but, so far so I can see, the steel frame isn't too bad. Putting everything together, I'll probably be able before long to make some sort of calculation of the date. But for now we'll have to call it 'X,' and let it go at that. "

"The year X!" she whispered under her breath. "Good Heavens, am I as old as that?"

He made no answer, but only drew her to him protectingly, while all about them the warm summer wind swept onward to the sea, out over the sparkling expanses of the bay—alone unchanged in all that universal wreckage.

In the breeze her heavy masses of hair stirred luringly. He felt its silken caress on his half-naked shoulder, and in his ears the blood began to pound with strange insistence.

Quite gone now the daze and drowsiness of the first wakening. Stern did not even feel weak or shaken. On the contrary, never had life bounded more warmly, more fully, in his veins.

The presence of the girl set his heart throbbing heavily, but he bit his lip and restrained every untoward thought.

Only his arm tightened a little about that warmly clinging body. Beatrice did not shrink from him. She needed his protection as never since the world began had woman needed man.

To her it seemed that come what might, his strength and comfort could not fail. And, despite everything, she could not—for the moment—find unhappiness within her heart.

Quite vanished now, even in those brief minutes since their awakening, was all consciousness of their former relationship—employer and employed.

The self-contained, courteous, yet unapproachable engineer had disappeared.

Now, through all the extraneous disguise of his outer self, there lived and breathed just a man, a young man, thewed with the vigor of his plentitude. All else had been swept clean away by this great change.

The girl was different, too. Was this strong woman, eager-eyed and brave, the quiet, low-voiced stenographer he remembered, busy only with her machine, her file-boxes, and her carbon-copies? Stern dared not realize the transmutation. He ventured hardly fringe it in his thoughts.

To divert his wonderings and to ease a situation which oppressed him, he began adjusting the "level" telescope to his eye.

With his back planted firmly against the tower, he studied a wide section of the dead and buried world so very far below them. With astonishment he cried:

"It *is* true, Beatrice! Everything's swept clean away. Nothing left, nothing at all—no signs of life!

"As far as I can reach with these lenses, universal ruin. We're all alone in this whole world, just you and I—and everything belongs to us!"

"Everything—all ours?"

"Everything! Even the future—the future of the human race!"

Suddenly he felt her tremble at his side. Down at her he looked, a great new tenderness possessing him. He saw that tears were forming in her eyes.

Beatrice pressed both hands to her face and bowed her head. Filled with strange emotions, the man watched her for a moment.

Then in silence, realizing the uselessness of any words, knowing that in this monstrous Ragnarök of all humanity no ordinary relations of life could bear either cogency or meaning, he took her in his arms.

And there alone with her, far above the ruined world, high in the pure air of mid-heaven, he comforted the girl with words till then unthought-of and unknown to him.

CHAPTER IV

THE CITY OF DEATH

PRESENTLY Beatrice grew calmer. For though grief and terror still weighed upon her soul, she realized that this was no fit time to yield to any weakness—now when a thousand things were pressing for accomplishment, if their own lives, too, were not presently to be snuffed out in all this universal death.

"Come, come," said Stern reassuringly. "I want you, too, to get a complete idea of what has happened. From now on you must know all, share all, with me." And, taking her by the hand he led her along the crumbling and uncertain platform.

Together, very cautiously, they explored the three sides of the platform still unchoked by ruins.

Out over the incredible mausoleum of civilization they peered. Now and again they fortified their vision by recourse to the telescope.

Nowhere, as he had said, was any slightest sign of life to be discerned. Nowhere a thread of smoke arose; nowhere a sound echoed upward.

Dead lay the city, between its rivers, whereon now no sail glinted in the sunlight, no tug puffed vehemently with plumy jets of steam, no liner idled at anchor or nosed its slow course out to sea.

The Jersey shore, the Palisades, the Bronx and Long Island all lay buried in dense forests of conifers and oak, with only here and there some skeleton mockery of a steel structure jutting through.

The islands in the harbor, too, were thickly overgrown. On Ellis, no sign of the immigrant station remained. Castle William was quite gone. And with a gasp of dismay and pain, Beatrice pointed out the fact that no longer Liberty held her bronze torch aloft.

Save for a black, misshapen mass protruding through the tree-tops, the huge gift of France was no more.

Fringing the water-front, all the way round, the mournful remains of the docks and piers lay in a mere sodden jumble of decay, with an occasional hulk sunk alongside.

Even over these wrecks of liners, vegetation was growing rank and green. All the wooden ships, barges and schooners had utterly vanished.

The telescope showed only a stray, lolling mast of steel, here or yonder, thrusting up from the desolation, like a mute appealing hand raised to a Heaven that responded not.

"See," remarked Stern, "up-town almost all the buildings seem to have crumbled in upon themselves, or to have fallen outward into the streets. What an inconceivable tangle of detritus those streets must be!

"And, do you notice the park hardly shows at all? Everything's so over-grown with trees you can't tell where it begins or ends. Nature has her revenge at last, on man!"

"The universal claim, made real," said Beatrice. "Those rather clearer lines of green, I suppose, must be the larger streets. See how the avenues stretch away and away, like ribbons of green velvet!

"Everywhere that roots can hold at all, Mother Nature has set up her flags again. Hark! What's that?"

A moment they listened intently. Up to them, from very far, rose a wail-ing cry, tremulous, long-drawn, formidable.

"Oh! Then there *are* people, after all?" faltered the girl, grasping Stern's arm.

He laughed.

"No, hardly!" answered he. "I see you don't know the wolf-cry. I didn't till I heard it in the Hudson Bay country, last winter—that is, last winter, plus X. Not very pleasant, is it?"

"Wolves! Then—there are—"

"Why not? Probably all sorts of game on the island now. Why, shouldn't there be? All in Mother Nature's stock-in-trade, you know.

"But come, come, don't let that worry you. We're safe, for the present. Time enough to consider hunting later. Let's creep around here to the other side of the tower, and see what we can see."

Silently she acquiesced. Together they reached the southern part of the platform, making their way as far as the jumbled rocks of the fallen railing would permit.

Very carefully they progressed, fearful every moment lest the support break beneath them and hurl them down along the sloping side of the pinnacle to death.

"Look!" bade Stern, pointing. "That very long green line there used to be Broadway. Quite a respectable Forest of Arden now, isn't it?" He swept his hand far outward.

"See those steel cages, those tiny, far-off ones with daylight shining through? You know them—the Park Row, the Singer, the Woolworth and all the rest. And the bridges, look at those!"

She shivered at the desolate sight. Of the Brooklyn Bridge only the towers were visible.

The watchers, two isolated castaways on their island in the sea of uttermost desolation, beheld a dragging mass of wreckage that drooped from these towers on either shore, down to the sparkling flood.

The other bridges, newer and stronger far, still remained standing. But even from that distance Stern could quite plainly see, without the telescope, that the Williamsburg Bridge had "buckled" downward and that the farther span of the Blackwell's Island Bridge was in ruinous disrepair.

"How horrible, how ghastly is all this waste and ruin!" thought the engineer. "Yet, even in their overthrow, how wonderful are the works of man!"

A vast wonder seized him as he stood there gazing; a fierce desire to rehabilitate all this wreckage, to set it right, to start the wheels of the world-machinery running once more.

At the thought of his own powerlessness a bitter smile curled his lips.

Beatrice seemed to share something of his wonder.

"Can it be possible," whispered she, "that you and—and I—are really like Macaulay's lone watcher of the world-wreck on London Bridge?"

"That we are actually seeing the thing so often dreamed of by prophets and poets? That 'All this mighty heart is lying still,' at last—forever? The heart of the world, never to beat again?"

He made no answer, save to shake his head; but fast his thoughts were running.

So then, could he and Beatrice, just they two, be in stern reality the sole survivors of the entire human race? That race for whose material welfare he had, once on a time, done such tremendous work?

Could they be destined, he and she, to witness the closing chapter in the long, painful, glorious Book of Evolution? Slightly he shivered and glanced round.

Till he could adjust his reason to the facts, could learn the truth and weigh it, he knew he must not analyze too closely; he felt he must try not to think. For *that* way lay madness!

Far out she gazed.

The sun, declining, shot a broad glory all across the sky. Purple and gold and crimson lay the light-bands over the breast of the Hudson.

Dark blue the shadows streamed across the ruined city with its crowding forests, its blank-staring windows and sagging walls, its thousands of gaping vacancies, where wood and stone and brick had crumbled down— the city where once the tides of human life had ebbed and flowed, roaring resistlessly.

High overhead drifted a few rosy clouds, part of that changeless nature which alone did not repel or mystify these two beleaguered waifs, these chance survivors, this man, this woman, left alone together by the hand of fate.

They were dazed, fascinated by the splendor of that sunset over a world devoid of human life, for the moment giving up all efforts to judge or understand.

Stern and his mate peered closer, down at the interwoven jungles of Union Square, the leafy frond-masses that marked the one-time course of Twenty-Third Street, the forest in Madison Square, and the truncated column of the tower where no longer Diana turned her huntress bow to every varying breeze.

They heard their own hearts beat. The intake of their breath sounded strangely loud. Above them, on a broken cornice, some resting swallows twittered.

All at once the girl spoke.

"See the Flatiron Building over there!" said she. "What a hideous wreck!"

From Stern she took the telescope, adjusted it, and gazed minutely at the shattered pile of stone and metal.

Blotched as with leprosy stood the walls, whence many hundreds of blocks had fallen into Broadway forming a vast moraine that for some distance choked that thoroughfare.

In numberless places the steel frame peered through. The whole roof had caved in, crushing down the upper stories, of which only a few sparse upstanding metal beams remained.

The girl's gaze was directed at a certain spot which she knew well.

"Oh, I can even see—into some of the offices on the eighteenth floor!" cried she. "There, *look?*" And she pointed. "That one near the front! I-I used to know—"

She broke short off. In her trembling hands the telescope sank. Stern saw that she was very pale.

"Take me down!" she whispered. "I can't stand it any longer—I can't, possibly! The sight of that wrecked office! Let's go down where I can't see *that!*"

Gently, as though she had been a frightened child, Stern led her round the platform to the doorway, then down the crumbling stairs and so to the wreckage and dust-strewn confusion of what had been his office.

And there, his hand upon her shoulder, he bade her still be of good courage.

"Listen now, Beatrice," said he. "Let's try to reason this thing out together, let's try to solve this problem like two intelligent human beings.

"Just what's happened, we don't know; we can't know yet a while, till I investigate. We don't even know what year this is.

"Don't know whether anybody else is still alive, anywhere in the world. But we can find out—after we've made provision for the immediate present and formed some rational plan of life.

"If all the rest *are* gone, swept away, wiped out clean like figures on a slate, then why *we* should have happened to survive whatever it was that struck the earth, is still a riddle far beyond our comprehension.

He raised her face to his, noble despite all its grotesque disfigurements; he looked into her eyes as though to read the very soul of her, to judge whether she could share this fight, could brave this coming struggle.

"All these things may yet be answered. Once I get the proper data for this series of phenomena, I can find the solution, never fear!

"Some vast world-duty may be ours, far greater, infinitely more vital than anything that either of us has ever dreamed. It's not our place, now, to mourn or fear! Rather it is to read this mystery, to meet it and to conquer!"

Through her tears the girl smiled up at him, trustingly, confidingly. And in the last declining rays of the sun that glinted through the window-pane, her eyes were very beautiful.

CHAPTER V

EXPLORATION

CAME now the evening, as they sat and talked together, talked long and earnestly, there within that ruined place. Too eager for some knowledge of the truth, they, to feel hunger or to think of their lack of clothing.

Chairs they had none, nor even so much as a broom to clean the floor with. But Stern, first-off, had wrenched a marble slab from the stairway.

And with this plank of stone still strong enough to serve, he had scraped all one corner of the office floor free of rubbish. This gave them a preliminary camping-place wherein to take their bearings and discuss what must be done.

"So then," the engineer was saying as the dusk grew deeper, "so then, we'll apparently have to make this building our headquarters for a while.

"As nearly as I can figure, this is about what must have happened. Some sudden, deadly, numbing plague or cataclysm must have struck the earth, long, long ago.

"It may have been an almost instantaneous onset of some new and highly fatal micro-organism, propagating with such marvelous rapidity that it swept the world clean in a day—doing its work before any resistance could be organized or thought of.

"Again, some poisonous gas may have developed, either from a fissure in the earth's crust, or otherwise. Other hypotheses are possible, but of what practical value are they now?

"We only know that here, in this uppermost office of the Tower, you and I have somehow escaped with only a long period of completely suspended animation. How long? God alone knows! That's a query I can't even guess the answer to as yet."

"Well, to judge by all the changes," Beatrice suggested thoughtfully, "it can't have been less than a hundred years. Great Heavens!" and she burst into a little satiric laugh. "Am *I* a hundred and twenty-four years old? Think of that!"

"You underestimate," Stern answered. "But no matter about the time question for the present; we can't solve it now.

"Neither can we solve the other problem about Europe and Asia and all the rest of the world. Whether London, Paris, Berlin, Rome, and every other city, every other land, all have shared this fate, we simply don't know.

"All we *can* have is a feeling of strong probability that life, human life I mean, is everywhere extinct—save right here in this room!

"Otherwise, don't you see, men would have made their way back here again, back to New York, where all these incalculable treasures seem to have perished, and—"

He broke short off. Again, far off, they heard a faint reechoing roar. For a moment they both sat speechless. What could it be? Some distant wall toppling down? A hungry beast scenting its prey? They could not tell. But Stern smiled.

"I guess," said he, "guns will be about the first thing I'll look for, after food. There ought to be good hunting down in the jungles of Fifth Avenue and Broadway!

"You shoot, of course? No? Well, I'll soon teach you. Lots of things both of us have got to learn now. No end of them!"

He rose from his place on the floor, went over to the window and stood for a minute peering out into the gloom. Then suddenly he turned.

"What's the matter with me, anyhow?" he exclaimed with irritation. "What right have I to be staying here, theorizing, when there's work to do? I ought to be busy this very minute!

"In some way or other I've got to find food, clothing, tools, arms—a thousand things. And above all, water! And here I've been speculating about the past, fool that I am!"

"You—you aren't going to leave me—not to-night?" faltered the girl.

Stern seemed not to have heard her, so strong the imperative of action lay upon him now. He began to pace the floor, sliding and stumbling through the rubbish, a singular figure in his tatters and with his patriarchal hair and beard, a figure dimly seen by the faint light that still gloomed through the window.

"In all that wreckage down below," said he, as though half to himself, "in all that vast congeries of ruin which once was called New York, surely enough must still remain intact for our small needs. Enough till we can reach the land, the country, and raise food of our own!"

"Don't go *now!*" pleaded Beatrice. She, too, stood up, and out she stretched her hands to him. "Don't, please! We can get along some way or other till morning. At least, *I* can!"

"No, no, it isn't right! Down in the shops and stores, who knows but we might find—"

"But you're unarmed! And in the streets—in the forest, rather—"

"Listen!" he commanded rather abruptly. "This is no time for hesitating or for weakness. I know you'll stand your share of all that we must suffer, dare and do together.

"Some way or other I've got to make you comfortable. I've got to locate food and drink immediately. Got to get my bearings. Why, do you think I'm going to let you, even for one night, go fasting and thirsty, sleep on bare cement, and all that sort of thing?

"If so, you're mistaken! No, you must spare me for an hour or two. Inside of that time I ought to make a beginning!"

"A whole hour?"

"Two would probably be nearer it. I promise to be back inside of that time."

"But," and her voice quivered just a trifle, "but suppose some wolf or bear—"

"Oh, I'm not quite so foolhardy as all that!" he retorted. "I'm not going to venture outside till to-morrow. My idea is that I can find at least a few essentials right here in this building.

"It's a city in itself—or was. Offices, stores, shops, everything right here together in a lump! It can't possibly take me very long to go down and rummage out something for your comfort.

"Now that the first shock and surprise of our awakening are over, we can't go on in this way, you know—h'm!—dressed in—well, such exceedingly primitive garb!"

Silently she looked at his dim figure in the dusk. Then she stretched out her hand.

"I'll go too," said she quite simply.

"You'd better stay. It's safer here."

"No, I'm going."

"But if we run into dangers?"

"Never mind. Take me with you."

Over to her he came. He took her hand. In silence he pressed it. Thus for a moment they stood. Then, arousing himself to action, he said: "First of all, a light."

"A light? How can you make a light? Why, there isn't a match left anywhere in this whole world."

"I know, but there are other things. Probably my chemical flasks and vials aren't injured. Glass is practically imperishable. And if I'm not mistaken, the bottles must be lying somewhere in that rubbish heap over by the window."

He left her wondering, and knelt among the litter. For a while he silently delved through the triturated bits of punky wood and rust-red metal that now represented the remains of his chemical cabinet.

All at once he exclaimed: "Here's one! And here's another! This certainly *is* luck! H-m! Shouldn't wonder if I got almost all of them back."

One by one he found a score of thick, ground-glass vials. Some were broken, probably by the shock when they and the cabinet had fallen, but a good many still remained intact.

Among these were the two essential ones. By the last dim ghost of light through the window, and by the sense of touch, Stern was able to make out the engraved symbols "P" and "S" on these bottles.

"Phosphorus and sulphur," he commented. "Well, what more could I reasonably ask? Here's alcohol, too, hermetically sealed. Not too bad, eh?"

While the girl watched, with wondering admiration, Stern thought hard a moment. Then he set to work.

First he took a piece of the corroded metal framework of the cabinet, a steel strip about eighteen inches long, frail in places, but still sufficiently strong to serve his purpose.

Tearing off some rags from his coat-sleeve, he wadded them together into a ball as big as his fist. Around this ball he twisted the metal strip, so that it formed at once a holder and a handle for the rag-mass.

With considerable difficulty he worked the glass stopper out of the alcohol bottle, and with the fluid saturated the rags. Then, on a clear bit of the floor, he spilled out a small quantity of the phosphorus and sulphur.

"This beats getting fire by friction all hollow," he cheerfully remarked. "I've tried that, too, and I guess it's only in books a white man ever succeeds at it. But this way, you see, it's simplicity itself."

Very moderate friction, with a bit of wood from the wreckage of the door, sufficed to set the phosphorus ablaze. Stern heaped on a few tiny lumps of sulphur. Then, coughing as the acrid fumes arose from the sputter of blue flame, he applied the alcohol-soaked torch.

Instantly a puff of fire shot up, colorless and clear, throwing no very satisfactory light, yet capable of dispelling the thickest of the gloom.

The blaze showed Stern's eager face, long-bearded and dusty, as he bent over this crucial experiment.

The girl, watching closely, felt a strange new thrill of confidence and solace. Some realization of the engineer's resourcefulness came to her, and in her heart she had confidence that, though the whole wide world had crumbled into ruin, yet *he* would find a way to smooth her path, to be a strength and refuge for her.

But Stern had no time for any but matters of intensest practicality. From the floor he arose, holding the flambeau in one hand, the bottle of alcohol in the other.

"Come now," bade he, and raised the torch on high to light her way, "You're still determined to go?"

For an answer she nodded. Her eyes gleamed by the uncanny light.

And so, together, he leading out of the room and along the wrecked hall, they started on their trip of exploration out into the unknown,

CHAPTER VI

Treasure-Trove

Never before had either of them realized just what the meaning of forty-eight stories might be. For all their memories of this height were associated with smooth-sliding elevators that had whisked them up as though the tremendous height had been the merest trifle.

This night, however, what with the broken stairs, the débris-cumbered hallways, the lurking darkness which the torch could hardly hold back from swallowing them, they came to a clear understanding of the problem.

Every few minutes the flame burned low and Stern had to drop on more alcohol, holding the bottle high above the flame to avoid explosion.

Long before they had compassed the distance to the ground floor the girl lagged with weariness and shrank with nameless fears.

Each black doorway that yawned along their path seemed ominous with memories of life that had perished there, of death that now reigned all-supreme.

Each corner, every niche and crevice, breathed out the spirit of the past and of the mystic tragedy which in so brief a time had wiped the human race from earth, "as a mother wipes the milky lips of her child."

And Stern, though he said little save to guide Beatrice and warn her of unusual difficulties, felt the somber magic of the place. No poet, he; only a man of hard and practical details. Yet he realized that, were he dowered with the faculty, here lay matter for an Epic of Death such as no Homer ever dreamed, no Virgil ever could have penned.

Now and then, along the corridors and down the stairways, they chanced on curious little piles of dust, scattered at random in fantastic shapes.

These for a few minutes puzzled Stern, till stooping, he stirred one with his hand. Something he saw there made him start back with a stifled exclamation.

"What is it?" cried the girl, startled. "Tell me!"

But he, realizing the nature of his discovery—for he had seen a human incisor tooth, gold-filled, there in the odd little heap—straightened up quickly and assumed to smile.

"It's nothing, nothing at all!" he answered. "Come, we haven't got any time to waste. If we're going to provide ourselves with even a few necessaries before the alcohol's all gone, we've got to be at work!"

And onward, downward, ever farther and farther, he led her through the dark maze of ruin, which did not even echo to their barefoot tread.

Like disheveled wraiths they passed, soundlessly, through eery labyrinths and ways which might have served as types of Coleridge's "caverns measureless to man," so utterly drear they stretched out in their ghostly desolation.

At length, after an eternal time of weariness and labor, they managed to make their way down into the ruins of the once famous and beautiful arcade which had formerly run from Madison Avenue to the square.

"Oh, how horrible!" gasped Beatrice, shrinking, as they clambered down the stairs and emerged into this scene of chaos, darkness, death.

Where long ago the arcade had stretched its path of light and life and beauty, of wealth and splendor, like an epitome of civilization all gathered in that constricted space, the little light disclosed stark horror.

Feeble as a will-o'-the-wisp in that enshrouding dark, the torch showed only hints of things—here a fallen pillar, there a shattered mass of wreckage where a huge section of the ceiling had fallen, yonder a gaping aperture left by the disintegration of a wall.

Through all this rubbish and confusion, over and through a score of the little dust-piles which Stern had so carefully avoided explaining to Beatrice, they climbed and waded, and with infinite pains slowly advanced.

"What we need is more light!" exclaimed the engineer presently. "We've got to have a bonfire here!"

And before long he had collected a considerable pile of wood, ripped from the door-ways and window-casings of the arcade. This he set fire to, in the middle of the floor.

Soon a dull, wavering glow began to paint itself upon the walls, and to fling the comrades' shadows, huge and weird, in dancing mockery across the desolation.

Strangely enough, many of the large plate-glass windows lining the arcade still stood intact. They glittered with the uncanny reflections of the fire as the man and woman slowly made way down the passage.

"See," exclaimed Stern, pointing. "See all these ruined shops? Probably almost everything is worthless. But there must be some things left that we can use.

"See the post-office, down there on the left? Think of the millions in real money, gold and silver, in all these safes here and all over the city—in the banks and vaults! Millions! Billions!

"Jewels, diamonds, wealth simply inconceivable! Yet now a good water supply, some bread, meat, coffee, salt, and so on, a couple of beds, a gun or two and some ordinary tools would outweigh them all!"

"Clothes, too," the girl suggested. "Plain cotton cloth is worth ten million dollars an inch now."

"Right," answered Stern, gazing about him with wonder. "And I offer a bushel of diamonds for a razor and a pair of scissors." Grimly he smiled as he stroked his enormous beard.

"But come, this won't do. There'll be plenty of time to look around and discuss things in the morning. Just now we've got a definite errand. Let's get busy!"

Thus began their search for a few prime necessities of life, there in that charnel-house of civilization, by the dull reflections of the firelight and the pallid torch glow.

Though they forced their way into ten or twelve of the arcade shops, they found no clothing, no blankets or fabric of any kind that would serve for coverings or to sleep upon. Everything at all in the nature of cloth had either sunk back into moldering annihilation or had at best grown far too fragile to be of the slightest service.

They found, however, a furrier's shop, and this they entered eagerly.

From rusted metal hooks a few warped fragments of skins still hung, moth-eaten, riddled with holes, ready to crumble at the merest touch.

"There's nothing in any of these to help us," judged Stern. "But maybe we might find something else in here."

Carefully they searched the littered place, all dust and horrible disarray, which made sad mockery of the gold-leaf sign still visible on the window: "Lange, Importer. All the Latest Novelties."

On the floor Stern discovered three more of those little dust-middens which meant human bodies, pitiful remnants of an extinct race, of unknown people in the long ago. What had he now in common with them? The remains did not even inspire repugnance in him.

All at once Beatrice uttered a cry of startled gladness.

"Look here! A storage chest!"

True enough, there stood a cedar box, all seamed and cracked and bulging, yet still retaining a semblance of its original shape.

The copper bindings and the lock were still quite plainly to be seen, as the engineer held the torch close, though green and corroded with incredible age.

One effort of Stern's powerful arms sufficed to tip the chest quite over. As it fell it burst. Down in a mass of pulverized, worm-eaten splinters it disintegrated.

Out rolled furs, many and many of them, black, and yellow, and striped— the pelts of the grizzly, of the leopard, the chetah, the royal Bengal himself.

"Hurray!" shouted the man, catching up first one, then another, and still a third. "Almost intact. A little imperfection here and there doesn't matter. Now we've got clothes and beds.

"What's that? Yes, maybe they are a trifle warm for this season of the year, but this is no time to be particular. See, now, how do you like *that?*"

Over the girl's shoulders, as he spoke, he flung the tiger-skin.

"Magnificent!" he judged, standing back a pace or two and holding up the torch to see her better. "When I find you a big gold pin or clasp to fasten that with at the throat you'll make a picture of another and more splendid Boadicea!"

He tried to laugh at his own words, but merriment sat ill there in that place, and with such a subject. For the woman, thus clad, had suddenly assumed a wild, barbaric beauty.

Bright gleamed her gray eyes by the light of the flambeau; limpid, and deep, and earnest, they looked at Stern. Her wonderful hair, shaken out in bewildering masses over the striped, tawny savagery of the robe, made colorful contrasts, barbarous, seductive.

Half hidden, the woman's perfect body, beautiful as that of a wood-nymph or a pagan dryad, roused atavistic passions in the engineer.

He dared speak no other word for the moment, but bent beside the shattered chest again and fell to looking over the furs.

A polar-bear skin attracted his attention, and this he chose. Then, with it slung across his shoulder, he stood up.

"Come," said he, steadying his voice with an effort, "come, we must be going now. Our light won't hold out very much longer. We've got to find food and drink before the alcohol's all gone; got to look out for practical affairs, whatever happens. Let's be going."

Fortune favored them.

In the wreck of a small fancy grocer's booth down toward the end of the arcade, where the post-office had been, they came upon a stock of goods in glass jars.

All the tinned foods had long since perished, but the impermeable glass seemed to have preserved fruits and vegetables of the finer sort, and chipped beef and the like, in a state of perfect soundness.

Best of all, they discovered the remains of a case of mineral water. The case had crumbled to dust, but fourteen bottles of water were still intact.

"Pile three or four of these into my fur robe here," directed Stern. "Now, a few of the other jars—that's right. To-morrow we'll come down and clean up the whole stock. But we've got enough for now."

"We'd best be getting back up the stairs again," said he. And so they started.

"Are you going to leave that fire burning?" asked the girl, as they passed the middle of the arcade.

"Yes. It can't do any harm. Nothing to catch here; only old metal and cement. Besides, it would take too much time and labor to put it out."

Thus they abandoned the gruesome place and began the long, exhausting climb.

It must have taken them an hour and a half at least to reach their aerie. Both found their strength taxed to the utmost.

Before they were much more than halfway up, the ultimate drop of alcohol had been burned.

The last few hundred feet had to be made by slow, laborious feeling, aided only by such dim reflections of the gibbous moon as glimmered through a window, cobweb-hung, or through some break in the walls.

At length, however—for all things have an end—breathless and spent, they found their refuge. And soon after that, clad in their savage robes, they supped.

Allan Stern, consulting engineer, and Beatrice Kendrick, stenographer, now king and queen of the whole wide world domain (as they feared), sat together by a little blaze of punky wood fragments that flickered on the eroded floor.

They ate with their fingers and drank out of the bottles, *sans* apology. Strange were their speculations, their wonderings, their plans—now discussed specifically, now half-voiced by a mere word that thrilled them both with sudden, poignant emotion.

And so an hour passed, and the night deepened toward the birth of another day. The fire burned low and died, for they had little to replenish it with.

Down sank the moon, her pale light dimming as she went, her faint illumination wanly creeping across the disordered, wrack-strewn floor.

And at length Stern, in the outer office, Beatrice in the other, they wrapped themselves within their furs and laid them down to sleep.

Despite the age-long trance from which they both had but so recently emerged, a strange lassitude weighed on them.

Yet long after Beatrice had lost herself in dreams, Stern lay and thought strange thoughts, yearning and eager thoughts, there in the impenetrable gloom.

CHAPTER VII

The Outer World

Before daybreak the engineer was up again, and active. Now that he faced the light of morning, with a thousand difficult problems closing in on every hand, he put aside his softer moods, his visions and desires, and—like the scientific man he was—addressed himself to the urgent matters in hand.

"The girl's safe enough alone, here, for a while," thought he, looking in upon her where she lay, calm as a child, folded within the clinging masses of the tiger-skin.

"I must be out and away for two or three hours, at the very least. I hope she'll sleep till I get back. If not—what then?"

He pondered a moment; then, coming over to the charred remnants of last night's fire, chose a bit of burnt wood. With this he scrawled in large, rough letters on a fairly smooth stretch of the wall:

"Back soon. All O. K. Don't worry."

Then, turning, he set out on the long, painful descent again to the earth-level.

Garish now, and doubly terrible, since seen with more than double clearness by the graying dawn, the world-ruin seemed to him.

Strong of body and of nerve as he was, he could not help but shudder at the numberless traces of sudden and pitiless death which met his gaze.

Everywhere lay those dust-heaps, with here or there a tooth, a ring, a bit of jewelry showing—everywhere he saw them, all the way down the stairs, in every room and office he peered into, and in the time-ravished confusion of the arcade.

But this was scarcely the time for reflections of any sort. Life called, and labor, and duty; not mourning for the dead world, nor even wonder or pity at the tragedy which had so mysteriously befallen.

And as the man made his way over and through the universal wreckage, he took counsel with himself.

"First of all, water!" thought he. "We can't depend on the bottled supply. Of course, there's the Hudson; but it's brackish, if not downright salt. I've got to find some fresh and pure supply, close at hand. That's the prime necessity of life.

"What with the canned stuff, and such game as I can kill, there's bound to be food enough for a while. But a good water-supply we must have, and at once!"

Yet, prudent rather for the sake of Beatrice than for his own, he decided that he ought not to issue out, unarmed, into this new and savage world, of which he had as yet no very definite knowledge. And for a while he searched, hoping to find some weapon or other.

"I've got to have an ax, first of all," said he. "That's man's first need, in any wilderness. Where shall I find one?"

He thought a moment.

"Ah! In the basements!" exclaimed he. "Maybe I can locate an engine-room, a store-room, or something of that sort. There's sure to be tools in a place like that." And, laying off the bear-skin, he prepared to explore the regions under the ground-level.

He used more than half an hour, through devious ways and hard labor, to make his way to the desired spot. The ancient stair-way, leading down, he could not find.

But by clambering down one of the elevator-shafts, digging toes and fingers into the crevices in the metal framework and the cracks in the concrete, he managed at last to reach a vaulted sub-cellar, festooned with webs, damp, noisome and obscure.

Considerable light glimmered in from a broken sidewalk-grating above, and through a gaping, jagged hole near one end of the cellar, beneath which lay a badly-broken stone.

The engineer figured that this block had fallen from the tower and come to rest only here; and this awoke him to a new sense of ever-present peril. At any moment of the night or day, he realized, some such mishap was imminent.

"Eternal vigilance!" he whispered to himself. Then, dismissing useless fears, he set about the task in hand.

By the dim illumination from above, he was able to take cognizance of the musty-smelling place, which, on the whole, was in a better state of repair than the arcade. The first cellar yielded nothing of value to him, but, making his way through a low vaulted door, he chanced into what must have been one of the smaller, auxiliary engine-rooms.

This, he found, contained a battery of four dynamos, a small seepage-pump, and a crumbling marble switch-board with part of the wiring still comparatively intact.

At sight of all this valuable machinery scaled and pitted with rust, Stern's brows contracted with a feeling akin to pain. The engineer loved mechanism of all sorts; its care and use had been his life.

And now these mournful relics, strange as that may seem, affected him more strongly than the little heaps of dust which marked the spots where human beings had fallen in sudden, inescapable death. Yet even so, he had no time for musing.

"Tools!" cried he, peering about the dim-lit vault "Tools—I must have some. Till I find tools, I'm helpless!"

Search as he might, he discovered no ax in the place, but in place of it he unearthed a sledge-hammer. Though corroded, it was still quite service-able. Oddly enough, the oak handle was almost intact.

"Kyanized wood, probably," reflected he, as he laid the sledge to one side and began delving into a bed of dust that had evidently been a work-bench. "Ah! And here's a chisel! A spanner, too! A heap of rusty old wire nails!"

Delightedly he examined these treasures.

"They're worth more to me," he exulted, "than all the gold between here and what's left of San Francisco!"

He found nothing more of value in the litter. Everything else was rusted beyond use. So, having convinced himself that nothing more remained, he gathered up his finds and started back whence he had come.

After some quarter-hour of hard labor, he managed to transport every-thing up into the arcade.

"Now for a glimpse of the outer world!" quoth he.

Gripping the sledge well in hand, he made his way through the con-fused nexus of ruin. Disguised as everything now was, fallen and disjoint-ed, moldering, blighted by age incalculable, still the man recognized many familiar features.

Here, he recalled, the telephone-booths had been; there, the information desk. Yonder, again, he remembered the little curved counter where once upon a time a man in uniform had sold tickets to such as had wanted to visit the tower.

Counter now was dust; ticket-man only a crumble of fine, grayish powder. Stern shivered slightly, and pressed on.

As he approached the outer air, he noticed that many a grassy tuft and creeping vine had rooted in the pavement of the arcade, up-prying the marble slabs and cracking the once magnificent floor.

The doorway itself was almost choked by a tremendous Norway pine which had struck root close to the building, and now insolently blocked that way where, other-time, many thousand men and women every day had come and gone.

But Stern clambered out past this obstacle, testing the floor with his sledge, as he went, lest he fall through an unseen weak spot into the depths of coal-cellars below. And presently he reached the outer air, unharmed.

"But—but, the sidewalk?" cried he, amazed. "The street—the Square? Where are they?" And in astonishment he stopped, staring.

The view from the tower, though it had told him something of the changes wrought, had given him no adequate conception of their magnitude.

He had expected some remains of human life to show upon the earth, some semblance of the metropolis to remain in the street. But no, nothing was there; nothing at all on the ground to show that he was in the heart of a city.

He could, indeed, catch glimpses of a building here or there. Through the tangled thickets that grew close up to the age-worn walls of the Metropolitan, he could make out a few bits of tottering construction on the south side of what had been Twenty-Third Street.

But of the street itself, no trace remained—no pavement, no sidewalk, no curb. And even so near and so conspicuous an object as the wreck of the Flatiron was now entirely concealed by the dense forest.

Soil had formed thickly over all the surface. Huge oaks and pines flourished there as confidently as though in the heart of the Maine forest, crowding ash and beech for room.

Under the man's feet, even as he stood close by the building—which was thickly overgrown with ivy and with ferns and bushes rooted in the crannies—the pine-needles bent in deep, pungent beds.

Birch, maple, poplar and all the natives of the American woods shouldered each other lustily. By the state of the fresh young leaves, just bursting their sheaths, Stern knew the season was mid-May.

Through the wind-swayed branches, little flickering patches of morning sunlight met his gaze, as they played and quivered on the forest moss or over the sere pine-spills.

Even upon the huge, squared stones which here and there lay in disorder, and which Stern knew must have fallen from the tower, the moss grew very thick; and more than one such block had been rent by frost and growing things.

"How long has it been, great Heavens! How long?" cried the engineer, a sudden fear creeping into his heart. For this, the reasserted dominance of nature, bore in on him with more appalling force than anything he had yet seen.

About him he looked, trying to get his bearings in that strange *milieu*.

"Why," said he, quite slowly, "it's—it's just as though some cosmic jester, all-powerful, had scooped up the fragments of a ruined city and tossed them pell-mell into the core of the Adirondacks! It's horrible—ghastly—incredible!"

Dazed and awed, he stood as in a dream, a strange figure with his mane of hair, his flaming, trailing beard, his rags (for he had left the bear-skin in the arcade), his muscular arm, knotted as he held the sledge over his shoulder.

Well might he have been a savage of old times; one of the early barbarians of Britain, perhaps, peering in wonder at the ruins of some deserted Roman camp.

The chatter of a squirrel high up somewhere in the branches of an oak, recalled him to his wits. Down came spiralling a few bits of bark and acorn-shell, quite in the old familiar way.

Farther off among the woods, a robin's throaty morning notes drifted to him on the odorous breeze. A wren, surprisingly tame, chippered busily. It hopped about, not ten feet from him, entirely fearless.

Stern realized that it was now seeing a man for the first time in its life, and that it had no fear. His bushy brows contracted as he watched the little brown body jumping from twig to twig in the pine above him.

A deep, full breath he drew. Higher, still higher he raised his head. Far through the leafy screen he saw the overbending arch of sky in tiny patches of turquoise.

"The same old world, after all—the same, in spite of everything—thank God!" he whispered, his very tone a prayer of thanks.

And suddenly, though why he could not have told, the grim engineer's eyes grew wet with tears that ran, unheeded, down his heavy-bearded cheeks.

CHAPTER VIII

A Sign of Peril

STERN'S weakness—as he judged it—lasted but a minute. Then, realizing even more fully than ever the necessity for immediate labor and exploration, he tightened his grip upon the sledge and set forth into the forest of Madison Square.

Away from him scurried a cotton-tail. A snake slid, hissing, out of sight under a jungle of fern. A butterfly, dull brown and ocher, settled upon a branch in the sunlight, where it began slowly opening and shutting its wings.

"H-m! That's a *Danaus plexippus*, right enough," commented the man. "But there are some odd changes in it. Yes, indeed, certainly some evolutionary variants. Must be a tremendous time since we went to sleep, for sure; probably very much longer than I dare guess. That's a problem I've got to go to work on, before many days!"

But now for the present he dismissed it again; he pushed it aside in the press of urgent matters. And, parting the undergrowth, he broke his crackling way through the deep wood.

He had gone but a few hundred yards when an exclamation of surprised delight burst from his lips.

"Water! Water!" he cried. "What? A spring, so close? A pool, right here at hand? Good luck, by Jove, the very first thing!"

And, stopping where he stood, he gazed at it with keen, unalloyed pleasure.

There, so near to the massive bulk of the tower that the vast shadow lay broadly across it, Stern had suddenly come upon as beautiful a little watercourse as ever bubbled forth under the yews of Arden or lapped the willows of Hesperides.

He beheld a roughly circular depression in the woods, fern-banked and fringed with purple blooms; at the bottom sparkled a spring, leaf-bowered, cool, Elysian.

From this, down through a channel which the water must have worn for itself by slow erosion, a small brook trickled, widening out into a pool some fifteen feet across; whence, brimming over, it purled away through the young sweet-flags and rushes with tempting little woodland notes.

"What a find!" cried the engineer. Forward he strode. "So, then? Deer-tracks?" he exclaimed, noting a few dainty hoof-prints in the sandy margin. "Great!" And, filled with exultation, he dropped beside the spring.

Over it he bent. Setting his bearded lips to the sweet water, he drank enormous, satisfying drafts.

Sated at last, he stood up again and peered about him. All at once he burst out into jovious laughter.

"Why, this is certainly an old friend of mine, or I'm a liar!" he cried out. "This spring is nothing more or less than the lineal descendant of Madison Square fountain, what? But good Lord, what a change!

"It would make a splendid subject for an article in the 'Annals of Applied Geology.' Only—well, there aren't any annals, now, and what's more, no readers!"

Down to the wider pool he walked.

"Stern, my boy," said he, "here's where you get an A-I, first-class dip!"

A minute later, stripped to the buff, the man lay splashing vigorously in the water. From top to toe he scrubbed himself vigorously with the fine, white sand. And when, some minutes later, he rose up again, the tingle and joy of life filled him in every nerve.

For a minute he looked contemptuously at his rags, lying there on the edge of the pool. Then with a grunt he kicked them aside.

"I guess we'll dispense with those," judged he. "The bear-skin, back in the building, there, will be enough." He picked up his sledge, and, heaving a mighty breath of comfort, set out for the tower again.

"Ah, but that was certainly fine!" he exclaimed. "I feel ten years younger, already. Ten, from what? X minus ten, equals—?"

Thoughtfully, as he walked across the elastic moss and over the pine-needles, he stroked his beard.

"Now, if I could only get a hair-cut and shave!" said he. "Well, why not? Wouldn't that surprise *her*, though?"

The idea strong upon him, he hastened his steps, and soon was back at the door close to the huge Norway pine. But here he did not enter. Instead, he turned to the right.

Plowing through the woods, climbing over fallen columns and shattered building-stones, flushing a covey of loud-winged partridges, parting the bushes that grew thickly along the base of the wall, he now found himself in what had long ago been Twenty-Third Street.

No sign, now of paving or car-tracks—nothing save, on the other side of the way, crumbling lines of ruin. As he worked his way among the detritus of the Metropolitan, he kept sharp watch for the wreckage of a hardware store.

Not until he had crossed the ancient line of Madison Avenue and penetrated some hundred yards still further along Twenty-Third Street, did he find what he sought.

"Ah!" he suddenly cried. "Here's something now!"

And, scrambling over a pile of grass-grown rubbish with a couple of time-bitten iron wheels peering out—evidently the wreckage of an electric car—he made his way around a gaping hole where a side-walk had caved in and so reached the interior of a shop.

"Yes, prospects here, certainly prospects!" he decided, carefully inspecting the place. "If this didn't use to be Currier & Brown's place, I'm away off my bearings. There ought to be *something* left."

"Ah! Would you?" and he flung a hastily-snatched rock at a rattlesnake that had begun its dry, chirring defiance on top of what once had been a counter.

The snake vanished, while the rock rebounding, crashed through glass.

Stern wheeled about with a cry of joy. For there, he saw, still stood near the back of the shop a showcase from within which he caught a sheen of tarnished metal.

Quickly he ran toward this, stumbling over the loose flooring, mossy and grass-grown. There in the case, preserved as you have seen Egyptian relics two or three thousand years old, in museums, the engineer beheld incalculable treasures. He thrilled with a savage, strange delight.

Another blow, with the sledge, demolished the remaining glass.

He trembled with excitement as he chose what he most needed.

"I certainly do understand now," said he, "why the New Zealanders took Captain Cook's old barrel-hoops and refused his cash. Same here! All the money in this town couldn't buy this rusty knife—" as he seized a corroded blade set in a horn handle, yellowed with age. And eagerly he continued the hunt.

Fifteen minutes later he had accumulated a pair of scissors, two rubber combs, another knife, a revolver, an automatic, several handfuls of cartridges and a Cosmos bottle.

All these he stowed in a warped, mildewed remnant of a Gladstone bag, taken from a corner where a broken glass sign, "Leather Goods," lay among the rank confusion.

"I guess I've got enough, now, for the first load," he judged, more excited than if he had chanced upon a blue-clay bed crammed with Cullinan diamonds. "It's a beginning, anyhow. Now for Beatrice!"

Joyously as a schoolboy with a pocketful of new-won marbles, he made his exit from the ruins of the hardware store, and started back toward the tower.

But hardly had he gone a hundred feet when all at once he drew back with a sharp cry of wonder and alarm.

There at his feet, in plain view under a little maple sapling, lay something that held him frozen with astonishment.

He snatched it up, dropping the sledge to do so.

"What? *What?*" he stammered; and at the thing he stared with widened, uncomprehending eyes.

"Merciful God! How—what—?" cried he.

The thing he held in his hand was *a broad, flat, flint assegai-point!*

CHAPTER IX

HEADWAY AGAINST ODDS

STERN gazed at this alarming object with far more trepidation than he would have eyed a token authentically labeled: "Direct from Mars."

For the space of a full half-minute he found no word, grasped no coherent thought, came to no action save to stand there, thunder-struck, holding the rotten leather bag in one hand, the spear-head in the other.

Then, suddenly, he shouted a curse and made as though to fling it clean away. But ere it had left his grasp, he checked himself.

"No, there's no use in *that,*" said he, quite slowly. "If this thing is what it appears to be, if it isn't merely some freakish bit of stone weathered off somewhere, why, it means—my God, what *doesn't* it mean?"

He shuddered, and glanced fearfully about him; all his calculations already seemed crashing down about him; all his plans, half-formulated, appeared in ruin.

New, vast and unknown factors of the struggle broadened rapidly before his mental vision, *if* this thing were really what it looked to be.

Keenly he peered at the bit of flint in his palm. There it lay, real enough, an almost perfect specimen of the flaker's art, showing distinctly where the wood had been applied to the core to peel off the many successive layers.

It could not have been above three and a half inches long, by one and a quarter wide, at its broadest part. The haft, where it had been hollowed to hold the lashings, was well marked.

A diminutive object and a skilfully-formed one. At any other time or place, the engineer would have considered the finding a good fortune; but now—!

"Yet after all," he said aloud, as if to convince himself, "it's only a bit of stone! What can it prove?"

His subconsciousness seemed to make answer: "So, too, the sign that Robinson Crusoe found on the beach was only a human foot-mark. Do not deceive yourself!"

In deep thought the engineer stood there a moment or two. Then, "Bah!" cried he. "What does it matter, anyhow? Let it come—whatever it is! If I hadn't just happened to find this, I'd have been none the wiser." And he dropped the bit of flint into the bag along with the other things.

Again he picked up his sledge, and, now more cautiously, once more started forward.

"All I can do," he thought, "is just to go right ahead as though this hadn't happened at all. If trouble comes, it comes, that's all. I guess I can meet it. Always *have* got away with it, so far. We'll see. What's on the cards has got to be played to a finish, and the best hand wins!"

He retraced his way to the spring, where he carefully rinsed and filled the Cosmos bottle for Beatrice. Then back to the Metropolitan he came, donned his bear-skin, which he fastened with a wire nail, and started the long climb. His sledge he carefully hid on the second floor, in an office at the left of the stairway.

"Don't think much of this hammer, after all," said he. "What I need is an ax. Perhaps this afternoon I can have another go at that hardware place and find one.

"If the handle's gone, I can haft it with green wood. With a good ax and these two revolvers—till I find some rifles—I guess we're safe enough, spear-heads or not!"

About him he glanced at the ever-present molder and decay. This office, he could easily see, had been both spacious and luxurious, but now it offered a sorry spectacle. In the dust over by a window something glittered dully.

Stern found it was a fragment of a beveled mirror, which had probably hung there and, when the frame rotted, had dropped. He brushed it off and looked eagerly into it.

A cry of amazement burst from him.

"Do I look like *that?*" he shouted. "Well, I won't, for long!"

He propped the glass up on the steel beam of the window-opening, and got the scissors out of the bag. Ten minutes later, the face of Allan Stern bore some resemblance to its original self. True enough, his hair remained a bit jagged, especially in the back, his brows were somewhat uneven, and the point to which his beard was trimmed was far from perfect.

But none the less his wild savagery had given place to a certain aspect of civilization that made the white bearskin over his shoulders look doubly strange.

Stern, however, was well pleased. He smiled in satisfaction.

"What will *she* think, and say?" he wondered, as he once more took up the bag and started on the long, exhausting climb.

Sweating profusely, badly "blown,"—for he had not taken much time to rest on the way—the engineer at last reached his offices in the tower.

Before entering, he called the girl's name.

"Beatrice! Oh, Beatrice! Are you awake, and visible?"

"All right, come in!" she answered cheerfully, and came to meet him in the doorway. Out to him she stretched her hand, in welcome; and the smile she gave him set his heart pounding.

He had to laugh at her astonishment and naïve delight over his changed appearance; but all the time his eyes were eagerly devouring her beauty.

For now, freshly-awakened, full of new life and vigor after a sound night's sleep, the girl was magnificent.

The morning light disclosed new glints of color in her wondrous hair, as it lay broad and silken on the tiger-skin. This she had secured at the throat and waist with bits of metal taken from the wreckage of the filing-cabinet.

Stern promised himself that ere long he would find her a profusion of gold pins and chains, in some of the Fifth Avenue shops, to serve her purposes till she could fashion real clothing.

As she gave him her hand, the Bengal skin fell back from her round, warm, cream-white arm.

At sight of it, at vision of that massy crown of hair and of those gray, penetrant, questioning eyes, the man's spent breath quickened.

He turned his own eyes quickly away, lest she should read his thought, and began speaking—of what? He hardly knew. Anything, till he could master himself.

But through it all he knew that in his whole life, till now self-centered, analytical, cold, he never had felt such real, spontaneous happiness.

The touch of her fingers, soft and warm, dispelled his every anxiety. The thought that he was working, now, for her; serving her; striving to preserve and keep her, thrilled him with joy.

And as some foregleam of the future came to him, his fears dropped from him like those outworn rags he had discarded in the forest.

"Well, so we're both up and at it, again," he exclaimed, commonplacely enough, his voice a bit uncertain. Stern had walked narrow girders six hundred feet sheer up; he had worked in caissons under tide-water, with the air-pumps driving full tilt to keep death out.

He had swung in a bosun's-chair down the face of the Yosemite Cañon at Cathedral Spires. But never had he felt emotions such as now. And greatly he marveled.

"I've had luck," he continued. "See here, and here?"

He showed her his treasures, all the contents of the bag, except the spear-point. Then, giving her the Cosmos bottle, he bade her drink. Gratefully she did so, while he explained to her the finding of the spring.

Her face aglow with eagerness and brave enthusiasm, she listened. But when he told her about the bathing-pool, an envious expression came to her.

"It's not fair," she protested, "for you to monopolize that. If you'll show me the place—and just stay around in the woods, to see that nothing hurts me—"

"You'll take a dip, too?"

Eagerly she nodded, her eyes beaming.

"I'm just dying for one!" she exclaimed. "Think! I haven't had a bath, now, for x years!"

"I'm at your service," declared the engineer. And for a moment a little silence came between them, a silence so profound that they could even hear the faint, far cheepings of the mud-swallows in the tower stair, above.

At the back of Stern's brain still lurked a haunting fear of the wood, of what the assegai-point might portend, but he dispelled it.

"Well, come along down," bade he. "It's getting late, already. But first, we must take just one more look, by this fresh morning light, from the platform up above, there?"

She assented readily. Together, talking of their first urgent needs, of their plans for this new day and for this wonderful, strange life that now confronted them, they climbed the stairs again. Once more they issued out on to the weed-grown platform of red tiles.

There they stood a moment, looking out with wonder over that vast, still, marvelous prospect of life-in-death. Suddenly the engineer spoke.

"Tell me," said he, "where did you get that line of verse you quoted last night? The one about this vast city-heart all lying still, you know?"

"That? Why, that was from Wordsworth's Sonnet on London Bridge, of course," she smiled up at him. "You remember it now, don't you?"

"No-o," he disclaimed a trifle dubiously. "I—that is, I never *was* much on poetry, you understand. It wasn't exactly in my line. But never mind. How did it go? I'd like to hear it, tremendously."

"I don't just recall the whole poem," she answered thoughtfully. "But I know part of it ran:

> '......*This city now doth like a garment wear*
> *The beauty of the morning. Silent, bare,*

Ships, towers, domes, theaters, and temples lie
Open unto the fields and to the sky
All bright and glittering in the smokeless air.'

A moment she paused to think. The sun, lancing its long and level rays across the water and the vast dead city, irradiated her face.

Instinctively, as she looked abroad over that wondrous panorama, she raised both bare arms; and, clad in the tiger-skin alone, stood for a little space like some Parsee priestess, sun-worshiping, on her tower of silence.

Stern looked at her, amazed.

Was this, could this indeed be the girl he had employed, in the old days—the other days of routine and of tedium, of orders and specifications and dry-as-dust dictation? As though from a strange spell he aroused himself.

"The poem?" exclaimed he. "What next?"

"Oh, that? I'd almost forgotten about that; I was dreaming. It goes this way, I think:

'Never did the sun more beautifully steep
In his first splendor valley, rock, or hill,
Ne'er saw I, never felt a calm so deep;
The river glideth at his own sweet will.
Dear God! the very houses seem asleep,
And all this mighty heart is standing still!......'

She finished the tremendous classic almost in a whisper.

They both stood silent a moment, gazing out together on that strange, inexplicable fulfilment of the poet's vision.

Up to them, through the crystal morning air, rose a faint, small sound of waters, from the brooklet in the forest. The nesting birds, below, were busy "in song and solace"; and through the golden sky above, a swallow slanted on sharp wing toward some unseen, leafy goal.

Far out upon the river, faint specks of white wheeled and hovered—a flock of swooping gulls, snowy and beautiful and free. Their pinions flashed, spiraled and sank to rest on the wide waters.

Stern breathed a sigh. His right arm slipped about the sinuous, fur-robed body of the girl.

"Come, now!" said he, with returning practicality. "Bath for you, breakfast for both of us—then we must buckle down to work. *Come!*"

CHAPTER X

TERROR

NOON found them far advanced in the preliminaries of their hard adventuring.

Working together in a strong and frank companionship—the past temporarily forgotten and the future still put far away—half a day's labor advanced them a long distance on the road to safety.

Even these few hours sufficed to prove that, unless some strange, untoward accident befell, they stood a more than equal chance of winning out.

Realizing to begin with, that a home on the forty-eighth story of the tower was entirely impractical, since it would mean that most of their time would have to be used in laborious climbing, they quickly changed their dwelling.

They chose a suite of offices on the fifth floor, looking directly out over and into the cool green beauty of Madison Forest. In an hour or so, they cleared out the bats and spiders, the rubbish and the dust, and made the place very decently presentable.

"Well, that's a good beginning, anyhow," remarked the engineer, standing back and looking critically at the finished work.

"I don't see why we shouldn't make a fairly comfortable home out of this, for a while. It's not too high for ease, and it's high enough for safety—to keep prowling bears and wolves and—and other things from exploring us in the night."

He laughed, but memories of the spear-head tinged his merriment with apprehension. "In a day or two I'll make some kind of an outer door, or barricade. But first, I need that ax and some other things. Can you spare me for a while, now?"

"I'd *rather* go along, too," she answered wistfully, from the window-sill where she sat resting.

"No, not this time, please!" he entreated. "First I've got to go 'way to the top of the tower and bring down my chemicals and all the other things up there.

"Then I'm going out on a hunt for dishes, a lamp, some oil and no end of things. You save your strength for a while; stay here and keep house and be a good girl!"

"All right," she acceded, smiling a little sadly. "But really, I feel quite able to go."

"This afternoon, perhaps; now now. Good-by!" And he started for the door. Then a thought struck him. He turned and came back.

"By the way," said he, "if we we can fix up some kind of a holster, I'll take one of those revolvers. With the best of this leather here," nodding at the Gladstone bag, "I should imagine we could manufacture something serviceable."

They planned the holster together, and he cut it out with his knife, while she slit leather thongs to lash it with. Presently it was done, and a strap to tie it round his waist with—a crude, rough thing, but just as useful as though finished with the utmost skill.

"We'll make another for you when I get home this noon," he remarked picking up the automatic and a handful of cartridges. Quickly he filled the magazine. The shells were green with verdigris, and many a rust-spot disfigured the one-time brightness of the arm.

As he stepped over to the window, aimed and pulled the trigger, a sharp and welcome report burst from the weapon. And a few leaves, clipped from an oak in the forest, zigzagged down in the bright, warm sunlight.

"I guess she'll do all right!" he laughed, sliding the ugly weapon into his new holster. "You see, the powder and fulminate, sealed up in the cartridges, are practically imperishable. Here, let me load yours, too.

"If you want something to do, you can practise on that dead limb out there, see? And don't be afraid of wasting ammunition. There must be millions of cartridges in this old burg—millions—all ours!"

Again he laughed, and handing her the other pistol, now fully loaded, took his leave. Before he had climbed a hundred feet up the tower stair, he heard a slow, uneven pop—pop—popping, and with satisfaction knew that Beatrice was already perfecting herself in the use of the revolver.

"And she may need it, too—we both may, badly—before we know it!" thought he, frowning, as he kept upon his way.

This reflection weighed in so heavily upon him, all due to the flint assegai-point, that he made still another excuse that afternoon and so got out of taking the girl into the forest with him on his exploring trip.

The excuse was all the more plausible inasmuch as he left her enough work at home to do, making some real clothing and some sandals for them both. This task, now that the girl had scissors to use, was not too hard.

Stern brought her great armfuls of the furs from the shop in the arcade, and left her busily and happily employed.

He spent the afternoon in scouting through the entire neighborhood from Sixth Avenue as far east as Third and from Twenty-Seventh Street down through Union Square.

Revolver in his left hand, knife in his right to cut away troublesome bush or brambles, or to slit impeding vine-masses, he progressed slowly and observantly.

He kept his eyes open for big game, but—though he found moose-tracks at the corner of Broadway and Nineteenth—he ran into nothing more formidable than a lynx, which snarled at him from a tree overhanging the mournful ruins of the Farragut monument.

One shot sent it bounding and screaming with pain, out of view. Stern noted with satisfaction that blood followed its trail.

"Guess I haven't forgotten how to shoot in all these x years!" he commented, stooping to examine the spoor. "That may come in handy later!"

Then, still wary and watchful, he continued his exploration.

He found that the city, as such, had entirely ceased to be.

"Nothing but lines and monstrous rubbish-heaps of ruins," he sized up the situation, "traversed by lanes of forest and overgrown with every sort of vegetation.

"Every wooden building completely wiped out. Brick and stone ones practically gone. Steel alone standing, and *that* in rotten shape. Nothing at all intact but the few concrete structures.

"Ha! ha!" And he laughed satirically. "If the builders of the twentieth century could have foreseen this they wouldn't have thrown quite such a chest, eh? And *they* talked of engineering!"

Useless though it was, he felt a certain pride in noting that the Osterhaut Building, on Seventeenth Street, had lasted rather better than the average.

"*My* work!" said he, nodding with grim satisfaction, then passed on.

Into the Subway he penetrated at Eighteenth Street, climbing with difficulty down the choked stairway, through bushes and over masses of ruin that had fallen from the roof. The great tube, he saw, was choked with litter.

Slimy and damp it was, with a mephitic smell and ugly pools of water settled in the ancient road-bed. The rails were wholly gone in places. In others only rotten fragments of steel remained.

A goggle-eyed toad stared impudently at him from a long tangle of rubbish that had been a train—stalled there forever by the final block-signal of death.

Through the broken arches overhead the rain and storms of ages had beaten down, and lush grasses flourished here and there, where sunlight could penetrate.

No human dust-heaps here, as in the shelter of the arcade. Long since every vestige of man had been swept away. Stern shuddered, more depressed by the sight here than at any other place so far visited.

"And they boasted of a work for all time!" whispered he, awed by the horror of it. "They boasted—like the financiers, the churchmen, the merchants, everybody! Boasted of their institutions, their city, their country. And *now*—"

Out he clambered presently, terribly depressed by what he had witnessed, and set to work laying in still more supplies from the wrecked shops. Now for the first time, his wonder and astonishment having largely abated, he began to feel the horror of this loneliness.

"No life here! Nobody to speak to—except the girl!" he exclaimed aloud, the sound of his own voice uncanny in that woodland street of death. "All gone, everything! My Heavens, suppose I didn't have *her*? How long could I go on alone, and keep my mind?"

The thought terrified him. He put it resolutely away and went to work. Wherever he stumbled upon anything of value he eagerly seized it.

The labor, he found, kept him from the subconscious dread of what might happen to Beatrice or to himself if either should meet with any mishap. The consequences of either one dying, he knew, must be horrible beyond all thinking for the survivor.

Up Broadway he found much to keep—things which he garnered in the up-caught hem of his bearskin, things of all kinds and uses. He found a clay pipe—all the wooden ones had vanished from the shop—and a glass jar of tobacco.

These he took as priceless treasures. More jars of edibles he discovered, also a stock of rare wines. Coffee and salt he came upon. In the ruins of the little French brass-ware shop, opposite the Flatiron, he made a rich haul of cups and plates and a still serviceable lamp.

Strangely enough, it still had oil in it. The fluid hermetically sealed in, had not been able to evaporate.

At last, when the lengthening shadows in Madison Forest warned him that day was ending, he betook himself, heavy laden, once more back past the spring, and so through the path which already was beginning to be visible back to the shelter of the Metropolitan.

"Now for a great surprise for the girl!" thought he, laboriously toiling up the stair with his burden: "What will she say, I wonder, when she sees all these housekeeping treasures?" Eagerly he hastened.

But before he had reached the third story he heard a cry from above. Then a spatter of revolver-shots punctured the air.

He stopped, listening in alarm.

"Beatrice! Oh, Beatrice!" he hailed, his voice falling flat and stifled in those ruinous passages.

Another shot.

"Answer!" panted Stern. "What's the matter *now?*"

Hastily he put down his burden, and, spurred by a great terror, bounded up the broken stairs.

Into their little shelter, their home, he ran, calling her name.

No reply came!

Stern stopped short, his face a livid gray.

"Merciful Heaven!" stammered he.

The girl was gone!

CHAPTER XI

A THOUSAND YEARS!

SICKENED with a numbing anguish of fear such as in all his life he had never known, Stern stood there a moment, motionless and lost.

Then he turned. Out into the hall he ran, and his voice, re-echoing wildly, rang through those long-deserted aisles.

All at once he heard a laugh behind him—a hail.

He wheeled about, trembling and spent. Out his arms went, in eager greeting. For the girl, laughing and flushed, and very beautiful, was coming down the stair at the end of the hall.

Never had the engineer beheld a sight so wonderful to him as this woman, clad in the Bengal robe; this girl who smiled and ran to meet him.

"What? Were you frightened?" she asked, growing suddenly serious, as he stood there speechless and pale, "Why—what could happen to me here?"

His only answer was to take her in his arms and whisper her name. But she struggled to be free.

"Don't! you mustn't!" she exclaimed. "I didn't mean to alarm you. Didn't even know you were here!"

"I heard the shots—I called—you didn't answer. Then—"

"You found me gone? I didn't hear you. It was nothing, after all. Nothing—much!"

He led her back into the room.

"What happened? Tell me!"

"It was really too absurd!"

"What was it?"

"Only this," and she laughed again. "I was getting supper ready, as you see," with a nod at their provision laid out upon the clean-brushed floor. "When—"

"Yes?"

"Why, a blundering great hawk swooped in through the window there, circled around, pounced on the last of our beef and tried to fly away with it."

Stern heaved a sigh of relief. "So that was all?" asked he. "But the shots? And your absence?"

"I struck at him. He showed fight. I blocked the window. He was determined to get away with the food. I was determined he *shouldn't*. So I snatched the revolver and opened fire."

"And then?"

"That confused him. He flapped out into the hall. I chased him. Away up the stairs he circled. I shot again. Then I pursued. Went up two stories. But he must have got away through some opening or other. Our beef's all gone!" And Beatrice looked very sober.

"Never mind, I've got a lot more stuff down-stairs. But tell me, did you wing him?"

"I'm afraid not," she admitted. "There's a feather or two on the stairs, though."

"Good work!" cried he laughing, his fear all swallowed in the joy of having found her again, safe and unhurt. "But please don't give me another such panic, will you? It's all right this time, however.

"And now if you'll just wait here and not get fighting with any more wild creatures, I'll go down and bring my latest finds. I like your pluck," he added slowly, gazing earnestly at her.

"But I don't want you chasing things in this old shell of a building. No telling what crevice you might fall into or what accident might happen. *Au revoir!*"

Her smile as he left her was inscrutable, but her eyes, strangely bright, followed him till he had vanished once more down the stairs.

*****

Broad strokes, a line here, one there, with much left to the imagining—such will serve best for the painting of a picture like this—a picture wherein every ordinary bond of human life, the nexus of man's society, is shattered. Where everything must strive to reconstruct itself from the dust. Where the future, if any such there may be, must rise from the ashes of a crumbling past.

Broad strokes, for detailed ones would fill too vast a canvas. Impossible to describe a tenth of the activities of Beatrice and Stern the next four days. Even to make a list of their hard-won possessions would turn this chapter into a mere catalogue.

So let these pass for the most part. Day by day the man, issuing forth sometimes alone, sometimes with Beatrice, labored like a Titan among the ruins of New York.

Though more than ninety percent of the city's one-time wealth had long since vanished, and though all standards of worth had wholly changed, yet much remained to harvest.

Infinitudes of things, more or less damaged, they bore up to their shelter, up the stairs which here and there Stern had repaired with rough-hewn logs.

For now he had an ax, found in that treasure-house of Currier & Brown's, brought to a sharp edge on a wet, flat stone by the spring, and hafted with a sapling.

This implement was of incredible use, and greatly enheartened the engineer. More valuable it was than a thousand tons of solid gold.

The same store yielded also a well-preserved enameled water-pail and some smaller dishes of like ware, three more knives, quantities of nails, and some small tools; also the tremendous bonanza of a magazine rifle and a shotgun, both of which Stern judged would come into shape by the application of oil and by careful tinkering. Of ammunition, here and elsewhere, the engineer had no doubt he could unearth unlimited quantities.

"With steel," he reflected, "and with my flint spearhead, I can make fire at any time. Wood is plenty, and there's lots of 'punk.' So the first step in reëstablishing civilization is secure. With fire, everything else becomes possible.

"After a while, perhaps, I can get around to manufacturing matches again. But for the present my few ounces of phosphorus and the flint and steel will answer very well."

Beatrice, like the true woman she was, addressed herself eagerly to the fascinating task of making a real home out of the barren desolation of the fifth floor offices. Her splendid energy was no less than the engineer's. And very soon a comfortable air pervaded the place.

Stern manufactured a broom for her by cutting willow withes and lashing them with hide strips onto a trimmed branch. Spiders and dust all vanished. A true housekeeping appearance set in.

To supplement the supply of canned food that accumulated along one of the walls, Stern shot what game he could—squirrels, partridges and rabbits.

Metal dishes, especially of solid gold, ravished from Fifth Avenue shops, took their place on the crude table he had fashioned with his ax. Not for esthetic effect did they now value gold, but merely because that metal had perfectly withstood the ravages of time.

In the ruins of a magnificent store near Thirty-First Street, Stern found a vault burst open by frost and slow disintegration of the steel.

Here something over a quart of loose diamonds, big and little, rough and cut, were lying in confusion all about. Stern took none of these. Their value now was no greater than that of any pebble.

But he chose a massive clasp of gold for Beatrice, for that could serve to fasten her robe. And in addition he gathered up a few rings and one-time costly jewels which could be worn. For the girl, after all, was one of Eve's daughters.

Bit by bit he accumulated many necessary articles, including some tooth-brushes which he found sealed in glass bottles, and a variety of gold toilet articles. Use was his first consideration now. Beauty came far behind.

In the corner of their rooms, after a time, stood a fair variety of tools, some already serviceable, others waiting to be polished, ground and hafted, and in some cases re-tempered. Two rough chairs made their appearance.

The north room, used only for cooking, became their forge and oven all in one. For here, close to a window where the smoke could drift out, Stern built a circular stone fireplace.

And here Beatrice presided over her copper casseroles and saucepans from the little shop on Broadway. Here, too, Stern planned to construct a pair of skin bellows, and presently to set up the altars of Vulcan and of Tubal Cain once more.

Both of them "thanked whatever gods there be" that the girl was a good cook. She amazed the engineer by the variety of dishes she managed to concoct from the canned goods, the game that Stern shot, and fresh dandelion greens dug near the spring. These edibles, with the blackest of black coffee, soon had them in fine fettle.

"I certainly have begun to put on weight," laughed the man after dinner on the fourth day, as he lighted his fragrant pipe with a roll of blazing birchbark.

"My bearskin is getting tight. You'll have to let it out for me, or else stop such magic in the kitchen!"

She smiled back at him, sitting there at ease in the sunshine by the window, sipping her coffee out of a gold cup with a solid gold spoon.

Stern, feeling the May breeze upon his face, hearing the bird-songs in the forest depths, felt a well-being, a glow of health and joy such as he had never in his whole life known—the health of outdoor labor and sound sleep and perfect digestion, the joy of accomplishment and of the girl's near presence.

"I suppose we do live pretty well," she answered, surveying the remnants of the feast. "Potted tongue and peas, fried squirrel, partridge and coffee ought to satisfy anybody. But still—"

"What is it?"

"I *would* like some buttered toast and some cream for my coffee, and some sugar."

Stern laughed heartily.

"You don't want much!" he exclaimed, vastly amused, the while he blew a cloud of Latakia smoke. "Well, you be patient, and everything will come, in time.

"You mustn't expect me to do magic. On the fourth day you don't imagine I've had time enough to round up the ten thousandth descendant of the erstwhile cow, do you?

"Or grow cane and make sugar? Or find grain for seed, clear some land, plow, harrow, plant, hoe, reap, winnow, grind and bolt and present you with a bag of prime flour? Now really?"

She pouted at his raillery. For a moment there was silence, while he drew at his pipe. At the girl he looked a little while. Then, his eyes a bit far-away, he remarked in a tone he tried to render casual:

"By the way, Beatrice, it occurs to me that we're doing rather well for old people—very old."

She looked up with a startled glance.

"*Very?*" she exclaimed. "You know how old then?"

"Very, indeed!" he answered. "Yes, I've got some sort of an idea about it. I hope it won't alarm you when you know."

"Why—how so? Alarm me?" she queried with a strange expression.

"Yes, because, you see, it's rather a long time since we went to sleep. Quite so. You see, I've been doing a little calculating, off and on, at odd times. Been putting two and two together, as it were.

"First, there was the matter of the dust in sheltered places, to guide me. The rate of deposition of what, in one or two spots, can't have been anything less than cosmic or star-dust, is fairly certain.

"Then again, the rate of this present deterioration of stone and steel has furnished another index. And last night I had a little peek at the pole-star, through my telescope, while you were asleep.

"The good old star has certainly shifted out of place a bit. Furthermore, I've been observing certain evolutionary changes in the animals and plants about us. Those have helped, too."

"And—and what have you found out?" asked she with tremulous interest.

"Well, I think I've got the answer, more or less correctly. Of course it's only an approximate result, as we say in engineering. But the different items check up with some degree of consistency.

"And I'm safe in believing I'm within at least a hundred years of the date one way or the other. Not a bad factor of safety, that, with my limited means of working."

The girl's eyes widened. From her hand fell the empty gold cup; it rolled away across the clean-swept floor.

"What?" cried she. "You've got it, within a hundred years! Why, then—you mean it's *more* than a hundred?"

Indulgently the engineer smiled.

"Come, now," he coaxed. "Just guess, for instance, how old you really are—and growing younger every day? How old?"

"Two hundred maybe? Oh surely not as old as that! It's horrible to think of!"

"Listen," bade he. "If I count your twenty-four years, when you went to sleep, you're now—"

"What?"

"You're now at the very minimum calculation, just about one thousand and twenty-four! Some age, that, eh?"

Then, as she stared at him wide-eyed he added with a smile.

"No disputing that fact, no dodging it. The thing's as certain as that you're now the most beautiful woman in the whole wide world!"

CHAPTER XII

DRAWING TOGETHER

DAYS passed, busy days, full of hard labor and achievement, rich in experience and learning, in happiness, in dreams of what the future might yet bring.

Beatrice made and finished a considerable wardrobe of garments for them both. These, when the fur had been clipped close with the scissors, were not oppressively warm, and, even though on some days a bit uncomfortable, the man and woman tolerated them because they had no others.

Plenty of bathing and good food put them in splendid physical condition, to which their active exercise contributed much. And thus, judging partly by the state of the foliage, partly by the height of the sun, which Stern determined with considerable accuracy by means of a simple, home-made quadrant—they knew mid-May was past and June was drawing near.

The housekeeping by no means took up all the girl's time. Often she went out with him on what he called his "pirating expeditions," that now sometimes led them as far afield as the sad ruins of the wharves and piers, or to the stark desolation and wreckage of lower Broadway and the one-time busy hives of newspaperdom, or up to Central Park or to the great remains of the two railroad terminals.

These two places, the former tide-gates of the city's life, impressed Stern most painfully of anything. The disintegrated tracks, the jumbled remains of locomotives and luxurious Pullmans with weeds growing rank upon them, the sunlight beating down through the caved-in roof of the Pennsylvania station "concourse," where millions of human beings once had trod in all the haste of men's paltry, futile affairs, filled him with melancholy, and he was glad to get away again leaving the place to the jungle, the birds and beasts that now laid claim to it.

"*Sic transit gloria mundi!*" he murmured, as with sad eyes he mused upon the downtumbled columns along the façade, the overgrown entrance-way, the cracked and falling arches and architraves. "And *this,* they said, was builded for all time!"

It was on one of these expeditions that the engineer found and pocketed—unknown to Beatrice—another disconcerting relic.

This was a bone, broken and splintered, and of no very great age, gnawed with perfectly visible tooth-marks. He picked it up, by chance, near the west side of the ruins of the old City Hall.

Stern recognized the manner in which the bone had been cracked open with a stone to let the marrow be sucked out. The sight of this gruesome relic revived all his fears, tenfold more acutely than ever, and filled him with a sense of vague, impending evil, of peril deadly to them both.

This was the more keen, because the engineer knew at a glance that the bone was the upper end of a human femur—human, or, at the very least, belonging to some highly anthropoid animal. And of apes or gorillas he had, as yet, found no trace in the forests of Manhattan.

Long he mused over his find. But not a single word did he ever say to Beatrice concerning it or the flint spear-point. Only he kept his eyes and ears well open for other bits of corroborative evidence.

And he never ventured a foot from the building unless his rifle and revolver were with him, their magazines full of high-power shells.

The girl always went armed, too, and soon grew to be such an expert shot that she could drop a squirrel from the tip of a fir, or wing a heron in full flight.

Once her quick eyes spied a deer in the tangles of the one-time Gramercy Park, now no longer neatly hedged with iron palings, but spread in wild confusion that joined the riot of growth beyond.

On the instant she fired, wounding the creature.

Stern's shot, echoing hers, missed. Already the deer was away, out of range through the forest. With some difficulty they pursued down a glen-like strip of woods that must have once been Irving Place.

Two hundred yards south of the park they sighted the animal again. And the girl with a single shot sent it crashing to earth.

"Bravo, Diana!" hurrahed Stern, running forward with enthusiasm. The "deer fever" was on him, as strong as in his old days in the Hudson Bay country. Hot was the pleasure of the kill when that meant food. As he ran he jerked his knife from the skin sheath the girl had made for him.

Thus they had fresh venison to their heart's content—venison broiled over white-hot coals in the fireplace, juicy and savory-sweet beyond all telling.

A good deal of the meat they smoked and salted down for future use. Stern undertook to tan the hide with strips of hemlock bark laid in a water pit dug near the spring. He added also some oak-bark, nut-galls and a good quantity of young sumac shoots.

"I guess *that* ought to hit the mark if anything will," remarked he, as he immersed the skin and weighted it down with rocks.

"It's like the old 'shotgun' prescriptions of our extinct doctors—a little of everything, bound to do the trick, one way or another."

The great variety of labors now imposed upon him began to try his ingenuity to the full. In spite of all his wealth of practical knowledge and his scientific skill, he was astounded at the huge demands of even the simplest human life.

The girl and he now faced these, without the social coöperation which they had formerly taken entirely for granted, and the change of conditions had begun to alter Stern's concepts of almost everything.

He was already beginning to realize how true the old saying was: "One man is no man!" and how the world had *been* the world merely because of the interrelations, the interdependencies of human beings in vast numbers.

He was commencing to get a glimpse of the vanished social problems that had enmeshed civilization, in their true light, now that all he confronted and had to struggle with was the unintelligent and overbearing dominance of nature.

All this was of huge value to the engineer. And the strong individualism (essentially anarchistic) on which he had prided himself a thousand years ago, was now beginning to receive some mortal blows, even during these first days of the new, solitary, unsocialized life.

But neither he nor the girl had very much time for introspective thought. Each moment brought its immediate task, and every day seemed busier than the last had been.

At meals, however, or at evening, as they sat together by the light of their lamp in the now homelike offices, Stern and Beatrice found pleasure in a little random speculation. Often they discussed the catastrophe and their own escape.

Stern brought to mind some of Professor Raoul Pictet's experiments with animals, in which the Frenchman had suspended animation for long periods by sudden freezing. This method seemed to answer, in a way, the girl's earlier questions as to how they had escaped death in the many long winters since they had gone to sleep.

Again, they tried to imagine the scenes just following the catastrophe, the horror of that long-past day, and the slow, irrevocable decay of all the monuments of the human race.

Often they talked till past midnight, by the glow of their stone fireplace, and many were the aspects of the case that they developed. These hours seemed to Stern the happiest of his life.

For the *rapprochement* between this beautiful woman and himself at such times became very close and fascinatingly intimate, and Stern felt, little by little, that the love which now was growing deep within his heart for her was not without its answer in her own.

But for the present the man restrained himself and spoke no overt word. For that, he understood, would immediately have put all things on a different basis—and there was urgent work still waiting to be done.

"There's no doubt in my mind," said he one day as they sat talking, "that you and I are absolutely the last human beings—civilized I mean—left alive anywhere in the world.

"If anybody else had been spared, whether in Chicago or San Francisco, in London, Paris or Hong-Kong, they'd have made some determined effort before now to get in touch with New York. This, the prime center of the financial and industrial world, would have been their first objective point."

"But suppose," asked she, "there *were* others, just a few here or there, and they'd only recently waked up, like ourselves. Could they have succeeded in making themselves known to us so soon?"

He shook a dubious head.

"There may be some one else, somewhere," he answered slowly, "but there's nobody else in this part of the world, anyhow. Nobody in this particular Eden but just you and me. To all intents and purposes I'm Adam. And you—well, you're Eve! But the tree? We haven't found that—yet."

She gave him a quick, startled glance, then let her head fall, so that he could not see her eyes. But up over her neck, her cheek and even to her temples, where the lustrous masses of hair fell away, he saw a tide of color mount.

And for a little space the man forgot to smoke. At her he gazed, a strange gleam in his eyes.

And no word passed between them for a while. But their thoughts—?

CHAPTER XIII

THE GREAT EXPERIMENT

THE idea that there might possibly be others of their kind in far-distant parts of the earth worked strongly on the mind of the girl. Next day she broached the subject again to her companion.

"Suppose," theorized she, "there might be a few score of others, maybe a few hundred, scattered here and there? They might awaken one by one, only to die, if less favorably situated than we happen to be. Perhaps thousands may have slept, like us, only to wake up to starvation!"

"There's no telling, of course," he answered seriously. "Undoubtedly that may be very possible. Some may have escaped the great death, on high altitudes—on the Eiffel Tower, for instance, or on certain mountains or lofty plateaus. The most we can do for the moment is just to guess at probabilities. And—"

"But if there *are* people elsewhere," she interrupted eagerly, her eyes glowing with hope, "isn't there any way to get in touch with them? Why should we expect them to seek us out? Why don't *we* hunt? Suppose only one or two in each country should have survived; if we could get them all together again in a single colony—don't you see?"

"You mean the different languages and arts and all the rest might still be preserved? The colony might grow and flourish, and mankind again take possession of the earth and conquer it, in a few decades? Yes, of course. But even though there shouldn't be anybody else, there's no cause for despair. Of that, however, we won't speak now."

"But why don't we try to find out about it?" she persisted. "If there were only the remotest chance—"

"By Jove, I *will* try it!" exclaimed the engineer, fired with a new thought, a fresh ambition. "How? I don't know just yet, but I'll see. There'll be a way, right enough, if I can only think it out!"

That afternoon he made his way down Broadway, past the copper-shop, to the remains of the telegraph office opposite the Flatiron.

Into it he penetrated with some difficulty. A mournful sight it was, this one-time busy ganglion of the nation's nerve-system. Benches and counters were quite gone, instruments corroded past recognition, everything in hideous disorder.

But in a rear room Stern found a large quantity of copper wire. The wooden drums on which it had been wound were gone; the insulation had vanished, but the coils of wire still remained.

"Fine!" said the explorer, gathering together several coils. "Now when I get this over to the Metropolitan, I think the first step toward success will have been taken."

By nightfall he had accumulated enough wire for his tentative experiments. Next day he and the girl explored the remains of the old wireless station on the roof of the building, overlooking Madison Avenue.

They reached the roof by climbing out of a window on the east side of the tower and descending a fifteen-foot ladder that Stern had built for the purpose out of rough branches.

"You see it's fairly intact as yet," remarked the engineer, gesturing at the broad expanse. "Only, falling stones have made holes here and there. See how they yawn down into the rooms below! Well, come on, follow me. I'll tap with the ax, and if the roof holds me you'll be safe."

Thus, after a little while, they found a secure path to the little station.

This diminutive building, fortunately constructed of concrete, still stood almost unharmed. Into it they penetrated through the crumbling door. The winds of heaven had centuries ago swept away all trace of the ashes of the operator.

But there still stood the apparatus, rusted and sagging and disordered, yet to Stern's practised eye showing signs of promise. An hour's careful overhauling convinced the engineer that something might yet be accomplished.

And thus they set to work in earnest.

First, with the girl's help, he strung his copper-wire antennæ from the tiled platform of the tower to the roof of the wireless station. Rough work this was, but answering the purpose as well as though of the utmost finish.

He connected up the repaired apparatus with these antennæ, and made sure all was well. Then he dropped the wires over the side of the building to connect with one of the dynamos in the sub-basement.

All this took two and a half days of severe labor, in intervals of food-getting, cooking and household tasks. At last, when it was done—

"Now for some power!" exclaimed the engineer. And with his lamp he went down to inspect the dynamos again and to assure himself that his belief was correct, his faith that one or two of them could be put into running order.

Three of the machines gave little promise, for water had dripped in on them and they were rusted beyond any apparent rehabilitation. The fourth, standing nearest Twenty-Third Street, had by some freak of chance been protected by a canvas cover.

This cover was now only a mass of rotten rags, but it had at least safeguarded the machine for so long that no very serious deterioration had set in.

Stern worked the better part of a week with such tools as he could find or make—he had to forge a wrench for the largest nuts—"taking down" the dynamo, oiling, filing, polishing and repairing it, part by part.

The commutator was in bad shape and the brushes terribly corroded. But he tinkered and patched, hammered and heated and filed away, and at last putting the machine together again with terrible exertion, decided that it would run.

"Steam now!" was his next watchword, when he had wired the dynamo to connect with the station on the roof. And this was on the eighth day since he had begun his labor.

An examination of the boiler-room, which he reached by moving a ton of fallen stone-work from the doorway into the dynamo-room, encouraged him still further. As he penetrated into this place, feeble-shining lamp held on high, eyes eager to behold the prospect, he knew that success was not far away.

Down in these depths, almost as in the interior of the great Pyramid of Gizeh—though the place smelled dank and close and stifling—time seemed to have lost much of its destructive power. He chose one boiler that looked sound, and began looking for coal.

Of this he found a plentiful supply, well-preserved, in the bunkers. All one afternoon he labored, wheeling it in a steel barrow and dumping it in front of the furnace.

Where the smoke-stack led to and what condition it was in he knew not. He could not tell where the gases of combustion would escape to; but this he decided to leave to chance.

He grimaced at sight of the rusted flues and the steam-pipes connecting with the dynamo-room—pipes now denuded of their asbestos packing and leaky at several joints.

A strange, gnome-like picture he presented as he poked and pried in those dim regions, by the dim rays of the lamp. Spiders, roaches and a great gray rat or two were his only companions—those, and hope.

"I don't know but I'm a fool to try and carry this thing out," said he, dubiously surveying the pipe. "I'm liable to start something here that I can't stop. Water-glasses leaky, gauges plugged up, safety-valve rusted into its seat—the devil!"

But still he kept on. Something drove him inexorably forward. For he was an engineer—and an American.

His next task was to fill the boiler. This he had to do by bringing water, two pails at a time from the spring. It took him three days.

Thus, after eleven days of heart-breaking lonely toil in that grimy dungeon, hampered for lack of tools, working with rotten materials, naked and sweaty, grimed, spent, profane, exhausted, everything was ready for the experiment—the strangest, surely, in the annals of the human race.

He lighted up the furnace with dry wood, then stoked it full of coal. After an hour and a half his heart thrilled with mingled fear and exultation at sight of the steam, first white, then blue and thin, that began to hiss from the leaks in the long pipe.

"No way to estimate pressure, or anything" remarked he. "It's bull luck whether I go to hell or not!" And he stood back from the blinding glare of the furnace. With his naked arm he wiped the sweat from his streaming forehead.

"Bull luck!" repeated he. "But by the Almighty, I'll send that Morse, or bust!"

CHAPTER XIV

The Moving Lights

Panting with exhaustion and excitement, Stern made his way back to the engine-room. It was a strangely critical moment when he seized the corroded throttle-wheel to start the dynamo. The wheel stuck, and would not budge.

Stern, with a curse of sheer exasperation, snatched up his long spanner, shoved it through the spokes, and wrenched.

Groaning, the wheel gave way. It turned. The engineer hauled again.

"Go on!" shouted the man. "Start! Move!"

With a hissing plaint, as though rebellious against this awakening after its age-long sleep, the engine creaked into motion.

In spite of all Stern's oiling, every journal and bearing squealed in anguish. A rickety tremble possessed the engine as it gained speed. The dynamo began to hum with wild, strange protests of racked metal. The ancient "drive" of tarred hemp strained and quivered, but held.

And like the one-hoss shay about to collapse, the whole fabric of the resuscitated plant, leaking at a score of joints, creaking, whistling, shaking, voicing a hundred agonized mechanic woes, revived in a grotesque, absurd and shocking imitation of its one-time beauty and power.

At sight of this ghastly resurrection, the engineer (whose whole life had been passed in the love and service of machinery) felt a strange and sad emotion.

He sat down, exhausted, on the floor. In his hand the lamp trembled. Yet, all covered with sweat and dirt and rust as he was, this moment of triumph was one of the sweetest he had ever known.

He realized that this was now no time for inaction. Much yet remained to be done. So up he got again, and set to work.

First he made sure the dynamo was running with no serious defect and that his wiring had been made properly. Then he heaped the furnace full of coal, and closed the door, leaving only enough draft to insure a fairly steady heat for an hour or so.

This done, he toiled back up to where Beatrice was eagerly awaiting him in the little wireless station on the roof.

In he staggered, all but spent. Panting for breath, wild-eyed, his coal-blackened arms stretching out from the whiteness of the bear-skin, he made a singular picture.

"It's going!" he exclaimed. "I've got current—it's good for a while, anyhow. Now—now for the test!"

For a moment he leaned heavily against the concrete bench to which the apparatus was clamped. Already the day had drawn close to its end. The glow of evening had begun to fade a trifle, along the distant skyline; and beyond the Palisades a dull purple pall was settling down.

By the dim light that filtered through the doorway, Beatrice looked at his deep-lined, bearded face, now reeking with sweat and grimed with dust and coal. An ugly face—but not to her. For through that mask she read the dominance, the driving force, the courage of this versatile, unconquerable man.

"Well," suddenly laughed Stern, with a strange accent in his voice, "well then, here goes for the operator in the Eiffel Tower, eh?"

Again he glanced keenly, in the failing light, at the apparatus there before him.

"She'll do, I guess," judged he, slipping on the rusted head-receiver. He laid his hand upon the key and tried a few tentative dots and dashes.

Breathless, the girl watched, daring no longer to question him. In the dielectric, the green sparks and spurts of living flame began to crackle and to hiss like living spirits of an unknown power.

Stern, feeling again harnessed to his touch the life-force of the world that once had been, exulted with a wild emotion. Yet, science-worshiper that he was, something of reverent awe tinged the keen triumph. A strange gleam dwelt within his eyes; and through his lips the breath came quick as he flung his very being into this supreme experiment.

He reached for the ondometer. Carefully, slowly, he "tuned up" the wavelengths; up, up to five thousand metres, then back again; he ran the whole gamut of the wireless scale.

Out, ever out into the thickening gloom, across the void and vacancy of the dead world, he flung his lightnings in a wild appeal. His face grew hard and eager.

"Anything? Any answer?" asked Beatrice, laying a hand upon his shoulder—a hand that trembled.

He shook his head in negation. Again he switched the roaring current on; again he hurled out into ether his cry of warning and distress, of hope, of invitation—the last lone call of man to man—of the last New Yorker to any other human being who, by the merest chance, might possibly hear him in the wreck of other cities, other lands. "S. O. S.!" crackled the green flame. "S. O. S. S. O. S.!—"

Thus came night, fully, as they waited, as they called and listened; as, together there in that tiny structure on the roof of the tremendous ruin, they swept the heavens and the earth with their wild call—in vain.

Half an hour passed and still the engineer, grim as death, whirled the chained lightnings out and away.

"Nothing yet?" cried Beatrice at last, unable to keep silence any longer. "Are you quite sure you can't—"

The question was not finished.

For suddenly, far down below them, as though buried in the entrails of the earth, shuddered a stifled, booming roar.

Through every rotten beam and fiber the vast wreck of the building vibrated. Some wall or other, somewhere, crumbled and went crashing down with a long, deep droning thunder that ended in a sliding diminuendo of noise.

"The boiler!" shouted Stern.

Off he flung the head-piece. He leaped up; he seized the girl.

Out of the place he dragged her. She screamed as a huge weight from high aloft on the tower smashed bellowing through the roof, and with a shower of stones ripped its way down through the rubbish of the floors below, as easily as a bullet would pierce a newspaper.

The crash sent them recoiling. The whole roof shook and trembled like honey-combed ice in a spring thaw.

Down below, something rumbled, jarred, and came to rest.

Both of them expected nothing but that the entire structure would collapse like a card-house and shatter down in ruins that would be their death.

But though it swayed and quivered, as in the grasp of an earthquake, it held.

Stern circled Beatrice with his arm.

"Courage, now! Steady, now *steady!*" cried he.

The grinding, the booming of down-hurled stones and walls died away; the echoes ceased. A wind-whipped cloud of steam and smoke burst up, fanlike, beyond the edge of the roof. It bellied away, dim in the night, upon the stiff northerly breeze.

"Fire?" ventured the girl.

"No! Nothing to burn. But come, come; let's get out o' this anyhow. There's nothing doing, any more. All through! Too much risk staying up here, now."

Silent and dejected, they made their cautious way over the shaken roof. They walked with the greatest circumspection, to avoid falling through some new hole or freshly opened crevasse.

To Stern, especially, this accident was bitter. After nearly a fortnight's exhausting toil, the miserable fiasco was maddening.

"Look!" suddenly exclaimed the engineer, pointing. A vast, gaping cañon of blackness opened at their very feet—a yawning gash forty feet long and ten or twelve broad, with roughly jagged edges, leading down into unfathomed depths below.

Stern gazed at it, puzzled, a moment, then peered up into the darkness above.

"H-m!" said he. "One of the half-ton hands of the big clock up there has just taken a drop, that's all. One drop too much, I call it. Now if we—or our rooms—had just happened to be underneath? Some excitement, eh?"

They circled the opening and approached the tower wall. Stern picked up the rough ladder, which had been shaken down from its place, and once more set it to the window through which they were to enter.

But even as Beatrice put her foot on the first rung, she started with a cry. Stern felt the grip of her trembling hand on his arm.

"What is it?" exclaimed he.

"Look! *Look!*"

Immobile with astonishment and fear, she stood pointing out and away, to westward, toward the Hudson.

Stern's eyes followed her hand.

He tried to cry out, but only stammered some broken, unintelligible thing.

There, very far away and very small, yet clearly visible in swarms upon the inky-black expanse of waters, a hundred, a thousand little points of light were moving.

CHAPTER XV

Portents of War

Stern and Beatrice stood there a few seconds at the foot of the ladder, speechless, utterly at a loss for any words to voice the turmoil of confused thoughts awakened by this inexplicable apparition.

But all at once the girl, with a wordless cry, sank on her knees beside the vast looming bulk of the tower. She covered her face with both hands, and through her fingers the tears of joy began to flow.

"Saved—oh, we're saved!" cried she. "There *are* people—and they're coming for us!"

Stern glanced down at her, an inscrutable expression on his face, which had grown hard and set and ugly. His lips moved, as though he were saying something to himself; but no sound escaped them.

Then, quite suddenly, he laughed a mirthless laugh. To him vividly flashed back the memory of the flint spear-head and the gnawed leg-bone, cracked open so the marrow could be sucked out, all gashed with savage tooth-marks.

A certain creepy sensation began to develop along his spine. He felt a prickling on the nape of his neck, as the hair stirred there. Instinctively he reached for his revolver.

"So, then," he sneered at himself, "we're up against it, after all? And all my calculations about the world being swept clear, were so much punk? Well, well, this *is* interesting! Oh, I see it coming, all right—good and plenty—and soon!"

But the girl interrupted his ugly thoughts as he stood there straining his eyes out into the dark.

"How splendid! How glorious!" cried she. "Only to think that we're going to see people again! Can you imagine it?"

"Hardly."

"Why, what's the matter? You—speak as though you weren't—*saved!*"

"I didn't mean to. It's—just surprise, I guess."

"Come! Let's signal them with a fire from the tower top. *I'll* help carry wood. Let's hurry down and run and meet them!"

Highly excited, the girl had got to her feet again, and now, clutched the engineer's arm in burning eagerness.

"Let's go! Go—at once! This minute!"

But he restrained her.

"You don't really think that would be quite prudent, do you?" asked he. "Not just yet?"

"Why not?"

"Why, can't you see? We—that is, there is no way to tell—"

"But they're coming to save us, can't you see? Somehow, somewhere, they must have caught that signal! And shall we wait, and perhaps let them lose us, after all?"

"Certainly not. But first we—why, we ought to make quite sure, you understand. Sure that they—they're really civilized, you know."

"But they *must* be, to have read the wireless!"

"Oh, you're counting on that, are you? Well, that's a big assumption. It won't do. No, we've got to go slow in this game. Got to wait. Wait, and see. Easy does it!"

He tried to speak boldly and with nonchalance, but the girl's keen ear detected at least a little of the emotion that was troubling him. She kept a moment's silence, while the quivering lights drew on and on, steadily, slowly, like a host of fireflies on the bosom of the night.

"Why don't you get the telescope, and see?" she asked, at length.

"No use. It isn't a night-glass. Couldn't see a thing."

"But anyhow, those lights mean *men*, don't they?"

"Naturally. But until we know what kind, we're better off right where we are. I'm willing to welcome the coming guest, all right, if he's peaceful. Otherwise, it's powder and ball, hot water, stones and things for him!"

The girl stared a moment at the engineer, while this new idea took root within her brain.

"You—you don't mean," she faltered at last, "that these may be—*savages?*"

He started at the word. "What makes you think that?" he parried, striving to spare her all needless alarm.

She pondered a moment, while the fire-dots, like a shoal of swimming stars, drew slowly nearer, nearer the Manhattan shore.

"Tell me, *are* they savages?"

"How do *I* know?"

"It's easy enough to see you've got an opinion about it. You *think* they're savages, don't you?"

"I think it's very possible."

"And if so—what then?"

"What then? Why, in case they aren't mighty nice and kind, there'll be a hot time in the old town, that's all. And somebody'll get hurt. It won't be *us!*"

Beatrice asked no more, for a minute or two, but the engineer felt her fingers tighten on his arm.

"I'm with you, till the end!" she whispered.

Another pregnant silence, while the nightwind stirred her hair and wafted the warm feminine perfume of her to his nostrils. Stern took a long, deep breath. A sort of dizziness crept over him, as from a glass of wine on an empty stomach. The Call of Woman strove to master him, but he repelled it. And, watching the creeping lights, he spoke; spoke to himself as much as to the girl; spoke, lest he think too much.

"There's a chance, a mere possibility," said he, "that those boats, canoes, coracles or whatever they may be, belong to white people, far descendants of the few supposititious survivors of the cataclysm. There's some slight chance that these people may be civilized, or partly so.

"Why they're coming across the Hudson, at this time o' night, with what object and to what place, we can't even guess. All we can do is wait, and watch and—be ready for anything."

"For anything!" she echoed. "You've seen me shoot! You know!"

He took her hand, and pressed it. And silence fell again, as the long vigil started, there in the shadow of the tower, on the roof.

For some quarter of an hour, neither spoke. Then at last, said Stern:

"See, now! The lights seem to be winking out. The canoes must have come close in toward the shore of the island. They're being masked behind the trees. The people—whoever they are—will be landing directly now!"

"And then?"

"Wait and see!"

They resigned themselves to patience. The girl's breath came quickly, as she watched. Even the engineer felt his heart throb with accelerated haste.

Now, far in the east, dim over the flat and dreary ruins of Long Island, the sky began to silver, through a thin veil of cirrus cloud. A pallid moon was rising. Far below, a breeze stirred the tree-fronds in Madison Forest. A bat staggered drunkenly about the tower, then reeled away into the gloom; and, high aloft, an owl uttered its melancholy plaint.

Beatrice shuddered.

"They'll be here pretty soon!" whispered she. "Hadn't we better go down, and get our guns? In case—"

"Time enough," he answered. "Wait a while."

"Hark! What's that?" she exclaimed suddenly, holding her breath.

Off to northward, dull, muffled, all but inaudible, they both heard a rhythmic pulsing, strangely barbaric.

"Heavens!" ejaculated Stern. "War-drums! Tom-toms, as I live!"

CHAPTER XVI

THE GATHERING OF THE HORDES

"TOM-TOMS? So they *are* savages?" exclaimed the girl, taking a quick breath. "But—what *then?*"

"Don't just know, yet. It's a fact, though; they're certainly savages. Two tribes, one with torches, one with drums. Two different kinds, I guess. And they're coming in here to parley or fight or something. Regular powwow on hand. Trouble ahead, whichever side wins!"

"For us?"

"That depends. Maybe we'll be able to lie hidden, here, till this thing blows over, whatever it may be. If not, and if they cut off our water-supply, well—"

He ended with a kind of growl. The sound gave Beatrice a strange sensation. She kept a moment's silence, then remarked:

"They're up around Central Park now, the drums are, don't you think so? How far do you make that?"

"Close on to two miles. Come, let's be moving."

In silence they climbed the shaky ladder, reached the tower stairs and descended the many stories to their dwelling.

Here, the first thing Stern did was to strike a light, which he masked in a corner, behind a skin stretched like a screen from one wall to the other. By this illumination, very dim yet adequate, he minutely examined all their firearms.

He loaded every one to capacity and made sure all were in working order. Then he satisfied himself that the supply of cartridges was ample. These he laid carefully along by the windows overlooking Madison Forest, by the door leading into the suite of offices, and by the stair-head that gave access to the fifth floor.

Then he blew out the light again.

"Two revolvers, one shotgun, and one rifle, all told," said he. "All magazine arms. I guess that'll hold them for a while, if it comes down to brass tacks! How's your nerve, Beatrice?"

"Never better!" she whispered, from the dark. He saw the dim white blur that indicated her face, and it was very dear to him, all of a sudden—dearer, far, than he had ever realized.

"Good little girl!" he exclaimed, giving her the rifle. A moment his hand pressed hers. Then with a quick intake of the breath, he strode over to the window and once more listened. She followed.

"Much nearer, now!" judged he. "Hear *that*, will you?"

Again they listened.

Louder now the drums sounded, dull, ominous, pulsating like the hammering of a fever-pulse inside a sick man's skull. A dull, confused hum, a noise as of a swarming mass of bees, drifted down-wind.

"Maybe they'll pass by?" whispered Beatrice.

"It's Madison Forest they're aiming at!" returned the engineer. "See there!"

He pointed to westward.

There, far off along the forest-lane of Fourteenth Street, a sudden gleam of light flashed out among the trees, vanished, reappeared, was joined by two, ten, a hundred others. And now the whole approach to Madison Forest, by several streets, began to sparkle with these *feux-follets,* weaving and flickering unsteadily toward the square.

Here, there, everywhere through the dense masses of foliage, the watchers could already see a dim and moving mass, fitfully illuminated by torches that now burned steady, now flared into red and smoky tourbillons of flame in the night-wind.

"Like monster glow-worms, crawling among the trees!" the girl exclaimed. "We *could* mow them down, from here, already! God grant we sha'n't have to fight!"

"S-h-h-h! Wait and see what's up!"

Now, from the other horde, coming from the north, sounds of warlike preparation were growing ever louder.

With quicker beats the insistent tom-toms throbbed their rhythmic melancholy rune, hollow and dissonant. Then all at once the drums ceased; and through the night air drifted a minor chant; a wail, that rose, fell, died, and came again, lagging as many strange voices joined it.

And from the square, below, a shrill, high-pitched, half-animal cry responded. Creeping shudders chilled the flesh along the engineer's backbone.

"What I need, now," thought he, "is about a hundred pounds of high-grade dynamite, or a gallon of nitroglycerin. Better still, a dozen capsules of my own invention, my 'Pulverite!'

"I guess *that* would settle things mighty quick. It would be the joker in this game, all right! Well, why not make some? With what chemicals I've got left, couldn't I work up a half-pint? Bottled in glass flasks, I guess it would turn the trick on 'em!"

"Why, they look black!" suddenly interrupted the girl. "See there—and there?"

She pointed toward the spring. Stern saw moving shadows in the dark. Then, through an opening, he got a blurred impression of a hand, holding a torch. He saw a body, half-human.

The glimpse vanished, but he had seen enough.

"Black—yes, blue-black! They seem so, anyhow. And—why, did you see the *size* of them? No bigger than apes! Good Heaven!"

Involuntarily he shuddered. For now, like a dream-horde of hideous creatures seen in a nightmare, the torch-bearers had spread all through the forest at the base of the Metropolitan.

Away from the building out across by the spring and even to Fifth Avenue the mob extended, here thick, there thin, without order or coherence—a shifting, murmuring, formless, seemingly planless congeries of dull brutality.

Here or there, where the swaying of the trees parted the branches a little, the wavering lights brought some fragment of the mass to view.

No white thing showed anywhere. All was dark and vague. Indistinctly, waveringly as in a vision, dusky heads could be made out. There showed a naked arm, greasily shining for a second in the ruddy glow which now diffused itself through the whole wood. Here the watchers saw a glistening back; again, an out-thrust leg, small and crooked, apelike and repulsive.

And once again the engineer got a glimpse of a misshapen hand, a long, lean, hideous hand that clutched a spear. But, hardly seen, it vanished into obscurity once more.

"Seems as though malformed human members, black and bestial, had been flung at random into a ghastly kaleidoscope, turned by a madman!" whispered Stern. The girl answering nothing, peered out in fascinated horror.

Up, up to the watchers rose a steady droning hum; and from the northward, ever louder, ever clearer, came now the war-song of the attacking party. The drums began again, suddenly. A high-pitched, screaming laugh echoed and died among the woods beyond the ruins of Twenty-eighth street.

Still in through the western approaches of the square, more and more lights kept straggling. Thicker and still more thick grew the press below. Now the torch-glow was strong enough to cast its lurid reflections on the vacant-staring wrecks of windows and of walls, gaping like the shattered skulls of a civilization which was no more. To the nostrils of the man and woman upfloated an acrid, pitchy smell. And birds, dislodged from sleep, began to zigzag about, aimlessly, with frightened cries. One even dashed against the building, close at hand; and fell, a fluttering, broken thing, to earth.

Stern, with a word of hot anger, fingered his revolver. But Beatrice laid her hand upon his arm.

"Not yet!" begged she.

He glanced down at her, where she stood beside him at the empty embrasure of the window. The dim light from the vast and empty overarch of sky, powdered with a wonder of stars, showed him the vague outline of her face. Wistful and pale she was, yet very brave. Through Stern welled a sudden tenderness.

He put his arm around her, and for a moment her head lay on his breast. But only a moment.

For, all at once, a snarling cry rang through the wood; and, with a northward surge of the torch-bearers, a confused tumult of shrieks, howls, simian chatterings and dull blows, the battle joined between those two vague, strange forces down below in the black forest.

CHAPTER XVII

STERN'S RESOLVE

How long it lasted, what its meaning, its details, the watchers could not tell. Impossible, from that height and in that gloom, broken only by an occasional pale gleam of moonlight through the drifting cloud-rack, to judge the fortunes of this primitive war.

They knew not the point at issue nor yet the tide of victory or loss. Only they knew that back and forth the torches flared, the war-drums boomed and rattled, the yelling, slaughtering, demoniac hordes surged in a swirl of bestial murder-lust.

And so time passed, and fewer grew the drums, yet the torches flared on; and, as the first gray dawn went fingering up the sky there came a break, a flight, a merciless pursuit.

Dimly the man and woman, up aloft, saw things that ran and shrieked and were cut down—saw things, there in the forest, that died even as they killed, and mingled the howl of triumph with the bubbling gasp of dissolution.

"Ugh! A beast war!" shuddered the engineer, at length, drawing Beatrice away from the window. "Come, it's getting light, again. It's too clear, now—come away!"

She yielded, waking as it were from the horrid fascination that had held her spell-bound. Down she sat on her bed of furs, covered her eyes with her hands, and for a while remained quite motionless. Stern watched her. And again his hand sought the revolver-butt.

"I ought to have waded into that bunch, long ago," thought he. "We both ought to have. What it's all about, who could tell? But it's an outrage against the night itself, against the world, even dead though it be. If it hadn't been for wasting good ammunition for nothing—!"

A curious, guttural whine, down there in the forest, attracted his attention. Over to the window he strode, and once again peered down.

A change had come upon the scene, a sudden, radical change. No more the sounds of combat rose; but now a dull, conclamant murmur as of victory and preparation for some ghastly rite.

Already in the center of the wood, hard by the spring, a little fire had been lighted. Even as Stern looked, dim, moving figures heaped on wood. The engineer saw whirling droves of sparks spiral upward; he saw dense smoke, followed by a larger flame.

And, grouped around this, already some hundreds of the now paling torches cast their livid glare.

Off to one side he could just distinguish what seemed to be a group engaged in some activity—but what this might be, he could not determine. Yet, all at once a scream of pain burst out, therefrom; and then a gasping cry that ended quickly and did not come again.

Another shriek, and still a third; and now into the leaping flames some dark, misshapen things were flung, and a great shout arose.

Then rose, also, a shrill, singsong whine; and suddenly drums roared, now with a different cadence.

"Hark!" said the engineer. "The torchmen must have exterminated the other bunch, and got possession of the drums. They're using 'em, themselves—and badly!"

By the firelight vague shapes came and went, their shadows grotesquely flung against the leafy screens. The figures quickened their paces and their gestures; then suddenly, with cries, flung themselves into wild activity. And all about the fire, Stern saw a wheeling, circling, eddying mob of black and frightful shapes.

"The swine!" he breathed. "Wait—wait till I make a pint or two of Pulverite!"

Even as he spoke, the concourse grew quiet with expectancy. A silence fell upon the forest. Something was being led forward toward the fire—something, for which the others all made way.

The wind freshened. With it, increased the volume of smoke. Another frightened bird, cheeping forlornly, fluttered above the tree-tops.

Then rose a cry, a shriek long-drawn and ghastly, that climbed till it broke in a bubbling, choking gasp.

Came a sharp clicking sound, a quick scuffle, a grunt; then silence once more.

And all at once the drums crashed; and the dance began again, madder, more obscenely hideous than ever.

"Voodoo!" gulped Stern. "Obeah-work! And—and the quicker I get my Pulverite to working, the better!"

Undecided no longer, determined now on a course of definite action without further delay, the engineer turned back into the room. Upon his forehead stood a cold and prickling sweat, of horror and disgust. But to his lips he forced a smile, as, in the half light of the red and windy dawn, he drew close to Beatrice.

Then all at once, to his unspeakable relief, he saw the girl was sleeping.

Utterly worn out, exhausted and spent with the long strain, the terrible fatigues of the past thirty-six hours, she had lain down and had dropped off to sleep. There she lay at full length. Very beautiful she looked, half seen in the morning gloom. One arm crossed her full bosom; the other pillowed her cheek. And, bending close, Stern watched her a long minute.

With strange emotion he heard her even breathing; he caught the perfume of her warm, ripe womanhood. Never had she seemed to him so perfect, so infinitely to be loved, to be desired.

And at thought of that beast-horde in the wood below, at realization of what *might* be, if they two should chance to be discovered and made captive, his face went hard as iron. An ugly, savage look possessed him, and he clenched both fists.

For a brief second he stooped still closer; he laid his lips soundlessly, gently upon her hair. And when again he stood up, the look in his eyes boded scant good to anything that might threaten the sleeping girl.

"So, now to work!" said he.

Into his own room he stepped quietly, his room where he had collected his various implements and chemicals. First of all he set out, on the floor, a two-quart copper tea-kettle; and beside this, choosing carefully, he ranged the necessary ingredients for a "making" of his secret explosive.

"Now, the wash-out water," said he, taking another larger dish.

Over to the water-pail he walked. Then he stopped, suddenly, frowning a black and puzzled frown.

"What?" he exclaimed. "But—there isn't a pint left, all together! H-m! Now then, here *is* a situation."

Hastily he recalled how the great labors of the previous day, the wireless experiments and all, had prevented him from going out to the spring to replenish his supply. Now, though he bitterly cursed himself for his neglect, that did no good. The fact remained, there was no water.

"Scant pint, maybe!" said he. "And I've got to have a gallon, at the very least. To say nothing of drink for two people! *And* the horde, there, camping round the spring. Je-*ru*-salem!"

Softly he whistled to himself; then, trying to solve this vital, unexpected problem, fell to pacing the floor.

Day, slowly looming through the window, showed his features set and hard. Close at hand, the breath of morning winds stirred the treetops. But of the usual busy twitter and gossip of birds among the branches, now there was none. For down below there, in the forest, the ghoulish vampire revels still held sway.

Stern, at a loss, swore hotly under his breath.

Then suddenly he found himself; he came to a decision. "*I'm* going down," he vowed. "I'm going down, to *see!*"

CHAPTER XVIII

THE SUPREME QUESTION

Now that his course lay clear before him, the man felt an instant and a huge relief. Whatever the risks, the dangers, this adventuring was better than a mere inaction, besieged there in the tower by that ugly, misshapen horde.

First of all, as he had done on the first morning of the awakening, when he had left the girl asleep, he wrote a brief communication to forestall any possible alarm on her part. This, scrawled with charcoal on a piece of smooth hide, ran:

"Have had to go down to get water and lay of the land. Absolutely neces-
sary. Don't be afraid. Am between you and them, well armed. Will leave you
both the rifle and the shotgun. Stay here, and have no fear. Will come back as
soon as possible.   ALLAN."

He laid this primitive letter where, on awakening, she could not fail to
see it. Then, making sure again that all the arms were fully charged, he put
the rifle and the gun close beside his "note," and saw to it that his revolvers
lay loosely and conveniently in the holsters she had made for him.

One more reconnaissance he made at the front window. This done, he
took the water-pail and set off quietly down the stairs. His feet were noiseless as a cat's.

At every landing he stopped, listening intently. Down, ever down, story
by story he crept.

To his chagrin—though he had half expected worse—he found that the
boiler-explosion of the previous night had really made the way impassible,
from the third story downward. These lowest flights of steps had been so
badly broken, that now they gave no access to the arcade.

All that remained of them was a jumbled mass of wreckage, below the
gaping hole in the third-floor hallway.

"That means," said Stern to himself, "I've got to find another way down.
And quick, too!"

He set about the task with a will. Exploration of several lateral corridors resulted in nothing; but at last good fortune led him to stairs that had
remained comparatively uninjured. And down these he stole, pail in one
hand, revolver ready in the other, listening, creeping, every sense alert.

He found himself, at length, in the shattered and dismembered wreckage of the once-famed "Marble Court." Fallen now were the carved and
gilded pillars; gone, save here or there for a fragment, the wondrous balustrade. One of the huge newel-posts at the bottom lay on the cracked floor
of marble squares; the other, its metal chandelier still clinging to it, lolled
drunkenly askew.

But Stern had neither time nor inclination to observe these woful changes. Instead, he pressed still forward, and, after a certain time of effort, found
himself in the arcade once more.

Here the effects of the explosion were very marked. A ghastly hole
opened into the subcellar below; masses of fallen ceiling blocked the way;

and every pane of glass in the shop-fronts had shattered down. Smoke had blackened everything. Ashes and dirt, *ad infinitum,* completed the dreary picture, seen there by the still insufficient light of morning.

But Stern cared nothing for all this. It even cheered him a trifle.

"In case of a mix-up," thought he, "there couldn't be a better place for ambushing these infernal cannibals—for mowing them down, whole-sale—for sending them sky-hooting to Tophet, in bunches!"

And with a grim smile, he worked his way cautiously toward Madison Forest and the pine-tree gate.

As he drew near, his care redoubled. His grip on the revolver-butt tightened.

"They mustn't see me—*first!*" said he to himself.

Into a littered wreck of an office at the right of the exit he silently crept. Here, he knew, the outer wall of the building was deeply fissured. He hoped he might be able to find some peep-hole where, unseen, he could peer out on the bestial mob.

He set his water-pail down, and on hands and knees, hardly breathing, taking infinite pains not to stir the loose rubbish on the floor, not even to crunch the fallen lumps of mortar, forward he crawled.

Yes, there *was* a glimmer of light through the crack in the wall. Stern silently wormed in between a corroded steel I-beam and a cracked granite block, about the edges of which the small green tendrils of a vine had laid their hold.

This way, then that, he craned his neck. And all at once, with a sharp breath, he grew rigid in horrified, eager attention.

"Great Lord!" he whispered. "*What?*"

Though, from the upper stories and by torch-light, he had already formed some notion of the Horde, he had in no wise been prepared for what he now was actually beholding through a screen of sumacs that grew along the wall outside.

"Why—why, this can't be real!" thought he. "It—must be some damned hallucination. Eh? Am I awake? What the deuce!"

Paling a little, his eyes staring, mouth agape, the engineer stayed there for a long minute unable to credit his own senses. For now he, he, the only white man living in the twenty-eighth century, was witnessing the strangest sight that ever a civilized being had looked upon in the whole history of the world.

No vision of DeQuincey, no drug-born dream of Poe could equal it for grisly fascination. Frankenstein, de Maupassant's "Horla," all the fantastic literary monsters of the past faded to tawdry, childish bogeys beside the actual observations of Stern, the engineer, the man of science and cold fact.

"Why—what *are* these?" he asked himself, shuddering despite himself at the mere sight of what lay outside there in the forest. "What? Men? Animals? Neither! God help me, what—*what are these things?*"

CHAPTER XIX

THE UNKNOWN RACE

An almost irresistible repugnance, a compelling aversion, more of the spirit than of the flesh, instantly seized the man at sight of even the few members of the Horde which lay within his view.

Though he had been expecting to see something disgusting, something grotesque and horrible, his mind was wholly unprepared for the real hideousness of these creatures, now seen by the ever-strengthening light of day.

And slowly, as he stared, the knowledge dawned on him that here was a monstrous problem to face, far greater and more urgent than he had foreseen; here were factors not yet understood; here, the product of forces till then not even dreamed of by his scientific mind.

"I—I certainly did expect to find a small race," thought he. "Small, and possibly misshapen, the descendants, maybe, of a few survivors of the cataclysm. But *this—!*"

And again, fascinated by the ghastly spectacle, he laid his eye to the chink in the wall, and looked.

A tenuous fog still drifted slowly among the forest trees, veiling the deeper recesses. Yet, near at hand, within the limited segment of vision which the engineer commanded, everything could be made out with reasonable distinctness.

Some of the Things (for so he mentally named them, knowing no better term) were squatting, lying or moving about, quite close at hand. The fire by the spring had now almost died down. It was evident that the revel had ceased, and that the Horde was settling down to rest—glutted, no doubt, with the raw and bleeding flesh of the conquered foe.

Stern could easily have poked his pistol muzzle through the crack in the wall and shot down many of them. For an instant the temptation lay strong upon him to get rid of at least a dozen or a score; but prudence restrained his hand.

"No use!" he told himself. "Nothing to be gained by that. But, once I get my proper chance at them—!"

And again, striving to observe them with the cool and calculating eye of science, he studied the shifting, confused picture out there before him.

Then he realized that the feature which, above all else, struck him as ghastly and unnatural, was the *color* of the Things.

"Not black, not even brown," said he. "I thought so, last night, but daylight corrects the impression. Not red, either, or copper-colored. *What* color, then? For Heaven's sake, what?"

He could hardly name it. Through the fog, it struck him as a dull slate-gray, almost a blue. He recalled that once he had seen a child's modeling-clay, much-used and very dirty, of the same shade, which certainly had no designation in the chromatic scale. Some of the Things were darker, some a trifle lighter—these, no doubt, the younger ones—but they all partook of this same characteristic tint. And the skin, moreover, looked dull and sickly, rather mottled and wholly repulsive, very like that of a Mexican dog.

Like that dog's hide, too, it was sparsely overgrown with whitish bristles. Here or there, on the bodies of some of the larger Things, bulbous warts had formed, somewhat like those on a toad's back; and on these warts the bristles clustered thickly. Stern saw the hair, on the neck of one of these creatures, crawl and rise like a jackal's, as a neighbor jostled him; and from the Thing's throat issued a clicking grunt of purely animal resentment.

"Merciful Heavens! What *are* they?" wondered Stern, again, utterly baffled for any explanation. "What *can* they be?"

Another, in the group close by, attracted his attention. It was lying on its side, asleep maybe, its back directly toward the engineer. Stern clearly saw the narrow shoulders and the thin, long arms, covered with that white bristling hair.

One sprawling, spatulate, clawlike hand lay on the forest moss. The twisted little apelike legs, disproportionately short, were curled up; the feet, prehensile and with a well-marked thumb on each, twitched a little now and then. The head, enormously too big for the body, to which it was joined by a thin neck, seemed to be scantily covered with a fine, curling down, of a dirty yellowish drab color.

"What a target!" thought the engineer. "At this distance, with my .38, I could drill it without half trying!"

All at once, another of the group sat up, shoved away a burned-out torch, and yawned with a noisy, doglike whine. Stern got a quick yet definite glimpse of the sharp canine teeth; he saw that the Thing's fleshless lips and retreating chin were caked with dried blood. The tongue he saw was long and lithe and apparently rasped.

Then the creature stood up, balancing on its absurd bandy legs, a spear in its hand—a flint-pointed spear of crude workmanship.

At full sight of the face, Stern shrank for a moment.

"I've known savages, as such," thought he. "I understand them. I know animals. They're animals, that's all. But *this* creature—merciful Heaven!"

And at the realization that it was neither beast nor man, the engineer's blood chilled within his veins.

Yet he forced himself still to look and to observe, unseen. There was practically no forehead at all. The nose was but a formless lump of cartilage, the ears large and pendulous and hairy. Under heavy brow-ridges, the dull, lackluster eyes blinked stupidly, bloodshot and cruel. As the mouth closed, Stern noted how the under incisors closed up over the upper lip, showing a gleam of dull yellowish ivory; a slaver dripped from the doglike corner of the mouth.

Stern shivered, and drew back.

He realized now that he was in the presence of an unknown semihuman type, different in all probability from any that had ever yet existed. It was less their bestiality that disgusted him, than their utter, hopeless, age-long degeneration from the man-standard.

What race had they descended from? He could not tell. He thought he could detect a trace of the Mongol in the region of the eye, in the cheek-bones and the general contour of what, by courtesy, might be called the face. There were indications, also, of the negroid type, still stronger. But the color—whence could *that* have come? And the general characteristics, were not these distinctly simian?

Again he looked. And now one of the pot-bellied little horrors, shambling and bulbous-kneed, was scratching its warty, blue hide with its black

claws as it trailed along through the forest. It looked up, grinning and jabbering; Stern saw the teeth that should have been molars. With repulsion
he noted that they were not flat-crowned, but sharp like a dog's. Through
the blue lips they clearly showed.

"Nothing herbivorous here," thought the scientist. "All flesh-food of—
who knows what sort!"

Quickly his mind ran over the outlines of the problem. He knew at
once that these Things were lower than any human race ever recorded,
far lower even that the famed Australian bushmen, who could not even
count as high as five. Yet, strange and more than strange, they had the use
of fire, of the tom-tom, of some sort of voodooism, of flint, of spears, and
of a rude sort of tanning—witness the loin-clouts of hide which they all
wore.

"Worse than any troglodyte!" he told himself. "Far lower than De Qua-
trefage's Neanderthal man, to judge from the cephalic index—worse than
that Java skull, the *pithecanthropus erectus,* itself! And I—am with my living eyes beholding them!"

A slight sound, there behind him in the room, set his heart flailing
madly.

His hand froze to the butt of the automatic as he drew back from the
cleft in the wall, and, staring, whirled about, ready to shoot on the second.

Then he started back. His jaw dropped, his eyes widened and limply fell
his arm. The pistol swung loosely at his side.

"*You?—*" he soundlessly breathed, "*You—here?*"

There at the door of the great empty room, magnificent in her tiger-skin,
the Krag gripped in her supple hand, stood Beatrice.

CHAPTER XX

The Curiosity of Eve

At him the girl peered eagerly, a second, as though to make quite sure he
was not hurt in any way, to satisfy herself that he was safe and sound.

Then with a little gasp of relief, she ran to him. Her sandled feet lightly
disturbed the rubbish on the floor; dust rose. Stern checked her with an
upraised hand.

"Back! Back! Go back, quick!" he formed the words of command on his trembling lips. The idea of this girl's close proximity to the beast-horde terrified him, for the moment. "Back! What on earth are you *here* for?"

"I—I woke up. I found you gone!" she whispered.

"Yes, but didn't you read my letter? *This* is no place for you!"

"I had to come! How could I stay up there, alone, when you—were—oh! maybe in danger—maybe in need of me?"

"Come!" he commanded, in his perturbation heedless of the look she gave him. He took her hand. "Come, we must get out of this! It's too—too near the—"

"The *what?* What *is* it, Allan? Tell me, have you seen them? Do you know?"

Even excited as the engineer was, he realized that for the first time the girl had called him by his Christian name. Not even the perilous situation could stifle the thrill that ran through him at the sound of it. But all he answered was:

"No, I don't know *what* to call them. Have no idea, as yet. I've seen them, yes; but what they are, Heaven knows—maybe!"

"Let me see, too!" she pleaded eagerly. "Is it through that crack in the wall? Is that the place to look?"

She moved toward it, her face blanched with excitement, eyes shining, lips parted. But Stern held her back. By the shoulder he took her.

"No, no, little girl!" he whispered. "You—you mustn't! Really must *not,* you know. It's too awful!"

Up at him she looked, knowing not what to think or say for a moment. Their eyes met, there in that wrecked and riven place, lighted by the dull, misty, morning gray. Then Stern spoke, for in her gaze abode questions unnumbered.

"I'd much rather you wouldn't look out at them, not just yet," said he, speaking very low, fearful lest the murmur of his voice might penetrate the wall. "Just what they are, frankly, there's no telling."

"You mean—?"

"Come back into the arcade, where we'll be safer from discovery, and we can talk. Not here. Come!"

She obeyed. Together they retreated to the inner court.

"You see," he commented, nodding at the empty water-pail. "I haven't been to the spring yet. Not very likely to get there for a while, either, unless—well, unless something pretty radical happens. I think these chaps have settled down for a good long stay in their happy hunting-ground, after the fight and the big feast. It's sort of a notion I've got, that this place, here, is some ancient, ceremonial ground of theirs."

"You mean, on account of the tower?"

He nodded.

"Yes, if they've got any religious ideas at all, or rather superstitions, such would very likely center round the most conspicuous object in their world. Probably the spring is a regular voodoo hangout. The row, last night, must have been a sort of periodic argument to see who was going to run the show."

"But," exclaimed the girl, in alarm—"but if they *do* stay a while, what about us? We simply must have water!"

"True enough. And, inasmuch as we can't drink brine and don't know where there's any other spring, it looks as though we'd either have to make up to these fellows or wade into them, doesn't it? But we'll get water safe enough, never fear. Just now, for the immediate present, I want to get my bearings a little, before going to work. *They* seem to be resting up, a bit, after their pleasant little *soirée*. Now, if they'd only all go to sleep, it'd be a walk-over!"

The girl looked at him, very seriously.

"You mustn't go out there alone, whatever happens!" she exclaimed. "I just won't let you! But tell me," she questioned again, "how much have you really found out about them—whatever they are?"

"Not much. They seem to be part of a nomadic race of half-human things, that's about all I can tell as yet. Perhaps all the white and yellow peoples perished utterly in the cataclysm, leaving only a few scattered blacks. You know blacks *are* immune to several germ-infections that destroy other races."

"Yes. And you mean—?"

"It's quite possible these fellows are the far-distant and degenerate survivors of that other time."

"So the whole world may have gone to pieces the way Liberia and Haiti and Santo Domingo once did, when white rule ceased?"

"Yes, only a million times more so. I see you know your history! *If* my hypothesis is correct, and only a few thousand blacks escaped, you can easily imagine what must have happened."

"For a while, maybe fifty or a hundred years, they may have kept some sort of dwindling civilization. Probably the English language for a while continued, in ever more and more corrupt forms. There may have been some pretense of maintaining the school system, railroads, steamship lines, newspapers and churches, banks and all the rest of that wonderfully complex system we once knew. But after a while—"

"Yes? What *then?*"

"Why, the whole false shell crumbled, that's all. It must have! History shows it. It didn't take a hundred years after Toussaint L'Ouverture and Dessalines, in Haiti, for the blacks to shuck off French civilization and go back to grass huts and human sacrifice—to make another little Central Africa out of it, in the backwoods districts, at any rate. And *we*—have had a thousand, Beatrice, since the white man died!"

She thought a moment, and shook her head.

"What a story," she murmured, "what an incredible, horribly fascinating story that would make, if it could ever be known, or written! Think of the ebb-tide of everything! Railroads abandoned and falling to pieces, cities crumbling, ships no longer sailing, language and arts and letters forgotten, agriculture shrinking back to a few patches of corn and potatoes, and then to nothing at all, everything changing, dying, stopping—and the ever-increasing yet degenerating people leaving the city ruins, which they could not rebuild—taking to the fields, the forests, the mountains—going down, down, back toward the primeval state, down through barbarism, through savagery, to—what?"

"To what we see!" answered the engineer, bitterly. "To animals, retaining by ghastly mockery some use of fire and of tools. All this, according to *one* theory."

"Is there another?" she asked eagerly.

"Yes, and I wish we had the shade of Darwin, of Haeckel or of Clodd here with us to help us work it out!"

"How do you imagine it?"

"Why, like this. Maybe, after all, even the entire black race was swept out along with the others, too. Perhaps you and I were really the only two human beings left alive in the world."

"Yes, but in that case, how—?"

"How came *they* here? Listen! May they not be the product of some entirely different process of development? May not some animal stock, under changed environment, have easily evolved them? May not some other semi-human or near-human race be now in process of arising, here on earth, eventually to conquer and subdue it all again?"

For a moment she made no answer. Her breath came a little quickly as she tried to grasp the full significance of this tremendous concept.

"In a million years, or so," the engineer continued, "may not the descendants of these things once more be men, or something very like them? In other words, aren't we possibly witnessing the recreation of the human type? Aren't *these* the real *pithecanthropi erecti,* rather than the brown-skinned, reddish-haired creatures of the biological text-books? There's our problem!"

She made no answer, but a sudden overmastering curiosity leaped into her eyes.

"Let me see them for myself! I must! I will!"

And before he could detain her, the girl had started back into the room whence they had come.

"No, no! No, Beatrice!" he whispered, but she paid no heed to him. Across the littered floor she made her way. And by the time Stern could reach her side, she had set her face to the long, crumbling crack in the wall and with a burning eagerness was peering out into the forest.

CHAPTER XXI

Eve Becomes an Amazon

STERN laid a hand on her shoulder, striving to draw her away. This spectacle, it seemed to him, was no fit sight for her to gaze on. But she shrugged her shoulders as if to say: "I'm not a child! I'm your equal, now, and I must see!" So the engineer desisted. And he, too, set his eye to the twisting aperture.

At sight of the narrow segment of forest visible through it, and of the several members of the Horde, a strong revulsion came upon him.

Up welled a deep-seated love for the memory of the race of men and women as they once had been—the people of the other days. Stern almost seemed to behold them again, those tall, athletic, straight-limbed men; those lithe, deep-breasted women, fair-skinned and with luxuriant hair; all alike now plunged for a thousand years in the abyss of death and of eternal oblivion.

Never before had the engineer realized how dear, how infinitely close to him his own race had been. Never had he so admired its diverse types of force and beauty, as now, now when all were but a dream.

"Ugh!" thought he, disgusted beyond measure at the sight before him. "And all *these* things are just as much alike as so many ants in a hill! I question if they've got the reason and the socialized intelligence of ants!"

He heard the girl breathe quick, as she, too, watched what was going on outside. A certain change had taken place there. The mist had somewhat thinned away, blown by the freshening breeze through Madison Forest and by the higher-rising sun. Both watchers could now see further into the woods; and both perceived that the Horde was for the most part disposing itself to sleep.

Only a few vague, uncertain figures were now moving about, with a strangely unsteady gait, weak-kneed and simian.

In the nearest group, which Stern had already had a chance to study, all save one of the creatures had lain down. The man and woman could quite plainly hear the raucous and bestial snoring of some half-dozen of the gorged Things.

"Come away, you've seen enough, more than enough!" he whispered in the girl's ear.

She shook her head.

"No, no!" she answered, under her breath. "How horrible—and yet, how wonderful!"

Then a misfortune happened; trivial yet how direly pregnant!

For Stern, trying to readjust his position, laid his right hand on the wall above his head.

A little fragment of loose marble, long since ready to fall, dislodged itself and bounced with a sharp click against the steel I-beam over which they were both peeking.

The sound, perhaps, was no greater than you would make in snapping an ordinary lead-pencil in your fingers; yet on the instant three of the Things raised their bulbous and exaggerated heads in an attitude of intense, suspicious listening. Plain to see that their senses, at least, excelled those of the human being, even as a dog's might.

The individual which, alone of them all, had been standing, wheeled suddenly round and made a step or two toward the building. Both watchers saw him with terrible distinctness, there among the sumacs and birches, with the beauty of which he made a shocking contrast.

Plain now was the simian aspect, plain the sidelong and uncertain gait, bent back and crooked legs, the long, pendulous arms and dully ferocious face.

And as the Thing listened, its hair bristling, it thrust its villainous, ape-like head well forward. Open fell the mouth, revealing the dog-teeth and the blue, shriveled-looking gums.

A wrinkle creased the low, dull brow. Watching with horrified fascination, Stern and Beatrice beheld—and heard—the creature sniff the air, as though taking up some scent of danger or of the hunt.

Then up came the right arm; they saw the claw-hand with a spear, poise itself a moment. From the open mouth burst with astounding force and suddenness a snarling yowl, inarticulate, shrill, horrible beyond all thinking.

An instant agitation took place all through the forest. The watchers could see only a small, fan-like space of it—and even this, only a few rods from the building—yet by the confused, vague noise that began, they knew the alarm had been given to the whole Horde.

Here, there, the cry was repeated. A shifting, moving sound began. In the visible group, the Things were getting to their handlike feet, standing unsteadily on their loose-skinned, scaly legs, gawping about them, whining and clicking with disgusting sounds.

Sudden, numbing fear seized Beatrice. Now for the first time she realized the imminent peril; now she regretted her insistence on seeing the Horde at close range.

She turned, pale and shaken; and her trembling hand sought the engineer's.

He still, for a moment, kept his eye to the crack, fascinated by the very horror of the sight. Then all at once another figure shambled into view.

"A female one!" he realized, shuddering. Too monstrously hideous, this sight, to be endured. With a gasp, the man turned back.

About Beatrice he drew his arm. Together, almost as soundlessly as wraiths, they stole away, out through the office, out to the hallway, into the dim light of the arcade once more.

Here, for a few moments, they knew that they were safe. Retreat through the Marble Court and up the stairs was fairly clear. There was but one entrance open into the arcade, the one through Pine Tree Gate; and this was blocked so narrowly by the giant bole that Stern knew there could be no general mob-rush through it—no attack which he could not for a while hold back, so long as his ammunition and the girl's should last.

Thus they breathed more freely now. Most of the tumult outside had been cut off from their hearing, by the retirement into the arcade. They paused, to plan their course.

At Stern the girl looked eagerly.

"Oh, oh, Allan—how horrible!" she whispered. "It was all my fault for having been so headstrong, for having insisted on a look at them! Forgive me!"

"S-h!" he cautioned again. "No matter about that. The main thing, now, is whether we attack or wait?"

"Attack? Now?"

"I don't think much of going up-stairs without that pail of water. We'll have a frightful time with thirst, to say nothing of not being able to make the Pulverite. Water we must have! If it weren't for your being here, I'd mighty soon wade into that bunch and see who wins! But—well, I haven't any right to endanger—"

Beatrice seized his hand and pulled him toward the doorway.

"Come on!" cried she. "If you and I aren't a match for *them*, we don't deserve to live, that's all. You know how I can shoot now! Come along!"

Her eyes gleamed with the light of battle, battle for liberty, for life; her cheeks glowed with the tides of generous blood that coursed beneath the skin. Never had Stern beheld her half so beautiful, so regal in that clinging, barbaric Bengal robe of black and yellow, caught at the throat with the clasp of raw gold.

A sudden impulse seized him, dominant, resistless. For a brief moment he detained her; he held her back; about her supple body his arm tightened.

She raised her face in wonder. He bent, a little, and on the brow he kissed her rapturously.

"Thank God for such a comrade and a—friend!" said he.

CHAPTER XXII

GODS!

SOME few minutes later, together they approached Pine Tree Gate, leading directly out into the Horde.

The girl, rosier than ever, held her Krag loosely in the hollow of her bare, warm right arm. One of Stern's revolvers lay in its holster. The other balanced itself in his right hand. His left held the precious water-pail, so vital now to all their plans and hopes.

Girt in his garb of fur, belted and sandaled, well over six feet tall and broad of shoulder, the man was magnificent. His red beard and mustache, close-cropped, gave him a savage air that now well fitted him. For Stern was mad—mad clear through.

That Beatrice should suffer in any way, even from temporary thirst, raised up a savage resentment in his breast. The thought that perhaps it might *not* be possible to gain access to the spring at all, that these foul Things might try to blockade them and siege them to death, wrought powerfully on him.

For himself he cared nothing. The girl it was who now preoccupied his every thought. And as they made their way through the litter of the explosion, toward the exit, slowly and cautiously, he spied out every foot of the place for possible danger.

If fight he must, he knew now it would be a brutal, utterly merciless fight—slaughter, extermination without any limit, to the end.

But there was scant time for thought. Already they could see daylight glimmering in through the gate, past the massive column of the conifer. Daylight—and with it came a thin and acrid smoke—and sounds of the uproused Horde in Madison Forest.

"Slow! Slow, now!" whispered Stern. "Don't let 'em know a thing until we've got 'em covered! If we surprise 'em just right, who knows but the whole infernal mob may duck and run? Don't shoot till you have to; but when you *do*—!"

"I know!" breathed she.

Then, all at once, there they were at the gate, at the big tree, standing out there in the open, on the thick carpet of pine-spills.

And before them lay the mossy, shaded forest aisles—with what a horror camped all through that peaceful, wondrous place!

"Oh!" gasped Beatrice. The engineer stopped as though frozen. His hand tightened on the revolver-butt till the knuckles whitened. And thus, face to face with the Horde, they stood for a long minute.

Neither of them realized exactly the details of that first impression. The narrow slit of view which they had already got through the crack in the wall had only very imperfectly prepared them for any understanding of what these Things really were, *en masse.*

But both Beatrice and the engineer understood, even at the first moment of their exit there, that they had entered an adventure whereof the end could not be foreseen; that here before them lay possibilities infinitely more serious than any they had contemplated.

For one thing, they had underestimated the numbers of the Horde. They had thought, perhaps, there might be five hundred in all.

The torches had certainty numbered no more than that. But now they realized that the torch-bearers had been but a very small fraction of the whole; for, as their eyes swept out through the forest, whence the fog had almost wholly risen, they beheld a moving, swarming mass of the creatures on every hand. A mass that seemed to extend on, on to indefinite vistas. A mass that moved, clicked, shifted, grunted, stank, snarled, quarreled. A mass of frightful hideousness, of inconceivable menace.

The girl's first impulse was to turn, to retreat back into the building once more; but her native courage checked it. For Stern, she saw, had no such purpose.

Surprised though he was, he stood there like a rock, head up, revolver ready, every muscle tense and ready for whatsoever might befall. And through the girl flashed a thrill of admiration for this virile, indomitable man, coping with every difficulty, facing every peril—for her sake.

Yet the words he uttered now were not of classic heroism. They were simple, colloquial, inelegant. For Stern, his eyes blazing, said only:

"We're in bad, girl! They're on—we've got to bluff—bluff like the devil!"

Have you ever seen a herd of cattle on the prairie, a herd of thousands, shift and face and, as by instinct, lower their horned heads against some enemy—a wolf-pack, maybe?

You know then, how this Horde of dwarfish, blue, warty, misformed little horrors woke to the presence of the unknown enemy.

Already half alarmed by the warning given by the one, which, near the crack in the wall, had sniffed the intruders and had howled, the pack now broke into commotion. Stern and Beatrice saw a confused upheaving, a shifting and a tumult. They heard a yapping outcry. The long, thin spears began to bristle.

And all at once, as a dull, ugly hornet-hum rose through the wood, they knew the moment for quick action was upon them.

"Here goes!" cried Stern, raging. "Let's see how *this* will strike the hell-hounds!"

His face white with passion and with loathing hate, he raised the automatic. He aimed at none of the pack, for angry as he was he realized that the time was not yet come for killing, if other means to reach the spring could possibly avail.

Instead he pointed the ugly blue muzzle up toward the branches of a maple, under which a dense swarm of the Horde had encamped and now was staring, apelike, at him.

Then his finger sought the trigger. And five crackling spurts of flame, five shots spat out into the calm and misty air of morning. A few severed leaves swayed down, idly, with a swinging motion. A broken twig fell, hung suspended a moment, then detached itself again and dropped to earth.

"Good Lord! Look a' *that*, will you?" cried Stern.

A startled cry broke from the girl's lips.

Both of them had expected some effect from the sudden fusillade, but nothing like that which actually resulted.

For, as the quick shots echoed to stillness again, and even before the first of the falling leaves had spiraled to the ground, an absolute, unbroken silence fell upon that vile rabble of beast-men—the silence of a numbing, paralyzing, sheer brute terror.

Some stood motionless, crouching on their bandy legs, holding to whatsoever tree or bush was nearest, staring with wild eyes.

Others dropped to their knees.

But by far the greater part, thousands on thousands of the little monstrosities, fell prone and grovelling. Their hideous masklike faces hidden, there they lay on the moss and all among the undergrowth, the trampled, desecrated, befouled undergrowth of Madison Forest.

Then all at once, over and beyond them, Stern saw the blue-curling smudge of the remains of the great fire by the spring.

He knew that, for a few brief, all-precious moments, the way might possibly be clear to come and go—to get water—to save Beatrice and himself from the thirst-tortures—to procure the one necessary thing for the making of his Pulverite.

His heart gave a great, up-bounding leap.

"Look, Beatrice!" cried he, his voice ringing out over the terror-stricken things. "Look—we're gods! While this lasts—*gods!* Come, now's our only chance! *Come on!*—"

CHAPTER XXIII

THE OBEAH

TOGETHER, as in a dream—a nightmare, dazed, incredible, grotesque—they advanced out into the dim-shaded forest aisles.

"Don't look!" Stern exclaimed, shuddering at sight of the unspeakable hideousness of the Things, at glimpses of gnawed bones, grisly bits of flesh, dried gouts of blood upon the woodland carpet. "Don't think—just come along!

"Five minutes, and we're safe, there and back again. S-h-h-h! Don't hurry! Count, now—count your steps—one, two, three—four, five, six—so—steady, steady!—"

Now they were ten yards from the tower, now twenty. Bravely they walked, now straight ahead among the trees, now circling some individual, some horrid group. Stern held the water-pail firmly. He gripped the revolver in a grasp of iron. The magazine-rifle lay in both the girl's hands, ready for instant use.

Suddenly Stern fired again, three shots.

"Some of 'em are moving, over there!" he said in a crisp, ugly tone. "I guess a little lead close to their ears will fix 'em for a while!"

His voice went to a hoarse whisper.

"Gods!" he repeated. "Don't forget it, for a moment; don't lose that thought, for it may pull us through! These creatures here, *if* they're descended from the blacks, must have some story, some tradition of the white man. Of his mastery, his power! We'll use it now, by Heaven, as it never yet was used!"

Then he began to count again; and so, tense, watching with eager-burning eyes and taut muscles, the man and woman made their way of frightful peril.

A snuffling howl rose.

"You will, will you?" Stern cried, adding another kick to the one he had just dealt to one of the creatures, who had ventured to look up at their approach. "Lie down, ape!" And with the clangorous metal pail he smote the ugly, brutish skull.

Beatrice gasped with fear; but the bluff made good. The creature grovelled, and again the pair strode forward, masterfully. Masterfully they had to go, or not at all. Masterfully, or die. For now their all-in-all lay just in that grim, steel-hard sense of mastery.

Before the girl's eyes a sort of haze seemed forming. Her heart beat thick and heavy. Stern's counting sounded very far away and strange; she hardly recognized his voice. To her came wild, disjointed, confused impressions—now a bony and distorted back, now a simian head; again a group that crouched and cowered in its filthy squalor, hideously.

Then all at once, there right before her she saw the little woodland path that, slightly descending, led past a big oak she well knew, down to the margin of the pool.

"Steady, girl, steady!" came the engineer's warning, tense as piano-wire. "Almost there, now. What's *that?*"

For a brief instant he hesitated. The girl felt his arm grow even more taut, she heard his breath catch. Then she, too, looked—and saw.

It was enough, that sight, to have smitten with sick horror the bravest man who ever lived. For there, beside the smouldering embers of the great feast-fire, littered with bones and indescribable refuse, a creature was squatting on its hams—one of the Horde, indeed, yet vastly different, tremendously more venomous, more dangerous of aspect.

Stern knew at once that here, not prostrate nor yet crouching, was the chief of the blue Horde.

He knew it by the superior size and strength of the Thing, by the almost manlike cunning of the low, gorilla face, the gleam of intelligence in the reddened eye, the crude wreath of maple-leaves upon the head, the necklace of finger-bones strung around the neck.

But most of all, he knew it by a thing that shocked him more than the sight of stark, outright cannibalism would have done. A simple thing, yet how ominous! A thing that argued reason in this reversion from the human; a thing that sent the shuddering chills along the engineer's spine.

For the chief, the obeah-man of this vile drove, rising now from beside the fire with a gibbering chatter and a look of bestial malice, held between his fangs a twisted brown leaf!

Stern knew at a glance the leaf was the rudely cured product of some degenerated tobacco-plant. He saw a glow of red at the tip of the close-rolled tobacco. Vapor issued from the chief's slit-mouth.

"Good Lord—he's—*smoking!*" stammered the engineer. "And *that* means—means an almost human brain. And—quick, Beatrice, the water! I didn't expect this! Thought they were all alike. Back to the tower, quick! Here, fill the pail—I'll keep him covered!"

Up he brought the automatic, till the bead lay fair upon the naked, muscular breast of the obeah.

Beatrice handed Stern the rifle, then snatching the pail, dipped it, filled it to the brim. Stern heard the water lap and gurgle. He knew it was but a few seconds, yet it seemed an hour to him, at the very least.

Keener than ever before in his whole life, his mental pictures now limned themselves with lightning rapidity upon his brain.

Stamped on his consciousness was this lithe, lean, formidable body, showing beyond dispute its human ancestry; the right hand that held *a steel-pointed* spear; the horrible ornament (a withered little smoked hand) that dangled from the left wrist by a cord of platted fiber.

Vividly Stern beheld a deep gash or scar that ran from the chief's right eye—a dull, fishlike eye, evidently destroyed by that wound—down across the leathery cheek, across the prognathous jaw; a reddish-purple wale, which on that clay-blue skin produced an effect indescribably repulsive.

Then the chief grunted, and moved forward, toward them. Stern saw that the gait was almost human, not shuffling and uncertain like that of the others, but firm and vigorous. He estimated the height at more than five feet, eight inches; the weight at possibly one hundred and forty pounds. Even at that juncture, his scientific mind, always accustomed to judging, instinctively registered these data, with the others.

"Here, you, get back there!" shouted Stern, as the girl rose again from filling the pail.

The cry was instinctive, for even as he uttered it, he knew it could not be understood. A thousand years of rapid degeneration had long wiped all traces of English speech from the brute-men, who now, at most, chattered some bestial gibberish. Yet the warning echoed loudly through Madison Forest; and the obeah hesitated.

The tone, perhaps, conveyed some meaning to that brain behind the sloping forehead. Perhaps some dim, racial memory of human speech still lingered in that mind, in that strange organism which, by some freak of atavism, had "thrown back" out of the mire of returning animality almost to the human form and stature once again.

However that may have been, the creature-chief halted in his advance. Undecided he stood a moment, leaning upon his spear, sucking at the rude mockery of a cigar. Stern remembered having seen Consul, the trained chimpanzee, smoke in precisely the same manner, and a nameless loathing filled him at his mockery of the dead, buried past.

"Let me carry the pail!" said he. "We've got to hurry—hurry—or it may be too late!"

"No, no—I'll keep the water!" she answered, panting. "You need both hands clear! Come!"

Thus they turned, and, with a shuddering glance behind, started back for the tower again.

But the obeah, with a whining plaint, spat away his tobacco-leaf. They heard a shuffle of feet. And, looking round again, both saw that he had crossed the little brook.

There he stood now, his right hand out, palm upward, his lips curled in the ghastly imitation of a smile, blue gums and yellow tushes showing, a sight to freeze the blood with horror. Yet through it all, the meaning was most clearly evident.

Beatrice, laden as she was with the heavy water-bucket, more precious now to them than all the wealth of the dead world, would still have retreated, but with a word of stern command he bade her wait. He stopped short in his tracks.

"Not a step!" commanded he. "Hold on! If he makes friends with us—with gods—that's a million times better every way! Hold on—wait, no—this is *his* move!"

He faced the obeah. His left hand gripped the repeating rifle, his right the automatic, held in readiness for instant action. The muzzle sight never for a second left its aim at the chief's heart.

And for a second silence fell there in the forest. Save for the rustling murmur of the Horde, and a faint, woodland trickle of the stream, you might have thought the place untouched by life.

Yet death lurked there, and destiny—the destiny of the whole world, the future, the human race, forever and ever without end; and the cords of Fate were being loosed for a new knitting.

And Stern, with Beatrice there at his side, stood harsh and strong and very grim; stood like an incarnation of man's life, waiting.

And slowly, step by step, over the yielding, noiseless moss, the grinning, one-eyed, ghastly obeah-man came nearer, nearer still.

CHAPTER XXIV

THE FIGHT IN THE FOREST

Now the Thing was close, very close to them, while a hush lay upon the watching Horde and on the forest. So close, that Stern could hear the soughing breath between those hideous lips and see the twitching of the wrinkled lid over the black, glittering eye that blinked as you have often seen a chimpanzee's.

All at once the obeah stopped. Stopped and leered, his head craned forward, that ghastly rictus on his mouth.

Stern's hot anger welled up again. Thus to be detained, inspected and seemingly made mock of by a creature no more than three-quarters human, stung the engineer to rage.

"What do *you* want?" cried he, in a thick and unsteady voice. "Anything I can do for you? If not, I'll be going!"

The creature shook its head. Yet something of Stern's meaning may have won to its smoldering intelligence. For now it raised a hand. It pointed to the pail of water, then to its own mouth; again it indicated the pail, then stretched a long, repulsive finger at the mouth of Stern.

The meaning seemed clear. Stern, even as he stood there in anger—and in wonder, too, at the fearlessness of this superthing—grasped the significance of the action.

"Why, he must mean," said he, to Beatrice, "he must be trying to ask whether we intend to drink any of the water, what? Maybe it's poisoned, now, or something! Maybe he's trying to warn us!"

"Warn us? Why should he?"

"How can I tell? It isn't entirely impossible that he still retains some knowledge of his human ancestors. Perhaps that tradition may have been handed down, some way, and still exists in the form of a crude beast-religion."

"Yes, but then—?"

"Perhaps he wants to get in touch with us, again; learn from us; try to struggle up out of the mire of degeneration, who knows? If so—and it's possible—of course he'd try to warn us of a poisoned spring!"

Acting on this hypothesis, of which he was now half-convinced, Stern nodded. By gesture-play he answered: Yes. Yes, this woman and he intended to drink of the water. The obeah-man, grinning, showed signs of lively interest. His eyes brightened, and a look of craft, of wizened cunning crept over his uncanny features.

Then he raised his head and gave a long, shrill, throaty call, ululating and unspeakably weird.

Something stirred in the forest. Stern heard a rustle and a creeping murmur; and quick fear chilled his heart.

To him it seemed as though a voice were calling, perhaps the inner, secret voice of his own subjective self—a voice that cried:

"You, who must drink water—now *he* knows you are not gods, but mortal creatures. Tricked by his question and your answer, your peril now is on you! *Flee!*"

The voice died. Stern found himself, with a strange, taut eagerness tingling all through him, facing the obeah and—and *not daring to turn his back.*

Retreat they must, he knew. Retreat, at once! Already in the forest he understood that heads were being lifted, beastlike ears were listening, brute eyes peering and ape-hands clutching the little, flint-pointed spears. Already the girl and he should have been half-way back to the tower; yet still, inhibited by that slow, grinning, staring advance of the chief, there the engineer stood.

But all at once the spell was broken.

For with a cry, a hoarse and frightful yell of passion, the obeah leaped— leaped like a huge and frightfully agile ape—leaped the whole distance intervening.

Stern saw the Thing's red-gleaming eyes fixed on Beatrice. In those eyes he clearly saw the hell-flame of lust. And as the woman screamed in terror, Stern pulled trigger with a savage curse.

The shot went wild. For at the instant—though he felt no pain—his arm dropped down and sideways.

Astounded, he looked. Something was wrong! What? His trigger-finger refused to serve. It had lost all power, all control.

For God's sake, what could it be?

Then—all this taking but a second—Stern saw; he knew the truth. Staring, pale and horrified, he understood.

There, through the fleshy part of his forearm, thrust clean from side to side by a lightning-swift stroke, he saw the obeah's spear!

It dangled strangely in the firm muscles. The steel barb and full eighteen inches of the shaft were red and dripping.

Yet still the engineer felt no slightest twinge of pain.

From his numbed, paralyzed hand the automatic dropped, fell noiselessly into the moss.

And with a formless roar of killing-rage, Stern swung on the obeah, with the rifle.

Stern felt his heart about to burst with hate. He did not even think of the second revolver in the holster at his side. With only his left hand now to use, the weapon could only have given clumsy service.

Instead, the man reverted instantly to the jungle stage, himself—to the law of claw and fang, of clutching talon, of stone and club.

The beloved woman's cry, ringing in his ears, drove him mad. Up he whirled the Krag again, up, up, by the muzzle; and down upon that villainous skull he dashed it with a force that would have brained an ox.

The obeah, screeching, reeled back. But he was not dead. Not dead, only stunned a moment. And Stern, horrified, found himself holding only a gun-barrel. The stock, shattered, had whirled away and vanished among the tall and waving ferns.

Beatrice snatched up the fallen revolver. She stumbled; and the pail was empty. Spurting, splashing away, the precious water flew. No time, now, for any more.

For all about them, behind them and on every hand, the Things were closing in.

They had seen blood—had heard the obeah's cry; they knew! Not gods, now, but mortal creatures! *Not gods!*

"Run! *Run!*" gasped Beatrice.

The spear still hanging from his arm, Stern wheeled and followed. High and hard he swung the rifle-barrel, like a war-club.

No counting of steps, now; no play at divinity. Panting, horror-stricken, frenzied with rage, bleeding, they ran, It was a hunt—the hunt of the last two humans by the nightmare Horde.

In front, a bluish and confused mass seemed to dance and quiver through the forest; and a pattering rain of spears and little arrows began to fall about the fugitives.

Then the girl's revolver sputtered in a quick volley; and again, for a space, silence fell. The way again was clear. But in the path, silent and still, or writhing horribly, lay a few of the Things. And the pine-needles and soft moss were very red, in spots.

Stern had his pistol out too, by now. For behind and on his flanks, like ferrets hanging to a hunted creature, the swarm was closing in.

The engineer, his face very white and drawn, veins standing out on his sweat-beaded forehead, heard Beatrice cry out to him, but he could not understand her words.

Yet as they ran, he saw her level the pistol and snap the hammer twice, thrice, with no result. The little dead *click* sounded like a death-warrant to him.

"Empty?" cried he. "Here, take this one! You can shoot better now than I can!" And into her hand he thrust the second revolver.

Something stung him on the left shoulder. He glanced round. A dart was hanging there.

With an oath, the engineer wheeled about. His eyes burned and his lips drew back, taut, from his fine white teeth.

There, already recovered from the blow which would have killed a man ten times over, he saw the obeah snarling after him. Right down along the path the monster was howling, beating his breast with both huge fists. And, now feeling fear no more than pain, Stern crouched to meet his onslaught.

CHAPTER XXV

The Goal, and Through It

It all happened in a moment of time, a moment, long—in seeming—as an hour. The girl's revolver crackled, there behind him. Stern saw a little round bluish hole take shape in the obeah's ear, and red drops start.

Then with a ghastly screaming, the Thing was upon him.

Out struck the engineer, with the rifle-barrel. All the force of his splendid muscles lay behind that blow. The Thing tried to dodge. But Stern had been too quick.

Even as it sprang, with talons clutching for the man's throat, the steel barrel drove home on the jaw.

An unearthly, piercing yell split the forest air. Then Stern saw the obeah, his jaw hanging oddly awry, all loose and shattered, fall headlong in the path.

But before he could strike again, could batter in the base of the tough skull, a moan from Beatrice sent him to her aid.

"Oh, God!" he cried, and sank beside her on his knees.

On her forehead, as she lay gasping among the bushes, he saw an ugly welt.

"A stone? They've hit her with a stone! *Killed her, perhaps?*"

Kneeling there, up he snatched the revolver, and in a deadly fire he poured out the last spitting shots, point-blank in the faces of the crowding rabble.

Up he leaped. The rifle barrel flashed and glittered as he whirled it. Like a reaper, laying a clean swath behind him, the engineer mowed down a dozen of the beast-men.

Shrieks, grunts, snarls, mingled with his execrations.

Then fair into a jabbering ape-face he flung the bloodstained barrel. The face fell, faded, vanished, as hideous illusions fade in a dream.

And Stern, with a strength he never dreamed was his, caught up the fainting girl in his left arm, as easily as though she had been a child.

Still dragging the spear which pierced his right—his right that yet protected her a little—he ran.

Stones, darts, spears, clattered in about him. He heard the swish and tang of them; heard the leaves flutter as the missiles whirled through.

Struck? Was he struck again?

He knew not, nor cared. Only he thought of shielding Beatrice. Nothing but that, just that!

"The gate—oh, let me reach the gate! God! The gate—"

And all of a sudden, though how he could not tell, there he seemed to see the gate before him. Could it be? Or was that, too, a dream? A cruel, vicious mockery of his disordered mind?

Yes—the gate! It must be! He recognized the giant pine, in a moment of lucidity. Then everything began to dance again, to quiver in the mocking sunlight.

"The gate!" he gasped once more, and staggered on. Behind him, a little trail of blood-drops from his wounded arm fell on the trampled leaves.

Something struck his bent head. Through it a blinding pain darted. Thousands of beautiful and tiny lights of every color began to quiver, to leap and whirl.

"They've—set the building on fire!" thought he; yet all the while he knew it was impossible, he understood it was only an illusion.

He heard the rustle of the wind through the forest. It blent and mingled with a horrid tumult of grunts, of clicking cries, of gnashing teeth and little bestial cries.

"The—gate!" sobbed Stern, between hard-set teeth, and stumbled forward, ever forward, through the Horde. To him, protectingly, he clasped the beautiful body in the tiger-skin.

Living? Was she living yet? A great, aching wonder filled him. Could he reach the stair with her, and bear her up it? Hurl back these devils? Save her, after all?

The pain had grown exquisite, in his head. Something seemed hammering there, with regular strokes—a red-hot sledge upon an anvil of white-hot steel.

To him it looked as though a hundred, a thousand of the little blue fiends were leaping, shrieking, circling there in front of him. Ten thousand! And he must break through.

Break through!

Where had he heard those words? Ah! Yes!

To him instantly recurred a distant echo of a song, a Harvard football-song. He remembered. Now he was back again. Yale, 0; Harvard, 17—New Haven, 1898. And see the thousands of cheering spectators! The hats flying through the air—flags waving—red, most of them! Crimson—like blood!

Came the crash and boom of the old Harvard Band, with big Joe Foley banging the drum till it was fit to burst; with Marsh blowing his lungs out on the cornet, and all the other fellows raising Cain.

Uproar! Cheering! And again the music. Everybody was singing now, everybody roaring out that brave old fighting chorus:

"......Now—all to-geth-er,
Smash them—*and*—break—*through!*"

And see! Look there! The goal!

The scene shifted, all at once, in a quite unaccountable and puzzling manner.

Somehow, victory wasn't quite won, after all. Not quite yet. What was the matter, then? What was wrong? Where *was* he?

Ah, the Goal!

Yes, there through the ruck and mass of the Blues, he saw it, again, quite clearly. He was sure of *that*, anyhow.

The goal-posts seemed a trifle near together, and they were certainly made of crumbling stone, instead of straight wooden beams. Odd, that!

He wondered, too, why the management allowed trees to grow on the field, trees and bushes—why a huge pine should be standing right there by the left-hand post. That was certainly a matter to be investigated and complained of, later. But now was no time for kicks.

"Probably some Blue trick," thought Stern. "No matter, it won't do 'em any good, this time!"

Ah! An opening! Stern's head went lower still. He braced himself for a leap.

"Come on, come on!" he yelled defiance.

Again he heard the cheering, once more, roaring downwind like a chorus of mad devils.

An opening? No, he was mistaken. Instead, the Blues were massing there by the Goal.

Bitterly he swore. Under his arm he tightened the ball. He ran!

What?

They were trying to tackle?

"Damn you!" he cried, in boiling anger. "I'll—I'll show you a trick or two—yet!"

He stopped, circled, dodged the clutching hands, feinted with a tactic long unthought of, and broke into a straight, resistless dash for the posts.

As he ran, he yelled:

"*Smash* them—and—*break through!*......"

All his waning strength upgathered for that run. Yet how strangely tired he felt—how heavy the ball was growing!

What was the matter with his head? With his right arm? They both ached hideously. He must have got hurt, some way, in one of the "downs." Some dirty work, somewhere. Rotten sport!

He ran. Never in all his many games had he seen such a peculiar grid-iron, all tangled and overgrown. Never, such a host of tackles. Hundreds of them! Where were the Crimsons? What? No support, no interference? Hell!

Yet the Goal was surely just there, now right ahead. He ran.

"Foul!" he shouted savagely, as a Blue struck at him, then another and another, and many more. The taste of blood came to his tongue. He spat. "Foul!"

Right and left he dashed them, with a giant's strength. They scattered in panic, with strange and unintelligible cries.

"The goal!"

He reached it. And, as he crossed the line, he fell.

"*Down,* down!" sobbed he.

CHAPTER XXVI

BEATRICE DARES

An hour later, Stern and Beatrice sat weak and shaken in their stronghold on the fifth floor, resting, trying to gather up some strength again, to pull together for resistance to the siege that had set in.

With the return of reason to the engineer—his free bleeding had some-what checked the onset of fever—and of consciousness to the girl, they began to piece out, bit by bit, the stages of their retreat.

Now that Stern had barricaded the stairs, two stories below, and that for a little while they felt reasonably safe, they were able to take their bearings, to recall the flight, to plan a bit for the future, a future dark with menace, seemingly hopeless in its outlook.

"If it—hadn't been for you," Beatrice was saying, "if you hadn't picked me up and carried me, when that stone struck, I—I—"

"How's the ache now?" Stern hastily interrupted, in a rather weak yet brisk voice, which he was trying hard to render matter-of-fact. "Of course the lack of water, except that half-pint or so, to bathe your bruise with, is a rank barbarity. But if we haven't got any, we haven't—that's all. All—till we have another go at 'em!"

"Oh, Allan!" she exclaimed, tremulously. "Don't think of *me!* Of me, when your back's gashed with a spear-cut, your head's battered, arm pierced, and we've neither water nor bandages—nothing of any kind to treat your wounds with!"

"Come now, don't you bother about me!" he objected, trying hard to smile, though racked with pain. "I'll be O. K., fit as a fiddle, in no time. Perfect health and all that sort of thing, you know. It'll heal right away.

"Head's clear again already, in spite of that whack with the war-club, or whatever it was they landed with. But for a while I certainly was seeing things. I had 'em—had 'em bad! Thought—well, strange things.

"My back? Only a scratch, that's all. It's begun to coagulate already, the blood has, hasn't it?" And he strove to peer over his own shoulder at the slash. But the pain made him desist. He could hardly keep back a groan. His face twitched involuntarily.

The girl sank on her knees beside him. Her arm encircled him; her hand smoothed his forehead; and with a strange look she studied his unnaturally pale face.

"It's your arm I'm thinking about, more than anything," said she. "We've *got* to have something to treat that with. Tell me, does it hurt you very much, Allan?"

He tried to laugh, as he glanced down at the wounded arm, which, ligatured about the spear-thrust with a thong, and supported by a rawhide sling, looked strangely blue and swollen.

"Hurt me? Nonsense! I'll be fine and dandy in no time. The only trouble is, I'm not much good as a fighter this way. Southpaw, you see. Can't shoot worth a—a cent, you know, with my left. Otherwise, I wouldn't mind."

"Shoot? Trust *me* for that now!" she exclaimed. "We've still got two revolvers and the shotgun left, and lots of ammunition. I'll do the shooting—if there's got to be any done!"

"You're all right, Beatrice!" exclaimed the wounded man fervently. "What would I do without you? And to think how near you came to—but never mind. That's over now; forget it!"

"Yes, but what next?"

"Don't know. Get well, maybe. Things might be worse. I might have a broken arm, or something; laid up for weeks—slow starvation and all that. What's a mere puncture? Nothing! Now that the spear's out, it'll begin healing right away.

"Bet a million, though, that What's-His-Name down there, Big Chief the Monk, won't get out of *his* scrape in a hurry. His face is certainly scrambled, or I miss my guess. You got him through the ear with one shot, by the way. Know that? Fact! Drilled it clean! Just a little to the right and you'd have *had* him for keeps. But never mind, we'll save him for the encore—if there is any."

"You think they'll try again?"

"Can't say. They've lost a lot of fighters, killed and wounded, already. And they've had a pretty liberal taste of our style. That ought to hold them for a while! We'll see, at any rate. And if luck stays good, we'll maybe have a thing or two to show them if they keep on hanging round where they aren't wanted!"

Came now a little silence. Beside Stern the girl sat, half supporting his wounded body with her firm, white arm. Thirst was beginning to torment them both, particularly Stern, whose injuries had already given him a marked temperature. But water there was absolutely none. And so, still planless, glad only to recuperate a little, content that for the present the Horde had been held back, they waited. Waiting, they both thought. The girl's thoughts were all of him; but he, man-fashion, was trying to piece out what had happened, to frame some coherent idea of it all, to analyze the urgent necessities that lay upon them both.

Here and there, a disjointed bit recurred to him, even from out of the delirium that had followed the blow on the head. From the time he had recovered his senses in the building, things were clearer.

He knew that the Horde, temporarily frightened by his mad rush, had given him time to stumble up again and once more lift the girl, before they had ventured to creep into the arcade in search of their prey.

He remembered that the spear had been gone then. Raving, he must have broken and plucked it out. The blood, he recalled, was spurting freely as he had carried Beatrice through the wreckage and up to the first landing, where she had regained partial consciousness.

Then he shuddered at recollection of that stealthy, apelike creeping of the Horde scouts in among the ruins, furtive and silent; their sniffing after the blood-track; their frightful agility in clambering with feet and hands alike, swinging themselves up like chimpanzees, swarming aloft on the death-hunt.

He had evaded them, from story to story. Beatrice, able now to walk, had helped him roll down balustrades and building-stones, fling rocks, wrench stairs loose and block the way.

And so, wounding their pursuers, yet tracked always by more and ever more, they had come to the landing, where by aid of the rifle barrel as a lever they had been able to bring a whole wall crashing down, to choke the passage. That had brought silence. For a time, at least, pursuit had been abandoned. In the sliding, dusty avalanche of the wall, hurled down the stairway, Stern knew by the grunts and shrieks which had arisen that some of the Horde had surely perished—how many, he could not tell. A score or two at the very least, he ardently hoped.

Fear, at any rate, had been temporarily injected into the rest. For the attack had not yet been renewed. Outside in the forest, no sign of the Horde, no sound. A disconcerting, ominous calm had settled like a pall. Even the birds, recovered from their terrors, had begun to hop about and take up their twittering little household tasks.

As in a kind of clairvoyance, the engineer seemed to know there would be respite until night. For a little while, at least, there could be rest and peace. But when darkness should have settled down—

"If they'd only show themselves!" thought he, his leaden eyes closing in an overmastering lassitude, a vast swooning weakness of blood-loss and exhaustion. Not even his parched thirst, a veritable torture now, could keep his thoughts from wandering. "If they'd tackle again, I could score with—with lead—what's *that* I'm thinking? I'm not delirious, am I?"

For a moment he brought himself back with a start, back to a full realization of the place. But again the drowsiness gained on him.

"We've got guns now; guns and ammunition," thought he. "We—could pick them off—from the windows. Pick them—off—pick—them—off—"

He slept. Thus, often, wounded soldiers sleep, with troubled dreams, on the verge of renewed battle which may mean their death, their long and wakeless slumber.

He slept. And the girl, laying his gashed head gently back upon the pile of furs, bent over him with infinite compassion. For a long minute, hardly breathing, she watched him there. More quickly came her breath. A strange new light shone in her eyes.

"Only for me, those wounds!" she whispered slowly. "Only for me!"

Taking his head in both her hands, she kissed him as he lay unconscious. Kissed him twice, and then a third time.

Then she arose.

Quickly, as though with some definite plan, she chose from among their store of utensils a large copper kettle, one which he had brought her the week before from the little Broadway shop.

She took a long rawhide rope, braided by Stern during their long evenings together. This she knotted firmly to the bale of the kettle.

The revolvers, fully reloaded, she examined with care. One of them she laid beside the sleeper. The other she slid into her full, warm bosom, where the clinging tiger skin held it ready for her hand.

Then she walked noiselessly to the door leading into the hallway.

Here for a moment she stood, looking back at the wounded man. Tears dimmed her eyes, yet they were very glad.

"For your sake, now, everything!" she said. "Everything—all! Oh, Allan, if you only knew! And now—good-by!"

Then she was gone.

And in the silent room, their home, which out of wreck and chaos they had made, the fevered man lay very still, his pulses throbbing in his throat.

Outside, very far, very faint in the forests, a muffled drum began to beat again.

And the slow shadows, lengthening across the floor, told that evening was drawing nigh.

CHAPTER XXVII

TO WORK!

THE engineer awoke with a start—awoke to find daylight gone, to find that dusk had settled, had shrouded the whole place in gloom.

Confused, he started up. He was about to call out, when prudence muted his voice. For the moment he could not recollect just what had happened or where he was; but a vast impending consciousness of evil and of danger weighed upon him. It warned him to keep still, to make no outcry. A burning thirst quickened his memory.

Then his comprehension returned. Still weak and shaken, yet greatly benefited by his sleep, he took a few steps toward the door. Where was the girl? Was he alone? What could all this mean?

"Beatrice! Oh, Beatrice!" he called thickly, in guarded tones. "Where are you? Answer me!"

"Here—coming!" he heard her voice. And then he saw her, dimly, in the doorway.

"What is it? Where have you been? How long have I been asleep?"

She did not answer his questions, but came quickly to him, took his hand, and with her own smoothed his brow.

"Better, now?" asked she.

"Lots! I'll be all right in a little while. It's nothing. But what have *you* been doing all this time?"

"Come, and I'll show you." She led him toward the other room.

He followed, in growing wonder.

"No attack, yet?"

"None. But the drums have been beating for a long time now. Hear *that?*"

They listened. To them drifted a dull, monotonous sound, harbinger of war.

Stern laughed bitterly, chokingly, by reason of his thirst.

"Much good their orchestra will do them," said he, "when it comes to facing soft-nosed .38's! But tell me, what was it you were going to show me?"

Quickly she went over to their crude table, took up a dish and came back to him.

"Drink this!" bade she.

He took it, wondering.

"What? *Coffee?* But—?"

"Drink! I've had mine, already. Drink!"

Half-stupefied, he obeyed. He drained the whole dish at a draft, then caught his breath in a long sigh.

"But this means water!" cried he, with renewed vigor. "And—?"

"Look here," she directed, pointing. There on the circular hearth stood the copper kettle, three-quarters full.

"Water! You've got *water?*" He started forward in amazement. "While I've been sleeping? Where—?"

She laughed with real enjoyment.

"It's nothing," she disclaimed. "After what you've done for me, this is the merest trifle, Allan. You know that big cavity made by the boiler-explosion? Yes? Well, when we looked down into it, before we ventured out to the spring, I noticed a good deal of water at the bottom, stagnant water, that had run out of the boiler and settled on the hard clay floor and in among the cracked cement. I just merely brought up some, and strained and boiled it, that's all. So you see—"

"But, my Lord!" burst out the man, "d'you mean to say you—you went down *there—alone?*"

Once more the girl laughed.

"Not alone," she answered. "One of the automatics was kind enough to bear me company. Of course the main stairway was impassable. But I found another way, off through the east end of the building and down some stairs we haven't used at all, yet. They may be useful, by the way, in case of—well—a retreat. Once I'd reached the arcade, the rest was easy. I had that leather rope tied to the kettle handle, you see. So all I had to do was—"

"But the Horde! The Horde?"

"None of them down there, now—that is, alive. None when I was there. All at the war-council, I imagine. I just happened to strike it right, you see. It wasn't anything. We simply *had* to have water, so I went and got some, that's all."

"That's all?" echoed Stern, in a trembling voice. That's—*all!*"

Then, lest she see his face even by the dim light through the window, he turned aside a minute. For the tears in his eyes, he felt, were a weakness which he would not care to reveal.

But presently he faced the girl again.

"Beatrice," said he, "words fall so flat, so hopelessly dead; they're so inadequate, so anticlimatic at a time like this, that I'm just going to skip them all. It's no use thanking you, or analyzing this thing, or saying any of the commonplace, stupid things. Let it pass. You've got water, that's enough. You've made good, where I failed. Well—"

His voice broke again, and he grew silent. But she, peering at him with wonder, laid a hand upon his shoulder.

"Come," said she, "you must eat something, too. I've got a little supper ready. After that, the Pulverite?"

He started as though shot.

"That's so! I *can* make it now!" cried he, new life and energy suffusing him. "Even with my one hand, if you help me, I can make it! Supper? No, no! *To work!*"

But she insisted, womanlike; and he at last consented to a bite. When this was over, they began preparations for the manufacture of the terrible explosive, Stern's own secret and invention, which, had not the cataclysm intervened, would have made him ten times over a millionaire. More precious now to him, that knowledge, than all the golden treasures of the dead, forsaken world!

"We've got to risk a light," said he. "If it's turned low, and shaded, maybe they won't learn our whereabouts. But however that may be, we can't work in the dark. It would be too horribly perilous. One false move, one wrong combination, even the addition of one ingredient at the improper moment, and—well—you understand."

She nodded.

"Yes," said she. "And we don't want to quit—just *yet!*"

So they lighted the smaller of their copper lamps, and set to work in earnest.

On the table, cleared of dishes and of food, Stern placed in order eight glass bottles, containing the eight basic chemicals for his reaction.

Beside him, at his left hand, he set a large metal dish with three quarts of water, still warm. In front of him stood his copper tea-kettle—the strangest retort, surely in which the terrific compound ever had been distilled.

"Now our chairs, and the lamp," said he, "and we're ready to begin. But first," and, looking earnestly at her, "first, tell me frankly, wouldn't you just a little rather have me carry out this experiment alone? You could wait elsewhere, you know. With these uncertain materials and all the crude conditions we've got to work under, there's no telling what—might happen.

"I've never yet found a man who would willingly stand by and see me build Pulverite, much less a woman. It's frightful, this stuff is! Don't be ashamed to tell me; are you afraid?"

For a long moment the girl looked at him.

"Afraid—with *you?*" said she.

CHAPTER XXVIII

THE PULVERITE

AN hour passed. And now, under the circle of light cast by the hooded lamp upon the table, there in that bare, wrecked office-home of theirs, the Pulverite was coming to its birth.

Already at the bottom of the metal dish lay a thin yellow cloud, something that looked like London fog on a December morning. There, covered with the water, it gently swirled and curdled, with strange metallic glints and oily sheens, as Beatrice with a gold spoon stirred it at the engineer's command.

From moment to moment he dropped in a minute quantity of glycerin, out of a glass test-tube, graduated to the hundredth of an ounce. Keenly, under the lamp-shine, he watched the final reaction; his face, very pale and set, reflected a little of the mental stress that bound him.

Along the table-edge before him, limp in its sling, his wounded arm lay useless. Yet with his left hand he controlled the sleeping giant in the dish. And as he dropped the glycerin, he counted.

"Ten, eleven, twelve—fifteen, sixteen—twenty! Now! Now pour the water off, quick! *Quick!*"

Splendidly the girl obeyed. The water ran, foaming strangely, out into a glass jar set to receive it. Her hands trembled not, nor did she hesitate. Only, a line formed between her brows; and her breath, half-held, came quickly through her lips.

"*Stop!*"

His voice rang like a shot.

"Now, decant it through this funnel, into the vials!"

Again, using both hands for steadiness, she did his bidding.

And one by one as she filled the little flasks of chained death, the engineer stoppered them with his left hand.

When the last was done, Stern drew a tremendous sigh, and dashed the sweat from his forehead with a gesture of victory.

Into the residue in the dish he poured a little nitric acid.

"*That's* got no kick left in it, now, anyhow," said he relieved. "The HNO3 tames it, quick enough. But the bottles—take care—don't tip one over, as you love your life!"

He stood up, slowly, and for a moment remained there, his face in the shadow of the lamp-shade, holding to the table-edge for support, with his left hand.

At him the girl looked.

"And now," she began, "now—?"

The question had no time for completion. For even as she spoke, a swift little something flicked through the window, behind them.

It struck the opposite wall with a sharp *crack!* then fell slithering to the floor.

Outside, against the building, they heard another and another little shock; and all at once a second missile darted through the air.

This hit the lamp. Stern grabbed the shade and steadied it. Beatrice stooped and snatched up the thing from where it lay beside the table.

Only one glance Stern gave at it, as she held it up. A long reed stem he saw wrapped at its base with cotton fibers—a fish-bone point, firm-lashed—and on that point a dull red stain, a blotch of something dry and shiny.

"Blow-gun darts!" cried he. "Poisoned! They've seen the light—got our range! They're up there in the tree-tops—shooting at us!"

With one puff, the light was gone. By the wrist he seized Beatrice. He dragged her toward the front wall, off to one side, out of range.

"The flasks of Pulverite! Suppose a dart should hit one?" exclaimed the girl.

"That's so! Wait here—I'll get them!"

But she was there beside him as, in the thick dark, he cautiously felt for the deadly things and found them with a hand that *dared not* tremble. And though here, there, the little venom-stings whis-s-shed over them and past them, to shatter on the rear wall, she helped him bear the vials, all nine of them, to a place of safety in the left-hand front corner where by no possibility could they be struck.

Together then, quietly as wraiths, they stole into the next room; and there, from a window not as yet attacked, they spied out at the dark tree-tops that lay in dense masses almost brushing the walls.

"See? See there?" whispered Stern in the girl's ear. He pointed where, not ten yards away and below, a blacker shadow seemed to move along a hemlock branch. Forgotten now, his wounds. Forgotten his loss of blood, his fever and his weakness. The sight of that creeping stealthy attack nerved him with new vigor. And, even as the girl looked, Stern drew his revolver.

Speaking no further word, he laid the ugly barrel firm across the sill.

Carefully he sighted, as best he could in that gloom lit only by the stars. Coldly as though at a target-shot, he brought the muzzle-sight to bear on that deep, crawling shadow.

Then suddenly a spurt of fire split the night. The crackling report echoed away. And with a bubbling scream, the shadow loosened from the limb, as a ripe fruit loosens. Vaguely they saw it fall, whirl, strike a branch, slide off, and disappear.

All at once a pattering rain of darts flickered around them. Stern felt one strike his fur jacket and bounce off. Another grazed the girl's head. But to their work they stood, and flinched not.

Now her revolver was speaking, in antiphony with his; and from the branches, two, three, five, eight, ten of the ape-things fell.

"Give it to 'em!" shouted the engineer, as though he had a regiment behind him. "*Give* it to 'em!" And again he pulled trigger.

The revolver was empty.

With a cry he threw it down, and, running to where the shotgun stood, snatched it up. He scooped into his pocket a handful of shells from the box where they were stored; and as he darted back to the window, he cocked both hammers.

"Poom! *Poom!*"

The deep baying of the Lefever roared out in twin jets of flame.

Stern broke the gun and jacked in two more shells.

Again he fired.

"Good Heaven! How many of 'em *are* there in the trees?" shouted he.

"Try the Pulverite!" cried Beatrice. "Maybe you might hit a branch!"

Stern flung down the gun. To the corner where the vials were standing he ran.

Up he caught one—he dared not take two lest they should by some accident strike together.

"Here—here, now, take *this!*" he bellowed.

And from the window, aiming at a pine that stood seventy-five feet away—a pine whose branches seemed to hang thick with the Horde's blowgun-men—he slung it with all the strength of his uninjured arm.

Into the gloom it vanished, the little meteorite of latent death, of potential horror and destruction.

"If it hits 'em, they'll think we *are* gods, after all, what?" cried the engineer, peering eagerly. But for a moment, nothing happened.

"Missed it!" he groaned. "If I only had my right arm to use now, I might—"

Far below, down there a hundred feet beneath them and out a long way from the tower base, night yawned wide in a burst of hellish glare.

A vast conical hole of flame was gouged in the dark. For a fraction of a second every tree, limb, twig stood out in vivid detail, as that blue-white glory shot aloft.

All up through the forest the girl and Stern got a momentary glimpse of little, clinging Things, crouching misshapen, hideous.

Then, as a riven and distorted whirl burst upward in a huge geyser of annihilation, came a detonation that ripped, stunned, shattered; that sent both the defenders staggering backward from the window.

Darkness closed again, like a gaping mouth that shuts. And all about the building, through the trees, and down again in a titanic, slashing rain fell the wreckage of things that had been stone, and earth, and root, and tree, and living creatures—that had been—that now were but one indistinguishable mass of ruin and of death.

After that, here and there, small dark objects came dropping, thudding, crashing down. You might have thought some cosmic gardener had shaken his orchard, his orchard where the plums and pears were rotten-ripe.

"*One!*" cried the engineer, in a strange, wild, exultant voice.

CHAPTER XXIX

THE BATTLE ON THE STAIRS

ALMOST like the echo of his shout, a faint snarling cry rose from the corridor, outside. They heard a clicking, sliding, ominous sound; and, with instant comprehension, knew the truth.

"They've got up, some of them—somehow!" Stern cried. "They'll be at our throats, here, in a moment! Load! *Load!* You shoot—*I'll* give 'em Pulverite!"

No time, now, for caution. While the girl hastily threw in more cartridges, Stern gathered up all the remaining vials of the explosive.

These, garnered along his wounded arm which clasped them to his body, made a little bristling row of death. His left hand remained free, to fling the little glass bombs.

"Come! Come, meet 'em—they mustn't trap us, here!"

And together they crept noiselessly into the other room and thence to the corridor-door.

Out they peered.

"Look! Torches!" whispered he.

There at the far end of the hallway, a red glare already flickered on the wall around the turn by the elevator-shaft. Already the confused sounds of the attackers were drawing near.

"They've managed to dig away the barricade, somehow," said Stern. "And now they're out for business—clubs, poisoned darts and all—and fangs, and claws! How many of 'em? God knows! A swarm, that's all!"

His mouth felt hot and dry, with fever, and the mad excitement of the impending battle. His skin seemed tense and drawn, especially upon the forehead. As he stood there, waiting, he heard the girl's quick breathing. Though he could hardly see her in the gloom, he felt her presence and he loved it.

"Beatrice," said he, and for a moment his hand sought hers, "Beatrice, little girl o' mine, if this is the big finish, if we both go down together and there's no to-morrow, I want to tell you now—"

A yapping outcry interrupted him. The girl seized his arm. Brighter the torchlight grew.

"Allan!" she whispered. "Come back, back, away from here. We've got to get up those stairs, there, at the other end of the hall. This is no kind of place to meet them—we're exposed, here. There's no protection!"

"You're right," he answered. "Come!"

Like ghosts they slid away, noiselessly, through the enshrouding gloom.

Even as they gained the shelter of the winding stairway, the scouts of the Horde, flaring their torches into each room they passed, came into view around the corner at the distant end.

Shuffling, hideous beyond all words by the fire-gleam, bent, wizened, blue, the Things swarmed toward them in a vague and shifting mass, a ruck of horror.

The defenders, peering from behind the broken balustrade, could hear the guttural jabber of their beast-talk, the clicking play of their fangs; could see the craning necks, the talons that held spears, bludgeons, blow-guns, even jagged rocks.

Over all, the smoky gleams wavered in a ghastly interplay of light and darkness. Uncanny shadows leaped along the walls. From every corner and recess and black, empty door, ghoulish shapes seemed creeping.

Tense, now, the moment hung.

Suddenly the engineer bent forward, staring.

"The chief!" he whispered. And as he spoke, Beatrice aimed.

There, shambling among the drove of things, they saw him clearly for a moment. Uglier, more incredibly brutal than ever he looked, now, by that uncanny light.

Stern saw—and rejoiced in the sight—that the obeah's jaw hung surely broken, all awry. The quick-blinking, narrow-lidded eyes shuttled here, there, as the creature sought to spy out his enemies. The nostrils dilated, to catch the spoor of man. Man, no longer god, but mortal.

One hand held a crackling pine-knot. The other gripped the haft of a stone ax, one blow of which would dash to pulp the stoutest skull.

This much Stern noted, as in a flash; when at his side the girl's revolver spat.

The report roared heavily in that constricted space. For a moment the obeah stopped short. A look of brute pain, of wonder, then of quintupled rage passed over his face. A twitching grin of passion distorted the huge, wounded gash of the mouth. He screamed. Up came the stone ax.

"Again!" shouted Stern. "Give it to him again!"

She fired on the instant. But already, with a chattering howl, the obeah was running forward. And after him, screaming, snarling, foaming till their lips were all a slaver, the pack swept toward them.

Stern dragged the girl away, back to the landing.

"Up! *Up!*" he yelled.

Then, turning, he hurled the second bomb.

A blinding glare dazzled him. A shock, as of a suddenly unleashed volcano, all but flung him headlong.

Dazed, choked by the gush of fumes that burst in a billowing cloud out along the hall and up the stairs, he staggered forward. Tightly to his body he clutched the remaining vials. Where was Beatrice? He knew not. Everything boomed and echoed in his stunned ears. Below, there, he heard thunderous crashes as wrecked walls and floors went reeling down. And ever, all about him, eddied the strangling smoke.

Then, how long after he knew not, he found himself gasping for air beside a window.

"Beatrice!" he shouted with his first breath. Everything seemed strangely still. No sound of pursuit, no howling now. Dead calm. Not even the drumbeat in the forest, far below.

"*Beatrice!* Where—are you? *Beatrice!*"

His heart leaped gladly as he heard her answer.

"Oh! Are you safe? Thank God! I—I was afraid—I didn't know—"

To him she ran along the dark passageway.

"No more!" she panted. "No more Pulverite here in the building!" pleaded she. "Or the whole tower will fall—and bury us! No more!"

Stern laughed. Beatrice was unharmed; he had found her.

"I'll sow it broadcast outside," he answered, in a kind of exaltation, almost a madness from the strain and horror of that night, the weakness of his fever and his loss of blood. "Maybe the others, down there still, may need it. Here goes!"

And, one by one, all seven of the bombs he hurled far out and away, to right, to left, straight ahead, slinging them in vast parabolas from the height.

And as they struck one by one, night blazed like noonday; and even to the Palisades the crashing echoes roared.

The forest, swept as by a giant broom, became a jack-straw tangle of destruction.

Thus it perished.

When the last vial of wrath had been out-poured, when silence had once more dropped its soothing mantle and the great brooding dark had come again, "girdled with gracious watchings of the stars," Stern spoke.

"Gods!" he exclaimed exultantly. "Gods we are now to them—to such of them as may still live. Gods we are—gods we shall be forever!

"Whatever happens now, *they* know us. The Great White Gods of Terror! They'll flee before our very look! Unarmed, if we meet a thousand, we'll be safe. *Gods!*"

Another silence.

Then suddenly he knew that Beatrice was weeping.

And forgetful of all save that, forgetful of his weakness and his wounds, he comforted her—as only a man can comfort the woman he loves, the woman who, in turn, loves him.

CHAPTER XXX

Consummation

After a while, both calmer grown, they looked again from the high window.

"See!" exclaimed the engineer, and pointed.

There, far away to westward, a few straggling lights—only a very few— slowly and uncertainly were making their way across the broad black breast of the river.

Even as the man and woman watched, one vanished. Then another winked out, and did not reappear. No more than fifteen seemed to reach the Jersey shore, there to creep vaguely, slowly away and vanish in the dense primeval woods.

"Come," said Stern at last. "We must be going, too. The night's half spent. By morning we must be very far away."

"What? We've got to leave the city?"

"Yes. There's no such thing as staying here now. The tower's quite untenable. Racked and shaken as it is, it's liable to fall at any time. But, even if it should stand, we can't live here any more."

"But—where now?"

"I don't just know. Somewhere else, that's certain. Everything in this whole vicinity is ruined. The spring's gone. Nothing remains of the forest, nothing but horror and death. Pestilence is bound to sweep this place in the wake of such a—such an affair.

"The sights all about here aren't such as you should see. Neither should I. We mustn't even think of them. Some way or other we can find a path down out of here, away—away—"

"But," she cried anxiously, "but all our treasures? All the tools and dishes, all the food and clothing, and everything? All our precious, hard-won things?"

"Nothing left of them now. Down on the fifth floor, at that end of the building, I'm positive there's nothing but a vast hole blown out of the side of the tower. So there's nothing left to salvage. Nothing at all."

"Can you replace the things?"

"Why not? Wherever we settle down we can get along for a few days on what game I can snare or shoot with the few remaining cartridges. And after that—"

"Yes?"

"After that, once we get established a little, I can come into the city and go to raiding again. What we've lost is a mere trifle compared to what's left in New York. Why, the latent resources of this vast ruin haven't been even touched yet! We've got our lives. That's the only vital factor. With those everything else is possible. It all looks dark and hard to you now, Beatrice. But in a few days—wait and see!"

"Allan!"

"What, Beatrice?"

"I trust you in everything. I'm in your hands. Lead me."

"Come, then, for the way is long before us. Come!"

Two hours later, undaunted by the far howling of a wolf-pack, as the wan crescent of the moon came up the untroubled sky, they reached the brink of the river, almost due west of where the southern end of Central Park had been.

This course, they felt, would avoid any possible encounter with stragglers of the Horde. Through Madison Forest—or what remained of it—they had not gone; but had struck eastward from the building, then northward, and so in a wide détour had avoided all the horrors that they knew lay near the wreck of the tower.

The river, flowing onward to the sea as calmly as though pain and death and ruin and all the dark tragedy of the past night, the past centuries, had never been, filled their tired souls and bodies with a grateful peace. Slowly, gently it lapped the wooded shore, where docks and slips had all gone back to nature; the moonlit ripples spoke of beauty, life, hope, love.

Though they could not drink the brackish waters, yet they laved their faces, arms and hands, and felt refreshed. Then for some time in silence they skirted the flood, ever northward, away from the dead city's heart. And the moon rose even higher, higher still, and great thoughts welled within their hearts. The cool night breeze, freshening in from the vast salt wastes of the sea—unsailed forever now—cooled their cheeks and soothed the fever of their thoughts.

Where the grim ruin of Grant's Tomb looked down upon the river, they came at length upon a strange, rude boat, another, then a third—a whole flotilla, moored with plaited ropes of grass to trees along the shore.

"These must certainly be the canoes of the attacking force from northward, the force that fought the Horde the night before *we* took a hand in the matter; fought, and were beaten, and—devoured," said Stern.

And with a practical eye, wise and cool even despite the pain of his wounded arm, he examined three or four of the boats as best he could by moonlight.

The girl and he agreed on one to use.

"Yes, this looks like the most suitable," judged the engineer, indicating a rough, banca-like craft nearly sixteen feet long, which had been carved and scraped and burned out of a single log.

He helped Beatrice in, then cast off the rope. In the bottom lay six paddles of the most degraded state of workmanship. They showed no trace of decoration whatsoever, and the lowest savages of the pre-cataclysmic era had invariably attempted some crude form of art on nearly every implement.

The girl took up one of the paddles.

"Which way? Up-stream?" asked she. "No, no, you mustn't even try to use that arm."

"Why paddle at all?" Stern answered. "See here."

He pointed where a short and crooked mast lay, unstepped, along the side. Lashed to it was a sail of rawhides, clumsily caught together with thongs, heavy and stiff, yet full of promise.

Stern laughed.

"Back to the coracle stage again," said he. "Back to Cæsar's time, and way beyond!" And he lifted one end of the mast. "Here we've got the Seuvian *pellis pro velis,* the 'skins for sails' all over again—only more so. Well, no matter. Up she goes!"

Together they stepped the mast and spread the sail. The engineer took his place in the stern, a paddle in his left hand. He dipped it, and the ripples glinted away.

"Now," said he, in a voice that left no room for argument, "now, *you* curl up in the tiger-skin and go to sleep! This is my job."

The sail caught the breath of the breeze. The banca moved slowly forward, trailing its wake like widening lines of silver in the moonlight.

And Beatrice, strong in her trust of him, her confidence and love, lay down to sleep while the wounded man steered on and on, and watched her and protected her. And over all the stars, a glory in the summer sky, kept silent vigil.

Dawn broke, all a flame of gold and crimson, as they landed in a sheltered little bay on the west shore.

Here, though the forest stood unbroken in thick ranges all along the background, it had not yet invaded the slope that led back from the pebbly beach. And through the tangle of what once must have been a splendid orchard, they caught a glimpse of white walls overgrown with a mad profusion of wild roses, wistarias and columbines.

"This was once upon a time the summer-place, the big concrete bungalow and all, of Harrison Van Amburg. You know the billionaire, the wheat man? It used to be all his in the long ago. He built it for all time of a material that time can never change. It was his. Well, it's ours now. Our home!"

Together they stood upon the shelving beach, lapped by the river. Somewhere in the woods behind them a robin was caroling with liquid harmony.

Stern drew the rude boat up. Then, breathing deep, he faced the morning.

"You and I, Beatrice," said he, and took her hand. "Just you—and I!"

"And love!" she whispered.

"And hope, and life! And the earth reborn. The arts and sciences, language and letters, truth, 'all the glories of the world' handed down through us!

"Listen! The race of men, our race, must live again—shall live! Again the forests and the plains shall be the conquest of our blood. Once more shall cities gleam and tower, ships sail the sea, and the world go on to greater wisdom, better things!

"A kinder and a saner world this time. No misery, no war, no poverty, woe, strife, creeds, oppression, tears—for we are wiser than those other folk, and there shall be no error."

He paused, his face irradiate. To him recurred the prophecy of Ingersoll, the greatest orator of that other time. And very slowly he spoke again:

"Beatrice, it shall be a world where thrones have crumbled and where kings are dust. The aristocracy of idleness shall reign no more! A world without a slave. Man shall at last be free!

"'A world at peace, adorned by every form of art, with music's myriad voices thrilled, while lips are rich with words of love and truth. A world in which no exile sighs, no prisoner mourns; a world on which the gibbet's shadow shall not fall.

"'A race without disease of flesh or brain, shapely and fair, the wedded harmony of form and function. And as I look, life lengthens, joy deepens, and over all in the great dome shines the eternal star of human hope!'"

"And love?" she smiled again, a deep and sacred meaning in her words. Within her stirred the universal motherhood, the hope of everything, the call of the unborn, the insistent voice of the race that was to be.

"And love!" he answered, his voice now very tender, very grave.

Tired, yet strong, he looked upon her. And as he looked his eyes grew deep and eager.

Sweet as the honey of Hymettus was the perfume of the orchard, all a powder of white and rosy blooms, among which the bees, pollen-dusted, labored, at their joyous, fructifying task. Fresh, the morning breeze. Clear, warm, radiant, the sun of June; the summer sun uprising far beyond the shining hills.

Life everywhere—and love!

Love, too, for them. For this man, this woman, love; the mystery, the pleasure and the eternal pain.

With his unhurt arm he circled her. He bent, he drew her to him, as she raised her face to his.

And for the first time his mouth sought hers.

Their lips, long hungry for this madness, met there and blended in a kiss of passion and of joy.

BOOK II
BEYOND THE GREAT OBLIVION

CHAPTER I

BEGINNINGS

A THOUSAND years of darkness and decay! A thousand years of blight, brutality, and atavism; of Nature overwhelming all man's work, of crumbling cities and of forgotten civilization, of stupefaction, of death! A thousand years of night!

Two human beings, all alone in that vast wilderness—a woman and a man.

The past, irrevocable; the present, fraught with problems, perils, and alarms; the future—what?

A thousand years!

Yet, though this thousand years had seemingly smeared away all semblance of the world of men from the cosmic canvas, Allan Stern and Beatrice Kendrick thrilled with as vital a passion as though that vast, oblivious age lay not between them and the time that was.

And their long kiss, there in sight of their new home-to-be—alone there in that desolated world—was as natural as the summer breeze, the liquid melody of the red-breast on the blossomy apple-bough above their heads, the white and purple spikes of odorous lilacs along the vine-grown stone wall, the gold and purple dawn now breaking over the distant reaches of the river.

Thus were these two betrothed, this sole surviving pair of human beings.

Thus, as the new day burned to living flame up the inverted bowl of sky, this woman and this man pledged each other their love and loyalty and trust.

Thus they stood together, his left arm about her warm, lithe body, clad as she was only in her tigerskin. Their eyes met and held true, there in the

127

golden glory of the dawn. Unafraid, she read the message in the depths of his, the invitation, the command; and they both foreknew the future.

Beatrice spoke first, flushing a little as she drew toward him.

"Allan," she said with infinite tenderness, even as a mother might speak to a well-loved son, "Allan, come now and let me dress your wound. That's the first thing to do. Come, let me see your arm."

He smiled a little, and with his broad, brown hand stroked back the spun silk of her hair, its mass transfixed by the raw gold pins he had found for her among the ruins of New York.

"No, no!" he objected. "It's nothing—it's not worth bothering about. I'll be all right in a day or two. My flesh heals almost at once, without any care. You don't realize how healthy I am."

"I know, dear, but it must hurt you terribly!"

"Hurt? How could I feel any pain with your kiss on my mouth?"

"Come!" she again repeated with insistence, and pointed toward the beach where their banca lay on the sand.

"Come, I'll dress your wound first. And after I find out just how badly you're injured—"

He tried to stop her mouth with kisses, but she evaded him.

"No, no!" she cried. "Not now—not now!"

Allan had to cede. And now presently there he knelt on the fine white sand, his bearskin robe opened and flung back, his well-knit shoulder and sinewed arm bare and brown.

"Well, is it fatal?" he jested. "How long do you give me to survive it?" as with her hand and the cold limpid water of the Hudson she started to lave the caked blood away from his gashed triceps.

At sight of the wound she looked grave, but made no comment. She had no bandages; but with the woodland skill she had developed in the past weeks of life in close touch with nature, she bound the cleansed wound with cooling leaves and fastened them securely in place with lashings of leather thongs from the banca.

Presently the task was done. Stern slipped his bearskin back in place. Beatrice, still solicitous, tried to clasp the silver buckle that held it; but he, unable to restrain himself, caught her hand in both of his and crushed it to his lips.

Then he took her perfect face between his palms, and for a long moment studied it. He looked at her waving hair, luxuriant and glinting rich brown gleams in the sunlight; her thick, arched brows and hazel eyes, liquid and full of mystery as woodland pools; her skin, sun-browned and satiny, with abundant tides of life-blood coursing vigorously in its warm flush; her ripe lips. He studied her, and loved and yearned toward her; and in him the passion leaped up like living flames.

His mouth met hers again.

"My belovèd!" breathed he.

Her rounded arm, bare to the shoulder, circled his neck; she hid her face in his breast.

"Not yet—not yet!" she whispered.

On the white and pink flowered bough above, the robin, unafraid, gushed into a very madness of golden song. And now the sun, higher risen, had struck the river into a broad sheet of spun metal, over which the swallows—even as in the olden days—darted and spiraled, with now and then a flick and dash of spray.

Far off, wool-white winding-sheets of mist were lifting, lagging along the purple hills, clothed with inviolate forest.

Again the man tried to raise her head, to burn his kisses on her mouth. But she, instilled with the eternal spirit of woman, denied him.

"No, not now—not yet!" she said; and in her eyes he read her meaning. "You must let me go now, Allan. There's so much to do; we've got to be practical, you know."

"Practical! When I—I love—"

"Yes, I know, dear. But there's so much to be done first." Her womanly homemaking instinct would not be gainsaid. "There's so much work! We've got the place to explore, and the house to put in order, and—oh, thousands of things! And we must be very sensible and very wise, you and I, boy. We're not children, you know. Now that we've lost our home in the Metropolitan Tower, everything's got to be done over again."

"Except to learn to love you!" answered Stern, letting her go with reluctance.

She laughed back at him over her fur-clad shoulder as her sandaled feet followed the dim remnants of what must once have been a broad driveway from the river road along the beach, leading up to the bungalow.

Through the encroaching forest and the tangle of the degenerate apple-trees they could see the concrete walls, with here or there a bit of white still gleaming through the enlacements of ancient vines that had enveloped the whole structure—woodbine, ivy, wistarias, and the maddest jungle of climbing roses, red and yellow, that ever made a nest for love.

"Wait, I'll go first and clear the way for you," he said cheerily. His big bulk crashed down the undergrowth. His hands held back the thorns and briers and the whipping hardhacks. Together they slowly made way toward the house.

The orchard had lost all semblance of regularity, for in the thousand years since the hand of man had pruned or cared for it Mother Nature had planted and replanted it times beyond counting. Small and gnarled and crooked the trees were, as the spine-tree souls in Dante's *dolorosa selva.*

Here or there a pine had rooted and grown tall, killing the lesser tribe of green things underneath.

Warm lay the sun there. A pleasant carpet of last year's leaves and pine-spills covered the earth.

"It's all ready and waiting for us, all embowered and carpeted for love," said Allan musingly. "I wonder what old Van Amburg would think of his estate if he could see it now? And what would he say to our having it? You know, Van was pretty ugly to me at one time about my political opinion—but that's all past and forgotten now. Only this is certainly an odd turn of fate."

He helped the girl over a fallen log, rotted with moss and lichens. "It's one awful mess, sure as you're born. But as quick as my arm gets back into shape, we'll have order out of chaos before you know it. Some fine day you and I will drive our sixty horse-power car up an asphalt road here, and—"

"A car? Why, what do you mean? There's not such a thing left in the whole world as a car!"

The engineer tapped his forehead with his finger.

"Oh, yes, there is. I've got several models right here. You just wait till you see the workshop I'm going to install on the bank of the river with current-power, and with an electric light plant for the whole place, and with—"

Beatrice laughed.

"You dear, big, dreaming boy!" she interrupted. Then with a kiss she took his hand.

"Come," said she. "We're home now. And there's work to do."

CHAPTER II

SETTLING DOWN

TOGETHER, in the comradeship of love and trust and mutual understanding, they reached the somewhat open space before the bungalow, where once the road had ended in a stone-paved drive. Allan's wounded arm, had he but sensed it, was beginning to pain more than a little. But he was oblivious. His love, the fire of spring that burned in his blood, the lure of this great adventuring, banished all consciousness of ill.

Parting a thicket, they reached the steps. And for a while they stood there, hand in hand, silent and thrilled with vast, strange thoughts, dreaming of what must be. In their eyes lay mirrored the future of the human race. The light that glowed in them evoked the glories of the dawn of life again, after ten centuries of black oblivion.

"Our home now!" he told her, very gently, and again he kissed her, but this time on the forehead. "Ours when we shall have reclaimed it and made it ours. See the yellow roses, dear? They symbolize our golden future. The red, red roses? Our passion and our pain!"

The girl made no answer, but tears gathered in her eyes—tears from the deepest wells of the soul. She brought his hand to her lips.

"Ours!" she whispered tremblingly.

They stood there together for a little space, silent and glad. From an oak that shaded the porch a squirrel chippered at them. A sparrow—larger now than the sparrows they remembered in the time that was—peered out at them, wondering but unafraid, from its nest under the eaves; at them, the first humans it had ever seen.

"We've got a tenant already, haven't we?" smiled Allan. "Well, I guess we sha'n't have to disturb her, unless perhaps for a while, when I cut away this poison ivy here." He pointed at the glossy triple leaf. "No poisonous thing, whether plant, snake, spider, or insect, is going to stay in this Eden!" he concluded, with a laugh.

Together, with a strange sense of violating the spirit of the past, they went up the concrete steps, untrodden now by human feet for ten centuries.

The massive blocks were still intact for the most part, for old Van Amburg had builded with endless care and with no remotest regard for cost.

Here a vine, there a sapling had managed to insinuate a tap-root in some crack made by the frost, but the damage was trifling. Except for the falling of a part of a cornice, the building was complete. But it was hidden in vines and mold. Moss, lichens and weeds grew on the steps, flourishing in the detritus that had accumulated.

Allan dug the toe of his sandal into the loose drift of dead leaves and pine-spills that littered the broad piazza.

"It'll need more than a vacuum cleaner to put this in shape!" said he. "Well, the sooner we get at it, the better. We'd do well to take a look at the inside."

The front door, one-time built of oaken planks studded with hand-worked nails and banded with huge wrought-iron hinges, now hung there a mere shell of itself, worm-eaten, crumbling, disintegrated.

With no tools but his naked hands Stern tore and battered it away. A thick, pungent haze of dust arose, yellow in the morning sunlight that presently, for the first time in a thousand years, fell warm and bright across the cobwebbed front hallway, through the aperture.

Room by room Allan and Beatrice explored. The bungalow was practically stripped bare by time.

"Only moth and rust," sighed the girl. "The same story everywhere we go. But—well, never mind. We'll soon have it looking homelike. Make me a broom, dear, and I'll sweep out the worst of it at once."

Talking now in terms of practical detail, with romance for the hour displaced by harsh reality, they examined the entire house.

Of the once magnificent furnishings, only dust-piles, splinters and punky rubbish remained. Through the rotted plank shutters, that hung drunkenly awry from rust-eaten hinges, long spears of sunlight wanly illuminated the wreck of all that had once been the lavish home of a billionaire.

Rugs, paintings, furniture, *bibelots,* treasures of all kinds now lay commingled in mournful decay. In what had evidently been the music room, overlooking the grounds to southward, the grand piano now was only a mass of rusted frame, twisted and broken fragments of wire and a considerable heap of wood-detritus, with a couple of corroded pedals buried in the pile.

"And *this* was the famous hundred-thousand-dollar harp of Sara, his daughter, that the papers used to talk so much about, you remember?"

asked the girl, stirring with her foot a few mournful bits of rubbish that lay near the piano.

"*Sic transit gloria mundi!*" growled Stern, shaking his head. "You and she were the same age, almost. And now—"

Silent and full of strange thoughts they went on into what had been the kitchen. The stove, though heavily bedded in rust, retained its form, for the solid steel had resisted even the fearful lapse of vanished time.

"After I scour that with sand and water," said Stern, "and polish up these aluminum utensils and reset that broken pane with a piece of glass from up-stairs where it isn't needed, you won't know this place. Yes, and I'll have running water in here, too—and electricity from the power-plant, and—"

"Oh, Allan," interrupted the girl, delightedly, "this must have been the dining room." She beckoned from a doorway. "No end of dishes left for us! Isn't it jolly? This is luxury compared to the way we had to start in the tower!"

In the dining-room a good number of the more solid cut-glass and china pieces had resisted the shock of having fallen, centuries ago, to the floor, when the shelves and cupboards of teak and mahogany had rotted and gone to pieces. Corroded silverware lay scattered all about; and there was gold plate, too, intact save for the patina of extreme age—platters, dishes, beakers. But of the table and the chairs, nothing remained save dust.

Like curious children they poked and pried.

"Dishes enough!" exclaimed she. "Gold, till you can't rest. But how about something to put *on* the dishes? We haven't had a bite since yesterday noon, and I'm about starved. Now that the fighting's all over, I begin to remember my healthy appetite!"

Stern smiled.

"You'll have some breakfast, girlie," promised he. "There'll be the where-withal to garnish our 18-k, never fear. Just let's have a look up-stairs, and then I'll go after something for the larder."

They left the down-stairs rooms, silent save for a fly buzzing in a spider's web, and together ascended the dusty stairs. The railing was entirely gone; but the concrete steps remained.

Stern helped the girl, in spite of the twinge of pain it caused his wounded arm. His heart beat faster—so, too, did hers—as they gained the upper story. The touch of her was, to him, like a lighted match flung into a powder magazine; but he bit his lip, and though his face paled, then flushed, he held his voice steady as he said:

"So then, bats up here? Well, how the deuce do they get in and out? Ah! That broken window, where the elm-branch has knocked out the glass—I see! That's got to be fixed at once!"

He brushed webs and dust from the remaining panes, and together they peered out over the orchard, out across the river, now a broad sheet of molten gold. His arm went about her; he drew her head against his heart, fast-beating; and silence fell.

"Come, Allan," said the girl at length, calmer than he. "Let's see what we've got here to do with. Oh, I tell you to begin with," and she smiled up frankly at him, "I'm a tremendously practical sort of woman. You may be an engineer, and know how to build wireless telegraphs and bridges and—and things; but when it comes to home-building—"

"I admit it. Well, lead on," he answered; and together they explored the upper rooms. The sense of intimacy now lay strong upon them, of unity and of indissoluble love and comradeship. This was quite another venture than the exploration of the tower, for now they were choosing a home, *their* home, and in them the mating instinct had begun to thrill, to burn.

Each room, despite its ruin and decay, took on a special charm, a dignity, the foreshadowing of what must be. Yet instrinsically the place was mournful, even after Stern had let the sunshine in.

For all was dark desolation. The rosewood and mahogany furniture, pictures, rugs, brass beds, all alike lay reduced to dust and ashes. A gold clock, the porcelain fittings of the bath-room, and some fine clay and meerschaum pipes in what had evidently been Van Amburg's den—these constituted all that had escaped the tooth of time.

In a front room that probably had been Sara's, a mud-swallow had built its nest in the far corner. It flew out, frightened, when Stern thrust his hand into the aperture to see if the nest were tenanted, fluttered about with scared cries, then vanished up the broad fireplace.

"Eggs—warm!" announced Stern. "Well, this room will have to be shut up and left. We've got more than enough, anyhow. Less work for you, dear," he added, with a smile. "We might use only the lower floor, if you like. I don't want you killing yourself with housework, you understand."

She laughed cheerily.

"You make me a broom and get all the dishes and things together," she answered, "and then leave the rest to me. In a week from now you won't know this place. Once we clear out a little foothold here we can go back to the tower and fetch up a few loads of tools and supplies—"

"Come on, come on!" he interrupted, taking her by the hand and leading her away. "All such planning will do after breakfast, but I'm starving! How about a five-pound bass on the coals, eh? Come on, let's go fishing."

CHAPTER III

The Maskalonge

With characteristic resourcefulness Stein soon manufactured adequate tackle with a well-trimmed alder pole, a line of leather thongs and a hook of stout piano wire, properly bent to make a barb and rubbed to a fine point on a stone. He caught a dozen young frogs among the sedges in the marshy stretch at the north end of the landing-beach, and confined them in the only available receptacle, the holster of his automatic.

All this hurt his arm severely, but he paid no heed.

"Now," he announced, "we're quite ready for business. Come along!"

Together they pushed the boat off; it glided smoothly out onto the breast of the great current.

"I'll paddle," she volunteered. "You mustn't, with your arm in the condition it is. Which way?"

"Up—over there into that cove beyond the point," he answered, baiting up his hook with a frog that kicked as naturally as though a full thousand years hadn't passed since any of its progenitors had been handled thus. "This certainly is far from being the kind of tackle that Bob Davis or any of that gang used to swear by, but it's the best we can do for now. When I get to making lines and hooks and things in earnest, there'll be some sport in this vicinity. Imagine water untouched by the angler for ten hundred years or more!"

He swung his clumsy line as he spoke, and cast. Far across the shining water the circles spread, silver in the morning light; then the trailing line cut a long series of V's as the girl paddled slowly toward the cove. Behind

the banca a rippling wake flashed metallic; the cold, clear water caressed
the primitive hull, murmuring with soft cadences, in the old, familiar music of the time when there were men on earth. The witchery of it stirred
Beatrice; she smiled, looked up with joy and wonder at the beauty of that
perfect morning, and in her clear voice began to sing, very low, very softly,
to herself, a song whereof—save in her brain—no memory now remained
in the whole world—

> "*Stark wie der Fels,*
> *Tief wie das Meer,*
> *Muss deine Liebe, muss deine Liebe sein—*"

"*Ah!*" cried the man, interrupting her.

The alder pole was jerking, quivering in his hands; the leather line was
taut.

"A strike, so help me! A big one!"

He sprang to his feet, and, unmindful of the swaying of the banca, began
to play the fish.

Beatrice, her eyes a-sparkle, turned to watch; the paddle lay forgotten
in her hands.

"Here he comes! Oh, *damn!*" shouted Stern. "If I only had a reel now—"

"Pull him right in, can't you?" the girl suggested.

He groaned, between clenched teeth—for the strain on his arm was torture.

"Yes, and have him break the line!" he cried. "There he goes, under the
boat, now! Paddle! Go ahead—paddle!"

She seized the oar, and while Stern fought the monster she set the banca in motion again. Now the fish was leaping wildly from side to side,
zig-zagging, shaking at the hook as a bull-dog shakes an old boot. The
leather cord hummed through the water, ripping and vibrating, taut as a
fiddle-string. A long, silvery line of bubbles followed the vibrant cord.

Flash!

High in air, lithe and graceful and very swift, a spurt of green and
white—a long, slim curve of glistening power—a splash; and again the
cord drew hard.

"Maskalonge!" Stern cried. "Oh, we've got to land him—got to! Fifteen
pounds if he's an ounce!"

Beatrice, flushed and eager, watched the fight with fascination.

"If I can bring him close, you strike—hit hard!" the man directed. "Give it to him! He's our breakfast!"

Even in the excitement of the battle Stern realized how very beautiful this woman was. Her color was adorable—rose-leaves and cream. Her eyes were shot full of light and life and the joy of living; her loosened hair, wavy and rich and brown, half hid the graceful curve of her neck as she leaned to watch, to help him.

And strong determination seized him to master this great fish, to land it, to fling it at the woman's feet as his tribute and his trophy.

He had, in the days of long ago, fished in the Adirondack wildernesses. He had fished for tarpon in the Gulf; he had cast the fly along the brooks of Maine and lured the small-mouthed bass with floating bait on many a lake and stream. He had even fished in a Rocky Mountain torrent, and out on the far Columbia, when failure to succeed meant hunger.

But this experience was unique. Never had he fished all alone in the world with a loved woman who depended on his skill for her food, her life, her everything.

Forgotten now the wounded arm, the crude and absurd implements; forgotten everything but just that sole, indomitable thought: "I've got to win!"

Came now a lull in the struggles of the monster. Stern hauled in. Another rush, met by a paying-out, a gradual tautening of the line, a strong and steady pull.

"He's tiring," exulted Stern. "Be ready when I bring him close!"

Again the fish broke cover; again it dived; but now its strength was lessening fast.

Allan hauled in.

Now, far down in the clear depths, they could both see the darting, flickering shaft of white and green.

"Up he comes now! Give it to him, hard!"

As Stern brought him to the surface, Beatrice struck with the paddle—once, twice, with magnificent strength and judgment.

Over the gunwale of the banca, in a sparkle of flying spray, silvery in the morning sun, the maskalonge gleamed.

Excited and happy as a child, Beatrice clapped her hands. Stern seized the paddle as she let it fall. A moment later the huge fish, stunned and dying, lay in the bottom of the boat, its gills rising, falling in convulsive gasps, its body quivering, scales shining in the sunlight—a thing of wondrous beauty, a promise of the feast for two strong, healthy humans.

Stern dried his brow on the back of his hand and drew a deep breath, for the morning was already warm and the labor had been hard.

"Now," said he, and smiled, "now a nice little pile of dead wood on the beach, a curl of birch-bark and a handful of pine punk and grass—a touch of the flint and steel! Then *this,*" and he pointed at the maskalonge, "broiled on a pointed stick, with a handful of checkerberries for dessert, and I think you and I will be about ready to begin work in earnest!"

He knelt and kissed her—a kiss that she returned—and then, slowly, happily, and filled with the joy of comradeship, they drove their banca once more to the white and gleaming beach.

CHAPTER IV

THE GOLDEN AGE

STERN'S plans of hard work for the immediate present had to be deferred a little, for in spite of his perfect health, the spear-thrust in his arm—lacking the proper treatment, and irritated by his labor in catching the big fish—developed swelling and soreness. A little fever even set in the second day. And though he was eager to go out fishing again, Beatrice appointed herself his nurse and guardian, and withheld permission.

They lived for some days on the excellent flesh of the maskalonge, on clams from the beach—enormous clams of delicious flavor—on a new fruit with a pinkish meat, which grew abundantly in the thickets and somewhat resembled breadfruit; on wild asparagus-sprouts, and on the few squirrels that Stern was able to "pot" with his revolver from the shelter of the leafy little camping-place they had arranged near the river.

Though Beatrice worked many hours all alone in the bungalow, sweeping it with a broom made of twigs lashed to a pole, and trying to bring the place into order, it was still no fit habitation.

She would not even let the man try to help her, but insisted on his keeping quiet in their camp. This lay under the shelter of a thick-foliaged oak at the southern end of the beach. The perfect weather and the presence of a three-quarters moon at night invited them to sleep out under the sky.

"There'll be plenty of time for the bungalow," she said, "when it rains. As long as we have fair June weather like this no roof shall cover me!"

Singularly enough, there were no mosquitoes. In the thousand years that had elapsed, they might either have shifted their habitat from eastern America, or else some obscure evolutionary process might have wiped them out entirely. At any rate, none existed, for which the two adventurers gave thanks.

Wild beasts they feared not. Though now and then they heard the yell of a wildcat far back in the woods, or the tramping of an occasional bulk through the forest, and though once a cinnamon bear poked his muzzle out into the clearing, sniffed and departed with a grunt of disapproval, they could not bring themselves to any realization of animals as a real peril. Their camp-fire burned high all night, heaped with driftwood and windfalls; and beyond this protection, Stern had his automatic and a belt nearly full of cartridges. They discussed the question of a possible attack by some remnants of the Horde; but common sense assured them that these creatures would—such as survived—give them a wide berth.

"And in any event," Stern summed it up, "if anything happens, we have the bungalow to retreat into. Though in its present state, without any doors or shutters, I think we're safer out among the trees, where, on a pinch, we could go aloft."

Thus his convalescence progressed in the open air, under the clouds and sun and stars and lustrous moon of that deserted world.

Beatrice showed both skill and ingenuity in her treatment. With a clam-shell she scraped and saved the rich fat from under the skins of the squirrels, and this she "tried out" in a golden dish, over the fire. The oil thus got she used to anoint his healing wound. She used a dressing of clay and leaves; and when the fever flushed him she made him comfortable on his bed of spruce-tips, bathed his forehead and cheeks, and gave him cold water from a spring that trickled down over the moss some fifty feet to westward of the camp.

Many a long talk they had, too—he prone on the spruce, she sitting beside him, tending the fire, holding his hand or letting his head lie in her lap, the while she stroked his hair. Ferns, flowers in profusion—lilacs and clover and climbing roses and some new, strange scarlet blossoms—bowered their nest. And through the pain and fever, the delay and disappointment, they both were glad and cheerful. No word of impatience or haste or repining escaped them. For they had life; they had each other; they had love. And those days, as later they looked back upon them, were among the happiest, the most purely beautiful, the sweetest of their whole wondrous, strange experience.

He and she, perfect friends, comrades and lovers, were inseparable. Each was always conscious of the other's presence. The continuity of love, care and sympathy was never broken. Even when, at daybreak, she went away around the wooded point for her bath in the river, he could hear her splashing and singing and laughing happily in the cold water.

It was the Golden Age come back to earth again—the age of natural and pure simplicity, truth, trust, honor, faith and joy, unspoiled by malice or deceit, by lies, conventions, sordid ambitions, or the lust of wealth or power. Arcady, at last—in truth!

Their conversation was of many things. They talked of their awakening in the tower and their adventures there; of the possible cause of the world-catastrophe that had wiped out the human race, save for their own survival; the Horde and the great battle; their escape, their present condition, and their probable future; the possibility of their ever finding any other isolated human beings, and of reconstituting the fragments of the world or of renewing the human race.

And as they spoke of this, sometimes the girl would grow strangely silent, and a look almost of inspiration—the universal mother-look of the race—would fill her wondrous eyes. Her hand would tremble in his; but he would hold it tight, for he, too, understood.

"Afraid, little girl?" he asked her once.

"No, not afraid," she answered; and their eyes met. "Only—so much depends on us—on you, on me! What strength we two must have, what courage, what endurance! The future of the human race lies in our hands!"

He made no answer; he, too, grew silent. And for a long while they sat and watched the embers of the fire; and the day waned. Slowly the sun set in its glory over the virgin hills; the far eastern spaces of the sky grew bathed in tender lavenders and purples. Haze drew its veils across the world, and the air grew brown with evenfall.

Presently the girl arose, to throw more wood on the fire. Clad only in her loose tiger-skin, clasped with gold, she moved like a primeval goddess. Stern marked the supple play of her muscles, the unspoiled grace and strength of that young body, the swelling warmth of her bosom. And as he looked he loved; he pressed a hand to his eyes; for a while he thought—it was as though he prayed.

Evening came on—the warm, dark, mysterious night. Off there in the shallows gradually arose the million-voiced chorus of frogs, shrill and monotonous, plaintive, appealing—the cry of new life to the overarching, implacable mystery of the universe. The first faint silvery powder of the stars came spangling out along the horizon. Unsteady bats began to reel across the sky. The solemn beauty of the scene awed the woman and the man to silence. But Stern, leaning his back against the bole of the great oak, encircled Beatrice with his arm.

Her beautiful dear head rested in the hollow of his throat; her warm, fragrant hair caressed his cheek; he felt the wholesome strength and sweetness of this woman whom he loved; and in his eyes—unseen by her—tears welled and gleamed in the firelight.

Beatrice watched, like a contented child, the dancing showers of sparks that rose, wavering and whirling in complex sarabands—sparks red as passion, golden as the unknown future of their dreams. From the river they heard the gentle lap-lap-lapping of the waves along the shore. All was rest and peace and beauty; this was Eden once again—and there was no serpent to enter in.

Presently Stern spoke.

"Dear," said he, "do you know, I'm a bit puzzled in some ways, about—well, about night and day, and temperature, and gravitation, and a number of little things like that. Puzzled. We're facing problems here that we don't realize fully as yet."

"Problems? What problems, except to make our home, and—and live?"

"No, there's more to be considered than just that. In the first place, although I have no timepiece, I'm moderately certain the day and night are shorter now than they used to be before the smash-up. There must be a difference of at least half an hour. Just as soon as I can get around to it, I'll build a clock, and see. Though if the force of gravity has changed, too, that, of course, will change the time of vibration of any pendulum, and so of course will invalidate my results. It's a hard problem, right enough."

"You think gravitation has changed?"

"Don't you notice, yourself, that things seem a trifle lighter—things that used to be heavy to lift are now comparatively easy?"

"*M-m-m-m-m*—I don't know. I thought maybe it was because I was feeling so much stronger, with this new kind of outdoor life."

"Of course, that's worth considering," answered Stern, "but there's more in it than that. The world is certainly smaller than it was, though how, or why, I can't say. Things are lighter, and the time of rotation is shorter. Another thing, the pole-star is certainly five degrees out of place. The axis of the earth has been given an astonishing twist, some way or other.

"And don't you notice a distinct change in the climate? In the old days there were none of these huge, palm-like ferns growing in this part of the world. We had no such gorgeous butterflies. And look at the new varieties of flowers—and the breadfruit, or whatever it is, growing on the banks of the Hudson in the early part of June!

"Something, I tell you, has happened to the earth, in all these centuries; something big! Maybe the cause of it all was the original catastrophe; who knows? It's up to us to find out. We've got more to do than make our home, and live, and hunt for other people—if any are still alive. We've got to solve these world-problems; we've got work to do, little girl. Work—big work!"

"Well, you've got to rest *now*, anyhow," she dictated. "Now, stop thinking and planning, and just rest! Till your wound is healed, you're going to keep good and quiet."

Silence fell again between them. Then, as the east brightened with the approach of the moon, she sang the song he loved best—"Ave Maria, Gratia Plena"—in her soft, sweet voice, untrained, unspoiled by false conventions. And Stern, listening, forgot his problems and his plans; peace came to his soul, and rest and joy.

The song ended. And now the moon, with a silent majesty that shamed human speech, slid her bright silver plate up behind the fret of trees on the far hills. Across the river a shimmering path of light grew, broadening; and the world beamed in holy beauty, as on the primal night.

And their souls drank that beauty. They were glad, as never yet. At last Stern spoke.

"It's more like a dream than a reality, isn't it?" said he. "Too wonderful to be true. Makes me think of Alfred de Musset's 'Lucie.' You remember the poem?

> "'*Un soit, nous étions seuls,*
> *J'étais assis près d'elle ...*'"

Beatrice nodded.

"Yes, I know!" she whispered. "How could I forget it? And to think that for a thousand years the moon's been shining just the same, and nobody—"

"Yes, but *is* it the same?" interrupted Stern suddenly, his practical turn of mind always reasserting itself. "Don't you see a difference? You remember the old-time face in the moon, of course. Where is it now? The moon always presented only one side, the same side, to us in the old days. How about it now? If I'm not mistaken, things have shifted up there. We're looking now at some other face of it. And if that's so it means a far bigger disarrangement of the solar system and the earth's orbit and lots of things than you or I suspect!

"Wait till we get back to New York for half a day, and visit the tower and gather up our things. Wait till I get hold of my binoculars again! Perhaps some of these questions may be resolved. We can't go on this way, surrounded by perpetual puzzles, problems, mysteries! We must—"

"Do nothing but rest now!" she dictated with mock severity.

Stern laughed.

"Well, you're the boss," he answered, and leaned back against the oak. "Only, may I propound one more question?"

"Well, what is it?"

"Do you see that dark patch in the sky? Sort of a roughly circular hole in the blue, as it were—right there?" He pointed. "Where there aren't any stars?"

"Why—yes. What about it?"

"It's moving, that's all. Every night that black patch moves among the stars, and cuts their light off; and one night it grazed the moon—passed before the eastern limb of it, you understand. Made a partial eclipse. You were asleep; I didn't bother you about it. But if there's a new body in the sky, it's up to us to know why, and what about it, and all. So the quicker—"

"The quicker you get well, the better all around!"

She drew his head down and kissed him tenderly on the forehead with that strange, innate maternal instinct which makes women love to "mother" men even ten years older than themselves.

"Don't you worry your brains about all these problems and vexations tonight, Allan. Your getting well is the main thing. The whole world's future hangs on just that! Do you realize what it means? Do you?"

"Yes, as far as the human brain *can* realize so big a concept. Languages, arts, science, all must be handed down to the race by us. The world can't begin again on any higher plane than just the level of our collective intelligence. All that the world knows to-day is stored in your brain-cells and mine! And our speech, our methods, our ideals, will shape the whole destiny of the earth. Our ideals! We must keep them very pure!"

"Pure and unspotted," she answered simply. Then with an adorable and feminine anticlimax:

"Dear, does your shoulder pain you now? I'm awfully heavy to be leaning on you like this!"

"You're not hurting me a bit. On the contrary, your touch, your presence, are life to me!"

"Quite sure you're comfy, boy?"

"Positive."

"And happy?"

"To the limit."

"I'm so glad. Because I am, too. I'm awfully sleepy, Allan. Do you mind if I take just a little, tiny nap?"

For all answer he patted her, and smoothed her hair, her cheek, her full, warm throat.

Presently by her slow, gentle breathing he knew she was asleep.

For a long time he half-lay there against the oak, softly swathed in his bear-skin, on the odorous bed of fir, holding her in his arms, looking into the dancing firelight.

And night wore on, calm, perfumed, gentle; and the thoughts of the man were long, long thoughts—thoughts "that do often lie too deep for tears."

CHAPTER V

DEADLY PERIL

PAGES on pages would not tell the full details of the following week—the talks they had, the snaring and shooting of small game, the fishing, the cleaning out of the bungalow, and the beginnings of some order in the estate, the rapid healing of Stern's arm, and all the multifarious little events of their new beginnings of life there by the river-bank.

But there are other matters of more import than such homely things; so now we come to the time when Stern felt the pressing imperative of a return to the tower. For he lacked tools in every way; he needed them to build furniture, doors, shutters; to clear away the brush and make the place orderly, rational and beautiful; to start work on his projected laboratory and power-plant; for a thousand purposes.

He wanted his binoculars, his shotgun and rifles, and much ammunition, as well as a boat-load of canned supplies and other goods. Instruments, above all, he had to have.

So, though Beatrice still, with womanly conservatism, preferred to let well enough alone for the present, and stay away from the scene of such ghastly deeds as had taken place on the last day of the invasion by the Horde, Stern eventually convinced and overargued her; and on what he calculated to be the 16th day of June, 2912—the tenth day since the fight—they set sail for Manhattan.

A favoring northerly breeze, joined with a clear sky and sunshine of unusual brilliancy, made the excursion a gala time for both. As they put their supplies of fish, squirrel-meat and breadfruit aboard the banca and shoved the rude craft off the sand, both she and he felt like children on an outing.

Allan's arm was now so well that he permitted himself the luxury of a morning plunge. The invigoration of this was still upon him as, with a song, he raised the clumsy skin sail upon the rough-hewn mast. Beatrice curled down in her tiger-skin at the stern, took one of the paddles, and made ready to steer. He settled himself beside her, the thongs of his sail in his hand. Thus happy in comradeship, they sailed away to southward, down the blue wonder of the river, flanked by headlands, wooded heights, crags, cliffs and Palisades, now all alike deserted.

Noon found them opposite the fluted columns of gray granite that once had borne aloft the suburbs of Englewood. Stern recognized the conformation of the place; but though he looked hard, could find no trace of the Interstate Park road that once had led from top to bottom of the Palisades, nor any remnant of the millionaires' palaces along the heights there.

"Stone and brick have long since vanished as structures," he commented. "Only steel and concrete have stood the gaff of uncounted years! Where all that fashion, wealth and beauty once would have scorned to notice us, girl, now what's left? Hear the cry of that gull? The barking of that fox? See that green flicker over the pinnacle? Some new, bright bird, never dreamed of in this country! And even with the naked eye I can make out the palms and the lianas tangled over the verge of what must once have been magnificent gardens!"

He pointed at the heights.

"Once," said he, "I was consulted by a sausage-king named Breitkopf, who wanted to sink an elevator-shaft from the top to the bottom of this very cliff, so he could reach his hundred-thousand-dollar launch in ease. Breitkopf didn't like my price; he insulted me in several rather unpleasant ways. The cliff is still here, I see. So am I. But Breitkopf is—elsewhere."

He laughed, and swept the river with a glance.

"Steer over to the eastward, will you?" he asked. "We'll go in through Spuyten Duyvil and the Harlem. That'll bring us much nearer the tower than by landing on the west shore of Manhattan."

Two hours later they had run past the broken arches of Fordham, Washington, and High Bridges, and following the river—on both banks of which a few scattered ruins showed through the massed foliage—were drawing toward Randall's and Ward's islands and Hell Gate.

Wind and tide still favored them. In safety they passed the ugly shoals and ledges. Here Stern took the paddle, while Beatrice went to the bow and left all to his directing hand.

By three o'clock in the afternoon they were drawing past Blackwell's Island. The Queensboro Bridge still stood, as did the railway bridges behind them; but much wreckage had fallen into the river, and in one place formed an ugly whirlpool, which Stern had to avoid by some hard work with the paddle.

The whole structure was sagging badly to southward, as though the foundations had given way. Long, rusted masses of steel hung from the spans, which drooped as though to break at any moment. Though all the flooring had vanished centuries before, Stern judged an active man could still make his way across the bridge.

"That's their engineering," gibed he, as the little boat sailed under and they looked up like dwarfs at the legs of a Colossus. "The old Roman bridges are good for practically eternity, but these jerry steel things, run up for profits, go to pieces in a mere thousand years! Well, the steel magnates are gone now, and their profits with them. But this junk remains as a lesson and a warning, Beta; the race to come must build better than this, and sounder, every way!"

On, on they sailed, marveling at the terrific destruction on either hand—
the dense forests now grown over Brooklyn and New York alike.

"We'll be there before long now," said Allan. "And if we have any luck at
all, and nothing happens, we ought to be started for home by nightfall. You
don't mind a moonlight sail up the Hudson, do you?"

It was past four by the time the banca nosed her way slowly in among
the rotten docks and ruined hulks of steamships, and with a gentle rustling
came to rest among the reeds and rushes now growing rank at the foot of
what had once been Twenty-Third Street.

A huge sea-tortoise, disturbed, slid off the sand-bank where he had been
sunning himself and paddled sulkily away. A blue heron flapped up from
the thicket, and with a frog in its bill awkwardly took flight, its long neck
crooked, legs dangling absurdly.

"Some mighty big changes, all right," commented Stern. "Yes, there's got
to be a deal of work done here before things are right again. But there's time
enough, time enough—there's all the time we need, we and the people who
shall come after us!"

They made the banca fast, noting that the tide was high and that the
leather cord was securely tied to a gnarled willow that grew at the water's
edge. Half an hour later they had made their way across town to Madison
Avenue.

It was with strange feelings they once more approached the scene of
their battle against such frightful odds with the Horde. Stern was especially
curious to note the effect of his Pulverite, not only on the building itself but
on the square.

This effect exceeded his expectations. Less than two hundred feet of the
tower now stood and the whole western façade was but a mass of cracked
and gaping ruin.

Out on the Square the huge elms and pines had been uprooted and flung
in titanic confusion, like a game of giants' jack-straws. And vast conical
excavations showed, here and there, where vials of the explosive had struck
the earth. Gravel and rocks had even been thrown over the Metropolitan
Building itself into the woodland glades of Madison Avenue. And, worse,
bits of bone—a leg-bone, a shoulder-blade, a broken skull with flesh still
adhering—here or there met the eye.

"Mighty good thing the vultures have been busy here," commented
Stern. "If they hadn't, the place wouldn't be even approachable. Gad! I

thank my stars what we've got to do won't take more than an hour. If we had to stay here after dark I'd surely have the creeps, in spite of all my scientific materialism! Well, no use being retrospective. We're living in the present and future now; not the past. Got the plaited cords Beatrice? We'll need them before long to make up our bundle with."

Thus talking, Stern kept the girl from seeing too much or brooding over what she saw. He engaged her actively on the work in hand. Until he had assured himself there was no danger from falling fragments in the shattered halls and stairways that led up to the gaping ruin at the truncated top of the tower he would not let her enter the building, but set her to fashioning a kind of puckered bag with a huge skin taken from the furrier's shop in the Arcade, while he explored.

He returned after a while, and together they climbed over the débris and ruins to the upper rooms which had been their home during the first few days after the awakening.

The silence of death that lay over the place was appalling—that and the relics of the frightful battle. But they had their work to do; they had to face the facts.

"We're not children, Beta," said the man. "Here we are for a purpose. The quicker we get our work done the better. Come on, let's get busy!"

Stifling the homesick feeling that tried to win upon them they set to work. All the valuables they could recover they collected—canned supplies, tools, instruments, weapons, ammunition and a hundred and one miscellaneous articles they had formerly used.

This flotsam of a former civilization they carried down and piled in the skin bag at the broken doorway. And darkness began to fall ere the task was done.

Still trickled the waters of the fountain in Madison Forest through the dim evening aisles of the shattered forest. A solemn hush fell over the dead world; night was at hand.

"Come, let's be going," spoke the man, his voice lowered in spite of himself, the awe of the Infinite Unknown upon him. "We can eat in the banca on the way. With the tide behind us, as it will be, we ought to get home by morning. And I'll be mighty glad never to see this place again!"

He slung a sack of cartridges over his shoulder and picked up one of the cord loops of the bag wherein lay their treasure-trove. Beatrice took the other.

"I'm ready," said she. Thus they started.

All at once she stopped short.

"Hark! What's that?" she exclaimed under her breath.

Far off to northward, plaintive, long-drawn and inexpressibly mournful, a wailing cry reëchoed in the wilderness—fell, rose, died away, and left the stillness even more ghastly than before.

Stern stood rooted. In spite of all his aplomb and matter-of-fact practicality, he felt a strange thrill curdle through his blood, while on the back of his neck the hair drew taut and stiff.

"What is it?" asked Beatrice again.

"That? Oh, some bird or other, I guess. It's nothing. Come on!"

Again he started forward, trying to make light of the cry; but in his heart he knew it well.

A thousand years before, far in the wilds near Ungava Bay, in Labrador, he had heard the same plaintive, starving call—and he remembered still the deadly peril, the long fight, the horror that had followed.

He knew the cry; and his soul quivered with the fear of it; fear not for himself, but for the life of this girl whose keeping lay within the hollow of his hand.

For the long wail that had trembled across the vague spaces of the forest, affronting the majesty and dignity of night and the coming stars with its blood-lusting plaint of famine, had been none other than the summons to the hunt, the news of quarry, the signal of a gathering wolf-pack on their trail.

CHAPTER VI

TRAPPED!

"THAT'S not the truth you're telling me, Allan," said Beatrice very gravely. "And if we don't tell each other the whole truth always, how can we love each other perfectly and do the work we have to do? I don't want you to spare me anything, even the most terrible things. That's not the cry of a bird—it's wolves!"

"Yes, that's what it is," the man admitted. "I was in the wrong. But, you see—it startled me at first. Don't be alarmed, little girl! We're well armed you see, and—"

"Are we going to stay here in the tower if they attack?"

"No. They might hold us prisoners for a week. There's no telling how many there may be. Hundreds, perhaps thousands. Once they get the scent of game, they'll gather for miles and miles around; from all over the island. So you see—"

"Our best plan, then, will be to make for the banca?"

"Assuredly! It's only a matter of comparatively few minutes to reach it, and once we're aboard, we're safe. We can laugh at them and be on our homeward way at the same time. The quicker we start the better. Come on!"

"Come!" she repeated. And they made their second start after Stern had assured himself his automatic hung easily in reach and that the guns were loaded.

Together they took their way along the shadowy depths of the forest where once Twenty-Third Street had lain. Bravely and strongly the girl bore her half of the load as they broke through the undergrowth, clambered over fallen and rotten logs, or sank ankle-deep in mossy swales.

Even though they felt the danger, perhaps at that very moment slinking, sneaking, crawling nearer off there in the vague, darkling depths of the forest, they still sensed the splendid comradeship of the adventure. No longer as a toy, a chattel, an instrument of pleasure or amusement did the idea of woman now exist in the world. It had altered, grown higher, nobler, purer—it had become that of mate and equal, comrade, friend, the indissoluble other half of man.

Beatrice spoke.

"You mustn't take more of the weight than I do, Allan," she insisted, as they struggled onward with their burden. "Your wounded arm isn't strong enough yet to—"

"S-h-h-h!" he cautioned. "We've got to keep as quiet as possible. Come on—the quicker we get these things aboard and push off the better! Everything depends on speed!"

But speed was hard to make. The way seemed terribly long, now that evening had closed in and they could no longer be exactly sure of their path. The cumbersome burden impeded them at every step. In the gloom they stumbled, tripped over vines and creepers, and became involved among the close-crowding boles.

Suddenly; once again the wolf-cry burst out, this time reëchoed from another and another savage throat, wailing and plaintive and full of frightful portent.

So much nearer now it seemed that Beatrice and Allan both stopped short. Panting with their labors, they stood still, fear-smitten.

"They can't be much farther off now than Thirty-Fifth Street," the man exclaimed under his breath. "And we're hardly past Second Avenue yet— and look at the infernal thickets and brush we've got to beat through to reach the river! Here, I'd better get my revolver ready and hold it in my free hand. Will you change over? I can take the bag in my left. I've got to have the right to shoot with!"

"Why not drop everything and run for the banca?"

"And desert the job? Leave all we came for? And maybe not be able to get any of the things for Heaven knows how long? I guess not!"

"But, Allan—"

"No, no! What? Abandon all our plans because of a few wolves? Let 'em come! We'll show 'em a thing or two!"

"Give me the revolver, then—you can have the rifle!"

"That's right—here!"

Each now with a firearm in the free hand, they started forward again. On and on they lunged, they wallowed through the forest, half carrying, half dragging the sack which now seemed to have grown ten times heavier and which at every moment caught on bushes, on limbs and among the dense undergrowth.

"Oh, look—look there!" cried Beatrice. She stopped short again, pointing the revolver, her finger on the trigger.

Allan saw a lean, gray form, furtive and sneaking, slide across a dim open space off toward the left, a space where once First Avenue had cut through the city from south to north.

"There's another!" he whispered, a strange, choked feeling all around his heart. "And look—three more! They're working in ahead of us. Here, I'll have a shot at 'em, for luck!"

A howl followed the second spurt of flame in the dusk. One of the gray, gaunt portents of death licked, yapping, at his flank.

"Got you, all right!" gibed Stern. "The kind o' game you're after isn't as easy as you think, you devils!"

But now from the other side, and from behind them, the slinking creatures gathered. Their eyes glowed, gleamed, burned softly yellow through the dusk of the great wilderness that once had been the city's heart. The two last humans in the world could even catch the flick of ivory fangs, the lolling wet redness of tongues—could hear the soughing breath through those infernal jaws.

Stern raised the rifle again, then lowered it.

"No use," said he quite calmly. "God knows how many there are. I might use up all our ammunition and still leave enough of 'em to pick our bones. They'll be all around us in a minute; they'll be worrying at us, dragging us down! Come on—come on, the boat!"

"Light a torch, Allan. They're afraid of fire."

"Grand idea, little girl!"

Even as he answered he was scrabbling up dry-kye. Came the rasp of his flint.

"Give 'em a few with the automatic, while I get this going!" he commanded.

The gun spat twice, thrice. Then rose a snapping, snarling wrangle. Off there in the gloom a hideous turmoil grew.

It ended in screams of pain and rage, suddenly throttled, choked, and torn to nothing. A worrying, rending, gnashing told the story of the wounded wolf's last moment.

Stern sprang up, a dry flaming branch of resinous fir in his hand. The rifle he thrust back into the bag.

"Ate him, still warm, eh?" he cried. "Fine! And five shots left in the gun. You won't miss, Beta! You can't!"

Forward they struggled once more.

"Gad, we'll hang to this bag *now*, whatever happens!" panted Stern, jerking it savagely off a jagged stub. "Five minutes more and we'll—arrh! *would* you?"

The flaring torch he dashed full at a grisly muzzle that snapped and slavered at his legs. To their nostrils the singe of burned hair wafted. Yelping, the beast swerved back.

But others ran in and in at them; and now the torch was failing. Both of them shouted and struck; and the revolver stabbed the night with fire.

Pandemonium rose in the forest. Cries, howls, long wails and snuffling barks blent with the clicking of ivories, the pad-pad-pad of feet, the crackling of the underbrush.

All around, wolves. On either side, behind, in front, the sliding, bristling, sneaking, suddenly bold horrors of the wild.

And the ring was tightening; the attack was coming, now, more and more concertedly. The swinging torch could not now drive them back so fast, so far.

Strange gleams shot against the tree-trunks, wavered through the dusk, lighted the harsh, rage-contracted face of the man, fell on the laboring, skin-clad figure of the woman as they still fought on and on with their precious burden, hoping for a glimpse of water, for the river, and salvation.

"Take—a tree?" gasped Beatrice.

"And maybe stay there a week? And use up—all our ammunition? Not yet—no—no! The boat!"

On, ever on, they struggled.

A strange, unnatural exhilaration filled the girl, banishing thoughts of peril, sending the blood aglow through every vein and fiber of her wonderful young body.

Stern realized the peril more keenly. At any moment now he understood that one of the devils in gray might hurl itself at the full throat of Beatrice or at his own.

And once the taste of blood lay on those crimson tongues—good-bye!

"The boat—the boat!" he shouted, striking right and left like mad with the smoky, half-extinguished flare.

"There—the river!" suddenly cried Beatrice.

Through the columns of the forest she had seen at last the welcome gleam of water, starlit, beautiful and calm. Stern saw it, too. A demon now, he charged the snarling ring. Back he drove them; he turned, seized the bag, and again plunged desperately ahead.

Together he and Beatrice crashed out among the willows and the alders on the sedgy shore, with the vague, shifting, bristling horror of the wolf-pack at their heels.

"Here, beat 'em off while I cut the cord—while I get the bag in—and shove off!" panted Stern.

She seized the torch from his hand. Up he snatched the rifle again, and with a pointblank volley flung three of the grays writhing and yelling all in the mud and weeds and trampled cattails on the river verge.

Down he threw the gun. He turned and swept the dark shore, there between the ruins of the wharves, with a keen reconnoitering glance.

What? What was this?

There stood the aged willow to which the banca had been tied. But the boat—where was it?

With a cry Stern leaped to the tree. His clutching hands fumbled at the trunk.

"My God! Here's—here's the cord!" he stammered. "But it's—been cut! The boat—*the boat's gone!*"

CHAPTER VII

A NIGHT OF TOIL

AN hour later, from the gnarled branches of the willow—up into which Stern had fairly flung her, and where he had himself clambered with the beasts ravening at his legs—the two sole survivors of the human race watched the glowering eyes that dotted the velvet gloom.

"I estimate a couple of hundred, all told," judged Allan. "Odd we never ran across any of them before to-night. Must be some kind of a migration under way—maybe some big shift of game, of deer, or buffalo, or what-not. But then, in that case, they wouldn't be so starved, so dead-set on white meat as they seem to be."

Beta shifted her place on a horizontal limb.

"It's awfully hard for a *soft* wood," she remarked. "Do you think we'll have to stay here long, dear?"

"That depends. I don't see that the fifteen we've killed since roosting here have served as any terrible examples to the others. And we're about twenty cartridges to the bad. They're not worth it, these devils. We've got to save our ammunition for something edible till I can get my shop to running and begin making my own powder. No; must be there's some other and better way."

"But what?" asked the girl. "We're safe enough here, but we're not getting any nearer home—and I'm *so* hungry!"

"Same here," Stern coincided. "And the lunch was all in the boat; worse luck! Who the deuce could have cut her loose? I thought we'd pretty effectually cleared out those Hinkmatinks, or whatever the Horde consisted of. But evidently something, or somebody, is still left alive with a terrific grudge against us, or an awful longing for navigation."

At any moment now, one of the gray devils might hurl itself at their throats.
And once the taste of blood lay on those crimson tongues—good-bye!

See page 153

"Was the cord broken or cut?"

"I'll see."

Stern clambered to a lower branch. With the trigger-guard of his rifle he was able to catch the cord. All about the trunk, meanwhile, the wolves leaped snarling. The fetid animal smell of them was strong upon the air—that, and the scent of blood and raw meat, where they had feasted on the slain.

With the severed cord, Allan climbed back to where Beatrice sat.

"Hold the rifle, will you?" asked he. A moment, and by the quick showers of sparks that issued from his flint and steel, he was examining the leather thong.

"*Cut!*"

"Cut? But then, then—"

"No tide or wind to blame. Some intelligence, even though rudimentary, has been at work here—is at work—opposed to us."

"But what?"

"No telling. There may be more things in this world yet than either of us dream. Perhaps we committed a very grave error to leave the apparently peaceful little nook we've got, up there on the Hudson, and tackle this place again. But who could ever have thought of anything like this after that terrible slaughter?"

They kept silence a few minutes. The wolves now had sunk to a plane of comparative insignificance. At the very worst Stern could annihilate them, one by one, with a lavish expenditure of his ammunition. Unnoticed now, they yelped, and scratched and howled about the tree, sat on their haunches, waiting in the gloom, or sneaked—vague shadows—among the deeper dusks of the forest.

And once again the east began to glow, even as when he and she had watched the moon rise over the hills beyond the Hudson; and their hearts beat with joy for even that relief from the dark mystery of solitude and night.

After a while the man spoke.

"It's this way," said he. "Whoever cut that cord and either let the banca float away or else stole it, evidently doesn't want to come to close quarters for the present, so long as these wolves are making themselves friendly.

"Perhaps, in a way, the wolves are a factor in our favor; perhaps, without them, we might have had a poisoned arrow sticking into us, or a spear or two, before now. My guess is that we'll get a wide berth so long as the wolves stay in the neighborhood. I think the anthropoids, or whoever they were, must have been calculating on ambushing us as we came back, and expected to 'get' us while we were hunting for the boat.

"They didn't reckon on this little diversion. When they heard it they probably departed for other regions. They won't be coming around just yet, that's a safe wager. Mighty lucky, eh? Think what A1 targets we'd make, up here in this willow, by moonlight!"

"You're right, Allan. But when it comes daylight we'll make better ones. And I don't know that I enjoy sitting up here and starving to death, with a body-guard of wolves to keep away the Horde, very much more than I would taking a chance with the arrows. It's two sixes, either way, and not a bit nice, is it?"

"Hang the whole business! There must be some other way—some way out of this infernal pickle! Hold on—wait—I—I almost see it now!"

"What's your plan, dear?"

"Wait! Let me think a minute!"

She kept silence. Together they sat among the spreading branches in the growing moonlight. A bat reeled overhead, chippering weakly. Far away a whippoorwill began its fluty, insistent strain. A distant cry of some hunting beast echoed, unspeakably weird, among the dead, deserted streets buried in oblivion. The brush crackled and snapped with the movements of the wolf-pack; the continued snarling, whining, yapping, stilled the chorus of the frogs along the sedgy banks.

"If I could only snare a good, lively one!" suddenly broke out Stern.

"What for?"

"Why, don't you see?" And with sudden inspiration he expounded. Together, eager as children, they planned. Beatrice clapped her hands with sheer delight.

"But," she added pensively, "it'll be a little hard on the wolf, won't it?"

Stern had to laugh.

"Yes," he assented; "but think how much he'll learn about the new kind of game he tried to hunt!"

Half an hour later a grim old warrior of the pack, deftly and securely caught by one hind leg with the slip-noosed leather cord, dangled inverted from a limb, high out of reach of the others.

Slowly he swung, jerking, writhing, frothing as he fought in vain to snap his jaws upon the cord he could not touch. And night grew horrible with the stridor of his yells.

"Now then," remarked Stern calmly, "to work. The moonlight's good enough to shoot by. No reason I should miss a single target."

Followed a time of frightful tumult as the living ate the dying and the dead, worrying the flesh from bones that had as yet scarcely ceased to move. Beatrice, pale and silent, yet very calm, watched the slaughter. Stern, as quietly methodical as though working out a reaction, sighted, fired, sighted, fired. And the work went on apace. The bag of cartridges grew steadily lighter. The work was done long before all the wolves had died. For the survivors, gorged to repletion, some wounded, others whole, slunk gradually away and disappeared in the dim glades, there to sleep off their cannibal debauch.

At last Stern judged the time was come to descend.

"Bark away, old boy!" he exclaimed. "The louder the better. You're our danger-signal now. As long as those poor, dull anthropoid brains keep sensing you I guess we're safe!"

To Beatrice he added:

"Come now, dear. I'll help you down. The quicker we tackle that raft and away, the sooner we'll be home!"

"Home!" she repeated. "Oh, how glad I'll be to see our bungalow again! How I hate the ruins of the city now! Look out, Allan—you'll have to let me take a minute or two to straighten out in. You don't know how awfully cramped I am!"

"Just slide into my arms—there, that's right!" he answered, and swung her down as easily as though she had been a child. Her arms went round his neck; their lips met and thrilled in a long kiss.

But not even the night-breeze and the moon could now beguile them to another. For there was hard, desperate work to do, and time was short.

A moment they stood there together, under the old tree wherein the wolf was dangling in loud-mouthed rage.

"Well, here's where I go at it!" exclaimed the man.

He opened the big sack. Fumbling among the tools, he quickly found the ax.

"You, Beta," he directed, "get together all the plaited rope you can take off the bag, and cut me some strips of hide. Cut a lot of them. I'll need all you can make. We've got to work fast—got to clear out of here before sunrise or there may be the devil to pay!"

It was a labor of extraordinary difficulty, there in those dense and dim-lit thickets, felling a tall spruce, limbing it out and cutting it into three sections. But Stern attacked it like a demon. Now and again he stopped to listen or to jab the suspended wolf with the ax-handle.

"Go on there, you alarm-signal!" he commanded. "Let's have plenty of music, good and loud, too. Maybe if you deliver the goods and hold out—well, you'll get away with your life. Otherwise, not!"

Robinson Crusoe's raft had been a mere nothing to build compared with this one that the engineer had to construct there at the water's edge, among the sedges and the reeds. For Crusoe had planks and beams and nails to help him, while Stern had naught but his ax, the forest, and some rough cordage.

He had to labor in the gloom, as well, listening betimes for sounds of peril or stopping to stimulate the wolf. The dull and rusty ax retarded him; blisters rose upon his palms, and broke, and formed again. But still he toiled.

The three longitudinal spruce timbers he lashed together with poles and with the cords that Beatrice prepared for him. On these, again, he laid and lashed still other poles, rough-hewn.

In half an hour's hard work, while the moon began to sink to the westward, he had stepped a crude mast and hewed a couple of punt-poles.

"No use our trying to row this monstrosity," he said to Beatrice, stopping a moment to dash the sweat off his forehead with a shaking hand. "We either rig the skin sack in some way as a sail, or we drift up with the tide, tie at the ebb, and so on—and if we make the bungalow in three days we're lucky!

"Come on now, Beatrice. Lend a hand here and we'll launch her! Good thing the tide's coming up—she almost floats already. Now, one, two, three!"

The absurd raft yielded, moved, slid out upon the marshy water and was afloat!

"Get aboard!" commanded Allan. "Go forward to the *salon de luxe*. I'll stow the bag aft, so."

He lifted her in his arms and set her on the raft. The bag he carefully deposited at what passed for the stern. The raft sank a bit and wallowed, but bore up.

"Now then, all aboard!" cried Stern.

"The wolf, Allan, the wolf! How about *him?*"

"That's right, I almost plumb forgot! I guess he's earned his life, all right enough."

Quickly he slashed the cord. The wolf dropped limp, tried to crawl, but could not, and lay panting on its side, tongue lolling, eyes glazed and dim.

"He'll be a horrible example all his life of what it means to monkey with the new kind of meat," remarked Allan, clambering aboard. "If wolves or anthropoids can learn, they ought to learn from him!"

Strongly, steadily, they poled the raft out through the marshy slip, on, on, past the crumbling wreckage of the pier-head.

"Now the tide's got us," exclaimed Allan with satisfaction, as the moonlit current, all silver and rippling with calm beauty, swung them up-stream.

Beatrice, still strong, and full of vigorous, pulsing life, in spite of the long vigil in the tree and the hard night of work, curled up at the foot of the rough mast, on the mass of fir-tips Stern had piled there.

"You steer, boy," said she, "and I'll go to work on making some kind of sail out of the big skin. By morning we ought to have our little craft under full control.

"It's one beautiful boat, isn't it?" mocked Stern, poling off from a gaunt hulk that barred the way.

"It mayn't be very beautiful," she answered softly, "but it carries the greatest, purest, noblest love that ever was since the world began—it carries the hope of the whole world, of all the ages—and it's taking us home!"

CHAPTER VIII

THE REBIRTH OF CIVILIZATION

A MONTH had hardly gone, before order and peace and the promise of bountiful harvests dwelt in and all about Hope Lodge, as they had named the bungalow.

From the kitchen, where the stove and the aluminum utensils now shone bright and free from rust, to the bedrooms where fir-tips and soft skin rugs made wondrous sleeping places, the house was clean and sweet and beautiful again. Rough-hewn chairs and tables, strong, serviceable and eloquent of nature—through which this rebirth of the race all had to come—adorned the rooms. Fur rugs covered the floors.

In lieu of pictures, masses of flowers and great sprays of foliage stood in clay pots of Stern's own manufacture and firing. And on a rustic book-case in their living room, where the big fireplace was, and where the southern sun beat warmest in, stood their chief treasure—a set of encyclopedias.

Stern had made leather bindings for these, with the deft help of Beatrice. The original bindings had vanished before the attacks of time and insects centuries before. But the leaves were still intact. For these were thin sheets of nickel, printed by the electrolysis process.

"Just a sheer streak of luck," Stern remarked, as he stood looking at this huge piece of fortune with the girl. "Just a kindly freak of fate, that Van Amburg should have bought one of Edison's first sets of nickel-sheet books.

"Except for the few sets of these in existence, here and there, not a book remains on the surface of this entire earth. The finest hand-made linen paper has disintegrated ages ago. And parchment has probably crinkled and molded past all recognition. Besides, up-to-date scientific books, such as we need, weren't done on parchment. We're playing into gorgeous luck with these cyclopedias, for everything I need and can't remember is in them. But it certainly was one job to sort those scattered sheets out of the rubbish-pile in the library and rearrange them."

"Yes, that *was* hard work, but it's done now. Come on out into the garden, Allan, and see if our crops have grown any during the night!"

The grounds about the bungalow were a delight to them. Like two children they worked, day by day, to enlarge and beautify their holdings, their lands won back from nature's greed.

Though wild fruits—some new, others familiar—and fish and the plentiful game all about them offered abundant food, to be had for the mere seeking, they both agreed on the necessity of reëstablishing agriculture. For they disliked the thought of being driven southward, with the return of each successive winter. They wanted, if advisable, to be able to winter in the bungalow. And this meant some provision for the unproductive season.

"It won't always be summer here, you know," Stern told her. "This Eden will sometime lie wet and dreary under the winter rains that I expect now take the place of snow. And the eternal curse of Adam—toil—is not yet lifted even from us two survivors of the fifteen hundred million that once ruled the earth. We, and those who shall come after, must have the old-time foods again. And that means work!"

They had cleared a patch of black, virgin soil, in a sunny hollow. Here Stern had transplanted all the wild descendants of the vegetables and grains of other time which in his still limited explorations he had come across.

The work of clearing away the thorns and bushes, the tangled lianas and tall trees, was severe; but it strengthened him and hardened his whip-cord muscles till they ridged his skin like iron. He burned and pulled the stumps, spaded and harrowed and hoed all by hand, and made ready the earth for the reception of its first crop in a thousand years.

He recalled enough of his anthropology and botany from university days to recognize the reverted, twisted and stringy little degenerate wild-potato root which had once served the Aztecs and Pueblo Indians for food, and could again, with proper cultivation, be brought back to full perfection. Likewise with the maize, the squash, the wild turnip, and many other vegetable forms.

"Three years of cultivation," he declared, "and I can win them back to edibility. Five, and they'll be almost where they were before the great catastrophe. As for the fruits, the apple, cherry, and pear, all they need is care and scientific grafting.

"I predict that ten years from today, orchards and cornfields and gardens shall surround this bungalow, and the heritage of man shall be brought back to this old world!"

"Always giving due credit to the encyclopedia," added Beatrice.

"And to *you!*" he laughed happily. "This is all on your account, anyhow. If I were alone in the world, you bet there'd be no gardens made!"

"No, I don't believe there would," she agreed, a serious look on her face. "But, then," she concluded, smiling again, "you aren't alone, Allan. You've got *me!*"

He tried to catch her in his arms, but she evaded him and ran back toward the bungalow.

"No, no, you've got to work," she called to him from the porch. "And so have I. Good-by!" And with a wave of the hand, a strong, brown hand now, slim and very beautiful, she vanished.

Stern stood in thought a moment, then shook his head, and, with a singular expression, picked up his hoe, and once more fell to cultivating his precious little garden-patch, on which so infinitely much depended. But something lay upon his mind; he paused, reflecting; then picked up a stone and weighed it in his hand, tried another, and a third.

"I'm damned," he remarked, "if these feel right to me! I've been wondering about it for a week now—there's got to be some answer to it. A stone of this size in the old days would certainly have weighed more. And that big boulder I rooted out from the middle of the field—in the other days I couldn't have more than stirred it.

"Am I so very much stronger? So much as all that? Or have things grown lighter? Is that why I can leap farther, walk better, run faster? What's it all about, anyhow?"

He could not work, but sat down on a rock to ponder. Numerous phenomena occurred to him, as they had while he had lain wounded under the tree by the river during their first few days at the bungalow.

"My observations certainly show a day only twenty-two hours and fifty-seven minutes long; that's certain," he mused. "So the earth is undoubtedly smaller. But what's that got to do with the mass of the earth? With weight? Hanged if I can make it out at all!

"Even though the earth has shrunk, it ought to have the same power of gravitation. If all the molecules and atoms really were pressed together, with no space between, probably the earth wouldn't be much bigger than a football, but it would weigh just that much, and a body would fall toward it from space just as fast as now. Quite a hefty football, eh? For the life of me I can't see why the earth's having shrunk has affected the weight of everything!"

Perplexed, he went back to his work again. And though he tried to banish the puzzle from his mind it still continued to haunt and to annoy him.

Each day brought new and interesting activities. Now they made an expedition to gather a certain kind of reeds which Beatrice could plat into cordage and basketry; now they peeled quantities of birch-bark, which on rainy days they occupied themselves in splitting into thin sheets for paper. Stern manufactured a very excellent ink in his improvised laboratory on the second floor, and the split and pointed quills of a wild goose served them for pens in taking notes and recording their experiences.

"Paper will come later, when we've got things a little more settled," he told her. "But for now this will have to do."

"I guess if you can get along with skin clothing for a while, I can do with birch-bark for my correspondence," she replied laughing. "Why not catch some of those wild sheep that seem so plentiful on the hills to westward? If we could domesticate them, that would mean wool and yarn and cloth— and milk, too, wouldn't it? And if milk, why not butter?"

"Not so fast!" he interposed. "Just wait a while—we'll have cattle, goats, and sheep, and the whole business in due time; but how much can one pair of human beings undertake? For the present we'll have to be content with what mutton-chops and steaks and hams I can get with a gun—and we're mighty lucky to have those!"

Singularly enough, and contrary to all beliefs, they felt no need of salt. Evidently the natural salts in their meat and in the fruits they ate supplied their wants. And this was fortunate, because the quest of salt might have been difficult; they might even had had to boil sea-water to obtain it.

They felt no craving for sweets, either; but when one day they came upon a bee-tree about three-quarters of a mile back in the woods to westward of the river, and when Stern smoked out the bees and gathered five pounds of honey in the closely platted rush basket lined with leaves, which they always carried for miscellaneous treasure-trove, they found the flavor delicious. They decided to add honey to their menu, and thereafter always kept it in a big pottery jar in their kitchen.

Stern's hunting, fishing and gardening did not occupy his whole time. Every day he made it a rule to work at least an hour, two if possible, on the thirty-foot yawl that had already begun to take satisfactory shape on the timber ways which now stood on the river bank.

All through July and part of August he labored on this boat, building it stanch and true, calking it thoroughly, fitting a cabin, stepping a fir mast, and making all ready for the great migration which he felt must inevitably be forced upon them by the arrival of cool weather.

He doubted very much, in view of the semitropic character of some of the foliage, whether even in January the temperature would now go below freezing; but in any event he foresaw that there would be no fruits available, and he objected to a winter on flesh foods. In preparation for the trip he had built a little "smoke-house" near the beach, and here he smoked considerable quantities of meat—deer-meat, beef from a wild steer which he was so fortunate as to shoot during the third week of their stay at the bungalow, and a good score of hams from the wild pigs which rooted now and then among the beech growth half a mile downstream.

Often the girl and he discussed this coming trip, of an evening, sitting together by the river to watch the stars and moon and that strange black wandering blotch that now and then obscured a portion of the night sky—or perchance leaning back in their huge, rustic easy chairs lined with furs on the broad piazza; or again, if the night were cool or rainy, in front of their blazing fire of pine knots and driftwood, which burned with gorgeous blues and greens and crimsons in the vast throat of Hope Lodge fireplace.

Other matters, too, they talked of—strange speculations, impossible to solve, yet filling them with vague uneasiness, with wonder and a kind of mighty awe in face of the vast, unknowable mysteries surrounding them; the forces and phenomena which might, though friendly in their outward aspect, at any time precipitate catastrophe, ruin and death upon them and extinguish in their persons all hopes of a world reborn.

The haunting thought was never very far away: "Should either one of us be killed—what then?"

One day Stern voiced his fear.

"Beatrice," he said, "if anything should ever happen to me, and you be left alone in a world which, without me, would become instantly hostile and impossible, remember that the most scientific way out is a bullet. That's *my* way if anything happens to *you!* Understand?"

She nodded, and for a long time that day the silence of a great pact weighed upon their souls.

CHAPTER IX

PLANNING THE GREAT MIGRATION

STERN rigged a tripod for the powerful field-glasses he had rescued from the Metropolitan Building, and by an ingenious addition of a wooden tube and another lens carefully ground out of rock crystal, succeeded in producing (on the right-hand barrel of the binoculars) a telescope of reasonably high power. With this, of an evening, he often made long observations, after which he would spend hours figuring all over many sheets of the birch bark, which he then carefully saved and bound up with leather strings for future reference.

In Van's set of encyclopedias he found a fairly large celestial map and thorough astronomic data. The results of his computations were of vital interest to him.

He said to Beatrice one evening:

"Do you know, that wandering black patch in the sky moves in a regular orbit of its own? It's a solid body, dark, irregular in outline, and certainly not over five hundred miles above the surface of the earth."

"What can it be, dear?"

"I don't know yet. It puzzles me tremendously. Now, if it would only appear in the daytime once in a while, we might be able to get some information or knowledge about it; but, coming only at night, all it records itself as is just a black, moving thing. I'm working on the size of it now, making some careful studies. In a while I shall probably know its area and mass and density. But what it is I cannot say—not yet."

They both pondered a while, absorbed in wonder. At last the engineer spoke again.

"Beta," said he, "there's another curious fact to note. The axis of the earth itself has shifted more than six degrees, thirty minutes!"

"It has? Well—what about it?" And she went on with her platting of reed cordage.

"You don't seem much concerned about it!"

"I'm not. Not in the least. It can shift all it wants to, for all of me. What hurt does it do? Doesn't it run just as well that way?"

Stern looked at her a moment, then laughed.

"Oh, yes; it runs all right," he answered. "Only I thought the announcement that the pole-star had thrown up its job might startle you a bit. But I see it doesn't. So far as practical results go, it accounts for the warmer climate and the decreased inclination to the plane of the ecliptic; or, rather, the decreased—"

"Please, please, don't!" she begged. "There's nothing really wrong, is there?"

"Well, that depends on how you define it. Probably an astronomer might think there was something very much wrong. I make it that the orbit of the earth has altered its relative length and width by—"

"No figures, Allan, there's a dear. You know I'm awfully bad at arithmetic. Tell me what it means, won't you?"

"Well, it means, for one thing, that we've maybe spent a far longer time on this earth since the cataclysm than we even dare suspect. It may be that what we've been calculating as about a thousand years, is twice that, or even five times that—no telling. For another thing, I'm convinced by all these changes, and by the diminution of gravity and by the accelerated rate of revolution of the earth—"

"Allan dear, please hand me those scissors, won't you?"

Stern laughed again.

"Here!" said he. "I guess I'm not much good as a lecturer. But I tell you one thing I'm going to do, and that's a one best bet. I'm going to have a try at some really big telescope before a year's out, and know the truth of this thing!"

"A big telescope! Build one, you mean?"

"Not necessarily. All I need is a chance to make some accurate observations, and I can find out all I need to know. Even though I have been out of college for—let's see—"

"Fifteen hundred years, at a guess," she suggested.

"Yes, all of that. Even so, I remember a good bit of astronomy. And I've got my mind set on peeking through a first-class tube. If the earth has broken in two, or anything like that, and our part is skyhooting away toward the unknown regions of outer space beyond the great ring of the Milky Way and is getting into an unchartered place in the universe—as it seems to be—why, we ought to have a good look at things. We ought to know what's what, eh?

"Then there's the moon I want to investigate, too. No living man except myself has even seen the side that's now turned toward the earth. No telling what a good glass mightn't show.

"That's so, dear," she answered. "But where can you find the sort of telescope you need?"

"In Boston—in Cambridge, rather. The Harvard observatory has the biggest one within striking distance. What do you say to our making our trial trip in the boat, up the Sound and around Cape Cod, to Boston? We can spend a week there, then slant away for wherever we may decide to pass the winter. How does that suit you, Beta?"

She put away her work, and for a moment sat looking in at the flames that went leaping up the huge boulder chimney. The room glowed with warmth and light that drove away the cheerlessness of a foggy, late August drizzle.

"Do you really think we're wise to—to leave our home, with winter coming on?" she asked at length, pensively, the firelight casting its glow across her cheek and glinting in her eyes.

"Wise? Yes. We can't stay here, that's certain. And what is there to fear out in the world? With our firearms and our knowledge of fire itself, our science and our human intelligence, we're far more than a match for all enemies, whether of the beast-world or of that race of the Horde. I hate, in a way, to revisit the ruins of New York, for more ammunition and canned stuffs. The place is too ghastly, too hideous, now, after the big fight.

"Boston will be a clean ground for us, with infinite resources. And as I said before, there's the Cambridge observatory. It's only two or three miles back in the forest, from the coast; maybe not more than half a mile from some part of the Charles River. We can sail up, camp on Soldiers' Field, and visit it easily. Why not?"

He sat down on the tiger-rug before the fire, near the girl. She drew his head down into her lap; then, when he was lying comfortably, began playing with his thick hair, as he loved so well to have her do.

"If you think it's all right, Allan," said she, "we'll go. I want what you want."

"That's my good girl!" exclaimed the engineer. "We'll be ready to start in a few days now. The boat's next thing to finished. What with the breadfruit, smoked steer and buffalo meat, hams and canned goods now on our shelves, we've certainly got enough supplies to stock her a two months' trip.

"Even with less, we'd be safe in starting. You see, the world's lain untouched by mankind for so many centuries that all the blighting effect of man's folly and greed and general piracy has vanished.

"The soil's got back to its natural state, animal life abounds, and so long as I still have a good supply of cartridges, we can live almost anywhere. Anthropoids? I don't think there's much danger. Oh, yes, I remember the line of blue smoke we saw yesterday over the hills to westward; but what does that prove? Lightning may have started a fire—there's no telling. And we can't always stay here, Beta, just because there may be dangers out yonder!"

He flung one arm toward the vast night, beyond the panes where the mist and storm were beating cheerlessly.

"No, we can't camp down here indefinitely. Now's the time to start. As I say, we've got all of sixty days' of downright civilized food on hand, for a good cruise in the Adventure. The chance of finding other people some-where is too precious not to make any risk worth while."

Silence fell between them for a few minutes. Each saw visions in the flames. The man's thoughts dwelt, in particular, on this main factor of a possible rediscovery of other human beings somewhere.

More than the girl, he realized the prime importance of this possibility. Though he and she loved each other very dearly, though they were all in all each to the other, yet he comprehended the loneliness she felt rather than analyzed—the infinite need of man for man, of woman for woman—the old social, group-instinct of the race beginning to reassert itself even in their Eden.

Each of them longed, with a longing they hardly realized as yet, to hear some other human voice, to see another face, clasp another hand and again feel the comradeship of man.

During the past week or so, Stern had more than once caught himself listening for some other sound of human life and activity. Once he had found the girl standing on a wooded point among the pines, shading her eyes with her hand and watching down-stream with an attitude of hope which spoke more fluently than words. He had stolen quietly away, saying nothing, careful not to break her mood. For he had understood it; it had been his very own.

The mood expressed itself, at times, in long talks together of the seeming dream-age when there had been so many millions of men and women in the world. Beatrice and Stern found themselves dwelling with a peculiar pleasure on memories and descriptions of throngs.

They would read the population statistics in Van's encyclopedia, and wonder greatly at them, for now these figures seemed the unreal chimeras of wild imaginings.

They would talk of the crowded streets, the "L" crushes and the jams at the Bridge entrance; of packed cars and trains and overflowing theaters; of great concourses they had seen; of every kind and condition of affairs where thousands of their kind had once rubbed elbows, all strangers to each other, yet all one vast kin and family ready in case of need to succor one another, to use the collective intelligence for the benefit of each.

Sometimes they indulged in fanciful comparisons, trying to make their present state seem wholly blest.

"This is a pretty fine way to live, after all," Stern said one day, "even if it is a bit lonesome at times. There's no getting up in the morning and rushing to an office. It's a perpetual vacation! There are no appointments to keep, no angry clients kicking because I can't make water run up-hill or make cast-iron do the work of tool-steel. No saloons or free-lunches, no subways to stifle the breath out of us, no bills to pay and no bill collectors to dodge; no laws except the laws of nature, and such as we make ourselves; no bores and no bad shows; no politics, no yellow journals, no styles—"

"Oh, dear, how I'd like to see a milliner's window again!" cried Beatrice, rudely shattering his thin-spun tissue of optimism. "These skin-clothes, all the time, and no hats, and no chiffons and no—no nothing, at all—! Oh, I never half appreciated things till they were all taken away!"

Stern, feeling that he had tapped the wrong vein, discreetly withdrew; and the sound of his calking-hammer from the beach, told that he was expending a certain irritation on the hull of the Adventure.

One day he found a relic that seemed to stab him to the heart with a sudden realization of the tremendous gap between his own life and that which he had left.

Hunting in the forest, to westward of the bungalow, he came upon what at first glance seemed a very long, straight, level Indian mound or earth-work; but in a moment his trained eye told him it was a railway embankment.

With an almost childish eagerness he hunted for some trace of the track; and when, buried under earth-mold and rubbish, he found some rotten splinters of metal, they filled him with mingled pleasure and depression.

"My God!" he exclaimed, "is it possible that here, right where I stand, countless thousands of human beings once passed at tremendous velocity, bent on business and on pleasure, now ages long vanished and meaningless and void? That mighty engines whirled along this bank, where now the forest has been crowding for centuries? That all, all has perished—forever?

"It shall not be!" he cried hotly, and flung his hands out in passionate denial. "All shall be thus again! All shall return—only far better! The world's death shall not, cannot be!"

Experiences such as these, leaving both of them increasingly irritated and depressed as time went on, convinced Stern of the imperative necessity for exploration. If human beings still existed anywhere in the world, he and she must find them, even at the risk of losing life itself. Years of migration, he felt, would not be too high a price to pay for the reward of coming once again in contact with his own species. The innate gregariousness of man was torturing them both.

Now that the hour of departure was drawing nigh, a strange exultation filled them both—the spirit of conquest and of victory.

Together they planned the last details of the trip.

"Is the sail coming along all right, Beta?" asked Stern, the night when they decided to visit Cambridge. "You expect to have it done in a day or two?"

"I can finish it to-morrow. It's all woven now. Just as soon as I finish binding one edge with leather strips, it'll be ready for you."

"All right; then we can get a good, early start, on Monday morning. Now for the details of the freight."

They worked out everything to its last minutiæ. Nothing was forgotten, from ammunition to the soap which Stern had made out of moose-fat and wood-ashes and had pressed into cakes; from fishing-tackle and canned goods to toothbrushes made of stiff vegetable fibers set in bone; from provisions even to a plentiful supply of birch-bark leaves for taking notes.

"Monday morning we're off," Stern concluded, "and it will be the grandest lark two people ever had since time began! Built and stocked as the Adventure is, she's safe enough for anything from here to Europe.

"Name the place you want to see, and it's yours. Florida? Bermuda? Mediterranean? With the compass I've made and adjusted to the new magnetic variations, and with the maps out of Van's set of books, I reckon we're good for anything, including a trip around the world.

"The survivors will be surprised to see a fully stocked yawl putting in to rescue them from savagery, eh? Imagine doing the Captain Cook stunt, with white people for subjects!"

"Yes, but I'm not counting on their treating us the way Captain Cook was; are you? And what if we shouldn't find anybody, dear? What then?"

"How can we help finding people? Could a billion and a half human beings die, all at once, without leaving a single isolated group somewhere or other?"

"But you never succeeded in reaching them with the wireless from the Metropolitan, Allan."

"Never mind—they weren't in a condition to pick up my messages; that's all. We surely must find somebody in all the big cities we can reach by water, either along the coast or by running up the Mississippi or along the St. Lawrence and through the lakes. There's Boston, of course, and Philadelphia, New Orleans, San Francisco, St. Louis, Chicago—dozens of others—no end of places!"

"Oh, if they're only not all like New York!"

"That remains to be seen. There's all of Europe, too, and Africa and Asia—why, the whole wide world is ours! We're so rich, girl, that it staggers the imagination—we're the richest people that have ever lived, you and I. The 'plutes' in the old days owned their millions; but we own—*we own the whole earth!*"

"Not if there's anybody else alive, dear."

"That's so. Well, I'll be glad to share it with 'em, for the sake of a handshake and a 'howdy,' and a chance to start things going again. Do you know, I rather count on finding a few scattered remnants of folk in London, or Paris, or Berlin?

"Just the same as in our day, a handful of ragged shepherds descended from the Mesopotamian peoples—extinct save for them—were tending their sheep at Kunyunjik, on those Babylonian ruins where once a mighty metropolis stood, and where five million people lived and moved, trafficked, loved, hated, fought, conquered, died—so now to-day, perhaps, we may run across a handful of white savages crouching in caves or rude huts among the débris of the Place de l'Opéra, or Unter den Linden, or—"

"And civilize them, Allan? And bring them back and start a colony and make the world again? Oh, Allan, do you think we could?" she exclaimed, her eyes sparkling with excitement.

"My plans include nothing less," he answered. "It's mighty well worth trying for, at any rate. Monday morning we start, then, little girl."

"Sunday, if you say so."

"Impatient, now?" he laughed. "No, Monday will be time enough. Lots of things yet to put in shape before we leave. And we'll have to trust our precious crops to luck, at that. Here's hoping the winter will bring nothing worse than rain. There's no help for it, whatever happens. The larger venture calls us."

They sat there discussing many many other factors of the case, for a long time. The fire burned low, fell together and dwindled to glowing embers on the hearth.

In the red gloom Allan felt her vague, warm, beautiful presence. Strong was she; vigorous, rosy as an Amazon, with the spirit and the beauty of the great outdoors; the life lived as a part of nature's own self. He realized that never had a woman lived like her.

Dimly he saw her face, so sweet, so gentle in its wistful strength, shadowed with the hope and dreams of a whole race—the type, the symbol, of the eternal motherhood.

And from his hair he drew her hand down to his mouth and kissed it; and with a thrill of sudden tenderness blent with passion he knew all that she meant to him—this perfect woman, his love, who sometime soon was now to be his bride.

CHAPTER X

TOWARD THE GREAT CATARACT

PLEASANT and warm shone the sun that Monday morning, the 2d of September, warm through the greenery of oak and pine and fern-tree. Golden it lay upon the brakes and mosses by the river-bank; silver upon the sands.

Save for the chippering of the busy squirrels, a hush brooded over nature. The birds were silent. A far blue haze veiled the distant reaches of the stream. Over the world a vague, premonitory something had fallen; it was summer still, but the first touch of dissolution, of decay, had laid the shadow of a pall upon it.

And the two lovers felt their hearts gladden at thought of the long migration out into the unknown, the migration that might lead them to southern shores and to perpetual plenty, perhaps to the great boon of contact once again with humankind.

From room to room they went, making all tight and fast for the long absence, taking farewell of all the treasures that during their long weeks of occupancy had accumulated there about them.

Though Stern was no sentimentalist, yet he, too, felt the tears well in his eyes, even as Beta did, when they locked the door and slowly went down the broad steps to the walk he had cleared to the river.

"Good-by," said the girl simply, and kissed her hand to the bungalow. Then he drew his arm about her and together they went on down the path. Very sweet the thickets of bright blossoms were; very warm and safe the little garden looked, cut out there from the forest that stood guard about it on all sides.

They lingered one last moment by the sun-dial he had carved on a flat boulder, set in a little grassy lawn. The shadow of the gnomon fell athwart the IX and touched the inscription he had graved about the edge:

I MARK NO HOURS BUT BRIGHT ONES.

Beatrice pondered.

"We've never had any other kind, together—not one," said she, looking up quickly at the man as though with a new sort of self-realization. "Do you know that, dear? In all this time, never one hour, never one single moment of unhappiness or disagreement. Never a harsh word, an unkind look or thought. 'No hours but bright ones!' Why, Allan, that's the motto of our lives!"

"Yes, of our lives," he repeated gravely. "Our lives, forever, as long as we live. But come, come—time's slipping on. See, the shadow's moving ahead already. Come, say good-by to everything, dear, until next spring. Now let's be off and away!"

They went aboard the yawl, which, fully laden, now lay at a little stone wharf by the edge of the sweet wild wood, its mast overhung by arching branches of a Gothic elm.

Allan cast off the painter of braided leather, and with his boat-hook pushed away. He poled out into the current, then raised the sail of woven rushes like that of a Chinese junk.

The brisk north wind caught it, the sail crackled, filled and bellied hugely. He hauled it tight. A pleasant ripple began to murmur at the stern as the yawl gathered speed.

"Boston and way-stations!" cried he. But through his jest a certain sadness seemed to vibrate. As the wooded point swallowed up their bungalow and blotted out all sight of their garden in the wilderness, then as the little wharf vanished, and nothing now remained but memories, he, too, felt the solemnity of a leave-taking which might well be eternal.

Beatrice pressed a spray of golden-rod to her lips.

"From our garden," said she. "I'm going to keep it, wherever we go."

"I understand," he answered. "But this is no time, now, for retrospection. Everything's sunshine, life, hope—we've got a world to win!"

Then as the yawl heeled to the breeze and foamed away down stream with a speed and ease that bore witness to the correctness of her lines, he struck up a song, and Beatrice joined in, and so their sadness vanished and a great, strong, confident joy thrilled both of them at prospect of what was yet to be.

By mid-afternoon they had safely navigated Harlem River and the upper reaches of East River, and were well up toward Willett's Point, with Long Island Sound opening out before them broadly.

Of the towns and villages, the estates and magnificent palaces that once had adorned the shores of the Sound, no trace remained. Nothing was visible but unbroken lines of tall, blue forest in the distance; the Sound appeared to have grown far wider, and what seemed like a strong current set eastward in a manner certainly not produced by the tide, all of which puzzled Stern as he held the little yawl to her course, sole alone in that vast blue where once uncounted thousands of keels had vexed the brine.

Nightfall found them abreast the ruins of Stamford, still holding a fair course about five or six miles off shore.

Save for the gulls and one or two quick-scurrying flights of Mother Carey's chickens (now larger and swifter than in the old days), and a single "V" of noisy geese, no life had appeared all that afternoon. Stern wondered at this. A kind of desolation seemed to lie over the region.

"Ten times more living things in our vicinity back home on the Hudson," he remarked to Beatrice, who now lay 'midships, under the shelter of the cabin, warmly wrapped in furs against the keen cutting of the night wind. "It seems as though something had happened around here, doesn't it? I should have thought the Sound would be alive with birds and fish. What can the matter be?"

She had no hypothesis, and though they talked it over, they reached no conclusion. By eight o'clock she fell asleep in her warm nest, and Stern steered on alone, by the stars, under promise to put into harbor where New Haven once had stood, and there himself get some much-needed sleep.

Swiftly the yawl split the waters of the Sound, for though her sail was crude, her body was as fine and speedy as his long experience with boats could make it. Something of the vast mystery of night and sea penetrated his soul as he held the boat on her way.

The night was moonless; only the great untroubled stars wondered down at this daring venture into the unknown.

Stern hummed a tune to keep his spirits up. Running easily over the monotonous dark swells with a fair following breeze, he passed an hour or two. He sat down, braced the tiller, and resigned himself to contemplation of the mysteries that had been and that still must be. And very sweet to him was the sense of protection, of guardianship, wherein he held the sleeping girl, in the shelter of the little cabin.

He must have dozed, sitting there inactive and alone. How long? He could not tell. All that he knew was, suddenly, that he had wakened to full consciousness, and that a sense of uneasiness, of fear, of peril, hung about him.

Up he started, with an exclamation which he suppressed just in time to avoid waking Beatrice. Through all, over all, a vast, dull roar was making itself heard—a sound as though of mighty waters rushing, leaping, echoing to the sky that droned the echo back again.

Whence came it? Stern could not tell. From nowhere, from everywhere; the hum and vibrant blur of that tremendous sound seemed universal.

"My God, what's that?" Allan exclaimed, peering ahead with eyes widened by a sudden stabbing fear. "I've got Beatrice aboard, here; I can't let anything happen to her!"

The gibbous moon, red and sullen, was just beginning to thrust its strangely mottled face above the uneasy moving plain of waters. Far off to southward a dim headland showed; even as Stern looked it drifted backward and away.

Suddenly he got a terrifying sense of speed. The headland must have lain five miles to south of him; yet in a few moments, even as he watched, it had gone into the vague obliteration of a vastly greater distance.

"What's happening?" thought Stern. The wind had died; it seemed as though the waters were moving with the wind, as fast as the wind; the yawl was keeping pace with it, even as a floating balloon drifts in a storm, unfeeling it.

Deep, dull, booming, omnious, the roar continued. The sail flapped idle on the mast. Stern could distinguish a long line of foam that slid away, past the boat, as only foam slides on a swift current.

He peered, in the gloom, to port; and all at once, far on the horizon, saw a thing that stopped his heart a moment, then thrashed it into furious activity.

Off there in a direction he judged as almost due northeast, a tenuous, rising veil of vapor blotted out the lesser stars and dimmed the brighter ones.

Even in that imperfect light he could see something of the sinuous drift of that strange cloud.

Quickly he lashed the tiller, crept forward and climbed the mast, his night-glasses slung over his shoulder.

Holding by one hand, he tried to concentrate his vision through the glasses, but they failed to show him even as much as the naked eye could discern.

The sight was paralyzing in its omen of destruction. Only too well Stern realized the meaning of the swift, strong current, the roar—now ever increasing, ever deepening in volume—the high and shifting vapor veil that climbed toward the dim zenith.

"Merciful Heaven!" gulped he. "There's a cataract over there—a terrible chasm—a plunge—to what? And we're drifting toward it at express-train speed!"

CHAPTER XI

THE PLUNGE!

DAZED though Stern was at his first realization of the impending horror, yet through his fear for Beatrice, still asleep among her furs, struggled a vast wonder at the meaning, the possibility of such a phenomenon.

How could a current like that rush up along the Sound? How could there be a cataract, sucking down the waters of the sea itself—whither could it fall? Even at that crisis the man's scientific curiosity was aroused; he felt, subconsciously, the interest of the trained observer there in the midst of deadly peril.

But the moment demanded action.

Quickly Stern dropped to the deck, and, noiseless as a cat in his doe-skin sandals, ran aft.

But even before he had executed the instinctive tactic of shifting the helm, paying off, and trying to beat up into the faint breeze that now drifted over the swirling current, he realized its futility and abandoned it.

"No use," thought he. "About as effective as trying to dip up the ocean with a spoon. Any use to try the sweeps? Maybe she and I together could swing away out of the current—make the shore—nothing else to do—I'll try it, anyhow."

Beside the girl he knelt.

"Beta! Beta!" he whispered in her ear. He shook her gently by the arm. "Come, wake up, girlie—there's work to do here!"

She, submerged in healthy sleep, sighed deeply and murmured some unintelligible thing; but Stern persisted. And in a minute or so there she was, sitting up in the bottom of the yawl among the furs.

In the dim moonlight her face seemed a vague sweet flower shadowed by the dark, wind-blown masses of her hair. Stern felt the warmth, scented the perfume of her firm, full-blooded flesh. She put a hand to her hair; her tiger-skin robe, falling back to the shoulder, revealed her white and beautiful arm.

All at once she drew that arm about the man and brought him close to her breast.

"Oh, Allan!" she breathed. "My boy! Where are we? What is it? Oh, I was sleeping so soundly! Have we reached harbor yet? What's that noise—that roaring sound? Surf?"

For a moment he could not answer. She, sensing some trouble, peered closely at him.

"What is it, Allan?" cried she, her woman's intuition telling her of trouble. "Tell me—is anything wrong?"

"Listen, dearest!"

"Yes, what?"

"We're in some kind of—of—"

"What? Danger?"

"Well, it may be. I don't know yet. But there's something wrong. You see—"

"Oh, Allan!" she exclaimed, and started up. "Why didn't you waken me before? What is it? What can I do to help?"

"I think there's rough water ahead, dear," the engineer answered, trying to steady his voice, which shook a trifle in spite of him. "At any rate, it sounds like a waterfall of some kind or other; and see, there's a line, a drift of vapor rising over there. We're being carried toward it on a strong current."

Anxiously she peered, now full awake. Then she turned to Allan.

"Can't we sail away?"

"Not enough wind. We might possibly row out of the current, and—and perhaps—"

"Give me one of the sweeps quick, quick!"

He put the sweeps out. No sooner had he braced himself against a rib of the yawl and thrown his muscles against the heavy bar than she, too, was pulling hard.

"Not too strong at first, dear," he cautioned. "Don't use up all your strength in the first few minutes. We may have a long fight for it!"

"I'm in it with you—till the end—whichever way it ends," she answered; and in the moonlight he saw the untrammeled swing and play of her magnificent body.

The yawl came round slowly till it was crosswise to the current, headed toward the mainland shore. Now it began to make a little headway. But the breeze slightly impeded it.

Stern whipped out his knife and slashed the sheets of platted rush. The sail crumpled, crackled and slid down; and now under a bare pole the boat cradled slowly ahead transversely across the foam-streaked current that ran swiftly soughing toward the dim vapor-swirls away to the northeast.

No word was spoken now. Both Beatrice and Stern lay to the sweeps; both braced themselves and put the full force of back and arms into each long, powerful stroke. Yet Stern could see that, at the rate of progress they were making over that black and oily swirl, they could not gain ten feet while the current was carrying them a thousand.

In his heart he knew the futility of the fight, yet still he fought. Still Beatrice fought for life, too, there by his side. Human instinct, the will to live, drove them on, on, where both understood there was no hope.

For now already the current had quickened still more. The breeze had sprung up from the opposite direction; Stern knew the boiling rush of waters had already reached a speed greater than that of the wind itself. No longer the stars trembled, reflected, in the waters. All ugly, frothing, broken, the swift current foamed and leaped, in long, horrible gulfs and crests of sickening velocity.

And whirlpools now began to form. The yawl was twisted like a straw, wrenched, hurled, flung about with sickening violence.

"Row! *Row!*" Stern cried none the less. And his muscles bunched and hardened with the labor; his veins stood out, and sweat dropped from his brow, ran into his eyes, and all but blinded him.

The girl, too, was laboring with all her might. Stern heard her breath, gasping and quick, above the roar and swash of the mad waters. And all at once revulsion seized him—rage, and a kind of mad exultation, a defiance of it all.

He dropped the sweep and sprang to her.

"Beta!" he shouted, louder than the droning tumult. "No use! No use at all! Here—come to me!"

He drew the sweep inboard and flung it in the bottom of the yawl.

Already the vapors of the cataract ahead were drifting over them and driving in their faces. A vibrant booming shuddered through the dark air, where now even the moon's faint light was all extinguished by the whirling mists.

Heaven and sea shook with the terrible concussion of falling waters. Though Stern had shouted, yet the girl could not have heard him now.

In the gloom he peered at her; he took her in his arms. Her face was pale, but very calm. She showed no more fear than the man; each seemed inspired with some strange exultant thought of death, there with the other.

He drew her to his breast and covered her face; he knelt with her among the heaped-up furs, and then, as the yawl plunged more violently still, they sank down in the poor shelter of the cabin and waited.

His arms were about her; her face was buried on his breast. He smoothed her hair; his lips pressed her forehead.

"Good-by!" he whispered, though she could not hear.

They seemed now to hover on the very brink.

A long, racing sluicelike incline of black waters, streaked with swirls of white, appeared before them. The boat plunged and whirled, dipped, righted, and sped on.

Behind, a huge, rushing, wall-like mass of lathering, leaping surges. In front, a vast nothingness, a black, unfathomable void, up through which gushed in clouds the mighty jets of vapor.

Came a lurch, a swift plunge.

The boat hung suspended a moment.

Stern saw what seemed a long, clear, greenish slant of water. Deafened and dazed by the infernal pandemonium of noise, he bowed his head on hers, and his arms tightened.

Suddenly everything dropped away. The universe crashed and bellowed. Stern felt a heavy dash of brine—cold, strangling, irresistible. All grew black.

"*Death!*" thought he, and knew no more.

CHAPTER XII

TRAPPED ON THE LEDGE

CONSCIOUSNESS won back to Allan Stern—how long afterward he could not tell—under the guise of a vast roaring tumult, a deafening thunder that rose, fell, leaped aloft again in huge, titanic cadences of sound.

And coupled with this glimmering sense-impression, he felt the drive of water over him; he saw, vaguely as in the memory of a dream, a dim gray light that weakly filtered through the gloom.

Weak, sick, dazed, the man realized that he still lived; and to his mind the thought "Beatrice!" flashed back again.

With a tremendous effort, gasping and shaken, weak, unnerved and wounded, he managed to raise himself upon one elbow and to peer about him with wild eyes.

A strange scene that. Even in the half light, with all his senses distorted by confusion and by pain, he made shift to comprehend a little of what he saw.

He understood that, by some fluke of fate, life still remained in him; that, in some way he never could discover, he had been cast upon a ledge of rock there in the cataract—a ledge over which spray and foam hurled, seething, yet a ledge which, parting the gigantic flood, offered a chance of temporary safety.

Above him, sweeping in a vast smooth torrent of clear green, he saw the steady downpour of the falls. Out at either side, as he lay there still unable to rise, he caught glimpses through the spume-drive, glimpses of swift white water, that broke and creamed as it whirled past; that jetted high; that, hissing, swept away, away, to unknown depths below that narrow, slippery ledge.

Realization of all this had hardly forced itself upon his dazed perceptions when a stronger recrudescence of his thought about the girl surged back upon him.

"Beatrice! Beatrice!" he gasped, and struggled up.

On hands and knees, groping, half-blinded, deafened, he began to crawl; and as he crawled, he shouted the girl's name, but the thundering of the vast tourbillions and eddies that swirled about the rock, white and ravening, drowned his voice. Vague yet terrible, in the light of the dim moon that filtered through the mists, the racing flood howled past. And in Stern's heart, as he now came to more and better understanding, a vast despair took shape, a sickening fear surged up.

Again he shouted, chokingly, creeping along the slippery ledge. Through the driving mists he peered with agonized eyes. Where was the yawl now? Where the girl? Down there in that insane welter of the mad torrent— swept away long since to annihilation? The thought maddened him.

Clutching a projection of the rock, he hauled himself up to his feet, and for a moment stood there, swaying, a strange, tattered, dripping figure in the dim moonlight, wounded, breathless and disheveled, with bloodshot eyes that sought to pierce the hissing spray.

All at once he gulped some unintelligible thing and staggered forward.

There, wedged in a crevice, he had caught sight of something—what it was he could not tell, but toward it now he stumbled.

He reached the thing. Sobbing with realization of his incalculable loss and of the wreckage of all their hopes and plans and all that life had meant, he fell upon his knees beside the object.

He groped about it as though blind; he felt that formless mass of débris, a few shattered planks and part of the woven sail, now jammed into the fissure in the ledge. And at touch of all that remained to him, he crouched there, ghastly pale and racked with unspeakable anguish.

But hope and the indomitable spirit of the human heart still urged him on. The further end of the ledge, over-dashed with wild jets of spray and stinging drives of brine, still remained unexplored. And toward this now he crept, bit by bit, fighting his way along, now clinging as some more savage surge leaped over, now battling forward on hands and knees along the perilous strip of stone.

One false move, he knew, one slip and all was over. He, too, like the yawl itself, and perhaps like Beatrice, would whirl and fling away down, down, into the nameless nothingness of that abyss.

Better thus, he dimly realized, better, after all, than to cling to the ledge in case he could not find her. For it must be only a matter of time, and no very long time at that, when exhaustion and starvation would weaken him and when he must inevitably be swept away.

And in his mind he knew the future, which voiced itself in a half-spoken groan:

"If she's not there, or if she's there, but dead—good-by!"

Even as he sensed the truth he found her. Sheltered behind a jutting spur of granite, Beatrice was lying, where the shock of the impact had thrown her when the yawl had struck the ledge.

Drenched and draggled in her water-soaked tiger-skin, her long hair tangled and disheveled over the rock, she lay as though asleep.

"*Dead?*" gasped Allan, and caught her in his arms, all limp and cold. Back from her brow he flung the brine-soaked hair; he kissed her forehead and her lips, and with trembling hands began to chafe her face, her throat, her arms.

To her breast he laid his ear, listening for some flicker of life, some promise of vitality again.

And as he sensed a slight yet rhythmic pulsing there—as he detected a faint breath, so vast a gratitude and love engulfed him that for a moment all grew dazed and shaken and unreal.

He had to brace himself, to struggle for self-mastery.

"Beta! Beta!" he cried. "Oh, my God! You live—you live!"

Dripping water, unconscious, lithe, she lay within his clasp, now strong again. Forgotten his weakness and his pain, his bruises, his wounds, his fear. All had vanished from his consciousness with the one supreme realization—"*She lives!*"

Back along the ledge he bore her, not slipping now, not crouching, but erect and bold and powerful, nerved to that effort and that daring by the urge of the great love that flamed through all his veins.

Back he bore her to the comparative safety of the other end, where only an occasional breaker creamed across the rock and where, behind a narrow shelf that projected diagonally upward and outward, he laid his precious burden down.

And now again he called her name; he rubbed and chafed her.

Only joy filled his soul. Nothing else mattered now. The total loss of their yawl and all its precious contents, the wreck of their expedition almost at its very start, the fact that Beatrice and he were now alone upon a narrow ledge of granite in the midst of a stupendous cataract that drained the ocean down to unknown, unthinkable depths, the knowledge that she and he now were without arms, ammunition, food, shelter, fire, anything at all, defenseless in a wilderness such as no humans ever yet had faced—all this meant nothing to Allan Stern.

For he had *her;* and as at last her lids twitched, then opened, and her dazed eyes looked at him; as she tried to struggle up while he restrained her; as she chokingly called his name and stretched a tremulous hand to him, there in the thunderous half light of the falls, he knew he could not ask for greater joy, though all of civilization and of power might be his, without her.

In his own soul he knew he would choose this abandonment and all this desperate peril with Beatrice, rather than safety, comfort, luxury, and the whole world as it once had been apart from her.

Yet, as sometimes happens in the supreme crises of life, his first spoken word was commonplace enough.

"There, there, lie still!" he commanded, drawing her close to his breast. "You're all right, now—just keep quiet, Beatrice!"

"What—what's happened—" she gasped. "*Where*—?"

"Just a little accident, that's all," he soothed the frightened girl. Dazed by the roaring cadence of the torrent, she shuddered and hid her face against him; and his arms protected her as he crouched there beside her in the scant shelter of the rocky shelf.

"We got carried over a waterfall, or something of that sort," he added. "We're on a ledge in the river, or whatever it is, and—"

"You're hurt, Allan?"

"No, no—are *you?*"

"It's nothing, boy!" She looked up again, and even in the dim light he saw her try to smile. "Nothing matters so long as we have each other!"

Silence between them for a moment, while he drew her close and kissed her. He questioned her again, but found that save for bruises and a cruel blow on the temple, she had taken no hurt in the plunge that had stunned her. Both, they must have been flung from the yawl when it had gone to pieces. How long they had lain upon the rock they knew not. All they could know was that the light woodwork of the boat had been dashed away with their supplies and that now they again faced the world empty-handed—provided even that escape were possible from the midst of that mad torrent.

An hour or so they huddled in the shelter of the rocky shelf till strength and some degree of calm returned and till the growing light far off to eastward through the haze and mist told them that day was dawning again.

Then Allan set to work exploring once more carefully their little islet in the swirling flood.

"You stay here, Beta," said he. "So long as you keep back of this projection you're safe. I'm going to see just what the prospect is."

"Oh, be careful, Allan!" she entreated. "Be so very, very careful, won't you?"

He promised and left her. Then, cautiously, step by step, he made his way along the ledge in the other direction from that where he had found the senseless girl.

To the very end of the ledge he penetrated, but found no hope. Nothing was to be seen through the mists save the mad foam-rush of the waters that leaped and bounded like white-maned horses in a race of death. Bold as the man was, he dared not look for long. Dizziness threatened to overwhelm him with sickening lure, its invitation to the plunge. So, realizing that nothing was to be gained by staying there, he drew back and once more sought Beatrice.

"Any way out?" she asked him, anxiously, her voice sounding clear and pure through the tumult of the rushing waters.

He shook his head, despairingly. And silence fell again, and each sat thinking long, long thoughts, and dawn came creeping grayly through the spume-drive of the giant falls.

More than an hour must have passed before Stern noted a strange phenomenon—an hour in which they had said few words—an hour in which both had abandoned hopes of life—and in which, she in her own way, he in his, they had reconciled themselves to the inevitable.

But at last, "What's that?" exclaimed the man; for now a different tone resounded in the cataract, a louder, angrier note, as though the plunge of waters at the bottom had in some strange, mysterious way drawn nearer. "What's that?" he asked again.

Below there somewhere by the tenebrous light of morning he could see—or thought that he could see—a green, dim, vaguely tossing drive of waters that now vanished in the whirling mists, now showed again and now again grew hidden.

Out to the edge of the rocky shelf he crept once more. Yes, for a certainty, now he could make out the seething plunge of the waters as they roared into the foam-lashed flood below.

But how could this be? Stern's wonder sought to grasp analysis of the strange phenomenon.

"If it's true that the water at the bottom's rising," thought he, "then there must either be some kind of tide in that body of water or else the cavity itself must be filling up. In either case, what if the process continues?"

And instantly a new fear smote him—a fear wherein lay buried like a fly in amber a hope for life, the only hope that had yet come to him since his awakening there in that trap sealed round by sluicing maelstroms.

He watched a few moments longer, then with a fresh resolve, desperate yet joyful in its strength, once more sought the girl.

"Beta," said he, "how brave are you?"

"How brave? Why, dear?"

He paused a moment, then replied: "Because, if what I believe is true, in a few minutes you and I have got to make a fight for life—a harder fight than any we've made yet—a fight that may last for hours and may, after all, end only in death. A battle royal! Are you strong for it? Are you brave?"

"Try me!" she answered, and their eyes met, and he knew the truth, that come what might of life or death, of loss or gain, defeat or victory, this woman was to be his mate and equal to the end.

"Listen, then!" he commanded. "This is our last, our only chance. And if it fails—"

CHAPTER XIII

ON THE CREST OF THE MAELSTROM

STERN'S observation of the rising flood proved correct. By whatever theory it might or might not be explained, the fact was positive that now the water there below them was rising fast, and that inside of half an hour at the outside the torrent would engulf their ledge.

It seemed as though there must be some vast, rhythmic ebb and flux in the unsounded abysses that yawned beneath them, some incalculable regurgitation of the sea, which periodically spewed forth a part, at least, of the enormous torrent that for hours poured into that titanic gulf.

And it was upon this flux, stormy and wild and full of seething whirlpools, that Allan Stern and the girl now built their only possible hope of salvation and of life.

"Come, we must be at work!" he told her, as together they peered over the edge and now beheld the weltering flood creeping up, up along the thunderous plunge of the waterfall till it was within no more than a hundred feet of their shelter.

As the depth of the fall decreased the spray-drive lessened, and now, with the full coming of day, some reflection of the golden morning sky crept through the spray. Yet neither to right nor left could they see shore or anything save that long, swift, sliding wall of brine, foam-tossed and terrible.

"To work!" said he again. "If we're going to save ourselves out of this inferno we've got to make some kind of preparation. We can't just swim and trust to luck.

We shall have to make a float of some sort or other, I think."

"Yes, but what with?" asked she.

"With what remains of the yawl!"

And even as he spoke he led the way to the crevice where the splintered boards and the torn sail had been wedged fast.

"A slim hope, I know," he admitted, "but it's all we've got now."

Driven home as the wreckage was by the terrific impact of the blow, Stern had a man's work cut out for him to get it clear; but his was as the strength of ten, and before half an hour had passed he had, with the girl's help, freed all the planks and laid them out along the rock-shelf, the most sheltered spot of the ledge.

Another hour later the planks had been lashed into a rough sort of float with what cordage remained and with platted strips of the mat sail.

"It's not half big enough to hold us up altogether," judged the man, "but if we merely use it to keep our heads out of water it will serve, and it's got the merit of being unsinkable, anyhow. God knows how long we may have to be in the water, little girl. But whatever comes we've got to face it. There's no other chance at all!"

They waited now calmly, with the resignation of those who have no alternative to hardship. And steadily the flood mounted up, up, toward the ledge, and now the seethe was very near. Now already the leaping froth of the plunge was dashing up against their rock. In a few moments the shelter would be submerged.

He put his lips close to her ear, for now his voice could not carry.

"Let's jump for it!" he cried. "If we wait till the flood reaches us here we'll be crushed against the rock. Come on, Beatrice, we've got to plunge!"

She answered with her eyes; he knew the girl was ready. To him he drew her and their kiss was one that spoke eternal farewell. But of this thought no word passed their lips.

"Come!" bade the man once more.

How they leaped into that vortex of mad waters, how they vanished in that thunderous welter, rose, sank, fought, strangled, rose again and caught the air, and once more were whirled down and buried in that crushing avalanche; how they clung to the lashed planks and with these spiraled in mad sarabands among the whirlpools and green eddies; how they were flung out into smoother water, blinded and deafened, yet with still the spark of life and consciousness within them, and how they let the frail raft bear them, fainting and dazed, all their senses concentrated just on gripping this support—all this they never could have told.

Stern knew at last, with something of clarity, that he was floating easily along an oily current which ran, undulating, beneath a slate-gray mist; he realized that with one hand he was grasping the planks, with the other arm upbearing the girl.

Pale and with closed eyes, she lay there in the hollow of his arm, her face free from water, her long hair floating out upon the tide.

He saw her lids twitch and knew she lived. Yet even as he thanked God and took a firmer hold on her, consciousness lapsed again, and with it all realization of time or of events.

Yet though the moments—or were they hours?—which followed left no impress on his brain, some intelligence must have directed Stern. For when once more he knew, he found the mist and fog all gone; he saw a golden sun that weltered all across the heaving flood in a brave splendor; and, off to northward, a wooded line of hills, blue in the distance, yet beautiful with their promise of salvation.

Stern understood, then, what must have happened. He saw that the up-filling of the abyss, whatever might have caused it, had flung them forth; he perceived that the temporary flood which had taken place before once more another terrific down-draft should pour into the gaping chasm, had cast them out, floated by their raft of planks, even as match-straws might be flung and floated on the outburst of a geyser.

He understood; he knew that, fortune favoring, life still beckoned there ahead.

And in his heart resolve leaped up.

"Life! Life!" he cried. "Oh, Beatrice, look! See! There's land ahead, there—*land!*"

But the girl, still circled by his arm, lay senseless. Allan knew he could make no progress in that manner. So by dint of great labor, he managed to draw her somewhat onto the float and there to lash her with a loose end of cordage in such wise that she could breathe with no danger of drowning.

Himself he summoned all his forces, and now began to swim through the smooth tides, which, warm with some grateful heat, vastly unlike the usual ocean chill, stretched lazily rolling away and away to that far off shore.

That day was long and bitter, an agony of toil, hope, despair, labor and struggle, and the girl, reviving, shared it toward the end. Only their frail raft fenced death away, but so long as the buoyant planks held together they could not drown.

Thirst and exhaustion tortured them, but there was no hope of appeal to any help. In this manless world there could be no rescue. Here, there, a few gulls wheeled and screamed above the flood; and once a school of porpoises, glistening as they curved their shining backs in long leaps through the brine, played past. Allan and the girl envied the creatures, and renewed their fight for life.

The south wind favored, and what seemed a landward current drew them on. Their own strength, too, in spite of the long fast and the incredible hardships, held out well. For now that civilization was a thing of the oblivious past, they shared the vital forces and the very powers of Mother Nature herself. And, like two favored children of that all-mother, they slowly made their way to land.

Night found them utterly exhausted and soaked to the marrow, yet alive, stretched out at full length, inert, upon the warm sands of a virgin beach. There they lay, supine, above high tide, whither they had dragged themselves with terrible exertion. And the stars wheeled overhead; and down upon them the strange-featured moon wondered with her pallid gleam.

Fireless, foodless and without shelter, unprotected in every way, possessing nothing now save just their own bodies and the draggled garments that they wore, they lay and slept. In their supreme exhaustion they risked attack from wild beasts and from anthropoids. Sleep to them was now the one vital, inevitable necessity.

Thus the long night hours passed and strength revived in them, up-welling like fresh tides of life; and once more a new day grayed the east, then transmuted to bright gold and blazoned its insignia all up the eastern sky.

Stern woke first, dazed with the long sleep, toward mid-morning. A little while he lay as though adream, trying to realize what had happened;

but soon remembrance knitted up the fabric of the peril and the close escape. And, arising stiffly from the sand, he stretched his splendid muscles, rubbed his eyes, and stared about him.

A burning thirst was tormenting him. His tongue clave to the roof of his mouth; he found, by trial, that he could scarcely swallow.

"Water!" gasped he, and peered at the deep green woods, which promised abundant brooks and streams.

But before he started on that quest he looked to see that Beatrice was safe and sound. The girl still slept. Bending above her he made sure that she was resting easily and that she had taken no harm. But the sun, he saw, was shining in her face.

"That won't do at all!" he thought; and now with a double motive he strode off up the beach, toward the dense forest that grew down to the line of shifting sands.

Ten minutes and he had discovered a spring that bubbled out beneath a moss-hung rock, a spring whereof he drank till renewed life ran through his vigorous body. And after that he sought and found with no great labor a tree of the same species of breadfruit that grew all about their bungalow on the Hudson.

Then, bearing branches of fruit, and a huge, fronded tuft of the giant fern-trees that abounded there, he came back down the beach to the sleeping girl, who still lay unconscious in her tiger-skin, her heavy hair spread drying on the sands, her face buried in the warm, soft hollow of her arm.

He thrust the stalk of the fern-tree branch far down into the sand, bending it so that the thick leaves shaded her. He ate plentifully of the fruit and left much for her. Then he knelt and kissed her forehead lightly, and with a smile upon his lips set off along the beach.

A rocky point that rose boldly against the morning, a quarter-mile to southward, was his objective.

"Whatever's to be seen round here can be seen from there," said he. "I've got *my* job cut out for me, all right—here we are, stranded, without a thing to serve us, no tools, weapons or implements or supplies of any kind— nothing but our bare hands to work with, and hundreds of miles between us and the place we call home. No boat, no conveyance at all. Unknown country, full of God knows what perils!"

Thinking, he strode along the fine, smooth, even sands, where never yet a human foot had trodden. For the first time he seemed to realize just what this world now meant—a world devoid of others of his kind. While the girl and he had been among the ruins of Manhattan, or even on the Hudson, they had felt some contact with the past; but here, Stern's eye looked out over a world as virgin as on the primal morn. And a vast loneliness assailed him, a yearning almost insupportable, that made him clench his fists and raise them to the impassive, empty sky that mocked him with its deep and azure calm.

But from the rocky point, when he had scaled its height, he saw far off to westward a rising column of vapor which for a while diverted his thoughts. He recognized the column, even though he could not hear the distant roaring of the cataract he knew lay under it. And, standing erect and tall on the topmost pinnacle, eyes shaded under his level hand, he studied the strange sight.

"Yes, the flood's rushing in again, down that vast chasm," he exclaimed. "The chasm that nearly proved a grave to us! And every day the same thing happens—but how and why? By Jove, here's a problem worthy a bigger brain than mine!

"Well, I can't solve it now. And there's enough to do, without bothering about the maelstrom—except to avoid it!"

He swept the sea with his gaze. Far off to southward lay a dim, dark line, which at one time must have been Long Island; but it was irregular now, and faint, and showed that the island had been practically submerged or swept away by the vast geodetic changes of the age since the catastrophe.

A broken shore-line, heavily wooded, stretched to east and west. Stern sought in vain for any landmark which might give him position on a shore once so familiar to him. Whether he now stood near the former site of New Haven, whether he was in the vicinity of the one-time mouth of the Connecticut River, or whether the shore where he now stood had once been Rhode Island, there was no means of telling. Even the far line of land on the horizon could not guide him.

"If that *is* some remnant of Long Island," he mused, "it would indicate that we're no further east than the Connecticut; but there's no way to be sure. Other islands may have been heaved up from the ocean floor. There's nothing definite or certain about anything now, except that we're both alive, without a thing to help us but our wits, and that I'm starving for something more substantial than that breadfruit!"

Wherewith he went back to Beatrice.

He found her, awake at last, sitting on the beach under the shadow of the fern-tree branch, shaking out her hair and braiding it in two thick plaits. He brought her water in a cup deftly fashioned from a huge leaf; and when she had drunk and eaten some of the fruit they sat and talked a while in the grateful warmth of the sun.

She seemed depressed and disheartened, at last, as they discussed what had happened and spoke of the future.

"This last misfortune, Allan," said she, "is too much. There's nothing now except life—"

"Which is everything!" he interrupted, laughing. "If we can weather a time like that, nothing in store for us can have any terrors!" His own spirits rose fast while he cheered the girl.

He drew his arm about her as they sat together on the beach.

"Just be patient, that's all," bade he. "Just give me a day or so to find out our location, and I'll get things going again, never fear. A week from now we may be sailing into Boston Harbor—who knows?"

And, shipwrecked and destitute though they were, alone in the vast emptiness of that deserted world, yet with his optimism and his faith he coaxed her back to cheerfulness and smiles again.

"The whole earth is ours, and the fulness thereof!" he cried, and flung his arms defiantly outward. "This is no time for hesitance or fear. Victory lies all before us yet. To work! To work!"

CHAPTER XIV

A Fresh Start

Indomitably the human spirit, temporarily beaten down and crushed by misfortunes beyond all calculation, once more rose in renewed strength to the tremendous task ahead. And, first of all, Stern and the girl made a camping place in the edge of the forest, close by the spring under the big rock.

"We've got to have a base of supplies, or something of that sort," the man declared. "We can't start trekking away into the wilderness at once, without consideration and at least some definite place where we can store a few necessaries and to which we can retreat, in case of need. A camp, and—if possible—a fire, these are our first requisites."

Their camp they built (regardless of the protests of birds and squirrels and many little woodland folk) roughly, yet strongly enough to offer protection from the rain, under a thick-leaved oak, which in itself gave shelter. This oak, through whose branches darted many a gay-plumaged bird of species unknown to Stern, grew up along the overhanging face of Spring Rock, as they christened it.

By filling in the space between the rock and the bole of the oak with moss and stones, and then by building a heavy lean-to roof of leafy branches, thatched with lashed bundles of marsh-grass, they constructed in two days a fairly comfortable shack, hard by an abundant, never-failing supply of the finest water ever a human set lip to.

Here Stern piled fragrant grasses in great quantity for the girl's bed. He himself volunteered to sleep at the door-way, on guard with his only weapon—a jagged boulder lashed with leather thongs to a four-foot haft, even in the very fashion of the neolithic ancestors of man.

Their food supply reverted to such berries and fruits as they could gather in the fringes of the forest, for as yet they dared not penetrate far from the shore. To these they added a plentiful supply of clams, which they dug with sharp sticks, at low tide, far out across the sand-flats—toiling for all the world like two of the identical savages who in the long ago, a thousand or five thousand years before the white man came to America, had left shell-heap middens along the north Atlantic coast.

This shell-fish gathering brought the action of the tides to their careful attention. The tide, they found, behaved in an erratic manner. Instead of two regular flows a day there was but one. And at the ebb more than two miles of beach and sea-bottom lay exposed below the spot where they had landed at the flood. Stern analyzed the probable cause of this phenomenon.

"There must be two regular tides," he said, "only they're lost in the far larger flux and reflux caused by the vortex we escaped from. Any marine geyser like that, able to suck down water enough from the sea to lay bare two miles of beach every day and capable of throwing a column of mist and spray like *that* across the sky, is worth investigating. Some day you and I are going to know more about it—a lot more!"

And that was truth; but little the engineer suspected how soon, or under what surpassingly strange circumstances, the girl and he were destined to behold once more the workings of that terrible and mighty force.

On the third day Stern set himself to work on the problem of making fire. He had not even flint-and-steel now, nor any firearm. Had he possessed a pistol he could have collected a little birch-bark, sought out a rotten pine-stump, and discharged his weapon into the "punk," then blown the glow to a flame, and almost certainly have got a blaze. But he lacked everything, and so was forced back to primitive man's one simplest resource—friction.

As an assistant instructor in anthropology at Harvard University, he had now and then produced fire for his class of expectant students by using the Peruvian fire-drill; but even this simple expedient required a head-strap and a jade bearing, a well-formed spindle and a bow. Stern had none of these things, neither could he fashion them without tools. He had, therefore, to resort to the still more primitive method of "fire-sawing," such as long, long ago the Australian bushmen had been wont to practise.

He was a strong man, determined and persistent; but two days more had passed, and many blisters covered his palms ere—after innumerable experiments with different kinds of woods and varying strokes—the first tiny glow fell into the carefully scraped sawdust. And it was with a fast-beating heart and tremulous breath that he blew his spark to a larger one, then laid on his shredded strips of bark and blew again, and so at last, with a great up-welling triumph in his soul, beheld the flicker of a flame once more.

Exhausted, he carefully fed that precious fire, while the girl clapped her hands with joy. In a few moments more the evening air in the dim forest aisles was gladdened by the ruddy blaze of a camp-fire at the door of the lean-to, and for the first time smoke went wafting up among the branches of that primeval wood.

"Now for some real meat!" cried Stern with exultation. "To-morrow I go hunting!"

That evening they sat for hours feeding their fire with deadfalls, listening to the trickle of the little spring and to the night sounds of the forest, watching the bats flicker among the dusky spaces, and gazing at the slow and solemn march of the stars beyond the leafy fretwork overhead. Stern slept but little that night, in his anxiety to keep the fire fed; and morning found him eager to be at his work with throwing-sticks among the vistas of the wilderness.

Together they hunted that day. She carried what his skilful aim brought down from the tangled greenery above. Birds, squirrels, chipmunks, all were welcome. Noon found them in possession of more than thirty pieces of small game, including two hedgehogs. And for the first time in almost a week they tasted flesh again, roasted on a sharp stick over the glowing coals.

Stern hunted all that day and the next. He dressed the game with an extraordinarily large and sharp clamshell, which he whetted from time to time on a rock beside the spring. And soon the fire was overhung with much meat, being smoked with a pine-cone smudge in preparation for the journey into the unknown.

"Inside of a week, at this rate," he judged, "we'll be able to start again. You must set to work platting a couple of sacks. The grass along the brook is tough and long. We can carry fifty or seventy-five pounds of meat, for emergencies. Fruits we can gather on the way."

"And fire? Can we carry that?"

"We can take a supply of properly dried-out wood, with punk. I've already had practise enough, so I ought to be able to get fire at any time inside of half an hour."

"Weapons?"

"I'll make you a battle-ax like my own, only lighter. That's the best we can do for the present, till we strike some ruin or other where a city used to be."

"And you're still bent on reaching Boston?"

"Yes. I reckon we're more than half-way there by now. It's the nearest big ruin, the nearest place where we can refit and recoup the damage done, get supplies and arms and tools, build another boat, and in general take a fresh start. If we can make ten miles a day, we can reach it in ten days or less. I think, all things considered, the Boston plan's the wisest possible one."

She gazed into the fire a moment before replying. Then, stirring the coals with a stick, said she:

"All right, boy; but I've got a suggestion to make."

"What is it?"

"We'll do better to follow the shore all the way round."

"And double the distance?"

"Yes, even so. You know, this shore is—or used to be—flat and sandy most of the way. We can make better progress along beaches and levels than we can through the forest. And there's the matter of shell-fish to consider; and most important of all—"

"Well, what?"

"The sea will guide us. We can't get lost, you understand. With the exception of cutting across the shank of Cape Cod, if the cape still exists, we needn't ever get out of sight of salt water. And it will bring us surely to the Hub."

"By Jove, you're right!" he cried enthusiastically. "The shore-line has it! And tomorrow morning at sunup we begin preparations in earnest. You'll weave the knapsacks while I go after still more meat. Gad! Now that everything's decided, the quicker we're on our way the better. I'm keen to see old Tremont Hill again, and get my hands on a good stock of arms and ammunition once more!"

That night, long after Beatrice was sleeping soundly on her bed of odorous grasses, Allan lay musing by the lean-to door, in the red glow of the fire. He was thinking of the long and painful history of man, of the great catastrophe and of the terrible responsibility that now lay on his own shoulders.

As in a panorama, he saw the emergence of humanity from the animal stage, the primitive savagery of his kind; then the beginnings of the family, the nomadic epoch, the stone age, and the bronze age, and the age of iron; the struggle up to agriculturalism, and communism, and the beginnings of the village groups, with all their petty tribal wars.

He saw the slow formation of small states, the era of slavery, then feudalism and serfdom, and at last the birth of modern nations, the development of machinery, and the vast nexus of exploitation known as capitalism—the stage which at one blow had been utterly destroyed just as it had been transmuting into collectivism.

And at thought of this Stern felt a pang of infinite regret.

"The whole evolutionary process wiped out," mused he, "just as it was about to pass into its perfect form, toward which the history of all the ages had conspired, for which oceans of blood had been spilled and millions of men and women—billions!—lived and toiled and died!

"All gone, all vanished—it's all been in vain, the woe and travail of the world since time began, unless she and I, just we two, preserve the memory and the knowledge of the world's long, bitter fight, and hand them down to strong descendants.

"Our problem is to bridge this gap, to keep the fires of science and of truth alive, and, if that be possible, to start the world again on a higher plane, where all the harsh and terrible phases will no longer have to be lived through again. Our problem and our task! Were ever two beings weighed by such a one?"

And as he pondered, in the firelight, his thoughts and dreams and hopes all centered in the sleeping girl, there in the lean-to sheltered by his watchful care. But what those dreams were, what his visions of the future—who shall set forth or fully understand?

CHAPTER XV

LABOR AND COMRADESHIP

FOUR days later, having hastened all their preparations and worked with untiring energy, they broke camp for the long, perilous trek in quest of the ruins of a dead and buried city.

It was at daylight that they started from the little shack in the edge of the forest. Both were refreshed by a long sleep and by a plunge in the curling breakers that now, at high tide, were driven up the beach by a stiff seabreeze.

The morning, which must have been toward the end of September—Stern had lost accurate count but reckoned the day at about the twenty-fifth—dawned clear and bracing, with just a tang of winelike exhilaration in the air. Before them the beach spread away and away to eastward, beyond the line of vision, a broad and yellow road to bid them travel on.

"Come, girl, *en marche!*" cried the man cheerily, as he adjusted Beta's knapsack so that the platted cord should not chafe her shoulders, then swung his own across his back. And with a buoyant sense of conquest, yet a regret at leaving the little camp which, though crude and rough, had yet been a home to them for a week, they turned their faces to the rising sun and set out on the journey into the unexplored.

Much altered were they now from those days at Hope Villa, when they had been able to restore most of the necessities and even some of the refinements of civilization. Now the girl's hair hung in two thick braids down over her worn tiger-skin, each braid as big as a strong man's wrist, for she lacked any means to do it up; she had not so much as a comb, nor could Stern, without a knife, fashion one for her. Their sandals hung in tatters.

Stern had tried to repair them with strips of squirrel-skin clumsily hacked out with the sharp clam-shell, but the result was crude.

Long were his hair and beard, untrimmed now, unkempt and red. Clad in his ragged fur garment, bare legged and bare armed, with the grass-cloth sack slung over his sinewy shoulder and the heavy stone-ax in his hand, he looked the very image of prehistoric man—as she, too, seemed the woman of that distant age.

But though their outward guise was that of savages far cruder than the North American Indian was when Columbus first beheld him, yet in their brains lay all the splendid inheritance of a world-civilization. And as the fire-materials in Stern's sack contained, in germ, all the mechanic arts, so their joint intelligence presaged everything that yet might be.

They traveled at an easy pace, like voyagers who foresee many hard days of journeying and who are cautious not at first to drain their strength. Five hours they walked, with now and then a pause. Stern calculated they had made twelve miles or more before they camped beside a stream that flowing thinly from the wood, sank into the sand and was lost before it reached the sea.

Here they ate and rested till the sun began to pass its meridian, when once more they started on their pilgrimage. That night, after a day wherein they had met no other sign of life than gulls and crows ravaging the mussel-beds, they slept on piles of sun-dried kelp which they heaped into some crevices under an overhanging brow of low cliffs on a rocky point. And dawn found them again, traveling steadily eastward, battle-axes swinging, hopes high, in perfect comradeship and faith.

Toward what must have been about ten o'clock of that morning they reached the mouth of a river, something like half a mile wide where it joined the sea. By following this up a mile or so they reached a narrow point; but even here, burdened as they were, swimming was out of the question.

"The only thing to do," said Stern, "will be to wait till the tide backs up and gives us quiet water, then make our way across on a log or two"—a plan they put into effect with good success. Mid-afternoon, and they were on their way again, east-bound.

"Was that the Connecticut?" asked Beatrice. "Or do you think we've passed that already?"

"More likely to be the Thames," he answered. "I figure that what used be New London is less than five miles from here."

"Why not visit the ruins? There might be something there."

"Not enough to bother with. We mustn't be diverted from the main is-sue, Boston! Forward, march!"

Next day Stern descried a point jutting far out to sea, which he declared was none other than Watch Hill Point, on the Rhode Island boundary. And on the afternoon of the following day they reached what was indisputably Point Judith and Narragansett Bay.

Here they were forced to turn northward; and when camping time came, after they had dug their due allowance of clams and gathered their bread-fruit and made their fire in the edge of the woods, they held conclave about their future course.

The bay was, indeed, a factor neither Stern nor she had reckoned on. To follow its détours all the way around would add seventy to a hundred miles to their journey, according as they hugged the shore or made straight cuts across some of the wooded promontories.

"And from Providence, at the head of the bay, to Boston, is only forty miles in a direct line northwest-by-north," said he, poking the fire contem-platively.

"But if we miss our way?"

"How can we, if we follow the remains of the railroad? The cuts and em-bankments will guide us all the way."

"I know; but the forest is so thick!"

"Not so thick but we can make at least five miles a day. That is, inside of eight days we can reach the Hub. And we shall have the help of tools and guns, remember. In a place the size of Providence there must be a few ruins still containing something of value. Yes, by all means the overland route is best, from now on. It means forty miles instead of probably two hundred."

Thus they agreed upon it; and, having settled matters, gave them no more thought, but prepared for rest. And sunset came down once more; it faded, smoldering along the forest-line to westward; it burned to dull um-bers and vague purples, then went out. And "the wind that runs after the sun awoke and sang softly among the tree-tops, a while, like the intoning of a choir invisible, and was silent again."

There by the firelight he half saw, half sensed her presence, vague and beautiful despite the travel-worn, tattered skin that clothed her. He felt her warm, vital nearness; his hand sought hers and pressed it, and the pressure was returned. And with a thrill of overwhelming tenderness he realized what this girl was to him and what his love meant and what it all portended.

Until long after dark they sat and talked of the future, and of life and death, and of the soul and of the great mystery that had swept the earth clean of all of their kind and had left them, alone, of all those fifteen hundred million human creatures.

And overhead, blotting out a patch of sky and stars, moved slowly the dark object which had so puzzled Stern since the first time he had observed it—the thing he meant to know about and solve, once he could reach the Cambridge Observatory. And of this, too, they talked; but neither he nor she could solve the riddle of its nature.

Their talk together, that night, was typical of the relationship that had grown up between them in the long weeks since their awakening in the Tower. Almost all, if not quite all, the old-time idea of sex had faded—the old, false assumption on the part of the man that he was by his very nature the superior of woman.

Stern and Beatrice now stood on a different footing; their friendship, comradeship and love were based on the tacit recognition of absolute equality, save for Stern's accidental physical superiority. It was as though they had been two men, one a little stronger and larger than the other, so far as the notion of equality went; though this by no means destroyed that magnetic sex-emotion which, in other aspects, thrilled and attracted and infused them both.

Their love never for a moment obscured Stern's recognition of the girl as primarily a human being, his associate on even terms in this great game that they were playing together, this tremendous problem they were laboring to solve—the vastest and most vital problem that ever yet had confronted the human race, now represented in its totality by these two living creatures.

And as Beatrice recalled the world of other times, with all its false conventions, limitations and pettily stupid gallantries, she shuddered with repulsion. In her heart she knew that, had the choice been hers, she would not have gone back to that former state of half-chattel patronage, half-hypocritical homage and total misconception.

Contrasting her present state with her past one, and comparing this man—all ragged, unshaven and long-haired as he was, yet a true man in every inch of his lithe, virile body—with others she remembered, she found up-welling in her a love so deep and powerful, grounded on such broad bases of respect and gratitude, mutual interest and latent passion, that she herself could not yet understand it in all its phases and its moods.

The relation which had grown up between them, comrades and partners in all things, partook of a fine tolerance, an exquisite and never-failing tenderness, a wealth of all intimate, yet respectful adoration. It held elements of brotherhood and parenthood; it was the love of coworkers striving toward a common goal, of companions in life and in learning, in striving, doing, accomplishing, even failing. Failure mattered nothing; for still the comradeship was there.

And on this soil was growing daily and hourly a love such as never since the world began had been equaled in purity and power, faith, hope, integrity. It purified all things, made easy all things, braved all things, pardoned all things; it was long-suffering and very kind.

They had no need to speak of it; it showed in every word and look and act, even in the humblest and most commonplace of services each for each. Their love was *lived,* not talked about.

All their trials and tremendous hardships, their narrow passes with death, and their hard-won escapes, the vicissitudes of a savage life in the open, with every imaginable difficulty and hard expedient, could not destroy their illusions or do aught than bind them in closer bonds of unity.

And each realized when the time should ripen for another and a more vital love, that, too, would circle them with deeper tenderness, binding them in still more intense and poignant bonds of joy.

CHAPTER XVI

FINDING THE BIPLANE

THE way up the shores of Narragansett Bay was full of experiences for them both. Animal life revealed itself far more abundantly here than along the open sea.

"Some strange blight or other must lie in the proximity of that terrific maelstrom," judged Stern, "something that repels all the larger animals. But skirting this bay, there's life and to spare. How many deer have we seen today? Three? And one bull-buffalo! With any kind of a gun, or even a revolver,

I could have had them all. And that big-muzzled, shaggy old moose we saw drinking at the pool, back there, would have been meat for us if we had had a rifle. No danger of starving here, Beatrice, once we get our hands on something that'll shoot again!"

The night they camped on the way, Stern kept constant guard by the fire, in case of possible attack by wolves or other beasts. He slept only an hour, when the girl insisted on taking his place; but when the sun arose, red and huge through the mists upon the bay, he started out again on the difficult trail as strong and confident as though he had not kept nine hours of vigil.

Everywhere was change and desolation. As the travelers came into a region which had at one time been more densely populated, they began to find here and there mournful relics of the life that once had been—traces of man, dim and all but obliterated, but now and then puissant in their revocation of the distant past.

Twice they found the ruins of villages—a few vague hollows in the earth, where cellars had been, hollows in which huge trees were rooted, and where, perhaps, a grass-grown crumble of disintegrated brick indicated the one-time presence of a chimney. They discovered several farms, with a few stunted apple-trees, the distant descendants of orchard growths, struggling against the larger forest strength, and with perhaps a dismantled well-curb, a moss-covered fireplace or a few bits of iron that had possibly been a stove, for all relics of the other age. Mournful were the long stone walls, crumbling down yet still discernible in places—walls that had cost the labor of generations of farmers and yet now lay useless and forgotten in the universal ruin of the world.

On the afternoon of the fifth day since having left their lean-to by the shore of Long Island Sound, they came upon a cañon which split the hills north of the site of Greenwich, a gigantic "fault" in the rocks, richly striated and stratified with rose and red and umber, a great cleft on the other side of which the forest lay somber and repellent in the slanting rays of the September sun.

"By Jove, whatever it was that struck the earth," said Stern, "must have been good and plenty. The whole planet seems to be ripped up and broken and shattered. No wonder it knocked down New York and killed everybody and put an end to civilization. Why, there's ten cubic miles of material gouged out right here in sight; here's a regular Panama Canal, or bigger, all scooped out in one piece! What the devil could have happened?"

There was no answer to the question. After an hour spent in studying the formations along the lip of the cleft they made a détour eastward to the shore, crossed the fjord that ran into the cañon, and again kept to the north. Soon after this they struck a railroad embankment, and this they followed now, both because it afforded easier travel than the shore, which now had grown rocky and broken, and also because it promised to guide them surely to the place they sought.

It was on the sixth day of their exploration that they at last penetrated the ruins of Providence. Here, as in New York, pavements and streets and squares were all grassed over and covered with pines and elms and oaks, rooting among the stones and shattered brickwork that lay prone upon the earth. Only here or there a steel or concrete building still defied the ravages of time.

"The wreckage is even more complete here than on Manhattan Island," Stern judged as he and the girl stood in front of the ruins of the post-office surveying the débris. "The smaller area, of course, would naturally be covered sooner with the inroads of the forest. I doubt whether there's enough left in the whole place to be of any real service to us."

"To-morrow will be time enough to see," answered the girl. "It's too late now for any more work to-day."

They camped that night in an upper story of the Pequot National Bank Building on Hampstead Street. Here, having cleared out the bats and spiders, they made themselves an aerie secure from attack, and slept long and soundly. Dawn found them at work among the overgrown ruins, much as—three months before—they had labored in the Metropolitan Tower and about it. Less, however, remained to salvage here. For the smaller and lighter types of buildings had preserved far less of the relics of civilization than had been left in the vast and solid structures of New York.

In a few places, none the less, they still came upon the little piles of the gray ash that marked where men and women had fallen and died; but these occurred only in the most sheltered spots. Stern paid no attention to them. His energies and his attention were now fixed on the one task of getting skins, arms, ammunition and supplies. And before nightfall, by a systematic looting of such shops as remained—perhaps not above a score in all could even be entered—the girl and he had gathered more than enough to last them on their way to Boston. One find which pleased him immensely was a dozen sealed glass jars of tobacco.

"As for a pipe," said he, "I can make that easily enough. What's more I will!" More still, he did, that very evening, and the gloom was redolent again of good smoke. Thereafter he slept as not for a long, long time.

They spent the next day in fashioning new garments and sandals; in putting to rights the two rifles Stern had chosen from the basement of the State armory, and in making bandoliers to carry their supply of cartridges. The possession of a knife once more, and of steel wherewith readily to strike fire, delighted the man enormously. The scissors they found in a hardware shop, though rusty, enabled him to trim his beard and hair. Beatrice hailed a warped hard-rubber comb with joy.

But the great discovery still awaited them, the one supreme find which in a moment changed every plan of travel, opened the world to them, and at a single stroke increased their hopes ten thousandfold—the discovery of the old Pauillac monoplane!

They came upon this machine, pregnant with such vast possibilities, in a concrete hangar back of the Federal courthouse on Anderson Street. The building attracted Stern's attention by its unusual state of preservation. He burst in one of the rusted iron shutters and climbed through the window to see what might be inside.

A moment later Beatrice heard a cry of astonishment and joy.

"Great Heavens!" the man exclaimed, appearing at the window. "Come in! Come in—see what I've found!"

And he stretched out his hands to help her up and through the aperture.

"What is it, boy? More arms? More—"

"An aeroplane! Good God, think o' that, will you?"

"An aeroplane? But it's all to pieces, of course, and—"

"Come on in and look at it, I say!" Excitedly he lifted her through the window. "See there, will you? Isn't that the eternal limit? And to think I never even thought of trying to find one in New York!"

He gestured at the dust-laden old machine that, forlorn and in sovereign disrepair, stood at the other end of the hangar. Together they approached it.

"If it will work," the man exclaimed thickly; "*if it will only work—*"

"But will it?" the girl exclaimed, her eyes lighting with the excitement of the find, heart beating fast at thought of what it might portend. "Can you put it in shape, boy? Or—"

"I don't know. Let me look! Who knows? Maybe—"

And already he was kneeling, peering at the mechanism, feeling the frame, the gear, the stays, with hands that trembled more than ever they had trembled since their great adventure had begun.

As he examined the machine, while Beatrice stood by, he talked to himself.

"Good thing the framework is aluminum," said he, "or it wouldn't be worth a tinker's dam after all this time. But as it is, it's taken no harm that I can see. Wire braces all gone, rusted out and disappeared. Have to be rewired throughout, if I can find steel wire; if not, I'll use braided leather thongs. Petrol tank and feed pipe O. K. Girder boom needs a little attention. Steering and control column intact—they'll do!"

Part by part he handled the machine, his skilled eye leaping from detail to detail.

"Canvas planes all gone, of course. Not a rag left; only the frame. But, no matter, we can remedy *that*. Wooden levers, skids, and so on, gone. Easily replaced, Main thing is the engine. Looks as though it had been carefully covered, but, of course, the covering has rotted away. No matter, we'll soon see. Now, this carbureter—"

His inspection lasted half an hour, while the girl, lost among so many technicalities, sat down on the dusty concrete floor beside the machine and listened in a kind of dazed admiration.

He gave her, finally, his opinion.

"This machine *will go* if properly handled," said he, rising triumphantly and slapping the dust off his palms. "The chassis needs truing up, the equilibrator has sagged out of plumb, and the ailerons have got to be readjusted, but it's only a matter of a few days at the outside before she'll be in shape.

"The main thing is the engine, and so far as I can judge, that's pretty nearly O. K. The magneto may have to be gone over, but that's a mere trifle. Odd, I never thought of either finding one of these machines in New York, or building one! When I think of all the weary miles we've tramped it makes me sick!"

"I know," she answered; "but how about fuel? And another thing—have you ever operated one? Could you—"

"Run one?" He laughed aloud. "I'm the man who first taught Carlton Holmes to fly—you know Holmes, who won the Gordon-Craig cup for altitude record in 1916. I built the first—"

"I know, dear; but Holmes was killed at Schenectady, you remember, and this machine is different from anything you're used to, isn't it?" Beatrice asked.

"It won't be when I'm through with it! I tell you, Beatrice, we're going to fly. No more hiking through the woods or along beaches for *us*. From now on we travel in the air—and the world opens out to us as though by magic.

"Distance ceases to mean anything. The whole continent is ours. If there's another human creature on it we find him! And if there isn't then, perhaps we may find some in Asia or in Europe, who knows?"

"You mean you'd dare to attack the Atlantic with a patched-up machine more than a thousand years old?"

"I mean that eventually I can and will build one that'll take us to Alaska, and so across the fifty-mile gap from Cape Prince of Wales to East Cape. The whole world lies at our feet, girl, with this new idea, this new possibility in mind!"

She smiled at his enthusiasm.

"But fuel?" asked she, practical even in her joy. "I don't imagine there's any gasoline left now, do you? A stuff as volatile as that, after all these centuries? What metal could contain it for a thousand years?"

"There's alcohol," he answered. "A raid on the ruins of a few saloons and drug-stores will give me all I need to carry me to Boston, where there's plenty, never fear. A few slight adjustments of the engine will fit it for burning alcohol. And as for the planes, good stout buckskin, well sewn together and stretched on the frames, will do the trick as well as canvas—better, maybe."

"But—"

"Oh, what a little pessimist it is to-day!" he interrupted. "Always coming at me with objections, eh?" He took her in his arms and kissed her. "I tell you Beta, this is no pipe-dream at all, or anything like it; the thing's reality—we're going to fly! But it'll mean the most tremendous lot of sewing and stitching for you!"

"You're a dear!" she answered inconsequentially. "I do believe if the whole world fell apart you could put it together again."

"With your help, yes," said he. "What's more, I'm going to—and a better world at that than ever yet was dreamed of. Wait and see!"

Laughing, he released her.

"Well, now, we'll go to work," he concluded. "Nothing's accomplished by mere words. Just lay hold of that lateral there, will you? And we'll haul this old machine out where we can have a real good look at her, what do you say? Now, then, one, two, three—"

CHAPTER XVII

All Aboard for Boston!

Nineteen days from the discovery of the biplane, a singular happening for a desolate world took place on the broad beach that now edged the city where once the sluggish Providence River had flowed seaward.

For here, clad in a double suit of leather that Beatrice had made for him, Allan Stern was preparing to give the rehabilitated Pauillac a try-out.

Day by day, working incessantly when not occupied in hunting or fishing, the man had rebuilt and overhauled the entire mechanism. Tools he had found a-plenty in the ruins, tools which he had ground and readjusted with consummate care and skill. Alcohol he had gathered together from a score of sources. All the wooden parts, such as skids and levers and propellers, long since vanished and gone, he had cleverly rebuilt.

And now the machine, its planes and rudders covered with strongly sewn buckskin, stretched as tight as drum heads, its polished screw of the Chauvière type gleaming in the morning sun, stood waiting on the sands, while Stern gave it a painstaking inspection.

"I think," he judged, as he tested the last stay and gave the engine its final adjustment. "I think, upon my word, this machine's better to-day than when she was first built. If I'm not mistaken, buckskin's a better material for planes than ever canvas was—it's far stronger and less porous, for one thing—and as for the stays, I prefer the braided hide. Wire's so liable to snap.

"This compass I've rigged on gimbals here, beats anything Pauillac himself ever had. What's the matter with my home-made gyrostat and anemometer? And hasn't this aneroid barometer got cards and spades over the old-style models?"

Enthusiastic as a boy, Stern shook his head and smiled delightedly at Beatrice as he expounded the merits of the biplane and its fittings. She, half glad, half anxious at the possible outcome of the venture, stood by and listened and nodded as though she understood all the minutiæ he explained.

"So then, you're ready to go up this morning?" she asked, with just a quiver of nervousness in her voice. "You're quite certain everything's all right—no chance of accident? For if anything happened—"

"There, there, nothing can happen, nothing will!" he reassured her. "This motor's been run three hours in succession already without skipping an explosion. Everything's in absolute order, I tell you. And as for the human, personal equation, I can vouch for that myself!"

Stern walked around to the back of the machine, picked up a long, stout stake he had prepared, took his ax, and at a distance of about twelve feet behind the biplane drove the stake very deep into the hard sand.

He knotted a strong leather cord to the stake, brought it forward and secured it to the frame of the machine.

"Now, Beatrice," he directed, "when I'm ready you cut the cord. I haven't any corps of assistants to hold me back till the right moment and then give me a shove, so the best I can do is this. Give a quick slash right here when I shout. And whatever happens don't be alarmed. I'll come back to you safe and sound, never fear. And this afternoon it's 'All Aboard for Boston!'"

Smiling and confident, he cranked the motor. It caught, and now a chattering tumult filled the air, rising, falling, as Stern manipulated throttle and spark to test them once again.

Into the driver's seat he climbed, strapped himself in and turned to smile at Beatrice.

Then with a practised hand he threw the lever operating the friction-clutch on the propeller-shaft. And now the great blades began to twirl, faster, faster, till they twinkled and buzzed in the sunlight with a hum like that of a gigantic electric fan.

The machine, yielding to the urge, tugged forward, straining at its bonds like a whippet eager for a race. Beatrice, her face flushed with excitement, stood ready with the knife.

Louder, faster whirled the blades, making a shiny blur; a breeze sprang out behind them; it became a wind, blowing the girl's hair back from her beautiful face.

Stern settled himself more firmly into the seat and gripped the wheel.

The engine was roaring like a battery of Northrup looms. Stern felt the pull, the power, the life of the machine. And his heart leaped within him at his victory over the dead past, his triumph still to be!

"All right!" he cried. "Let go—*let go!*"

The knife fell. The parted rope jerked back, writhing, like a wounded serpent.

Gently at first, then with greater and greater speed, shaking and bouncing a little on the broad, flat wheels that Stern had fitted to the alighting gear, the plane rolled off along the firm-beaten sands.

Stern advanced the spark and now the screw sang a louder, higher threnody. With ever-accelerating velocity the machine tooled forward down the long stretch, while Beatrice stood gazing after it in rapt attention.

Then all at once, when it had sped some three hundred feet, Stern rotated the rising plane; and suddenly the machine lifted. In a long smooth curve, she slid away up the air as though it had been a solid hill—up, up, up—swifter and swifter now, till a suddenly accelerated rush cleared the altitude of the tallest pines in the forest edging the beach, and Stern knew his dream was true!

With a great shout of joy, he leaped the plane aloft! Its rise had all the exhilarating suddenness of a seagull flinging up from the foam-streaked surface of the breakers. And in that moment Stern felt the bliss of conquest.

Behind him, the spruce propellers were making a misty haze of humming energy. In front, the engine spat and clattered. The vast spread of the leather wings, sewn, stretched and tested, crackled and boomed as the wind got under them and heaved them skyward.

Stern shouted again. The machine, he felt, was a thing of life, friendly and true. Not since that time in the tower, months ago, when he had repaired the big steam-engine and actually made it run, had he enjoyed so real a sense of mastery over the world as now; had he sensed so definite a connection with the mechanical powers of the world that was, the world that still should be.

No longer now was he fighting the forces of nature, all barehanded and alone. Now back of him lay the energy of a machine, a metal heart, throbbing and inexhaustible and full of life! Now he had tapped the vein of Power! And in his ears the ripping volley of the exhaust sounded as sweetly as might the voice of a long-absent and beloved girl returning to her sweetheart.

For a moment he felt a choking in his throat, a mist before his eyes. This triumph stirred him emotionally, practical and cool and keen though he was. His hand trembled a second; his heart leaped, throbbing like the motor itself.

But almost immediately he was himself once more. The weakness passed. And with a sweep of his clear eyes, he saw the speeding landscape, woods, hills, streams, that now were running there beneath him like a fluid map.

"My God, it's grand, though!" he exclaimed, swerving the plane in a long, ascending spiral. All the art, the knack of flight came back to him, at the touch of the wheel, as readily as swimming to an expert in the water. Fear? The thought no more occurred to him than to you, reading these words.

Higher he mounted, higher still, his hair whipping out behind in the wild wind, till he could see the sparkle of Narragansett Bay, there in the distance where the river broadened into it. At him the wind tore, louder even than the spitting crackle of the motor. He only laughed, and soared again.

But now he thought of Beatrice; and, as he banked and came about, he peered far down for sight of her.

Yes, there she stood, a tiny dot upon the distant sand. And though he knew she could not hear, in sheer animal spirits and overwhelming joy he shouted once again, a wild, mad triumphant hurrah that lost itself in empty space.

The test he gave the Pauillac convinced him she would carry all the load they would need put upon her, and more. He climbed, swooped, spiraled, volplaned, and rose again, executing a series of evolutions that would have won him fame at any aero meet. And when, after half an hour's exhaustive trial, he swooped down toward the beach again, he found the plane alighted as easily as she had risen.

Like a sea-bird sinking with flat, outstretched wings, coming to rest with perfect ease and beauty on the surface of the deep, the Pauillac slid down the long hill of air. Stern cut off power. The machine took the sand with no more than vigorous bound, and, running forward perhaps fifty yards, came to a stand.

Stern had no sooner leaped from the seat than Beatrice was with him.

"Oh, glorious!" she cried, her face alight with joy and fine enthusiasm. All her spontaneity, her love and admiration were aroused. And she kissed him with so frank and glad a love that Stern felt his heart jump wildly. He thought she never yet had been so beautiful.

But all he said was:

"Couldn't run finer, little girl! Barring a little stiffness here and there, she's perfect. So, then, when do we start, eh? To-morrow morning, early?"

"Why not this afternoon? I'm sure we can get ready by then."

"Afternoon it is, if you say so! But we've got to work, to do it!"

By noon they had gathered together all the freight they meant to carry, and—though the sun had dimmed behind dull clouds of a peculiar slaty gray, that drifted in from eastward—had prepared for the flight to Boston. After a plentiful dinner of venison, berries and breadfruit, they loaded the machine.

Stern calculated that, with Beatrice as a passenger, he could carry seventy-five or eighty pounds of freight. The two rifles, ammunition, knives, ax, tools and provisions they packed into the skin sack Beatrice had prepared, weighed no more than sixty. Thus Stern reckoned there would be a fair "coefficient of safety" and more than enough power to carry them with safety and speed.

It was at 1:15 that the girl took her place in the passenger's seat and let Stern strap her in.

"Your first flight, little girl?" he asked smiling, yet a trifle grave. The barking motor almost drowned his voice.

She nodded but did not speak. He noted the pulse in her throat, a little quick, yet firm.

"You're positive you're not going to be afraid?"

"How could I, with you?"

He made all secure, climbed up beside her, and strapped himself in his seat.

Then he threw in the clutch and released the brake.

"Hold fast!" cried he. "All aboard for Boston! Hold fast!"

CHAPTER XVIII

THE HURRICANE

SOARING strongly even under the additional weight, humming with the rush of air, the plane made the last turn of her spiral and straightened out at the height of twelve hundred feet for her long northward run across the unbroken wilderness.

Stern preferred to fly a bit high, believing the air-currents more depend-able there. Even as he rose above the forest-level, his experienced eye saw possible trouble in the wind-clouds banked to eastward and in the fall of the barometer. But with the thought, "At this rate we'll make Boston in three-quarters of an hour at the outside, and the storm can't strike so soon," he pushed the motor to still greater speed and settled to the urgent business of steering a straight course for Massachusetts Bay.

Only once did he dare turn aside his eyes even so much as to glance at Beatrice. She, magnificently unafraid on the quivering back of this huge airdragon, showed the splendid excitement of the moment by the sparkle of her glance, the rush of eloquent blood to her cheeks.

Stern's achievement, typical of the invincible conquest of the human soul over matter, time and space, thrilled her with unspeakable pride. And as she breathed for the first time the pure, thin air of those upper regions, her strong heart leaped within her breast, and she knew that this man was worthy of her most profound, indissoluble love.

Far down beneath them now the forest sped away to southward. The gleam of the river, dulled by the sunless sky, showed here and there through the woods, which spread their unbroken carpet to the horizon, impenetra-ble and filled with nameless perils. At thought of how he was cheating them all, Stern smiled to himself with grim satisfaction.

"Good old engine!" he was thinking, as he let her out another notch. "Some day I'll put you in a boat, and we'll go cruising. With you, there's no limit to the possibilities. The world is really ours now, with your help!"

Behind them now lay the débris of Pawtucket. Stern caught a glimpse of a ruined building, a crumpled-in gas-tank with an elm growing up through the stark ribs of it, a jumble of wreckage, all small and toylike, there below; then the plane swooped onward, and all lay deep buried in the wilderness again.

"A few minutes now," he said to himself, "and we'll be across what used to be the line, and be spinning over Massachusetts. This certainly beats walking all hollow! Whew!" as the machine lurched forward and took an ugly drop. He jerked the rising-plane lever savagely. "Still the same kind of unreliable air, I see, that we used to have a thousand years ago!"

For a few minutes the biplane hummed on and on in long rising and fall-ing slants, like a swallow skimming the surface of a lake. The even staccato of the exhaust, echoless in that height and vacancy, rippled with cadences like a monster mowing-machine. And Stern was beginning to consider himself as good as in Boston already—was beginning to wonder where the best place might be to land, whether along the shore or on the Common, where, perhaps, some open space still remained—when another formidable air-pocket dropped him with sickening speed.

He righted the plane with a wrench that made her creak and tremble.

"I've got to take a higher level, or a lower," he thought. "Something's wrong here, that's certain!"

But as he shot the biplane sharply upward, hoping to find a calmer lane, a glance at the sky showed trouble impending.

Over the gray background of wind-clouds, a fine-shredded drive was beginning to scud. The whole east had grown black. Only far off to westward did a little patch of dull blue show; and even this was closing up with singular rapidity. And, though the motion of the machine made this hard to estimate, Stern thought to see by the lateral drift of the country below, that they were being carried westward by what—to judge from the agitation of the tree-tops far below—must already be a considerable gale.

For a moment the engineer cursed his foolhardiness in having started in face of such a storm as now every moment threatened to break upon them.

"I should have known," he told himself, "that it was suicidal to attempt a flight when every indication showed a high wind coming. My infernal impatience, as usual! We should have stayed safe in Providence and let this blow itself out, before starting. But now—well, it's too late."

But was it? Had he not time enough left to make a wide sweep and circle back whence he had come? He glanced at the girl. If she showed fear he would return. But on her face he saw no signs of aught but confidence and joy and courage. And at sight of her, his own resolution strengthened once again.

"Why retreat?" he pondered, holding the machine to her long soaring rise. "We must have made a good third of the distance already—perhaps a half. In ten or fifteen minutes more we ought to sight the blue of the big bay. No use in turning back now. And as for alighting and letting the storm blow over, that's impossible. Among these forests it would mean only total wreckage. Even if we could land, we never could start again. No; the only thing to do is to hold her to it and plow through, storm or no storm. I guess the good old Pauillac can stand the racket, right enough!"

Thus for a few moments longer he held the plane with her nose to the northeast-by-north, his compass giving him direction, while far, far below, the world slid back and away in a vast green carpet of swaying trees that stretched to the dim, dun horizon.

Stern could never afterward recall exactly how or when the hurricane struck them. So stunning was the blow that hurled itself, shrieking, in a tumult of mad cross-currents, air maelstroms and frenzied whirls, all across the sky; so overpowering the chill tempest that burst from those inky clouds; so sudden the darkness that fell, the slinging hail volleys that lashed and pelted them, that any clear perception of their plight became impossible.

All the man knew was that direction and control had been knocked clean from his hands; that the world had suddenly vanished in a black drive of cloud and hail and wild-whipping vapor; that he no longer knew north from south, or east from west; but that—struggling now even to breathe, filled with sick fears for the safety of the girl beside him—he was fighting, wrenching, wrestling with the motor and the planes and rudders, to keep the machine from up-ending, from turning turtle in mid-air, from sticking her nose under an air-layer and swooping, hurtling over and over, down, down, like a shattered rocket, to dash herself to pieces on the waiting earth below.

The first furious onset showed the engineer he could not hope to head up into that cyclone and live. He swung with it, therefore; and now, driving across the sky like a filament of cloud-wrack, rode on the crest of the great storm, his motor screaming its defiance at the shrieking wind.

Did Beatrice shout out to him? Did she try to make him hear? He could not tell. No human voice could have been audible in such a turmoil. Stern had no time to think even of her at such a moment of deadly peril.

As a driver with a runaway stallion jerks and saws and strains upon the leather to regain control, so now the man wrestled with his storm-buffeted machine. A less expert aeronaut must have gone down to death in that mad nexus of conflicting currents; but Stern was cool and full of craft and science. Against the blows of the huge tempest he pitted his own skill, the strength of the stout mechanism, the trained instincts of the born mechanician.

And, storm-driven, the biplane hurtled westward, ever westward, through the gloom. Nor could its two passengers by any sight or sound determine what speed they traveled at, whither they went, what lay behind, or what ahead.

Concepts of time, too, vanished. Did it last one hour or three? Five hours, or even more? Who could tell? Lacking any point of contact with reality, merged and whelmed in that stupendous chill nightmare, all wrought of savage gale, rain, hail-blasts, cloud and scudding vapor, they sensed nothing but the fight for life itself, the struggle to keep aloft till the cyclone should have blown itself out, and they could seek the shelter of the earth once more.

Reality came back with a reft in the jetty sky, the faint shine of a little pale blue there, and—a while later—a glimpse of water, or what seemed to be such, very far below.

More steady now the currents grew. Stern volplaned again; and as the machine slid down toward earth, came into a calmer and more peaceful stratum.

Down, down through clouds that shifted, shredded and reassembled, he let the plane coast, now under control once more; and all at once there below him, less than three thousand feet beneath, he saw, dim and vague as though in the light of evening, a vast sheet of water that stretched away, away, till the sight lost it in a bank of low-hung vapors on the horizon.

"*The sea?*" thought Stern, with sudden terror. Who could tell? Perhaps the storm, westbound, had veered; perhaps it might have carried them off the Atlantic coast! This might be the ocean, a hundred or two hundred miles from land. And if so, then good-by!

Checking the descent, he drove forward on level wings, peering below with wide eyes, while far above him the remnants of the storm fled, routed, and let a shaft of pallid sunlight through.

Stern's eye caught the light of that setting beam, which still reached that height, though all below, on earth, was dusk; and now he knew the west again and found his sense of direction.

The wind, he perceived, still blew to westward; and with a thrill of relief he felt, as though by intuition, that its course had not varied enough to drive him out to sea.

Though he knew the ripping clatter of the engine drowned his voice, he shouted to the girl:

"Don't be alarmed! Only a lake down there!" and with fresh courage gave the motor all that she would stand.

A lake! But what lake? What sheet of water, of this size, lay in New England? And if not in New England, then where were they?

A lake? One of the Great Lakes? Could that be? Could they have been driven clear across Massachusetts, its whole length, and over New York State, four hundred miles or more from the sea, and now be speeding over Erie or Ontario?

Stern shuddered at the thought. Almost as well be lost over the sea as over any one of these tremendous bodies! Were not the land near, nothing but death now faced them; for already the fuel-gage showed but a scant two gallons, and who could say how long the way might be to shore?

For a moment the engineer lost heart, but only for a moment.

His eye, sweeping the distance, caught sight of a long, dull, dark line on the horizon.

A cloud-bank, was it? Land, was it? He could not tell.

"I'll chance it, anyhow," thought he, "for it's our only hope now. When I don't know where I am, one direction's as good as any other. We've got no other chance but that! Here goes!"

Skilfully banking, he hauled the plane about, and settled on a long, swift slant toward the dark line.

"If only the alcohol holds out, and nothing breaks!" his thought was. *"If only that's the shore, and we can reach it in time!"*

CHAPTER XIX

WESTWARD HO!

FATE meant that they should live, those two lone wanderers on the face of the great desolation; and, though night had gathered now and all was cloaked in gloom, they landed with no worse than a hard shake-up on a level strip of beach that edged the confines of the unknown lake.

Exhausted by the strain and the long fight with death, chilled by that sojourn in the upper air, drenched and stiffened and half dead, they had no strength to make a camp.

The most that they could do was drag themselves down to the water's edge and—finding the water fresh, not salt—drink deeply from hollowed palms. Then, too worn-out even to eat, they crawled under the shelter of the biplane's ample wings, and dropped instantly into the long and dream-less sleep of utter weariness.

Mid-morning found them, still lame and stiff but rested, cooking break-fast over a cheery fire on the beach near the machine. Save for here and there a tree that had blown down in the forest, some dead branches scat-tered on the sands, and a few washed-out places where the torrent of yes-terday's rain had gullied the earth, nature once more seemed fair and calm.

The full force of the terrific wind-storm had probably passed to north-ward; this land where they now found themselves—whatever it might be—had doubtless borne only a small part of the attack. But even so, and even through the sky gleamed clear and blue and sunlit once again, Stern and the girl knew the hurricane had been no ordinary tempest.

"It must have been a cyclone, nothing less," judged the engineer, as he finished his meal and reached for his comforting pipe. "And God knows where it's driven us to! So far as judging distances goes, in a hurricane like that it's impossible. This may be any one of the Great Lakes; and, again, it may not. For all we know, we may be up in the Hudson Bay region some-where. This may be Winnipeg, Athabasca, or Great Slave. With the kind of storms that happen nowadays, anything's possible."

"Nothing matters, after all," the girl assured him, "except that we're alive and unhurt; and the machine can still travel, for—"

"Travel!" cried Stern. "With about a quart of fuel or less! How far, I'd like to know?"

"That's so; I never thought of that!" the girl replied, dismayed. "Oh, dear, what shall we do now?"

Stern laughed.

"Hunt for a town, of course," he reassured her. "There, there, don't wor-ry! If we find alcohol, we're all right, anyhow. If not, we're better off than we were after the maelstrom almost got us, at any rate. *Then* we had no arms, ammunition, tools, or means to make fire, while *now* we've got them all. Forgive my speaking as I did, little girl. Don't worry—everything will come right in the end."

Reassured, she sat before the fire, and for an hour or more they drew maps and diagrams in the sand, made plans, and laid out their next step in this long campaign against the savage power of a deserted world.

At last, their minds made up, they wheeled the plane back to the forest, where Stern cut out among the trees a space for its protection. And, leaving it here, covered with branches of the thick-topped fern-tree, they took provisions and once more set out on their exploration.

But this time they had an ax and their two rifles, and as they strode northward along the shore they felt a match for any peril.

An hour's walk brought them to the ruins of a steel recreation-pier, with numerous traces of a town along the lake behind it.

"That settles the Hudson Bay theory," Stern rejoiced, as they wandered among the débris. "This is certainly one of the Great Lakes, though which one, of course, we can't tell as yet. And now if we can round up some alcohol we'll be on our way before very long."

They found no alcohol, for the only ruin where drugs or liquors had evidently been sold had caved in, a mass of shattered brickwork, smashing every bottle in the place. Stern found many splintered shards of glass; but that was all, so far as fuel was concerned. He discovered something else, however, that proved of tremendous value—the wreck of a printing-office.

Presses and iron of all kind had gone to pieces, but some of the larger lead types and quads still were recognizable. And, the crucial thing, he turned up a jagged bit of stereotype-sheet from under the protection of a concrete plinth that had fallen into the cellar.

All corroded and discolored though it was, he still could make out a few letters.

"A newspaper head, so help me!" he exclaimed, as with a trembling finger he pointed the letters out to Beatrice : "Here's an ' H'—here's ' mbur'—here's ' aily,' and ' ronicl'! Eh, what? 'Chronicle,' it must have been! By Jove, you're right! And the whole thing used to spell 'Hamburg Daily Chronicle,' or I'm a liar!"

He thought a moment—thought hard—then burst out:

"Hamburg, eh? Hamburg, by a big lake? Well, the only Hamburg by a lake that I know of used to be Hamburg, New York. I ought to remember. I drew the plans for the New York Central bridge, just north of here, over the Spring Creek ravine.

"Yes, sir, this certainly is Hamburg, New York. And this lake must be Erie. Now, if I'm correct, just back up there on that hill we'll find the remains of the railway cut, and less than ten miles north of here lies all that's left of Buffalo. Some luck, eh? Cast away, only fifteen miles or so from a place like that. And we might have gone to Great Bear Lake, or to—h-m!—to any other place, for all the cyclone cared.

"Well, come on now, let's see if the railway cut is still there, and my old bridge; and if so, it's Buffalo for ours!"

It was all as he had said. The right-of-way of the railroad still showed distinctly, in spite of the fact that ties and rails had long since vanished. Of the bridge nothing was left but some rusted steel stringers lying entangled about the disintegrated concrete piers. But Stern viewed them with a melancholy pride and interest—his own handiwork in the very long ago.

They had no time, however, for retrospection; but, once more taking the shore, kept steadily northward. And before noon they reached the débris of Buffalo, stark and deserted by the lake where once its busy commerce and its noisy life had thronged. By four o'clock that afternoon they had collected fuel enough for the plane to do that distance on, and more. Late that night they were again back at the spot where they had landed the night before.

And here, in high spirits and with every hope of better fortune now to follow evil, they cooked their meal and spent an hour in planning their next move, then slept the sleep of well-earned rest.

They had now decided to abandon the idea of visiting Boston. This seeming change of front was not without its good reasons.

"We're half-way to Chicago as it is," Stern summed up next morning. "Conditions are probably similar all along the Atlantic coast; there's no life to be found there. On the other hand, if we strike for the West there's at least a chance of running across survivors. If we don't find them there, then we probably sha'n't find them anywhere. In Chicago we can live and restock for further explorations, and as for locating a telescope, the University of Chicago ruins are as promising as those of Harvard. Chicago, by all means!"

They set out at nine o'clock, and, having made a good start, reached Buffalo by twenty minutes past, flying easily along the shore at not more than five hundred feet elevation.

Gaily the lake sparkled and wimpled in the morning sun, unvexed now by any steamer's prow, unshaded by any smoke from cities or roaring mills along its banks.

Despite the lateness of the season, the morning was warm; a mild breeze swayed the treetops and set the little whitecaps foaming here and there over the broad expanse of blue. Beatrice and Stern felt the joy of life reborn in them at that sight.

"Magnificent!" cried the engineer. "Now for a swing up past Niagara, and we're off!"

The river, they found as the plane swept onward, had dwindled to a brook that they could almost leap across. The rapids now were but a dreary waste of blackened rocks, and the Falls themselves, dry save for a desolate trickle down past Goat Island, presented a spectacle of death—the death of the world as Beatrice and Stern had known it, which depressed them both.

That this tremendous cataract could vanish thus; that the gorge and the great Falls which for uncounted centuries had thundered to the rush and tumult of the mighty waters could now lie mute and dry and lifeless, saddened them both beyond measure.

And they were glad when, with a wide sweep of her wings, the Pauillac veered to westward again along the north shore of Lake Erie and settled into the long run of close on two hundred and fifty miles to Detroit, where Stern counted on making his first stop.

Without mishap, yet without sighting a single indication of the presence of man, they coasted down the shore and ate their dinner on the banks of Lake Saint Clair, near the ruins of Windsor, with those of Detroit on the opposite side. For some reason or other, impossible to solve, the current now ran northward toward Huron, instead of south to Erie. But this phenomenon they could do little more than merely note, for time lacked to give it any serious study.

Mid-afternoon found them getting under way again westbound.

"Chicago next," said Stern, making some slight but necessary adjustment of the air-feed in the carbureter. "And here's hoping there'll be some natives to greet us!"

"Amen to that!" answered the girl. "If any life has survived at all, it ought to be on the great central plain of the country, say from Indiana out through Nebraska. But do you know, Allan, if it should come right down to meeting any of our own kind of people—savages, of course, I mean, but white—I really believe I'd be awfully afraid of them. Imagine white savages dressed in skins—"

"Like us!" interrupted Stern, laughing.

"And painted with woad, whatever woad is; I remember reading about it in the histories of England; all the early Britons used it. And carrying nice, knobby stone cleeks to stave in our heads! It *would* be nice to meet a hundred or a thousand of them, eh? Rather a different matter from dealing with a horde of those anthropoid creatures, I imagine."

Stern only smiled, then answered:

"Well, I'll take *my* chances with 'em. Better a fight, say I, with my own kind, than solitude like this—you and I all alone, girl, getting old some time and dying with never a hand-clasp save perhaps such as it may please fate to give us from whatever children are to be. But come, come, girl. No time for gloomy speculations of trouble. In you get now, and off we go—westward bound again."

Only half an hour out of Detroit it was that they first became aware of some strange disturbance of the horizon, some inexplicable appearance such as neither of them had ever seen, a phenomenon so peculiar that, though both observed it at about the same time, neither Stern could believe his own senses nor Beatrice hers.

For all at once it seemed to them the sky-line was drawing suddenly nearer; it seemed that the horizon was approaching at high speed.

The dark, untrodden forest mass still stretched away, away, until it vanished against the dim blue of the sky; but now, instead of that meeting-line being forty miles off, it seemed no farther than twenty, and minute by minute it indubitably was rushing toward them with a speed equal to their own.

Stern, puzzled and alarmed at this unusual sight, felt an impulse to slow, to swerve, to test the apparition in some way; but second thought convinced him it must be deception of some sort.

"Some peculiar state of the atmosphere," thought he, "or perhaps we're approaching a high ridge, on the other side of which lie clouds that cut away the farther view. Or else—no, hang it! the world seems to end right there, with no clouds to veil it—nothing, only—what?"

He saw the girl pointing in alarm. She, too, was clearly stirred by the appearance.

What to do? Stern felt indecision for the first time since he had started on this long, adventurous journey. Shut off and descend? Impossible among those forests. Swing about and return? Not to be thought of. Keep on and meet perils perhaps undreamed of? Yes—at all hazards he would keep on.

And with a tightening of the jaw he drove the Pauillac onward, ever onward—toward the empty space that yawned ahead.

"End o' the world?" thought he. "All right, the old machine is good for it, and so are we. Here goes!"

CHAPTER XX

ON THE LIP OF THE CHASM

VERY near, now, was the strange apparition. On, on, swift as a falcon, the plane hurtled. Stern glanced at Beatrice. Never had he seen her more beautiful. About her face, rosy and full of life, the luxuriant loose hair was whipping. Her eyes sparkled with this new excitement, and on her full red lips a smile betrayed her keen enjoyment. No trace of fear was there—nothing but confidence and strength and joy in the adventure.

The phenomenon of the world's end—for nothing else describes it adequately—now appeared distinctly as a jagged line, beyond which nothing showed. It differed from the horizon line, inasmuch as it was close at hand. Already the adventurers could peer down upon it at an acute angle.

Plainly could they see the outlines of trees growing along the verge. But beyond them, nothing.

It differed essentially from a cañon, because there was no other side at all. Strain his eye as he might, Stern could detect no opposite wall. And now, realizing something of the possibilities of such a chasm, he swung the Pauillac southward. Flying parallel to the edge of this tremendous barrier, he sought to solve the mystery of its true nature.

"If I go higher, perhaps I may be able to get some notion of it," thought he, and swinging up-wind, he spiraled till the barometer showed he had gained another thousand feet.

But even this additional view profited him nothing. Half a mile to westward the ragged tree-line still showed as before, with vacancy behind it, and as far as Stern could see to north, to south, it stretched away till the dim blue of distance swallowed it. Yet, straight across the gulf, no land appeared. Only the sky itself was visible there, as calm and as unbroken as in the zenith, yet extending far below where the horizon-line should have been—down, in fact, to where the tree-line cut it off from Stern's vision.

The effect was precisely that of coming to the edge of a vast plain, beyond which nothing lay, save space, and peering over.

"The end of the world, indeed!" thought the engineer, despite himself. "But what can it mean? What can have happened to the sphere to have changed it like this? Good Heavens, what a marvel—what a catastrophe!"

Determined at all hazards to know more of this titanic break or "fault," or whatsoever it might be, he banked again, and now, on a descending slant, veered down toward the lip of the chasm.

"Going out over it?" cried Beatrice.

He nodded.

"It may be miles deep!"

"You can't get killed any deader falling a hundred miles than you can a hundred feet!" he shouted back, above the droning racket of the motor.

And with a fresh grip on the wheel, head well forward, every sense alert and keen to meet whatever conditions might arise, to battle with cross-currents, "air-holes," or any other vortices swirling up out of those unknown depths, he skimmed the Pauillac fair toward the lip of the monstrous vacancy.

Now as they rushed almost above the verge he could see conclusively they were not dealing here with a cañon like the Yosemite or like any other he had ever seen or heard of in the old days.

There was positively no bottom to the terrific thing!

Just a sheer edge and beyond that—nothing.

Nowhere any sign of an opposite bank; nowhere the faintest trace of land. Far, far below, even a few faint clouds showed floating there as if in mid-heaven.

The effect was ghastly, unnerving and altogether terrible. Not that Stern feared height. No, it was the unreality of the experience, the inexplicable character of this yawning edge of the world that almost overcame him.

Only by a strong exercise of will-power could he hold the biplane to her course. His every instinct was to veer, to retreat back to solid earth, and land somewhere, and once more, at all hazards, get the contact of reality.

But Stern resisted all these impulses, and now already had driven the Pauillac right to the lip of the vast nothingness.

Now they were over!

"My God!" he cried, stunned by the realization of this thing. "Sheer space! No bottom anywhere!"

For all at once they had shot, as it were, out into a void which seemed to hold no connection at all with the earth they now were quitting.

Stern caught a glimpse of the tall forest growing up to within a hundred yards of the edge, then of smaller trees, dwindling to bushes and grasses, and strange red sand that bordered the gap—sand and rocks, barren as though some up-draft from the void had killed off vegetable growth along the very brink.

Then all slid back and away. The red-ribbed wall of the great chasm, shattered and broken as by some inconceivable disaster, some cosmic cataclysm, fell away and away, downward, dimmer and more dim, until it faded gradually into a blue haze, then vanished utterly.

And there below lay nothingness—and nothingness stretched out in front to where the sight lost itself in pearly vapors that overdimmed the sky.

Beatrice glanced at Stern as the Pauillac sped true as an arrow in its flight, out into this strange and incomprehensible vacuity.

Just a shade paler now he seemed. Despite the keen wind, a glister of sweat-drops studded his forehead. His jaw was set, set hard; she could see the powerful maxillary muscles knotted there where the throat-cords met the angle of the bone. And she understood that, for the first time since their tremendous adventure had begun, the man felt shaken by this latest and greatest of all the mysteries they had been called upon to face.

Already the verge lay far behind; and now the sense of empty space above and on all sides and there below was overpowering.

Stern gasped with a peculiar choking sound. Then all at once, throwing the front steering plane at an angle, he brought the machine about and headed for the distant land.

He spoke no word, nor did she; but they both swept the edge of the chasm with anxious eyes, seeking a place to light.

It was with tremendous relief that they both saw the solid earth once more below them. And when, five minutes later, having chosen a clear and sand-barren on the verge, some two miles southward along the abyss, Stern brought the machine to earth, they felt a gratitude and a relief not to be voiced in words.

"By Jove!" exclaimed the man, lifting Beatrice from the seat, "if that isn't enough to shake a man's nerve and upset all his ideas, geological or otherwise, I'd like to know what is!"

"Going to try to cross it?" she asked anxiously; "that is, if there is any other side? I know, of course, that if there is you'll find out, some way or other!"

"You overestimate me," he replied. "All I can do, for now, is to camp down here and try to figure the problem out—with your help. Whatever this thing is, it's evident it stands between us and our plan. Either Chicago lies on the other side—(provided, of course, as you say, that there *is* one)—or else it's been swallowed up, ages ago, by whatever catastrophe produced this yawning gulf.

"In either event we've got to try to discover the truth, and act accordingly. But for now, there's nothing we can do. It's getting late already. We've had enough for one day, little girl. Come on, let's make the machine ready for the night, and camp down here and have a bite to eat. Perhaps by tomorrow we may know just what we're up against!"

The moon had risen, flooding the world with spectral light, before the two adventurers had finished their meal. All during it they had kept an unusual silence. The presence of that terrible gulf, there not two hundred feet away to westward of them, imposed its awe upon their thoughts.

And after the meal was done, by tacit understanding they refrained from trying to approach it or to peer over. Too great the risks by night. They spoke but little, and presently—exhausted by the trying events of the day—sought sleep under the vanes of the Pauillac.

But for an hour, tired as he was, the engineer lay thinking of the chasm, trying in vain to solve its problem or to understand how they were to follow any further the search for the ruins of Chicago, where fuel was to be had, or carry on the work of trying to find some living members of the human race.

Morning found them revived and strengthened. Even before they made their fire or prepared their breakfast they were exploring along the edge of the gigantic cleft.

Going first to make sure no rock should crumble under the girl's tread, no danger threaten, Stern tested every foot of the way to the very edge of the sheer chasm.

"Slowly, now!" he cautioned, taking her hand. "We've got to be careful here. My God, what a drop!"

Awed, despite themselves, they stood there on a flat slab of schist that projected boldly over the void. Seen from this point, the immense nothingness opened out below them even more terrible than it had seemed from the biplane.

The fact is common knowledge that a height, viewed from a balloon or aeroplane, is always far less dizzying than from a lofty building or a monument. Giddiness vanishes when no solid support lies under the feet. This fact Stern and the girl appreciated to the full as they peered over the edge.

Ten times more ominous and frightful the vast blue mystery beneath them now appeared than it had seemed before.

"Let's look sheer down," said the girl. "By lying flat and peering over, there can't be any danger."

"All right, but only on condition that I keep tight hold of you!"

Cautiously they lay down and worked their way to the edge. The engineer circled Beta's supple waist with his arm.

"Steady, now!" he warned. "When you feel giddy, let me know, and we'll go back."

The effect of the chasm, from the very edge of the rock, was terrifying. It was like nothing ever seen by human eyes. Peering down into the Grand Cañon of the Colorado would have been child's play beside it. For this was no question of looking down a half-mile, a mile, or even five, to some solid bottom.

Bottom there was none—nothing save dull purple haze, shifting vapors, and an unearthly dim light which seemed to radiate upward as though the sun's rays, reflected, were striving to beat up again.

"There must be miles and miles of air below us," said Stern, "to account for this curious light-effect. Air, of course, will eventually cut off the vision. Given a sufficiently thick layer, say a few hundred miles, it couldn't be seen through. So if there *is* a bottom to this place, be it one hundred or even five hundred miles down, of course we couldn't see it. All we could see would be the air, which would give this sort of blue effect."

"Yes; but in that case how can we see the sun, or the moon, or stars?"

"Light from above only has to pierce forty or fifty miles of really dense air. Above that height it's excessively rarified. While down below earth-level, of course, it would get more and more dense all the time, till at the bottom of a five-hundred-mile drop the density and pressure would be tremendous."

Beatrice made no answer. The spectacle she was gazing at filled her with solemn thoughts. Jagged, rent and riven, the rock extended downward. Here vast and broken ledges ran along its flanks—red, yellow, black, all seared and burned and vitrified as by the fire of Hell; there huge masses, up-piled, seemed about to fall into the abyss.

A quarter-mile to southward, a rivulet had found its way over a projecting ledge. Spraying and silvery it fell, till, dissipated by the up-draft from the abyss, it dissolved in mist.

The ledge on which they were lying extended downward perhaps three hundred yards, then sloped backward, leaving sheer empty space beneath them. They seemed to be poised in mid-heaven. It was totally unlike the sensation on a mountain-top, or even floating among the clouds; for a moment it seemed to Stern that he was looking *up* toward an unfathomable, infinite dome above him.

He shuddered, despite his cool and scientific spirit of observation.

"Some chemical action going on somewhere down there," said he, half to divert his own attention from his thoughts. "Smell that sulphur? If this place wasn't once the scene of volcanic activities, I'm no judge!"

A moderate yet very steady wind blew upward from the chasm, freighted with a scent of sulphur and some other substance new to Stern.

Beatrice, all at once overcome by sudden giddiness, drew back and hid her face in both hands.

"No bottom to it—no end!" she said in a scared tone. "Here's the end of the world, right here, and beyond this very rock—nothing!"

Stern, puzzled, shook his head.

"That's really impossible, absurd and ridiculous, of course," he answered. "There *must* be something beyond. The way this stone falls proves that."

He pitched a two-pound lump of granite far out into the air. It fell vertically, whirling, and vanished with the speed of a meteor.

"If a whole side of the earth had split off, and what we see down below there were really sky, of course the earth's center of gravity would have shifted," he explained, "and that rock would have fallen in toward the cliff below us, not straight down."

"How can you be sure it doesn't fall that way after the impulse you gave it has been lost?"

"I shall have to make some close scientific tests here, lasting a day or two, before I'm positive; but my impression is that this, after all, is only a cañon—a split in the surface—rather than an actual end of the crust."

"But if it were a cañon, why should blue sky show down there at an angle of forty-five degrees?"

"I'll have to think that out, later," he replied. "Directly under us, you see all seems deep purple. That's another fact to consider. I tell you, Beatrice, there's more to be figured out here than can be done in half an hour.

"As I see it, some vast catastrophe must have rent the earth, a thousand or fifteen hundred years ago, as a result of which everybody was killed except you and me. We're standing now on the edge of the scar left by that explosion, or whatever it was. How deep or how wide that scar is, I don't know. Everything depends on our finding out, or at least on our guessing it with some degree of accuracy."

"How so?"

"Because, don't you see, this chasm stands between us and Chicago and the West, and all our hopes of finding human life there. And—"

"Why not coast south along the edge here, and see if we can't run across some ruined city or other where we can refill the tanks?"

"I'll think it over," the engineer answered. "In the meantime we can camp down here a couple of days or so, and rest; and I can make some calculations with a pendulum and so on."

"And if you decide there's probably another side to this gulf, what then?"

"We cross," he said; then for a while stood silent, musing as he peered down into the bottomless abyss that stretched there hungrily beneath their narrow observation-rock.

"We cross, that's all!"

CHAPTER XXI

LOST IN THE GREAT ABYSS

FOR two days they camped beside the chasm, resting, planning, discussing, while Stern, with improvised transits, pendulums and other apparatus, made tests and observations to determine, if possible, the properties of the great gap.

During this time they developed some theories regarding the catastrophe which had swept the world a thousand years ago.

"It seems highly and increasingly probable to me," the engineer said, after long thought, "that we have here the actual cause of the vast blight of death that left us two alone in the world. I rather think that at the time of the great explosion which produced this rent, certain highly poisonous gases were thrown off, to impregnate the entire atmosphere of the world. Everybody must have been killed at once. The poison must have swept the earth clean of human life."

"But how did *we* escape?" asked the girl.

"That's hard telling. I figure it this way: The mephitic gas probably was heavy and dense, thus keeping to the lower air-strata, following them, over plain and hill and mountain, like a blanket of death.

"Just what happened to us, who can tell? Probably, tightly housed up there in the tower, the very highest inhabited spot in the world, only a very slight infiltration of the gas reached us. If my theory won't work, can you suggest a better one? Frankly, I can't; and until we have more facts, we've got to take what we have. No matter, the condition remains—we're alive and all the rest are dead; and I'm positive this cleft here is the cause of it."

"But if everybody's dead, as you say, why hunt for men?"

"Perhaps a handful may have survived among the highlands of the Rockies. I imagine that after the first great explosion there followed a series of terrible storms, tornadoes, volcanic eruptions, tidal waves and so on. You remember how I found the bones of a whale in lower Broadway; and many of the ruins in New York show the action of the sea—they're laid flat in such a manner as to indicate that the island was washed on one or two occasions by monster waves.

"Well, all these disturbances probably finished up what few survivors escaped, except possibly among the mountains of the West. A few scattered colonies may have survived a while—mining camps, for instance, or isolated prospectors, or what-not. They may all have died out, or again, they may have come together and reëstablished some primitive form of barbarous or even savage life by this time. There's no telling. Our imperative problem is to reach that section and explore it thoroughly. For there, if anywhere, we'll find survivors of our race."

"How about that great maelstrom that nearly got us?" asked the girl. "Can you connect that with the catastrophe?"

"I think so. My idea is that, in some way or other, the sea is being sucked down into the interior of the earth and then hurled out again; maybe there's a gradual residue being left; maybe a great central lake or sea has formed. Who knows? At any rate all the drainage system of the country seems to have been changed and reversed in the most curious and unaccountable manner. I think we should find, if we could investigate everything thoroughly, that this vast chasm here is intimately connected with the whole thing."

These and many other questions perplexed the travelers, but most of all they sought to know the breadth of the vast gap and to determine if it had, as they hoped, another side, or if it were indeed the edge of an enormous mass split bodily off the earth.

Stern believed he had an answer to this problem on the afternoon of the second day. For many hours he had hung his pendulums over the cliff, noted deflections, taken triangulations, and covered the surface of the smooth stone with X's, Y's, Z's, sines and cosines and abstruse formulæ— all scrawled with charcoal, his only means of writing.

At last he finished the final equation, and, with a smile of triumph and relief, got to his feet again.

Back to the girl, who was cooking over an odorous fire of cedar, he made his way, rejoicing.

"I've got it!" he shouted gladly. "Making reasonable allowances for depth, I've got it!"

"Got what?"

"The probable width!"

"Oh!" And she stood gazing at him in admiration, beautiful and strong and graceful. "You mean to say—"

"I'm giving the chasm a hundred miles' depth. That's more than anybody could believe possible—twice as much. On that assumption, my tests show the distance to the other side—and there *is* another side, by the way!— can't be over—"

"Five hundred miles?"

"Nonsense! Not over one hundred to one-fifty. I'm going on a liberal allowance for error, too. It may not be over seventy-five. The—"

"But if that's as far as it is, why can't we see the other side?"

"With all that chemicalized vapor rising constantly? Who knows what elements may be in it? Or what polarization may be taking place?"

"Polarization?"

"I mean, what deflection and alteration of light? No wonder we can't see! But we can fly! And we're going to, what's more!"

"Going to make a try for Chicago, then?" she asked, her eyes lighting up joyfully at thought of the adventure.

"To-morrow morning, sure!"

"But the alcohol?"

"We've still got what we started with from Detroit, minus only what we've burned reaching this place. And we reckoned when we set out that it would far more than be enough. Oh, that part of it's all right!"

"Well, you know best," she answered. "I trust you in all things, Allan. But now just look at this roast partridge; come, dear, let to-morrow take care of itself. It's supper-time now!"

After the meal they went to the flat rock and sat for an hour while the sun went down beyond the void. Its disappearance seemed to substantiate the polarization theory. There was no sudden obliteration of the disk by a horizon. Rather the sun faded away, redder and duller; then slowly losing form and so becoming a mere blur of crimson, which in turn grew purple and so gradually died away to nothing.

For a long time they sat in the deepening gloom, their rifles close at hand, saying little, but thinking much. The coming of night had sobered them to a sense of what now inevitably lay ahead. The solemn purple pall that adumbrated the world and the huge nothingness before them, so silent, so immutable and pregnant with terrible mysteries, brought them close together.

The vague, untrodden forest behind them, where the night-sounds of the wild dimly reëchoed now and then, filled them with indefinable emotions. And that night sleep was slow in coming.

Each realized that, despite all caculations and all skill, the morrow might be their last day of life. But the morning light, golden and clear above the eastern sky-line of tall conifers, dispelled all brooding fears. They were both up early and astir, in preparation for the crucial flight. Stern went over the edge of the chasm, while Beatrice prepared breakfast, and made some final observations of wind, air currents and atmosphere density.

An eagle which he saw soaring over the abyss, more than half a mile from its edge, convinced him a strong upward current existed to-day, as on the day when they had made their short flight over the void. The bird soared and circled and finally shot away to northward, without a wing-flap, almost in the manner of a vulture. Stern knew an eagle could not imitate the feat without some aid in the way of an up-draft.

"And if that draft is steady and constant all the way across," thought he, "it will result in a big saving of fuel. Given a sufficient rising current, we could volplane all the way across with a very slight expenditure of alcohol. It looks now as though everything were coming on first-rate. Couldn't be better. And what a day for an excursion!"

By nine o'clock all was ready. Along the land a mild south wind was blowing. Though the day was probably the 5th of October or thereabout, no signs of autumn yet were blazoned in the forest. The morning was perfect, and the travelers' spirits rose in unison with the abounding beauty of the day.

Stern had given the Pauillac another final going over, tightening the stays and laterals, screwing up here a loosened nut, there a bolt, making certain all was in perfect order.

At nine-fifteen, after he had had a comforting pipe, they made a clean getaway, rising along the edge of the chasm, then soaring in huge spirals.

"I want all the altitude I can get," Stern shouted at the girl as they climbed steadily higher. "We may need it to coast on. And from a mile or two up maybe we can get a glimpse of the other side."

But though they ascended till the aneroid showed eight thousand five hundred feet, nothing met their gaze but the same pearly blue vapor which veiled the mystery before them. And Stern, satisfied now that nothing could be gained by any further ascent, turned the machine due west, and sent her skimming like a swallow out over the tremendous nothingness below.

As the earth faded behind them they began to feel distinctly a warm and pungent wind that rose beneath—a steady current, as from some huge chimney that lazily was pouring out its monstrous volume of hot vapors.

Away and away behind them slid the lip of this gigantic gash across the world; and now already with the swift rush of the plane the solid earth had begun to fade and to grow dim.

Stern only cast a glance at the sun and at his compass, hung there in gimbals before him, and with firm hand steadied the machine for the long problematical flight to westward. Behind them the sun kept even with their swift pace; and very far below and ahead, at times they thought to see the fleeing shadow of the biplane cast now and then on masses of formless vapor that rose from the unsounded deeps.

Definitely committed now to this tremendous venture, both Stern and the girl settled themselves more firmly in their seats. No time to feel alarm, no time for introspection, or for thoughts of what might lie below, what fate theirs must be if the old Pauillac failed them now!

No time save for confidence in the stout mechanism and in the skill of hand and brain that was driving the great planes, with a roaring rush like a gigantic gull, a swooping rise and fall in long arcs over the hills of air, across the vast enigma of that space!

Stern's whole attention was fixed on driving, just on the manipulation of the swift machine. Exhaust and interplay, the rhythm of each whirling cam and shaft, the chatter of the cylinders, the droning diapason of the blades, all blent into one intricate yet perfect harmony of mechanism; and as a leader knows each instrument in the great orchestra and follows each, even as his eye reads the score, so Stern's keen ear analyzed each sound and action and reaction and knew all were in perfect tune and resonance.

The machine—no early and experimental model, such as were used in the first days of flying, from 1900 to 1915, but one of the perfected and self-balancing types developed about 1920, the year when the Great Death had struck the world—responded nobly to his skill and care. From her landing-skids to the farthest tip of her ailerons she seemed alive, instinct with conscious and eager intelligence.

Stern blessed her mentally with special pride and confidence in her mercury equalizing balances. Proud of his machine and of his skill, superb like Phaeton whirling the sun-chariot across the heavens, he gave her more and still more speed.

Below nothing, nothing save vapors, with here and there an open space where showed the strange dull purple of the abyss. Above, to right, to left, nothing—absolute vacant space.

Gone now was all sight of the land that they had left. Unlike balloonists who always see dense clouds or else the earth, they now saw nothing. All alone with the sun that rushed behind them in their skimming flight, they fled like wraiths across the emptiness of the great void.

Stern glanced at the barometer, and grunted with surprise.

"H'm! Twelve thousand four hundred and fifty feet—and I've been jockeying to come down at least five hundred feet already!" thought he. "How the devil can *that* be?"

The explanation came to him. But it surprised him almost as much as the noted fact.

"Must be one devil of a wind blowing up out of that place," he pondered, "to carry us up nearly four thousand feet, when I've been trying to descend. Well, it's all right, anyhow—it all helps."

He looked at the spinning anemometer. It registered a speed of ninety-seven miles an hour. Yet now that they were out of sight of any land, only the rush of the wind and the enormous vibration of the plane conveyed an idea of motion. They might as well have been hung in mid-space, like Mohammed's tomb, as have been rushing forward; there was no visible means of judging what their motion really might be.

"Unique experience in the history of mankind!" shouted Stern to the girl. "The world's invisible to us."

She nodded and smiled back at him, her white teeth gleaming in the strange, bluish light that now enveloped them.

Stern, keenly attentive to the engine, advanced the spark another notch, and now the needle crept to 102½.

"We'll be across before we know it," thought he. "At this rate, I shouldn't be surprised to sight land any minute now."

A quarter-hour more the Pauillac swooped along, cradling in her swift flight to westward.

But all at once the man started violently. Forward he bent, staring with widened eyes at the tube of the fuel-gage.

He blinked, as though to convince himself he had not seen aright, then stared again; and as he looked a sudden grayness overspread his face.

"*What?*" he exclaimed, then raised his head and for a moment sniffed, as though to catch some odor, elusive yet ominous, which he had for some time half sensed yet paid no heed to.

Then suddenly he knew the truth; and with a cry of fear bent, peering at the fuel-tank.

There, quivering suspended from the metal edge of the aluminum tank, hung a single clear white drop—*alcohol!*

Even as Stern looked it fell, and at once another took its place, and was shaken off only to be succeeded by a third, a fourth, a fifth!

The man understood. The ancient metal, corroded almost through from the inside, had been eaten away. That very morning a hole had formed in the tank. And now a leak—existing since what moment he could not tell— was draining the very life-blood of the machine.

"The alcohol!" cried Stern in a hoarse, terrible voice, his wide eyes denoting his agitation. With a quivering hand he pointed.

"My God! It's all leaked out—there's not a quart left in the tank! *We're lost—lost in the bottomless abyss!*"

CHAPTER XXII

LIGHTS!

AT realization of the ghastly situation that confronted them, Stern's heart stopped beating for a moment. Despite his courage, a sick terror gripped his soul; he felt a sudden weakness, and in his ears the rushing wind seemed shouting mockeries of death.

As in a dream he felt the girl's hand close in fear upon his arm, he heard her crying something—but what, he knew not.

Then all at once he fought off the deadly horror. He realized that now, if ever, he needed all his strength, resource, intelligence. And, with a violent effort, he flung off his weakness. Again he gripped the wheel. Thought returned. Though the end might be at hand, thank God for even a minute's respite!

Again he looked at the indicator.

Yes, only too truly it showed the terrible fact! No hallucination, this. Not much more than a pint of the precious fluid now lay in the fuel tank. And though the engine still roared, he knew that in a minute or two it must slacken, stop and die.

What then?

Even as the question flashed to him, the engine barked its protest. It skipped, coughed, stuttered. Too well he knew the symptoms, the imperative cry: "More fuel!"

But he had none to give. In vain for him to open wide the supply valve. Vain to adjust the carburetor. Even as he made a despairing, instinctive motion to perform these useless acts—while Beatrice, deathly pale and shaking with terror, clutched at him—the engine spat forth a last, convulsive bark, and grew silent.

The whirling screws hummed a lower note, then ceased their song and came to rest.

The machine lurched forward, swooped, spiraled, and with a sickening rush, a flailing tumult of the stays and planes, plunged into nothingness!

Had Stern and the girl not been securely strapped to their seats, they must have been precipitated into space by the violent, erratic dashes, drops, swerves and rushes of the uncontrolled Pauillac.

For a moment or two, instinctively despite the knowledge that it could do no good, Stern wrenched at the levers. A thousand confused, wild, terrible impressions surged upon his consciousness.

Swifter, swifter dropped the plane; and now the wind that seemed to rise had grown to be a hurricane! Its roaring in their ears was deafening. They had to fight even for breath itself.

Beatrice was leaning forward now, sheltering her face in the hollow of her arm. Had she fainted? Stern could not tell. He still was fighting with the mechanism, striving to bring it into some control. But, without headway, it defied him. And like a wounded hawk, dying even as it struggled, the Pauillac staggered wildly down the un-plumbed abyss.

How long did the first wild drop last? Stern knew not. He realized only that, after a certain time, he felt a warm sensation; and, looking, perceived that they were now plunging through vapors that sped upward—so it seemed—with vertiginous rapidity.

No sensation now was there of falling. All motion seemed to lie in the uprushing vapors, dense and warm and pale violet in hue. A vast and rhythmic spiraling had possessed the Pauillac. As you have seen a falling leaf turn in air, so the plane circled, boring with terrific speed down, down, down through the mists, down into the unknown!

Nothing to be seen but vapors. No solid body, no land, no earth to mark their fall and gauge it. Yet slowly, steadily, darkness was shrouding them. And Stern, breathing with great difficulty even in the shelter of his arms, could now hardly more than see as a pale blur the white face of the girl beside him.

The vast wings of the machine, swirling, swooping, plunging down, loomed hugely vague in the deepening shadows. Dizzy, sick with the monstrous caroming through space, deafened by the thunderous roaring of the up-draft, Stern was still able to retain enough of his scientific curiosity to peer upward. The sun! Could he still see it?

Vanished utterly was now the glorious orb! There, seeming to circle round and round in drunken spirals, he beheld a weird, diffused, angry-looking blotch of light, tinted a hue different from any ever seen on earth by men. And involuntarily, at sight of this, he shuddered.

Already with the prescience of death full upon him, with a numb despair clutching his soul, he shrank from that ghastly, hideous aspect of what he knew must be his last sight of the sun.

Around the girl he drew his right arm; she felt his muscles tauten as he clasped her to him. Useless now, he knew, any further struggles with the aeroplane. Its speed, its plummetlike drop checked only by the huge sweep of its parachute wings, Stern knew now it must fall clear to the bottom of the abyss—if bottom there were. And if not—what then?

Stern dared not think. All human concepts had been shattered by this stupendous catastrophe. The sickly and unnatural hue of the rushing vapors that tore and slatted the planes, confused his senses; and, added to this, a stifling, numbing gas seemed diffused through the inchoate void.

He tried to speak, but could not. Against the girl's cheek he pressed his own. Hers was cold!

In vain he struggled to cry out. Even had his parched tongue been able to voice a sound, the howling tempest they themselves were creating as they fell, would have whipped the shout away and drowned it in the gloom.

In Stern's ears roared a droning as of a billion hornets. He felt a vast, tremendous lassitude. Inside his head it seemed as though a huge, merciless pressure were grinding at his very brain. His breath came only slowly and with great difficulty.

"My God!" he panted. "Oh, for a little fuel! Oh, for a chance—a chance to fight—for life!"

But chance there was none, now. Before his eyes there seemed to darken, to dazzle, a strange and moving curtain. Through it, piercing it with a supreme effort of the will, he caught dim sight of the dial of the chronometer. Subconsciously he noted that it marked 11.25.

How long had they been falling? In vain his wavering intelligence battered at the problem. Now, as in a delirium, he fancied it had been only minutes; then it seemed hours. Like an insane man he laughed—he tried to scream—he raved. And only the stout straps that had held them both prevented him from leaping free of the hurtling machine.

"Crack!"

A lashing had given way! Part of the left hand plane had broken loose. Drunkenly, whirling head over like an albatross shot in mid-air, the Pauillac plunged.

It righted, swerved, shot far ahead, then once again somersaulted.

Stern had disjointed, crazy thoughts of air-pressure, condensation and compression, resistance, abstruse formulæ. To him it seemed that some gigantic problem in stress-calculation were being hurled at him, to solve—it seemed that, blind, deaf, dumb, some sinister and ghoul-like demon were flailing him until he answered—and that he could not answer!

He had a dim realization of straining madly at his straps till the veins started big and swollen in his hammering brows. Then consciousness lapsed.

Lapsed, yet came again—and with it pain. An awful pain in the ear-drums, that roared and crackled without cease.

Breath! He was fighting for breath!

It was a nightmare—a horrible dream of darkness and a mighty boom-ing wind—a dream of stifling vapors and an endless void that sucked them down, down, down, eternally!

Delusions came, and mocking visions of safety. Both hands flung out as though to clutch the roaring gale, he fought the intangible.

Again he lost all knowledge.

And once again—how long after, how could he know?—he came to some partial realization of tortured existence.

In one of the mad downward rushes—rushes which ended in a long spiral slant—his staring, bloodshot eyes that sought to pierce the murk, seemed to behold a glimmer, a dull gleam of light.

The engineer screamed imprecations, mingled with wild, demoniac laughter.

"Another hallucination!" was his thought. "But if it's not—if it's Hell—then welcome, Hell! Welcome even that, for a chance to stop!"

A sweep of the Pauillac hid the light from view. Even that faintest ray vanished. But—what? It came again! Much nearer now, and brighter! And—another gleam! Another still! Three of them—*and they were real!*

With a tremendous effort, Stern fixed his fevered eyes upon the lights.

Up, up at a tremendous rate they seemed speeding. Blue and ghastly through the dense vapors, spinning in giddy gyrations, as the machine wheeled, catapulted and slid from one long slant to another, their relative positions still remained fixed.

And, with a final flicker of intelligence, Stern knew they were no figment of his brain.

"Lights, Beatrice! Lights, lights, real lights!" he sought to scream.

But even as he fought to shake her from the swoon that wrapped her senses, his own last fragment of strength deserted him.

He had one final sense impression of a swift upshooting of the lights, a sudden brightening of those three radiant points.

Then came a sudden gleam as though of waters, black and still.

A gleam, blue and uncanny, across the inky surface of some vast, mysterious, hidden sea.

Up rushed the lights at him; up rushed the sea of jetty black!

Stern shouted some wild, incoherent thing.

Crash!

A shock! A frightful impact, swift, sudden, annihilating!

Then in a mad and lashing struggle, all knowledge and all feeling vanished utterly. And the blackness of oblivion received him into its insensate bosom.

CHAPTER XXIII

THE WHITE BARBARIANS

WARMTH, wetness, and a knowledge of great weakness—these, joined with a singular lassitude, oppression of the lungs and stifling of the breath, were Allan Stern's sensations when conscious life returned.

Pain there was as well. His body felt sorely bruised and shaken. His first thought, his intense yearning wonder for the girl's welfare and his sickening fear lest she be dead, mingled with some attempt to analyze his own suffering; to learn, if possible, what damage he had taken in flesh and bone.

He tried to move, but found he could not. Even lying inert, as he now found himself, so great was the exertion to breathe that only by a fight could he keep the breath of life in his shaken frame.

He opened his eyes.

Light! Could it be? Light in that place?

Yes, the light was real, and it was shining directly in his face.

At first all that his disturbed, half-delirious vision could make out was a confused bluish glare. But in a moment this resolved itself into a smoking, blazing cresset. Stern could now distinctly see the metal bands of the fire-basket in which it lay, as well as a supporting staff, about five feet long, that seemed to vanish downward in the gloom.

And, understanding nothing, filled with vague, half-insane hallucinations and wild wonders, he tried to struggle upward with a babbling cry:

"Beatrice! Oh, Beatrice—*where are you?*"

To his intense astonishment, a human hand, bluish in the strange glare, laid itself upon his breast and pushed him down again.

Above him he saw a face, wrinkled, bearded and ghastly blue. And as he struggled still he perceived by the unearthly light that a figure was bending over him.

"A man!" he gulped. "Man! *Man!* Oh, my God! At last—*a man!*"

He tried to raise himself upon his elbow, for his whole soul was flooded with a sudden gratitude and love and joy in presence of that long-sought goal. But instantly, as soon as his dazed senses could convey the terrible impression to his brain, his joy was curdled into blank astonishment and fear and grief.

For to his intense chagrin, strive as he might, he could move neither hand nor foot!

During his unconsciousness, which had lasted he could not tell how long, he had been securely bound. And now, awakening slowly, once more, fighting his way up into consciousness, he found himself a prisoner!

A prisoner! With whom? Among what people—with what purpose? After the long quest, the frightful hardships and the tremendous fall into the abyss, a prisoner!

"Merciful God!" groaned Stern, and in his sudden anguish, strained against the bonds, that drawn tight and fast, were already cutting painfully into his swollen, water-sodden flesh.

In vain did he struggle. Terrible thoughts that Beatrice, too, might be subjected to this peril and humiliation branded themselves upon his brain. He shouted wildly, calling her name, with all the force of his spent lungs; but naught availed. There came no answer but the shrouding fogs.

The strange man bent above him, peering from beneath wrinkled brows. Stern heard a few words in a singular, guttural tone—words rendered dull by the high compression of the air. What the words might be he could not tell, yet their general sound seemed strangely familiar and their command was indubitable.

But, still half-delirious, Stern tried again to stretch up his arms, to greet this singular being, even as a sick man recovering from etherization raves and half sees the nurses and doctors, yet dreams wild visions in the midst of pain.

The man, however, only shook his head, and with a broad, firm hand, again held the engineer from trying to sit up. Stern, understanding nothing clearly, relapsed to quietude. To him the thought came: "This is only another delusion after all!" And then a vast and poignant woe possessed him—a wonder where the girl might be. But under the compulsion of that powerful hand, he lay quite still.

Half consciously he seemed to realize that he was lying prone in the bottom of some strange kind of boat, rude and clumsy, strangely formed of singular materials, yet safe and dry and ample.

To his laboring nostrils penetrated a rank and pungent odor of fish, with another the like of which he never had known—an odor not unpleasant, yet keenly penetrant and all-pervading. Wet through, the engineer lay reeking in heat and steam, wrapped in his suit of heavy furs. Then he heard a ripple of water and felt the motion of the craft as it was driven forward.

Another voice spoke now and the strange man answered briefly. Again the engineer half seemed to comprehend the meaning, though no word was intelligible.

"Where's the girl, you?" he shouted with all his might "What have you done with her? If you hurt her, damn you, you'll be sorry! *Where—where is she?*"

No answer. It was evident that English speech conveyed no meaning to his captors. Stern relapsed with a groan of anguish and sheer pain.

The boat rocked. Another man came creeping forward, holding to the gunwale to steady himself. Stern saw him vaguely through the drifting vapor by the blue-green light of the cresset at the bow.

He was clad in a coarse kind of brownish stuff, like the first, roughly and loosely woven. His long hair, pure white, was twisted up in a kind of topknot and fastened there by pins of dull gold. Bearded he was, but not one hair upon his head or chin was other than silvery white—a color common to all these folk, as Stern was soon to know.

This man, evidently seeing with perfect clarity by a light which permitted the engineer only partial vision, also examined Stern and made speech thereto and nodded with satisfaction.

Then he put half a dozen questions to the prisoner with evident slowness and an attempt to speak each word distinctly, but nothing came of this. And with a contemptuous grunt he went back to his paddle.

"Hold on, there!" cried Stern. "Can't you understand? There were two of us, in a—machine, you know! We fell. Fell from the surface of the earth—

fell all the way down into this pit of hell, whatever it is. Where's the girl? For God's sake, *tell me!*"

Neither man paid any heed, but the elder suddenly set hollowed palms to his lips and hailed; and from across the waters dully drifted another answering cry.

He shouted a sentence or two with a volume of noise at which the engineer marveled, for so compressed was the air that Stern's best effort could hardly throw a sound fifty feet. This characteristic of the atmosphere he well recognized from work he had often done in bridge and tunnel caissons. And a wonder possessed him, despite his keen anxiety, how any race of men could live and grow and develop the evident physical force of these people under conditions so unnatural.

Turning his head and wrenching his neck sidewise, he was able to catch a glimpse of the water, over the low gunwale—a gunwale made, like the framework of the boat itself, of thin metallic strips cleverly riveted.

There, approaching through the mists, he got sight of another boat, also provided with its cresset that flung an uncanny shaft of blue across the jetty expanse—a boat now drawing near under the urge of half-seen oarsmen. And farther still another torch was visible; and beyond that a dozen, a score or more, all moving with dim and ghostly slowness, through the blind abyss of fog and heat and drifting vapors.

Stern gathered strength for another appeal.

"Who *are* you people?" cried he passionately. "What are you going to do with us? Where are we—and what kind of a place are we in? Any way to get out, out to the world again? And the girl—that girl! Oh, great God! *Can't* you answer something?"

No reply. Only that same slow, strong paddling, awful in its purposeful deliberation. Stern questioned in French, Spanish and German, but got not even the satisfaction of attracting their attention. He flung what few phrases of Latin and Esperanto he had at them. No result. And a huge despair filled his soul, a feeling of utter and absolute helplessness.

For the first time in his life—that life which had covered a thousand years or more—he found himself unable to make himself intelligible. He had not now even recourse to gestures, to sign language. Bound hand and foot, trussed like a fowl, ignored by his captors (who, by all rules, should have been his hosts and shown him every courtesy), he felt a profound and terrible anger growing in his heart.

A sudden rage, unreasoning and insensate, blazed within him. His fists clenched; once more he tugged, straining at his stout bonds. He called down maledictions on those two strange, impassive, wraithlike forms hardly more than half seen in the darkness and fog.

Then, as delirium won again over his tortured senses and disjointed thoughts, he shouted the name of Beatrice time after time out into the echoing dark that brooded over the great waters.

All at once he heard her voice, trembling and faint and weak, but still hers!

From the other boat it came, the boat now drawing very near. And as the craft loomed up through the vapors that rose incessantly from that Stygian sea, he made a mighty effort, raised himself a little and suddenly beheld her—dim, vague, uncertain in the shuddering bluish glare, yet still alive!

She was crouching midships of the canoe and, seemingly, was not bound. At his hail she stretched forth a hand and answered with his name.

"Oh, Allan! Allan!" Her voice was tremulous and very weak.

"Beatrice! You're safe? Thank God!"

"Hurt? Are you hurt?"

"No—nothing to speak of. These demons haven't done you any damage, have they? If so—"

"Demons? Why, Allan! They've rescued us, haven't they?"

"Yes—and now they've got me tied here, hand and foot! I can't more than just move about two or three inches, blast them! They haven't tied you, have they?"

"No," she answered. "Not yet! But—what an outrage! I'll free you, never fear. You and I together—"

"Can't do anything, now, girl. There may be hundreds of these people. Thousands, perhaps. And we're only two—two captives, and—well—hang it, Beatrice! I don't mean to be pessimistic or anything like that, but it certainly looks bad!"

"But who are they, boy? Who can they be? And where are we?"

"Hanged if I know! This certainly beats any dream I ever had. For sheer outrageous improbability—"

He broke off short. Beatrice had leaned her head upon her arms, along the gunwale of the other canoe which now was running parallel to Stern's, and he knew the girl was weeping.

"There, there!" he cried to her. "Don't you be afraid, little girl! I've got my automatic yet; I can feel it under me, as I lie here in this infernal boat. They haven't taken yours away?"

"No!" she answered, raising her head again. "And before they ever do, I'll use it, that's all!"

"Good girl!" he cheered her, across the space of water. "That's the way to talk! Whatever happens, shoot straight if you have to shoot at all—and remember, at worst, the last cartridge is for yourself!"

CHAPTER XXIV

The Land of the Merucaans

"I'll remember," she answered simply, and for a little space there came silence between them.

A vast longing possessed the man to take her in his arms and hold her tight, tight to his fast-throbbing heart. But he lay bound and helpless. All he could do was call to her again, as the two canoes now drew on, side by side and as still others, joining them, made a little fleet of strange, flare-lighted craft.

"Beatrice!"

"Yes—what is it?"

"Don't worry, whatever happens. Maybe there's no great harm done, after all. We're still alive and sound—that's ninety-nine percent of the battle."

"How *could* we have fallen like that and not been killed? A miracle!"

"The machine must have struck the surface on one of its long slants. If it had plunged straight down—well, we shouldn't be here, that's all. These infernal pirates, whoever they are, must have been close by, in their boats, and cut us loose from our straps before the machine sank, and got us into their canoes. But—"

"Without the machine, how are we ever going to get out of here again?"

"Don't bother about that now! We've got other more important things to think of. It's all a vast and complex problem, but we'll meet it, never fear. You and I, together, are going to win! We've got to—for the sake of the world!"

"Oh, if they'd only take us for gods, as the Horde did!"

"Gods nothing! They're as white as we are—whiter, even. People that can make boats like these, out of iron bars covered with pitched fabric, and weave cloth like this they're wearing, and use oil-flares in metal baskets, aren't mistaking us for gods. The way they've handled me proves it. Might be a good thing if they weren't so devilish intelligent!"

He relapsed into silence, and for a while there came no sound but the cadenced dipping of many paddles as the boats, now perhaps a score in number, all slowly moved across the unfathomed black as though toward some objective common point. Each craft bore at its bow a fire-basket filled with some spongy substance, which, oil-soaked, blazed smokily with that peculiar blue-green light so ghostly in its wavering reflections.

Many of the folk sat in these boats, among their brown fiber nets and long, iron-tipped lances. All alike were pale and anemic-looking, though well-muscled and of vigorous build. Even the youngest were white-haired. All wore their hair twisted in a knot upon the crown of the head; none boasted anything even suggesting a hat or cap.

By contrast with their chalky skins, white eyebrows and lashes, their pinkish eyes—for all the world like those of an albino—blinked oddly as they squinted ahead, as though to catch some sign of land. Every one wore a kind of cassock of the brown coarse material; a few were girdled with belts of skin, having well-wrought metal buckles. Their paddles were not of wood. Not one trace of wood, in fact, was anywhere to be seen. Light metal blades, well-shaped and riveted to iron handles, served for propulsion.

Stern lay back, still faint and sick with the shock of the fall and with the pain, humiliation and excitement of the capture. Yet through it all he rejoiced that the girl and he had escaped with life and were both still sound of limb and faculty.

Even the loss of the machine could not destroy all his natural enthusiasm, or kill his satisfaction in this great adventuring, his joy at having found after all, a remnant of the human race once more.

"Men, by the Almighty!" thought he, peering keenly at such as he could see through the coiling, spiraling wreaths of mist that arose from the black water into the dun air. "Men! *White* men, too! Given such stock to work with—provided I get the chance—who shall say anything's impossible? If only there's some way out of this infernal hole, what may not happen?"

And, as he watched, he thrilled with nascent pride, with consciousness of a tremendous mission to perform; a sense that here—here in the actual living flesh—dwelt the potentialities of all his dreams, of all the many deep and noble plans which he and Beatrice had laid for a regenerated world!

Men they certainly were, white men, Caucasians, even like himself. Despite all changes of superficial character, their build and cast of features bore witness that these incredible folk, dwellers upon that nameless and buried sea, were the long-distant descendants of Americans!

"Americans, so help me!" he pondered as the boats drew onward toward what goal he knew not. "Barbarians, yet Americans, still. And with half a chance at them, God! we'll work miracles yet, she and I!"

Again he raised his voice, calling to Beatrice:

"Don't be afraid, little girl! They're our own people, after all—Americans!"

At sound of that word a startled cry broke from the lips of Stern's elder boatman, a cry which, taken up from boat to boat, drifted dully through the fog, traversed the whole fleet of strange, slow-moving craft, and lost itself in the vague gloom.

"*Merucaans! Merucaans!*" the shout arose, with other words whereof Stern knew not the meaning; and closer pressed the outlying boats. The engineer felt a thrill run through the strange, mysterious folk.

"They knew their name, anyhow! Hurrah!" he exulted. "God! If we had the Stars and Stripes here, I wager a million they'd go mad about it! Remember? You bet they'll remember, when I learn their lingo and tell them a few things! Just wait till I get a chance at 'em, that's all!"

Forgotten now his bonds and all his pain. Forgotten even the perilous situation. Stern's great vision of a reborn race had swallowed minor evils. And with a sudden glow of pride that some of his own race had still survived the vast world catastrophe, he cheered again, eager as any schoolboy.

Suddenly he heard the girl's voice calling to him:

"Something ahead, Allan—land, maybe. A big light through the mist!"

He wrenched his head a trifle up and now perceived that through the vapors a dim yet steady glow was beginning to shine, and on each side of it there stretched a line of other, smaller, blue-green lights. These, haloed by the vapor with the most beautiful prismatic rings, extended in an irregular row high above water level.

Lower down other lights were moving slowly to and fro, gathering for the most part at a point toward which the boats were headed.

"A settlement, Beatrice! A town, maybe! At last—men, *men!*" he cried.

Forward the boats moved, faster now, as the rowers bent to their tasks; and all at once, spontaneously, a song rose up. First from one boat, then another, that weird, strange melody drifted through the dark air. It blended into a spectral chorus, a vague, tremulous, eery chant, ghostlike and awful, as though on the black stream of Acheron the lost souls of a better world had joined in song.

Nothing could Stern catch of the words; but like some faint and far re-echoing of a half-heard melody, dream-music perhaps, a vaguely reminiscent undertone struck to his heart with an irresistible, melancholy, penetrant appeal.

"That tune! I know it—if I could only think!" the engineer exclaimed. "Those words! I almost seem to know them!"

Then, with the suddenness characteristic of all that drew near in the fog, the shore-lights grew rapidly bigger and more bright.

The rowers lay back on their paddles at a sharp word of command from one of the oarsmen in Stern's boat.

Came a grating, a sliding of keels on pebbles. The boat stopped. Others came up to land. From them men began clambering.

The song died. A sound of many voices rose, as the boatmen mingled with those who, bearing torches, now began gathering about the two canoes where Stern and Beatrice still were.

"Well, we're here, anyhow, wherever *here* is!" exclaimed the engineer. "Hey, you fellows, let me loose, will you? What kind of a way is this to treat a stranger, I'd like to know?"

Two of the men waded through the water, tepid as new milk, to where Stern lay fast-bound, lifted him easily and carried him ashore. Black though the water was, Stern saw that it was clear. As the torch-light struck down through it, he could distinguish the clean and sandy bottom shining with metallic luster.

A strange hissing sound pervaded all the air, now sinking to a dull roar, now rising shrill as a vast jet of escaping steam.

As the tone lowered, darkness seemed to gain, through the mists; its rising brought a clearer light. But what the phenomenon was, Stern could not tell. For the source of the faint, diffused illumination that verberated through the vapor was hidden; it seemed to be a huge and fluctuating glow, off there somewhere beyond the fog-curtain that veiled whatever land this strange weird place might be.

Vague, silent, dim, the wraithlike men stood by, peering with bent brows, just as Dante described the lost souls in Hell peering at Virgil in the eternal night. A dream-crew they seemed. Even though Stern felt the vigorous muscles of the pair who now had borne him up to land, he could scarce realize their living entity.

"Beatrice! Beatrice!" he called. "Are you all right? Don't mind about me—just look out for yourself! If they hurt you in any way, shoot!"

"I'm all right, I'm coming!" He heard her voice, and then he saw the girl herself. Unaided she had clambered from her boat; and now, breaking through the throng, she sought to reach him. But hands held her back, and words of hard command rose from a score of lips.

Stern had only time to see that she was as yet unharmed when with a quick slash of a blade somebody cut the thongs that bound his feet.

Then he was pushed forward, away from the dim and ghostly sea up an acclivity of smooth black pebbles all wet with mist.

Limping stiffly, by reason of his cramped muscles, he stumbled onward, while all about him and behind him—as about the girl, who followed— came the throng of these strange people.

Their squinting, pinkish eyes and pallid faces showed ghastly by the torch-glare, as, murmuring among themselves in their incomprehensible yet strangely familiar tongue, they climbed the slope.

Even then, even there on that unknown beach beside an uncharted sea at the bottom of the fathomless abyss, Stern thought with joy of his revolver which still swung on his hip.

"God knows how we're going to talk to these people," reflected he, "or what sort of trouble they've got ready to hand out to us. But, once I get my right hand free—I'm ready for whatever comes!"

CHAPTER XXV

THE DUNGEON OF THE SKELETONS

As the two interlopers from the outer world moved up the slippery beach toward the great, mist-dimmed flare, escorted by the strange and spectral throng, Stern had time to analyze some factors of the situation.

It was evident that diplomacy was now—unless in a sharp crisis—the only rôle to play. How many of these people there might be he could not tell. The present gathering he estimated at about a hundred and fifty or a hundred and seventy-five; and moment by moment more were coming down the slope, looming through the vapor, each carrying a cresset on a staff or a swinging light attached to a chain.

"The village or settlement, or whatever it is," thought he, "may contain hundreds of them, thousands perhaps. And *we* are only two! The last thing in the world we want is a fight. But if it comes to fighting, Beatrice and I with our backs to the wall could certainly make a mighty good showing against barbarians such as these.

"It's evident from the fact that they haven't taken our revolvers away they don't know the use of firearms. Ages ago they must have forgotten even the tradition of such weapons. Their culture status seems to be a kind of advanced barbarism. Some job, here, to bring them up to civilization again."

Slow-moving, unemotional, peering dimly through the hot fog, their wraithlike appearance (as more and more came crowding) depressed and saddened Stern beyond all telling.

And at thought that these were the remnants of the race which once had conquered a vast continent, built tall cities and spanned abysses with steel—the remnants of so many million keen, energetic, scientific people—he groaned despairingly.

"What does all this mean?" he exclaimed in a kind of passionate outburst. "Where are we? How did you get here? *Can't* you understand me? We're Americans, I tell you—Americans! For God's sake, *can't you understand?*"

Once more the word *"Merucaans"* passed round from mouth to mouth; but beyond this Stern got no sign of comprehension.

"Village! Houses!" shouted he. "Shelter! Rest, eat, sleep!"

They merely shoved him forward up the slope, together with the girl; and now Stern saw a curious kind of causeway, paved with slippery, wet, black stones that gleamed in the torchlight, a causeway slanting sharply upward, its further end hidden in the dense vapor behind which the great and unknown light shone with ever-clearer glowing.

This road was bordered on either hand by a wall of carefully cut stone about three and a half feet high; and into the wall, at equal distances of twenty feet or so, iron rods had been let. Each rod bore a fire-basket, some only dully flickering, some burning bright and blue.

Numbers of the strange folk were loitering on the causeway or coming down to join the throng which now ascended; many clambered lithely up onto the wall, and, holding to the rods or to each other—for the stones, like everything here, were wet and glairy—watched with those singular-hued and squinting eyes of theirs the passage of the strangers.

Stern and Beatrice, their breathing now oppressed by the thickening smoke which everywhere hung heavy, as well as by this fresh exertion in the densely compressed air, toiled, panting, up the steep incline.

The engineer was already bathed in a heavy sweat. The intense heat, well above a hundred degrees, added to the humidity, almost stifled him. His bound arms pained almost beyond endurance. Unable to balance himself, he slipped and staggered.

"Beatrice!" he called chokingly. "Try to make them understand I want my hands freed. It's bad enough trying to clamber up this infernal road, anyhow, without having to go at it all trussed up this way."

She, needing no second appeal, raised her free arms, pointed to her wrists and then at his, and made a gesture as of cutting. But the elder boatman of Stern's canoe—seemingly a person of some authority—only shook his head and urged the prisoners upward, ever upward toward the great and growing light.

Now they had reached the top of the ascent.

On either hand, vanishing in shadows and mist, heavy and high walls extended, all built of black, cut stone surmounted by cressets.

Through a gateway the throng passed, and the prisoners with them—a gateway built of two massive monoliths of dressed stone, octagonal and highly polished, with a huge, straight plinth that Stern estimated at a glance never could have weighed less than ten tons.

"Ironwork, heavy stonework, weaving, fisheries—a good beginning here to work on," thought the engineer. But there was little time for analysis. For now already they were passing through a complex series of inner gateways, passages, détours and labyrinthic defenses which—all well lighted from above by fire-baskets—spoke only too plainly the character of the enclosure within.

"A walled town, heavily fortified," Stern realized as he and Beatrice were thrust forward through the last gate. "Evidently these people are living here in constant fear of attack by formidable foes. I'll wager there's been some terrible fighting in these narrow ways—and there may be some more, too, before we're through with it. God, what a place! Makes me think of the *machicoulis* and posterns at old Carcassonne. So far as this is concerned, we're back again in the Dark Ages—dark, dark as Erebus!"

Then, all at once, out they issued into so strange a scene that, involuntarily, the two captives stopped short, staring about them with wide eyes.

Stretching away before them till the fog swallowed it—a fog now glowing with light from some source still mist-hidden—an open plaza stretched. This plaza was all surrounded, so far as they could see, with singular huts, built of dressed stone, circular for the most part, and with conical roofs like monster beehives. Windows there were none, but each hut had an open door facing the source of the strange, blue-green light.

Stern could now see the inside of the wall, topped with torches; its crest rose some five feet above the level of the plaza; and, where he could catch a glimpse of its base between the huts and through the crowding folk, he noticed that huge quantities of boulders were piled as though for instant use in case of attack.

A singular dripping of warmish water, here a huge drop, there another, attracted his attention; but though he looked up to determine its source, if possible, he could see nothing except the glowing mist. The whole floor of the enclosure seemed to be wet and shining with this water; and all the roughly clad folk, now coming from the huts and concentrating toward the captives, from every direction, were wet as well, as though with this curious, constant, sparsely scattered rain.

Not a quadruped of any kind was to be seen. Neither cat nor dog was there, neither goat nor pig nor any other creature such as in the meanest savage villages of other times might have been found upon the surface of the earth. But, undisturbed and bold, numbers of a most extraordinary fowl—a long-legged, red-necked fowl, wattled and huge of beak—gravely waddled here and there or perched singly and in solemn rows upon the huts.

"Great Heavens, Beatrice," exclaimed the engineer, "what are we up against? Of all the incredible places! That light! That roaring!"

He had difficulty in making himself even heard. For now the hissing roar which they had perceived from afar off seemed to fill the place with a tremendous vibrant blur, rising, falling, as the light waxed and waned.

Terribly confusing all these new sense-impressions were to Stern and Beatrice in their unnerved and weakened state. And, staring about them as they went, they slowly moved along with the motion of their captors toward the great light.

All at once Stern stopped, with a startled cry.

"The infernal devils!" he exclaimed, and recoiled with an involuntary shudder from the sight that met his eyes.

The girl, too, cried out in fear.

Some air-current, some heated blast of vapor from the vast flame they now saw shooting upward from the stone flooring of the plaza, momently dispelled the thick, white vapors.

Stern got a glimpse of a circular row of stone posts, each about nine feet high—he saw not the complete circle, but enough of it to judge its diameter as some fifty feet. In the center stood a round and massive building, and from each post to that building stretched a metal rod perhaps twenty feet in length.

"Look! *Look!*" gasped Beatrice, and pointed.

Then, deadly pale, she hid her face in both her hands and crouched away, as though to blot the sight from her perception.

Each metal bar was sagging with a hideous load—a row of human skeletons, stark, fleshless, frightful in their ghastliness. All were headless. All, suspended by the cervical vertebræ, swayed lightly as the blue-green light glared on them with its weird, unearthly radiance.

Before either Stern or the girl had time even to struggle or so much as recover from the shock of this fell sight, they were both pushed roughly between two of the posts into the frightful circle.

Stern saw a door yawn black before them in the massive hut of stone.

Toward this the Folk of the Abyss were thrusting them.

"No, you don't, damn you!" he howled with sudden passion. "None o' that for *us!* Shoot, Beta! *Shoot!*"

But even as her hand jerked at the butt of the automatic, in its rawhide holster on her hip, an overmastering force flung them both forward into the foul dark of the round dungeon. A metal door clanged shut. Absolute darkness fell.

"My God!" cried Stern. "Beta! Where are you? Beta! *Beta!*"

But answer there was none. The girl had fainted.

CHAPTER XXVI

"You Speak English!"

EVEN in his pain and rage and fear, Stern did not lose his wits. Too great the peril, he subconsciously realized, for any false step now. Despite the fact that the stone prison could measure no more than some ten feet in diameter, he knew that in its floors some pit or fissure might exist, frightfully deep, for their destruction.

And other dangers, too, might lie hidden in this fearful place. So, restraining himself with a strong effort, he stood there motionless a few seconds, listening, trying to think. Severe now the pain from his lashed wrists had grown, but he no longer felt it. Strange visions seemed to dance before his eyes, for weakness and fever were at work upon him. In his ears still sounded, though muffled now, the constant hissing roar of the great flame, the mysterious and monstrous jet of fire which seemed to form the center · of this unknown, incomprehensible life in the abyss.

"Merciful Heavens!" gasped he. "That fire—those skeletons—this black cell—what can they mean?" He found no answer in his bewildered brain. Once more he called, "Beatrice! *Beatrice!*" but only the close echo of the prison replied.

He listened, holding his breath in sickening fear. Was there, in truth, some waiting, yawning chasm in the cell, and had she, thrust rudely forward, been hurled down it? At the thought he set his jaws with terrible menace and swore, to the last drop of his blood, vengeance on these inhuman captors.

But as he listened, standing there with bound hands in the thick gloom, he seemed to catch a slow and sighing sound, as of troubled breathing. Again he called. No answer. Then he understood the truth. And, unable to grope with his hands, he swung one foot slowly, gently, in the partial circumference of a circle.

At first he found nothing save the smooth and slippery stone of the floor, but, having shifted his position very cautiously and tried again, he experienced the great joy of feeling his sandaled foot come in contact with the girl's prostrate body.

Beside her on the floor he knelt. He could not free his hands, but he could call to her and kiss her face. And presently, even while the joy of this discovery was keen upon him, obscuring the hot rage he felt, she moved, she spoke a few vague words, and reached her hands up to him; she clasped him in her arms.

And there in the close, fetid dark, imprisoned, helpless, doomed, they kissed again, and once more—though no word was spoken—plighted their love and deep fidelity until the end.

"Hurt? Are you hurt?" he panted eagerly, as she sat up on the hard floor and with her hands smoothed back the hair from his hot, aching head.

"I feel so weak and dizzy," she answered. "And I'm afraid—oh, Allan, I'm afraid! But, no, I'm not *hurt.*"

"Thank God for that!" he breathed fervently. "Can you untie these infernal knots? They're almost cutting my hands off!"

"Here, let me try!"

And presently the girl set to work; but even though she labored till her fingers ached, she could not start the tight and water-soaked ligatures.

"Hold on, wait a minute," directed he. "Feel in my right-hand pocket. Maybe they forgot to take my knife."

She obeyed.

"They've got it," she announced. "Even if they don't know the meaning of revolvers, they understand knives all right. It's gone."

"Pest!" he ejaculated hotly. Then for a moment he sat thinking, while the girl again tried vainly to loosen the hard-drawn knots.

"Can you find the iron door they shoved us through?" asked he at length.

"I'll see!"

He heard her creeping cautiously along the walls of stone, feeling as she went.

"Look out!" he warned. "Keep testing the floor as you go. There may be a crevice or pit or something of that kind."

All at once she cried: "Here it is! I've found it!"

"Good! Now, then, feel it all over and see if there's any rough place on it. Any sharp edge of a plate, or anything of that kind, that I could rub the cords on."

Another silence. Then the girl spoke.

"Nothing of that kind here," she answered depairingly. "The door's as smooth as if it had been filed and polished. There's not even a lock of any kind. It must be fastened from the outside in some way."

"By Heaven, this is certainly a hard proposition!" exclaimed the engineer, groaning despite himself. "What the deuce are we going to do *now?*"

For a moment he remained sunk in a kind of dull and apathetic respair. But suddenly he gave a cry of joy.

"I've got it!" he exclaimed. "Your revolver, quick! Aim at the opposite wall, there, and fire!"

"Shoot, in here?" she queried, astonished. "Why—what for?"

"Never mind! Shoot!"

Amazed, she did his bidding. The crash of the report almost deafened them in that narrow room. By the stabbing flare of the discharge they glimpsed the black and shining walls, a deadly circle all about them.

"Again?" asked she.

"No. That's enough. Now, find the bullet. It's somewhere on the floor. There's no pit; it's all solid. The bullet—find the bullet!"

Questioning no more, yet still not understanding, she groped on hands and knees in the impenetrable blackness. The search lasted more than five minutes before her hand fell on the jagged bit of metal.

"Ah!" cried she. "Here it is!"

"Good! Tell me, is the steel jacket burst in any such way as to make a jagged edge?"

A moment's silence, while her deft fingers examined the metal. Then said she:

"I think so. It's a terribly small bit to saw with, but—"

"To work, then! I can't stand this much longer."

With splendid energy the girl attacked the tough and water-soaked bonds. She worked half an hour before the first one, thread by thread yielding, gave way. The second followed soon after; and now, with torn and bleeding fingers, she released the final bond.

"Thank Heaven!" he breathed as she began chafing his numb wrists and arms to bring the circulation back again; and presently, when he had regained some use of his own hands, he also rubbed his arms.

"No great damage done, after all," he judged, "so far as this is concerned. But, by the Almighty, we're in one frightful fix every other way! Hark! Hear those demons outside there? God knows what they're up to now!"

Both prisoners listened.

Even through the massive walls of the circular dungeon they could hear a dull and gruesome chant that rose, fell, died, and then resumed, seemingly in unison with the variant roaring of the flame.

Thereto, also, an irregular metallic sound, as of blows struck on iron, and now and then a shrill, high-pitched cry. The effect of these strange sounds, rendered vague and unreal by the density of the walls, and faintly penetrating the dreadful darkness, surpassed all efforts of the imagination.

Beatrice and Stern, bold as they were, hardened to rough adventurings, felt their hearts sink with bodings, and for a while they spoke no word. They sat there together on the floor of polished stone—perceptibly warm to the touch and greasy with a peculiarly repellent substance—and thought long thoughts which neither one dared voice.

But at length the engineer, now much recovered from his pain and from the oppression of the lungs caused by the compressed air, reached for the girl's hand in the dark.

"Without you where should I be?" he exclaimed. "My good angel now, as always!"

She made no answer, but returned the pressure of his hand. And for a while silence fell between them there—silence broken only by their troubled breathing and the cadenced roaring of the huge gas-well flame outside the prison wall.

At last Stern spoke.

"Let's get some better idea of this place," said he. "Maybe if we know just what we're up against we'll understand better what to do."

And slowly, cautiously, with every sense alert, he began exploring the dungeon. Floor and walls he felt of, with minute care, reaching as high as he could and eagerly seeking some possible crevice, some promise—no matter how remote—of ultimate escape.

But the examination ended only in discouragement. Smooth almost as glass the walls were, and the floor as well, perhaps worn down by countless prisoners.

The iron door, cleverly let into the wall, lay flush with it, and offered not the slightest irregularity to the touch. So nicely was it fitted that not even Stern's finger-nail could penetrate the joint.

"Nothing doing in the escape line," he passed judgment unwillingly. "Barbarians these people certainly are, in some ways, but they've got the

arts of stone and iron working down fine. I, as an engineer, have to appreciate *that*, and give the remote descendants of our race credit for it, even if
it works our ruin. Gad, but they're clever, though!"

Discouraged, in spite of all his attempted optimism, he sought the girl
again, there in the deep and velvet dark. To himself he drew her; and, his
arm about her sinuous, supple body, tried to comfort her with cheering
speech.

"Well, Beatrice, they haven't got us *yet!* We're better off, on the whole,
than we had any right to hope for, after having fallen one or two hundred
miles—maybe five hundred, who knows? If I can manage to get a word or
two with these confounded barbarians, I'll maybe save our bacon yet! And,
at worst—well, we're in a mighty good little fort here. I pity anybody that
tries to come in that door and get us."

"Oh, Allan—those skeletons, those headless skeletons!" she whispered;
and in his arms he felt her shudder with unconquerable fear.

"I know; but they aren't going to add *us* to their little collection, you
mark my words! These men are white; they're our own kind, even though
they have slid back into barbarism. They'll listen to reason, once I get a
chance at them."

Thus, talking of the abyss and of their fall—now of one phase, now another, of their frightful position—they passed an hour in the stifling dark.

And, joining their observations and ideas, they were able to get some
general idea of the conditions under which these incredible folk were
dwelling.

From the warmth of the sea and the immense quantities of vapor that
filled the abyss, they concluded that it must be at a tremendous depth in
the earth—perhaps as far down as Stern's extreme guess of five hundred
miles—and also that it must be of very large extent.

Beatrice had noted also that the water was salt. This led them to the conclusion that in some way or other, perhaps intermittently, the oceans on the
surface were supplying the subterranean sea.

"If I'm not much mistaken," judged the engineer, "that tremendous
maelstrom near the site of New Haven—the cataract that almost got us,
just after we started out—has something very vital to do with this situation.

"In that case, and if there's a way for water to come *down,* why mayn't
there be a way for us to climb *up?* Who knows?"

"But if there were," she answered, "wouldn't these people have found it, in all these hundreds and hundreds of years?"

They discussed the question, pro and con, with many another that bore on the folk—this strange and inexplicable imprisonment, the huge flame at the center of the community's life, the probable intentions of their captors, and the terrifying rows of headless skeletons.

"What those mean I don't know," said Stern. "There may be human sacrifice here, and offerings of blood to some outlandish god they've invented. Or these relics may be trophies of battle with other peoples of the abyss.

"To judge from the way this place is fortified, I rather think there must be other tribes, with more or less constant warfare. The infernal fools! When the human race is all destroyed, as it is, except a few handfuls of albino survivors, to make war and kill each other! It's on a par with the old Maoris of New Zealand, who practically exterminated each other—fought till most of the tribes were wiped clean out and only a remnant was left for the British to subdue!"

"I'm more interested in what they're going to do with *us* now," she answered, shuddering, "than in how many or how few survive! *What are we going to do, Allan? What on earth can we do now?*"

He thought a moment, while the strange chant, dimly heard, rose and fell outside, always in unison with the gigantic flame. Then said he:

"Do? Nothing, for the immediate present. Nothing, except wait, and keep all the nerve and strength we can. No use in our shouting and making a row. They'd only take that as an admission of fear and weakness, just as any barbarians would. No use hammering on the iron door with our revolver-butts, and annoying our white brothers by interrupting their song services.

"Positively the only thing I can see to do is just to make sure both automatics are crammed full of cartridges, keep our wits about us, and plug the first man that comes in through that door with the notion of making sacrifices of us. I certainly don't hanker after martyrdom of that sort, and, by God! the savage that lays hands on you, dies inside of one second by the stop-watch!"

"I know, boy; but against so many, what are two revolvers?"

"They're everything! My guess is that a little target practise would put the fear of God into their hearts in a most extraordinary manner!"

He tried to speak lightly and to cheer the girl, but in his breast his heart lay heavy as a lump of lead.

"Suppose they *don't* come in, what then?" suddenly resumed Beatrice. "What if they leave us here till—"

"There, there, little girl! Don't you go borrowing any trouble! We've got enough of the real article, without manufacturing any!"

Silence again, and a long, dark, interminable waiting. In the black cell the air grew close and frightfuly oppressive. Clad as they both were in fur garments suitable to outdoor life and to aeroplaning at great altitudes, they were suffering intensely from the heat.

Stern's wrists and arms, moreover, still pained considerably, for they had been very cruelly bruised with the ropes, which the barbarians had drawn tight with a force that bespoke both skill and deftness. His need of some occupation forced him to assure himself, a dozen times over, that both revolvers were completely filled. Fortunately, the captors had not known enough to rob either Beatrice or him of the cartridge-belts they wore.

How long a time passed? One hour, two, three?

They could not tell.

But, overcome by the vitiated air and the great heat, Beatrice slept at last, her head in the man's lap. He, utterly spent, leaned his back against the wall of black and polished stone, nodding with weariness and great exhaustion.

He, too, must have dropped off into a troubled sleep, for he did not hear the unbolting of the massive iron cell-door.

But all at once, with a quick start, he recovered consciousness. He found himself broad awake, with the girl clutching at his arm and pointing.

With dazzled eyes he stared—stared at a strange figure standing framed in a rectangle of blue and foggy light.

Even as he shouted: "Hold on, there! Get back out o' that, you!" and jerked his ugly pistol at the old man's breast—for very aged this man seemed, bent and feeble and trembling as he leaned upon an iron staff—a voice spoke dully through the half-gloom, saying:

"Peace, friends! Peace be unto you!"

Stern started up in wild amaze.

From his nerveless fingers the pistol dropped. And, as it clattered on the floor, he cried:

"English? You speak *English?* Who *are* you? *English! English! Oh, my God!*"

CHAPTER XXVII

Doomed!

The aged man stood for a moment as though tranced at sound of the engineer's voice. Then, tapping feebly with his staff, he advanced a pace or two into the dungeon. And Stern and Beatrice—who now had sprung up, too, and was likewise staring at this singular apparition—heard once again the words:

"Peace, friends! Peace!"

Stern snatched up the revolver and leveled it.

"Stop there!" he shouted. "Another step and I—I—"

The old man hesitated, one hand holding the staff, the other groping out vacantly in front of him, as though to touch the prisoners. Behind him, the dull blue light cast its vague glow. Stern, seeing his bald and shaking head, lean, corded hand, and trembling body wrapped in its mantle of coarse brown stuff, could not finish the threat.

Instead, his pistol-hand dropped. He stood there for a moment as though paralyzed with utter astonishment. Outside, the chant had ceased. Through the doorway no living beings were visible—nothing but a thin and tenuous vapor, radiant in the gas-flare which droned its never-ending roar.

"In the name of Heaven, who—what—*are* you?" cried the engineer, at length. "A man who speaks English, *here? Here?*"

The aged one nodded slowly, and once again groped out toward Stern.

Then, in his strangely hollow voice, unreal and ghostly, and with uncertain hesitation, an accent that rendered the words all but unintelligible, he made answer:

"A man—yea, a living man. Not a ghost. A man! and I speak the English. Verily, I am ancient. Blind, I go unto my fathers soon. But not until I have had speech with you. Oh, this miracle—English speech with those to whom it still be a living tongue!"

He choked, and for a space could say no more. He trembled violently. Stern saw his frail body shake, heard sobs, and knew the ancient one was weeping.

"Well, great Scott! What d'you think of *that?*" exclaimed the engineer. "Say, Beatrice—am I dreaming? Do you see it, too?"

"Of course! He's a survivor, don't you understand?" she answered, with quicker intuition than his. "He's one of an elder generation—he remembers more! Perhaps he can help us!" she added eagerly. And without more ado, running to the old man, she seized his hand and pressed it to her bosom.

"Oh, father!" cried she. "We are Americans in terrible distress! You understand us—you, alone, of all these people here. Save us, if you can!"

The patriarch shook his head, where still some sparse and feeble hairs clung, snowy-white.

"Alas!" he answered, intelligibly, yet still with that strange, hesitant accent of his—"alas, what can I do? I am sent to you, verily, on a different mission. They do not understand, my people. They have forgotten all. They have fallen back into the night of ignorance. I alone remember; I only know. They mock me. But they fear me, also.

"Oh, woman!"—and, dropping his staff a-clatter to the floor, he stretched out a quivering hand—"oh, woman! and oh, man from above—speak! Speak, that I may hear the English from living lips!"

Stern, blinking with astonishment there in the half-gloom, drew near.

"English?" he queried. "Haven't you ever heard it spoken?"

"Never! Yet, all my life, here in this lost place, have I studied and dreamed of that ancient tongue. Our race once spoke it. Now it is lost. That magnificent language, so rich and pure, all lost, forever lost! And we—"

"But what *do* you speak down here?" exclaimed the engineer, with eager interest. "It seemed to me I could almost catch something of it; but when it came down to the real meaning, I couldn't. If we could only talk with these people here, your people, they might give us some kind of a show! Tell me!"

"A—a show?" queried the blind man, shaking his head and laying his other hand on Stern's shoulder. "Verily, I cannot comprehend. An entertainment, you mean? Alas, no, friends; they are not hospitable, my people. I fear me; I fear me greatly that—that—"

He did not finish, but stood there blinking his sightless eyes, as though with some vast effort of the will he might gain knowledge of their features. Then, very deftly, he ran his fingers over Stern's bearded face. Upon the engineer's lips his digits paused a second.

"Living English!" he breathed in an awed voice. "These lips speak it as a living language! Oh, tell me, friends, *are* there now men of your race—once our race—still living, up yonder? *Is* there such a place—is there a sky, a sun, moon, stars—verily such things now? Or is this all, as my people say, deriding me, only the babbling of old wives' tales?"

A thousand swift, conflicting thoughts seemed struggling in Stern's mind. Here, there, he seemed to catch a lucid bit; but for the moment he could analyze nothing of these swarming impressions.

He seemed to see in this strange ancient-of-days some last and lingering relic of a former generation of the Folk of the Abyss, a relic to whom perhaps had been handed down, through countless generations, some vague and wildly distorted traditions of the days before the cataclysm. A relic who still remembered a little English, archaic, formal, mispronounced, but who, with the tenacious memory of the very aged, still treasured a few hundred words of what to him was but a dead and forgotten tongue. A relic, still longing for knowledge of the outer world—still striving to keep alive in the degenerated people some spark of memory of all that once had been!

And as this realization, not yet very clear, but seemingly certain in its general form, dawned on the engineer, a sudden interest in the problem and the tragedy of it all sprang up in him, so keen, so poignant in its appeal to his scientific sense, that for a moment it quite banished his distress and his desire for escape with Beatrice.

"Why, girl," he cried, "here's a case parallel, in real life, to the wildest imaginings of fiction! It's as though a couple of ancient Romans had walked in upon some old archeologist who'd given his life to studying primitive Latin! Only you'd have to imagine he was the only man in the world who remembered a word of Latin at all! Can you grasp it? No wonder he's overcome!

"Gad! If we work this right," he added in a swift aside, "this will be good for a return ticket, all right!"

The old man withdrew his hand from the grasp of Beatrice and folded both arms across his breast with simple dignity.

"I rejoice that I have lived to this time," he stammered slowly, gropingly, as though each word, each distorted and mispronounced syllable had to be sought with difficulty. "I am glad that I have lived to touch you and to hear your voices. To know it is no mere tradition, but that, verily, there *was* such a race and such a language! The rest, also, must be true—the earth, and the sun, and everything! Oh, this is a wonder and a miracle! Now I can die in a great peace, and they will know I have spoken truth to their mocking!"

He kept silence a space, and the two captives looked fixedly at him, strangely moved. On his withered cheeks they could see, by the dull bluish glow through the doorway, tears still wet. The long and venerable beard of spotless white trembled as it fell freely over the coarse mantle.

"What a subject for a painter—if there were any painters left!" thought Stern.

The old man's lips moved again.

"Now I can go in peace to my appointed place in the Great Vortex," said he, and bowed his head, and whispered something in that other speech they had already heard but could not understand.

Stern spoke first.

"What shall we call your name, father?" asked he.

"Call me J'hungaav," he answered, pronouncing a name which neither of them could correctly imitate. When they had tried he asked:

"And yours?"

Stern gave both the girl's and his own. The old man caught them both readily enough, though with a very different accent.

"Now, see here, father," the engineer resumed, "you'll pardon us, I know. There's a million things to talk about. A million we want to ask, and that we can tell *you!* But we're very tired. We're hungry. Thirsty. Understand? We've just been through a terrible experience. You can't grasp it yet; but I'll tell you we've fallen, God knows how far, in an aeroplane—"

"Fallen? In an—an—"

"No matter. We've fallen from the surface. From the world where there's a sky, and sun, and stars, and all the rest of it. So far as we know, this woman and I are the only two people—the original kind of people, I mean; the people of the time before—er—hang it!—it's mighty hard to explain!"

"I understand. You are the only two now living of our former race? And you have come from above? Verily, this is strange!"

"You bet it is! I mean, verily. And now we're here, your people have thrown us into this prison, or whatever it is. And we don't like the look of those skeletons on the iron rods outside a little bit! We—"

"Oh, I pray! I pray!" exclaimed the patriarch, thrusting out both hands. "Speak not of those! Not yet!"

"All right, father. What we want to ask is for something to eat and drink, some other kind of clothes than the furs we're wearing, and a place to sleep—a house, you know—we've got to rest! We mean no harm to your people. Wouldn't hurt a hair of their heads! Overjoyed to find 'em! Now, I ask you, as man to man, can't you get us out of this, and manage things so that we shall have a chance to explain?

"I'll give you the whole story, once we've recuperated. You can translate it to your people. I ask some consideration for myself, and I *demand* it for this woman! Well?"

The old man stood in silent thought a moment. Plain to see, his distress was very keen. His face wrinkled still more, and on his breast he bowed his majestic head, so eloquent of pain and sorrow and long disappointment.

Stern, watching him narrowly, played his trump-card.

"Father," said he, "I don't know why you were sent here to talk with us, or how they knew you *could* talk with us even. I don't know what any of this treatment means. But I *do* know that this girl and I are from the world of a thousand years ago—the world in which your ancient forefathers used to dwell!

"She and I know all about that world. We know the language which to you is only a precious memory, to us a living fact. We can tell you hundreds, thousands of things! We can teach you everything you want to know! For a year—if you people *have* years down here—we can sit and talk to you, and instruct you, and make you far, far wiser than any of your Folk!

"More, we can teach your Folk the arts of peace and war—a multitude of wonderful and useful things, We can raise them from barbarism to civilization again! We can save them—save the world! And I appeal to you, in the name of all the great and mighty past which to you is still a memory, if not to them—*save us now!*"

He ceased. The old man sighed deeply, and for a while kept silence. His face might have served as the living personification of intense and hopeless wo.

Stern had an idea.

"Father," he added—"here, take this weapon in your hand!" He thrust the automatic into the patriarch's fingers. "This is a revolver. Have you ever heard that word? With this, and other weapons even stronger, our race, your race, used to fight. It can kill men at a distance in a twinkling of an eye. It is swift and very powerful! Let this be the proof that we are what we say, survivors from the time that was! And in the name of that great day, and in the name of what we still can bring to pass for you and yours, save us from whatever evil threatens!"

A moment the old man held the revolver. Then, shuddering as with a sudden chill, he thrust it back at Stern.

"Alas!" cried he. "What am I against a thousand? A thousand, sunk in ignorance and fear and hate? A thousand who mock at me? Who believe you, verily, to be only some new and stronger kind of Lanskaarn, as we call our ancient enemies on the great islands in the sea.

"What can I do? They have let me have speech with you merely because they think me so old and so childish! Because they say my brain is soft! Whatever I may tell them, they will only mock. Wo upon me that I have known this hour! That I have heard this ancient tongue, only now forever to lose it! That I know the truth! That I know the world of old tradition *was* true and *is* true, only now to have no more, after this moment, any hope ever to learn about it!"

"The devil you say!" cried Stern, with sudden anger. "You mean they won't listen to reason? You mean they're planning to butcher us, and hang us up there along with the rest of the captured Lanskaarns, or whatever you call them? You mean they're going to take us—*us*, the only chance they've got ever to get out of this, and stick us like a couple of pigs, eh? Well, by God! You tell them—you tell—"

In the doorway appeared another form, armed with an iron spear. Came a quick word of command.

With a cry of utter hopelessness and heartbreak, a wail that seemed to pierce the very soul, the patriarch turned and stumbled to the door.

He paused. He turned, and, stretching out both feeble arms to them—to them, who meant so infinitely much to him, so absolutely nothing to his barbarous race—cried:

"Fare you well, O godlike people of that better time! Fare you well! Before another tide has risen on our accursed black beach, verily both of you, the last survivors—"

With a harsh word of anger, the spearsman thrust him back and away.

Stern leaped forward, revolver leveled.

But before he could pull trigger the iron door had clanged shut.

Once more darkness swallowed them.

Black though it was, it equaled not the blackness of their absolute despair.

CHAPTER XXVIII

THE BATTLE IN THE DARK

FOR a time no word passed between them. Stern took the girl in his arms and comforted her as best he might; but his heart told him there was now no hope.

The old man had spoken only too truly. There existed no way of convincing these barbarians that their prisoners were not of some hated, hostile tribe. Evidently the tradition of the outer world had long since perished as a belief among them. The patriarch's faith in it had come to be considered a mere doting second childhood vagary, just as the tradition of the Golden Age was held to be by the later Greeks.

That Stern and Beatrice could in any way convince their captors of the truth of this outer world and establish their identity as real survivors of the other time, lay wholly outside the bounds of the probable.

And as the old man's prophecy of evil—interrupted, yet frightfully ominous—recurred to Stern's mind, he knew the end of everything was very close at hand.

"They won't get us, though, without a stiff fight, damn them!" thought he. "That's one satisfaction. If they insist on extermination—if they want war—they'll get it, all right enough! And it'll be what Sherman said war always was, too—*Hell!*"

Came now a long, a seemingly interminable wait. The door remained fast-barred. Oppression, heat, thirst, hunger tortured them, but relief there was none.

And at length the merciful sleep of stupefaction overcame them; and all their pain, their anguish and forebodings were numbed into a welcome oblivion.

They were awakened by a confused noise—the sound of cries and shouts, dulled by the thick walls, yet evidently many-voiced—harsh commands, yells, and even some few sharp blows upon the prison stones.

The engineer started up, wide-eyed and all alert now in the gloom.

Gone were his lassitude, his weakness and his sense of pain. Every sense acute, he waited, hand clutching the pistol-butt, finger on trigger.

"Ready there, Beatrice!" cried he. "Something's started at last! Maybe it's our turn now. Here, get behind me—but be ready to shoot when I tell you! Steady now, steady for the attack!"

Tense as coiled springs they waited. And all at once a bar slid, creaking. Around the edge of the metal door a thin blue line of light appeared.

"*Stand back, you!*" yelled Stern. "*The first man through that door's a dead one!*"

The line of light remained a moment narrow; then suddenly it broadened. From without a pandemonium of sound burst in—howls, shrieks, imprecations, cries of pain.

Even in that perilous moment a quick wonder darted through Stern's brain, what the meaning of this infernal tumult might be, and just what ghastly fate was to be theirs—what torments and indignities they might still have to face before the end.

"Remember, Beatrice," he commanded, "if I'm killed, use the revolver on yourself before you let them take you!"

"I know!" she cried. And, crouching beside him in the half light, she, too, awaited what seemed the inevitable.

The door swung open.

There stood the patriarch again, arms extended, face eager with a passionate hope and longing, a great pride even at that strange and pregnant moment.

"Peace, friends!" he cried. "I give you peace! Strike me not down with those terrible weapons of yours! For verily I bring you hope again!"

"Hope? What d'you mean?" shouted Stern.

Through the opened door he caught vague glimpses in the luminous fog of many spearmen gathered near—of excited gestures and the wild waving of arms—of other figures that, half seen, ran swiftly here and there.

"Speak up, you! What's the matter? What's wanted?" demanded the engineer, keeping his automatic sighted at the doorway. "What's all this infernal row? If your people there think they're going to play horse with us, they're mightily mistaken! You tell them the first man that steps through that door to get us never'll take another step! *Quick! What's up?*"

"Come!" answered the aged man, his voice high and tremulous above the howling tumult and the roar of the great gas-well. "Come, now! The *Lanskaarn*—they attack! *Come!* I have spoken of your weapons to my people. *Come, fight for us!* And verily, if we win—"

"What kind of a trick are you putting up on us, anyhow?" roared Stern with thrice-heated rage. "None o' that now! If your people want us, let 'em come in here and get us! But as for being fooled that way and tricked into coming out—"

"I swear the truth!" supplicated the patriarch, raising his withered hand on high. "If you come not, you must verily die, oh, friends! But if you come—"

"Your own life's the first to pay for any falsehood now."

"I give it gladly! *The truth, I swear it!* Oh, listen, while there is still time, and come! *Come!*"

"What about it, girl?" cried Stern. "Are you with me? Will you take a chance on it?"

"There's nothing else to do, Allan. They've got us, anyway. And—and I think the old man's telling the truth. Hear *that*, now—"

Off somewhere toward the fortification wall that edged the beach, sounds of indisputable conflict were arising. The howls, cries, shrieks, blows were not to be mistaken.

Stern's resolution was instant.

"I'm with you, old man!" he shouted. "But remember your promise. And if you fail me—it's your finish!

"Come, Beta! Stick close to me! If we fall, we'll go down together. It's both or neither. *Come on—come on!*"

Out into the glare of the great flame they issued warily, out into the strangely glowing mist that covered the incredible village as with a virescent pall.

Blinking, they stared about them, not knowing for a moment whither to run or where to shoot.

But the patriarch had Stern by the arm now; and in the midst of a confused and shouting mass of the Folk—all armed with spears and slings, knobbed clubs and battle-maces—was pushing him out through the circle of those ghastly posts whence dangled the headless skeletons.

"Where? Which way?" cried Stern. "Show me—I'll do the rest!"

"Thither!" the old man directed, pointing with one hand, while with the other he shoved the engineer forward. Blind though he was, he knew the right direction. *"Thither—to the wall!"*

For a second Stern had the thought of leaving Beatrice in the cell, where she might at least be safe from the keen peril of battle; but greater dangers threatened her, he knew, in his absence.

At all hazards they must keep together. And with a cry: "Come! Come— stick close to me!" once more he broke into a run toward the sea.

Through the mists, which grew darker as he neared the wall with Beatrice close beside him and the troop that followed them, he could catch
glimpses of the battle.

Every hut seemed to have poured forth its inhabitants, for now the plaza swarmed with life—men, women, even children, running this way and
that, some with weapons rushing towards the wall, others running wildly
hither and yon with unintelligible cries.

A spear pierced the vapors; it fell clashing at Stern's feet and slid rattling away over the black stones, worn smooth and greasy by uncounted
feet.

Past him as he ran a man staggered; the whole side of his head was
bashed in, as though by a frightful blow from a mace. Up the wounded
man flung both arms, and fell twitching.

The fog covered him with its drifting folds. Stern shuddered that
Beatrice should see such hideous sights; but even now he almost fell over
another prostrate body, hideously wounded in the back, and still kicking.

"Ready, now!" panted Stern. "Ready with the pistols!"

Where was the patriarch?

He no longer knew. About him the Folk pressed, but none molested either him or Beatrice.

In the confusion, the rush of the outskirts of battle, he could have
shot down a score of them, but he was reserving his fire. It might, perhaps, be true, who could tell—that safety lay in battling now against the
Lanskaarn!

All at once the captives saw vague fire-lights in the gloom—seemingly
blazing comets of blue, that tossed and hurled and disappeared.

Then came the nearer sound of shouting and the clash of arms.

Stern, with the atavistic instincts of even the most civilized man, scented
the kill. And with a roar he whirled into the confused and sweltering mass
of men which now, emerging from the darkening mists, had suddenly become visible by the uncanny light of the cressets on the wall.

Beside him the girl, her face aglow, nostrils dilated, breath quick, held
her revolver ready.

And then, quite suddenly, they found themselves at the wall.

"Shoot! Shoot!" bellowed Stern, and let drive, point-blank, at an ugly,
grinning face that like a nightmare-vision all at once projected over the
crest. His own revolver-fire was echoed by hers. The face vanished.

All down there, below him on the beach, he caught a dim, confused impression of the attacking swarm.

Subconsciously he realized that he—he a man of the twentieth century—was witnessing again a scene such as made the whole history of the Middle Ages sanguinary—a siege, by force of human strength and rage!

Even as he vaguely saw the swift and supple men, white-skinned yet larger than the Folk, which crowded the whole beach as far as he could pierce the mists with his straining sight, he knew that here was a battle of huge scope and terrible danger.

Up from the sea the attackers, the Lanskaarn, were swarming, from their dimly seen canoes. The place was alive with them.

At the base of the wall they were clotted in dense hordes; and siege-ladders were being raised; and now up the ladders the lithe men of darkness were running like so many ants.

Automatically as the mechanism of his own gun which he pumped into that dense mass as fast as he could pull trigger—while beside him the girl was shooting hard and straight, as well—he seemed to be recording these wonderful impressions.

Here he caught a glimpse of a siege-ladder hurled backward by the Folk, backward and down to the beach. Amid frightful yells and screams it fell; and a score of crushed and mangled men lay writhing there under the uncanny glare of the cressets.

There he saw fire-bales being hurled down from the walls—these, the comet-like apparitions he had seen from a distance—hurled, blazing, right into the brown of the mob.

Beyond, a party had scaled the wall, and there the fight was hand to hand—with gruntings, thrustings of spears, slashings of long knives that dripped red and cut again and rose and fell with hideous regularity!

He jacked his pistol full of shells once more and thrust it into the girl's hand—for she, excited beyond all control, was snapping the hammer of her weapon on empty steel.

"Give it to 'em! Shoot! Kill!" he yelled. "Our only chance now! If they—get in—we're dead!"

He snatched her weapon, reloaded, and again rained the steel-jacketed bolts of death against the attackers.

In the tumult and wild maelstrom of the fight the revolvers' crackling seemed to produce little effect. If Stern expected that this unknown weapon would at once bring panic and quick victory he reckoned without the berserker madness and the stern mettle of this horde of raging Lanskaarn.

White men, like himself, they yielded not; but with strange cries and frightful yells, pressed on and on, up to the walls, and up the ladders ever; and now came flights of spears, hissing through the dark air—and now smooth black rocks from the beach, flung with terrible strength and skill by the slingers below, mowed down the defenders.

Here, there, men of the Folk were falling, pierced by the iron spears, shattered by the swift and heavy rocks.

The place was becoming a shambles where the blood of attackers and attacked mingled horribly in the gloom.

One ladder, pushed outward, dragged half a dozen of the Merucaans with it; and at the bottom of the wall a circling eddy of the Lanskaarn despatched the fighting Folkmen who had been hauled to their destruction by the grappling besiegers.

Blows, howls and screams, hurtling fire-bales and great rocks flung from above—the rocks he had already noted laid along the inside of the wall—these, and the smell of blood and fire, the horrid, sweaty contact of struggling bodies, the press and jam of the battle that surged round them, all gave Stern a kaleidoscopic picture of war—war as it once was, in the long ago—war, naked and terrible, such as he had never even dreamed!

But, mad with the lust of the kill, he heeded nothing now.

"Shoot! Shoot!" he kept howling, beside himself; and, tearing open the bandoliers where lay his cartridges, he crammed them with feverish fingers into the girl's weapon and his own—weapons now burning hot with the quick, long-continued firing.

The battle seemed to dance, to waver there before his eyes, in the haze of mist and smoke and stifling air. The dark scene, blue-lit by the guttering torches, grew ever more sanguinary, more incredibly hideous. And still the attackers swarmed along the walls and up them, in front and on both sides, till the swirling mists hid them and the defenders from view.

He heard Beatrice cry out with pain. He saw her stagger and fall back.

To her he leaped.

"Wounded?" he gasped.

She answered nothing, but fell limp.

"God of Battles!" he howled. "Revenge!"

He snatched her automatic from beneath the trampling, crowding feet; he bore her back, away from the thick press. And in the shelter of a massive hut he laid her down.

Then, stark-mad, he turned and leaped into the battle-line that swayed and screamed along the wall.

Critical now the moment. In half a dozen places the besiegers had got their ladders planted. And, while dense masses of the Lanskaarn—unminding fire-balls and boulders rained down upon them—held these ladders firm, up the attackers came with a rush.

Stern saw the swing and crushing impact of the maces and iron clubs; he saw the stabbing of the spears on both sides.

Slippery and red the parapet became.

Men, killed there, crawled and struggled and fell both outward and inside, and were trampled in indiscriminate heaps, besieged and besiegers alike, still clawing, tearing, howling even in their death agony.

Now one of the ladders was down—another fell, with horrid tumult—a third!

An automatic in each hand, Stern scrambled to the glairy summit of the fortification.

A mace swung at him. He leaped sidewise, firing as he sprang. With a scream the ax-man doubled up and fell, and vanished in the gloom below the wall.

Raking the parapet with a hail of lead, he mowed down the attackers on top of the fourth ladder. With a mighty shout, those inside staved it away with iron grapples. It, too, swayed drunkenly, held below, pushed madly above. It reeled—then fell with a horrible, grinding crash!

"Hurray, boys! One more down! Give 'em Hell!" he screamed. "One more!"

He turned. Subconsciously he felt that his right hand was wet, and hot, and dripping, but he felt no pain.

"One more! Now for another!"

And in the opposite direction along the wall he emptied his other revolver.

Before the stinging swarm of the steel-jacketed wasps of death the Lanskaarn writhed and melted down with screams such as Dante in his wildest vision never even dreamed.

Stern heard a great howl of triumph break from the mass of defenders fighting to overthrow the fifth ladder.

"Hold 'em! Hold 'em!" he bellowed. "Wait till I load up again—I'll—"

A swift and crashing impact dashed sheaves of radiant fire through his brain.

Everything leaped and whirled.

He flung up both hands.

Clutching at empty air, then suddenly at the slippery parapet which seemed to have leaped up and struck him in the face, he fell.

Came a strange numbness, then a stabbing pain.

And darkness quenched all knowledge and all consciousness.

CHAPTER XXIX

SHADOWS OF WAR

A BLUE and flickering gleam of light, dim, yet persistent, seemed to enhalo a woman's face; and as Stern's weary eyes opened under languid lids, closed, then opened again, the wounded engineer smiled in his weakness.

"Beatrice!" he whispered, and tried to stretch a hand to her, as she sat beside his bed of seaweed covered with the coarse brown fabric. "Oh, Beatrice! Is this—is this another—hallucination?"

She took the hand and kissed it, then bent above him and kissed him again, this time fair upon the lips.

"No, boy," she answered. "No hallucination, but reality! You're all right now—and I'm all right! You've had a little fever and—and—well, don't ask any questions, that's all. Here, drink this now and go to sleep!"

She set a massive golden bowl to his mouth, and very gently raised his head.

Unquestioningly he drank, as though he had been a child and she his mother. The liquid, warm and somewhat sweet, had just a tang of some new taste that he had never known. Singularly vitalizing it seemed, soothing yet full of life. With a sigh of contentment, despite the numb ache in his right temple, he lay back and once more closed his eyes. Never had he felt such utter weakness. All his forces seemed drained and spent; even to breathe was very difficult.

Feebly he raised his hand to his head.

"Bandaged?" he whispered. "What does *that* mean?"

"It means you're to go to sleep now!" she commanded. "That's all—just go to sleep!"

He lay quiet a moment, but sleep would not come. A score, a hundred thoughts confusedly crowded his brain.

And once more looking up at her in the dim blue gloom of the hut where they were, he breathed a question:

"Were you badly hurt, dear, in—in the battle?"

"No, Allan. Just stunned, that's all. Not even wounded. Be quiet now or I'll scold!"

He raised his arms to her and, weak though he was, took her to his breast and held her tight, tight.

"Thank God!" he whispered. "Oh, I love you! I love you so! If you'd been killed—"

She felt his tears hot upon his wasted cheeks, and unloosened his arms.

"There, there!" she soothed him. "You'll get into a fever again if you don't lie still and try not to think! You—"

"When was it? Yesterday?" he interrupted.

"*Sh-h-h-h!* No more questions now."

"But I want to know! And what happened to me? And the—the Lanskaarn? What about them? And—"

"Heavens, but you're inquisitive for a man that's just missed—I mean, that's been as sick as you have!" she exclaimed, taking his head in both hands and gazing down at him with eyes more deeply tender than he had ever seen them. "Now do be good, boy, and don't worry about all these things, but go to sleep—there's a dear. And when you wake up next time—"

"No, no!" he insisted with passionate eagerness. "I'm not that kind! I'm not a child, Beta! I've got to know—I can't go to sleep without knowing. Tell me a little about it, about what happened, and then—then I'll sleep as long as you say!"

She pondered a moment, weighing matters, then made answer:

"All right, boy, only remember your promise!"

"I will."

"Good! Now listen. I'll tell you what the old man told me, for naturally I don't remember the last part of the fight any better than you do.

"I was struck by a flying stone, and—well, it wasn't anything serious. It just stunned me for a while. I came to in a hut."

"Where I carried you, dearest, just before I—"

"Yes, I know, just before the battle-ax—"

"Was it an ax that hit me?"

"Yes. But it was only a glancing blow. Your long hair helped save you, too. But even so—"

"Skull cracked?"

"No, I guess concussion of the brain would be the right term for it." She took his groping hand in both her own warm, strong ones and kissed it tenderly. "But before you fell, your raking fire along the wall there—you understand—"

"Cleaned 'em out, eh?" he queried eagerly.

"That's about it. It turned the tide against the Lanskaarn. And after that—I guess it was just butchery. I don't know, of course, and the old man hasn't wanted to tell me much; but anyway, the ladders all went down, and the Folk here made a sortie from the gate, down the causeway, and—and—"

"And they've got a lot more of those infernal skeletons hanging on the poles by the fire?" he concluded in a rasping whisper.

She nodded, then kept a minute's silence.

"Did any of 'em get away in their canoes?"

"A few. But in all their history the Folk never won such a victory. Oh, it was glorious, glorious! And all because of you!"

"And you, dear!"

"And now—now," she went on, "we're not prisoners any more, but—"

"Everything coming our way? Is that it?"

"That's it. They dragged you out, after the battle, from under a big heap of bodies under the wall."

"Outside or inside?"

"Outside, on the beach. They brought you in, for dead, boy. And I guess they had an awful time about you, from what I've found out—"

"Big powwow, and all that?"

"Yes. If you'd died, they'd have gone on a huge war expedition out to the islands, wherever those are, and simply wiped out the rest of the Lanskaarn. But—"

"I'm glad I didn't," he interrupted. "No more killing from now on! We want all the living humans we can get; we need 'em in our business!"

Stern was growing excited; the girl had to calm him once more.

"Be quiet, Allan, or I'll leave you this minute and you shan't know another thing!" she threatened.

"All right, I'll be good," he promised. "What next? I'm the Big Chief now, of course? What I say now *goes?*"

She answered nothing, but a troubled wrinkle drew between her perfect brows. For a moment there was silence, save for the dull and distant roaring of the flame.

By the glow of the bluish light in the hut, Stern looked up at her. Never had she seemed so beautiful. The heavy masses of her hair, parted in the middle and fastened with gold pins such as the Folk wore, framed her wonderful face with twilight shadows. He saw she was no longer clad in fur, but in a loose and flowing mantle of the brown fabric, caught up below the breast with a gold-clasped girdle.

"Oh, Beatrice," he breathed, "kiss me again!"

She kissed him; but even in the caress he sensed an unvoiced anxiety, a hidden fear.

"What's wrong?" asked he anxiously.

"Nothing, dear. Now you *must* be quiet! You're in the patriarch's house here. You're safe—for the present, and—"

"For the present? What do you mean?"

"See here," the girl threatened, "if you don't stop asking questions, and go to sleep again, I'll leave you alone!"

"In that case I promise!"

And now obedient, he closed his eyes, relaxed, and let her soothingly caress him. But still another thought obtruded on his mind.

"Beatrice?"

"Yes, dearest."

"How long ago was that fight?"

"Oh, a little while. Never mind now!"

"Yes, but how long? Two days? Four? Five?"

"They don't have days down here," she evaded.

"I know. But reckoning our way—five days?"

"Nearer ten, Allan."

"*What?* But then—"

The girl withdrew her hand from him and arose.

"I see it's no use, Allan," she said decisively. "So long as I stay with you you'll ask questions and excite yourself. I'm going! Then you'll *have* to keep still!"

"Beta! Beta!" he implored. "I'll be good! Don't leave me—you *mustn't!*"

"All right; but if you ask me another question, a single one, mind, I'll truly go!"

"Just give me your hand, girlie, that's all! Come here—sit down beside me again—so!"

He turned on his side, on the rude couch of coarse brown fabric stuffed with dried seaweed, laid his hollow cheek upon her hand, and gave a deep sigh.

"Now, I'm off," he murmured. "Only, don't leave me, Beta!"

For half an hour after his deep, slow breathing told that the wounded man was sleeping soundly—half an hour as time was measured where the sun shone, for down in the black depths of the abyss all such divisions were as naught, Beatrice sat lovingly and tenderly beside the primitive bed. Her right palm beneath his face, she stroked his long hair and his wan cheek with her other hand; and now she smiled with pride and reminiscence, now a grave, troubled look crossed her features.

The light, a fiber wick burning in a stone cup of oil upon a stone-slab table in the center of the hut, guttered unsteadily, casting huge and dancing shadows up the black walls.

"Oh, my beloved!" whispered the girl, and bent above him till the loosened sheaves of her hair swept his face. "My love! Only for you, where should I be now? With you, how could I be afraid? And yet—"

She turned at a sound from a narrow door opposite the larger one that gave upon the plaza, a door, like the other, closed by a heavy curtain platted of seaweed.

There, holding the curtain back, stood the blind patriarch. His hut, larger than most in the strange village, boasted two rooms. Now from the inner one, where he had been resting, he came to speak with Beatrice.

"Peace, daughter!" said the old man. "Peace be unto you. He sleeps?"

"Yes, father. He's much better now, I think. His constitution is simply marvelous."

"Verily, he is strong. But far stronger are those terrible and wonderful weapons of yours! If our Folk only had such!"

"You're better off without them. But of course, if you want to understand them, he can explain them in due time. Those, and endless other things!"

"I believe that is truth." The patriarch advanced into the room, and for a minute stood by the bedside with venerable dignity. "The traditions, I remember, tell of so many strange matters. I shall know them, every one. All in time, all in time!"

"Your simple medicines, down here, are wonderful," said the girl admiringly. "What did you put into that draught I gave him to make him sleep this way?"

"Only the steeped root of our *n'gahar* plant, my daughter—a simple weed brought up from the bottom of this sea by our strong divers. It is nothing, nothing."

Came silence again. The aged man sat down upon a curved stone bench that followed the contour of the farther wall. Presently he spoke once more.

"Daughter," said he, "it is now ten sleeping-times—nights, the English speech calls them, if I remember what my grandfather taught me—since the battle. And my son, here, still lies weak and sick. I go soon to get still other plants for him. Stronger plants, to make him well and powerful again. For there is haste now—haste!"

"You mean—Kamrou?"

"Yea, Kamrou! I know the temper of that evil man better than any other. He and his boats may return from the great fisheries in the White Gulf beyond the vortex at any time, and—"

"But, father, after all we've done for the village here, and especially after what Allan's done? After this wonderful victory, I can't believe—"

"You do not know that man!" exclaimed the patriarch. "*I* know him! Rather would he and his slay every living thing in this community than yield one smallest atom of power to any other."

He arose wearily and gathered his mantle all about him, then reached for his staff that leaned beside the outer door.

"Peace!" he exclaimed. "Ah, when shall we have peace and learning and a better life again? The teaching and the learning of the English speech and all the arts you know, now lost to us—to us, the abandoned Folk in the abyss? When? When?"

He raised the curtain to depart; but even then he paused once more, and turned to her.

"Verily, you have spoken truth," said he, "when you have said that all, all *here* are with us, with you and this wondrous man now lying weak and wounded in my house. But Kamrou—is different. Alas, you know him not—you know him not!

"Watch well over my son, here! Soon must he grow strong again. Soon, soon! Soon, against the coming of Kamrou. For if the chief returns and my son be weak still, then woe to him, to you, to me! Woe to us all! Woe, Woe!"

The curtain fell. The patriarch was gone. Outside, Beatrice heard the *click-click-click* of his iron staff upon the smooth and flinty rock floor.

And to her ears, mingled with the far roaring of the flame, drifted the words:

"Woe, woe to him! Woe to us all—woe—woe!"

CHAPTER XXX

EXPLORATION

UNDER the ministering care of Beatrice and the patriarch, Stern's convalescence was rapid. The old man, consumed with terror lest the dreaded chief, Kamrou, return ere the stranger should have wholly recovered, spent himself in efforts to hasten the cure. And with deft skill he brewed his potions, made his salves, and concocted revivifying medicines from minerals which only he—despite his blindness—knew how to compound.

The blow that had so shrewdly clipped Stern's skull must have inevitably killed, as an ox is dropped in the slaughter-house, a man less powerfully endowed with splendid energies and full vitality.

Even Stern's wonderful physique had a hard fight to regain its finely ripened forces. But day by day he gained—we must speak of days, though there were only sleeping-times and waking-times—until at length, upon the fifth, he was able for the first time to leave his seaweed bed and sit a while weakly on the patriarch's bench, with Beatrice beside him.

Hand in hand they sat, while Stern asked many questions, and the old man, smiling, answered such as he saw fit. But of Kamrou neither he nor the girl yet breathed one syllable.

Next day and the next, and so on every day, Stern was able to creep out of the hut, then walk a little, and finally—sometimes alone, sometimes with one or both his nurses—go all among the wondering and admiring Folk, eagerly watch their labors of all kinds, try to talk with them in the few halting words he was able to pick up, and learn many things of use and deepest interest. A grave and serious Folk they were, almost without games or sports, seemingly without religious rites of any kind, and lacking festivals such as on the surface every barbarous people had always had.

Their fisheries, netmaking, weaving, ironwork, sewing with long iron needles and coarse fiber-thread keenly interested him. Accustomed now to the roaring of the flame, he seemed no longer to hear this sound which had at first so sorely disconcerted him.

He found out nothing concerning their gold and copper supply; but their oil, he discovered, they collected in pits below the southern wall of the village, where it accumulated from deep fissures in the rock. With joy he noted the large number of children, for this bespoke a race still vigorous and with all sorts of possibilities when trained.

Odd little, silent creatures the children were, white-faced and white-haired, playless and grave, laboring like their elders even from the age of five or six. They followed him about in little troops, watching him soberly; but when he turned and tried to talk with them they scurried off like frightened rabbits and vanished in the always-open huts of stone.

Thoroughly he explored every nook and corner of the village. As soon as his strength permitted, he even penetrated parts of the surrounding region. He thought at times to detect among the Folk who followed and surrounded him, unless he expressly waved them away, some hard looks here or there. Instinctively he felt that a few of the people, here one, there one, still held hate and bitterness against him as an alien and an interloper.

But the mass of them now outwardly *seemed* so eager to serve and care for him, so quick to obey, so grateful almost to adoration, that Stern felt ashamed of his own suspicions and of the revolver that he still always carried whenever outside the patriarch's hut.

And in his heart he buried his fears as unworthy delusions, as the imaginings of a brain still hurt. The occasional black looks of one or another of the people, or perchance some sullen, muttered word, he set down as the crude manners of a primitive and barbarous race.

How little, despite all his skill and wit, he could foresee the truth!

To Beatrice he spoke no word of his occasional uneasiness, nor yet to the old man. Yet one of the very first matters he attended to was the overhauling of the revolvers, which had been rescued out of the mêlée of the battle and been given to the patriarch, who had kept them with a kind of religious devotion.

Stern put in half a day cleaning and oiling the weapons. He found there still remained a hundred and six cartridges in his bandolier and the girl's. These he now looked upon as his most precious treasure. He divided them equally with Beatrice, and bade her never go out unless she had her weapon securely belted on.

Their life at home was simple in the extreme. Beatrice had the inner room of the hut for her own. Stern and the patriarch occupied the outer one. And there, often far into the hours of the sleeping-time, when Beatrice was resting within, he and the old man talked of the wonders of the past, of the outer world, of old traditions, of the abyss, and a thousand fascinating speculations.

Particularly did the old man seek to understand some notions of the lost machine on which the strangers had come from the outer world; but, though Stern tried most patiently to make him grasp the principle of the mechanism, he failed. This talk, however, set Stern thinking very seriously about the biplane; and he asked a score of questions relative to the qualities of the native oil, to currents in the sea, locations, depths, and so on.

All that he could learn he noted mentally with the precision of the trained engineer.

With accurate scientific observation he at once began to pile up information about the people and the village, the sea, the abyss—everything, in fact, that he could possibly learn. He felt that everything depended on a sound understanding of the topography and nature of the incredible community where he and the girl now found themselves—perhaps for a life stay.

Beatrice and he were clad now like the Folk; wore their hair twisted in similar fashion and fastened with heavy pins or spikes of gold, cleverly graven; were shod with sandals like theirs, made of the skin of a shark-like fish; and carried torches everywhere they went—torches of dried weed, close-packed in a metal basket and impregnated with oil.

This oil particularly interested Stern. Its peculiar blue flame struck him as singular in the extreme. It had, moreover, the property of burning a very long time without being replenished. A wick immersed in it was never consumed or even charred, though the heat produced was intense.

"If I can't set up some kind of apparatus to distil that into gas-engine fuel, I'm no engineer, that's all," said Stern to himself. "All in time, all in time—but first I must take thought how to raise the old Pauillac from the sea."

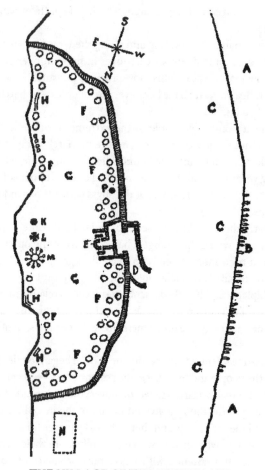

THE VILLAGE OF THE MERUCAANS

After sketch by Allan Stern, engineer. A. D. 2912

A—Sea	H—Cooking-places
B—Landing	I—Smithy
C—Beach	J—Cliff
D—Causeway	K—Boiling pit
E—Fortified gate	L—Flame
F—Huts	M—Dungeon of skeletons
G—Plaza	N—Graveyard
	P—Hut of Patriarch

The plaza is about forty feet above sea-level. Length of village, half a mile.

Already the newcomers' lungs had become absolutely accustomed to the condensed air, so that they breathed with entire ease and comfort. They even found this air unusually stimulating and revivifying, because of its greater amount of oxygen to the cubic unit; and thus they were able to endure greater exertions than formerly on the surface of the earth.

The air never grew foul. A steady current set in the direction that Stern's pocket-compass indicated as north. The heat no longer oppressed them; they were even getting used to the constant fog and to the darkness; and already could see far better than a fortnight previously, when they had arrived.

Stern never could have believed he could learn to do without sunlight and starlight and the free winds of heaven; but now he found that even these were not essential to human life.

Certain phenomena excited his scientific interest very keenly—such as the source of the great gas-flare in the village, the rhythmic variations in the air-current, the small but well-marked tides on the sea, the diminished force of gravitation—indicating a very great depth, indeed, toward the center of the earth—the greater density of the sea-water, the heavy vaporization, certain singular rock-strata of the cliffs near the village, and many other matters.

All these Stern promised himself he would investigate as soon as time and strength allowed.

The village itself, he soon determined, was about half a mile long and perhaps a quarter-mile across, measuring from the fortified gate directly back to the huge flame near the dungeon and the place of bones.

He found, incidentally, that more than one hundred and sixty freshly boiled and headless skeletons were now dangling from the iron rods, but wisely held his peace concerning them. Nor did the patriarch volunteer any information about the loss of life of the Folk in the battle. Stern estimated there were now some fifteen hundred people, men, women and children, still remaining in the community; but since he knew nothing of their number when he had arrived, he could not form more than a rough idea of the total slaughter.

He found, however, on one of his excursions outside the walls—which at a distance of two hundred and fifty yards from the sea stretched in a vast irregular arc abutting at each end against the cliff—the graveyard of the Folk.

This awesome and peculiar place consisted of heaps of smooth black boulders piled upon the dead, each heap surmounted by a stone with some crude emblem cut upon it, such as a circle, a square, a cluster of dots, even the rude figure of a bird, a fish, a tortoise, and so on.

Certain of the figures he could make nothing of; but he concluded rightly they were totem-signs, and that they represented all which still remained of the art of writing among those barbarous remnants of the once dominant, powerful and highly cultured race of Americans.

He counted more than two hundred freshly built piles of stone, but whether any of these contained more than one body of the Folk he could, of course, not tell. Allowing, however, that only two hundred of the Folk and one hundred and sixty of the Lanskaarn had fallen, he readily perceived that the battle had been, for intensity and high percentage of killing, sanguinary beyond all battles of his own time.

Under the walls, too, the vast numbers of boulders which had been thrown down, the débris of broken weapons, long and jaggedly barbed iron spear-points and so on, indicated the military ardor and the boldness of the fighting men he now had to dominate and master.

And in his soul he knew the problem of taming, civilizing, saving this rude and terrible people, was certainly the very greatest ever given into the hands of one man and one woman, since time began!

Along the beach he found a goodly number of empty revolver-shells. These he picked up, for possible reloading, in case he should be able at some later time to manufacture powder and some fulminating mixture.

He asked the patriarch to have search made for all such empty shells. The Folk eagerly and intelligently coöperated.

With interest he watched the weird sight of scores of men with torches rolling the great stones about, seeking for the precious cartridges. From the beach they tossed the shells up to him as he walked along the top of the fortifications so lately the scene of horrible combat; and despite him his heart swelled with pride in his breast, to be already directing them in some concerted labor, even so slight as this.

Save for some such interruption, the life of the community had now settled back into its accustomed routine.

With diminished numbers, but indomitable energy, the Folk went on with their daily tasks. Stern concluded the great funeral ceremony, which must have taken place over the fallen defenders, and the horrible rites attending the decapitation, boiling, and hanging up of the trophies of war, the Lanskaarn skeletons, certainly must have formed a series of barbaric pictures more ghastly than any drug-fiend's most diabolical nightmare. He thanked God that the girl had been spared these frightful scenes.

He could get the old man to tell him nothing concerning these terrific ceremonies. But he discovered, some thirty yards to southward of the circle of stone posts, a boiling geyserlike pool in the rock floor, whence the thick steam continually arose, and which at times burst up in terrific seething.

Here his keen eye detected traces of the recent rites. Here, he knew, the enemies' corpses—and perhaps even some living captives—had been boiled.

And as he stood on the sloping, slippery edge of the great natural caldron, a pit perhaps forty feet in diameter—its margins all worn smooth and greasy by innumerable feet—he shuddered in his soul.

"Good God!" thought he. "Imagine being flung in there!"

What was it, premonition or sheer repulsion, that caused him, brave as he was, to turn away with a peculiar and intense horror?

Try as he might, he could not banish from his mind the horrible picture of that boiling vat as it must have looked, crammed to the lip with the tumbling, crowding bodies of the dead.

He seemed still to hear the groans of the wounded, the shrieks of the prisoners being dragged thither, being hurled into the spumy, scalding water.

And in his heart he half despaired of ever bringing back to civilization a people so wild and warlike, so cruel, so barbarous as these abandoned People of the Abyss.

Could he have guessed what lay in store for Beatrice and himself should Kamrou, returning, find them still there, a keener and deadlier fear would have possessed his soul.

But of Kamrou he knew nothing yet. Even the chief's name he had not heard. And the patriarch, for reasons of his own, had not yet told the girl a tenth part of the threatening danger.

Even what he had told, he had forbidden her—for Allan's own sake—to let him know.

Thus in a false and fancied sense of peace and calm security, Stern made his observations, laid his plans, and day by day once more came back toward health and strength again.

And day by day the unknown peril drew upon them both.

CHAPTER XXXI

ESCAPE?

WHO could, indeed, suspect aught of this threatening danger? Outwardly all now was peaceful. Each waking-time the fishers put forth in their long boats of metal strips covered with fish-skins. Every sleeping-time they returned laden with the fish that formed the principal staple of the community.

The weaving of seaweed fiber, the making of mats, blankets, nets and slings went on as probably for many centuries before.

At forges here and there, where gas-wells blazed, the smiths of the Folk shaped their iron implements or worked most skillfully in gold and copper; and the ringing of the hammers, through the dim-lit gloom around the strange blue fires, formed a chorus fit for Vulcan or the tempering of Siegfried's master-sword.

Stern took occasion to visit many of the huts. They were all similar. As yet he could not talk freely with the Folk but he took keen interest in examining their household arrangements, which were of the simplest. Stone benches and tables, beds of weed, and coarse blankets, utensils of metal or bone—these completed the total.

Stern groaned inwardly at thought of all the arts he still must teach them before they should once more even approximate the civilization whence they had fallen since the great catastrophe.

Behind the village rose a gigantic black cliff, always dripping and running with water from the condensation of the fogs. This water the Folk very sensibly and cleverly drained down into large tanks cut in the rock floor. The tanks, always full, furnished their entire supply for drinking and cooking. Flat, warm and tasteless though it was, it seemed reasonably pure. None of this water was ever used for bathing. What little bathing the Folk ever indulged in took place at certain points along the shore, where the fine and jet-black sand made a good bottom.

Along the base of the vast cliff, which, broken and jagged, rose gleaming in the light of the great flame till it gradually faded in the luminous mist, they carried on their primitive cooking.

Over cracks in the stone, whence gas escaped steadily and burned with a blue flicker, hung copper pots fairly well fashioned, though of bizarre shapes. Here the communal cuisine went steadily forward, tended by the strange, white-haired, long-cloaked women; and odors of boiling and of frying, over hot iron plates, rose and mingled with the shifting, swirling vapors from the sea.

Beatrice tried, a few times, to take some part in this work. She was eager to teach the women better methods, but at last the patriarch told her to let them alone, as she was only irritating them. Unlike the men, who almost worshipped the revolvers, and would have handled them, and even quickly learned to shoot, if Stern had allowed, the women clung sternly to their old ways.

The patriarch had a special cooking place made for Beatrice, and got her a lot of the clumsy utensils. Here she busied herself preparing food for Allan and herself—and a strange sight that was, the American girl, dressed in her long, brown robe, her thick hair full of gold pins, cooking over natural gas in the Abyss, with heavy copper pans and kettles of incredible forms!

Almost at once, the old man abandoned the native cookery and grew devoted to hers. Anything that told him of the other and better times, the days about which he dreamed continually in his blindness, was very dear to him.

The Merucaans were, truly, barbarously dull about their ways of preparing food. Day after day they never varied. The menu was limited in the extreme. Stern felt astonished that a race could maintain itself in such fine condition and keep so splendidly energetic, so keen and warlike, on such a miserable diet. The food must, he thought, possess nutritive qualities far beyond any expectation.

Fish was the basis of all—a score of strange and unnatural-looking varieties, not one of which he had ever seen in surface waters. For the most part, they were gray or white; two or three species showed some rudiments of coloring. All were blind, with at most some faint vestigia of eye-structure, wholly degenerated and useless.

"Speaking of evolution," said the engineer, one day, to Beatrice, as they stood on the black boulder-beach and watched the fishermen toss their weird freight out upon the slippery stones—"these fish here give a magnificent example of it. You see, where the use for an organ ceases, the organ itself eventually perishes. But take these creatures and put them back into the surface-ocean—"

"The eyes would develop again?" she queried.

"Precisely! And so with everything! Take the Folk themselves, for instance. Now that they've been living here a thousand or fifteen hundred years, away from the sunlight, all the protecting pigmentation that used to shield the human race from the actinic sun rays has gradually faded out. So they've got white hair, colorless skins, and pinkish eyes. Out in the world again, they'd gradually grow normal again. How I wish some of my old-time opponents to the evolutionary theory could stand here with me today in the Abyss! I bet a million I could mighty soon upset their nonsense!"

Such of the fish as were not eaten in their natural state were salted down in vats hollowed in the rock, at the far end of the village. Still others were dried, strung by the gills on long cords of seaweed fiber, and hung in rows near the great flame. There were certain days for this process.

At other times no fish were allowed anywhere near the fire. Why this was, Stern could not discover. Even the patriarch would not tell him.

Beside the fish, several seaweeds were cooked and eaten in the form of leaves, bulbs, and roots, which some of the Folk dived for or dragged from the bottom with iron grapples. All the weeds tasted alike to Stern and Beatrice; but the old man assured them there were really great differences, and that certain of them were rare delicacies.

A kind of huge, misshapen sea-turtle was the chief prize of all. Three were taken during the strangers' first fortnight in the Abyss; but the fortunate boat-crews that brought them in devoured them, refusing to share even a morsel with any other of the people.

Stern and the girl were warned against tasting any weed, fish, or mussel on their own initiative. The patriarch told them certain deadly species existed—species used only in preparing venoms in which to dip the spear and lance-points of the fighting men.

Beyond these foods the only others were the flesh and eggs of the highly singular birds the strangers had seen on their first entry into the village. These tasted rankly of fish, and were at first very disagreeable. But gradually the newcomers were able to tolerate them when cooked by Beatrice in as near an approximation to modern methods as she could manage.

The birds made a peculiar feature of this weird, uncanny life. Long of leg, wattled and web-footed, with ungainly bodies, sparsely feathered, and bare necks, they were, Stern thought, absolutely the most hideous and unreal-appearing creatures he had ever seen. In size they somewhat re-sembled an albatross. The folk called them *kalamakee*. They were so fully domesticated as to make free with all the refuse of the village and even to waddle into the huts in croaking search of plunder; yet they nested among the broken rocks along the cliff to northward of the place.

There they built clumsy structures of weed for their eggs and their in-credibly ugly young. Every day at a certain time they took their flight out into the fog, with hoarse and mournful cries, and stayed the equivalent of some three hours.

Their number Stern could only estimate, but it must have mounted well toward five or six thousand. One of the most singular sights the newcom-ers had in the Abyss was the homecoming of the flight, the feeding of the young—by discharging half-digested fish—and the subsequent noisy powwow of the waddling multitude. All this, heard and seen by torch-light, produced a picture weirdly fascinating.

Fish, weeds, sea-fowl—these constituted the sum total of food sources for the Folk. There existed neither bread, flesh-meat, milk, fruit, sweets, or any of the abundant vegetables of the surface. Nor yet was there any plant which might be dried and smoked, like tobacco, nor any whence alcohol might be distilled. The folk had neither stimulants nor narcotics.

Stern blessed fate for this. If any such had existed, he knew human na-ture well enough to feel certain that, there in the eternal gloom and fog, the race would soon have given itself over to excesses and have miserably perished.

"To my mind," he said to Beatrice, one time, "the survival of our race under such conditions is one of the most marvelous things possibly to be conceived." Out toward the black and mist-hidden sea that rolled forever in the gloom he gestured from the wall where they were standing.

"Imagine!" he continued. "No sunlight—for centuries! Without that, nothing containing chlorophyl can grow; and science has always main-tained that human life must depend, at last analysis, on chlorophyl, on the green plants containing it. No grains, no soil, or agriculture, no mammals even! Why, the very Eskimo have to depend on mammals for their life!

"But these people here, and the Lanskaarn, and whatever other un-known tribes live in this vast Abyss, have to get their entire living from this tepid sea. They don't even possess wood to work with! If this doesn't prove the human race all but godlike in its skill and courage and adaptability, what does?"

She stood a while in thought, plainly much troubled. It was evident her mind was far from following his analysis. At last she spoke.

"Allan!" she suddenly exclaimed.

"Well?"

"It's still out there somewhere, isn't it? Out there, in those black, un-sounded depths—the biplane?"

"You mean—"

"Why couldn't we raise it again, and—"

"Of course! You know I mean to try as soon as I have these people under some control so I can get them to coöperate with me—get them to under-stand!"

"Not till then? No escape till then? But, Allan, it may be too late!" she burst out with passionate eagerness.

Puzzled, he turned and peered at her in the bluish gloom.

"Escape?" he queried. "Too late? Why, what do you mean? Escape from what? You mean that we should leave these people, here, before we've even begun to teach them? Before we've discovered some way out of the Abyss for them? Leave everything that means the regeneration of the human race, the world? Why—"

A touch upon his arm interrupted him.

He turned quickly to find the patriarch standing at his side. Silent and dim through the fog, he had come thither with sandaled feet, and now stood with a strange, inscrutable smile on his long-bearded lips.

"What keeps my children here," asked he, "when already it is long past the sleeping-hour? Verily, this should not be! Come," he commanded. "Come away! Tomorrow will be time for speech."

And, giving them no further opportunity to talk of this new problem, he spoke of other matters, and so led them back to his hospitable hut of stone.

But for a long time Allan could not sleep. Weird thoughts and new sus-picions now aroused, he lay and pondered many things.

What if, after all, this seeming friendliness and homage of the savage Folk were but a mask?

A vision of the boiling geyser-pit rose to his memory. And the dreams he dreamed that night were filled with strange, confused, disquieting images.

CHAPTER XXXII

PREPARATIONS

HE woke to hear a drumming roar that seemed to fill the spaces of the Abyss with a wild tumult such as he had never known—a steady thunder, wonderful and wild.

Starting up, he saw by the dim light that the patriarch was sitting there upon the stone, thoughtful and calm, apparently giving no heed to this singular tumult. But Stern, not understanding, put a hasty question.

"What's all this uproar, father? I never heard anything like that up in the surface-world!"

"That? Only the rain, my son," the old man answered. "Had you no rain there? Verily, traditions tell of rain among the people of that day!"

"Rain? Merciful Heavens!" exclaimed the engineer. Two minutes later he was at the fortifications, gazing out across the beach at the sea.

It would be hard to describe accurately the picture that met his eyes. The heaviest cloudburst that ever devastated a countryside was but a trickle compared with this monstrous, terrifying deluge.

Some five hundred miles of dense and saturated vapors, suddenly condensing, were precipitating the water, not in drops but in great solid masses, thundering, bellowing, crashing as they struck the sea, which, churned to a deep and raging froth, flung mighty waves even against the massive walls of the village itself.

The fog was gone now; but in its place the rushing walls of water blotted out the scene. Yet not a drop was falling in the village itself. Stern wondered for a moment. But, looking up, he understood.

The vast cliff was now dimly visible in the glare of the great flame, the steady roar of which was drowned by the tumult of the rain.

Stern saw that the village was sheltered under a tremendous overhang of the black rock; he understood why the ancestors of the Folk, coming to these depths after incredible adventurings and long-forgotten struggles, had settled here. Any exposed location would have been fatal; no hut could have withstood the torrent, nor could any man, caught in it, have escaped drowning outright.

Amazed and full of wonder at this terrific storm, so different from those on the surface—for there was neither wind nor lightning, but just that steady, frightful sluicing down of solid tons of rain—Stern made his way back to the patriarch's house.

There he met Beatrice, just awakened.

"No chance to raise the machine to-day!" she called to him as he entered. "He says this is apt to last for hours and hours!" She nodded toward the old man, much distressed.

"Patience!" he murmured. "Patience, friends—and peace!"

Stern thought a moment.

"Well," said he, at last, making himself heard only with difficulty, "even so, we can spend the day in making ready."

And, after the simple meal that served for breakfast, he sat down to think out definitely some plan of campaign for the recovery of the lost Pauillac.

Though Stern by no means understood the girl's anxiety to leave the Abyss, nor yet had any intention of trying to do so until he had begun the education of the Folk and had perfected some means of trying to transplant this group—and whatever other tribes he could find—to the surface again, he realized the all-importance of getting the machine into his possession once more.

For more than an hour he pondered the question, now asking a question of the patriarch—who seemed torn between desire to have the wonder-thing brought up, and fear lest he should lose the strangers—now designing grapples, now formulating a definite line of procedure.

At last, all things settled in his mind, he bade the old man get for him ten strong ropes, such as the largest nets were made of. These ropes which he had already seen coiled in huge masses along the wall at the northern end of the village, where they were twisted of the tough weed-fiber, averaged all of two hundred feet in length. When the patriarch had gone to see about having them brought to the hut, he himself went across the plaza, with Beatrice, to the communal smithy.

There he appropriated a forge, hammers, and a quantity of iron bars, and energetically set to work fashioning a huge three-pronged hook.

A couple of hours' hard labor at the anvil—labor which proved that he was getting back his normal strength once more—completed the task. Deftly he heated, shaped and reshaped the iron, while vast Brocken-shadows danced and played along the titanic cliff behind him, cast by the wavering blue gas-flames of the forge. At length he found himself in possession of a drag weighing about forty pounds and provided with a stout ring at the top of the shank six inches in diameter.

"Now," said he to Beatrice, as he surveyed the finished product, while all about them the inquisitive yet silent Folk watched them by the unsteady light, "now I guess we're ready to get down to something practical. Just as soon as this infernal rain lets up a bit, we'll go angling for the biggest fish that ever came out of this sea!"

But the storm was very far from being at an end. The patriarch told Stern, when he brought the grapple to the hut—followed by a silent, all-observant crowd—that sometimes these torrential downpours lasted from three to ten sleep-times, with lulls between.

"And nobody can venture on the sea," he added, "till we know—by certain signs we have—that the great rain is verily at an end. To do that would mean to court death; and we are wise, from very long experience. So, my son, you must have patience in this as in all things, and wait!"

Part of that afternoon of forced inactivity Stern spent in his favorite habit of going about among the Folk, closely mingling with them and watching all their industrial processes and social life, and trying, as usual, to pick up words and phrases of the very far-degenerated speech that once had been English but was now a grammarless and formless jumble of strange words.

Only a few of the most common words he found retained anything like their original forms—such as *w'hata,* water; *fohdu,* food; *yernuh,* iron; *vlaak,* black; *gomu,* come; *ghaa,* go; *fysha,* fish; and so on for about forty others.

Thousands upon thousands of terms, for which no longer any objects now existed among the Folk, had been of course utterly forgotten; and some hundreds of new words, relative to new conditions, had been invented.

The entire construction was altered; the language now bore no more resemblance to English than English had borne to the primitive Indo-Germanic of the Aryan forefathers. Now that writing had been lost, nothing retarded changes; and Stern realized that here—were he a trained philologist—lay a task incomparably interesting and difficult, to learn this Merucaan speech and trace its development from his own tongue.

But Stern's skill was all in other lines. The most that he could do was to make some rough vocabularies, learn a few common phrases, and here or there try to teach a little English. A deeper study and teaching, he knew, would come later, when more important matters had been attended to.

His attempts to learn and to talk with these people—by pointing at objects and listening to their names—were comparable to those, perhaps, of a prehistoric Goth turned loose in an American village of the twentieth century. Only the patriarch had retained the mother-tongue, and that in an archaic, imperfect manner, so that even his explanations often failed. Stern felt the baffling difficulties in his way; but his determination only grew.

The rain steadily continued to drum down, now lessened, now again in terrific deluges of solid black water churned to white as they struck the sea and flung the froth on high. The two Americans passed an hour that afternoon in the old man's hut, drawing up a calendar on which to check as accurately as possible, the passage of time as reckoned in the terms of life upon the surface.

They scratched this on a slab of slatelike rock, with a sharp iron awl; and, reckoning the present day as about October first, agreed that every waking-time they would cross off one square.

"For," said the engineer, "it's most important that we should keep track of the seasons up above. That may have much to do with our attempts to transplant this colony. It would never do to take a people like this, accustomed to heat and vapor, and carry them out into even the mild winter that now prevails in a present-day December. If we don't get them to the surface before the last of this month, at latest—"

"We'll have to wait until another spring?" asked she.

"Looks that way," he assented, putting a few final touches to the calendar. "So you see it's up to us to hurry—and certainly nothing more inopportune than this devilish rain could possibly have happened! Haste, haste! We must make haste!"

"That's so!" exclaimed Beatrice. "Every day's precious, now. We—"

"My children," hurriedly interrupted the patriarch, "I never yet have shown you my book—my one and greatest treasure. The book!

"You have told me many things, of sun and moon and stars, which are mocked at as idle tales by my unbelieving people; of continents and seas, mountains, vast cities, great ships, strange engines moved by vapor and by lightning, tall houses; of words thrown along metal threads or even through the air itself; of great nations and wars, of a hundred wondrous matters that verily have passed away even from the remotest memories of us in the Abyss!

"But of our history I have told you little; nor have you seen the book! Yet you must see it, for it alone remains to us of that other, better time. And though my folk mock at it as imposture and myth and fraud, you shall judge if it be true; you shall see what has kept the English speech alive in me, kept memories of the upper world alive. Only the book, the book!"

His voice seemed strangely agitated. As he spoke he raised his hands toward them, sitting on the stone bench in the hut, while outside the rain still thundered louder than the droning roar of the great flame. Stern, his curiosity suddenly aroused, looked at the old man with keen interest.

"The book?" he queried. "What book? What's the name of it? What date? What—who wrote it, and—"

"Patience, friends!"

"You mean you've really got an English book here in this village? A—"

"A book, verily, from the other days! But first, before I show you, let me tell you the old tradition that was handed down to me by my father and my father's fathers, down through centuries—I know not how many."

"You mean the story of this Lost Folk in the Abyss?"

"Verily! You have told me yours, of your awakening, of the ruined world and all your struggles and your fall down into this cursed pit. Listen now to mine!"

CHAPTER XXXIII

THE PATRIARCH'S TALE

"IN the beginning," he commanded, slowly and thoughtfully, "our people were as yours; they were the same. Our tradition tells that a great breaking of the world took place very many centuries ago. Out of the earth a huge portion was split, and it became as the moon you tell of, only dark. It circled about the earth—"

"By Jove!" cried Stern, and started to his feet. "That dark patch in the sky! That moving mystery we saw nights at the bungalow on the Hudson!"

"You mean—" the girl exclaimed.

"It's a new planetoid! Another satellite of the earth! It's the split-off part of the world!"

"Another satellite?"

"Of course! Hang it, yes! See now? The great explosion that liberated the poisonous gases and killed practically everybody in the world must have gouged this new planet out of the flank of Mother Earth in the latter part of 1920. The ejected portions, millions of millions of tons, hundreds of thousands of cubic miles of solid rock—and with them the ruins of Chicago, Milwaukee, St. Louis, Omaha, and hundreds of smaller cities—are now all revolving in a fixed, regular orbit, some few thousand miles or so from the surface!

"Think! Ours are the only living human eyes that have seen this new world blotting out the stars! This explains everything—the singular changes in the tides and in the direction of the magnetic pole, decreased gravitation and all the other strange things we noticed, but couldn't understand. By Gad! What a discovery!"

The patriarch listened eagerly while Stern and the girl discussed the strange phenomenon; but when their excitement had subsided and they were ready again to hear him, he began anew:

"Verily, such was the first result of the great catastrophe. And, as you know, millions died. But among the cañons of the Rocky Mountains—so says the tradition; is it right? *Were* there such mountains?"

"Yes, yes! Go on!"

"In those cañons a few handfuls of hardy people still survived. Some perished of famine and exposure; some ventured out into the lowlands and died of the gas that still hung heavy there. Some were destroyed in a great fire that the tradition says swept the earth after the explosion. But a few still lived. At one time the number was only eighteen men, twelve women and a few children, so the story goes."

"And then?"

"Then," continued the patriarch, his brow wrinkled in deep thought, "then came the terrible, swift cold. The people, still keeping their English tongue, now dead save for you two, and still with some tools and even a few books, retreated into caves and fissures in the cañons. And so they came to the great descent."

"The what?"

"The huge cleft which the story says once connected the upper world with this Abyss. And—"

"Is it open *now?*" cried Stern, leaning sharply forward.

"Alas, no; but you hurry me too much, good friend. You understand, for a long time they lived the cave-life partly, and partly the upper life. And they increased a great deal in the hundred years that followed the explosion. But they never could go into the plains, for still the gas hung there, rising from a thousand wells—ten thousand, mayhap, all very deadly. And so they knew not if the rest of the world lived or died."

"And then?" queried the engineer. "Let's have it all in outline. What happened?"

"This, my son: that a still greater cold came upon the world, and the life of the open became impossible. There were now ten or twelve thousand alive; but they were losing their skill, their knowledge, everything. Only a few men still kept the wisdom of reading or writing, even. For life was a terrible fight. And they had to seek food now in the cave-lakes; that was all remaining.

"After that, another fifty or a hundred years, came the second great explosion. The ways were closed to the outer world. Nearly all died. What happened even the tradition does not tell. How many years the handful of people wandered I do not know. Neither do I know how they came here.

"The story says only eight or ten altogether reached this sea. It was much smaller then. The islands of the Lanskaarn, as we call them now, were then joined to the land here. Great changes have taken place. Verily, all is different! Everything was lost—language and arts, and even the look of the Folk.

"We became as you see us. The tradition itself was forgotten save by a few. Sometimes we increased, then came pestilences and famines, outbreaks of lava and hot mud and gases, and nearly all died. At one time only seven remained—"

"For all the world like the story of Pitcairn Island and the mutineers of the 'Bounty'!" interrupted the engineer. "Yes, yes—go on!"

"There is little more to tell. The tradition says there was once a place of records, where certain of the wisest men of our Folk placed all their lore to keep it; but even this place is lost. Only one family kept any knowledge of the English as a kind of inheritance and the single book went with that family—"

"But the Lanskaarn and the other peoples of the Abyss, where did *they* come from?" asked Stern eagerly.

The patriarch shook his head.

"How can I tell?" he answered. "The tradition says nothing of them."

"Some other groups, probably," suggested Beatrice, "that came in at different times and through other ways."

"Possibly," Stern assented. "Anything more to tell?"

"Nothing more. We became as savages; we lost all thought of history or learning. We only fought to live! All was forgotten.

"My grandfather taught the English to my father and he to me, and I had no son. Nobody here would learn from me. Nobody cared for the book. Even the tradition they laughed at, and they called my brain softened when I spoke of a place where in the air a light shone half the time brighter even than the great flame! And in every way they mocked me!

"So I—I"—the old man faltered, his voice tremulous, while tears glittered in his dim and sightless eyes—"I ceased to speak of these things. Then I grew blind and could not read the book. No longer could I refresh my mind with the English. So I said in my heart: 'It is finished and will soon be wholly forgotten forever. This is the end.'

"Verily, I laid the book to rest as I soon must be laid to rest! Had you not come from that better place, my thought would have been true—"

"But it isn't, not by a jugful!" exclaimed the engineer joyously, and stood up in the dim-lit little room. "No, *sir!* She and I, we're going to change the face of things considerably! How? Never mind just yet. But let's have a look at the old volume, father. Gad! That must be some relic, eh? Imagine a book carried about for a thousand years and read by at least thirty generations of men! The book, father! The book!"

Already the patriarch had arisen and now he gestured at the heavy bench of stone.

"Can you move this, my son?" asked he. "The place of the book lies beneath."

"Under there, eh? All right!" And, needing no other invitation, he set his strength against the massive block of gneiss.

It yielded at the second effort and, sliding ponderously to one side, revealed a cavity in the stone floor some two feet long by about eighteen inches in breadth.

Over this the old man stooped.

"Help me, son," bade he. "Once I could lift it with ease, but now the weight passes my strength."

"What? The weight of a book? But—where is it? In this packet, here?"

He touched a large and close-wrapped bundle lying in the little crypt, dimly seen by the flicker of the oily wick.

"Yea. Raise it out that I may show you!" answered the patriarch. His hands trembled with eagerness; in his blind eyes a sudden fever seemed to burn. For here was his dearest, his most sacred treasure, all that remained to him of the long-worshipped outer world—the world of the vague past and of his distant ancestors—the world that Stern and Beatrice had really known and seen, yet which to him was only "all a wonder and a wild desire."

"Lay the book upon the bench," he ordered. "I will unwrap it!"

Complex the knots were, but his warped and palsied fingers deftly undid them as though long familiar with each turn and twist. Then off came many a layer of the rough brown seaweed fabric and afterward certain coverings of tough shark-skin neatly sewn.

"The book!" cried the patriarch. "Now behold it!"

"*That?*" exclaimed Beatrice. "I never saw a book of that shape!"

"Each page is separately preserved, wherefore it is so very thick," explained the old man. "See here?"

He turned the leaves reverently. Stern, peering closely by the dim light, saw that they were loosely hung together by loops of heavy gold wire. Each page was held between two large plates of mica, and these plates were securely sealed around the edges by some black substance like varnish or bitumen.

"Only thus," explained the patriarch, "could we hope to save this precious thing. It was done many hundreds of years ago, and even then the book was almost lost by age and use."

"I should say so!" ejaculated Stern. Even sealed in its air-tight covering, he saw that every leaf was yellow, broken, rotten, till the merest breath would have disintegrated it to powder. A sense of the infinitudes of time bridged by this volume overwhelmed him; he drew a deep breath, reached out his hand and touched the wondrous relic of the world that was.

"Long ago," continued the old man, "when the book began to crumble, one of my ancestors copied it on gold plates, word by word, letter by letter, every point and line. And our family used only that book of gold and put away the other. But in my grandfather's time the Lanskaarn raided our village and the gold plates went for loot to make them trinkets, so they were lost.

"My father meant to begin the task again, but was killed in a raid. I, too, in my fighting youth, had plans for the work; but blindness struck me before I could find peace to labor in. So now all that remains of the mother tongue here is my own knowledge and these tattered scraps. And, if you save us not, soon all, all will be lost forever!"

Much moved, the engineer made no reply, yet thoughts came crowding to his brain. Here visibly before him he beheld the final link that tied these lost Folk to the other time, the last and breaking thread. What history could this book have told? What vast catastrophies, famines, pestilences, wars, horrors had it passed through? In what unwritten cataclysms, in what anguish and despair and long degeneration had the human mind still clung to it and cherished it?

No one could tell; yet Stern felt the essence of its unknown story. An infinite pathos haloed the ancient volume. And reverently he touched its pages once again; he bent and by the guttering light tried to make out a few words here or there upon the crackled, all but perished leaves.

He came upon a crude old woodcut, vague and dim; then a line of text caught his eye.

"By Gad! 'Pilgrim's Progress'!" he exclaimed. "Look, Beatrice—'Pilgrim's Progress,' of all books! No wonder he says 'Verily' and talks archaic stuff and doesn't catch more than half we say. Well, I'll be—"

"Is this then not the English of your time?" asked the patriarch.

"Hardly! It was centuries old at the epoch of the catastrophe. Say, father, the quicker you forget this and take a few lessons in the up-to-date language of the real world that perished, the better! I see now why you don't get on to the idea of steamships and railroads, telephones and wireless and all the rest of it. God! but you've got a lot to learn!"

The old man closed up the precious volume and once more began wrapping it in its many coverings.

"Not for me, all this, I fear," he answered with deep melancholy. "It is too late, too late—I cannot understand."

"Oh, yes, you can, and will!" the engineer assured him. "Buck up, father! Once I get my biplane to humming again you'll learn a few things, never fear!"

He stepped to the door of the hut and peered out.

"Rain's letting up a bit," he announced. "How about it? Do the signs say it's ready to quit for keeps? If so—all aboard for the dredging expedition!"

CHAPTER XXXIV

The Coming of Kamrou

The storm, in fact, was now almost at an end, and when the engineer awoke next morning he found the rain had wholly ceased. Though the sea was still giving forth white vapors, yet these had not yet reached their usual density. From the fortifications he could see, by the reflected lights of the village and of the great flame, a considerable distance out across the dim, mysterious sea. He knew the time was come to try for the recovery of the machine, if ever.

"If I don't make a go of it to-day," said he, "I might as well quit for good. There'll never be a better opportunity. And if it's left down there very much longer, Heaven only knows what kind of shape it'll be in. I make good to-day or it's all off."

Beatrice eagerly seconded his plans. The old man, too, was impatient as a child to learn more of this wonder of the upper world. And, translating to the Folk the directions that Stern gave him, he soon had a great throng on the beach, where lay not only the Folk's canoes, but also many left by the slaughtered and dispersed Lanskaarn.

Two hours after the crude meal that must be called breakfast for want of a better name, the expedition was ready to start.

Twenty-five of the largest boats, some holding twelve men, set out, to the accompaniment of shouting and singing much like that when the captives had been brought in. Stern, Beatrice and the patriarch all sat in one canoe with eight paddlers. In the bottom lay Stern's heavy grapple with the ten long ropes, now twisted into a single cable, securely knotted to its ring.

To Stern it seemed impossible that any means existed for locating, even approximately, the spot where the machine had fallen. As the shore faded away and the village lights disappeared in the gloom and mist, all landmarks vanished. Everywhere about them the dim, oily sea stretched black and gloomy, with here and there the torches of the little fleet casting strange blue-green lights that wavered like ghostly will-o'-the-wisps over the water.

The boatman's song wailed high, sank low, trembled and ceased; and for a while came silence, save for the dipping of the paddles, the purling of the waters at the bow of the canoe. The engineer, despite his hard-headed practicality, shuddered a little and drew his mantle closer round him.

Beatrice, too, felt the eery mystery of the scene. Stern put an arm about her; she slid her hand into his, and thus in silence they sat thinking while the boats drew on and on.

"They really know where they're going, father?" the engineer asked at length. "It all looks alike to me. How can they tell?"

"Verily, I cannot explain that to you," the old man made answer. "We know, that is all."

"But—"

"Had I been always blind you could not expound sight to me. A deaf man cannot understand sound."

"You mean you've developed some new sense, some knowledge of direction and location that *we* haven't got?"

"Yea, it must be so. In all these many centuries among the dark mists we have to know. And this gloom, this night, are the same to us as you have told me a lake on the surface would be to you in the brightness of that sun which none of us have ever yet beheld."

"Is that so? Well, hanged if I get it! However, no matter about that just so they locate the place. Can they find the exact spot, father?"

"Perhaps not so. But they will come near to it, my son. Only have patience; you shall see!"

Stern and the girl relapsed into silence again, and for perhaps a quarter-hour the boats moved steadily forward through the vapors in a kind of crescent, the tips of which were hidden by the mist.

Then all at once a sharp cry rang from a boat off to the right, a cry taken up and echoed all along the line. The paddles ceased to ply; the canoes now drifted idly forward, their wakes trailing out behind in long "slicks" of greasy blackness flecked with sparkles from the reflected light of all those many torches.

Another word of command; the boatmen slowed their craft.

"Drop the iron here, son, and drag the bottom," said the patriarch.

"Good!" answered Stern, thrilled with excitement and wonder.

He pitched the dredge into the jetty sea. It sank silently as he payed out the cable. At a depth he estimated—from the amount of cable still left in the boat—as about thirty fathoms, it struck bottom.

He let out another five fathoms.

"All right, father!" he exclaimed sharply. "Tell our boatmen to give way!"

The old man translated the order: *"Ghaa vrouaad, m'yaun!"* (Go forward, men.) The paddles dipped again and Stern's canoe moved silently over the inky surface.

Every sense alert, the engineer at the gunwale held the cable. For a few seconds he felt nothing as the slack was taken up; then he perceived a tug and knew the grapple was dragging.

Now intense silence reigned, broken only by the sputter of the smoking torches. The canoes, spaced over the foggy sea, seemed floating in a void of nothingness; each reflected light quivered and danced with weird and tremulous patterns.

Stern played the cable as though it were a fish-line. All his senses centered on interpreting the message it conveyed. Now he felt that it was dragging over sand; now came rocks—and once it caught, held, then jerked free. His heart leaped wildly. Oh, had it only been the aeroplane!

The tension grew. Out, far out from the drifting line of boats the canoe went forward; it turned at a word from the patriarch and dragged along the front of the line. It criss-crossed on its path; Stern had to admire the skill and thoroughness with which the boatmen covered the area where their mysterious sixth sense of location told them the machine must lie.

All at once a tug, different from all others, yielding, yet firm, set his pulses hammering again.

"Got it!" he shouted, for he knew the truth. "Hold fast, there—*she's hooked!*"

"You've got it, Allan? Really got it?" cried the girl, starting up. "Oh—"

"Feel this!" he answered. "Grab hold and pull!"

She obeyed, trembling with eagerness.

"It's caught through one of the ailerons, or some yielding part, I think," he said. "Here, help me hold it tight, now; we mustn't let the hook slip out again!" To the patriarch he added: "Tell 'em to back up, there—easy—easy!"

The canoe backed, while Stern took up the slack again. When the pull from below was vertical he ordered the boat stopped.

"Now get nine other boats close in here," commanded he.

The old man gave the order. And presently nine canoes stood in near at hand, while all the rest lay irregularly grouped about them.

Now Stern's plan of the tenfold cable developed itself. Already he was untwisting the thick rope. One by one he passed the separate cords to men in the other boats. And in a few minutes he and nine other men held the ropes, which, all attached to the big iron ring below, spread upward like the ribs of an inverted umbrella.

The engineer's scheme was working to perfection. Well he had realized that no one boat could have sufficed to lift the great weight of the machine. Even the largest canoe would have been capsized and sunk long before a single portion of the Pauillac and its engine had been so much as stirred from the sandy bottom.

But with the buoyant power of ten canoes and twenty or thirty men all applied simultaneously, Stern figured he had a reasonable chance of raising the sunken aeroplane. The fact that it was submerged, together with the diminished gravitation of the Abyss, also worked in his favor. And as he saw the Folk-men grip the cords with muscular hands, awaiting his command, he thrilled with pride and with the sense of real achievement.

"Come, now, boys!" he cried. "Pull! Heave-ho, there! Altogether, lift her! *Pull!*"

He strained at the rope which he and two others held; the rest—each rope now held by three or four men—bent their back to the labor. As the ropes drew tense, the canoes crowded and jostled together. Those men who were not at the ropes, worked with the paddles to keep the boats apart, so that the ropes should not foul or bind. And in an irregular ring, all round the active canoes, the others drew. Lighted by so many torches, the misty waters glittered as broken waves, thrown out by the agitation of the canoes, radiated in all directions.

"Pull, boys, pull!" shouted the engineer again. "*Up* she comes! Now, all together!"

Came a jerk, a long and dragging resistance, then a terrific straining on the many cords. The score and a half of men breathed hard; on their naked arms the veins and muscles swelled; the torchlight gleamed blue on their sweating faces and bodies.

And spontaneously, as at all times of great endeavor among the Folk, a wailing song arose; it echoed through the gloom; it grew, taken up by the outlying boats; and in the eternal dark of the Abyss it rose, uncanny, soul-shaking, weird beyond all telling.

Stern felt the shuddering chills chase each other up and down his spine, playing a nervous accompaniment to their chant.

"Gad!" he muttered, shivering, "what a situation for a hard-headed, practical man like me! It's more like a scene from some weird pipe-dream magazine story of the remote past than solid reality!"

Again the Folk strained at the ropes, Stern with them; and now the great weight below was surely rising, inch by inch, up, up, toward the black and gleaming surface of the abysmal sea.

Stern's heart was pounding wildly. If only—incredible as it seemed—the Pauillac really were there at the end of the converging ropes; and if it were still in condition to be repaired again! If only the hook and the hard-taxed ropes held!

"Up, boys! Heave 'er!" he shouted, pulling till his muscles hardened like steel, and the canoe—balanced, though it was by five oarsmen and the patriarch all at the other gunwale—tipped crazily. "Pull! *Pull!*"

Beatrice sprang to the rope. Unable to restrain herself, she, too, laid hold on the taut, dripping cord; and her white hands, firm, muscular, shapely, gripped with a strength one could never have guessed lay in them.

And now the ropes were sliding up out of the water, faster, ever faster; and higher rose the song of all those laboring Folk and all who watched from the outlying ring of boats.

"Up with it, men! *Up!*" panted the engineer.

Even as he spoke the waters beneath them began to boil and bubble strangely, as though with the rising of a monstrous fish; and all at once, with a heave, a sloshing splatter, a huge, weed-covered, winglike object, sluicing brine, wallowed sharply out into the torchlight.

A great triumphal howl rose from the waiting Folk—a howl that drowned Stern's cheer and that of Beatrice, and for a moment all was confusion. The wing rose, fell, slid back into the water and again dipped upward. The canoes canted; some took water; all were thrown against each other in the central group; and cries, shouts, orders and a wild fencing off with paddles followed.

Stern yelled in vain orders that the old man could not even hear to translate; orders which would not, even though heard, have been obeyed. But after a moment or two comparative order was restored, and the engineer, veins standing out on his temples, eyes ablaze, bellowed:

"Hold fast, you! No more, nor more—don't pull up any more, damn you! Hey, stop that—you'll rip the hook clean out and lose it again!

"You, father—here—tell 'em to let it down a little, now—about six feet, so. Easy—does it—*easy!*"

Now the Pauillac, sodden with water, hanging thickly with the luxuriant weed clusters which even in a fortnight had grown in that warm sea, was suspended at the end of the ten cords about six or eight feet below the keels of the canoes.

"Tell 'em to let it stay that way now," continued the engineer. "Tell 'em all to hold fast, those that have the ropes. The others paddle for the shore as fast as they can—and damn the man that loafs *now!*"

The patriarch conveyed the essence of these instructions to the oarsmen, and now, convoyed by the outlying boats, the ten canoes moved very slowly toward the village.

Retarded by the vast, birdlike bulk that trailed below, they seemed hardly to make any progress at all. Stern ordered the free boats to hitch on and help by towing. Lines were passed, and after a while all twenty-five canoes, driven by the power of two hundred and fifty pairs of sinewy arms, were dragging the Pauillac shoreward.

Stern's excitement—now that the machine was really almost in his grasp again—far from diminishing, was every minute growing keener.

The delay until he could examine it and see its condition and its chances of repair, seemed interminable. Continually he urged the patriarch—himself profoundly moved—to force the rowers to still greater exertion. At a paddle he labored, throwing every ounce of strength into the toil. Each moment seemed an hour.

"Gad! If it's only possible to make it fly again!" thought he.

Half an hour passed, and now at length the dim and clustered lights of the village began to show vaguely through the mist.

"Come on, boys; now for it!" shouted Stern. "Land her for me and I'll show you wonders you never even dreamed of!"

They drew near the shore. Already Stern was formulating his plans for landing the machine without injuring it, when out from the beach a long and swift canoe put rapidly, driven by twenty men.

At sight of it the rowing in Stern's boats weakened, then stopped. Confused cries arose, altercations and strange shouts; then a hush of expectancy, of fear, seemed to possess the boat crews.

And ever nearer, larger, drew the long canoe, a two-pronged, blazing cresset at its bows.

Across the waters drifted a word.

"Go on, you! Row!" cried Stern. "Land the machine, I tell you! Say, father, what's the matter *now?* What are my men on strike for all of a sudden? Why don't they finish the job?"

The old man, perplexed, listened intently.

Between the group of canoes and the shore the single boat had stopped. A man was standing upright in it. Now came a clear hail, and now two or three sentences, peremptory, angry, harsh.

At sound of them consternation seized certain of the men. A number dropped the ropes, while others reached for the slings and spears that always lay in the bottoms of the canoes.

"What the devil *now?*" shouted Stern. "You all gone crazy, or what?"

He turned appealingly to the old man.

"For Heaven's sake, what's up?" he cried. "Tell me, can't you, before the idiots drop my machine and ruin the whole thing? What—"

"Misfortune, O my son!" cried the patriarch in a strange, trembling voice. "The worst that could befall! In our absence *he* has come back—*he*, Kamrou! And under pain of death he bids all men abandon every task and haste to homage. *Kamrou the Terrible is here!*"

CHAPTER XXXV

FACE TO FACE WITH DEATH

FOR a moment Stern stared, speechless with amazement, at the old man, as though to determine whether or not he had gone mad. But the commotion, the mingled fear and anger of the boat crews convinced him the danger, though unknown, was very real.

And, flaring into sudden rage at this untimely interruption just in the very moment of success, he jerked his pistol from its holster, and stood up in the boat.

"I'll have no butting in here!" he cried in a loud, harsh voice. "Who the devil is Kamrou, I'd like to know? Go on, *on, to shore!*"

"My son—"

"You order these men to grab those ropes again and go ashore or I warn you there's going to be a whole big heap of trouble!"

Over the waters drifted another hail, and the strange long boat, under the urge of vigorous arms, now began to move toward Stern's fleet. At the same time, mingled cries arose on shore. Stern could see lights moving back and forth; some confusion was under way there, though what, he could not imagine.

"Well," he cried, "are you going to order these men to go forward? Or shall I—with *this?*"

And menacingly he raised the grim and ugly gun.

"Oh my son!" exclaimed the patriarch, his lips twitching, his hands outstretched—while in the boats a babel of conflicting voices rose—"O my son, if I have sinned in keeping this from you, now let me die! I hid it from your knowledge, verily, to save my people—to keep you with us till this thing should be accomplished! My reckoning was that Kamrou and his men would stay beyond the Great Vortex, at their labor, until after—"

"*Kamrou?*" shouted Stern again. "What the deuce do I care about him? Who *is* he, anyhow? A Lanskaarn, or—"

The girl seized Allan's hand.

"Oh, listen, listen!" she implored. "I—"

"Did *you* know about this? And never told me?"

"Allan, he said our work could all be done before the—"

"So you *did* know, eh?"

"He said I must not tell you. Otherwise—"

"Oh, hang that! See here, Beatrice, what's the matter, anyhow? These people have all gone crazy, just in a second, the old man and all! If you know anything about it, for God's sake tell me! I can't stand much more!"

"I've got to get this machine to land before they go entirely nutty and drop it, and we lose all our work for nothing. What's up? Who's this Kamrou they're talking about? For Heaven's sake, tell me!"

"He's their chief. Allan—their chief! He's been gone a long time, he and his men. And—"

"Well, what do we care for *him?* We're running this village now, aren't we?"

"Listen. The old man says—"

"He's a hard nut, eh? And won't stand for us—is that it?" He turned to the patriarch. "This Kamrou you're talking about doesn't want us, or our new ideas, or anything? Well, see here. There's no use beating around the bush, now. *This thing's going through, this plan of ours!* And if Kamrou or anybody else gets in the way of it—*good-by for him!*"

"You mean war?"

"*War!* And I know who'll win, at that! And now, father, you get these men here to work again, or there'll be some sudden deaths round here!"

"Hearken, O my son! Already the feast of welcome to Kamrou is beginning, around the flame. See now, the boat of his messenger is close at hand, bidding all those in this party to hasten in, for homage. Kamrou will not endure divided power. Trust me now and I can save you yet. For the present, yield to him, or seem to, and—"

"*Yield nothing!*" fairly roared the engineer, angrier than he had ever been in his whole life. "This is *my* affair now! Nobody else butts in on it at all! To shore with these boats, you hear? or I begin shooting again! And if I do—"

"Allan!" cried the girl.

"Not a word! Only get your gun ready, that's all. We've got to handle this situation sharp, or it's all off! Come, father," he delivered his ultimatum to the patriarch; "come, order them ashore!"

The old man, anguished and tremulous, spoke a few words. Answers arose, here, there. He called something to the standing figure in the despatch-boat, which slackened, stopped, turned and headed for the distant beach.

With some confusion the oarsmen of the fleet took up their task again. And now, in a grim silence, more disconcerting even than the previous uproar, the boats made way toward land.

Ten minutes later—minutes during which the two Americans kept their revolvers ready for instant action—the aeroplane began to drag on the bottom. Despite the crowd now gathered on the beach, very near at hand and ominously silent, Stern would not let the machine lie even here, in shallow water, where it could easily have been recovered at any time. Like a bulldog with its jaws set on an object, he clung to his original plan of landing the Pauillac at once.

And, standing up in the boat with his pistol leveled, he commanded them, through the mediumship of the patriarch, to shorten the ropes and paddle in still closer.

When the beach was only a few rods distant he gave orders that all should land, carrying the ropes with them. He himself was one of the first to wade ashore, with Beatrice.

Ignoring the silent, expectant crowd and the tall figure of Kamrou's messenger—who now stood, arms crossed, amazed, indignant, almost at the water's edge—he gave quick commands:

"Now, clear these boats away on both sides! Make a free space, here—wider—so, that's right. Now, all you men get hold of the ropes—all of you, here, take hold, you! Ready, now? Give way, then! Out she comes! Out with her!"

The patriarch, standing in fear and keen anxiety beside him, transmitted the orders. Truly the old man's plight was hard, torn as he was between loyalty to the newcomers and terror of the implacable Kamrou. But Stern had no time to think of aught but the machine and his work.

For now already the great ungainly wings of the machine were wallowing up, up, out of the jetty waters; and now the body, now the engine showed, weed-festooned, smeared with mud and slime, a strange and awesome apparition in that blue and ghastly torch-flare, as the toiling men hauled it slowly, foot by foot, up the long slope of the beach.

Dense silence held the waiting throng; silence and awe, in face of this incomprehensible, tremendous thing.

Even the messenger spoke not a word. He had lost somewhat of his assurance, his pride and overbearing haughtiness. Perhaps he had already heard some tales of these interlopers' terrible weapons.

Stern saw the man's eyes follow the revolver, as he gestured with it; the high-lights gleaming along the barrel seemed to fascinate the tall barbarian. But still he drew no step backward. Still in silence, with crossed arms, he waited, watched and took counsel only with himself.

"Thank God, it's out at last!" exclaimed the engineer, and heaved a sigh of genuine, heartfelt relief. "See, Beatrice, there's our old machine again— and except for that broken rudder, this wing, here, bent, and the rent where the grapple tore the leather covering of the starboard plane, I can't see that it's taken any damage. Provided the engine's intact, the rest will be easy. Plenty of chance for metal-work, here, and—"

"Going to take it right up to the village, now?" queried she, anxiously glancing at the crowd of white and silent faces, all eagerly staring—staring like so many wraiths in a strange dream.

He shrugged his shoulders.

"That depends," he answered. He seemed already to have forgotten Kamrou and the threatening peril in the village, near the great flame. Even the sound of distant chanting and the thudding of dull drums stirred him not. Fascinated, he was walking all round the great mechanical bird, which now lay wounded, weed-covered, sodden and dripping, yet eloquent of infinite possibilities, there on that black, unearthly beach.

All at once he spoke.

"Up to the village with it!" he commanded, waving his pistol-hand toward the causeway and the fortified gates. "I can't risk leaving it here. Come, father, speak to them! It's got to go into the village right now!"

Then Kamrou's messenger, grasping the sense if not the words of the command, strode forward—a tall, lithe figure of a man, well-knit and hard of face. Under the torchlight the dilated pupils of his pinkish eyes seemed to shine as phosphorescent as a cat's.

Crying out something unintelligible to Stern, he blocked the way. Stern heard the name "Kamrou! Kamrou!"

"Well, what do you want now?" shouted the engineer, a huge and sudden anger seizing him. Already super-excited by the labors of the day and by the nervous strain of having recovered the sunken biplane, all this talk of Kamrou, all this persistent opposition just at the most inauspicious moment worked powerfully upon his irritated nerves.

Cool reason would have dictated diplomacy, parley, and, if possible, truce. But Stern could not believe the Folk, for so long apparently loyal to him and dominated by his influence, could work against their vital interest and his own by deserting him now.

And, all his saner judgment failing him, heeding nothing of the patriarch's entreaties or of the girl's remonstrance as she caught his arm and tried to hold him back, he faced this cooly insolent barbarian.

"You, damn you, what *d'you* want?" he cried again, his finger itching on the trigger of the automatic. "Think I'm going to quit for you, or Kamrou, or anybody? Quit, *now?*

"Think a civilized white man, sweating his heart out to save your people here, is going to knuckle under to any savage that happens to blow in and try to boss this job? If so, you've got another guess coming! Stand back, you, or you'll get cold lead in just one minute!"

Quick words passed from the old man to the messenger and back again. The patriarch cried again to him, and for a moment Stern saw the barbarian's eyes flicker uneasily toward the revolver. But the calm and cruel face never changed, nor did the savage take one step backward.

"All right, then!" shouted Stern, "seeing red" in his overpowering rage. "You want it—you'll get it—take it, so!"

Up he jerked the automatic, fair at the big barbarian's heart—a splendid target by the torch-light, not ten feet distant; a sure shot.

But before he could pull trigger the strange two-pronged torch was tossed on high by somebody behind the messenger, and through the dull and foggy gloom a wild, fierce, penetrant cry wailed piercingly.

Came a shooting, numbing pain in Stern's right elbow. The arm dropped, helpless. The boulder which, flung with accurate aim, had destroyed his aim, rolled at his feet. The pistol clattered over the wet, shining stones.

Stern, cursing madly, leaped and snatched for it with the other hand.

Before he could even reach it a swift foot tripped him powerfully. Headlong he fell. And in a second one of the very ropes that had been used to drag the Pauillac from the depths was lashed about his wrists, his ankles, his struggling, fighting body.

"Beatrice! Shoot! Kill!" he shouted. "Help here! *Help! The machine*—they'll wreck it! Everything—lost! *Help!*"

His speech died in a choking mumble, stifled by the wet and sodden gag they forced into his mouth.

About him the mob seethed. Through his brain a quick anguish thrilled, the thought of Beatrice unaided and alone. Then came a wonder when the death-stroke would fall—a frightful, sick despair that on the very eve of triumph, of salvation for this Folk and for the world as well as for Beatrice and himself, this unforeseen catastrophe should have befallen.

He struggled still to catch some glimpse of Beatrice, to cry aloud to her, to shield her; but, alone against five hundred, he was powerless.

Nowhere could he catch even a glimpse of the girl. In that shoving, pushing, shouting horde, nothing could be made out. He knew not even whether civil war had blazed or whether all alike had owned the rule of Kamrou the Terrible.

Like buoys tossing upon the surface of a raging sea, the flaring torches pitched and danced, rose, fell. And from a multitude of throats, from beach and causeway, walls and town, strange shouts rang up into the all-embracing, vague, enshrouding vapor.

Still striving to fight, bound as he was, he felt a great force driving him along, on, on, up the beach and toward the village.

Mute, desperate, stark mad, he knew the Folk were half carrying, half dragging him up the causeway.

As in a dark dream, he vaguely saw the great fortified gate with its huge, torch-lighted monolithic lintel. Even upon this some of the Folk were crowded now to watch the strange, incredible spectacle of the man who had once turned the tide of battle against the Lanskaarn and had saved all their lives, now haled like a criminal back into the community he had rescued in its hour of sorest need.

His mind leaped to their first entry into the village—it seemed months ago—also as prisoners. In a flash he recalled all that had happened since and bitterly he mocked himself for having dared to dream that their influence had really altered these strange, barbarous souls, or uplifted them, or taught them anything at all.

"Now, now just as the rescue of these people was at hand, just as the machine might have carried us and them back into the world, slowly, one by one—*now comes defeat and death!*"

An exceeding great bitterness filled his soul once more at this harsh, cynic turn of fate. But most of all he yearned toward Beatrice. That he should die mattered nothing; but the thought of this girl perishing at their hands there in the lost Abyss was dreadful as the pangs of all the fabled hells.

Again he fought to hold back, to try for some sight, even a fleeting glimpse of Beatrice; but the Folk with harsh cries drove him roughly forward.

He could not even see the patriarch. All was confusion, glare, smoke, noise, as he was thrust through the fortified gate, out into the thronged plaza.

Everywhere rose cries, shouts, vociferations, among which he could distinguish only one a thousand times repeated : "Kamrou! *Kamrou!*"

And through all his rage and bitter bafflement and pain, a sudden great desire welled up in him to see this chief of the Folk, at last—to lay eyes on this formidable, this terrible one—to stand face to face with him in whose hand now lay everything, Kamrou!

Across the dim, fog-covered expanse of the plaza he saw the blue-green shimmer of the great flame.

Thither, toward that strange, eternal fire and the ghastly circle of the headless skeletons the Folk were drifting now. Thither his captors were dragging him.

And there, he knew, Kamrou awaited Beatrice and him. There doom was to be dealt out to them. There, and at once!

Thicker the press became. The flame was very near now, its droning roar almost drowning the great and growing babel of cries.

On, on the Folk bore him. All at once he saw again that two-pronged torch raised before him, going ahead; and a way cleared through the press.

Along this way he was carried, no longer struggling, but eager now to know the end, to meet it bravely and with calm philosophy, "as fits a man."

And quite at once he found himself in sight of the many dangling skeletons. Now the quivering jet of the flame grew visible. Now, suddenly, he was thrust forward into a smooth and open space. Silence fell.

Before him he saw Kamrou, Kamrou the Terrible, at last.

CHAPTER XXXVI

GAGE OF BATTLE

THE chief of the People of the Abyss was seated at his ease in a large stone chair, over which heavy layers of weed-fabric had been thrown. He was flanked on either side by spearsmen and by drummers, who still held their iron sticks poised above their copper drums with shark-skin heads.

Stern saw at a glance that he was a man well over six feet tall, with whipcord muscles and a keen, eager, domineering air. Unlike any of the other Folk, his hair (snow-white) was not twisted into a fantastic knot and fastened with gold pins, but hung loose and was cut square off at about the level of his shoulders, forming a tremendous, bristly mass that reminded one of a lion's mane.

Across his left temple, and involving his left eye with a ghastly mutilation, ran a long, jagged, bright red scar, that stood out vividly against the milk-white skin. In his hands he held no mace, no symbol of power; they rested loosely on his powerful knees; and in their half-crooked fingers, large and long, Stern knew there lay a formidable, an all but irresistible strength.

At sight of the captives—for Beatrice, too, now suddenly appeared, thrust forward through another lane among the Folk—Kamrou's keenly cruel face grew hard. His lips curled with a sneer of scorn and hate. His pinkish eyes glittered with anticipation. Full on his face the flare of the great flame fell; Stern could see every line and wrinkle, and he knew that to beg mercy from this huge barbarian (even though he would have begged), were a task wholly vain and futile.

He glanced along the circle of expectant faces that ringed the chief at a distance of some fifteen feet. Surely, thought he, some of the many Folk that he and the girl had saved from butchery, some to whom they had taught the rudiments of the world's lost arts, would now show pity on them— would stand by them now!

But no; not one face of all that multitude—now that Kamrou had returned—evinced other than eager interest to see the end of everything. To Stern flashed the thought that here, despite their seeming half-civilization in the use of metals, fire, dwellings, fabrics and all the rest, dwelt within them a savagery even below that of the ancient, long-extinct American Indians.

And well he knew that if both he and Beatrice were not to die the death this day, only upon themselves they must depend!

Yes, one face showed pity. But only one—the patriarch's.

Stern suddenly caught sight of him, standing in the front rank of the circled crowd, about twenty feet away to the left, just beyond the girl. Tears gleamed in the old man's sightless eyes; his lips quivered; the engineer saw his hands tremble as he twisted the feeble, impotent fingers together in anguish.

And though he could catch no sound in that rising, falling, ever-roaring tumult of the flame, he knew the patriarch, with some vague and distant remnant of the old-time and vanished religion of the world, was striving to pray.

Stern's eyes met the girl's. Neither could speak, for she, too, was gagged with a rough band of fabric which cruelly cut her beautiful, her tender mouth. At sight of her humiliation and her pain, the man's heart leaped hotly; he strained against his bonds till the veins swelled, and with eyes of terrible rage and hate stared at Kamrou.

But the chief's gaze was now fixed insolently upon Beatrice. She, as she stood there, stripped even of her revolver and cartridge-belt, hands bound behind her, hair disheveled, had caught his barbarous fancy. And now in his look Stern saw the kindling of a savage passion so ardent, so consuming, that the man's heart turned sick within him.

"Ten thousand times better she should die!" thought he, racked at the thought of what might be. "Oh, God! If I only had my revolver for a single minute now! One shot for Kamrou—one for Beatrice—and after that, nothing would matter; nothing!"

Came a disturbance in the Folk. Heads craned; a murmur of voices rose.

The patriarch, no longer trembling, but with his head held proudly up, both hands outstretched, had stepped into the circle. And now, advancing toward Kamrou, he spoke in quick and eager sentences—he gestured at the engineer, raised his hand on high, bowed and stepped back.

And all at once a wild, harsh, swelling chorus of cries arose; every face turned toward Stern; the engineer, amazed, knew not what all this meant, but to the ultimate drop in the arteries he pledged his fighting-blood to one last, bitter struggle.

Silence again.

Kamrou had not stirred. Still his great hands rested on his knees; but a thin, venomous smile lengthened his lips. He, too, looked at the engineer, who gave the stare back with redoubled hate. Tense grew the expectation of the Folk.

"What the devil now?" thought Stern, tautening every muscle for the expected attack.

But attack there came none. Instead the patriarch asked a question of those who stood near him; and hands now guided the old man toward the place where Stern was standing, bound.

"O friend; O son!" exclaimed the old man when he had come close. "Now hearken! For, verily, this is the only way!

"It is an ancient custom of the Merucaans that any man, captive or free, can ever challenge our chief, whosoever he be, to the death-combat. If the chief wins, he remains chief. If he loses, the victor takes his place. Many hundreds of years, I know not how long, this has been our way. And many terrible combats have been seen here among our people.

"Kamrou has said that you must die, the girl must be his prize. Only one way remains to save her and yourself—you must struggle with Kamrou. I have delivered to him your challenge already. Let fate decide the issue!"

Everything seemed to whirl before Stern's eyes, and for a moment all grew black. In his ears sounded a great roaring, louder than the roar of the huge flame. Quick questions flashed through his mind. Fight Kamrou? But how? A duel with revolvers? Spears? Maces?

He knew not. Only he knew that in whatever way the ancient combats must be held he was ready!

"You affirm the challenge I have given in your behalf?" demanded the patriarch. "If you accept it, nod."

Stern nodded with all the vigor of his terrible rage. Kamrou's eyes narrowed; his smile grew fixed and hard, but in it Stern perceived the easy contempt of a bully toward any chance weakling. And through him thrilled a passion of hate such as he had never dreamed in all his life.

Came a quick word from the patriarch. Somebody was slashing the engineer's bonds. All at once the ropes gave way. Free and unfettered, he stepped forward, stretching his arms, opening and closing his cramped, numbed hands, out into the ring toward Kamrou, the chief.

Off came the gag. Stern could speak at last.

His first word was to the girl.

"Beatrice!" he called to her, "there's one chance left! I'm to fight this ruffian here. If I beat him we're free—we own this tribe, body and soul! If not—"

He broke off short. Even the possibility was not to be considered.

She looked at him and understood his secret thought. Well the man knew that Beatrice would die by her own hand before Kamrou should have his way with her.

The patriarch spoke again.

"My son," said he, "there is but one way for all these combats. It has been so these many centuries. By the smooth edge of the great boiling pit the fights are held. Man against man it is. Verily, you two with only your hands must fight! He who loses—"

"Goes into the pit?"

The old man nodded.

"There is no other way," he answered. "The new, terrible weapons you cannot use. The arrows, slings and spears are all forbidden by ancient custom. It is the naked grasp of the hands, the strong muscles of two men against each other! So we decide our chief!

"I, alas, can help you in nothing. I am powerless, weak, old. Were I to interfere now and try to change this way, my own body would only go to the pit, and my old bones hang, headless, in the place of captives and criminals. All lies in your hands, my son!

"All; everything! Our whole future, and the future of the world! If you lose, the wonderful machine will be destroyed and all its metal forged into spears and battle-axes. Barbarism will conquer; darkness will continue, and war, and death. All will be forever lost!

"The last ray of hope, of light, from the great past of the upper world, will vanish forever! Your own death, my son, and the fate of the girl, will be as nothing beside the terrible catastrophe, if you are beaten.

"For, verily, it will be the death of the world!

"And now, my son, now go to battle—to battle for this woman, for yourself, for us, for the future of our race, for everything!

"Kamrou is ready. The pit is boiling.

"Go now! Fight—and—and—"

His voice was lost in a great tumult of cries, yells, shouts. Spears brandished. Came a sound of shields struck with clubs and axes. The copper drums again began to throb and clang.

Kamrou had risen from his seat.

Stern knew the supreme moment of his life was at hand.

CHAPTER XXXVII

THE FINAL STRUGGLE

KAMROU flung off his long and heavy cloak. He stood there in the flame-light, broad-chested, beautifully muscled, lean of hip, the perfect picture of a fighting man. Naked he was, save for his loin-cloth. And still he smiled.

Stern likewise stripped away his own cloak. Clad only like the chief, he faced him.

"Well, now," said he, "here goes! And may the best man win!"

Kamrou waved the circle back at one side. It opened, revealing the great pit to southward of the flame. Stern saw the vapors rising, bluish in that strange light, from the perpetual boiling of the black waters in its depths. Oddly enough, even at that moment a stray bit of scientific thought nicked into his consciousness—the memory that under compressed air water boils only at very high temperatures. Down here, in this great pressure, the water must easily be over three hundred degrees to seethe like that.

He, too, smiled.

"So much the better," thought he. "The hotter, the sooner it's all over for the man who goes!"

Up rose numbers of the two-pronged torches. Stern got confused glimpses of the Folk—he saw the terrible, barbaric eagerness with which they now anticipated this inevitable tragedy of at least one human death in its most awful form.

Beatrice he no longer saw. Where was she? He knew not. But in a long, last cry of farewell he raised his voice. Then, with Kamrou, he strode toward the steaming, boiling pit in the smooth rock floor.

Two tall men broke through the tensely eager throng. In their hands they bore each a golden jar, curiously shaped and chiseled, and bearing a whimsical resemblance to a coffee-urn.

"What the devil now?" wondered Stern, eager to be at work. He saw at once the meaning of the jars. One of the bearers approached Kamrou. The other came to him. They raised the vessels, and over the antagonists' bare bodies poured a thin, warm stream of some rank-smelling oil. All over the skin they rubbed it, till the bodies glistened strangely in the flamelight. Then, with muttered words he could not catch, they withdrew.

All seemed confused and vague to Stern as in a painful dream. Images and pictures seemed to present themselves to his brain. The light, the fog and heat, the rising stream, the roaring of the flame, and over all the *throb-throb-throb* of those infernal copper drums worked powerfully on his senses.

Already he seemed to feel the grip of Kamrou, the pangs of the hard struggle, the sudden plunge into the vat of scalding death.

With a strong effort he flung off these fancies and faced his sneering foe, who now—his red-wealed face puckered into a malicious grin—stood waiting.

Stern all at once saw the patriarch once more.

"Go, son!" cried the old man. "Now is the moment! When the drums cease, lay hold of him!"

Even as he spoke, the great drums slowed their beat, then stopped.

Stern, with a final thought of Beatrice, advanced.

All the advantage lay with Kamrou. Familiar with the place was he, and with the rules of this incredible contest. Everywhere about him stood crowding hundreds of his Folk, owing him their allegiance, hostile to the newcomer, the man from another world. Out of all that multitude only two hearts beat in sympathy and hope for him; only two human beings gave him their thoughts and their support—a helpless girl; a feeble, blind old man.

Kamrou stood taller, too, than Stern, and certainly bulked heavier. He was in perfect condition, while Stern had not yet fully recovered from the fight in the Abyss, from the great change in living conditions there in the depths, and—more important still—from the harsh blow of the rock that had numbed his elbow on the beach.

His arms and hands, too, still felt the cramping of the cords that had bound him. He needed a few hours yet to work them into suppleness and perfect strength. But respite there was none.

He must fight now at once under all handicaps, or die—and in his death yield Beatrice to the barbaric passions of the chief.

Oddly enough there recurred to his mind, as he drew near the waiting, sneering Kamrou, that brave old warcry of the Greeks of Xenophon as they hurled themselves against the vastly greater army of the Persians—*"Zeus Sotor kaì Niké!*—Zeus Savior and victory!"

The shout burst from his lips. Forward he ran, on to the battle where either he or the barbarian must perish in the boiling pit—forward, *to what? To victory—to death?*

Kamrou stood fast till Stern's right hand had almost gripped his throat—for Stern, the challenger, had to deliver the first attack.

But suddenly he slipped aside; and as Stern swerved for him, made a quick leap.

With an agility, a strength and skill tigerlike and marvelous, he caught Stern round the waist, whirled him and would have dashed him toward the pit. But already the engineer's right arm was under Kamrou's left; the right hand had him by the throat, and Kamrou's head went sharply back till the vertebræ strained hard.

Eel-like, elusive, oiled, the chief broke the hold, even as he flung a leg about one of Stern's.

A moment they swayed, tugging, straining, panting. In the old days Stern would not for one moment have been a match for this barbaric athlete, but the long months of life close to nature had hardened him and toughened every fiber. And now a stab of joy thrilled through him as he realized that in his muscles lay at least a force to balk the savage for a little while.

To Stern came back his wrestling lore of the very long ago, the days of Harvard, in the dim, vanished past. He freed his left arm from the gorilla-like grip of Kamrou, and, quick as lightning, got a *jiu-jitsu* stranglehold.

The savage choked, gurgled, writhed; his face grew purple with stagnant blood. Then he leaped, dragging the engineer with him; they fell, rolled, twisted—and Stern's hold was broken.

A great shout rose as Kamrou struggled up and once more seized the American. He raised him like a child, and took a step, two, three, toward the infernal caldron in the rock floor.

Stern, desperate, wrenched his oiled arms clear. A second later they had closed again about the chief's throat—the one point of attack that Stern had chosen for his best.

The barbarian faltered. Grunting, panting, he shook the engineer as a dog shakes a rat, but the hold was secure. Kamrou's great arms wrapped themselves in a formidable "body-scissors" grip; Stern felt the breath squeezed from his body.

Then suddenly the chief's oily heel slipped on the smooth-worn rock, not ten feet from the lip of the bubbling vat—and for the second time both fell.

This time Stern was atop. Over they rolled, once, twice, straining with madness. Stern's thumbs were sunk deep in the throat of the barbarian at either side. As he gouged harder, deeper, he felt the terrific pounding of the chief's jugular. Hot on his own neck panted the choking breath of Kamrou. Oh, could he only hold that grip a minute longer—even a half-minute!

But already his own breath was gone. A buzzing filled his ears; sparkling lights danced, quivering before his eyes. The blood seemed bursting his brain; far off and vague he heard the droning of the flame, the shouts and cries of the great horde of watchers.

A whiff of steam—hot, damp, terrifying—passed across his face, in which the veins were starting from the oily skin. His eyes, half closed, bulged from the sockets. He knew the pit was very close now; dully he heard its steady bubbling.

"If I go—he goes, too!" the engineer swore to himself. *"He'll never have—Beatrice—anyway!"*

Over and over they rolled, their grips tight-locked as steel. Now Kamrou was on top, now Stern. But the chief's muscles were still strong as ever; Stern's already had begun to weaken.

Strive as he might, he could not get another hold, nor could he throw another ounce of power into that he already had. Up, up, slowly up slipped the chief's arms; Stern knew the savage meant to throttle him; and once those long, prehensile fingers reached his throat, good-by!

Then it seemed to him a voice, very far and small, was speaking to him, coolly, impersonally, in a matter-of-fact way as though suggesting an experiment.

Dazed as he was, he recognized that voice—it was the voice of Dr. Harbutt, who once had taught him many a wily trick upon the mat; Harbutt, dead and gone these thousand years or more.

"Why not try the *satsu-da*, Stern?" the voice was saying. "Excellent, at times."

Though Stern's face was black and swollen, eyes shut and mouth all twisted awry in this titanic struggle with the ape-hold of the huge chief, yet the soul within him calmly smiled.

The *satsu-da*—yes, he remembered it now, strongest and best of all the *jiu-jitsu* feats.

And, suddenly loosening his hands from the chief's throat, he clenched his right fist, hard as steel.

A second later the "killing-blow" had fallen on the barbarian's neck, just where the swelling protuberance behind the ear marked the vital spot.

Terrible was the force of that blow, struck for his own life, for the honor of Beatrice, the salvation of the world.

Kamrou gave a strange grunt. His head fell backward. Both eyes closed; the mouth lolled open and a glairy froth began to trickle down.

The frightful grip of the long, hairy arms relaxed. Exhausted, Stern fell prone right on the slippery edge of the boiling pit.

He felt a sudden scalding dash of water, steam and boiling spray; he heard a sudden splash, then a wild, barbarous, long-drawn howling of the massed Folk.

Lying there, spent, gasping, all but dead in the thick steam-drift of the vat, he opened his eyes.

Kamrou was nowhere to be seen.

Seemingly very distant, he heard the copper drums begin to beat once more with feverish haste.

A great, compelling lassitude enveloped him. He knew no more.

CHAPTER XXXVIII

The Sun of Spring

"What altitude now? Can you make-out, Allan?"

"No. The aneroid's only good up to five miles. We must have made two hundred, vertically, since this morning. The way the propeller takes hold and the planes climb in this condensed air is just a miracle!"

"Two passengers at that!" Beatrice answered, leaning back in her seat again. She turned to the patriarch, who, sitting in an extra place in the thoroughly overhauled and newly equipped Pauillac, was holding with nervous hands to the wire stays in front of him.

"Patience, father," she cheered him. "Two hours more—not over three, at the outside—and you shall breathe the upper air again! For the first time the sunlight shall fall upon your face!"

"The sun! The sun! Oh, is it possible?" murmured the aged man. "Verily, I had never thought to live until this day! *The sun!*"

Came silence between these three for a time, while the strong heart of the machine beat steadily; and the engineer, with deft and skilful hand, guided it in wide-swept spirals upward, ever up, up, up, back toward the realms of day, of life, once more; up through the fogs and clouds, away from heat and dark and mystery, toward the clear, pure, refreshing air of heaven again.

At last Stern spoke.

"Well, father," said he, "I never would have thought it; but you were right, after all! They're like so much clay in the potter's hand now, for me. I see I can do with them whatever I will.

"I was afraid some of them might object, after all, to any such proposition. It's one thing for them to accept me as boss down there, and quite another for them to consent to wholesale transplanting, such as we've got under way. But I can't see any possible reason why—with plenty of time and patience—the thing can't be accomplished all right. The main difficulty was their consent; and now we've got *that,* the rest is mere detail and routine work."

"Time and patience," repeated the girl. "Those are our watchwords now, boy. And we've got lots of both, haven't we?"

"Two passengers each trip," the engineer continued, more practical than she, "and three trips a week, at the most, makes six of the Folk landed on the surface weekly. In other words, it'll take—"

"No matter about that now!" interrupted Beatrice. "We've got all the time there is! Even if it takes five years, what of that? What are months or even years in the life-history of the world?"

Stern kept silence again. In his mind he was revolving a hundred vital questions of shelter, feeding, acclimatization for these men, now to be transported from a place of dark and damp and heat to the strange outer regions of the surface-world.

Plainly he saw it would be a task of unparalleled skill, delicacy, and difficult accomplishment; but his spirits rose only the higher as he faced its actual details. After all that he and Beatrice had been through since their wakening in the tower, he feared no failure to solve any questions that now might rise. By care, by keeping the Folk at first in caves, then gradually accustoming them to stronger and brighter light, more air, more cold, he knew he could bridge the gap of centuries in a few years.

Ever adaptable, the human body would respond to changed environments. Patience and time—these would solve all!

And as for this Folk's barbarism, it mattered not. Much better such stock to rebuild from than some mild, supine race of far higher culture. To fight the rough battles of life and re-establishment still ahead, the bold and warlike Merucaans were all that he could wish.

"Imagine *me* as a school-teacher," suddenly exclaimed the girl, laughing: "giving the children A B C and making them read: 'I see the cat'—when there *aren't* any cats nowadays—no tame ones, anyhow! Imagine—"

"*Sh-h-h!*" cautioned Stern. "Don't waste your energies imagining things just yet. There's more than enough real work, food-getting, house-building in caves, and all that, before we ever get to schools. That's years ahead yet, education is!"

Silence again, save for the strong and ceaseless chatter of the engine, that, noisy as a score of mowing machines, flung its indomitable challenge to gravitation out into the fathomless void on every hand.

"Allan! Allan! Oh, a star! Look, look! *A star!*"

The girl was first to see that blest and wondrous thing. Hours had passed, long, weary hours; steadily the air-pressure had sunk, the vapors thinned;

but light had not yet filtered through the mists. And Allan's mind had been sore troubled thereat. He had not thought of the simple reason that they were reaching the surface at night.

But now he knew, and as she cried to him "A star!" he, too, looked and saw it, and as though he had been a little child he felt the sudden tears start to his weary eyes.

"A star!" he answered. "Oh, thank God—a star!"

It faded almost at once, as vapors shrouded it; but soon it came again, and others, many more; and now the first breath of the cool and blessed outer air was wafted to them.

Used as they had been, all these long months—for now the year had turned again and early spring was coming up the world—used to the closed and stifling atmosphere of the Abyss, its chemicalized fogs and mists, the first effect of the pure surface-air was almost intoxicating as they mounted higher, higher, toward the lip of the titanic gulf.

The patriarch, trembling with eagerness and with exhaustion—for he was very old and now his vital forces were all but spent—breathed it only with difficulty. Rapid was his respiration; on either pallid cheek a strange and vivid patch of color showed.

Suddenly he spoke.

"Stars? You see them—really see them?" faltered he. "Oh, for my sight again! Oh, that I might see them once, only once, those wonderful things of ancient story! Then, verily, I should be glad to die!"

Midnight.

Hard-driven now for many hours, heated, yet still running true, the Pauillac had at length made a safe landing on the western verge of the Abyss. Again the voyagers felt solid earth beneath their feet. By the clear starlight Stern had brought the machine to earth on a little plateau, wooded in part, partly bare sand. Numb and stiff, he had alighted from the driver's seat, and had helped both passengers alight.

The girl, radiant with joy, had kissed him full upon the lips; the patriarch had fallen on his knees, and, gathering a handful of the sand—the precious surface of the earth, long fabled among his Folk, long worshipped in his deepest reveries—had clasped it to his thin and heaving breast.

If he had known how to pray he would have worshipped there. But even though his lips were silent, his attitude, his soul were all one vast and heartfelt prayer—prayer to the mother-earth, the unseen stars, the night, the wind upon his brow, the sweet and subtle airs of heaven that enfolded him like a caress.

Stern wrapped the old man in a spare mantle, for the night was chill, then made a crackling fire on the sands. Worn out, they rested, all. Little they said. The beauty and majesty of night now—seen again after long absence—a hundred times more solemn than they had ever known it, kept the two Americans from speech. And the old man, buried in his own thoughts, sat by the fire, burning with a fever of impatient longings for the dawn.

Five o'clock.

Now all across the eastern sky, shrouded as it was with the slow, silent mist-wreaths rising ghostly from the Abyss, delicate pink and pearl-gray tints were spreading, shading above to light blues and to purples of exquisite depth and clarity.

No cloud flecked the sky, the wondrous sky of early spring. Dawn, pure as on the primal day, was climbing from the eastern depths. And, thrilled by that eternal miracle, the man and woman, hand in hand, awaited the full coming of the light.

The patriarch spoke.

"Is the sun nigh arisen now?" he queried in a strange, awed voice, trembling with eagerness and deep emotion. "Is it coming, at last—the sun?"

"It'll be here now before long, father," answered Stern.

"From which direction does it come? Am I facing it?" he asked, with pitiful anxiety.

"You're facing it. The first rays will fall on you. Only be patient. I promise you it shall not fail!"

A pause. Then the aged man, spoke again.

"Remember, oh, my children," said he, with terrible earnestness, "all that I have told you, all that you must know. Remember how to deal with my people. They are as children in your hands. Be very patient, very firm and wise; all will be well.

"Remember my warnings of the Great Vortex, so very far below our sea, the Lanskaarn, and all those other perils of the Abyss whereof I have spoken. Remember, too, all the traditions of the Cave of Records. Some day, when all else is accomplished, you may find that cave. I have told you everything I know of its location. Seek it some day, and find the history of the dead, buried past, from the time of the great catastrophe to the final migration when my ancestors sought the lower sea."

Another silence. All three were too deeply moved for any speech. And ever mounting higher, brighter and more clear, dawn flung its glories wide across the sky.

"Help me that I may stand, to greet the day!" at last the patriarch said. "I cannot rise, alone."

Stern and the girl, each taking an arm, got him to his feet. He stood there facing the east, priestlike in venerable and solemn worship of the coming sun.

"Give me each a hand, my children," he commanded. In Stern's hand, strong, corded, toil-worn, he laid the girl's.

"Thus do I give you each to each," said he. "Thus do I make you one!"

Stern drew Beatrice into his arms. Blind though the old man was, he sensed the act, and smiled. A great and holy peace had shrouded him.

"Only that I may feel the sun upon my face!" breathed he.

All at once a thinning cloud-haze let the light glow through.

Beatrice looked at Stern. He shook his head.

"Not yet," he answered.

Swiftly uprose the sun. The morning wind dispelled the shrouding vapors.

"Oh, what is this warmth?" exclaimed the patriarch, trembling violently. "What is this warmth, this glow upon my face? This life, this—"

Out toward the east he stretched both hands. Instinctively the priestlike worship of the sun, old when the world was still in infancy, surged back to him again after the long, lost centuries of darkness and oblivion.

"The sun! *The sun!*" he cried, his voice triumphant as a trumpet-call. Tears coursed from his blind eyes; but on his lips a smile of joy unutterable was set.

"The sun! *At last! The—*"

Stern caught his feeble body as he fell.

Down on the sands they laid him. To the stilled heart Stern laid his ear.

Tears were in his eyes, too, and in the girl's, as Stern shook his head, silently.

Up over the time-worn, the venerable, the kindly face they drew the mantle, but not before each had reverently kissed the wrinkled forehead.

"Better thus," whispered the engineer. "Far better, every way. He had his wish; he felt the sunshine on his face; his outgoing spirit must be mingled with that worshipped light and air and sky—with dawn—with springtime—"

"With life itself!" said Beatrice.

And through her tears she smiled, while higher rose the warm, life-giving sun of spring.

Book III
The Afterglow

CHAPTER I

DEATH, LIFE, AND LOVE

LIFE! Life again, and light, the sun and the fresh winds of heaven, the perfect azure of a June sky, the perfume of the passionate red blooms along the lips of the chasm, the full-throated song of hidden birds within the wood to eastward—life, beauty, love—such, the sunrise hour when Allan and the girl once more stood side by side in the outer world, delivered from the perils of the black Abyss.

Hardly more real than a disordered nightmare now, the terrible fall into those depths, the captivity among the white barbarians, the battles and the ghastly scenes of war, the labors, the perilous escape.

All seemed to fall and fade away from these two lovers, all save their joy in life and in each other, their longing for the inevitable greater passion, pain and joy, their clear-eyed outlook into the vast and limitless possibilities of the future, their future and the world's.

And as they stood there, hand in hand beside the body of the fallen patriarch—he whose soul had passed in peace, even at the moment of his life's fulfilment, his knowledge of the sun—awe overcame them both. With a new tenderness, mingled with reverent adoration, Stern drew the girl once more to him.

Her face turned up to his and her arms tightened about his neck. He kissed her brow beneath the parted masses of her wondrous hair. His lips rested a moment on her eyes; and then his mouth sought hers and burned its passion into her very soul.

Suddenly she pushed him back, panting. She had gone white; she trembled in his clasp.

"Oh, your kiss—oh, Allan, what is this I feel?—it seems to choke me!" she gasped, clutching her full bosom where her heart leaped like a pris-

oned creature. "Your kiss—it is so different now! No, no—not again—
not yet!"

He released her, for he, too was shaking in the grip of new, fierce passions.

"Forgive me!" he whispered. "I—I forgot myself, a moment. Not yet—
no, not yet. You're right, Beatrice. A thousand things are pressing to be
done. And love—must wait!"

He clenched his fists and strode to the edge of the chasm, where, for a
while, he stood alone and silent, gazing far down and away, mastering himself, striving to get himself in leash once more.

Then suddenly he turned and smiled.

"Come, Beta," said he. "All this must be forgotten. Let's get to work. The
whole world's waiting for us, for our labor. It's eager for our toil!"

She nodded. In her eyes the fire had died, and now only the light of comradeship and trust and hope glowed once again.

"Allan?"

"Yes?"

"Our first duty—" She gestured toward the body of the patriarch, nobly
still beneath the rough folds of the mantle they had drawn over it.

He understood.

"Yes," murmured he. "And his grave shall be for all the future ages a
place of pilgrimage and solemn thought. Where first, one of lost Folk issued again into the world and where he died, this shall be a monument of
the new time now coming to its birth.

"His grave shall lie here on this height, where the first sun shall each day
for ages fall upon it, supreme in its deep symbolism. Forever it shall be a
memorial, not of death, but life, of liberty, of hope!"

They kept a moment's silence, then Stern added.

"So now, to work!" From the biplane he fetched the ax. With this he cut
and trimmed a branch from a near-by fir. He sharpened it to a flat blade
three or four inches across. In the deep red sand along the edge of the Abyss
he set to work, scooping the patriarch's grave.

In silence Beatrice took the ax and also labored, throwing the sand
away. Together, in an hour, they had dug a trench sufficiently deep and
wide.

"This must do, for now," said Stern, looking up at last. "Some time he
shall have fitting burial, but for the present we can do no more. Let us now

commit his body to the earth, the Great Mother which created and which waits always to give everlasting sleep, peace, rest."

Together, silently, they bore him to the grave, still wrapped in the cloak which now had become his shroud. Once more they gazed upon the noble face of him they had grown to love in the long weeks of the Abyss, when only he had understood them or seemed near.

"What is this, Allan?" asked the girl, touching a fine chain of gold about the patriarch's neck, till now unnoticed.

Allan drew at the chain, and a small golden cylinder was revealed, curiously carven. Its lightness told him it was hollow.

"Some treasure of his, I imagine," judged he.

"Some record, perhaps? Oughtn't we to look?"

He thought a moment in silence, then detached the chain.

"Yes," said he. "It can't help him now. It may help *us*. He himself would have wanted us to have it."

And into the pocket of his rough, brown cassock, woven of the weed-fiber of the dark sea, he slid the chain and golden cylinder.

A final kiss they gave the patriarch, each; then, carefully wrapping his face so that no smallest particle of sand should come in contact with it, stood up. At each other they gazed, understandingly.

"Flowers? Some kind of service?" asked the girl.

"Yes. All we can do for him will be too little!"

Together they brought armfuls of the brilliant crimson and purple blooms along the edge of the sands, where forest and barren irregularly met; and with these, fir and spruce boughs, the longer to keep his grave freshly green.

All about him they heaped the blossoms. The patriarch lay at rest among beauties he never had beheld, colors and fragrances that to him had been but dim traditions of antiquity.

"I can't preach," said Stern. "I'm not that kind, anyway, and in this new world all that sort of thing is out of place. Let's just say good-by, as to a friend gone on a long, long journey."

Beatrice could no longer keep back her grief. Kneeling beside the grave, she arranged the flowers and the evergreens, on which her tears fell shining.

"Dust unto dust!" Stern said. "To you, oh Mother Nature, we give back the body of this friend, your son. May the breeze blow gently here, the sun shine warm, and the birds forever sing his requiem. And may those who shall come after us, when we too sleep, remember that in him we had a friend, without whom the world never again could have hoped for any new birth, any life! To him we say good-by—eternally! Dust unto dust; good-by!"

"Good-by!" whispered the girl. Then, greatly overcome, she arose and walked away.

Stern, with his naked hands, filled the shallow grave and, this done, rolled three large boulders onto it, to protect it from the prowling beasts of the wild.

Beatrice returned. They strewed more flowers and green boughs, and in silence stood a while, gazing at the lowly bed of their one friend on earth.

Suddenly Stern took her hand and drew her toward him.

"Come, come, Beatrice," said he, "he is not dead. He still lives in our memories. His body, aged and full of pain, is gone, but his spirit still survives in us—that indomitable sold which, buried alive in blindness and the dark, still strove to keep alive the knowledge and traditions of the upper world, hopes of attaining it, and visions of a better time to be!

"Was ever greater human courage, faith or strength? Let us not grieve. Let us rather go away strengthened and inspired by this wonderful life that has just passed. In us, let all his hopes and aspirations come to reality.

"His death was happy. It was as he wished it, Beatrice, for his one great ambition was fully granted—to know the reality of the upper world, the winds of heaven and the sun! Impossible for him to have survived the great change. Death was inevitable and right. He wanted rest, and rest is his, at last.

"We must be true to all he thought us, you and I—to all he believed us, even demigods! He shall inspire and enlighten us, O my love; and with his memory to guide us, faith and fortitude shall not be lacking.

"Now, we must go. Work waits for us. Everything is yet to be planned and done. The world and its redemption lie before us. Come!"

He led the girl away. As by mutual understanding they returned to where the biplane lay, symbol of their conquest of nature, epitome of hopes.

Near it, on the edge of the Abyss, they rested, hand in hand. In silence they sat thinking, for a space. And ever higher and more warmly burned the sun; the breeze of June was sweet to them, long-used to fogs and damp and dark; the boundless flood of light across the azure thrilled them with aspiration and with joy.

Life had begun again for them and for the world, life, even there in the presence of death. Life was continuing, developing, expanding—life and its immortal sister, Love!

CHAPTER II

EASTWARD HO!

PRACTICAL matters now for a time thrust introspection, dreams and sentiment aside. The morning was already half spent, and in spite of sorrow, hunger had begun to assert itself; for since time was, no two such absolutely vigorous and healthy humans had ever set foot on earth as Beatrice and Allan.

The man gathered brush and dry-kye and proceeded to make a fire, not far from the precipice, but well out of sight of the patriarch's grave. He fetched a generous heap of wood from the neighboring forest, and presently a snapping blaze flung its smoke-banner down the breeze.

Soon after Beatrice had raided the supplies on board the Pauillac—fish, edible seaweed, and the eggs of the strange birds of the Abyss—and with the skill and speed of long experience was getting an excellent meal. Allan meantime brought water from a spring near by. And the two ate in silence, cross-legged on the warm, dry sand.

"What first, now?" queried the man, when they were satisfied. "I've been thinking of about fifteen hundred separate things to tackle, each one more important than all the others put together. How are we going to begin again? That's the question!"

She drew from her warm bosom the golden cylinder and chain.

"Before we make any move at all," she answered, "I think we ought to see what's in this record—if it *is* a record. Don't you?"

"By Jove, you're right! Shall I open it for you?"

But already the massively chased top lay unscrewed in her hand. Within the cylinder a parchment roll appeared.

A moment later she had spread it on her knee, taking care not to tear the ancient, crackling skin whereon faint lines of writing showed.

Stern bent forward, eager and breathless. The girl, too, gazed with anxious eyes at the dim script, all but illegible with age and wear.

"You're right, Allan," said she. "This *is* some kind of record, some direction as to the final history of the few survivors after the great catastrophe. Oh! Look, Allan—it's fading already in the sunlight. Quick, read it quick, or we shall lose it all!"

Only too true. The dim lines, perhaps fifteen hundred years old, certainly never exposed to sunlight since more than a thousand, were already growing weaker; and the parchment, too, seemed crumbling into dust. Its edges, where her fingers held it, already were breaking away into a fine, impalpable powder.

"Quick, Allan! Quick!"

Together they read the clumsy scrawl, their eyes leaping along the lines, striving to grasp the meaning ere it were too late.

TO ANY WHO AT ANY TIME MAY EVER REVISIT THE UPPER WORLD: Be it known that two records have been left covering our history from the time of the cataclysm in 1920 till we entered the Chasm in 1957. One is in the Great Cave in Medicine Bow Range, Colorado, near the ruins of Dexter. Exact location, 106 degrees, 11 minutes, 3 seconds west; 40 degrees, 22 minutes, 6 seconds north. Record is in left, or northern branch of Cave, 327 yards from mouth, on south wall, 4 feet 6 inches from floor. The other—

"Where? Where?" cried Beatrice. A portion of the record was gone; it had crumbled even as they read.

"Easy does it, girl! Don't get excited," Allan cautioned, but his face was pale and his hand trembled as he sought to steady and protect the parchment from the breeze.

Together they pieced out a few of the remaining words, for now the writing was but a pale blur, momently becoming dimmer and more dim.

. . . Cathedral on . . . known as Storm King . . . River . . . crypt under . . . this was agreed on . . . never returned but may possibly . . . signed by us on this 12th day . . .

They could read no more, for now the record was but a disintegrating shell in the girl's hands, and even as they looked the last of the writing vanished, as breath evaporates from a widow-pane.

Allan whirled toward the fire, snatched out a still-glowing stick, and in the sand traced figures.

"Quick! What was that? 106-11-3, West—Forty—"

"Forty, 22, north," she prompted.

"How many seconds? You remember?"

"No." Slowly she shook her head. "Five, wasn't it?"

Eagerly he peered at the record, but every trace was gone.

"Well, no matter about the seconds," he judged. "I'll enter these data on our diary, in the Pauillac, anyhow. We can remember the ruins of Dexter and Medicine Bow Range; also the cathedral on Storm King. Put the fragments of the parchment back into the case, Beta. Maybe we can yet preserve them, and by some chemical means or other bring out the writing again. As it is, I guess we've got the most important facts; enough to go on, at any rate."

She replaced the crumbled record in the golden cylinder and once more screwed on the cap. Allan got up and walked to the aeroplane, where, among their scanty effects, was the brief diary and set of notes he had been keeping since the great battle with the Lanskaarn.

Writing on his fish-skin tablets, with his bone stylus dipped in his little stone jar of cuttle-fish ink, he carefully recorded the geographical location. Then he went back to Beatrice, who still sat in the midmorning sunlight by the fire, very beautiful and dear to him.

"If we can find those records, we'll have made a long step toward solving the problem of how to handle the Folk. They aren't exactly what one would call an amenable tribe, at best. We need their history, even the little of it that the records must contain, for surely there must be names and events in them of great value in our work of trying to bring these people to the surface and recivilize them."

"Well, what's to hinder our getting the records now?" she asked seriously, with wonder in her gray and level gaze.

"*That,* for one thing!"

He gestured at the Abyss.

"It's a good six or seven hundred miles wide, and we already know how deep it is. I don't think we want to risk trying to cross it again and running out of fuel *en route!* Volplaning down to the village is quite a different proposition from a straight-away flight across!"

She sat pensive a moment.

"There must be some way around," said she at last. "Otherwise a party of survivors couldn't have set out for Storm King on the Hudson to deposit a set of records there!"

"That's so, too. But—remember? 'Never returned.' I figure it this way: A party of the survivors probably started for New York, exploring. The big, concrete cathedral on Storm King—it was new in 1916, you remember— was known the country over as the most massive piece of architecture this side of the pyramids. They must have planned to leave one set of records there, in case the east, too, was devastated. Well—"

"Do you suppose they succeeded?"

"No telling. At any rate, there's a chance of it. And as for this Rocky Mountain cache, that's manifestly out of the question, for now,"

"So then?" she queried eagerly.

"So then our job is to strike for Storm King. Incidentally we can revisit Hope Villa, our bungalow on the banks of the Hudson. It's been a year since we left it, almost—ten months, at any rate. Gad! What marvels and miracles have happened since then, Beta—what perils, what escapes! Wouldn't you like to see our little nest again? We could rest up and plan and strengthen ourselves for the greater tasks ahead. And then—"

He paused, a change upon his face, his eyes lighting with a sudden glow. She saw and understood; and her breast rose with sudden keen emotion.

"You mean," whispered she, "in our own home?"

"Where better?"

She paled as, kneeling beside her, he flung a powerful arm about her, and pulled her to him, breathing heavily.

"Don't! Don't!" she forbade. "No, no, Allan—there's so much work to do—you mustn't!"

To her a vision rose of dream-children—strong sons and daughters yet unborn. Their eyes seemed smiling, their fingers closing on hers. Cloud-like, yet very real, they beckoned her, and in her stirred the call of motherhood—of life to be. Her heart-strings echoed to that harmony; it seemed already as though a tiny head, downy-soft, was nestling in her bosom, while eager lips quested, quested.

"No, Allan! No!"

Almost fiercely she flung him back and stood up.

"Come!" said she. "Let us start at once. Nothing remains for us to do here. Let us go—home!"

An hour later the Pauillac spiralled far aloft, above the edge of the Abyss, then swept into its eastward tangent, and in swift, droning flight rushed toward the longed-for place of dreams, of rest, of love.

Before them stretched infinities of labor and tremendous struggle; but for a little space they knew they now were free for this, the consummation of their dreams, of all their hopes, their happiness, their joy.

CHAPTER III

Catastrophe!

Toward five o'clock next afternoon, from the swooping back of the air-dragon they sighted a far blue ribbon winding among wooded heights, and knew Hudson once more lay before them.

The girl's heart leaped for joy at thought of once again seeing Hope Villa, the beach, the garden, the sun-dial—all the thousand and one little happy and pleasant things that, made by them in the heart of the vast wilderness, had brought them such intimate and unforgetable delight.

"There it is, Allan!" cried she, pointing. "There's the river again. We'll soon be home now—home again!"

He smiled and nodded, watchful at the wheel, and swung the biplane a little to southward, in the direction where he judged the bungalow must lie.

Weary they both were, yet full of life and strength. The trip from the chasm had been tedious, merely a long succession of hours in the rushing air, with unbroken forest, hills, lakes, rivers, and ever more forest steadily rolling away to westward like a vast carpet a thousand feet below.

No sign of man, no life, no gap in nature's all-embracing sway. Even the occasional heap of ruins marking the grave of some forgotten city served only to intensify the old half-terror they had felt, when flying for the first time, at thought of the tremendous desolation of the world.

The shining plain of Lake Erie had served the first day as a landmark to keep them true to their course.

That night they had stopped at the ruins of Buffalo, where they had camped in the open, and where next morning Stern had fully replenished his fuel-tanks with the usual supplies of alcohol from the débris of two or three large drugstores.

From Buffalo eastward, over almost the same course along which the hurricane of ten months ago had driven them, battling at random with the gale, they steered by the compass. Toward mid-morning they saw a thin line of smoke arising in the far north, answered by still another on the hills beyond, but to these signs they gave no heed.

Already they had seen and scorned them during their first stay at the bungalow. They felt that nothing more was to be seriously feared from such survivors of the Horde as had escaped the great Battle of the Tower—a year and a half previously.

"Those chaps won't bother us again; I'm sure of that!" said Allan, nodding toward the smoke-columns that rose, lazily blue, on the horizon. "The scare we threw into them in Madison Forest will last them *one* while!"

Still in this confident, defiant mood it was that they sighted the river again and watched it rapidly broaden as the Pauillac, in a long series of flat arcs, spurned the June air and whirled them onward toward their goal.

Nearer the Hudson drew, and nearer still; and now its untroubled azure, calm save for a few cat's-paws of breeze that idled on the surface, stretched almost beneath them in their rapid flight.

"We're still a little too far north, I see," the man judged, and swept the biplane round to southward.

The ruins of Newburgh lay presently upon their right. Soon after the crumbled walls of West Point's pride slid past in silence, save for the chatter of the engines, the whirling roar of the propeller-blades' vast energy.

No boat now vexed the flood. Upon its bosom neither steam nor sail now plowed a furrow. Along the banks no speeding train flung its smoke-pennant to the wind. Primeval silence, universal calm, wrapped all things.

Beatrice shuddered slightly. Now that they were nearing "home" the desolation seemed more appalling.

"Oh, Allan, is it possible all this will ever be peopled again—*alive?*"

"Certain to be! Once we get those records and begin transplanting the Merucaans, the rest will be only a matter of time!"

She made no answer, but in her eyes shone pride that he could know such visions, have such faith.

Already they recognized the ruins of Nyack, and beyond them the point in the river behind which, they knew, lay Hope Villa, nestling in its gardens, its little sphere of cultivation hewn from the very heart of the dense wilderness.

Allan slackened speed, crossed to the eastern bank, and jockeyed for a safe landing.

The point slipped backward and away. There, right ahead, they caught a glimpse of the long white beach where they had fished and bathed and built their boat-house, and whence in their little yawl they had ten months before started on their trip of exploration—a trip destined to end so strangely in the Abyss.

"Home! Home!" cried Beta, the quick tears starting to her lids. "Oh, home again!"

Already the great plane was swooping downward toward the beach, hardly a mile away, when a harsh shout escaped the man.

"Look! Canoes! My God—*what*—"

As the drive of the Pauillac opened up the concave of the sand and brought its whole length to view, Stern and the girl suddenly became aware of trouble.

There, strung along the beach irregularly, they all at once made out ten, twenty, thirty boats. Still afar, they could see these were the same rough bancas such as they had seen after the battle—bancas in one of which they two had escaped up-river!

"*Boats! The Horde again!*"

Even as he shouted a tiny, black, misshapen little figure ran crouching out onto the sand. Another followed and a third, and now a dozen showed there, very distinct and hideous, upon the white crescent.

Stern's heart went sick within him. A terrible rage welled up—a hate such as he had never believed possible to feel.

Wild imprecations struggled to be voiced. He snapped his lips together in a thin line, his eyes narrowed, and his face went gray.

"The infernal little beasts!" he gritted. "Tried to trap us in the tower—cut our boat loose afterward—and now invading us! Don't know when they're licked, the swine!"

Beatrice had lost her color now. Milk-white her face was; her eyes grew wide with terror; she strove to speak, but could not.

Her hand went out in a wild, repelling gesture, as though by the very power of her love for home she could protect it now against the incursion of these foul, distorted, inhuman little monsters.

Stern acted quickly. He had been about to cut off power and coast for the beach; but now he veered suddenly to eastward again, rotated the rising-plane, and brought the Pauillac up at a sharp tilt. Banking, he advanced the spark a notch; the engine shrilled a half-tone higher, and with increased speed the aero lifted them bravely in a long and rising swoop.

He snatched his automatic from its holster on his hip and as the plane swept past the beach, down-stream, let fly a spatter of steel-jacketed souvenirs at the fast-thickening pack on the sand.

Far up to the girl and him, half heard through the clatter of the motors, they sensed a thin, defiant, barbarous yell—a yapping chorus, bestial and horrible.

Again Stern fired.

He could see quick spurts of water jet up along the edge of the sand, and one of the creatures fell, but this was only a chance shot.

At that distance, firing from a swift-skimming plane, he knew he could do no execution, and with a curse slid the pistol back again into its place.

"Oh, for a dirigible and a few Pulverite bombs, same as we had in the tower!" he wished. "I'd clean the blighters out mighty quick!"

But now Beatrice was pointing, with a cry of dismay, down, away at the bungalow itself, which had for a moment become visible at the far end of the clearing as the Pauillac scudded past.

Even as Stern thought: "Odd, but they're not afraid of us—a flying-machine means nothing to them, does not terrify them as it would human savages. They're too debased even to feel fear!"—even as this thought crossed his brain he, too, saw the terrible thing that the girl had cried out at sight of.

"My God!" he shouted. "This—this is too much!"

All about the bungalow, their home, the scene of such happy hours, so many dreams and hopes, such heart-enthralling labors, hundreds of the Horde were swarming.

Like vicious parasites attacking prey, they overran the garden, the grounds, even the house itself.

As in a flash, Stern knew all his work of months must be undone—the fruit-trees he had rescued from the forest be cut down or broken, the bulbs and roots in the garden uptorn, even the hedges and fences trampled flat.

Worse still, the bungalow was being destroyed! Rather, its contents, since the concrete walls defied the venomous troop.

They knew, at any rate, the use of fire, and not so swiftly skimmed the Pauillac as to prevent both Stern and Beatrice seeing a thin but ominous thread of smoke out-curling on the June air from one of the living-room windows.

With an imprecation of unutterable hate and rage, yet impotent to stay the ravishment of Hope Villa, Stern brought the machine round in a long spiral.

For a moment the wild, suicidal idea possessed him to land on the beach, after all, and charge the little slate-blue devils who had evidently piled all the furnishings together in the bungalow and were now burning them.

He longed for slaughter now; he lusted blood—the blood of the Anthropoid pack which from the beginning had hung upon his flank and been as a thorn unto his flesh.

He seemed to feel the joy of rushing them, an automatic in each hand spitting death, just as he had mown down the Lanskaarn in the Battle of the Wall, down below in the Abyss. Even though he knew the inevitable end—a poisoned spear-thrust, a wound with one of those terribly envenomed arrows—he felt no fear.

Revenge! If he could only feel its sweetness, death had no terrors.

Common sense instantly sobered him and dispelled these vain ideas. The bungalow, after all, was not vital to his future or the girl's. Barring the set of encyclopedias on metal plates, everything else could be replaced with sufficient labor. Only a madman would risk a fight with such a Horde in company with a woman.

Not now were he and Beatrice entrenched in a strong tower, with terrible explosives. Now they were in the open, armed only with revolvers. For the present there was no redress.

"Beta," cried he, "we're up against it this time for fair—and we can't hit back!"

"Our bungalow! Our precious home!"

"I know." He saw that she was crying: "It's a rotten shame and all that, but it isn't fatal."

He brought the Pauillac down-wind again, coasting high over the bungalow, whence smoke now issued ever more and more thickly.

"We're simply hamstrung this time, that's all. Where those devils have come from and how many there may be, God knows. Thousands, perhaps;

the woods may be full of 'em. It's lucky for us they didn't attack while we were there!

"Now—well, the only thing to do is let 'em have their way for the present. Eventually—"

"Oh, can't we *ever* get rid of the horrid little beasts for good?"

"We can and will!" He spoke very grimly, soaring the machine still higher over the river and once more coming round above the upper end of the beach. "One of these days there's got to be a final reckoning, but not yet!"

"So it's good-by to Hope Villa, Allan? There's no way?"

"It's good-by. Humanly speaking, none."

"Couldn't we land, blockade ourselves in the boat-house, and—"

Her eyes sparkled with the boldness of the plan—its peril, its possibilities. But Allan only shook his head.

"And expose the Pauillac on the beach?" he asked. "One good swing with a war-club into the motor and then a week's siege and slow starvation, with a final rush—interesting, but not practical, little girl. No, no; the better part of valor is to recognize *force majeure* and *wait!* Remember what we've said already? '*Je recule pour mieux sauter?*' Wait till we get a fresh start on these hell-hounds; we'll jump 'em far enough!"

The bungalow now lay behind. The whole clearing seemed alive with the little blue demons, like vermin crawling everywhere. Thicker and thicker now the smoke was pouring upward. The scene was one of utter desolation.

Then suddenly it faded. The plane had borne its riders onward and away from the range of vision. Again only dense forest lay below, while to eastward sparkled the broad reach where, in the first days of their happiness at Hope Villa, the girl and Allan had fished and bathed.

Her tears were unrestrained at last; but Allan, steadying the wheel with one hand, drew an arm about her and kissed and comforted her.

"There, there, little girl! The world's not ended yet, even if they *have* burned up our home-made mission furniture! Come, Beatrice, no tears—we've other things to think of now!"

"Where away, since our home's gone?" she queried pitifully.

"Where away? Why, Storm King, of course! And the cathedral and the records, and—*and*—"

CHAPTER IV

"To-Morrow is Our Wedding-Day"

Purple and gold the light of that dying day still glowed across the western sky when the stanch old Pauillac, heated yet throbbing with power, skimmed the last league and swung the last great bend of the river that hid old Storm King from the wanderers' eager sight.

Stern's eyes brightened at vision of that vast, rugged headland, forest-clad and superb in the approaching twilight. Beatrice, weary now and spent—for the long journeys, the excitements and griefs of the day had worn her down despite her strength—paled a little and grew pensive as the massive structure of the cathedral loomed against the sky-line.

What thoughts were hers now that the goal lay near—what longings, fears and hopes, what exultation and what pain? She shivered slightly; but perhaps the evening coolness at that height had pierced her cloak. Her hands clasped tightly, she tried to smile but could not.

Allan could notice nothing of all this. His gaze was anxiously bent on the earth below, to find a landing for the great machine. He skimmed the broad brow of the mountain, hardly a hundred feet above the spires of the massive concrete pile that still reared itself steadfastly upon the height facing the east.

All about it the dense unbroken forest spread impenetrable to the eye. Below the bold breast of the cliff a narrow strip of beach appeared.

"Hard job to land, that's one sure thing!" exclaimed the man, peering at the inhospitable contours of the land. "No show to make it on top of the mountain, and if we take the beach it means a most tremendous climb up the cliff or through the forest on the flank. Here *is* a situation, Beatrice! Now—ah—see there? Look! that barren ridge to westward!"

Half a mile back from the river on the western slope of the highlands, a spur of Storm King stretched water-worn and bare, a sandy spit dotted only sparsely with scrub-pine.

"It's that, or nothing!" cried the man, banking in a wide sweep.

"Can you make it? Even the clearest space at this end is terribly short!"

Allan laughed and cut off power. In the old days not for ten thousand dollars would he have tried so ticklish a descent, but now his mettle was of sterner stuff and his skill with the machine developed to a point where man and biplane seemed almost one organism.

With a swift rush the Pauillac coasted down. He checked her at precisely the right moment, as the sand seemed whirling up to meet them, swerved to dodge a fire-blasted trunk, and with a shout took the earth.

The plane bounced, creaked, skidded on the long runners he had fitted to her, and with a lurch came to rest not ten yards from an ugly stump dead ahead.

"Made it, by Heaven!" he exulted. "But a few feet more and it wouldn't have been—well, no matter. We're here, anyhow. Now, supper and a good sleep. And tomorrow, the cathedral!"

He helped the girl alight, for she was cramped and stiff. Presently their camp-fire cheered the down-drawing gloom, as so many other times in such strange places. And before long their evening meal was in course of preparation, close by a great glacial boulder at the edge of the sand-barren.

In good comradeship they ate, then wheeled the biplane over to the rock, and under the shelter of its wide-spreading wings made their camp for the night. An hour or so they sat talking of many things—their escape from the Abyss, the patriarch's death, their trip east again, the loss of their little home, their plans, their hopes, their work.

Beatrice seemed to grieve more than Stern over the destruction of the bungalow. So much of her woman's heart had gone into the making of that nest, so many thoughts had centered on a return to it once more, that now when it lay in ruins through the spiteful mischief of the Horde, she found sorrow knocking insistently at the gates of her soul. But Allan comforted her as best he might.

"Never you mind, little girl!" said he bravely. "It's only an incident, after all. A year from now another and a still more beautiful home will shelter us in some more secure location. And there'll be human companionship, too, about us. In a year many of the Folk will have been brought from the depths. In a year miracles may happen—even the greatest one of all!"

Her eyes met his a moment by the ruddy fire-glow and held true.

"Yes," answered she, "even the greatest in the world!"

A sudden tenderness swept over him at thought of all that had been and was still to be, at sight of this woman's well-loved face irradiated by the leaping blaze—her face now just a little wan with long fatigues and sad as though with realization, with some compelling inner sense of vast, impending responsibilities.

He gathered her in his strong arms, he drew her yielding body close, and kissed her very gently.

"To-morrow!" he whispered. "Do you realize it?"

"To-morrow," she made answer, her breath mingling with his. "To-morrow, Allan—one page of life forever closed, another opened. Oh, may it be for good—may we be very strong and very wise!"

Neither spoke for the space of a few heart-beats, while the wind made a vague, melancholy music in the sentinel tree-tops and the snapping sparks danced upward by the rock.

"Life, all life—just dancing sparks—then gone!" said Beatrice slowly. "And yet—yet it is good to have lived, Allan. Good to have lighted the black mystery of the universe, formless and endless and inscrutable, by even so brief a flicker!"

"Is it my little pessimist to-night?" he asked. "Too tired, that's all. In the morning things will look different. You must smile, then, Beta, and not think of formless mystery or—or anything sad at all. For to-morrow is our wedding-day."

He felt her catch her breath and tremble just a bit.

"Yes, I know. Our wedding-day, Allan. Surely the strangest since time began. No friends, no gifts, no witnesses, no minister, no—"

"There, there!" he interrupted, smiling. "How can my little girl be so wrong-headed? Friends? Why, everything's our friend! All nature is our friend—the whole life-process is our friend and ally! Gifts? What need have we of gifts? Aren't you my gift, surely the best gift that a man ever had since the beginning of all things? Am I not yours?

"Minister? Priest? We need none! The world-to-be shall have got far away from such, far beyond its fairy-tale stage, its weaknesses and fears of the Unknown, which alone explain their existence. Here on Storm King, under the arches of the old cathedral our clasped hands, our mutual words of love and trust and honor—these shall suffice. The river and the winds and forest, the sunlight and the sky, the whole infinite expanse of Nature herself shall be our priest and witnesses. And never has a wedding been so true, so solemn and so holy as yours and mine shall be. For you are mine, my Beatrice, and I am yours—forever!"

A little silence, while the flames leaped higher and the shadows deepened in the dim aisles of the fir-forest all about them. In the vast canopy of evening sky clustering star-points had begun to shimmer.

Redly the camp-fire lighted man and woman there alone together in the wild. For them there was no sense of isolation nor any loneliness. She was his world now, and he hers.

Up into his eyes she looked fairly and bravely, and her full lips smiled.

"Forgive me, Allan!" she whispered. "It was only a mood, that's all. It's passed now—it won't come back. Only forgive me, boy!"

"My dear, brave girl!" he murmured, smoothing the thick hair back from her brow. "Never complaining, never repining, never afraid!"

Their lips met again and for a time the girl's heart throbbed on his.

Afar a wolf's weird, tremulous call drifted down-wind. An owl, disturbed in its nocturnal quest, hooted upon the slope above to eastward; and across the darkening sky reeled an unsteady bat, far larger than in the old days when there were cities on the earth and ships upon the sea.

The fire burned low. Allan arose and flung fresh wood upon it, while sheaves of winking light gyrated upward through the air. Then he returned to Beatrice and wrapped her in his cloak.

And for a long, long time they both talked of many things—intimate, solemn, wondrous things—together in the night.

And the morrow was to be their wedding-day.

CHAPTER V

THE SEARCH FOR THE RECORDS

MORNING found them early astir, to greet the glory of June sunlight over the shoulder of Storm King. A perfect morning, if ever any one was perfect since the world began—soft airs stirring in the forest, golden robins' full-throated song, the melody of the scarlet tropic birds they had named "fire-birds" for want of any more descriptive title, the chatter of gray squirrels on the branches overhead, all blent, under a sky of wondrous azure, to tell them of life, full and abundant, joyous and kind.

Two of the squirrels had to die, for breakfast, which Beta cooked while Allan quested the edges of the wood for the ever-present berries. They drank from a fern-embowered spring a hundred yards or so to south of their camp in the forest, and felt the vigorous tides of life throb hotly through their splendid bodies.

Allan got together the few simple implements at their disposal for the expedition—his ax, a torch made of the brown weed of the Abyss, oil-soaked and bound with wire that fastened it to a metal handle, and a skin bag of the rude matches he had manufactured in the village of the Folk.

"Now then, *en marche!*" said he at length. "The old cathedral and the records are awaiting a morning call from us—and there are all the wedding preparations to make as well. We've got no time to lose!"

She laughed happily with a blush and gave him her hand.

"Lead on, Sir Knight!" she jested. "I'm yours by right of capture and conquest, as in the good old days!"

"The good new days will have better and higher standards," he answered gravely. "To-day, one age is closed, another opened for all time."

Hand in hand they ascended the barren spur to eastward, and presently reached the outposts of the forest that rose in close-ranked majesty over the brow of Storm King.

The going proved hard, for with the warmer climate that now favored the country, undergrowth had sprung up far more luxuriantly than in the days of the old-time civilization; but Stern and Beatrice were used to labor, and together—he ahead to break or cut a path—they struggled through the wood.

Half an hour's climb brought them to their first dim sight of the massive towers of the cathedral, rising beyond the tangle of trees, majestic in the morning sun.

Soon after they had made their way close up to the huge, lichen-crusted walls, and in the shadow of the gigantic pile slowly explored round to the vast portals facing eastward over the Hudson.

"Wonderful work, magnificent proportions and design," Stern commented, as they stopped at last on the broad, débris-littered steps and drew breath. "Brick and stone have long since perished. Even steel has crumbled. But concrete seems eternal. Why, the building's practically intact even to-day, after ten centuries of absolute abandonment. A week's work with a force of men would quite restore it. The damage it's suffered is absolutely insignificant. Concrete. A lesson to be learned, is it not, in our rebuilding of the world?"

The mighty temple stood, in fact, almost as men had left it in the long ago, when the breath of annihilation had swept a withering blast over the face of the earth. The broad grounds and driveways that had led up to the entrance had, of course, long since absolutely vanished under rank growths.

Grass flourished in the gutters and on the Gothic finials; the gargoyles were bearded with vines and fern-clusters; the flying buttresses and mullions stood green with moss; and in the vegetable mold that had for centuries accumulated on the steps and in the vestibule—for the oaken doors had crumbled to powder—many a bright-flowered plant raised its blossoms to the sun.

The tall memorial windows and the great rose-window in the eastern façade had long since been shattered out of their frames by hail and tempest. But the main body of the cathedral seemed yet as massively intact as when the master-builders of the twentieth century had taken down the last scaffold, and when the gigantic organ had first pealed its *"Laus Deo"* through the vaulted apse.

Together they entered the vast silent space, and—awed despite themselves—gazed in wonder at the beauties of this, the most magnificent temple ever built in the western hemisphere.

The marble floor was covered now with windrows of dead leaves and pine-spills, and with the litter from myriads of birds'-nests that sheltered themselves on achitraves and galleries, and on the lofty capitals of the fluted pillars which rose, vistalike, a hundred feet above the clearstory, spraying out into a wondrous complexity of ribs to sustain the marvelous concrete vaultings full two hundred feet in air.

Through the shattered windows broad slants of sunshine fell athwart the walls and floor. Swallows chirped and twittered far aloft, or winged their swift way through the dusky upper spaces, passing at will in or out the mullioned gaps whence all the painted glass had long since fallen.

An air of mystery, of long expectancy seemed brooding everywhere; it seemed almost as though the spirit of the past were waiting to receive them—waiting now, as it had waited a thousand years, patiently, inexorably, untiringly for those to come who should some day reclaim the hidden secrets in the crypt, once more awaken human echoes in the vault, and so redeem the world.

"Waiting!" breathed Stern, as if the thought hung pregnant in the very air. "Waiting all these long centuries—for *us!* For you, Beatrice, for me!

And we are here, at last, we of the newer time; and here we shall be one. The symbol of the pillars, mounting, ever mounting toward the infinite, the hope of life eternal, the majesty and mystery of this great temple, welcome us! Come!"

He took her hand again and now in silence they walked forward noiselessly over the thick leaf-carpet on the pavement of rare marble.

"Oh, Allan, I feel so very small in here!" she whispered, drawing close to him. "You and I, all alone in this tremendous place built for thousands—"

"You and I are *the world* to-day!" he answered very gravely; and so together they made way toward the vast transept, arched with a bewildering lacery of vaultings.

All save the concrete had long vanished. No traces now remained of pews, or railings, altars, pulpits, or any of the fittings of the vast cathedral.

Majestic in its naked strength, the building stood in light and shadow, here banded with strong sun, there lost in cool purple shade that foiled the eye far up among the hanging miracles of the roof.

At the transept-crossing they stood amazed; for here the flutings ran up five hundred feet inside the stupendous central spire, among a marvelous filigree of windows which diminished toward the top—a lacework as of frost-patterns etched into the solid substance of the *flèche.*

"Higher than that, more massive and more beautiful the buildings of the future shall arise," said Allan slowly after a pause. "But they shall not serve creed or faction. They shall be for all mankind, for the great race still to come. Beauty shall be its heritage, its right.

> "'*And loveliness shall crown the waiting world*
> *As with a garland of immortal joy!'*

"But come, come, Beatrice—there's work to do. The records, girl! We mustn't stand here admiring architecture and dreaming dreams while those records are still undiscovered. Down into the crypt we go, to dig among the relics of a vanished age!"

"The crypt, Allan? Where is it?"

"If I remember rightly—and at the time this cathedral was built I followed the plans with some care—the entrance is back of the main southern cluster of pillars over there at the transept-crossing. Come on, Beta. In a minute we can see whether thousand-year-old memories are any good or not!"

Quickly he led the way, ax and torch in hand, and as they rounded the group of massive buttresses whence sprang the pillars for the groin-vaults aloft, a cry of satisfaction escaped him, followed by a word of quick astonishment.

"What is it, Allan?" exclaimed the girl. "Anything wrong? Or—"

The man stood peering with wide eyes; then suddenly he knelt and began pawing over the little heap of vegetable drift that had accumulated along the wall.

"It's here, all right," said he. "There's the door, right in front of us—but what I don't understand is—*this!*"

"What, Allan? Is there anything wrong?"

"Not wrong, perhaps, but devilish peculiar!"

Speaking, he raised his hand to her. The fingers held an arrow-head of flint.

"There's been a battle here, that's sure," said he. "Look, spear-points— shattered!"

He had already uncovered three obsidian blades. The broken tips proved how forcibly they had been driven against the stone in the long ago.

"What? A—"

His fingers closed on a small, hollow shell of gold.

"A molar, so help me! All that's left of some forgotten white man who fell here, at the door, a thousand years ago!"

Speechless, the girl took the shell from him and examined it.

"You're right, Allan," she answered. "This certainly is a hollow gold crown. Any one can see *that,* in spite of the patina that's formed over the metal. Why—what can it all mean?"

"Search *me!* The patriarch's record gave the impression that this eastern expedition set out within thirty years or so of the catastrophe. Well, in that short time it doesn't seem possible there could have developed savages fighting with flints and so on. But that there certainly was a battle here at this door, and that the cathedral was used as a fort against some kind of invasion is positively certain.

"Why, look at the chips of concrete knocked off the jamb of the door here! Must have been some tall mace-work where you're standing, Beta! If we could know the complete story of this expedition, its probable failure to reach New York, its entrapment here, the siege and the inevitable tragedy of its end—starvation, sorties, repulses, hand-to-hand fighting at the outer gates, in the nave, here at the crypt door, perhaps on the stairs and in the vaults below—then defeat and slaughter and extinction—what a tremendous drama we could formulate!"

Beatrice nodded. Plain to see, the thought depressed her.

"Death, everywhere—" she began, but Allan laughed.

"Life, you mean!" he rallied. "Come, now, this does no good, poking in the rubbish of a distant tragedy. Real work awaits us. Come!"

He picked up the torch, and with his primitive but serviceable matches lighted it. The smoke rose through the silent air of the cathedral, up into a broad sunlit zone from a tall window in the transept, where it writhed blue and luminous.

A single blow of Allan's ax shattered the last few shreds of oaken plank that still hung from the eroded hinges of the door. In front of the explorers a flight of concrete steps descended, winding darkly to the crypt beneath.

Allan went first, holding the torch high to light the way.

"The records!" he exclaimed. "Soon, soon we shall know the secrets of the past!"

CHAPTER VI

TRAPPED!

SOME thirty steps the way descended, ending in a straight and very narrow passage. The air, though somewhat chill, was absolutely dry and perfectly respirable, thanks to the enormously massive foundation of solid concrete which formed practically one solid monolith six hundred feet long by two hundred and fifty broad—a monolith molded about the crypt and absolutely protecting it from every outside influence.

"Not even the Great Pyramid of Ghizeh could afford a more perfect— hello, what's *this?*"

Allan stopped short, staring downward at the floor. His voice reëchoed strangely in the restricted space.

"A skeleton, so help me!"

True indeed. At one side of the passage, lying in a position that strongly suggested death in a crouching, despairing attitude—death by starvation rather than by violence—a little clutter of human bones gleamed white under the torch-flare.

"A skeleton—the first one of our vanished race we've ever found!" exclaimed the man. "All the remains in New York, you remember, down in the subway or in any of the buildings, were invariably little piles of impalpable dust mixed with coins and bits of rusted metal. But this—it's absolutely intact!"

"The dry air and all—" suggested Beatrice.

Stern nodded.

"Yes," he answered, "Intact, so far. But—"

He stirred the skull with his foot. Instantly it vanished into powder.

"Just as I thought," said he. "No chance to give a decent burial to this or any other human remains we may come across here. The slightest disturbance totally disintegrates them. But with *this* it's different!"

He picked up a revolver, hardly rusted at all, that lay near at hand.

"Cartridges; look!" cried Beatrice, pointing.

"That's so, too—a score or more!"

Lying in an irregular oval that plainly told of a vanished cartridge-belt, a string of cartridges trailed on the concrete floor.

"H-m-m-m! Just for an experiment, let's see!" murmured the engineer.

Already he had slipped in a charge.

"Steady, Beatrice!" he cautioned, and, pointing down the passage, pulled trigger.

Flame stabbed the half-dark and the crashing detonation rang in their ears.

"What do you think of *that?*" cried Stern exultantly. "Talk about your miracles! A thousand years and—"

Beatrice grasped him by the arm and pointed downward. Astonished, he stared. The rest of the skeleton had vanished. In its place now only a few handfuls of dust lay on the floor.

"Well, I'll be—" the man exclaimed. "Even *that* does the trick, eh? H-m! It would be a joke, now, wouldn't it, if the records should act the same way? Come on, Beta; this is all very interesting, but it isn't getting us anywhere. We've got to be at work!"

He pocketed the new-found gun and cartridges and once more, torch on high, started down the passage, with the girl at his side.

"See here, Allan!"

"Eh?"

"On the wall here—a painted stripe?"

He held the torch close and scrutinized the mark.

"Looks like it. Pretty well gone by now—just a flake here and a daub there, but I guess it once was a broad band of white. A guide?"

They moved forward again. The strip ended in a blur that might once have been an inscription. Here, there, a letter faintly showed, but not one word could now be made out.

"Too bad," he mused. "It must have been mighty important or they wouldn't have—"

"Here's a door, Allan!"

"So? That's right. Now this looks like business at last!"

He examined the door by the unsteady flicker of the torch. It was of iron, still intact, and fastened by a long iron bar dropped into massive metal staples.

"Beat it in with the ax?" she queried.

"No. The concussion might reduce everything inside to dust. Ah! Here's a padlock and a chain!"

Carefully he studied the chain beneath bent brows.

"Here, Beta, you hold the torch, so. That's right. Now then—"

Already he had set the ax-blade between the padlock and the staple. A quick jerk—the lock flew open raspingly. Allan tried to lift the bar, but it resisted.

A tap of the ax and it gave, swinging upward on a pivot. Then a minute later the door swung inward, yielding to his vigorous push.

Together they entered the crypt of solid concrete, a chamber forty feet long by half as wide and vaulted overhead with arches, crowning perhaps twenty feet from the floor.

"More skeletons, so help me!"

Allan pointed at two more on the pavement at the left of the entrance.

"Why—how could *that* happen?" queried Beta, puzzled "The door was locked outside!"

"That's so. Either there must be some other exit from this place or there were dissensions and fightings among the party itself. Or these men were wounded and were locked in here for safe-keeping while the others made a sortie and never got back, or—*I* don't know! Frankly, it's too much for me. If I were a story-writer I might figure it out, but I'm not. No matter, they're here, anyhow; that's all. Here two of our own people died ten centuries ago, trying to preserve civilization and the world's history for future ages, if there were to be any such. Two martyrs. I salute them!"

In silence and awed sympathy they inspected the mournful relics of humanity a minute, but took good care not to touch them.

"And now the records!"

Even as Stern spoke he saw again a dimly painted line, this time upon the floor, all but invisible beneath the dust of centuries that had come from God knows where.

"Come, let's follow the line!" cried he.

It led them straight through the middle of the crypt and to a sort of tunnel-like vault at the far end. This they entered quickly and almost at once knew they had reached the goal of their long quest.

In front of them, about seven feet from the floor, a rough white star had been smeared. Directly below it a kind of alcove or recess appeared, lined with shelves of concrete. What its original purpose may have been it would be hard to say; perhaps it may have been intended as a storage-place for the cathedral archives.

But now the explorers saw it was partly filled with pile on pile of curiously crinkled parchment not protected in any way from the air, not covered or boxed in. To the right, however, stood a massive chest, seemingly of sheet-lead.

"Some sense to the lead," growled Stern; "but why they left their records open to the air, blest if I can see!"

He raised the torch and flared the light along the shelves, and then he understood. For here, there, copper nails glinted dully, lying in dust that once upon a time had been wood.

"I'm wrong, Beta; I apologize to them," Stern exclaimed. "These were all securely boxed once, but the boxes have gone to pieces long since. Dry-rot, you know. Well, let's see what condition the parchments are in!"

She held the torch while he tried to raise one, but it broke at the slightest touch. Again he assayed, and a third time. Same result.

"Great Scott!" he ejaculated, nonplused. "See what we're up against, will you? We've found 'em and they're ours, but—"

They stood considering a minute. All at once a dull metallic clang echoed heavily through the crypt. Despite herself, the girl shuddered. The eery depths, the gloom, the skeletons had all conspired to shake her nerves.

"What's *that?*" she whispered, gripping Allan by the arm.

"That? Oh—nothing! Now *how* the deuce are we going to get at these—"

"It *was* something, Allan! But what?"

He grew suddenly silent.

"By Jove—it sounded like—the door—"

"The door? Oh, Allan, quick!"

A sudden, irresistible fear fingered at the strings of the man's heart. At the back of his neck he felt the hair begin to lift. Then he smiled by very strength of will.

"Don't be absurd, Beatrice," he managed to say. "It couldn't be, of course. There's no one here. It—"

But already she was out of the alcove. With the torch held high in air, she stood there peering with wide eyes down the long blackness of the crypt, striving to pierce the dark.

Then suddenly he heard her cry of terror.

"The door, Allan! The door! *It's shut!*"

CHAPTER VII

THE LEADEN CHEST

NOT at any time since the girl and he had wakened in the tower, more than a year ago, had Allan felt so compelling a fear as overswept him then. The siege of the Horde at Madison Forest, the plunge down the cataract, the fall into the Abyss and the battle with the Lanskaarn had all taxed his courage to the utmost, but he had met these perils with more calm than he now faced the blank menace of that metal door.

For now no sky overhung him, no human agency opposed him, no counterplay of stress and strife thrilled his blood.

No; the girl and he now were far underground in a crypt, a tomb, walled round with incalculable tons of concrete, barred from the upper world, alone—and for the first time in his life the man knew something of the anguish of unreasoning fear.

Yet he was not bereft of powers of action. Only an instant he stood there motionless and staring; then with a cry, wordless and harsh, he ran toward the barrier.

Beneath his spurning feet the friable skeletons crumbled and vanished; he dashed himself against the door with a curse that was half a prayer; he strove with it—and staggered back, livid and shaken, for it held!

Now Beatrice had reached it, too. In her hand the torch trembled and shook. She tried to speak, but could not. And as he faced her, there in the tomblike vault, their eyes met silently.

A deathly stillness fell, with but their heart-beats and the sputtering of the torch to deepen it.

"Oh!" she gasped, stretching out a hand. "You—we—*can't*—"

He licked his lips and tried to smile, but failed.

"Don't—don't be afraid, little girl!" he stammered. "This can't hold us, possibly. The chain—I broke it!"

"Yes, but the bar, Allan—the bar! How did you leave the bar?"

"Raised!"

The one word seemed to seal their doom. A shudder passed through Beatrice.

"So then," she choked, "some air-current swung the door shut—and the bar—fell—"

A sudden rage possessed the engineer.

"Damn that infernal staple!" he gritted, and as he spoke the ax swung into air.

"Crash!"

On the metal plates it boomed and echoed thunderously. A ringing clangor vibrated the crypt.

"*Crash!*"

Did the door start? No; but in the long-eroded plates a jagged dent took form.

Again the ax swung high. Cold though the vault was, sweat globuled his forehead, where the veins had swelled to twisting knots.

"*Crash!*"

With a wild verberation, a scream of sundered metal and a clatter of flying fragments, the staple gave way. A crack showed round the edge of the iron barrier.

Stern flung his shoulder against the door. Creaking, it swung. He staggered through. One hand groped out to steady him, against the wall. From the other the ax dropped crashing to the floor.

Only a second he stood thus, swaying; then he turned and gathered Beta in his arms. And on his breast she hid her face, from which the roses all had faded quite.

He felt her fighting back the tears, and raised her head and kissed her.

"There, there!" he soothed. "It wasn't anything, after all, you see. But—if we hadn't brought the ax with us—"

"Oh, Allan, let's go now! This crypt—I can't—"

"We will go very soon. But there's no danger now, darling. We're not children, you know. We've still got work to do. We'll go soon; but first, those records!"

"Oh, how can you, after—after what might have been?"

He found the strength to smile.

"I know," he answered, "but it didn't happen, after all. A miss is worth a million miles, dear. That's what life seems to mean to us, and has meant ever since we woke in the tower, peril and risk, labor and toil—and victory! Come, come, let's get to work again, for there's so endlessly much to do."

Calmer grown, the girl found new courage in his eyes and in his strong embrace.

"You're right, Allan. I was a little fool to—"

He stopped her self-reproach with kisses, then picked up the torch from the floor where it had fallen from her nerveless hand.

"If you prefer," he offered. "I'll take you back into the sunlight, and you can sit under the trees and watch the river, while I—"

"Where you are, there am I! Come on, Allan; let's get it over with. Oh, what a coward you must think me!"

"I think you're a woman, and the bravest that ever lived!" he exclaimed vehemently. "Who but you could ever have gone through with me all that has happened? Who could be my mate and face the future as you're doing? Oh, if you only understood my estimate of you!

"But now let's get at those records again. Time's passing, and there must be still no end of things to do!"

He recovered his ax, and with another blow demolished the last fragment of the staple, so that by no possibility could the door catch again.

Then for the second time they penetrated the crypt and the tunnel and once more reached the alcove of the records.

"Beatrice!"

"What is it, Allan?"

"Look! Gone—all gone!"

"*Gone?* Why, what do you mean? They're—"

"Gone, I tell you! My God! Just a mass of rubbish, powder, dust—"

"But—but how—"

"The concussion of the ax! That must have done it! The violent sound-waves—the air in commotion!"

"But, Allan, it can't be! Surely there must be something left?"

"You see?"

He pointed at the shelves. She stood and peered, with him, at the sad havoc wrought there. Then she stretched out a tentative finger and stirred a little of the detritus.

"Catastrophe!" she cried.

"Yes and no. At any rate, it may have been inevitable."

"Inevitable?"

He nodded.

"Even if this hadn't happened, Beatrice, I'm afraid we never could have moved any of these parchments, or read them, or handled them in any way. Perhaps if we'd had all kinds of proper appliances, glass plates, transparent adhesives, and so on, *and* a year or two at our disposal, we might have made something out of them, but even so, it's doubtful.

"Of course, in detective stories, Hawkshaw can take the ashes right out of the grate and piece them together and pour chemicals on them and decipher the mystery of the lost rubies, and all that. But this isn't a story, you see; and what's more, Hawkshaw doesn't have to work with ashes nearly a thousand years old. Ten centuries of dry-rot—that's *some* problem!"

She stood aghast, hardly able to believe her eyes.

"But—but," she finally articulated, "there's the other cache out there in Medicine Bow Range. The cave, you know. And we have the bearings. And some time, when we've got all the leisure in the world and all the necessary appliances—"

"Yes, perhaps. Although, of course, you realize the earth is seventeen degrees out of its normal plane, and every reckoning's shifted. Still, it's a possibility. But for the present there's strictly nothing doing, after all."

"How about that leaden chest?"

She wheeled about and pointed at the other side of the alcove, where stood the metal box, sullen, defiant, secure.

"By Jove, that's so, too! Why, I'd all but forgotten that! You're a brick, Beta! The box, by all means. Perhaps the most important things of all are still in safety there. Who knows?"

"Open it, Allan, and let's see!"

Her recent terror almost forgotten in this new excitement, the girl had begun to get back some of her splendid color. And now, as she stood gazing at the metal chest which still, perhaps, held the most vital of the records, she felt again a thrill of excitement at thought of all its possibilities.

The man, too, gazed at it with keen emotion.

"We've got to be careful this time, Beatrice!" said he. "No more mistakes. If we lose the contents of this chest, Heaven only knows when we may be able to get another glimpse into the past. Frankly, the job of opening it, without ruining the contents, looks pretty stiff. Still, with care it may be done. Let's see, now, what are we up against here?"

He took the torch from her and minutely examined the leaden casket.

It stood on the concrete floor, massive and solid, about three and a half feet high by five long and four wide. So far as he could see, there were neither locks nor hinges. The cover seemed to have been hermetically sealed on. Still visible were the marks of the soldering-iron, in a ragged line, about three inches from the top.

"The only way to get in here is to cut it open," said Allan at last. "If we had any means of melting the solder, that would be better, of course, but there's no way to heat a tool in this crypt. I take it the men who did this work had a plumber's gasoline torch, or something of that sort. We have practically nothing. As for building a fire in here and heating one of the aeroplane tools, that's out of the question. It would stifle us both. No, we must cut. That's the best we can do."

He drew his hunting-knife from its sheath and, giving the torch back to Beatrice, knelt by the chest. Close under the line of soldering he dug the blade into the soft metal, and, boring with it, soon made a puncture through the leaden sheet.

"Only a quarter of an inch thick," he announced, with satisfaction. "This oughtn't to be such a bad job!"

Already he was at work, with infinite care not to shock or jar the precious contents within. In his powerful hands the knife laid back the metal

Giving the torch to Beatrice, Allan set to work. In his powerful hands the
hunting-knife laid back the metal of the mysterious leaden chest.

See page 361

in a jagged line. A quarter of an hour sufficed to cut across the entire front.

He rested a little while.

"Seems to be another chest inside, of wood," he told the girl. "Not decayed, either. I shouldn't wonder if the lead had preserved things absolutely intact. In that case this find is sure to be a rich one."

Again he set to work. In an hour from the time he had begun, the whole top of the lead box—save only that portion against the wall—had been cut off.

"Do you dare to move it out, Allan?" queried the girl anxiously.

"Better not. I think we can raise the cover as it is."

He slit up the front corners, and then with comparative ease bent the entire top upward. To the explorer's eyes stood revealed a chest of cedar, its cover held with copper screws.

"Now for it!" said the man. "We ought to have one of the screw-drivers from the Pauillac, but that would take too much time. I guess the knife will do."

With the blade he attacked the screws, one by one, and by dint of laborious patience in about an hour had removed all twenty of them.

A minute later he had pried up the cover, had quite removed it, and had set it on the floor.

Within, at one side, they saw a formless something swathed in oiled canvas. The other half of the space was occupied by eighty or a hundred vertical compartments, in each of which stood something carefully enveloped in the same material.

"Well, for all the world if it doesn't look like a set of big phonograph records!" exclaimed the man. He drew one of the objects out and very carefully unwrapped it.

"Just what they are—records! On steel. The new Chalmers-Enemarck process—new, that is, in 1917. So, then, that's a phonograph, eh?"

He pointed at the oiled canvas.

"Open it, quick, Allan!" Beatrice exclaimed. "If it *is* a phonograph, why, *we can hear the very voices of the past, the dead, a full thousand years ago!*"

With trembling fingers Stern slit the canvas wrappings.

"What a treasure! What a find!" he exulted. "Look, Beta—see what fortune has put into our hands!"

Even as he spoke he was lifting the great phonograph from the space where, absolutely uninjured and intact, it had reposed for ten centuries. A silver plate caught his eye. He paused to read:

METROPOLITAN OPERA HOUSE,

New York City.

This Phonograph and these Records were immured in the vault of this building September 28, 1918, by the Philavox Society, to be opened in the year 2000.

Non Pereat Memoria Musicae Nostrae.

"Let not the memory of our music perish!" he translated. "Why, I remember well when these records were made and deposited in the Metropolitan! A similar thing was done in Paris, you remember, and in Berlin. But how does this machine come *here?*"

"Probably the expedition reached New York, after all, and decided to transfer this treasure to a safer place where it might be absolutely safe and dry," she suggested. "It's here, anyhow; that's the main thing, and we've found it. What fortune!"

"It's lucky, all right enough," the man assented, setting the magnificent machine down on the floor of the crypt. "So far as I can see, the mechanism is absolutely all right in every way. They've even put in a box of the special fiber needles for use on the steel plates, Beta. Everything's provided for.

"Do you know, the expedition must have been a much larger one than we thought? It was no child's play to invade the ruins of New York, rescue all this, and transport it here, probably with savages dogging their heels every step. Those certainly were determined, vigorous men, and a goodly number at that. And the fight they must have put up in the cathedral, defending their cache against the enemy, and dying for it, must been terrifically dramatic!

"But all that's done and forgotten now, and we can only guess a bit of it here and there. The tangible fact is this machine and these records, Beatrice. They're real, and we've got them. And the quicker we see what they have to tell us the better, eh?"

She clapped her hands with enthusiasm.

"Put on a record, Allan, quick! Let's hear the voices of the past once more—human voices—the voices of the age that was!" she cried, excited as a child.

CHAPTER VIII

"TILL DEATH US DO PART"

"ALL right, my darling," he made answer. "But not here. This is no place for melody, down in this dark and gloomy crypt, surrounded by the relics of the dead. We've been buried alive down here altogether too long as it is. *Brrr!* The chill's beginning to get into my very bones! Don't you feel it, Beta?"

"I do, now I stop to think of it. Well, let's go up then. We'll have our music where it belongs, in the cathedral, with sunshine and air and birds to keep it company!"

Half an hour later they had transported the magnificent phonograph and the steel records out of the crypt and up the spiral stairway, into the vast, majestic sweep of the transept.

They placed their find on the broad concrete steps that in the old days had led up to the altar, and while Allan minutely examined the mechanism to make sure that all was right, the girl, sitting on the top step, looked over the records.

"Why, Allan, here are instrumental as well as vocal masterpieces," she announced with joy. "Just listen—here's Rossini's 'Barbier de Seville,' and Grieg's 'Anitra's Dance' from the 'Peer Gynt Suite,' and here's that most entrancing 'Barcarolle' from the 'Contes d'Hoffman'—you remember it?"

She began to hum the air, then, as the harmony flowed through her soul, sang a few lines, her voice like gold and honey:

> *Belle nuit, ô nuit d'amour, souris à nos ivresses!*
> *Nuit plus douce que le jour, ô belle nuit d'amour!*
> *Le temps fuit et sans retour emporte nos tendresses;*
> *Loin de cet heureux séjour le temps fuit sans retour!*
> > *Zéphyrs embrasés, versez-nous vos caresses!*
> > *Ah! Donnez-nous vos baisers!*

The echoes of Offenbach's wondrous air, a crystal stream of harmony, and of the passion-pulsing words, died through the vaulted heights. A moment Allan sat silent, gazing at the girl, and then he smiled.

"It lives in you again, the past!" he cried. "In you the world shall be made new once more! Beatrice, when I last heard that 'Barcarolle' it was sung by Farrar and Scotti at the Metropolitan, in the winter of 1913. And now— you waken the whole scene in me again!

"I seem to behold the vast, clear-lighted space anew, the tiers of gilded galleries and boxes, the thousands of men and women hanging eagerly on every silver note—I see the marvelous orchestra, many, yet one; the Venetian scene, the moonlight on the Grand Canal, the gondolas, the merrymakers—I hear Giulietta and Nicklausse blending those perfect tones! My heart leaps at the memory, beloved, and I bless you for once more awakening it!"

"With my poor voice?" she smiled. "Play it, play the record, Allan, and let us hear it as it should be sung!"

He shook his head.

"No!" he declared. "Not after you have sung it. Your voice to me is infinitely sweeter than any that the world of other days ever so much as dreamed of!"

He bent above her, caressed her hair and kissed her; and for a little while they both forgot their music. But soon the girl recalled him to the work in hand.

"Come, Allan, there's so much to do!"

"I know. Well now—let's see, what next?"

He paused, a new thought in his eyes.

"Beta!"

"Well?"

"You don't find Mendelssohn's 'Wedding March,' do you? Look, dearest, see if you can find it. Perhaps it may be there. If so—"

She eyed him, her gaze widening.

"You mean?"

He nodded.

"Just so! Perhaps, after all, you and I can—"

"Oh, come and help me look for it, Allan!" she cried enthusiastic as a child in the joy of his new inspiration. "If we only *could* find it, wouldn't that be glorious?"

Eagerly they searched together.

"'Ich Grolle Nicht,' by Schumann, no," Stern commented, as one by one they examined the records. "'Ave Maria,' Arcadelt-Liszt—no, though it's magnificent. That's the one you sing best of all, Beta. How often you've sung it to me! Remember, at the bungalow, how I used to lay my head in your lap while you played with my Samsonesque locks and sang me to sleep? Let's see—Brahms's 'Wiegenlied.' Cradle-song, eh? A little premature; that's coming later. Eh? Found it, by Jove! Here we are, the March itself, so help me! Shall I play it now?"

"Not yet, Allan. Here, see what *I've* found!"

She handed him a record as they sat there together in a broad ribbon of mid-morning sunlight that flooded down through one of the clearstory windows.

"'The Form of the Solemnization of Matrimony, by Bishop Gibson,'" he read. And silence fell, and for a long minute their eyes met.

"Beatrice!"

"I know; I understand! So, after all, these words—"

"Shall be spoken, O my love! Out of the dead past a voice shall speak to us and we shall hear! Beatrice, the words your mother heard, my mother heard, we shall hear, too. Come, Beatrice, for now the time is at hand!"

She fell a trembling, and for a moment could not speak. Her eyes grew veiled in tears, but through them he saw a bright smile break, like sunlight after summer showers.

She stood up and held out her hand to him.

"My Allan!"

In his arms he caught her.

"At last!" he whispered. "Oh, at last!"

When the majesty and beauty of the immortal marriage hymn climbed the high vaults of the cathedral, waking the echoes of the vacant spaces, and when it rolled, pealing triumphantly, she leaned her head upon his breast and, trembling, clung to him.

With his arm he clasped her; he leaned above her, shrouding her in his love as in an everlasting benison. And through their souls thrilled wonder, awe and passion, and life held another meaning and another mystery.

The words of solemn sacredness hallowed for centuries beyond the memory of man, rose powerful, heart-thrilling, deep with symbolism, strong with vibrant might—and, hand in hand, the woman and the man bowed their heads, listening:

"Dearly beloved, we are gathered here to join together this man and this woman in holy matrimony—reverently, discreetly, advisedly, soberly. Into this holy estate these two persons present now come to be joined."

His hand tightened upon her hand, for he felt her trembling. But bravely she smiled up at him and upon her hair the golden sunlight made an aureole.

The voice rose in its soul-shaking question—slow and powerful:

"Wilt thou have this woman to thy wedded wife, to live together in the holy estate of matrimony? Wilt thou love her, comfort her, honor, and keep her in sickness and in health, and keep thee only unto her, so long as ye both shall live?"

Allan's *"I will!"* was as a hymn of joy upon the morning air.

"Wilt thou have this man to thy wedded husband, to live together in the holy estate of matrimony? Wilt thou serve him, love, honor, and keep him in sickness and in health, and keep thee only unto him, so long as ye both shall live?"

She answered proudly, bravely:
"I will!"
Then the man chorused the voice and said:

"I, Allan, take thee, Beatrice, to my wedded wife, to have and to hold from this day forward for better, for worse, for richer, for poorer, in sickness and in health to love and to cherish, till death us do part, and thereto I plight thee my troth."

Her answer came, still led by the commanding voice, like an antiphony of love:

"I, Beatrice, take thee, Allan, to my wedded husband, to have and to hold from this day forward for better, for worse, for richer, for poorer, in sickness and in health to love and to cherish, till death us do part, and thereto I give thee my troth!"

Already Allan had drawn from his little finger the plain gold ring he had worn there so many centuries. Upon her finger he placed the ring and kissed it, and, following the voice, he said:

"With this ring I thee wed, and with all my worldly goods I thee endow. In the name of the Father, and of the Son, and of the Holy Ghost. Amen."

Forest, river, sky and golden sunlight greeted them as they stood on the broad porch of the cathedral, and the clear song of many birds, unafraid in the virgin wilderness, made music to their ears such as must have greeted the primal day.

Suddenly Allan caught and crushed her in his arms.

"My wife!" he whispered.

The satin of her skin from breast to brow surged into sudden flame. Her eyes closed and between her eager lips the breath came fast.

"Oh, Allan—*husband!* I feel—I hear—"

"The voice of the unborn, crying to us from out the dark, *'O father, mother, give us life!'*"

CHAPTER IX

At Settlement Cliffs

Ten days later the two lovers—now man and wife—were back again at the eastern lip of the Abyss. With them on the biplane they had brought the phonograph and records, all securely wrapped in oiled canvas, the same which had enveloped the precious objects in the leaden chest.

They made a camp, which was to serve them for a while as headquarters in their tremendous undertaking of bringing the Merucaans to the surface, and here carefully stored their treasure in a deep cleft of rock, secure from rain and weather.

They had not revisited the bungalow on the return trip. The sight of their little home and garden, now totally devastated, they knew would only sadden them unnecessarily.

"Let it pass, dearest, as a happy memory that was and is no more," Stern cheered the girl as he held her in his arms the first night of their stay in the new camp, and as together they watched the purple haze of sunset beyond the chasm. "Some day, perhaps, we may go back and once more restore Hope Villa and live there again, but for the present many other and far more weighty matters press. It will be wisest for a while to leave the East alone. Too many of the Horde are still left there. Here, west of the Ohio River Valley, they don't seem to have penetrated—and what's more, they never shall! Just now we must ignore them—though the day of reckoning will surely come! We've got our hands full for a while with the gigantic task ahead of us. It's the biggest and the hardest that one man and one woman ever tackled since the beginning of time!"

She drew his head down and kissed him, and for a little while they kept the silence of perfect comradeship. But at last she questioned:

"You've got it all worked out at last, Allan? You know just the steps to take? One false move—"

"There shall be no false moves. Reason, deliberation, care will solve this problem like all the others. Given some fifteen hundred people, at a depth of five hundred miles, and given an aeroplane and plenty of time—"

"Yes, of course, they can be brought to the surface. But after that, what? The dangers are tremendous! The patriarch died at the first touch of sunlight. We can't afford to take chances with the rest!"

"I've planned on all that. Our first move must be to locate a rocky ledge, a cave, or something of the sort, where the transplanting process can be carried out. There mustn't be any exposure to the actual daylight for a long time after they're on the surface. The details of food and water have all got to be arranged, too. It means work, work, *work!* God, what work! But—it's our task, Beta, all our own. And I glory in it. I thank Heaven for it—a man's-size labor! And if we're strong and brave enough, patient and wise enough, we're bound to win."

"Win? Of course we'll win!" she answered, her faith in him touching the sublime. "We must! The life of the whole world's at stake!"

Night came, and redder glowed the firelight in the gloom. They spoke of life, of love, of destiny; and over them seemed to brood the mystery of all that was to be.

The very purpose of the universe enwrapped itself about their passion, and the untroubled stars kept vigils till the dawn.

Daylight called them to begin the epic campaign they had mapped out—the rescue of a race.

After a visit to the patriarch's grave, which they decked anew with blossoms and fresh leaves, they prepared for the journey in search of a suitable temporary home for the Folk.

Nine o'clock found them once more on the wing. Stern laid a southerly course along the edge of the Abyss. He and Beatrice had definitely decided that the new home of humanity was not to be the distant regions of the East, involving so long and perilous a journey, but rather some location in the vast, warm, central plain of what had once been the United States.

They judged they were now somewhere in the one-time State of Indiana, not far from Indianapolis. So much warmer had the climate grown that for some months to come at least the Folk could without doubt accustom themselves to the change from the hot and muggy atmosphere of the Abyss to the semitropic heat.

The main object now was to discover suitable caves near a good water supply, where by night the Folk could prosecute their accustomed fisheries. Agriculture and the care of domestic animals by daylight would have to be postponed for some time, possibly for a year or more. Above all, the health of the prospective colonists must be safeguarded.

It was not until nearly nightfall of the next day, and after stops had been made at the ruins of two considerable but unidentified towns—for fuel, as well as to fit up an electric search-light and hooded lamps to illuminate the instruments in the Abyss—that the explorers found what they were seeking.

About half past five that afternoon they sighted a very considerable river, flowing westward down a rugged and irregular valley, in the direction of the chasm.

"This can't be the Ohio," judged Stern. "We must have long since passed its bed, now probably dried up. I don't remember any such hilly region as this in the old days along the Mississippi Valley. All these formations must be the result of the cataclysm. Well, no matter, just so we find what we're after."

"Where are we now?" she asked, peering downward anxiously. "Over what State—can you tell?"

"Probably Tennessee or northern Alabama. See the change in vegetation? No conifers here, but many palms and fern-trees, and new, strange growths. Fertile isn't the name for it! Once we clear some land here, crops will grow themselves! I don't think we'll do better than this, Beta. Shall we land and see?"

A quarter-hour later the Pauillac had safely deposited them on a high, rocky plateau about half a mile back from the edge of the river cañon. Stern, in his eagerness, was all for cave-hunting that very evening, but the girl restrained him.

"Not so impatient, dear!" she cautioned. "'Too fast arrives as tardy as too slow!' To-morrow's time enough."

"Ruling me with quotations from Shakespeare, eh?" he laughed, with a kiss. "All right, have your way—*Mrs.* Stern!"

She laughed, too, at this, the first time she had heard her new name. So they made camp and postponed further labors till daylight again.

Morning found them early astir and at work. Together they traversed the tropic-seeming woods, aflame with brilliant flowers, dank with ferns and laced with twining lianas.

In the treetops—strange trees, fruit laden—parrakeets and flashing green and crimson birds of paradise disturbed the little monkeyfolk that chattered at the intruders. Once a coral-red snake whipped away, hissing, but not quick enough to dodge a ball from Stern's revolver.

Stern viewed the ugly, triangular head with apprehension. Well he knew that venom dwelt there, but he said nothing. The one and only chance of successfully transplanting the Folk must be to regions warm as these. All dangers must be braved a time till they could grow acclimated to the upper air. After that—but the vastness of the future deterred even speculation. Perils were inevitable. The more there were to overcome the greater the victory.

"On to the cliffs!" said he, clasping the girl's hand in his own and making a path for her.

Thus presently they reached the edge of the cañon.

"Magnificent!" cried Beatrice as they came out on the overhang of the rock wall. "With these fruitful woods behind, that river in front, and these natural fortifications for our home, what more could we want?"

"Nothing except caves," Stern answered. "Let's call this New Hope River, eh? And the cliffs?"

"Settlement Cliffs!" she exclaimed.

"Done! Well, now let's see."

For the better part of the morning they explored the face of the palisade. Its height, they estimated, ranged from two to three hundred feet, shelving down in rough terraces to the rocky débris through and beyond which foamed the strong current of New Hope River, a stream averaging about two hundred yards in width.

Up-current a broader pool gave promise of excellent fishing. It overflowed into violent rapids, with swift, white waters noisily cascading.

"There, incidentally," Stern remarked, with the practical perception of the engineer, "there's power enough, when properly harnessed, to light a city and to turn machinery *ad libitum*. I don't see how we could better this site, do you?"

"Not if you think there are good chances for cave-dwellings," she made answer.

"From what we've seen already, it looks promising. Of course, there'll be a deal of work to do; but there are excellent possibilities here. First rate."

Fortune seemed bent on favoring them. The limestone cliff, fantastically eroded, offered a score of shelters, some shallow and needing to be walled up in front, others deep and tortuous. All was in utter confusion.

Stern saw that the terraces would have to be blasted and leveled, roads and stairs built along the face of the rock and down to the river, stalactites and stalagmites cut away, chambers fashioned, and a vast deal of labor done; but the rough framework of a cliff colony undeniably existed here. He doubted whether it would be possible to find a more favorable site without long and tedious travels.

"I guess we'll take the apartments and sign the lease," he decided toward noon, after they had clambered, pried, explored with improvised torches, and penetrated far into some of the grottoes. "The main thing to consider is that we can find darkness and humidity for the Folk by day. They mustn't be let out at first except in the night. It may be weeks or months before they can stand the direct sunlight. But that, too, will come. Patience, girl—patience and time—and all will yet be done."

Yet, even as he spoke, a strange anxiety, a prescience of tremendous difficulties, brooded in his soul. These were not cattle that he had to deal with, but *men*.

Could he and Beatrice, rulers of the Folk though they now were, could they—with their paltry knowledge of the people's language, superstitions, prejudices and inner life—really bring about this great migration?

Could they ravish a nation from its accustomed home, transplant it bodily, force new conditions on it, train, teach, civilize it? All this without rebellion, anarchy and failure?

"God!" thought the engineer. "The labors of Hercules were child's play beside this problem!"

His heart quaked at the thought of all that lay ahead; yet through everything, deep in the basic strata of his being, he knew that all should be and must be as he planned.

Barring death only, the seemingly impossible should come to pass.

"I swear it!" he murmured to himself. "For *her* sake, for theirs, and for the world's, I swear it shall be!"

At high noon they emerged once more from the caverns, climbed the steep cliff face, and again stood on the heights.

Facing northward, their gaze swept the lower river-bank opposite, and reached away, away, over the rolling hills and plains that lay, a virgin forest, to the dim horizon, brooding, mysterious, quivering with fertility and wild, strange life.

"Some time," he prophesied, sweeping his arm out toward the wilderness—"some time all *that*—and far beyond—shall be dotted with clearings and rich farms, with cottages, schools, towns, cities. Broad highways shall traverse it. The hum of motors, of machinery, of industry—of life itself—shall one day displace the cry of beast and bird.

"Some time the English tongue shall reign here again—here and beyond. Here strong men shall toil and build and reap and rest. Here love shall reign and women be called 'mother.' Here children shall play and learn and grow to manhood and to womanhood, secure and free.

"Some time all good things shall here come to realization. Oppression and slavery, alone, shall be undreamed of. These, and poverty and pain, shall never enter into the new world that is to be.

"Some time, here, 'all shall be better than well.' *Some time!*"

He circled her with his arm, and for a while they stood surveying this cradle of the new race. Much moved, Beatrice drew very close to him. They made no speech.

For the dreams they two were dreaming, as the golden sun irradiated all that vast, magnificent wilderness, passed any power of words.

Only she whispered "Some time!" too, and Allan knew she shared with him the glory of his vast, tremendous vision!

CHAPTER X

Separation

THEY spent the remainder of that day and all the next in hard work, making practical preparations for the arrival of the first settlers. Allan assured himself the waters of New Hope River were soft and pure and that an ample supply of fish dwelt in the pool as well as in the rapids—trout, salmon and pike of new varieties and great size, as well as other species.

Beatrice and he, working together, put the largest and darkest of the caves into habitable order. They also prepared, for their own use, a sunny grotto, which they thought could with reasonable labor be made into a comfortable temporary home.

"Though it isn't our own cozy bungalow, and never can be," she remarked rather mournfully, surveying the fireplace of roughly piled stones Allan had built. "Oh, dear, *if* we only could have had that to live in while—"

He stopped her yearning with a kiss.

"There, there, little girl," he cheered her, "don't be impatient. All in good time we'll have another, garden and sun-dial and everything. All in good time. The more we have to overcome, the more we'll appreciate results, eh? The only really serious matter to consider now is *you!*"

"Me, Allan? Why, what do you mean? What about me?"

He sat down on the rough-hewn bench of logs that he had fashioned and drew her to him.

"Listen, Beta. This is very serious."

"What, Allan? Has anything happened?"

"No, and nothing must, either. That's what's troubling me now. Our separation, I mean."

"Our—why, what—"

"Don't you see? Can't you understand? We've got to be apart a while. I must go alone—"

"Oh, no, no, Allan! You mustn't; I can't let you!"

"You've *got* to let me, darling! The machine will only carry, at most, three persons and a little freight. Now if you take the trip back into the Abyss I can only bring one, just one of the Folk back with me. And at that rate you can see for yourself how long it will take to make even a beginning at colonization. I figure three or four days for the round trip, at the inside. If you go we'll be all summer and more getting even twenty-five or thirty colonists here. Whereas, if you can manage to let me do this work alone, we'll have fifty in the caves by October. So you see—"

"You don't want to go and leave me, Allan?"

"God forbid! Shall I abandon the whole attempt and settle down with you here, all alone, and—"

"No, no, no! Not that, Allan!"

"I knew you'd say so. After all, the future of the race means more than our own welfare or comfort or anything. Even our safety has got to be risked for it. So you see—"

She thought a moment, clinging to him, somewhat pale and shaken, but with an indefinable courage in her eyes. Then asked she:

"Wouldn't it be possible in some way—for you can do anything, Allan—wouldn't it be possible for you to build another machine? Surely in the ruins of some city not too far away, in Nashville, Cincinnati, or Detroit, you could find materials! Couldn't you make another aeroplane and teach me how to fly, so I could help you? I'd learn, Allan! I'd dare, and be brave—awfully brave, for your sake, and theirs, and—"

He gravely shook his head in negation.

"I know you would, dearest, but you mustn't. Half my real reason for not wanting you to go with me is just this danger of flying. You'll be safer here. With plenty of supplies and your pistol you'll be all right. I know it seems heartless to talk of leaving you, even for three days, but, after all, it's far the wisest way. We'll build a barricade and make a regular fort for you and stock it with supplies. Then you can wait for me and the first two settlers. And after that you'll have company. Why, you'll have *subjects*—for, until they're educated, we've simply got to rule these people. It'll be only the first trip that will make you lonely, and it won't be long."

"I know; but suppose anything should happen to you!"

He laughed confidently.

"Nonsense!" he exclaimed. "You know nothing ever *does* happen to me! Everything will be all right, my best-beloved. Only a little patience and a little courage, that's all we need now. You'll see!"

Till late that night, sheltered in their cave, they talked of this momentous step. Redly their firelight glowed upon their walls and roof, where sparkled myriads of tiny rock-facets. Far below the rapids of New Hope River murmured a contra-bass to their voices.

And in the cañon the sighing of the night-wind, pierced now and then by some strange cry of beast-life from the forest beyond, heightened their pleasant sense of security. Only the knowledge of approaching separation weighed heavy on their souls.

From every possible standpoint they discussed the situation. Allan's plan, viewed with the eye of reason, was really the only sane one. Nothing could have been more absurdly wasteful of time and energy than the idea of carrying the girl down into the Abyss each time and bringing her up with every return.

Not only would it expose her needlessly to very grave perils, but it would bisect the efficiency of the Pauillac. Allan realized, moreover, that in the rebuilding of the world a time must inevitably come when he could not always stand by her side. She must learn self-reliance, harsh as that teaching might seem.

All this and much more he pointed out to her. And before midnight she, too, agreed. It was definitely decided that he was to undertake the transportation work alone.

Thus the matter was settled. But on that night there was little sleep for either of them. For, on the day after the morrow was to commence their first separation since the time they had awakened in the tower, more than a year ago.

Separation!

The thought weighed leaden on Allan's heart. As for Beatrice, though in the dark she hid her tears, she felt that grief could plumb no blacker depths save utter loss. Only the thought of the new world and all that it must mean steeled her to resignation.

Morning dawned, aflare with light and color, as only a June morning in that semitropic wilderness could glow. Allan and Beatrice, early at work, resolutely attacked their labor of preparation.

First of all they laid in adequate supplies of fruit and game, both of which, in that virgin wild, were to be had in a profusion undreamed of in the old days of civilization. With an improvised lance Allan also speared three salmon in the rapids. The game and fish he dressed for her and packed among green leaves in the cool recesses at the extreme inner end of the cavern.

"No need whatever for you to leave the cave while I'm gone," he warned her. "I'm not forbidding you to, because I'm not your master. All I say is I'll be far happier if you stay close at home. Will you promise me that, whatever happens, you won't wander from the cave?"

"I needn't promise, dearest. All I need to know is your wish. That's enough for me!"

Together they set about fortifying the place. They built a rough but strong barricade of rocks across the mouth of the cavern, leaving only one small aperture, just sufficient to admit a single person on hands and knees.

Allan fetched a rounded stone that she could roll into this door by night and arranged a stout sapling to brace the stone immovably. He supplied her well with fire-wood and saw to it that her bandoliers were full of cartridges. In addition, he left her the extra gun and ammunition they had found in the crypt under the cathedral.

With a torch he carefully explored every crevice of the cave to make sure no noxious spiders, centipedes, or serpents were sheltered there.

From the Pauillac he brought his own cloak, which he insisted on her keeping. This, with hers, would add to the comfort of the bed they had made with fragrant ferns and grasses.

He fashioned, out of the tenacious clay of an earth-bank about half a mile down stream, two large water-jars, and baked them for some hours in a huge fire on the terrace in front of the cave.

When properly hardened he scoured them carefully with river-sand and filled them one at a time, struggling up the hard ascent with a stout heart— for all this toil meant safety for the girl; it was all another step on the hard pathway toward the goal.

In her sleep that night he bent above her, kissed her tenderly, and realized how inexpressibly dear she was to him.

The thought: "To-morrow I must leave her!" weighed heavy on him. And for a long time he could not sleep, but lay listening to the night sounds of the forest and the brawling stream. Once a deep, booming roar echoed throughout the cañon, and thereto, hollow blows.

But Allan could not think their meaning. Only he knew the wild was full of perils; and in his mind he reviewed the precautions he had taken for her welfare. Bit by bit he analyzed them. He knew that he could do no more. Now Fate must solve the rest.

He slept at length, not to waken till morning with its garish eye peeped in around the crevices of the rock doorway. Returning from his swim in the pool, he found Beatrice already making breakfast. They ate in silence, overborne with sad and bodeful thoughts.

But now the decision had been made, nothing remained save to execute it. Such a contingency as backing out of an undertaking once begun lay far outside their scheme of things.

The leave-taking was not delayed. They both realized that an early start was necessary if he were to reach the village of the Folk before sleep should assail him. Still more, they dreaded the departure less than the suspense.

Together they provisioned the Pauillac, back there on the rocky barren, and made sure everything was in order. Allan assured himself especially that he had fuel enough to last four or five hours.

"In that time," he told the girl, "I can easily reach the rim of the Abyss. You see, I needn't fly northward to the point where we emerged. That would be only an unnecessary waste of time and energy. I'm positive the chasm extends all the way up and down what was once the Mississippi Valley, and that the Great Central Sea is fed by that and other rivers. In that case, by striking almost due west, I can reach the rim. After that I can volplane easily till I sight the water."

"And then?"

"Then the power goes on again and I scout for the west shore and the village. The sustaining power of that lower-level air is simply miraculous. I realize perfectly well it's no child's play, but I can do it, Beta. I can find the place again. You see, I'm perfectly familiar with conditions down there now. The first time it was all new and strange. This time, after all those months in the Abyss, why, it will be almost like getting back home again. It'll be quite a triumphal return, won't it? The chief getting back to his tribe, eh?"

He tried to speak lightly, but his lips refused to smile. She frankly wept.

"There, there, little girl," he soothed her. "Now let's go back to the cave and see that you're all right and safe. Then I'll be going. Remember on the third night to kindle the big fire we've agreed on just outside your door on the terrace—the beacon-fire, you know. I'll have to reckon by the chronometer, so as to make the return by night. The risk of bringing any of the Folk into daylight is prohibitive. And the fire will be tremendously important. I can sight it a long way off. It will guide me home—to you!"

She nodded silently, for she did not trust herself to speak. Hand in hand they returned along the path they had beaten through the rank half-tropic growth.

One last inspection he gave to all things necessary for her comfort. Then, standing in the warm, bright sunlight on the ledge before the new home, he took her in his arms.

A long embrace, a parting kiss that clung; then he was gone.

Not long after the girl, still standing there upon the windswept terrace overlooking New Hope River, heard the rapid chatter of the engine high in air and rapidly approaching.

A swift black shadow leaped the cañon and swept away across the plain. Far aloft she saw the skimming Pauillac, very small and black against the dazzling blue.

Did Allan wave a hand to her? Could she hear his farewell cry?

Impossible to tell. Her ears, confused by the roaring of the rapids, her eyes dazzled by the shimmer of the morning heavens and dimmed by burning tears, refused to serve her.

But bravely she waved her cloak on high. Bravely she strove to watch the arrow-flight of the swift bird-man till the tiny machine dwindled to a moving blur, a point, a mere speck on the far horizon, then vanished in the blue.

Choked with anguish, against which all her courage, all her philosophy could not make way, Beatrice sank down upon the rocky ledge and abandoned herself to grief.

Allan was gone at last! Gone—ever to return?

At last she was alone in the unbroken wilderness!

CHAPTER XI

"HAIL TO THE MASTER!"

ELEVEN hours of incessant labor, care, watchfulness and fatigue, three hours of flight and eight of coasting into the terrific depths, brought Allan once more through the fogs, the dark, the heat, to sight of the vast sunken sea, five hundred miles below the surface.

Throughout the whole stupendous labor he thanked Heaven the girl was safely left behind, nor forced to share this travail and exhaustion. Myriad anxieties and fears assailed him—fears he had taken good care not to let her know or dream of.

Always existed the chance that something might go wrong about the machine and it be hurled, with him, into that black and steaming sea; the possibility of landing not among the Folk, but in some settlement of the Lanskaarn on the rumored islands he had never seen; the menace of the Great Vortex, of which he knew nothing save the little that the patriarch had told him.

All these and many other perils sought to force themselves upon his mind. But Allan put them resolutely back and, guided by his instruments, his reason, and that marvelous sixth sense of location which his long months of battling with the wilderness had brought to birth in him, swiftly yet carefully slid in vast spirals down the purple, then the black and terrifying void that yawned interminably below.

The beam of his underslung searchlight, shifting at his will, shot its white ray in a long, fading pencil downward as he coasted. And hour after hour it found nothing whereon to rest. It, too, seemed lost forever in the welter of up-rushing, choking vapors from the pit.

"Ah! *At last!*"

The cry, dull in that compressed air, burst triumphantly from his lips as the light-ray, suddenly piercing a rift of cloud, sparkled dimly on a surface shiny-black as newly cleft anthracite.

Allan threw in the motor once more and quickly got the Pauillac under control. In a long downward slant he rushed, like some vast swallow skimming a pool, over the mysterious plain of steaming waters. And ever, peering eagerly ahead, he sought a twinkle of the fishermen's oil-flares wimpling across the sunken sea.

Moment by moment he consulted his instruments and the chart he had stretched before him under the gleam of the hooded bulbs.

"Inside of half an hour now," said he, "I ought to sight the first flash of the flares upon the parapet—the glow of the flaming well!"

And a singular eagerness all at once possessed him, a strange yearning to behold once more the strange, fog-shrouded, reeking City of the Lost People, almost as though it had been home, as though these white barbarians had been his own people.

Men! To see men once more! The idea leaped up and gripped him with a powerful fascination.

So it was that when in reality the first faint twinkle of the fishing-boats peeped through the mist—and beyond, a tiny necklace of gleaming points that he knew marked the walls of the town—his heart throbbed hotly and a cry of eager greeting welled from his soul.

Quickly the Pauillac swept him onward. Manœuvering cautiously, jockeying the great machine with that consummate skill he had acquired from long practise, he soon beheld the dim outlines of the vast cliff, the long walls, the dull reflections of the fire-plume, the slanting slope of beach.

And with keen exultation, thrilled with his triumph and his greeting to the Folk he came to rescue, he landed with a whir upon the reeking slope.

To him, even before he had been able to free his cramped body from the saddle, came swarming the people, with loud cries of welcome and rejoicing. Powerfully the automatics he and Beatrice had used in the Battle of the Walls had impressed their simple minds with almost superstitious reverence. More powerfully still his terrible fight with Kamrou, ending with the death of that great chief in the boiling vat. And now, acknowledging him their overlord and ruler, whom they had feared to lose forever, they trooped in wild, disordered throngs to do him reverence.

In from the sea, summoned by waving flares, the fishing-boats came plowing mightily, driven by many paddles in the hands of the strange, white-haired men.

Along the beach the townsfolk thronged, and down the causeway, beneath the vast monolithic plinth of the fortified gate, jostled and pushed an ever-growing multitude.

Cries of *"Kromno h'viat! Tai Kromno!"* reëchoed—"The chief has come back! The great master!"—and the confusion swelled to a mighty roar, close-pent under the heavy mists blued by the naphtha-torches.

But Stern noticed, and rejoiced to see it, that none prostrated themselves. None fell to earth or groveled in his presence. Disorderly and wild the greeting was, but it was the greeting of men, not slaves.

"Thank God, I've got a race of real men to deal with here!" thought he, surveying the pressing throng. "Hard they may be to rule, and even turbulent, but they're not servile. Rude, brave, bold—what better stock could I have hoped for in this great adventuring?"

For a while even thoughts of Beatrice were crowded back by the excitement of the arrival. In all his wonderful experience never before had he sensed a feeling such as this.

To be returning, master and lord of a race of long-buried people, his own people, after all—to be acknowledged chieftain—to hold their destinies within his hand for good or evil—the magnitude of the situation, the tremendous difficulties and responsibilities, almost overwhelmed him.

He felt a need to rest, and think, and plan, to recuperate from the long journey and to recover poise and strength.

And with relief, as he raised his hand for silence, he perceived the wrinkled face of one Vreenya, head councillor of Kamrou, his predecessor.

Him he summoned to come close, and to him gave his orders. With some degree of fluency—for in the months Beatrice and he had spent in the Abyss they had acquired much of the Merucaan tongue—he said:

"I greet you, Vreenya. I greet my people, all. Harken. I have made a long journey to return to you. I am tired and would rest. There be many things to tell you, but not now. I would sleep and eat. Is my house in readiness?"

"It is in readiness—the house of the *Kromno*. Your word is our law. It shall be as you have spoken."

"That is good. Now it is my will that this air-boat on which I ride should be carried close up to the walls and carefully covered with mantles, especially this part," and he gestured at the engines. "After that I rest."

"So it shall be," Vreenya made answer, while the Folk listened. "But, master, where is the woman? Where is the ancient man, J'hungaav, who sailed with you in the air-boat to those upper regions we know not of?"

"The woman is well. She awaits in a place we have prepared for you."

"It is well. And the ancient man?"

Stern thought quickly. To confess the patriarch's death would certainly be fatal to the undertaking. These simple minds would judge from it that certain destruction must be the portion of any who should dare venture into those mysterious upper regions which to them were but a myth, a strange tradition—almost a terror.

And though the truth was dear to him, yet under stress of the greater good he uttered falsehood by implication.

"The ancient man awaits you, too. He is resting in the far places. He would desire you to come to him."

"He is at peace? He found the upper world good?"

"He found it good, Vreenya. And he is at peace."

"It is well. Now the commands of *Tai Kromno* shall be done. His house is ready!"

While Stern clambered out of the machine and stretched his half-paralyzed limbs, the news ran, a murmur of many voices, through the massed Folk. Stern's heart swelled with pride at the success so far of his mission. If all should go as well from now on, his mighty object could and would be accomplished. But if not—

He shuddered slightly despite himself, for to his mind arose the ever-present possibility of the Folk's custom of trial by combat—the chance that some rebellious one might challenge him—that the outcome might another time turn against him.

He remembered still the scream of Kamrou as the deposed chieftain had plunged into the boiling pool. What if this fate should some time yet be *his?* And once more thoughts of Beatrice obtruded; and, despite himself, he felt the clutch of terror at his heart.

He put it resolutely away, however, for he realized that all depended now on maintaining good courage and a bold, commanding air. The slightest weakness might at any time prove fatal.

He understood enough of the barbarian psychology to know the value of dominance. And with a command to Vreenya: "Make way for me, your master!" he advanced through the lane which the crowding Folk made for him.

As, followed by the councillor and the elders, he climbed the slippery causeway and passed through the labyrinthine passes of the great gate, strange emotions stirred him.

The scene was still the same as when he first had witnessed it. Still flared the torches in the hands of the populace and along the walls, where, perched on the very ledge of the one-time battle with the Lanskaarn, the strange waterfowl still blinked their ghostly eyes.

No change was to be witnessed in the enclosure, the huts, the wide plaza, stretching away to the cliff, to the fire-pit, and the Dungeon of Skeletons. But still how different was it all!

Only too clearly he remembered the first time he and Beatrice had been thrust into this weird community, bound and captive; with only too vivid distinctness he recalled the frightful indignities, perils and hardships inflicted on them.

The absence of the kindly patriarch saddened him; and, too, the fact that now no Beatrice was with him there.

Slowly, wearily, he moved along the slippery rock-floor toward his waiting house, unutterably lonesome even in this pushing throng that now acclaimed him, yet thanking God that the girl, at least, was far from the buried town of such hard ways and latent perils.

At the door of the round, conical stone hut that had been Kamrou's and now was his—so long as he could hold the chieftainship by sheer force of will and power—he paused a moment and faced the eager throng.

"Peace to you, my people!" he exclaimed, once more raising his hand on high. "Soon I shall tell you many wonders and things strange to hear—many things of great import and good tidings.

"When I have slept I shall speak with you. Now I go to rest. Await me, for the day of your deliverance is at hand!"

A face caught his attention, a sinister and brutal face, doubly ominous in the flaring cresset-glare. He knew the man—H'yemba, the cunning iron-smith, one who in other days had before now crossed his will and, dog-like, snarled as much as he had dared. Now a peculiarly malevolent expression lay upon the evil countenance. The dead-white skin wrinkled evilly; the pink eyes gleamed with disconcerting malice.

But Stern, dead tired, only glanced at H'yemba for a second, then with Vreenya entered the hut and bade the door be closed.

All dressed as he was, he flung himself upon the rude bed of seaweed covered with the coarse brown stuff woven by the Folk.

"Sleep, master," Vreenya said. "I will sit here and watch. But before you sleep loosen the terrible fire-bow that shoots the bolts of lead and lay it near at hand."

"You mean—there may be trouble here?"

"Sleep!" was all the councillor would answer. "When you have rested there will be many things to ask and tell."

Spent beyond the power of any further effort, Stern laid his automatic handy and disposed himself to rest.

As his weary eyelids closed and the first outposts of consciousness began to fall before the attacking power of slumber, his thoughts, his love, his enduring passion, reverted to the girl, the wife, now so infinitely far away in the cavern beside the brawling cañon-stream. Yearning and tenderness unspeakable flooded his soul.

But once or twice her face faded from his mental vision and in its stead he seemed to see again the surly stare, the evil eyes, and venomously sinister expression of H'yemba, the resourceful man of fire and of steel.

CHAPTER XII

CHALLENGED!

AFTER many hours of profound and dreamless sleep, Allan awoke filled with fresh vigor for the tasks that lay ahead. His splendid vitality, quickly recuperating, calmed his mind; and now the problems, the anxieties and fears of the day before—to call it such, though there was neither night nor day in this strange place—seemed negligible.

Only a certain haunting uneasiness about the girl still clung to him. But, sending her many a thought of love, he reflected that soon he should be back again with her; and so, resolutely grasping the labor that now awaited him, he felt fresh confidence and hope.

After a breakfast of the familiar sea-weeds, bulbs, fish and eggs, he bade Vreenya (who seemed devotion incarnate) summon the folk for a great *charweg,* or tribal council, at the Place of Skeletons.

Here they gathered, men, women and children, all of fifteen hundred, in close-packed, silent masses, leaving only the inner circle under the stone posts and iron rods clear for Allan and for Vreenya and some half-dozen elders.

The rocky plaza-floor sloping upward somewhat from the dungeon, formed a very shallow natural amphitheater, so that the majority could see as well as hear.

No platform was there for their *Kromno* to speak from. He had not even a block of stone. In the true native style he was expected to address them on their own level, pacing back and forth the while.

In his early days among them he had seen one or two such gatherings. His quick wit prompted a close imitation of their ceremonies and ancient customs.

First, Vreenya sprinkled the open space between the poles and the dungeon with a kind of sea-weed swab dipped in the waters of the boiling vat, then with a bit of the coarse brown cloth washed Allan's lips—a pledge of truth.

The councillor raised both hands toward the roaring flame back there by the cliff, and all inclined themselves thereto, the only trace of any religious ceremony still remaining among them.

Allan likewise saluted the flame; then he faced the multitude.

"O my people," he began, striving to speak clearly above the noise of the fire-jet, his voice sounding dull and heavy in that compressed atmosphere, "O Folk of the Merucaans, I greet you! There be many things to tell that you must know and believe. I have come back to you with great peril in my flying-boat to tell you of the upper world and all its goodness.

"Easily could I have stayed in those places of light and plenty, but my heart was warm for my people. I thought of my people night and day. The woman Beatrice thought of you. The ancient man thought of you. Alone, we could not enjoy those happy places. So I returned to tell you and to show you the way to liberty. Thus have we proved our love for you, my folk!"

He paused. Silence overhung the assemblage save for the fretful cry of children here and there, squeezed in the press or clinging to their mothers' backs after the fashion of the Merucaans.

Afar, on the walls, the faint and raucous quarreling of the sea-birds drifted through the fog. Allan drew breath and began again:

"In those places, my people, those far places whence your forefathers came, are many wonders. Betimes it is dark, as always here. Betimes a great fire mounts into the upper air and make the whole world brighter than around your flaming well. In the dark time lesser fires travel in the air. Of birds there are many kinds, strangely colored. Of beasts, many kinds—I cannot make you understand because none of you have ever seen any animal but fish and bird. But I speak truth. There be many other creatures with good flesh to eat, and the skins of them are proper for soft clothing.

"Here you have only weeds of the sea. There we have tall growing things, many hundred *spedi* high, and rich fruit, delicious to the taste, grows on some kinds. In a few words, it is a place of wondrous plenty, where you can all live more easily than here, and with more pleasure—far—"

Again he ceased his discourse, but still continued to pace up and down the open space under the swaying skeletons on the poles above.

Through the dense press of the Folk murmurs were wandering. Man spoke to man, and many a new thought was coming now to birth among those white barbarians.

The elders, too, were whispering together: "So runs the ancient tradition. So said the ancient man! Can it be true, indeed?"

Stern continued, more and more earnestly, with the sweat now beginning to dot his brow:

"It were too long, my people, to tell you everything about that land of ours above. Only remember it is richer far and far more beautiful than this, your place of darkness and of clouds. It is the ancient home of your fathers in the very long ago. It is waiting for you once again, more fertile and more beautiful than ever. My errand is to carry you thither—two or three at a time. At last I shall be able to take you all.

"Then the world will begin to be as it once was, before the great explosion destroyed all but a few of your people, who were my people once. Will any of you—any two bold men—believe my words and go with me? Will any be as brave as—the patriarch?"

He flung the veiled taunt loudly at them, with a raising of both arms.

"I have spoken truth! Now answer!"

He ceased, and for a short minute there was silence. Then spoke Vreenya:

"O *Kromno*, master! We would question you!"

"I will answer and say only the thing that is."

"First, can our people live in that other, lighter air?"

"They can live. We have prepared caves for you. At first you shall not see the light. Only little by little you shall see it, and you and your children will change, till at last you shall be as I am and as your people were in the old days!"

Vreenya pondered, while tense interest held the elders and the Folk. Then he nodded, for his understanding—like that of all—was keen in spite of his savagery. "And we can eat, O *Kromno*? This flesh of beasts you speak of may be good. This strange fruit may be good. I know not. It may also be as the poison weeds of our sea to us. But, if so, there are fish in those waters of the upper world?"

"There are fish, Vreenya, and of the best, and many! Near the caves runs a river—"

"A what, master?"

"A going of the waters. In those waters live fish without number. At the dark times you can catch them with nets, even as here. The dark times are half of each day. You shall have many hours for the fishing. Even that will suffice to live; but the flesh and fruits will not hurt you. They are good. There will be food for all, and far more than enough for all!"

Vreenya pondered again.

"We would talk together, we elders," he said, simply.

"It meets my pleasure," answered Allan. "And when ye have talked, I desire your answer!"

He crossed his arms, faced the multitude, and waited, while the elders gathered in a little group by the dungeon and for some minutes conferred in low and earnest tones.

Outwardly, the man seemed calm, but his soul burned within him and his heart was racing violently.

For on this moment, he well knew, hung the world's destiny. Should they decide to venture forth into the outer world all would be well. If not, the long labor, the plans, the hopes were lost forever.

Well he knew the stubborn nature of the Folk. Once their minds set, nothing on earth could ever stir them.

"Thank God I managed that lie about the patriarch!" thought Allan quickly. "If I'd slipped up on that, and told them he died at the very minute the sunlight struck him, it would have been all off, world without end. Hope it doesn't make a row later. But if it does, I'll face it. The main and only thing now is to get 'em started. They've *got* to go, that's all there is about it.

"Gad! After all, it's a terrific proposition I'm putting up to these simple fishers of the Abyss. I'm asking them, just on my say-so, to root up the life, the habits, the traditions of more than a thousand years and make a leap into the dark—into the light, I mean.

"I'm asking them to leave everything they've ever known for thirty generations and take a chance on what to them must be the wildest and most hair-brained adventure possible to imagine. To risk homes, families, lives, everything, just on my unsupported word. Jove! Columbus's proposal to his men was a mere afternoon jaunt compared with *this!* If they refuse, how can I blame them? But if they accept—God! what stuff I'll know they're made of! With material like that to work with, the conquest of the world's in sight already."

His eyes, wandering nervously along the front ranks of the waiting Folk, dimly illumined by the dull blue glow of the fire-well that shone through the mist, suddenly stopped with apprehension. His brows contracted, and on his heart it seemed as though a gripping hand had suddenly laid hold.

"H'yemba, the smith, again! Damn him! H'yemba!" he muttered, in sudden anger strongly tinged with fear.

The smith, in fact, was standing there a little to the left of him, huge and sinewed hands loosely clasped in front of him, face sinister, eyes glowing like two malevolent evil fires.

Allan noted the defiant poise of the body, the vast breadth of the shoulders, the heavy hang of the arms, biceped like a gorilla's.

For a minute the two men looked each other steadfastly in the eye, each measuring the other. Then suddenly the voice of Vreenya broke the tension.

"O *Kromno,* we have spoken. Will you hear us?"

Stern faced him, a strange sinking at his heart, almost as though the foreman of a jury stood before him to announce either freedom or sentence of death.

But, holding himself in check, lest any sign of fear or nervousness betray him, he made answer:

"I will hear you. Speak!"

"We have listened to your words. We believe you speak truth. Yet—"

"Yet *what?* Out with it, man!"

"Yet will we not compel any man to go. All shall be free—"

"Thank God!" breathed Allan, with a mighty sigh.

"—Free to stay or go, as they will. Our village is too full, even now. We have many children. It were well that some should make room for others. Those who dare, have our consent. Now, speak *you* to the people, your people, O *Kromno,* and see who chooses the upper world with you!"

Once more Allan turned toward the assemblage. But before he had found time to frame the first question in this unfamiliar speech, a disturbance somewhat to the left interrupted him.

There came a jostling, a pushing, a sound of voices in amazement, anger, approbation, doubt.

Into the clear space stepped H'yemba, the smith. His powerful right hand he raised on high. And boldly, in a loud voice, he cried:

"*Folk of the Merucaans, this cannot be!*"

CHAPTER XIII

THE RAVISHED NEST

"IT cannot be? Who says it cannot be? *Who dares stand out and challenge me?*"

"I, H'yemba, the man of iron and of flame!"

Stern faced him, every nerve and fiber quivering with sudden passion. At realization that in the exact psychological moment when success lay almost in his hand, this surly brute might baffle him, he felt a wave of murderous hate.

He realized that the dreaded catastrophe had indeed come to pass. Now his sole claim to chieftainship lay in his power to defend the title. Failure meant—death.

"You?" he shouted, advancing on the smith.

His opponent only leered and grimaced offensively. Then without even having vouchsafed an answer, he swung toward the elders.

"I challenge!" he exclaimed. "I have the right of words!"

Vreenya nodded, fingering his long white beard.

"Speak on!" he answered. "Such is our ancient custom."

"Oh, people," cried the smith, suddenly facing the throng, "will ye follow one who breaks the tribal manners of our folk? One who disdains our law? Who has neglected to obey it? Will ye trust yourselves into hands stained with law-breaking of our blood?"

A murmur, doubtful, wondering, obscure, spread through the people. By the greenish flare-light Stern could see looks of wonder and dismay. Some frowned, others stared at him or at the smith, and many muttered.

"What the devil and all have I broken *now*?" wondered Allan. "Plague take these barbarous customs! Jove, they're worse than the taboos of the old Maoris, in the ancient days! What's up?"

He had not long to wonder, for of a sudden H'yemba wheeled on him, pointed him out with vibrant hands, and in a voice of terrible anger cried:

"The law, the law of old! *No man shall be chief who does not take a wife from out our people!* None who weds one of the Lanskaarn, the island folk, or the yellow-haired Skeri beyond the Vortex, none such shall ever rule us. Yet this man, this stranger who speaks such great things very hard to be believed, scorns our custom. No woman from among us he has taken, but instead, that *vuedma* of his own kind! What? Will ye—"

He spoke no further, for Allan was upon him with one leap. At sound of that word, the most injurious in their tongue, the fires of Hell burst loose in Stern.

Reckoning no consequences, staying for no parley or diplomacy, he sprang; and as he sprang, he struck.

The blow went home on the smith's jaw with a smash like a pile-driver. H'yemba, reeling, swung at him—no skill, no science, just a wild, barbaric, sledge-hammer sweep.

It would have killed had it landed, but Allan was not there. In point of tactics, the twentieth century met the tenth.

And as the smith whirled to recover, a terrible left-hander met him just below the short ribs.

With a grunt the man doubled, sprawled and fell. By some strange atavism, which he never afterward could understand, Allan counted, in the Folk's tongue: "*Hathi, ko, zem, baku—*" and so up to "*lamnu*"—ten.

Still the smith did not rise, but only lay and groaned and sought to catch the breath that would not come.

"I have won!" cried Allan in a loud voice. "Here, you people, take this *greun*, this child, away! And let there be no further idle talk of a dead law— for surely, in your custom, a law dies when its champion is beaten! Come, quick, away with him!"

Two stout men came forward, bowed to Allan with hands clasped upon their breasts in signal of fresh allegiance, and without ceremony took the insensible smith, neck-and-heels, and lugged him off as though he had only been a net heavily laden with fish.

The crowd opened in awed silence to let them pass. By the glare Allan noticed that the man's jaw hung oddly awry, even as the obeah's had hung, in Madison Forest.

"Jove, what a wallop that must have been!" thought he, now perceiving for the first time that his knuckles were cut and bleeding. "Old Monahan himself taught me that in the Harvard gym a thousand odd years ago— and it still works. *One* question settled, mighty quick; and H'yemba won't have much to say for a few weeks at least. Not till his jawbone knits again, anyhow!"

Upon his arm he felt a hand. Turning, he saw Vreenya, the aged counselor.

"Surely, O master, he shall not live, now you have conquered him? The boiling pit awaits. It is our custom—if you will!"

Allan only shook his head.

"All customs change, these times," he answered. "*I* am your law! This man's life is needed, for he has good skill with metals. He shall live, but never shall he speak before the Folk again. I have said it!"

To the waiting throng he turned again.

"Ye have witnessed!" he cried, in a loud voice. "Now, have fear of me, your master! Once in the Battle of the Walls ye beheld death raining from my fire-bow. Once ye watched me vanquish your ruler, even the great Kamrou himself, and fling him far into the pit that boils. And now, for the third time, ye have seen. Remember well!"

A stir ran through the multitude. He felt its potent meaning, and he understood.

"I am the law!" he flung at them once more. "Declare it, all! Repeat!"

The thousand-throated chorus: *"Thou art the law!"* boomed upward through the fog, rolled mightily against the towering cliff, and echoed thunderlike across the hot, black sea.

"It is well!" he cried. "One more sleep, and then—then I choose from among ye two for the journey, two of your boldest and best. And that shall be the first journey of many, up to the better places that await ye, far beyond the pit!"

Straining his eyes in the night, pierced only by the electric beam that ran and quavered rapidly over the broken forest-tops far below, Allan peered down and far ahead. The fire, the signal-fire he had told Beatrice to build upon the ledge—would he never sight it?

Eagerly he scanned the dark horizon only just visible in the star-shine. Warmly the rushing night wind fanned his cheek; the roar of the motor and propellers, pulsating mightily, made music to his ears. For it sang: "Home again! Beatrice, and love once more!"

Many long hours had passed since, his fuel-tanks replenished from the apparatus for distilling the crude naphtha, which he had installed during his first stay in the Abyss, he had risen a second time into that heavy, humid, purple-vapored air.

With him he now bore Bremilu, the strong, and Zangamon, most expert of all the fishermen. Slung in the baggage-crate aft lay a large seine, certain supplies of fish, weed and eggs, and—from time to time noisily squawking—some half-dozen of the strange sea-birds, in a metal basket.

The pioneers had insisted on taking these impedimenta with them, to bridge the gap of changed conditions, a precaution Stern had recognized as eminently sensible.

"Gad!" thought he, as the Pauillac swept its long, flat-arc'd trajectory through the night, "under any circumstances this must be a terrific wrench for them. Talk about nerve! If *they* haven't got it, who has? This trip of these subterranean barbarians, thus flung suddenly into midair, out into a world of which they know absolutely nothing, must be exactly what a journey to Mars would mean to me. More, far more, to their simple minds. I wonder myself at their courage in taking such a tremendous step."

And in his heart a new and keener admiration for the basic stamina of the Merucaans took root.

"They'll do!" he murmured, as he scanned his lighted chart once more, and cast up reckonings from the dials of his delicately adjusted instruments.

Half an hour more of rapid flight and he deemed New Hope River could not now be far.

"No use to try and hear it, though, with this racket of the propellers in my ears," thought he. "The searchlight might possibly pick up a gleam of water, if we fly over it. But even that's a small index to go by. The signal-fire must be my only real guide—and where is it, now, that fire?"

A vague uneasiness began to oppress him. The fire, he reckoned, should have shown ere now in the far distance. Without it, how find his way? And what of Beatrice?

His uneasy reflections were suddenly interrupted by a word from Zangamon, at his right.

"O *Kromno*, master, see?"

"What is it, now?"

"A fire, very distant, master!"

"Where?" queried Stern eagerly, his heart leaping with joy. "I see no fire. Your eyes, used to the dark places and the fogs, now far surpass mine, even as mine will yours when the time of light shall come. Where is the fire, Zangamon?"

The fisher pointed, a dim huge figure in the star-lit gloom.

"There, master. On thy left hand, thus."

Stern shifted his course to southwest by west, and for some minutes held it true, so that the needle hardly trembled on the compass dial.

Then all at once he, too, saw the welcome signal, a tiniest pin-prick of light far on the edge of the world, no different from the sixth-magnitude stars that hung just above it on the horizon, save for its redness.

A gush of gratitude and love welled in the fountains of his heart.

"Home!" he whispered. "Home—for where *you* are that's home to me! Oh, Beatrice, I'm coming—coming home to you!"

Slowly at first, then with greater and ever greater swiftness, the signal star crept nearer; and now even the flames were visible, and now behind them he caught dim sight of the rock-wall.

On and on, a very vulture of the upper air, planed the Pauillac. Stern shouted with all his strength. The girl might possibly hear him and might come out of their cave. She might even signal—and the nearness of her presence mounted upon him like a heady wine.

He swung the searchlight on the cañon, as they swept above it. He flung the pencil of radiance in a wide sweep up the cliff and down along the terrace.

It gave no sight, no sign of Beatrice.

"Sleeping, of course," he reflected.

And now, Hope River past, and the cañon swallowed by the dense forest, he flung his light once more ahead. With it he felt out the rocky barrens for a landing-place.

Not more than twenty minutes later, followed by Bremilu and Zangamon, Stern was making way through the thick-laced wood and jungle.

Awed, terrified by their first sight of trees and by the upper world which to them was naught but marvel and danger, the two Merucaans followed close behind their guide. Even so would you or I cling to the Martian who should land us on that ruddy planet and pilot us through some huge, inchoate and grotesque growth of things to us perfectly unimaginable.

"Oh, master, we shall see the patriarch soon?" asked Bremilu, in a strange voice—a voice to him astonishingly loud, in the clear air of night upon the surface of the world. "Soon shall we speak with him and—"

"Hark! What's that?" interrupted Stern, pausing, the while he gripped his pistol tighter.

From afar, though in which direction he could not say, a vague, dull roar made itself heard through the forest.

Sonorous, vibrant, menacing, it echoed and died; and then again, as once before, Stern heard that strange, hollow booming, as of some mighty drum struck by a muffled fist.

A cry? Was that a cry, so distant and so faint? Beast-cry, or call of nightbird, shrill and far?

Stern shuddered, and with redoubled haste once more pushed through the vague path he and Beatrice had made from the barrens to Settlement Cliffs.

Presently, followed by the two colonists who dared not let him for a moment out of their sight, he reached the brow of the cañon. His hand flashlamp showed him the rough path to the terrace.

With fast-beating heart he ran down it, unmindful of the unprotected edge or the sheer drop to the rocks of New Hope River, far below.

Bremilu and Zangamon, seeing perfectly in the gloom, hurried close behind, with words of awe, wonder and admiration in their own tongue.

"Beta! Oh, Beatrice! Home again!" Stern shouted triumphantly. "Where are you, Beta? Come! I'm home again!"

Quickly he scrambled along the broken terrace, stumbling in his haste over loose rocks and débris. Now he had reached the turn. The fire was in sight.

"Beta!" again he hailed. "*O-hé!* Beatrice!"

Still no answer, nor any sign from her. As he came to the fire he noted, despite his strong emotions, that it had for the most part burned down to glowing embers.

Only one or two resinous knots still flamed. It could not have been replenished for some time, perhaps two hours or more.

Again, his quick eye caught the fact that cinders, ashes and half-burned sticks lay scattered about in strange disorder.

"Why, Beatrice never makes a fire like that!" the thought pierced through his mind.

And—though as yet on no very definite grounds—a quick prescience of catastrophe battered at his heart.

"What's *this?*"

Something lying on the rock-ledge, near the fire, caught his eye. He snatched it up.

"What—what can *this* mean?"

The colonists stood, frightened and confused, peering at him in the dark. His face, in the ruddy fire-glow, as he studied the thing he now held in his hand, must have been very terrible.

"*Cloth!* Torn! But—but *then*—"

He flung from him the bit of the girl's cloak which, ripped and shredded as though by a powerful hand, cried disaster.

"Beatrice!" he shouted. "Where are you? Beatrice!"

To the doorway in the cliff he ran, shaken and trembling.

The stone had been pushed away; it lay inside the cave. Ominously the black entrance seemed staring at him in the dull gleam of the firelight.

On hands and knees he fell, and hastily crawled through. As he went, he flashed his lamp here, there, everywhere.

"Beatrice! *Beatrice!*"

No answer.

In the far corner still flickered some remainder of the cooking-fire. But there, too, ashes and half-burned sticks lay scattered all about.

To the bed he ran. It was empty and cold.

"Beatrice! Oh, my God!"

A glint of something metallic on the floor drew his bewildered, terror-smitten gaze.

He sprang, seized the object, and for a moment stood staring, while all about him the very universe seemed thundering and crashing down.

The object in his hand was the girl's gun. One cartridge, and only one, had been exploded.

The barrel had been twisted almost off, as though by the wrenching clutch of a hand inhuman in its ghastly power.

On the stock, distinctly nicked into the hard rubber as Stern held the flash-lamp to it, were the unmistakable imprints of teeth.

With a groan, Allan started backward. The revolver fell with a clatter to the cave floor.

His foot slid in something wet, something sticky.

"Blood!" he gasped.

Half-crazed, he reeled toward the door.

The flash-lamp in his hand flung its white brush of radiance along the wall.

With a chattering cry he recoiled.

There, roughly yet unmistakably imprinted on the white limestone surface, he saw the print, in crimson, of a huge, a horrible, a brutally distorted hand.

CHAPTER XIV

On the Trail of the Monster

STERN'S cry of horror as he scrambled from the ravaged, desecrated cave, and the ghastly horror of his face, seen by the firelight, brought Zangamon and Bremilu to him, in terror.

"Master! Master! What—"

"My God! The girl—she's gone!" he stammered, leaning against the cliff in mortal anguish.

"Gone, master? Where?"

"Gone! Dead, perhaps! Find her for me! Find her! You can see—in the dark! I—I am as though blind! Quick, on the trail!"

"But tell us—"

"Something has taken her! Some savage thing! Some wild man! Even now he may be killing her! *Quick—after them!*"

Bremilu stood staring for a moment, unable to grasp this catastrophe on the very moment of arrival. But Zangamon, of swifter wit, had already fallen on his knees, there by the mouth of the cave, and now—seeing clearly by the dim light which more than sufficed for him—was studying the traces of the struggle.

Stern, meanwhile, clutching his head between both hands, dumb-mad with agony, was choking with dry sobs.

"Master! See!"

Zangamon held up a piece of splintered wood, with the bark deeply scarred by teeth.

Stern snatched it.

"Part of the pole I gave her to brace the rock with," he realized. "Even that was of no avail."

"Master—this way they went!"

Zangamon pointed up along the rock-terrace. Stern's eyes could distinguish no slightest trace on the stone, but the Merucaan spoke with certainty. He added:

"There was fighting, all the way along here, master. And then, here, the girl was dragged."

Stern stumbled blindly after him as he led the way.

"There was fighting here? She struggled?"

"Yes, master."

"Thank God! She was alive here, anyhow! She wasn't killed in the cave. Maybe, in the open, she might—"

"Now there is no more fighting, master. The wild thing carried her here."

He pointed at the rock. Stern, trembling and very sick, flashed his electric-lamp upon it. With eyes of dread and horror he looked for blood-stains.

What? A drop! With a dull, shuddering groan, he pressed forward again.

Out he jerked his pistol and fired, straight up, their prearranged signal: One shot, then a pause, then two. Some bare possibility existed and that she still might live and hear and know that rescue came—if it could come before it were eternally too late!

"On, on!" cried Allan. "Go on, Zangamon! Quick! Lead me on the trail!"

The Merucaan, now aided by Bremilu, who had recovered his wits, scouted ahead like a blood-hound on the spoor of a fugitive. One gripped his stone ax, the other a javelin.

Bent half double, scrutinizing in the dark the stony path which Allan followed behind them only by the aid of his flash, they proceeded cautiously up toward the brow of the cliff again.

But ere they reached the top they branched off onto another lateral path, still rougher and more tortuous, that led along the breast of the cañon,

"This way, master. It was here, most surely, the thing carried her."

"What kind of marks? Do you see signs of claws?"

"Claws? What are claws?"

"Sharp, long nails, like our nails, only much larger and longer. Do you see any such marks?"

Zangamon paused a second to peer.

"I seem to see marks as of hands, master, but—"

"No matter! On! We must find her! Quick—lead the way!"

Five minutes of agonizing suspense for Allan brought him, still following the guides, without whom all would have been utterly lost, to a kind of thickly wooded dell that descended sharply to the edge of the cañon. Into this the trail led.

Even he himself could now here and there make out, by the aid of his light, a broken twig, trampled ferns and down-crushed grass. Once he distinguished a blood-stain on a limb—fresh blood, not coagulated. A groan burst from between his chattering teeth.

He turned his light on the grass beneath. All at once a blade moved.

"Oh, thank God!" he wheezed. "They passed here only a few minutes ago. They can't be far now!"

Something drew his attention. He snatched at a sapling.

"Hair!"

Caught in a roughness of the bark a few short, stiff, wiry-hairs, reddish-brown, were twisted.

"One of the Horde?" he stammered.

A lightning-flash of memory carried him back to Madison Forest, more than a year ago. He seemed to see again the obeah, as that monster advanced upon the girl, clutching, supremely hideous.

"The hair! The same kind of hair! In the power of the Horde!" he gasped.

A mental picture of extermination flashed before his mind's eye. Whether the girl lived or died, he knew now that his life work was to include a total slaughter of the Anthropoids. The destruction he had already wrought among them was but child's play to what would be.

And in his soul flamed the foreknowledge of a hunt *à l'outrance,* to the bitter end. So long as one, a single one of that foul breed should live, he would not rest from killing.

"Master! This way! Here, master!"

The voice of Zangamon sent him once more crashing through the jungle, after his questing guides. Again he fired the signal-shot, and now with the full power of his lungs he yelled.

His voice rang, echoing, through the black and tangled growths, startling the night-life of the depths. Something chippered overhead. Near-by a serpent slid away, hissing venomously. Death lurked on every hand.

Stern took no thought of it, but pressed forward, shouting the girl's name, hallooing, beating down the undergrowth with mad fury. And here, there, all about he flung the light-beam.

Perhaps she might yet hear his hails; perhaps she might even catch some distant glimmer of his light, and know that help was coming, that rescuers were fighting onward to her.

Silent, lithe, confident even among these new and terribly strange conditions, the two men of the Folk slid through the jungle.

No hounds ever trailed fugitive more surely and with greater skill than these strange, white barbarians from the underworld. Through all his fear and agony, Stern blessed their courage and their skill.

"Men, by God! They're *men!*" he muttered, as he thrashed his painful way behind them in the night.

Of a sudden, there somewhere ahead, far ahead in the wilderness—a cry?

Allan stopped short, his heart leaping.

Again he fired, and his voice set all the echoes ringing.

A cry! He knew it now. There could be no mistake—*a cry!*

"Beatrice!" he shouted in a terrible voice, leaping forward. The guides broke into a crouching run. All three crashed through the thickets, split the fern-masses, struggled through the tall saber-grass that here and there rose higher than their heads.

Allan cursed himself for a fool. That other cry he had heard while on his way from the Pauillac to Settlement Cliffs—that had been her cry for help—and he had neither known nor heeded.

"Fool that I was! Oh, damnable idiot that I was!" he panted as he ran.

From moment to moment he fired. He paused a few seconds to jack a fresh cartridge-clip into the automatic.

"Thank God I've got a belt full of ammunition!" thought he, and again smashed along with the two Merucaans.

All at once a formidable roar gave them pause.

Hollow, booming, deep, yet rising to a wild shriek of rage and horrid brutality, the beast-cry flung itself through the jungle.

And, following it, they heard again that muffled drumming, as though gigantic fists were flailing a tremendous tambour in the darkness.

"Master!" whispered Zangamon, recoiling a step. "Oh, Kromno, what is *that?*"

"Never have we heard such in our place!" added Bremilu, gripping his ax the tighter. "Is that a man-cry, or the cry of a beast—one of the beasts you told us of, that we have never seen?"

"Both! A man-beast! Kill! Kill!"

Now, Allan, sure of his direction, took the lead. No longer he flashed the light, and only once more he called: "Beatrice! O Beatrice! We're coming!"

Again he heard her cry, but suddenly it died as though swiftly choked in her very throat. Allan spat a blasphemy and surged on.

The two white barbarians followed, peering with those strange, pinkish eyes of theirs, courageous still, yet utterly at a loss to know what manner of thing they were now drawing near.

They burst through a thicket, waded a marshy swale and went splashing, staggering and slipping among tufts of coarse and knife-edged grasses, the haunt of unknown venomous reptiles.

Up a slope they won; and now, all at once the roar burst forth again close at hand, a rending tumult, wild, earth-shaking, inexpressibly terrible.

All three stopped.

"Beatrice! Are you there? Answer!" shouted Stern.

Silence, save for a peculiar mumbling snuffle off ahead, among the deeper shadows of a fern-tree thicket.

"Beatrice!"

No answer. With a groan Allan shot his light toward the thicket. He seemed to distinguish something moving. To his ears now came a sound of twigs and brushwood snapping.

Absolutely void of fear he pressed forward, and the two colonists with him, their weapons ready. Stern held his revolver poised for instant action. His heart was hammering, and his breath surged pantingly; but within him his consciousness and soul lay calm.

For he knew one of two things were now to happen. Either that beast ahead there in the gloom, or he, must die.

CHAPTER XV

IN THE GRIP OF TERROR

As the three pursuers steadily advanced, the thing roared once more, and again they heard the hammering, drumming boom. Zangamon whispered some unintelligible phrase.

Allan projected the light forward again, and at sight of a moving mass, vague and intangible, among the gigantic fronds, leveled his automatic.

But on the instant Bremilu seized his arm.

"O master! Do not throw the fire of death!" he warned. "You cannot see, but we can! Do not throw the fire!"

"Why not? What *is* that thing?"

"It seems a man, yet it is different, master. It is all hair, and very thick and strong, and hideous! Do not shoot, O Kromno!"

"Why not?"

"Behold! That strange man-thing holds the woman, Beatrice, in his left arm. Of a truth, you may kill her, and not the enemy."

Allan steadied himself against a palm. His brain seemed whirling, and for a moment all grew vague and like a dream.

She was there—Beatrice was there, and they could see her. There, in the clutches of some monster, horrible and foul! Living yet? *Dead?*

"Tell me! Does she live?"

"We cannot say, O Kromno. But do not shoot. We will creep close—we, ourselves, will slay, and never touch the woman."

"No, no! If you do he'll strangle her—provided she still lives! Don't go! Wait! Let me think a second."

With a tremendous effort Allan mastered himself. The situation far surpassed, in horror, any he had ever known.

There not a hundred yards distant in the dense blackness was Beatrice, in the grip of some unknown and hideous creature. Advance, Allan dared not, lest the creature rend her to tatters. Shoot, he dared not.

Yet something must be done, and quickly, for every second, every fraction of a second, was golden. The merest accident might now mean death or life—life, if the girl still lived!

"Zangamon!"

"Yea, master?"

"Be very bold! Do my bidding!"

"Speak only the word, Kromno, and I obey!"

"Go you, then, very quietly, very swiftly, to the other side of these great growing things—these trees, we call them. Then call, so that this thing shall turn toward you. Thus, I may shoot, and perhaps not kill the woman. It is the only way!"

"I hear, master. I go!"

Allan and Bremilu waited, while from the thicket came, at intervals, the savage snuffling, with now and then a grumbling mutter.

All at once a call sounded from far ahead.

"Come!" commanded Allan. Together he and Bremilu crept through the jungle toward the thicket.

Wide-eyed, yet seeing almost nothing, Allan crawled noiselessly, automatic in hand. The Merucaan slid along, silent as an Apache.

"Tell me if you see the thing again—if you see it turn!" whispered Stern. "Tell me, for you can see."

Now the distance was cut in half; now only a third of it remained. Before Stern it seemed a fathomless pit of black was opening. Under the close-woven arches of the giant fern-trees the night was impenetrable.

And as yet he dared not dart the light-beam into that pit of darkness, for fear of precipitating an unthinkable tragedy—if, indeed, the horror had not already been consummated.

But now Bremilu gripped his arm. Afar, on the other side of the thicket, they heard a singular commotion, cries, shouts, and the vigorous beating of the fern-trees.

"The thing has turned, master!" the Merucaan exclaimed, at Allan's side. "Now throw the fire-death! *Etvur!* Quickly, throw!"

Stern swept the thicket with his beam.

"Ah! There—*there!*"

The light caught a moving, hairy mass of brown—a huge, squat, terrible creature, its back now toward them. At one side Stern saw a vague blackness—the long, unbound hair of Beatrice!

He glimpsed a white arm dangling limp; and in his breast the heart flamed at white-heat of rage and passion.

But his hand was steel. Never in his life had he drawn so fine a bead.

"Hold the light for me!" he whispered, passing it to his companion. "I want both hands for this!"

Bremilu held the beam true, blinking strangely with his pink eyes. Stern, resting his pistol hand in the hollow of his left elbow, sighted true.

A fraction of a hair to the left, and the bullet might crash through the brain of Beatrice!

"Oh, God—if there be any God—speed the shot true!" he prayed, and fired.

A hideous yell, ripping the night to shreds, burst in a raw and rising discord through the forest—a scream as of a damned soul flung upon the brimstone.

Then, as he glimpsed the white arm falling and knew the thing had loosed its grip, the light died. Bremilu, starting at the sudden discharge close to his ear, had pressed the ivory button.

Stern snatched for the flash-lamp, fumbled it, and dropped it there among the lush growths underfoot.

Before he could more than stoop to feel for it a heavy crash through the wood told that the thing was charging.

With bubbling yells it came, trampling the undergrowth, drumming on its huge breast, gibbering with demoniac rage and pain—came swiftly, like the terrific things that people nightmares.

Behind it, shouts echoed. Stern heard the voice of Zangamon as, spear in hand, the Merucaan pursued.

He raised his revolver once more, but dared not fire.

Yet only an instant he hesitated, in the fear of killing Zangamon.

For, quick-looming through the darkness, a huge bulk, panting, snarling, chattering, sprang—an avalanche of muscle, bone, fur, mad with murder-rage.

Crack! spoke the automatic, point-blank at this rushing horror, this blacker shadow in the blackness.

The fire-stab revealed a grinning white-fanged face close to his own, and clutching hands, and terrible, thick, hairy arms.

Then something hurled itself on Stern; something bore him backward—something beside which his strength was as a baby's—something vast, irresistible, hideous beyond all telling.

Stern felt the flesh of his left arm ripped up. Crushed, doubled, impotent, he fell.

And at his throat long fingers clutched. A fetid, stinking breath gushed hot upon his face. He heard the raving chatter of ivories, snapping to rend him.

Up sprang another shadow. High it swung a weapon. The blow thudded hollow, smashing, annihilating.

Hot liquid gushed over Allan's hand as he sought to beat the monster back.

Then, fair upon him, fell a crushing weight.

Swooning, he knew no more.

CHAPTER XVI

A Respite from Toil

The bright beam of the flash-lamp in his face roused Allan to a consciousness that he was bruised and suffering, and that his left arm ached with dull insistence. Dazed, he brought it up and saw his sleeve of dull brown stuff was dripping red.

Beside him, in the trampled grass, he vaguely made out a hairy bulk, motionless and huge. Bremilu was kneeling beside his master, with words of cheer.

"It is dead, O Kromno! The man-beast is dead! My stone ax broke its skull. See, now it lies here harmless!"

The currents of thought began to flow once more. Allan struggled up, unmindful of his wounds.

"Beatrice! *Where is the girl?*" he gasped.

As though by way of answer, the tall growths swayed and crackled, and through them a dim figure loomed—a man with something in his arms.

"Zangamon!" panted Allan, springing toward him. "Have you got her? The girl—is she alive?"

"She lives, master!" replied a voice. "But as yet she remains without knowledge of aught."

"Wounded? Is she wounded?"

Already he had reached Zangamon, and, injured though he was, had taken the beloved form in his arms.

"Beatrice! Beatrice!" he called, pressing kisses to her brow, her eyes, her mouth—still warm, thank God!

He sank down among the underbrush and gathered her to his breast, cradling her, cherishing her to him as though to bring back life and consciousness.

To her heart he laid his ear. It beat! She breathed!

"The light, here! Quick!"

By its clear ray he saw her hair disheveled; her coarse mantle of brown stuff ripped and torn, and on her throat long scratches.

Bruises showed on her hands and arms, as from a terrible fight she had put up against the monster. And his heart bled; and to his lips rose execrations, mingled with the tenderest words of pity and love.

"We must get her back to the cave at once!" he exclaimed. "Quick! Break branches. Make a litter—a bed—to carry her on! Everything depends on getting her to shelter now!"

But the two Merucaans did not understand. All this was beyond their knowledge. Ignoring his hurts, Allan laid the girl down very gently, and with them set to work, directing the making of the litter.

They obeyed eagerly. In a few minutes the litter was ready—made of fern-tree branches thickly covered with leaves and odorous grasses.

On this he placed the girl.

"You, Zangamon, take these boughs here. Bremilu, those others. Now I will hold the light. Back to the cave, now—quick!"

"We need not the light, master. We see better without it. It dazzles our eyes. Use it for yourself. We need it not!" exclaimed Bremilu, stooping above the body of the dead monster to recover his ax.

Involuntarily Allan turned the beam upon the horrible creature. There stood Bremilu, his foot upon the hairy shoulder, tugging hard at the ax-handle. Thrice he had to pull with all his might to loosen the blade which had buried itself deep in the shattered skull.

"A giant gorilla, so help me!" he cried, shuddering; "My God, Beatrice— what a ghastly terror you've been through!"

Still grinning ferociously, in death, with blood-smeared face and glazed, staring eyes, the creature shocked and horrified even Allan's steady nerves. He gazed upon it only a moment, then turned away.

"Enough!" said he. "To the cave!"

A quarter-hour had passed before they reached shelter again. Allan bade the Merucaans heap dry wood on the embers in the cavern, while he himself laid Beatrice upon the bed.

With a piece of their brown cloth dipped in one of the water-jars he bathed her face and bruised throat.

"Fresh water! Fetch a jar of fresh water from the river below!" he commanded Zangamon.

But even as the white barbarian started to obey, the girl stirred, raised a hand, and feebly spoke.

"Allan—oh—are you here again? Allan—my love!"

He strained her to his breast and kissed her; and his eyes grew hot with tears.

"Beatrice!"

Her arms were round his neck, and their lips clung.

"Hurt? Are you hurt?" he cried. "Tell me—how—"

"Allan! The monster—is he dead?" she shivered, sitting up and staring wildly round at the cave walls on which the fresh-built fire was beginning to throw dancing lights.

"Dead, yes. But hush, Beta! Don't think of that now. Everything's all right—you're safe! I'm here!"

"Those men—"

"Two of our own Folk. I brought them back with me—just in time, darling. Without them—"

He broke short off. Not for worlds would he have told her how near the borderland she had been.

"You heard my shouts? You heard our signal?"

"Oh—I don't know Allan. I can't think, yet—it's all so terrible—so confused—"

"There, there, sweetheart; don't think about it any more. Just lie down and rest. Go to sleep. I'll watch here beside you. You're safe. Nothing can hurt you now!"

She lay back with a sigh, and for a while kept silence while he sat beside her, his uninjured arm beneath her head.

His one ambition, now that he found she was not seriously hurt in body, was to keep her from talking of the horrible affair—from exciting herself and rehearsing her terrors. Above all, she must be quieted and kept calm.

At last, in her own natural voice, she spoke again.

"Allan?"

"What is it, sweetheart?"

"I owe you my life once more! If I was yours before, I'm ten times more yours now!"

He bent and kissed her, and presently her deepened breathing told him she had drifted over the borderline into the sleep of exhaustion.

He blessed her strength and courage.

"No futility here," thought he. "No useless questions or hysterics; no scene. Strong! Gad, but she's strong! She realized she was safe and I was with her again; that sufficed. Was there ever another woman like her since the world began?"

Only now that the girl slept did he pay attention to the two Merucaans who, sitting by the cave door, were regarding him with troubled looks.

"Master!" said Zangamon, arising and coming toward him.

"Well, what is it now?"

"You are wounded, O Kromno! Your arm still bleeds. Let us bind it."

"It is nothing—only a scratch!"

But Zangamon insisted.

"Master," said he, "in this we cannot obey you. See! While you and the woman talked I fetched water, as you commanded. Now I must wash your hurts and bind them."

Allan had to accede. Together the two Merucaans examined the injuries with words of commiseration. The "scratch" turned out to be three severe lacerations of the forearm. The gorilla's teeth had missed the radial artery only by a fluke of fortune.

They bathed away the clotted blood and bandaged the arm not unskilfully. Allan pressed the hand of Zangamon, then that of his companion.

"No thanks of mine can tell you what I feel!" he exclaimed straight from the heart. "Only for you to guide me, to drive the man-brute, to strike it down when it was just about to throttle me—only for you, both *she* and *I*—"

He could not finish. The words choked him. He felt, as never before, a sudden, warm, human touch of kinship with the Merucaans—a strong, nascent affection. Till now they had been savages to him—inferiors.

Now he perceived their inner worth—the strong and manly stamina of soul and body; and through him thrilled a love for these strange men, his saviors and the girl's.

Once more he seemed to see a vision of the future—a world peopled by the descendants of this hardy and resourceful folk, "without disease of flesh or brain, shapely and fair, the married harmony of form and function"—and, as with a gesture, he dismissed them wondering, not understanding in the least why he should thank them, he knew the world already had begun once more to come back under the hand, under the strong control of man.

"Sleep now, master," Bremilu entreated. "We who are new to this strange world will sit outside the door upon the rock and watch those fires so far above that you call stars. And the big sun-fire that is coming, too—we would see that!"

"No, not yet!" Stern commanded. "You cannot bear it for a while. Stay within and roll the rock against the door and sleep. The great fire might injure you or even kill you, as it did the—"

He checked himself just in time, for "the patriarch" had all but escaped him. Zangamon, with sudden understanding, once more advanced toward him as he sat there by the girl.

"O master! You mean the ancient man? He is dead?"

Stern nodded.

"Yes," he answered. "He was so old and weak, the touch of the fire in the sky—he could not bear it. But his death was happy, for at least he felt its warmth upon his brow!"

The Merucaans kept silence for a moment, then Stern heard them murmuring together, and a vague uneasiness crept over him.

He strove, however, to put it away; though in his heart the shame of the lie he had been forced to tell would not be quieted.

The colonists, however, made no further speech, but presently rolled the rock in front of the cave entrance, then wrapped themselves in their long cloaks and lay down by the fire.

Soon, like the healthy savages they were, they were fast asleep, with vigorous snorings.

Thus the night passed, while Stern kept watch over the girl; and another day crept slowly up the sky, and in the cave now rested four human beings—the vanguard of the coming nation.

CHAPTER XVII

THE DISTANT MENACE

STERN never knew when he, too, drifted off to sleep; but he awoke to find Zangamon sitting beside him, with his cloak drawn over his head, while Beatrice and Bremilu still slept.

"The light, master—it is like knives to me! Like spears to my eyes, master! I cannot bear it!" whispered the Merucaan, pointing to where, around the interstices of the doorway, bright white gleams were streaming in.

Allan considered with perplexity.

"It hurts, you say?"

"Yes, Kromno! Once or twice I have tried to watch that strange fire, but I cannot. The pain is very great!"

"Humph!" thought Allan. "This may be a more serious factor than I've reckoned on. These people are albinos. White hair and pink eyes—not a particle of protecting pigmentation. For thirty or so generations they've been subjected to nothing but torchlight. The actinic rays of the sun are infinitely more penetrating than anything they've ever known. It may take months, years even, to accustom them to sunlight!"

And disquieting situations presented themselves to his mind. True, if it were necessary, the Folk could work and take the air only at night.

They could fish, hunt and till the soil by star and moonlight, and sleep by day; but this was by no means the veritable reëstablishment of a real, human civilization.

Then an idea struck him.

"The very thing!" cried he. "Once I can put it into effect, it will solve the question. And the second generation, at the outside, will be normal. They'll 'throw back' to remote ancestry under changed conditions. In time, even if only a long time, all will yet be well!"

But now immediate labors and difficult problems were pressing. The future would have to look out for itself.

Stern felt positive that to let the Merucaans out of the cave would not only blind them, but might also kill them outright as well.

Their unprotected skins would inevitably burn to a blister under the rays of the sun, and they would in all probability die. So said he:

"Listen, Zangamon! You must stay here till the dark comes again, which will not be very long. The woman and I will prepare another cave for your dwelling. When it is dark you can fish in the flowing water beneath. In the mean time we will bring you your accustomed food and your nets from the flying boat.

"You must be patient. In a short time all things shall be as you wish, and you shall see the wonderful and beautiful world up into which I have brought you!"

The man nodded, yet Stern clearly saw his face betrayed uneasiness, distrust and pain. In all fairness, the Merucaans' first experience of the upper world had been enough to shake the faith even of a philosopher—how much more so that of simple and untaught barbarians!

Terror, violence, slaughter and insecurity—these all had greeted the colonists; and now, in addition, they found the patriarch was dead. Above all, they were virtually prisoners in this gloomy cavern of the rock.

But Stern was very wise. He by no means thought of commiserating or excusing. His only course was to make light of trials and hardships, and, if need were, to command.

He arose, carefully stopped up the chinks around the rock at the doorway, and bade Zangamon replenish the fire with dry sticks. Then, Bremilu awakening, they prepared food.

Now Beatrice, too, awoke. Allan took her in his arms, unmindful of the newcomers, and there were words of love and joy, and self-reproaches, and a new faith plighted between them once again.

She was unharmed, except for a few bruises and scratches. Her nerves had already recovered something of their usual strength. But at sight of

Allan's bandaged arm she turned pale, and not even his assurances could comfort her.

They talked of the terrible adventure.

"It was all my fault, Allan—every bit my fault!" she exclaimed remorsefully. "It all came from my not obeying orders. You see, I was expecting you last night. Instead of staying in the cave, with the door barricaded, I lingered on the terrace, after having piled the signal-fire high with wood.

"I sat down and watched the sky, and listened to the river down below, and thought of you. I must have dozed a little, for all of a sudden I came wide-awake, shuddering with a terror I couldn't understand. Then I heard something moving down the path—something that grunted and snuffled savagely.

"I started up, ran for the cave, and just got inside when the brute reached it. I rolled the stone in place, Allan, but before I could brace it with the pole it was hurled back, and in crawled the gorilla, roaring and snapping like a demon!"

She hid her face in both hands, shuddering at the terrible memory. But, forcing herself to be calm, she went on again:

"I snatched up the pistol and fired. Then—"

"You hit him?"

"I must have, for he screeched most horribly and pawed at his breast—"

"So, then, that explains the blood-marks on the floor and the great hand-print on the wall?"

"Hand-print? Was there one?"

"Yes; but no matter now. Go on!"

"After that—oh, it was too ghastly! He seized me and I fought—I struggled against that huge, hairy chest; he gripped me like iron. My blows were no more than so many pats to him.

"I tried to fire again, but he wrenched the pistol away, and bent it in his huge teeth and flung it down. But, though he was raging, he didn't wound me—didn't try to kill me, or anything. He seemed to want to capture me alive—"

Allan shuddered. Only too well he understood. Gorilla nature had not changed in fifteen hundred years.

"After that?" he questioned eagerly.

"Oh, after that I don't remember much. I must have fainted. Next thing I knew, everything was dark and the forest was all about. I screamed and then again I knew nothing. Once more I seemed to sense things, and once more all grew black. And after that—"

"Well?"

"Why—I was here on the bed, and you were beside me, Allan—and these men of our Folk were here! But how it all happened, God knows!"

"I'll tell you some time. You shall have the story from our side some day, but not now. Only one thing—if it hadn't been for Zangamon here and Bremilu—well—"

"You mean they helped rescue me?"

He nodded.

"Without them I'd have been helpless as a child. They traced you in the dark, for they could see as plainly as we see by day. It was a blow from Bremilu's stone ax that killed the brute. *They* saved you, Beatrice! Not I!"

She kept a little silence, then said thoughtfully:

"How can I ever thank them, Allan? How can I thank them best?"

"You can't thank them. There's no way. I tried it, but they didn't understand. They only did what seemed natural to them. They're savages, remember; not civilized men. It's impossible to thank them! The only thing you can do, or I can do, is work for them now. The greatest efforts and sacrifices for these men will be small payment for their deed. And if—as I believe—the whole race is dowered with the same spirit and indomitable courage—the courage we certainly did see in the Battle of the Wall—then we need have no fear of our transplanted nation dying out!"

Much more there might have been to say, but now the meal was ready, and hunger spoke in no uncertain tones. All four of the adventurers ate in silence, thoughtful and grave, cross-legged, about the meat and drink, which lay on palm-leaves or in clay bowls hard-burned and red.

A kind of embarrassment seemed to rest on all, for this was the first time they had eaten together—these barbarians with the two folk of the upper world.

But the meal was soon at an end, and the prospect of labors to be undertaken cheered Allan's spirit. Despite his stiff and painful arm, he felt courage and energy throbbing in his veins, and longed to be at work.

"The very first thing we must do," said he, "is fix up a place for our guests. They've got to stay here, out of the light, till nightfall. That will give us plenty of time. I want to get them settled in their own quarters, and bring them into some regular routine of life and labor, before they have a chance to get homesick and dejected."

He warned the Merucaans to cover their heads with their cloaks while Beatrice and he opened the doorway.

He closed it then, with other rocks outside, and covered it with his own outer cloak; then, wearing only his belted tunic, he rejoined Beatrice halfway up the path to the cliff-top. Both were armed; he with his own automatic, she with the one they had found in the crypt.

"Our first move," said he, "will be to transport the various things from the aeroplane. It will be something of a task, but I don't dare leave them out there on the barrens till night, when the men themselves could bring them in. The sooner we get things to rights the better."

She agreed, and together they took the path toward the landing-place, which they had christened Newport Heights. Stern felt grateful that his right arm, his gun arm, was uninjured. The other mattered little for the present.

An idea crossed his mind to seek out the dead gorilla and make a trophy of the pelt; but he dismissed it at once. The beast was so repellant that the very thought of it fair sickened him.

They reached the plane in some few minutes, found everything uninjured, and loaded themselves with the Merucaans' goods and chattels. Stern took the bags of edible seaweed and the metal crate of fowl; she draped the big net over her shoulders, and together, not without difficulty, they returned to Settlement Cliffs.

Pass, now, all the minute details of the installation. By noon they had prepared a habitation for the newcomers, deep in a far recess of a winding gallery which thoroughly excluded all direct sunlight.

Only the dimmest glow penetrated even at high noon. Here they stowed the freight, built a rock fireplace, and threw down quantities of the long, fragrant grass for bedding.

They returned to their own cave, bade the colonists once more cover their heads, and entered, carefully closing the doorway after them. All four dined together, in true Merucaan style, on the familiar food of the Abyss. The colonists seemed a little more reassured, but talk languished none the less.

The afternoon was spent in preparing a second cave; for, in spite of all the girl's entreaties, Allan was determined to make another visit to the village of the Lost Folk as soon as his arm should permit.

"Nothing can happen this time, dear girl," he assured her as they sat resting by the mouth of the newly prepared dwelling. "You'll have two absolutely faithful and efficient guards always within call by night. By day you can barricade yourself with them, if there's any sign of danger."

"I know, Allan, but—"

"There's no other way! Our work is just begun!"

She nodded silently, then said in a low tone:

"Yours the labor; mine the waiting, the watching, and the fear!"

"The fear? Since when have *you* grown timid?"

"Only for you, Allan! Only for you! Suppose, some time, you should not come back!"

He laughed.

"We thrashed that all out the first time. It's old straw, Beta. My end of the task is getting these people here. Yours is waiting, watching—and being strong!"

Her hand tightened on his, and for a little while they sat quite still and without speech, watching the day draw to its close.

Far below, New Hope River chattered its incessant gossip to the vexing boulders. Above, in the sky, lazy June clouds, wool-white, drifted to westward, as though seeking the glory that there promised to transmute them into gold and crimson.

A pleasant wind swayed the forest, wherein the scarlet birds flitted like flashes of flame. The beauty of the outlook thrilled their hearts, leaving no room for words.

But suddenly Allan's eyes narrowed, and with a singular hardening of expression, a tightening of the jaw, he peered away at the dim, haze-shrouded line of far horizon to northeastward.

He cast a sidelong glance at Beatrice. She had noticed nothing.

One moment he made as though to speak, then repressed the words, and once more gazed at the horizon.

There, so vague as almost to leave a doubt in mind, yet, after all, only too terribly real, his keen sight had detected something which caused his heart to throb the quicker and his eye to gleam with hate.

For, at the very rim of the world, dim, pale, ominous, three tiny threads of smoke were hanging in the evening air.

CHAPTER XVIII

THE ANNUNCIATION

A WEEK later all was ready for Allan's second trip into the Abyss.

His arm had recovered its usual strength and suppleness, for his flesh, healthy as any savage's, now had the power of healing with a rapidity unknown to civilized men in the old days.

And his abounding vigor dictated action—always action, progress, and accomplishment. Only one thing depressed him—idleness.

It was on the second day of July, according to the rude calendar they were keeping, that he once more bade farewell to Beatrice and, borne by the Pauillac, headed for the village of the Lost Folk.

He left behind him all matters in a state of much improvement. Zangamon and Bremilu were now well installed in the new environment and seemingly content. By night they fished in New Hope Pool, making hauls such as their steaming sea had never yielded.

They wandered—not too far, however—in the forest, gradually making the acquaintance of the wondrous upper world, and with their strangely acute instincts finding fruits, bulbs and plants that well agreed with them for food.

Allan had carefully instructed them in the use of the wonderful "firebow"—the revolver—warning them, however, not to waste ammunition. They learned quickly, and now Beatrice found her larder supplied each night with game, which they dressed and brought her in the evening gloom, eager to serve their mistress in all possible ways.

They fished for her as well, and all the choicest fruits were her portion. She, in turn, cooked for them in their own cave. And for an hour or two each night she instructed them in English.

Short are the annals of peace—and peace reigned at Settlement Cliffs those few days at least. Progress!

She could feel it, see it, every hour. And her thoughts of Allan, now abandoning their melancholy hue, began to thrill with a new and even greater pride.

"Only he, only he could have brought these things to pass!" she murmured sometimes. "Only he could have planned all this, dreamed this dream, and brought it to reality; only he could labor for the future so strongly and so well!"

And in her heart the love that had been that of a girl became that of a woman. It broadened, deepened and grew calmer.

Its fever cooled into a finer, purer glow. It strengthened day by day, transmuting to a perfect trust and confidence and peace.

Allan returned safely inside the week with two more of the Folk—warriors and fishers both. Beatrice would have welcomed the arrival of even one woman to bear her some kind of company, but she realized the wisdom of his plan.

"The main thing at first," he explained, as they sat again on the terrace the evening of his return, "the very most essential thing is to build up even a small force of fighting men to hold the colony and protect it—a stalwart advance-guard, as if this were a military expedition. After that the women and children can come. But for the present there's no place for them."

Now that there were four Merucaans, all seemed more contented. The little group settled down into some real semblance of a community.

Work became systematized. Life was beginning to take firm root in the world again, and already the outlines of the future colony were commencing to be sketched in.

So far as Stern could discover, no disaffection as yet existed. The Folk, in any event, were singularly stolid, here as in their own home. If the colonists sometimes muttered together against conditions or concerning the lie Allan had told about the patriarch, he could never discover the fact.

He derived a singular sense of power and exaltation from watching his settlers at their work.

Strange figures they made in the upper world, descending the cliff at night, their torches flaring on their pure-white hair bound with gold ornaments, their nets slung over their brown-clad shoulders.

Strange, too, were the sensations of Beta and Allan as they beheld the flambeaux gleaming silently along the pool or over the surface when the Folk put forth on the rude rafts Allan had helped them build.

And as, with the same weird song they had used in the under world, the heavy-laden Merucaans clambered again up the terraces to their dwelling in the rock, something drew very powerfully at Allan's heart.

He analyzed it not, being a man of deeds rather than of introspection; yet it was "the strong man yearning toward his kind," the very love of his own race within him—the thrill, the inspiration of the master builder laying the foundations for better things to be.

Allan and the girl had long talks about the character of the future civilization they meant to raise.

"We must begin right this time at all hazards," he told her. "The world we used to know just happened; it just grew up, hit-or-miss, without scientific planning or thought or care. It was partly the result of chance, partly of ignorance and greed. The kind of human nature it developed was in essence a beast nature, with 'Grab!' for its creed.

"We must do better than that! From the very start, now, we must nip off the evil bud that might later blossom into private property and wealth, exploitation and misery. There shall be no rich men in our world now and no slaves. No idlers and no oppressed. 'Service' must be our watchword, and our motto 'Each for all and all for each!'

"While there are fish within the river and fruit upon the palm, none shall starve and none shall hoard. Superstition and dogma, fear and cruelty, shall have no place with us. We understand—you and I; and what we know we shall teach. And nothing shall survive of the world that was, save such things as were good. For the old order has passed away—and the new day shall be a better one."

Thus for hours at a time, by starlight and moonlight on the rock-terrace or by fire-glow in their cave—now homelike with rough-hewn furniture and mats of plaited grass—they talked and dreamed and planned.

And executed, too; for they drew up a few basic, simple laws, and these they taught their little colony even now, for from the very beginning they meant the germs of the new society should root in the hearts of the rescued race.

The third trip was delayed by a tremendous rain that poured with tropic suddenness and fury over the face of the world, driven on the breath of a wild-shouting tempest.

For the space of two days heaven and earth were blotted out by the gray, hurling sheets of wind-driven water, while down the cañon New Hope River roared and foamed in thunder cadences.

Beta and Allan, warmly and snugly sheltered in their cave, cared nothing for the storm. It only served to remind them of that other torrential downpour, soon after they had reached the village of the Folk; but now how altered the situation! Captives then, they were masters now; and the dread chasms of the Abyss were now exchanged for the beauties and the freedom of the upper world.

No wind could shake, no deluge invade, their house among the everlasting rock-ribs. Bright crackled their fire, and on the broad divan of cedar he had hewn and covered thick with furs, they two could lie and talk and dream, and let the storm rage, careless of its impotent fury.

"There's only one sorrow in my heart," whispered Beta, drawing his head down on her breast and smoothing his hair with that familiar, well-loved caress. "Just one, dear—can you guess it?"

"No millinery shops to visit, you mean?" he rallied her.

"Oh, Allan, when I'm so much in earnest, how can you?"

"Well, what's the trouble, sweetheart?"

"When the storm ends you're going to leave me again! I wish—I almost wish it would rain forever!"

He made no answer, and she, as one who sees strange and sad visions, gazed into the leaping flames, and in her deep gray eyes lay tears unshed.

"Sing to me!" he murmured presently.

Stroking his head and brow, she sang—as aforetime at the bungalow upon the Hudson:

> *Stark wie der Fels,*
> *Tief wie das Meer,*
> *Muss deine Liebe,*
> *Muss deine Liebe sein!*

The third trip was made in safety, and others after it, and steadily the colony took shape and growth.

More and more the caves came to be occupied. Stern set the Merucaans to work excavating the limestone, piercing tunnels and chimneys, making passageways and preparing for the ever-increasing number of settlers.

Their native arts and crafts began to flourish. In the gloomy recesses fires glowed hot. Ores began to be smelted, with primitive bellows and technique as in the Under-world, and through the night-stillness sounded the ring and clangor of anvils mightily smitten.

Palm-fibers yielded cordage for more nets or finer thread for the looms that now began to clack—for at last some few women had arrived, and even a couple of the strong, pale children, who had traveled stowed in crates like the water-fowl.

By night the pool and river gleamed more and more brightly. Boats navigated even the rapids, for these were hardy water-people, whose whole life had been semi-aquatic.

The strange fowl nested in the cliff below the settlement, hiding by day, flying abroad by night, swimming and diving in the river, even rearing their broods of squawking, naked little monsters in rough nests of twigs and mud.

Some of the hardier of the first-arrived colonists had already—far sooner than Allan had hoped—begun to tolerate a little daylight.

Following his original idea, he prepared some sets of brown mica eye-shields, and by the aid of these a number of the Merucaans were able to endure an hour or two of early dawn and late evening in the open air.

The children, he found, were far less sensitive to light than the adults—a natural sequence of the atavistic principle well known to all biologists.

He hoped that in a year or so many of the Folk might even bear the noon-day sun. Once he could get them to working with him by daylight his progress would leap forward mightily in many lines of activity that he had planned.

An occasional short raid with the Pauillac had stocked the colony with firearms, chemicals and necessary drugs, cutlery, ammunition and some glassware, from the dismantled cities of Nashville, Cincinnati, Indianapolis and other places unidentified.

Allan foresaw almost infinite possibilities in these raids. Civilization he felt, would surge onward with amazing rapidity fostered by this detritus of the distant past.

He also unearthed and brought back to Settlement Cliffs the phonographs and records, sealed in their oiled canvas and hidden in the rock-cleft near the patriarch's grave.

Thereafter of an evening the voices of other days sang in the cave. Around the entrance, now protected by stout and ample timber doors, gathered an eager, wondering, fascinated group, understanding the universal appeal of harmony, softened and humanized by the music of the world that was. And thus, too, was the education of the Folk making giant strides.

Progress, tremendous progress, toward the goal!

Autumn came down the world, and the sun paled a little as it sank to southward in the heavens. Warmth and luxuriant fertility, fecundity without parallel, still pervaded the earth, but a certain change had even so become well marked. Slowly the year was dying, that another might be born.

It was of a glorious purple evening late in October that Allan made the great discovery.

He had come in from working with two or three of the hardier Folk on the temporary hangar he was building for the Pauillac on New-port Heights, to which a broad and well-graded roadway now extended through the jungle.

Entering the home-cave suddenly—and it was home now indeed, with its broad stone fireplace, its comfortable furnishings, its furs, its mats of clean, sweet-smelling rushes—he stopped, toil-worn and weary, to view the well-loved place.

"Well, little wife! Busy, as usual? Always busy, sweetheart?"

At his greeting Beatrice looked up as though startled. She was sitting in a low easy-chair he had made for her of split bamboos cleverly lashed and softly cushioned.

At her left hand, on the palm-wood table, stood a heavy bronze lamp from some forgotten millionaire's palace in Atlanta. Its soft radiance illu-mined her face in profile, making a wondrous aureole of her clustered hair, as in old paintings of the Madonna at the Annunciation.

A presage gripped the man's heart, drawing powerfully at its strings with pain, yet with delicious hope and joy as she turned toward him.

For something in her face, some new, beatified, maternal loveliness, not to be analyzed or understood, betrayed her wondrous secret.

With a little gasp, she dropped into her lap the bit of needlework and sought to hide it with her hands—a gesture wholly girlish yet—to hide and guard it with those hands, so useful and beautiful, so precious and so dearly loved.

But Allan, breathing hard and deep, strode to her, his face aflame with hope and adoration. He caught them up together in the gentle strength of his rough hands and pressed them to his heart.

Beside her he knelt silently; he encircled her with his right arm. Then he took up the tiny garment, smiling.

For a long minute their eyes met.

His brimmed with sudden tears. Hers fell, and her head drooped down upon his breast, and—as once before, at the cathedral—an eloquent tide of crimson mounted from breast to throat, from cheek to tendrilled hair.

About his neck her arms slid, trembled, tightened.

No word was uttered there under the golden lamp-glow; but the strong kiss he pressed, reverently, proudly, upon her brow, renewed with ten-time depth their eternal sacrament of love.

CHAPTER XIX

THE MASTER OF HIS RACE

DAYS, busy days, lengthened into weeks, and these to months happy and full of labor; and in the ever-growing colony progress and change came steadily forward.

All along the cliff-face and the terraces the cave-dwellings now extended, and the smoke from a score of chimneys fashioned among the clefts rose on the temperate air of that sub-tropic winter.

At the doors, nets hung drying. On the pool, boats were anchored at several well-built stone wharfs. The terraces had been walled with palisades on their outer edge and smooth roadways fashioned, leading to all the dwellings as well as to the river below.

On top of the cliff and about three hundred yards back from the edge another palisade had been built of stout timbers set firmly in the earth, interlaced with cordage and propped with strong braces.

The enclosed space, bounded to east and west by the barrier which swung toward and touched the cañon, had all been cleared, save for a few palms and fern-trees left for shade.

Beside drying-frames for fish and game and a well-smoothed plaza for public assemblies and the giving of the Law, it now contained Stern's permanent hangar. The Pauillac had been brought along the road from Newport Heights and housed there.

This road passed through strong gates of hewn planks hinged with well-wrought ironwork forged by some of the Folk under the direction of H'yemba, the smith. For H'yemba, be it known, had been brought up by Stern early in December.

The man was essential to progress, for none knew so well as he the arts of smelting and of metal-work. Stern still felt suspicious of him, but by no word or act did the smith now betray any rebellious spirit, any animosity, or aught but faithful service.

Allan, however, could not trust him yet. No telling what fires might still be smoldering under the peaceful and industrious exterior. And the master's eye often rested keenly on the powerful figure of the blacksmith.

Across the cañon, from a point about fifty yards to eastward of Cliff Villa—as Beta and Allan had christened their home—a light bridge had been flung, connecting the northern with the southern bank and saving laborious toil in crossing via the river-bed.

This bridge, of simple construction, was merely temporary. Allan counted on eventually putting up a first-class cantilever; but for now he was content with two stout fiber cables anchored to palm-trunks, floored with rough boards lashed in place with cordage, and railed with strong rope.

This bridge opened up a whole new tract of country to northward and vastly widened the fruit and game supply. Plenty reigned at Settlement Cliffs; and a prosperity such as the Folk had never known in the Abyss, a well-being, a luxurious variety of foodstuffs—fruits, meats, wild vegetables—as well as a profusion of furs for clothing, banished discontent.

Barring a little temporary depression and lassitude due to the great alteration of environment, the Folk experienced but slight ill effects from the change.

And, once they grew acclimated, their health and vigor rapidly improved. Strangest of all, a phenomenon most marked in the children, Allan noticed that after a few weeks under the altered conditions of food and exposure to the actinic rays of the sun as reflected by the moonlight, pigmentation began to develop. A certain clouding of the iris began to show, premonitory of color-deposit. The skin lost something of its chalky hue, while at the roots of the hair, as it grew, a distinct infiltration of pigment-cells was visible. And at this sight Allan rejoiced exceedingly.

Beatrice did not now go much abroad with him, on account of her condition. She hardly ventured farther than the top of the cliff, and many days she sat in her low chair on the terrace, resting, watching the river and the forest, thinking, dreaming, sewing for the little new colonist soon to arrive. Some of their most happy hours were spent thus, as Allan sat beside her in the sun, talking of their future. The bond between them had grown closer and more intimate. They two, linked by another still unseen, were one.

"Will you be very angry with me, dear, if it's a girl?" she asked one day, smiling a little wistfully.

"Angry? Have I ever been angry with you, darling? Could I ever be?"

She shook her head.

"No; but you might if I disappointed you now."

"Impossible! Of course, the world's work demands a chief, a head, a leader, to come after me and take up the reins when they fall from my hands, but—"

"Even if it's a girl—only a girl—you'll love me just the same?"

His answer was a pressure of her hand, which he brought to his lips and held there a long minute. She smiled again, and in the following silence their souls spoke together though their lips were mute.

But Beta had her work to do those days as well as Allan.

While he planned the public works of the colony and directed their construction at night, or made his routine weekly trip into the Abyss for more and ever more of the Folk—a greatly shortened trip, now that he knew the way so well and needed stop below ground only long enough to rest a bit and take on oil and fuel—she was busy with her teaching of the people.

They had carefully discussed this matter, and had decided to impose English bodily and arbitrarily upon the colonists. Every evening Beatrice gathered a class of the younger men and women, always including the children, and for an hour or two drilled them in simple words and sentences.

She used their familiar occupations, and taught them to speak of fishing, metal-working, weaving, dyeing, and the preparation of food.

And always after they had learned a certain thing, in speaking to them she used English for that thing. The Folk, keen-witted and retentive of memory as barbarians often are, made astonishing strides in this new language.

They realized fully now that it was the speech of their remote and superior ancestors, and that it far surpassed their own crude and limited tongue.

Thus they learned with enthusiasm; and before long, among them in their own daily lives and labors, you could hear words, phrases, and bits of song in English. And at sound of this both Allan and the girl thrilled with pride and joy.

Allan felt confident of ultimate success along this line.

"We must teach the children, above all," he said to her one day. "English must come to be a secondary tongue to them, familiar as Merucaan. The next generation will speak English from birth and gradually the other language will decay and perish—save as we record it for the sake of history.

"It can't be otherwise, Beatrice. The superior tongue is always bound to replace the inferior. All the science and technical work I teach these people must be explained in English.

"They have no words for all these things. Bridges, flying-machines, engines, water-pipes for the new aqueduct we're putting in to supply the colony from the big spring up back there, tools, processes, everything of importance, will enforce English. The very trend of their whole evolution will drive them to it, even if they were unwilling, which they aren't."

"Yes, of course," she answered. "Yet, after all, we're only two—"

"We'll be three soon."

She blushed.

"Three, then, if you say so. So few among so many—it will be a hard fight, after all."

"I know, but we shall win. Old man Adams and one or two others, at the time of the mutiny of the 'Bounty' taught English to all their one or two score wives and numerous children on Pitcairn.

"The Tahitan was soon forgotten, and the brown half-breeds all spoke good English right up to the time of the catastrophe, when, of course, they were all wiped out. So you see, history proves the thing can be done—and will be."

Came an evening toward the beginning of spring again—an evening of surpassing loveliness, soft, warm, perfumed with the first crimson blossoms of the season—when Bremilu ran swiftly up the path to the cliff-top and sought Allan in the palisaded enclosure, working with his men on the new aqueduct.

"Come, master, for they seek you now!" he panted.

"Who?"

"The mistress and old Gesafam, the aged woman, skilled in all maladies! Come swiftly, O Kromno!"

Allan started, dropped his lantern, and turned very white.

"You mean—"

"Yea, master! Come!"

He found Beatrice in bed, the bronze lamp shining on her face, pale as his own.

"Come, boy!" she whispered. "Let me kiss you just once before—before—"

He knelt, and on her brow his lips seemed to burn. She kissed him, then with a smile of happiness in all her pain said:

"Go, dearest! You must go now!"

And, as he lingered, old Gesafam, chattering shrilly, seized him by the arm and pushed him toward the doorway.

Dazed and in silence he submitted. But when the door had closed behind him, and he stood alone there in the moonlight above the rushing river, a sudden exaltation thrilled him.

He knelt again by the rough sill and kissed the doorway of the house of pain, the house of life; and his soul flamed into prayer to whatsoever Principle or Power wrought the mysteries of the ever-changing universe.

And for hours, keeping all far away, he held his vigil; and the stars watched above him, too, mysterious and far.

But with the coming of the dawn, hark! a cry within! The cry—the thrilling, never-to-be-forgotten, heart-wringing cry of the first-born!

"Oh, God!" breathed Allan, while down his cheeks hot tears gushed unrestrained.

The door opened. Gesafam beckoned.

Trembling, weak as a child, the man faltered in. Still burned the lamp upon the table. He saw the heavy masses of Beta's hair upon the pillow of deerskin, and something in his heart yearned toward her as never until now.

"Allan!"

Choking, unable to formulate a word, shaking, he sank beside the bed, buried his face upon it, and with his hand sought hers.

"Allan, behold your son!"

Into his quivering arms she laid a tiny bundle wrapped in the finest cloth the Folk could weave of soft palm-fibers.

His son!

Against his face he held the child, sobbing. One hand sheltered it; the other pressed the weak and trembling hand of Beatrice.

And as the knowledge and the joy and pain of realization, of full achievement, of fatherhood, surged through him, the strong man's tears baptized the future master of the race!

CHAPTER XX

DISASTER!

THAT evening, the evening of the same day, Allan presented the man-child to his assembled Folk.

Eager, silent, awed, the white barbarians gathered on the terrace, all up and down the slope of it, before the door of their Kromno's house, waiting to behold the son of him they all obeyed, of him who was their law.

Allan took the child and bore it to the doorway; and in the presence of all he held it up, and in the yellow moonlight dedicated it to their service and the service of the world.

"Listen, O folk of the Merucaans!" he cried. "I show you and I give you, now, into your keeping and protection forever, this first-born child of ours!

"This is the first American, the first of the ancient race that once was, the same race whence you, too, have descended, to be born in the upper world! His name shall be my name—Allan. To him shall be taught all good and useful things of body and of mind. He shall be your master, but more than master; he shall be your friend, your teacher, your strength, your guide in the days yet to come! To you his life is given. Not for himself shall he live, not for power or oppression, but for service in the good of all!

"To you and your children is he given, to those who shall come after, to the new and better time. When we, his parents, and when you, too, shall all be gone from here, this man-child shall carry on the work with your descendants. His race shall be your race, his love and care all for your welfare, his every thought and labor for the common good!

"Thus do I consecrate and give him to you, O my Folk! And from this hour of his naming I give you, too, a name. No longer shall you be *Merucaans*, but now *Americans* again. The ancient name shall live once more. He, an American, salutes you, Americans! You are his elder brothers, and between you the bond shall never loosen till the end.

"I have spoken unto you. This is the Law!"

In silence they received it, in silence made obeisance; and, as Allan once more carried the child back to its mother, silently they all departed to their homes and labors.

From that moment Allan believed his rule established now by stronger bonds of love than any force could be. And through all the intoxication of success and consummated power he felt a love for Beatrice, who had rendered all this possible, such as no human words could ever say.

Allan, Junior, grew lustily, waxed strong, and filled the colony with joy. A new spirit pervaded Settlement Cliffs. The vital fact of new life born there, an augury of strength and increase and world-dominance once more, cemented all the social bonds.

An *esprit de corps,* an admirable and powerful coöperative sense developed, and the work of reconstruction, of learning, of progress went on more rapidly than ever.

Beatrice, seated at the door of Cliff Villa with the child upon her knee, made a veritable heart and center for all thought and labor. She and Allan, Junior, became objects almost of worship for the simple Folk.

It was heart-touching to see the eager interest, the love and veneration of the people, the hesitant yet fascinated way in which they contemplated this strange boy, blue-eyed and with yellow hair beginning to grow already; this, the first child they had ever seen to show them what the children of their one-time ancestors had been.

The hunters, now growing very expert in the use of firearms, fairly overloaded the larder of the villa with rare game-birds and venison. The fishers outdid themselves to catch choice fish for their master's family. And every morning fruits and flowers were piled at the doorway for their rulers' pleasure.

Even then, when so much still remained to do, it seemed as though the Golden Age of Allan's dreams already was beginning to take form. These were by far the happiest days Beta and he had ever lived. Love, work, hopes and plans filled their waking hours.

Put far away were all discouragements and fears. All dangers seemed forever to have vanished. Even the portent of the signal-fires, from time to time seen on the northern or eastern horizons, were ignored. And for a while all was peace and joy.

How little they foresaw the future; how little realized the terrible, the inevitable events now already closing down about them!

Allan made no further trips into the Abyss for about two months and a half. Before bringing any more of the people to the surface, he preferred to put all things in readiness for their reception.

He now had a working force of fifty-four men and twelve women. Including his own son, there were some seven children at Settlement Cliffs. The labor of civilization waxed apace.

With large plans in view, he dammed the rapids and set up a small mill and power-plant, the precursor of a far larger one in the future. Various short flights to the ruins of neighboring towns put him in possession, bit by bit, of machinery which he could adapt into needful forms.

In a year or two he knew he would have to clear land and make preparations for agriculture. A grist-mill would soon be essential. He could not always depend upon the woods and streams for food for the colony.

There must be cultivation of fruits and grains; the taming of wild fowl, cattle, horses, sheep and goats—but no swine; and a regular evolution up through the stages again by which the society of the past had reached its climax.

And to his ears the whirring of his turbine as the waters of New Hope River swirled through the penstocks, the spinning of the wheels, the slapping of the deerskin belting, made music only second to the voices of Beatrice and his son.

Allan brought piecemeal and fitted up a small dynamo from some extensive ruins to southeastward. He brought wiring and several still intact incandescent lights. Before long Cliff Villa shone resplendent, to the awe and marvel of the Folk.

But Allan made no mystery of it. He explained it all to Zangamon, Bremilu and H'yemba, the smith; and when they seemed to understand, bade them tell the rest.

Thus every day some new improvement was installed, or some fresh knowledge spread among the colonists.

June had drawn on again, and the hot weather had become oppressive, before Allan thought once more of still further trips into the Abyss. Beatrice tried to dissuade him. Her heart shrank from further separation, risk and fear.

"Listen, dearest," she entreated as they sat by young Allan's bedside, one sultry, breathless night. "I think you've risked enough; really I do. You've got a boy now to keep you here, even if I can't! Please don't go! Follow out the plan you spoke to me about yesterday, but don't go yourself!"

"The plan?"

"Yes, *you* know. Your idea of training three or four of the most intelligent men to fly, and perhaps building one or two more planes—that is, establishing a regular service to and from the Abyss. That would be so much wiser, Allan! Think how deadly imprudent it is for you, you personally, to take this risk every time! Why, if anything should happen—"

"But it won't! It can't!"

"—What would become of the colony? We haven't got anything like enough of a start to go ahead with, lacking you! I speak now without sentiment or foolish, womanly fears, but just on a common-sense, practical basis. Viewed at that angle, ought you to take the risk again?"

"There's no time now, darling, to build more planes! No time to teach flying! We've got to recruit the colony as fast as possible, in case of emergencies. Why, I haven't made a trip since—since God knows when! It's time I was off now!"

"Allan!"

"Well?"

"Suppose you *never* went again? With the population we now have, and the natural increase, wouldn't civilization reëstablish itself in time?"

"Undoubtedly. But think how long it would take! Every additional person imported puts us ahead tremendously. I may never be able to bring all the Folk, all the Lanskaarn, and those other mysterious yellow-haired people they talk about from beyond the Great Vortex. But I can do my share, anyhow. Our boy here may have to complete the process. It may take a lifetime to accomplish the rescue, but it must be done!"

"So you're determined to go again?"

"I am! I must!"

She seized his hand imploringly.

"And leave us? Leave your boy? Leave *me?*"

"Only to return soon, darling! Very soon!"

"But after this one trip, will you promise to train somebody else to go in your place?"

"I'll see, dearest!"

"No, no! Not that! Promise!"

She had drawn his head down, and now her face close to his, was trembling in her eagerness.

"Promise! Promise me, Allan! You must!"

Suddenly moved by her entreaty, he yielded.

"I promise, Beta!" he exclaimed. "Gad, I didn't know you were so deadly afraid of my little expeditions! If I'd understood, I might have been arranging otherwise already. But I certainly will change matters when I get back. Only let me go once more, darling—that'll be the last time, I swear it to you!"

She gave a great sigh of relief unspeakable and kept silence. But in her eyes he saw the shine of sudden tears.

Allan had been gone more than four days and a half before Beatrice allowed herself to realize or to acknowledge the sick terror that for some hours had been growing in her soul.

His usual time of return had hitherto been just a little over three days. Sometimes, with favorable winds to the brink of the Abyss, and unusually strong rising currents of vapors from the sunken sea—from the Vortex, perhaps?—he had been able to make the round trip in sixty hours.

But now over a hundred and eight hours had lagged by since Beatrice, carrying the boy, had accompanied him up the steep path to the hangar in the palisaded clearing.

How light-hearted, confident, strong he had been, filled with great dreams and hopes and visions! No thought of peril, accident, or possible failure had clouded his mind.

She recalled his farewell kiss given to the child and to herself, his careful inspection of the machine, his short and vigorous orders, and the supreme skill with which he had leaped aloft upon its back and gone whirring up the sky till distance far to the northwestward had swallowed him.

And since that hour no sign of return. No speck against the blue. No welcome chatter of the engine far aloft, no hum of huge blades beating the summer air! Nothing!

Nothing save ever-growing fear and anguish, vain hopes, fruitless peerings toward the dim horizon, agonizing expectations always frustrated, a vast and swiftly growing terror.

Beatrice cringed from her own thoughts. She dared not face the truth.

For that way, she felt instinctively, lay madness.

CHAPTER XXI

Allan Returns Not

Five days dragged past, then six, then seven, and still no sign of Allan came to lighten the terrible and growing anguish of the woman.

All day long now she would watch for him—save at such times as the care and nursing of her child mercifully distracted her attention a little while from the intolerable grief and woe consuming her.

She would stand for hours on the rock terrace, peering into the northwest; she would climb the steep path a dozen times a day, and in distraction pace the cliff-top inside the palisaded area, where now some few wild sheep and goats were penned in process of domestication.

Here she would walk, calling in vain his name to the uncaring winds of heaven. With the telescope she would untiringly sweep the far reaches of the horizon, hoping, ever hoping, that at each moment a vague and distant speck might spring to view, wing its swift way southeastward, resolve itself into that one and only blessed sight her whole soul craved and burned for—the Pauillac and her husband!

And so, till night fell, and her strained eyes could no longer distinguish anything but swimming mists and vapors, she would watch, her every thought a prayer, her every hope a torment—for each hope was destined only to end in disappointment bitterer far than death.

And when the shrouding dark had robbed her of all possibility for further watching she would descend with slow and halting steps, grief-broken, dazed, half-maddened, to the home-cavern—empty now, in spite of her child's presence there—empty, and terrible, and drear!

Then would begin the long night vigil. Daylight gave some simulacrum of relief in action, some slight deadening of pain in the very searching of the sky, the strong, determined hope against what had now become an inner conviction of defeat and utter loss. But night—

Night! Nothing, then, but to sit and think, and think, and think, to madness! Sleep was impossible. At most, exhausted nature snatched only a few brief spells of semi-consciousness.

Even the sight of the boy, lying there sunk in his deep and healthy slumber, only kindled fresh fires of woe. For he was Allan's child—he spoke to her by his mere presence of the absent, the lost, perhaps the dead man.

And at thought that now she might be already widowed and her boy fatherless, she would pace the rock-floor in terrible, writhen crises of agony, hands clenched till the nails pierced the delicate flesh, eyes staring, face waxen, only for the sake of the child suppressing the sobs and heart-torn cries that sought to burst from her overburdened soul.

"Oh, Allan! Allan!" she would entreat, as though he could know and hear. "Oh, come back to me! What has happened? Where are you? Come back, come back to your boy—to me!"

Then, betimes, she would catch up the child and strain it to her breast, even though it awakened. Its cries would mingle with her anguished weeping; and in the firelit gloom of the cave they two—she who knew, and he who knew not—would in some measure comfort one another.

On the eighth day she sustained a terrible shock, a sudden joy followed by so poignant a despair that for a moment it seemed to her human nature could endure no more and she must die.

For, eagerly watching the cloud-patched sky with the telescope, from the cliff-top—while on the terrace old Gesafam tended the child—she thought suddenly to behold a distant vision of the aeroplane!

A tiny spot in the heavens, truly, was moving across the field of vision!

With a cry, a sudden flushing of her face, now so wan and colorless, she seemed to throw all her senses into one sense, the power of sight. And though her hand began to shake so terribly that she could only with a great effort hold the glass, she steadied it against a fern-tree and thus managed to find again and hold the moving speck.

The Pauillac! Was it indeed the Pauillac and Allan?

"Merciful Heaven!" she stammered. "Bring him back—to me!"

Again she watched, her whole soul aflame with hope and eagerness and tremulous joy, ready to burst into a blaze of happiness—and then came disillusion and despair, blacker than ever and more terrible.

For suddenly the moving speck turned, wheeled and rose. One second she caught sight of wings. She knew now it was only some huge, tropic bird, afar on the horizon—some condor, vulture, or other creature of the air.

Then, as with a quick swoop, the vulture slid away and vanished behind a blue hill-shoulder, the woman dropped her glass, sank to earth, and—half-fainting—burst into a terrible, dry, sobbing plaint. Her tears, long since exhausted, would not flow. Grief could pass no further limits.

After a time she grew calmer, arose and thought of her child once more. Slowly she returned down the *via dolorosa* of the terrace-path, the walk where she and Allan had so often and so gaily trodden; the path now so barren, so hateful, so solitary.

To her little son she returned, and in her arms she cherished him—in her trembling arms—and the tears came at last, welcome and heart-stilling.

Old Gesafam, gazing compassionately with troubled eyes that blinked behind their mica shields, laid a comforting hand on the girl's shoulder.

"Do not weep, O Yulcia, mistress!" she exclaimed in her own tongue. "Weep not, for there is still hope. See, all things are going on, as before, in the colony!" She gestured toward the lower caves, whence the sounds of smithy-work and other toil drifted upward. "All is yet well with us. Only our *Kromno* is away. And he will yet come! He will come back to us—to the child, to you, to all who love and obey him!"

Beatrice seized the old woman's hand and kissed it in a burst of gratitude.

"Oh—if I could only believe you!" she sobbed.

"It will be so! What could happen to him, so strong, so brave? He must come back! He will!"

"What could happen? A hundred things, Gesafam! One tiny break in the flying boat and he might be hurled to earth or down the Abyss, to death! Or, among your Folk, he may have been defeated, for many of the Folk are still savage and very cruel! Or, the Horde—"

"The Horde? But the Horde, of which you have so often spoken, is now afar."

"No, Gesafam. Even to-day I saw their signal-fires on the horizon."

The old woman drew an arm about the girl. All barbarian that she was, the eternal, universal spirit of the feminine, pervading her, made her akin with the sorrowing wife.

"Go rest," she whispered. "I understand. I, too have wept and mourned, though that was very long ago in the Abyss. My man, my Nausaak, a very brave and strong catcher of fish, fought with the Lanskaarn—and he died. I understand, Yulcia! You must think no more of this now. The child needs your strength. You must rest. Go!"

Gently, yet with firmness that was not to be disputed, she forced Beatrice into the cave, made her lie down, and prepared a drink for her.

Though Beta knew it not, the wise old woman had steeped therein a few leaves of the *ronyilu* weed, brought from the Abyss, a powerful soporific. And presently a certain calm and peace began to win possession of her soul.

For a time, however, distressing visions still continued to float before her disordered mind. Now she seemed to behold the Pauillac, flaming and shattered, whirling down, over and over, meteor-swift, into the purple mists and vapors of the Abyss.

Now the scene changed; and she saw it, crushed and broken, lying on some far rock-ledge, amid impenetrable forests, while from beneath a formless tangle of wreckage protruded a hand—his hand—and a thin, dripping stream of red.

Gasping, she sought to struggle up and stare about her; but the drugged draft was too potent, and she could not move. Yet still the visions came again—and now it seemed that Allan lay there, in the woods, somewhere afar, transfixed with an envenomed spear, while in a crowding, hideous, jabbering swarm the distorted, beast-like anthropoids jostled triumphantly all about him, hacked at him with flints and knives, flayed and dismembered him, inflicted unimaginable mutilations—

She knew no more. Thanks to the wondrous beneficence of the *ronyilu,* she slept a deep and dreamless slumber. Even the child being laid on her breast by the old woman—who smiled, though in her eyes stood tears—even this did not arouse her.

She slept. And for a few blessed hours she had respite from woe and pain unspeakable.

At last her dreams grew troubled. She seemed caught in a thunder-storm, an earthquake. She heard the smashing of the lightning bolts, the roaring shock of the reverberation, then the crash of shattered buildings.

A sudden shock awoke her. She thought a falling block of stone had struck her arm. But it was only old Gesafam shaking her in terror.

"Oh, *Yulcia, noa!*" the nurse was crying in terror. "*Up! Waken! The cliff falls! Awake, awake!*"

Beatrice sat up in bed, conscious through all the daze of dreams quick broken, that some calamity—some vast and unknown peril—had smitten the colony at Settlement Cliffs.

CHAPTER XXII

The Treason of H'yemba

Not yet even fully awake, Beatrice was conscious of a sudden, vast responsibility laid on her shoulders. She felt the thrill of leadership and command, for in her hands alone now rested the fate of the community.

Out of bed she sprang, her grief for the moment crushed aside, aquiver now with the spirit of defense against all ills that might menace the colony and her child.

"The cliff falls?" she cried, starting for the doorway.

"Yea, mistress! Hark!"

Both women heard a grating, crushing sound. The whole fabric of the cavern trembled again, as though shuddering; then, far below, a grinding crash reëchoed—and now rose shouts, cries, wails of pain.

Already Beatrice was out of the door and running down the terrace.

"Yulcia! Yulcia!" the old woman stood screaming after her. "You must not go!"

She answered nothing, but ran the faster. Already she could see dust rising from the river-brink; and louder now the cries blended in an anguished chorus as she sped down the terrace.

What could have happened? How great was the catastrophe? What might the death-roll be?

Her terrors about Allan had at last been thrown into the background of her mind. She forgot the boy, herself, everything save the crushing fact of some stupendous calamity.

All at once she stopped with a gasp of terror.

She had reached the turn in the path whence now all the further reach of the cliff was visible. But, where the crag had towered, now appeared only a great and jagged rent in the limestone, through which the sky peered down.

An indescribable chaos of fragments, blocks, débris, detritus of all kinds half choked the river below; and the swift current, suddenly blocked, now foamed and chafed with lathering fury through the newly fallen obstacle.

Broken short off, the path stopped not a hundred yards in front of her.

As she stood there, dazed and dumb, harkening the terrible cries that rose from those still not dead in the ruins, she perceived some of the Folk gathered along the brink of the new chasm. More and more kept coming from the scant half of the caves still left. And all, dazed and numbed like herself, stood there peering down with vacant looks.

Beatrice first recovered wit. Dimly she understood the truth. The cavern digging of the Folk, the burrowing and honeycombing through the cliff, must have sprung some keystone, started some "fault," or broken down some vital rib of the structure.

With irresistible might it had torn loose, slid, crashed, leaped into the cañon, carrying with it how many lives she knew not.

All she knew now was that rescues must be made of such as still lived, and that the bodies of the dead must be recovered.

So with fresh strength, utterly forgetful of self, she ran once more down the steep terrace, calling to her folk:

"Men! My people! Down to the river, quickly! Take hammers, bars, tools—go swiftly! Save the wounded! Go!"

There was no sleep for any in the colony that day, that night, or the next day. The vast pile of débris rang with the sledge blows, louder than ever anvil rang; and the torches flared and sparkled over the jumble of broken rock, beneath which now lay buried many dead—none knew how many—nevermore to be seen of man. Great iron bars bent double with the prying of strong arms.

Beatrice herself, flambeau in hand, directed the labor. And as, one by one, the wounded and the broken were released, she ordered them borne to the great cave of Bremilu, the Strong.

Bremilu had been in the house of one Jukkos at the time of the catastrophe. His body was one of the first to be found. Beta transformed his cave into a hospital.

And there, working with the help of three or four women, hampered in every way for lack of proper materials, she labored hour after hour dressing wounds, setting broken bones, watching no few die, even despite the best that she could do.

Old Gesafam came to seek her there with news that the child cried of hunger. Dazed, Beta went to nurse it; and then returned, in spite of the old woman's pleadings; and so a long time passed—how long she never knew.

Disaster! This was her one clear realization through all those hours of dark and labor, anguish and despair. For the first time the girl felt beaten.

Till now, through every peril, exposure and hardship, she had kept hope and courage. Allan had always been beside her—wise, and very strong to counsel and to act.

But now, alone there—all alone in face of this sudden devastation—she felt at the end of her resources. She had to struggle to hold her reason, to use her native judgment, common sense and skill.

The work of rescue came to an end at last. All were saved who could be. All the bodies that could be reached had been carried into still another cave, not far from the path of the disaster. All the wounds and injuries had been dressed, and now Beatrice knew her force was at an end. She could do no more.

Drained of energy, spent, broken, she dragged herself up the path again. In front of the cave of H'yemba, the smith, a group of survivors had gathered.

Dimly she sensed that the ugly fellow was haranguing them with loud and bitter words. As she came past, the speech died; but many lowering and evil looks were cast on her, and a low murmur—sullen and ominous—followed her on up the terrace.

Too exhausted even to note it or to care, she staggered back to Cliff Villa, flung herself on the bed, and slept.

How long? She could not tell when she awoke again. Only she knew that a dim light, as of evening, was glimmering in at the doorway, and that her child was in the bed beside her.

"Gesafam!" she called, for she heard some one moving in the cave. "Bring me water!"

There came no answer. Beta repeated the command. A curious, sneering mockery startled her. Still clad in her loose brown cloak, belted at the waist—for she had thrown herself upon the bed fully clad—she sat up, peering by the light of the fireplace into the half dark of the room.

A third time she called the old woman.

"It is useless!" cried a voice. "She will not come to help you. See, I have bound her—and now she lies in that further chamber of the cave, helpless. For it is not with her I would speak, but with you. And you shall hear me."

"H'yemba!" cried Beatrice, startled, suddenly recognizing the squat and brutal figure that now, a threat in every gesture, approached the bed. "Out! Out of here, I say! How dare you enter my house? You shall pay heavily for this great insult when the master comes. Out and away!"

The ugly fellow only laughed menacingly.

"No, I shall not go, and there will be no payment," he retorted in his own speech. "And you must hear me, for now I, and not he, shall be the master here."

Beta sprang from the bed and faced him.

"Go, or I shoot you down like a dog!" she threatened.

He sneered.

"There will be no shooting," he answered coolly. "But there will be speech for you to hear. Now listen! *This* is what ye brought us here to? The man and you? *This?* To death and wo? To accidents and perishings?

"Ye brought us to hardship and to battle, not to peace! With lies, deceptions and false promises ye enticed us! We were safe and happy in our homes in the Abyss beside the sunless sea, till *ye* fell thither in your air-boat from these cursed regions. We—"

"For this speech ye shall surely die when the master comes!" cried she. "This is treason, and the penalty of it is death!"

He continued, paying no heed:

"We had no need of you, your ways, or your place. But the man Allan would rule or he would ruin. He overthrew and killed our chief, the great Kamrou himself—Kamrou the Terrible! To us he brought dissensions. From us he bore the patriarch away and slew him, and then made us a great falsehood in that matter.

"So he enticed us all. And ye behold the great disaster and the death! The man Allan has deserted us all to perish here. Coward in his heart, he has abandoned *you* as well. Gone once more to safety and ease, below in the Abyss, there to rule the rest of the Folk, there to take wives according to our law, while *we* die here!"

Menacingly he advanced toward the dumb-stricken woman, his face ablaze with evil passion.

"*Gremnya!*" (coward) he shouted. "Weakling at heart. Great boaster, doer of little deeds! Even you, who would be our mistress, he has abandoned—even his own son he has forsaken. A rotten breed, truly! And we die!

"But listen now. This shall not be! I, H'yemba, the smith, the strongest of all, will not permit it. I will be ruler here, if any live to be ruled! And you shall be my serving-maid—your son my slave!"

Aghast, struck dumb by this wild tempest of rebellion, Beatrice recoiled. His face showed like a white blur in the gloom.

"Allan!" she gasped. "My Allan—"

The huge smith laughed a venomous laugh that echoed through the cave.

"Ha! Ye call on the coward?" he mocked, advancing on her. "On the coward who cannot hear, and would not save you if he could? Behold now ye shall kneel to me and call me master! And my words from now ye shall obey!"

She snatched for her pistol. It was not there. In the excitement of the past hours she had forgotten to buckle it on. She was unarmed.

H'yemba already grasped for her, to force her down upon the floor, kneeling to him—to make her call him master.

Already his strong and hairy fingers had all but seized her robe.

But she, lithe and agile, evaded the grip. To the fire she sprang. She caught up a flaming stick that lay upon the hearth. With a cry she dashed it full into his glaring eyes.

So sudden was the attack that H'yemba had no time even to ward it off with his hands. Fair in the face the scorching flame struck home.

Howling, blinded, stricken, he staggered back; beat the air with vain blows and retreated toward the door.

As he went he poured upon her a torrent of the most hideous imprecations known to their speech—and they were many.

But she, undaunted now, feeling her power and her strength again, followed close. And like blows of a flail, the sputtering, flaring flame beat down upon his head, neck, shoulders.

His hair was blazing now; a smell of scorched flesh diffused itself through the cavern.

"Go! *Go, dog!*" she shouted, maddened and furious, in consuming rage and hate. "Coward! Slanderer and liar! Go, ere I kill you now!"

In panic-stricken fright, unable to see, trying in vain to ward off the devastating, torturing whip of flame and to extinguish the fire ravaging his hair, the brute half ran, half fell out of the cave.

Down the steep path he staggered, yelling curses; down, away, anywhere—away from this pursuing fury.

But the woman, outraged in all her inmost sacred tendernesses, her love for child and husband, still drove him with the blazing scourge—drove, till the torch was beaten to extinction—drove, till the smith took refuge in his own cave.

There, being spent and weary, she let him lie and howl. Exhausted, terribly shaken in body and soul, yet her eyes triumphant, she once more climbed the precipitous path to her own dwelling. The torch she flung away, down the cañon into the river.

She ran to the far recess of the cave, found Gesafam indeed bound and helpless, and quickly freed her.

The old woman was shaking like a leaf, and could give no coherent account of what had happened. Beta made her lie down on the couch, and herself prepared a bowl of hot broth for the faithful nurse.

Then she bethought herself of the pistol Allan had given her.

"I must never take that off again, whatever happens," said she. "But— where is it now?"

In vain she hunted for it on the table, the floor, the shelves, and in the closets Allan had built. In vain she ransacked the whole cave.

The pistol, belt, and cartridges—all were gone.

CHAPTER XXIII

THE RETURN OF THE MASTER

SUDDENLY finding herself very much alarmed and shaken, Beatrice sat down in the low chair beside her bed, and covering her face with both hands tried to think.

The old woman, somewhat recovered, moved about with words of pity and indignation, and sought to make speech with her, but she paid no heed. Now, if ever, she had need of self-searching—of courage and enterprise. And all at once she found that, despite everything, she was only a woman.

Her passion spent, she felt a desperate need of a man's strength, advice, support. In disarray she sat there, striving to collect her reason.

Her robe was torn, and her loosened hair, escaping from its golden pins, cascaded all about her shoulders. Loudly her heart throbbed; a certain shivering had taken possession of her, and all at once she noticed that her brow was burning.

Resolutely she tried to put her weakness from her, and marshalled her thoughts. In the bed her son still slept quietly, his fat fist protruding from the clothes, his ruddy, healthy little face half buried in the pillow.

A great, overpowering wave of mother-love swept her heart. She leaned forward, and through lids now tear-dimmed, with eyes no longer angry, peered at the child—her child and Allan's.

"For your sake—for yours if not for mine," she whispered, "I must be strong!"

She thought.

"Evidently some great conspiracy is going on here. Beyond and apart from the calamity of the landslide, some other and even greater peril menaces the colony!"

She reflected on the incident of her pistol and ammunition being stolen.

"There can be no doubt that H'yemba did that," she decided. "In the confusion of the catastrophe he has disarmed me. That means well-planned rebellion—and at this time it will be fatal! Now, above all else, we must work in harmony, stand fast, close up the ranks! This must not be!"

Yet she could see no way clear to crush the danger. What could she do against so many—nearly all provided with firearms? Why had H'yemba even taken the trouble to steal her weapon?

"Coward!" she exclaimed. "Afraid for his own life—afraid even to face me, so long as I had a pistol! As I live, and heaven is above me, in case of civil war he shall be the first to die!"

She summoned Gesafam.

"Go, now!" she commanded; "go among the remaining Folk and secretly find me a pistol, with ammunition. Steal them if you must. Say nothing, and return as quickly as you can. There be many guns among the Folk. I must have one. Go!"

"O, Yulcia, will there be fighting again?"

"I know not. Ask no questions, but obey!"

Trembling—shaking her head and muttering strange things, the old woman departed.

She returned in a quarter-hour with not only one, but two pistols and several ammunition-belts cleverly concealed beneath her robe. Beta seized them gladly with a sudden return of confidence.

But the old woman, though she said no word, eyed her mistress in a strange, disquieting manner. What had she heard, or seen, down in the caves? Beatrice had now neither time nor inclination to ask.

"Listen, old mother," she commanded. "I am now going to leave you and my son here together. After I am gone lock the door. Let no one in.

I alone shall enter. My signal shall be two knocks on the door, then a pause, then three. Do not open till you hear that signal. You understand me?"

"I understand and I obey, O Yulcia *noa!*"

"It is well. Guard my son as your life. Now I go to see the wounded and the sick again!"

The old woman let her out and carefully barred the door behind her. Beatrice, unafraid, with both her weapons lying loose in their holsters, belted under her robe, advanced alone down the terrace path.

Her hair had once more been bound up. She had recovered something of her poise and strength. The realization of her mission inspired her to any sacrifice.

"It's all for your sake, Allan," she whispered as she went. "All for yours—and our boy's!"

Far beneath her New Hope River purled and sparkled in the morning sun. Beyond, the far and vivid tropic forest stretched in wild beauty to the hills that marked the world's end—those hills beyond which—

She put away the thought, refusing to admit even the possibility of Allan's failure, or accident, or death.

"He will come back to me!" she said bravely and proudly, for a moment stopping to face the sun. "He will come back from beyond those hills and trackless woods! He will come back—to us!"

Again she turned, and descending some dozen steps in the terrace path, once more reached the doorway of the hospital cave.

Pausing not, hesitating not, she lifted the rude latch and pushed.

The door refused to give.

Again she tried more forcibly.

It still resisted.

Throwing all her strength against the barrier, she fought to thrust it inward. It would not budge.

"Barred!" she exclaimed, aghast.

Only too true. During her absence, though how or by whom she could not know, the door had been impassably closed to keep her out!

Who, now, was working against her will? Could it be that H'yemba, all burned and blinded as he was, could have returned so soon and once more set himself to thwart her? And if not the smith, then who?

"Rebellion!" she exclaimed. "It's spreading—growing—now, at the very minute when I should have help, faith and coöperation!"

"Open! Open, in the name of the law that has been given you—our law!" she cried loudly in the Merucaan tongue.

No answer.

She snatched out a pistol, and with the butt loudly smote the planks of palm-wood. Within, the echoes rumbled dully, but no human voice replied.

"Traitors! Cowards!" she defied the opposing power. "I, a woman, your mistress, am come to save you, and you bar me out! Wo on you! Wo!"

Waiting not, but now with greater haste, she ran down along the pathway toward the next door.

That, too, was sealed. And the next, and the fourth, and all, every one, both on the upper and the lower terrace, all—all were barricaded, even to the great gap made by the landslide.

From within no sound, no reply, no slightest sign that any heard or noticed her. Dumb, mute, passive, invincible rebellion!

In vain she called, commanded, pleaded, explained, entreated. No answer. The white barbarians, all banded against her now, had shut themselves up with their wounded and their dying, to wait their destiny alone.

How many were already dead? How many might yet be saved, who would die without her help? She could not tell. The uncertainty maddened her.

"If they den up, that way," she said, "pestilence may break out among them and all may die! And then what? If I'm left all alone in the wilderness with Gesafam and the boy—what then?"

The thought was too horrible for contemplation. So many blows had crashed home to her soul the past week—even the past few hours—that the girl felt numbed and dazed as in a nightmare.

It was, it must be, all some frightful unreality—Allan's absence, the avalanche, H'yemba's attack, and this widespread, silent defiance of her power.

Only a few days before Allan had been there with her—strong, vigorous, confident.

Authority had been supreme. Labor, content, prosperity had reigned. Health and life and vigor had been everywhere. On the horizon of existence no cloud; none over the sun of progress.

And now, suddenly—annihilation!

With a groan that was a sob, her face drawn and pale, eyes fixed and unseeing, Beatrice turned back up the terrace path, back up the steep, toward the only door still at her command—Hope Villa.

Back toward the only one of these strange Folk still loyal; back toward her child.

Her head felt strangely giddy. The depths at her left hand, below the parapet of stone, seemed to be calling—calling insistently. Before her sight something like a veil was drawn; and yet it was not a veil, but a peculiar haze, now and then intershot with sparkles of pale light.

Through her mind flittered for the first time something like an adequate realization of the vast, abysmal gulf in culture-status still yawning between these barbarians and Allan and herself.

"Civilization," she stammered in an odd voice; "why that means—generations!"

All at once she wondered if she were going to faint. A sudden pain had stabbed her temples; a humming had attacked her ears.

She put out her hand against the rock wall of the cliff at the right to steady herself. Her mouth felt hot and very dry.

"I—I must get back home," she said weakly. "I'm not at all well—this morning. Overexertion—"

Painfully she began to climb the stepped path toward the upper level and Cliff Villa. And again it seemed to her the depths were calling; but now she felt positive she heard a voice—a voice she knew but could not exactly place—a hail very far away yet near—all very strange, unreal and terrifying.

"Oh—am I going to be ill?" she panted. "No, no! I mustn't! For the boy's sake, I mustn't! I *can't!*"

With a tremendous effort, now crawling rather than walking—for her knees were as water—the girl dragged herself up the path almost to her doorway.

Again she heard the call, this time no hallucination, but reality.

"Beatrice! *Beatrice!*" the voice was shouting. *"O-hé! Beatrice!"*

His hail! Allan's!

Her heart stopped, a long minute, and then, leaping with joy, a very anguish of revulsion from long pain, thrashed terribly in her breast.

Gasping with emotion, burned with the first sudden onset of a consuming fever, half-blind, shivering, parched and in agony, the girl made a tremendous effort to hear, to see, to understand.

"Allan! Allan!" she shouted wildly. "Where are you? *Where?*"

"Beatrice! Here! On the bridge! *I'm coming!*"

She turned her dimming eyes toward the suspension-bridge hung high above the swift and lashing rapids of New Hope River—the bridge, a cobweb-strand in space, across the chasm.

There it seemed to her, though now she could be sure of nothing, so strangely did the earth and sky and cliffs, the bridge, the jungle, all dance and interplay—there, it seemed, she saw a moving figure.

Disheveled, torn, almost naked, lame and slow, yet with something still of power and command in its bearing, this figure was advancing over the swaying path of bamboo-rods lashed to the cables of twisted fiber.

Now it halted as in exhaustion and great pain; now, once more, it struggled forward, limping, foot by foot; crawling, hanging fast to the ropes like some great insect meshed in the wind-swung filaments.

She saw it, and she knew the truth at last.

"Allan! Allan—come quick! *Help me—help!*"

Then she collapsed. At her door she fell. All things blent and swirled, faded, darkened.

She knew no more.

CHAPTER XXIV

"The Boy Is Gone!"

The man, weak, wounded, racked with exhaustion from the terrible ordeal of the past days, felt fresh vigor leap through his spent veins at sight of her distress, afar.

He broke into a strange, limping run across the slight and shaking bridge; and as he ran he called to her, words of cheer and greeting, words of encouragement and love.

But when, having penetrated the palisaded area and stumbled down the terraces, he reached her side, he stopped short, shaking, speechless, with wide and terror-stricken eyes.

"Beatrice! Beta! My God, what's—*what's happened here?*" he stammered, kneeling beside her, raising her in his weakened arms, covering her pallid face with kisses, chafing her throat, her temples, her hands.

The girl gave no sign of returning consciousness. Allan stared about him, sensing a great and devastating change since his departure, but as yet unable to comprehend its nature.

Giddy himself with loss of blood and terrible fatigues, he hardly more than half saw what lay before him; yet he knew catastrophe had befallen Settlement Cliffs.

The river now foamed through strange new obstructions. A whole section of the cliff was gone. No sign of life at all was to be seen anywhere down the terraces or paths.

None of the Folk, their blinking eyes shielded by their mica glasses from the morning sun, were drying fish or fruit at the frames.

The nets hung brown, and stiff, and dry; they should, at this hour, have been limp and wet, from the night's fishing. The life of the colony, he knew, had suddenly and for some incomprehensible reason stopped, as a watch stops when the spring is broken.

And, worse than all, here Beatrice now lay in his arms, stricken by some strange malady. He could not know the cause—the sleepless nights, the terrible toil, the shattering nervous strain of catastrophe, of nursing, of the swift rebellion.

But he saw plainly now, the girl was burning with fever. And, raising his face to heaven, he uttered a cry, half a groan, half a sob—the cry of a soul racked too long upon the torture-wheel of fate.

"But—but where's the boy?" he asked himself, striving to recover his self-control; trying to understand, to act, to save. "What's happened here? God knows! An earthquake? Disaster, at any rate! Beatrice! Oh, my Beta! Speak to me!"

Unable to solve any of the terrible problems now beating in upon him, he raised her still higher in his arms.

Loudly he shouted for help down the terrace, calling on his Folk to show themselves; to come to him and to obey.

But though the shattered cliff rang with his commands, no one appeared. In all seeming as deserted and as void of human life as on the first day he and Beta had set foot there, the cañon brooded under the morning sun, and for all answer rose only the foaming tumult of the rapids far below.

"Merciful Heavens, I've got to do *something!*" cried Allan, forgetting his own lacerations and his pain, in this supreme crisis. "She—she's sick! She's got a fever! I've got to put her to bed anyhow! After that we'll see!"

With a strength he knew not lay now in his wasted arms, he lifted her bodily and carried her to the door of Cliff Villa, their home among the massive buttresses of rock.

But, to his vast astonishment and terror, he found the door refused to open. It was fast barred inside.

Even from his own house he found himself shut out, an exile and a stranger!

Loudly he shouted for admission, savagely beat upon the planks, all to no purpose. There came no sound from within, no answering word or sign.

Eagerly listening for perhaps the cry of his child, he heard nothing. A tomblike silence brooded there, as in all the stricken colony.

Then Allan, fired with a burning fury, laid the girl down again, and seizing a great boulder from the top of the parapet that guarded the terraced walk, dashed it against the door. The planks groaned and quivered, but held.

Recoiling, exhausted by even this single effort, the disheveled, wounded man stared with haggard eyes at the barrier.

The very strength he had put into that door to guard his treasures, his wife and his son, now defied him. And a curse, bitter as death, burst from his trembling lips.

But now he heard a sound, a word, a phrase or two of incoherent speech.

Whirling, he saw the girl's mouth move. In her delirium she was speaking.

He knelt again beside her, cradled her in his arms, kissed and cherished her—and he heard broken, disjointed words—words that filled him with passionate rage and overpowering wo.

"So many dead—so many!—And so many dying.—*You,* H'yemba! You beast! Let me go!—Oh, when the master comes!"

Allan understood at last. His mind, now clear, despite the maddening torments of the past week, grasped the situation in a kind of supersensitive clairvoyance.

As by a lightning-flash on a dark night, so now the blackness of his wonder, of this mystery, all stood instantly illumined. He understood.

"What incredible fiendishness!" he exclaimed, quite slowly, as though unable to imagine it in human bounds. "At a time of disaster and of death, such as has smitten the colony—what hellish villainy!"

He said no more, but in his eyes burned the fire that meant death, instant and without reprieve.

First he looked to his automatic; but, alas, not one cartridge remained either in its magazine or in the pouches of his belt. The fouled and blackened barrel told something of the terrible story of the past few days.

"Gone, all gone," he muttered; but, with sudden inspiration, bent over the girl.

"Ah! Ammunition again!"

Quickly he reloaded from her belts. One belt he buckled round his waist. Then, pistol in hand, he thought swiftly.

Thus his mind ran: "The first thing to do is look out for Beatrice, and make her comfortable—find out what the matter is with her, and give treatment. I need fresh water, but I daren't go down to the river for it and leave her here. At any minute H'yemba may appear. And when he does, I must see him first.

"Evidently the thing most necessary is to gain access to our home. How can it be locked, inside, when Beatrice is here? Heaven only knows! There may be enemies in there at this minute. H'yemba may be there—"

Anguish pierced his soul at thought of his son now possibly in the smith's power.

"By God!" he cried, "something has got to be done, and quick!"

His rage was growing by leaps and bounds.

He advanced to the door, and putting the muzzle of his automatic almost on the lock, shattered it with six heavy bullets.

Again he dashed the boulder against the door. It groaned and gave.

Reloading ere he ventured in, he now set his shoulder to the door and forced it slowly open, with the pistol always ready in his right hand.

Keenly his eyes sought out the darkened corners of the room. Here, there they pierced, striving to determine whether any ambushed foe were lying there in wait for him.

"Surrender!" he cried loudly in the Merucaan tongue. "If there be any here who war with me, surrender! *At the first sign of fight, you die!*"

No answer.

Still leaving the girl beside the broken door till he should feel positive there was no peril—and always filled with a vast wonder how the door could have been locked from within—Allan advanced slowly, cautiously, into their home.

He was cool now—cool and strong again. The frightful perils and exposures of the week past seemed to have fallen from him like an outworn mantle.

He ignored his pain and weakness as though such things were not. And, with index on trigger, eyes watchful and keen, he scouted down the cave-dwelling.

Suddenly he stopped.

"Who's there?" he challenged loudly.

At the left of the room, not far from the big fireplace, he had perceived a dim, vague figure, prone upon the floor.

"Answer, or I shoot!"

But the figure remained motionless. Allan realized there was no fight in it. Still cautiously, however, he advanced.

Now he touched the figure with his foot, now bent above it and peered down.

"Old Gesafam! Heaven above! Wounded! What does this mean?"

Starting back, he stared in horror at the old woman, stunned and motionless, with the blood coagulating along an ugly cut on her forehead.

Then, as though a prescience had swept his being, he sprang to the bed.

"My son! My boy! Where are you?" he shouted hoarsely.

With a shaking hand he flung down the bedclothes of finely woven palm fiber.

"My boy! My boy!"

The bed was empty. His son had disappeared.

CHAPTER XXV

THE FALL OF H'YEMBA

BLINDED with staggering grief and terror, stunned, stricken, all but annihilated, the man recoiled.

Then, with a cry, he sprang to the bed again, and now in a very passion of eagerness explored it. His trembling hands dragged all the bedding off and threw it broadcast. By the dim light he peered with wide and terror-smitten eyes.

"My boy!" he choked. *"My boy!"*

But beyond all manner of doubt the boy had been stolen.

Unable to understand, or think, or plan, Allan stood there, his face ghastly, his heart quivering within him.

What could have happened? How and why? If the door had been securely locked and the old nurse been with the child, how could the kidnapper have borne him away?

What? How? Why?

More, ever more, questions crowded the man's brain, all equally without answer.

But now, he dimly realized, was no time for solving problems. The minute demanded swift and drastic action. He must find, must save, his son! After that other riddles could he unraveled.

"H'yemba!" he cried hoarsely. "This is H'yemba's work! Revenge and hate have driven him to rebel again. To try to seize Beatrice! To steal my son! At this time of peril and affliction, above all others! H'yemba! The smith must die!"

But first he realized he must get Beatrice into safety.

In haste he ran to the door, picked up the girl and carried her to the bed. Here he disposed her at ease, covered her with the bedding, and bathed her face and hands with water from the cooling-jar.

The old nurse he laid upon the broad couch by the fire and likewise tended. He saw now she had been struck with a stone ax, a glancing blow, severe, but not necessarily fatal.

"Probably trying to defend the boy!" thought he. "Brave heart! Faithful even unto death—if death be your reward!"

Leaving her, he returned to his wife.

Now, he well understood, he had no time for emotion. There must be no false move. Even at the expense of a little time, he must plan the campaign with skill and execute it with relentless energy.

He alone now stood for power, rule, order, law, in this disintegrated community—this colony racked with disaster, anarchy and death.

Upon him alone now depended its whole fate and future, and, with it, the fate and future of the world.

"Merciful Lord, what a situation!" he whispered. "At home, disruption and savagery. Outside, the Horde—the Horde now pressing onward after me!"

He sat down beside the bed and forced himself to think. Weak as he was and wounded with a spear-thrust in the lower leg as well as a jagged cut across the breast, he felt that he might still keep strength enough for a few hours more of toil.

Of a sudden he realized an over-powering thirst. Till now he had not felt it. He arose, drank deeply from the jar, then—something cooler and more calm—once more returned to Beatrice.

"The first thing is to help her," he said. "No use in losing my wits and rushing out unprepared to find the boy. If H'yemba has stolen him it's certain the boy is hidden beyond my present power in some far recess of the inter-communicating rabbit-warren of caves below there in the cliff.

"I feel positive no bodily harm will be done the child. H'yemba will hold him for power over me. He will try to exact terms—even to leadership in the colony, even to possession of Beatrice. And the penalty of refusal may be the boy's death—"

He shuddered profoundly, and with both wasted hands covered his face. For a moment madness sought to possess him.

He felt a wild desire to shout imprecations, to rush out, fling himself against the cave-door of H'yemba and riddle it with bullets—but presently calm returned again. For in Stern's nature lay nothing of hysteria. Reason and calm judgment dominated. And before he acted he always reckoned every pro and con.

"It must be a battle of wits as well as force," thought he. "A little time will decide all that. For now Beatrice demands my first care and thought!"

Now he examined the girl once more. Closing the door and lighting the bronze lamp, he carefully studied the sick woman, noting her symptoms, pulse and respiration.

"What to do?" he asked himself. "What means to take?"

He arose and rummaged the stores for drugs. Above all, he must break the fever. He therefore prepared and administered a powerful febrifuge, covered the girl with all the available bedding, and determined, if possible, to make her sweat. This done, he found no further means at hand and now turned his attention once more to Gesafam.

Her wound he bathed and bandaged and, having given her a stiff drink of brandy, poured between resisting teeth which he had to separate with his knife-blade, he presently perceived some signs of returning consciousness.

But, though he questioned the old woman and tried desperately to make her answer, he could get no coherent information.

Only the name of H'yemba and some few disconnected mutterings of terror rewarded him. He knew now, however, with positive certainty that the smith was responsible for the kidnapping of his son.

"And that," said he, "means I must seek him out at once. All I ask is just one sight of him. One sight, one bullet—and the score is paid!"

He arose and, again making sure his automatic was in complete readiness, stood for a second in thought. Whatever he was now to do must be done quickly.

In a few hours, at the outside, he knew the vanguard of the pursuing Horde would enter the last valley on the other side of the cañon. By afternoon another battle might be on.

"Whatever happens, I must get my grip on the colony again at once!" he realized. "Such of the Folk as are still sound must be rallied. Otherwise nothing but annihilation awaits us all!"

But, even as he faced the exit of Cliff Villa, all at once the door was hurled violently open and a harsh, discordant cry of hatred and defiance burst into the cave.

Stern saw the detested figure of H'yemba standing there, loose-hung, powerful, barbaric, his eyes blinking evilly behind the mica screens that Allan himself had made for him.

With a cry Allan started forward.

"My son!" he gasped.

There, clutched in the smith's left arm, lay the boy!

Allan heard his child crying as in pain, and rage swept every caution to the winds.

He sprang toward H'yemba, cursing; but the smith, with a beast-laugh, raised his right hand.

"Master!" he mocked. "No nearer or ye die!"

Allan, aghast, saw the flicker of sunlight on a pistol-barrel. With only too true an aim, H'yemba had him covered.

Came a little pause, tense as steel wire. Somewhere down the terrace sounded a murmur of voices. Allan seemed to sense that the rebel had now gathered his forces and that a general attack was imminent.

Time! At all hazards he must gain a moment's time!

"H'yemba!" cried he. "What is your speech with me, your master?"

"Master?" sneered the smith again. "My slave! Power has passed from you to me. From you, who speak the false, who entrap us here to suffer and die, who slay and ruin us, to me, who will yet lead the people back to their far home, to safety and to life!"

"You lie, hound!"

The smith laughed bitterly.

"That shall be seen—who lies!" he gibed. "But now power is mine. I have your son in my hand. *Move only and I fling him from the cliff!*"

Allan felt his brain whirl; all things seemed to turn about him. But he fought off his faintness, and in a shaken voice once more demanded:

"What terms, H'yemba?"

"Slavery for you and yours! Your son shall be my serf; your woman my chattel! Ha, that woman! She has already fought me, like one of these strange woods-beasts you have made us kill! See! My hair is burned and my flesh blistered with her fire-beating! But when I hold her in these hands then she shall pay for all, the *vuedma!*"

Stern's hand twitched, with the automatic gripped in the fingers, but the blacksmith cried a warning.

"Raise not that hand, slave!" he ordered. "You cannot shoot without the danger of killing this vile spawn of yours! And remember, too, the river lies far below, and very sharp are the waiting rocks!

"Fool that you are, that think yourself so wise! To leave this place with me! With me, skilled in all labors of metal and stone, strong to cut passage-ways—"

"You devil! You hewed a way into my house?"

H'yemba laughed brutally.

"Silently, steadily, I labored!" he boasted. "And behold the reward! Power for me; eternal slavery for you and all your blood—if any live!"

Insane with rage and hate, Allan nevertheless realized that now all depended on keeping his thought and nerve.

One single premature move and his son would inevitably be hurled over the parapet, down two hundred and fifty feet to the river-bed below. At all hazards, he must keep cool!

The smith, after all only a barbarian and of limited intelligence, had not even thought of the obvious command to make Stern drop his pistol on the floor.

Upon this oversight now hung all Allan's hopes.

Even though the man's retainers might rush the cave and slaughter all, yet in Allan's heart burned a clear and steady flame of hot desire to compass H'yemba's death.

And as the smith now loudly boasted, insulted, vilified, in the true manner of the savage, imperceptibly, inch by inch, Allan was turning his pistol-barrel upward.

Higher, higher, bit by bit it crept toward the horizontal. Unaccustomed to shoot from the hip, Allan realized that right before him lay a supreme test of nerve and marksmanship and skill.

To shoot and kill his boy—the thought was too hideous even to be considered. His father-heart yearned toward the frightened, crying child there in the traitor's grip.

The unconscious form of Beatrice fever-burned and panting on the bed, seemed calling aloud to him: "Aim true, Allan! *Aim true!*"

For one false shot inevitably sealed the child's death. To wound H'yemba and not kill him meant the catastrophe. If the bullet failed to enter brain or heart, H'yemba—though mortally hurt—would of a surety, with his last quiver of strength, sling the boy outward over the dizzying parapet.

Allan prayed; yet his prayer was wordless, formless and unconscious.

He dared not glance down at the automatic. His eyes must hold the smith's. And he must speak, must parley, at all hazards must still gain another moment's respite.

What Allan said in those last terrible, eternal seconds he could never afterward recall.

He only knew he was treating with the enemy, making terms, listening, answering—all with mechanical sub-consciousness.

His real personality, his true ego, was absolutely absorbed in the one vital, all-deciding problem of that stiffening pistol-hand.

Suddenly something seemed to cry in his ear:

"*You have it now! Fire!*"

His hand leaped back with the crashing discharge, loud-echoing in the cave.

H'yemba did not even yell. But at the second when he seemed to crumple all together, falling as an empty sack falls, some involuntary jerk of his finger sent a bullet zooning into the cave.

It shattered beyond Allan in a little shower of steel and lead fragments, mingled with rock-dust.

Before these had even fallen Allan was upon him.

Neglecting for an instant the bruised and screaming child, who lay there struggling on the terrace-path, Allan seized the still-twitching body of the monstrous traitor.

With passionate strength he dragged it to the parapet.

Below, down the path, he caught a swift glimpse of grouped Folk, wondering, staring, aghast.

To them he gave no heed.

He lifted the body, dripping bright blood.

Silent, indomitable, disheveled, he raised it on high.

Then, with a cry: *"See, ye people, how I answer traitors!"* he whirled it outward into the void.

Over and over it gyrated through vacant space. Then, with an echoing splash, the river took it, and the swift current, white-foaming, boisterous, wild, rolled it and tumbled it away, away forever, into the unknown.

With harsh cries and a wild spatter of bullets aimed high above them, Allan drove the cowed and beaten partizans of H'yemba jostling, fleeing, howling for mercy, down the terrace-path between the cliff and parapet.

Only then, when he knew victory was secure and his own dominance once more sealed on them, did he run swiftly back to his boy.

Snatching up the child, he retreated into the home cave again; and now for the first time he realized his wan and sunken cheeks were wet with tears.

CHAPTER XXVI

The Coming of the Horde

Now that, for an hour or two at least, he felt himself free and master of the situation, Allan devoted himself with energy to the immediate situation in Cliff Villa.

Though still weak and dazed, old Gesafam had now recovered strength and wit enough to soothe and care for the child.

Allan heard from her, in a few disjointed words, all she knew of the kidnapping. H'yemba, she said, had suddenly appeared to her, from the remote end of the cave, and had tried to snatch the child.

With a cry, "See, ye people, how I answer traitors!" Stern whirled H'yemba's
body outward into the void. Over and over it gyrated through vacant space.

See page 456

She had fought, but one blow of his ax had stunned her. Beyond this, she remembered nothing.

Allan sought and quickly found the aperture made by the smith through the limestone.

"Evidently he'd been planning this coup for a long time," thought he. "The great catastrophe of the land-slide broke the last bonds of order and restraint, and gave him his opportunity. Well, it's his last villainy! I'll have this passageway cemented up. That's all the monument he'll ever get. It's more than he deserves!"

He returned to Beatrice. The girl still lay there, moaning a little in her fevered sleep. Allan watched her in anguish.

"Oh, if she should die—if she should die!" thought he, and felt the sweat start on his forehead. "She must not! She can't! I won't let her!"

A touch on his arm aroused him from his vigil. Turning, he saw Gesafam.

"The child, O Kromno, hungers. It is crying for food!"

Allan thought. He saw at once the impossibility of letting the boy come near its mother. Some other arrangement must be made.

"Ah!" thought he. "I have it!"

He gestured toward the door.

"Go," he commanded. "Go up the path, to the palisaded place. Take this rope. Bring back, with you a she-goat. Thus shall the child be fed!"

The old woman obeyed. In a quarter-hour she had returned, dragging a wild goat that bleated in terror.

Then, while she watched with amazement, Allan succeeded in milking the creature; though he had to lash securely all four feet and throw it to the cave-floor before it would submit.

He modified the milk with water and bade the old woman administer it by means of a bit of soft cloth. Allan, Junior, protested with yells, but had to make the best of hard necessity; and, after a long and painful process, was surfeited and dozed off. Gesafam put him to bed on the divan by the fire.

"A poor substitute," thought Allan, "but it will sustain life. He's healthy; he can stand it—he's *got* to. Thank God for that goat! Without it he might easily have starved."

He tied the animal at the rear of the cave, and had Gesafam fetch a good supply of grass. Thus for the present one problem at least was solved.

Beatrice's condition remained unchanged. Now and then she called for water, which he gave her plentifully. Once he thought she recognized him, but he could not be certain.

And day wore on; and now the hour of noon was at hand. Allan knew that other duties called him. He must go down among the Folk and save them, too, if possible.

Eating a little at random and making sure as always that his pistols were well loaded, he consigned Beatrice and the child into the old woman's keeping and left the cave.

On the terrace he stopped a moment, gazing triumphantly at the bloodmarks now thickly coagulated down the rocks.

Then, out over the cañon and the forest to northward he peered. His eyes caught the signal-fires he knew must be there now, not ten miles away; and with a nod he smiled.

"They've certainly trailed me close, the devils!" sneered he. "Since the minute they first attacked my two men and me, trying to repair the disabled Pauillac in that infernal valley so far to northward, they haven't given me an hour's respite! Before night there'll be war! Well, let them come. The quicker now the better!"

Then he turned, and with a determined step, still clad in his grotesque rags, descended toward the caves of the Folk, such as still were left.

Where all had been resistance and defiant surliness before, now all had become obedience and worship. He understood enough of the barbarian psychology to know that power, strength and dominance—and these alone—commanded respect with the Folk.

And among them all, those who had not seen as well as those that had, the sudden, dramatic, annihilating downfall of H'yemba had again cemented the bonds of solidarity more closely than ever.

The sight of that arch-rebel's body hurled from the parapet had effectually tamed them, every one. No longer was there any murmur in their caves, no thought save of obedience and worship.

"It's not what I want," reflected Allan. "I want intelligent coöperation, not adulation. I want democracy! But, damn it! if they can't understand, then I must rule a while. And rule I will—and they shall obey or die!"

Quickly he got in touch with the situation. From cave to cave he went, estimating the damage. At the great gap in the terrace he stood and carefully observed the wreckage in the river-bed below.

He visited the hospital-cave, administered medicines, changed dressings and labored for his Folk as though no shadow of rebellion ever had come 'twixt them and him.

The news of Bremilu's death moved him profoundly. Bremilu had been one of his two most competent and trusted followers, and Allan, too, felt a strong personal affection for the man who had saved his life that first night at the cliffs.

Beside the body he stood, in the morgue-cave whither it had been borne. With bowed head the master looked upon the man; and from his eyes fell tears; and in his heart he felt a vacant place not soon to be made whole.

With profound emotion he took Bremilu's cold hand in his—the hand that had so deftly and so powerfully stricken down the gorilla—and for a while held it, gazing on the dead man's face.

"Good-by," said he at length. "You were a brave heart and a true. Never shall you be forgotten. Good-by!"

He summoned a huge fellow named Frumuos, now the most intelligent of the Folk remaining, and together they directed the work of carrying the bodies up to the cliff-top and there burying them.

By the middle of the afternoon some semblance of order and control had become organized in the colony. He returned to Cliff Villa, leaving strict orders for Frumuos to call him in case of need.

Very beautiful the world was that afternoon. In the soft south wind the fronded palms across the river were bowing and nodding gracefully. Overhead, dazzling clouds drifted northward.

It seemed to him he could almost hear the rustle of the dry undergrowth, parched by the past fortnight of exceptionally hot weather; but, above all, rose the eternal babble of the rapids. High in air, a vulture wheeled its untiring spirals. At sight of it he frowned. It reminded him of the Pauillac, now wrecked far beyond the horizon, where the Horde had trapped him. He shuddered, for the memories of the past week were infinitely horrible, and he longed only to forget.

With a last glance at the scene, over which the ominous threads of smoke now drifted in considerable numbers, he frowned. He reëntered the villa.

"No matter *what* happens now," he muttered, "I've got to snatch a few minutes rest. Otherwise, I'm liable to drop in my tracks. And, above all, I must try to pull through. For on me, and me alone, now everything depends!"

He sat down by the bed again, too stupefied by the toxins of fatigue and exhaustion to do more than note that Beatrice was, at any rate, no worse.

Human effort and emotion had, in fact, reached their extreme climax in him. He felt numb all over, in body, mind and soul. A weaker man would have succumbed long ago to but half the hardships he had struggled through. Now he must rest a bit.

"Bring water, Gesafam!" he commanded. When she had obeyed, he let her wash his wounds and dress them with leaves and ointment. Then he himself bandaged them, his head nodding, eyes already drooping shut from moment to moment.

His head sank on the bed, and one hand sought the girl's. Despite his wonderful vitality and strength, Allan was on the verge of collapse.

Vague and confused thoughts wandered through his unsettled brain.

What was the destiny of the colony to be, now that the Pauillac was lost and so many of the Folk wiped out? Were there any hopes of ultimate success? And the Horde, what of that? How long a respite might be counted on before the inevitable, decisive battle?

A score, a hundred questions, more and more illusory, blent and faded and reformed in his overtaxed mind.

Then, blessed as a balm, sleep took him.

A violent shaking roused him from dead slumber. Old Gesafam stood there beside him. She had him by the arm.

"Waken, O master!" she was crying. "O Kromno, rouse! For now there is great need!"

Dazed, he started up.

"What—what is it now? More trouble?"

She pointed toward the door.

"Beyond there, master! Beyond the river there be many moving creatures! Darts and arrows have begun to fall against the cliff. See, one has even come into the cave! What shall be done, master?"

Broad awake now, Allan ran to the door and peered out.

Daylight was fading. He must have slept an hour or two; it had seemed but a second. In the west the sun was burning its way toward the horizon, through a thick set of haze that cloaked the rim of the earth.

"Here, master! See!"

Stooping, she picked up a long, slight object and handed it to him.

"One of their poisoned darts, so help me!" he exclaimed. "Cast that into the fire, Gesafam. And have a care lest it wound you, for the slightest scratch is death!"

While she, wondering, obeyed, he hastily reconnoitered the situation.

He had felt positive the Horde, after his escape from it by devious and terrible ways, would track him down.

He had known the army of the hideous little beast-folk, that for a year now had been slowly gathering from north and east for one final assault, would eventually find Settlement Cliffs and there make still another attempt to crush him and his.

But, knowing all this, knowing even that the whole region beyond the river now swarmed with these ghastly monstrosities, the actuality appalled him.

Now that the attack was really at hand, he felt a strange and sudden sense of helplessness.

And with a bitter curse he shook his fist at the dark forest across the cañon where—even as he looked—he saw a movement of crouching, furtive things; he heard a dull thump-thump as of clubs beating hollow logs.

"You devils!" he execrated. "Oh, for a ton of Pulverite to drop among you!"

"Look, master, look! The bridge! The bridge!"

He turned quickly as old Gesafam pointed up-stream.

There, clearly outlined against the sky, he saw a dozen—a score of little, crouching figures emerge from the forest on the north bank, and at a clumsy run defile along the swaying footpath high above the rapids.

CHAPTER XXVII

WAR!

At sight of the advance-guard of the Horde now already loping, crouched and ugly, over the narrow bridge to Settlement Cliffs Allan's first impulse was one of absolute despair.

He had expected an attack ere night, but at least he had hoped an hour's respite to recover a little of his strength and to muster all the still valid men of the Folk for resistance. Now, however, he saw even this was to be denied him. For already the leaders of the Horde scouts had passed the center of the bridge.

Three or four minutes more and they would be inside the palisade, upon the cliff!

"God! If they once get in there, we're gone!" cried Allan. "We're cut off from everything. Our animals will be slaughtered. The boy will die! They can bombard us with rocks from aloft. It means annihilation!"

Already he was running up the path toward the palisade. Not one second was to be lost. There was no time even to call a single man of the Folk to reën-force him. Single-handed and alone he must meet the invaders' first attack.

Panting, sweating, stumbling, he scrambled up the steep terrace. And as he ran his thoughts outdistanced him.

"Fool that I was to have left the bridge!" choked he. "My first act when I set foot on solid land should have been to cut the ropes and drop the whole thing into the rapids! I might have known this would happen—fool that I was!"

The safety, the life, of the whole colony, including his wife and son, now depended solely on his reaching the southern end of the bridge before the vanguard of the Horde.

With a heart-racking burst of energy he sprang to the defence, and as he ran he drew his hunting-knife.

Reeling with exhaustion, spent, winded, yet still in desperation strug-gling onward, he won the top of the cliff, swung to the left along the path that led to the bridge, and—more dead than alive—rushed onward in a last, supreme effort.

Already he saw the Anthropoids were within a hundred feet of the abut-ment. He could plainly see their squat, hideous bodies, their hairy and pen-dent arms, and the ugly shuffle of their preposterous legs, as at their best speed they made for the cliff.

Three or four poisoned darts fell clicking on the stones about him. Howls and yells of rage burst from the file of beast-men.

One of the horrible creatures even—with apelike agility—sprang up into the guy ropes of the bridge, clung there, and discharged an arrow from its bamboo blow-gun, chattering with rage.

Stern, running but the faster, plugged him with a forty-four. The An-thropoid, still clinging, yowled hideously, then all at once dropped off and vanished in the depths.

Full drive, Allan hurled himself toward the entrance of the bridge. It seemed to him the beasts were almost on him now.

Plainly he could hear the slavering click of their tushes and see the red, bleared winking of their deep-set eyes.

Now he was at the rope-anchorage, where the cables were lashed to two stout palms.

He emptied his automatic point-blank into the pack.

Pausing not to note effects, he slashed furiously at the left-hand rope.

One strand gave. It sprang apart and began untwisting. Again he hewed with mad rage.

"Crack!"

The cable parted with a report like a pistol-shot. From the bridge a wild, hideous tumult of yells and shrieks arose. The whole fabric, now unsupported on one side, dropped awry. Covered from end to end with Anthropoids, it swayed heavily.

Had *men* been on it, all must have been flung into the rapids by the shock. But these beast-things, used to arboreal work, to scaling cliffs, to every kind of dangerous adventuring, nearly all succeeded in clinging.

Only three or four were shaken off, to catapult over and over down into the foaming lash of the river.

And still, now creeping with hideous agility along the racked and swinging bridge that hung by but a single rope, they continued to make way, howling and screaming like damned souls.

One gained the shore! At Allan it bounded, crouching, ferocious, deadly. He saw, the tiny, venomous lance raised for the throw.

"Flick!"

He felt a twitch on his arm. Was he wounded? He knew not. Only he knew that with blind rage he had flung himself on the second rope, and now with demon-rage was hacking at it desperately.

The snapping whirl of the cable as it parted flung him backward.

He had an instant's vision of the whole bridge-structure crumpling. Then it vanished. From the depths rose the most awful scream, quickly smothered, that he had ever heard.

And as the bestial bodies went tumbling, rolling, fighting, down the rapids, he suddenly beheld the bridge footway hanging limp and swaying against the further cliff.

"Thank God! In time, in time!" he panted, staggering like a drunken man.

But all at once he beheld two of the Horde still there in front of him—the one that had flung the dart and another. They were advancing at a lope.

Allan turned and fled.

His ammunition was all spent, he knew that to face them was madness.

"I must load up again," thought he. "Then I'll make short work of them!"

Fortunately he could far outstrip them in flight. That, and that alone, had already saved him in the past week of horrible pursuit through the forests to northward. And quickly now he ran down the terrace again—down to the caves below. As he ran he shouted in Merucaan:

"Out, my people! Out with you! Out to battle! Out to war!"

Half way down to Cliff Villa he met Frumuos toiling upward. Him he greeted and quickly informed of the situation.

"The bridge is down!" he panted. "I cut it! The further shore is swarming with enemies. Two have reached this side!"

"What is this, O Kromno?" asked the man anxiously, pointing at Allan's shoulder. "Have they wounded you?"

Allan looked and saw a poisoned dart hanging loosely in his left sleeve. As he moved he could feel the point rubbing against his naked skin.

"Merciful Heaven!" he exclaimed. "Has it scratched me?"

With infinite precautions he loosened and threw off his outer garment. He flung it, with the dart still adhering, down over the cliff.

"Look, Frumuos!" he commanded. "Search carefully and see if there be any scratch on the skin!"

The man obeyed, making a minute inspection through his mica eye-shields. Then he shook his head.

"No, Kromno," he answered. "I see nothing. But the arrow came near, near!"

Stern, tremendously relieved, gestured toward the caves.

"Go swiftly!" he commanded. "Bring up every man who still can fight. All must have full burdens of cartridges. Even though the bridge be down, the enemy will still attack!"

"But how, since the great river lies between?"

"They can climb down those cliffs and swim the river and scramble up this side as easily as we can walk on level ground. Go swiftly! There is no time to lose!"

"I go, master. But tell me, the two who have already reached this side—shall we not first slay them?"

Allan thought. For the first time he now realized clearly the terrible peril that lay in these two Anthropoids already inside the limits of the colony.

He peered up the pathway. No sign of them above. Their animal cunning had warned them not to descend to certain death.

Now Allan knew they were at liberty inside the palisades, waiting, watching, constituting a deadly menace at every turn.

In any one of a thousand places they could lie ambushed, behind trees or bushes, or in the limbs aloft, and thence, unseen, they could discharge an indefinite number of darts.

It was now perilous in the extreme even to venture back to the palisade. Any moment might bring a flicking, stinging messenger of death. Those two, alone, might easily decimate the remaining men of the colony—and now each man was incalculably precious.

"Go, Frumuos," Allan again commanded. "For the moment we must leave those two up there. Go, muster all the fighting men and bring them up here along the terrace. I must think! Go!"

Suddenly, before the messenger had even had time to disappear round the first bend in the path, Allan found his inspiration.

"Regular warfare will never do it!" he exclaimed decisively. "They have thousands where we have tens. Before we could pick them off with our fire-arms they'd have exhausted all our ammunition and have rushed us—and everything would be all over.

"No; there must be some quicker and more drastic way! Even dynamite or Pulverite could never reach them all, swarming over there through miles of forest. Only one thing can stand against them—*fire!*

"With fire we must sweep and purge the world, even though we destroy it! *With fire we must sweep the world!*"

CHAPTER XXVIII

THE BESOM OF FLAME

STERN was not long in carrying out his plan.

Even before Frumuos had returned, with the seventeen men still able to bear arms, he was at work.

In Cliff Villa he hastily lashed up half a dozen fireballs, of coarse cloth, thoroughly soaked them in oil, and, with a blazing torch, brought them out to the terrace. Old Gesafam, at his command, bolted the door behind him. At all hazards, Beta and the child must be protected from any possibility of peril.

"Here, Frumuos!" cried Stern.

"Yes, master?"

"Run quickly! Fetch the strongest bow in the colony and many arrows!"

"I go, master!"

Once more the man departed, running.

"Gad! If I only had my oxygen-containing bullets ready!" thought Stern, his mind reverting to an unfinished experiment down there in his laboratory in the Rapids power-house. "*They* would turn the trick, sure enough! They'd burst and rain fire everywhere. But they aren't ready yet; and even if they were, nobody could venture down there now!"

For already, plainly visible on the farther edge of the cañon, scores and hundreds of the hideous little beast-men were beginning to swarm. Their cries, despite the contrary stiff wind, carried across the river; and here and there a dart broke against the cliff.

Already a few of the Anthropoids were beginning to scramble down the opposite wall of stone.

"Men!" cried Allan commandingly, "not one of those creatures must ever reach this terrace! Take good aim. Waste no single shot. Every bullet must do its work!"

Choosing six of the best marksmen, he stationed them along the parapet with rifles. The firing began at once.

Irregularly the shots barked from the line of sharpshooters; and the little stabs of smoke, drifting out across the river, blent in a thin blue haze. Every moment or two, one of the Horde would writhe, scream, fall—or hang there twitching, to the cliff, with terrible, wild yells.

Stern greeted the return of Frumuos with eagerness.

"Here!" he exclaimed, scattering the arrows among half a dozen men. "Bind these fireballs fast to the arrowheads!"

He dealt out cord. In a moment the task was done.

"*Sivad!*" he called a man by name. "You, the best bowman of all! Here quickly!"

Even as Sivad fitted the first arrow to the string, and Stern was about to apply the torch, a rattling crash from above caused all to cringe and leap aside.

Down, leaping, ricochetting, thundering, hurtled a great boulder, spurning the cliff-face with a tremendous uproar.

It struck the parapet like a thirteen-inch shell, smashed out two yards of wall, and vanished in the depths. And after it, sliding, rattling and bouncing down, followed a rain of pebbles, fragments and detritus.

"Those two above—they're attacking!" shouted Stern. "Quick—after them! *You, you, you!*"

He told off half a dozen men with rifles and revolvers.

"Quick, before they can hide! Look out for their darts! *Kill! Kill!*"

The detachment started up the path at a run, eager for the hunt.

Stern set the flaring torch to the first fireball. It burst into bright flame.

"Shoot, Sivad! Shoot!" he commanded. "Shoot high, shoot far. Plant your arrow there in the dry undergrowth where the wind whips the jungle! Shoot and fail not!"

The stout bowman drew his arrow to the head, back, back till the flame licked his left hand.

"Zing-g-g-g-g!"

The humming bowspring sang in harmony with the zooning arrow. A swift blue streak split the air, high above the river. In a quick trajectory it leaped.

It vanished in the wind-swept forest. Almost before it had disappeared, Sivad had snatched another flaming arrow and had planted it farther down stream.

One by one, till all were gone, the marksman sowed the seed of conflagration. And all the while, from the rifles along the parapet, death went spitting at the forefront of invasion.

Another boulder fell from aloft, this time working havoc; for as one of the riflemen sprang to dodge, it struck a shoulder of limestone, bounded, and took him fair on the back.

His cry was smashed clean out; he and the stone, together, plumbed the depths.

But, as though to echo it, shots began to clatter up above. Then all at once they ceased; and a cheer floated away across the cañon.

"*They're* done, those two up there, damn them!" shouted Stern. "And look, men, look! The fire takes! *The woods begin to burn!*"

True! Already in three places, coils of greasy smoke were beginning to writhe upward, as the resinous, dry undergrowth blossomed into red bouquets of flame.

Now another fire burst out; then the two remaining ones. From six centers the conflagration was already swiftly spreading.

Smoke-clouds began to drift downwind; and from the forest depths arose not only harsh cries from the panic-stricken Horde, but also beast and bird-calls as the startled fauna sought to flee this new, red terror.

Shouts and cheers of triumph burst from the little band of defenders on the terrace as the sweeping wind, flailing the flame through the sun-dried underbrush, whirled it crackling aloft in a quick-leaping storm of fire.

But Stern was silent as he watched the fierce and sudden onset of the conflagration. Between narrowed lids, as though calculating a grave problem, he observed the crazed birds taking sudden flight, launching into air and whirling drunkenly hither and yon with harsh cries for their last brief bit of life.

He listened to the animal calls in the forest and to the strange crashings of the underwood as the creatures broke cover and in vain sought safety.

Mingled with these sounds were others—yells, shrieks, and gibberings—the tumult of the perishing Horde.

Swiftly the fire spread to right and left, even as it ate northward from the river.

The mass of Anthropoids inevitably found themselves trapped; their slouching, awkward figures could here or there be seen in some clear space, running wildly. Then, with a gust of flame, that space, too, vanished, and all was one red glare.

The riflemen, meanwhile, were steadily potting such of the little demons as still were crawling up or down the cliffside opposite. Surely, relentlessly, they shot the invaders down. And, even as Stern watched, the enemy melted and vanished before his eyes.

Allan was thinking.

"What may this not result in?" he wondered as he observed the swift and angry leap of the forest-fire to northward. "It may ravage thousands of square miles before rain puts an end to it. It may devastate the whole country. A change in the wind may even drive it back on us, across the river, sweeping all before it. This may mean ruin!"

He paused a moment, then said aloud:

"Ruin, perhaps. Yes; but the alternative was death! There was no other way!"

Now none of the attackers remained save a few feebly twitching, writhing bodies caught on some protuberance of rock. Here, there, one of these fell, and like the rest was borne away down stream.

Through the heated air already verberated a strange roar as the forest-fire leaped up the opposite hillside in one clear lick of incandescence. This roar hummed through the heavens and trembled over the long reaches of the river.

The fire jumped a little valley and took the second hill, burning as clear as any furnace, with a swift onward, upward slant as the wind fanned it forward through the dry brush and among the crowded palms.

Now and then, with a muffled explosion, a sap-filled palm burst. Here, or yonder, some brighter flare showed where the fire had run at one clear leap right to the fronded top of a fern-tree.

Fire-brands and dry-kye, caught up by the swirl, spiralled through the thick air and fell far in advance of the main fire-army, each outpost colonizing into swift destruction.

Already the nearer portion of the opposite cliff-edge was barren and smoking, swept clean of life as a broom might sweep an ant-hill. Tourbillons of dense smoke obscured the sky.

The air flew thick with brands, live coals and flaring bits of bark, all whirling aloft on the breath of the fire-demon. Showers of burning jewels were sown broadcast by the resistless wind.

Stern, unspeakably saddened in spite of victory by this wholesale destruction of forest, fruit and game, turned away from the magnificent, the terrifying spectacle.

He left his riflemen staring at it, amazed and awed to silence by the splendor of the flame-tempest, which they watched through their eye-shields in absolute astonishment.

Back to Cliff Villa he returned, his step heavy and his heart like lead. In a few brief hours, how great, how terrible, how devastating the changes that had come upon Settlement Cliffs!

Attack, destruction, pestilence and flame had all worked their will there; and many a dream, a plan, a hope now lay in ashes, even like those smoldering cinder-piles across the river—those pyres that marked the death-field of the hateful, venomous, inhuman Horde!

Numb with exhaustion and emotions, he staggered up the path, knocked, and was admitted to his home by the old nurse.

He heard the crying of his son, vigorously protesting against some infant grievance, and his tired heart yearned with strong father-love.

"A hard world, boy!" thought he. "A hard fight, all the way through. God grant, before you come to take the burden and the shock, I may have been able to lighten both for you?"

The old woman touched his arm.

"O, master! Is the fighting past?"

"It is past and done, Gesafam. *That* enemy, at least, will never come again! But tell me, what causes the boy to cry?"

"He is hungered, master. And I—I do not know the way to milk the strange animal!"

Despite his exhaustion, pain and dour forebodings, Allan had to smile a second.

"That's one thing you've got to learn, old mother!" he exclaimed. "I'll milk presently. But not just yet!"

For first of all he must see Beatrice again. The boy must cry a bit, till he had seen her!

To the bed he hastened, and beside it fell on his knees. His eager eyes devoured the girl's face; his trembling hand sought her brow.

Then a glad cry broke from his lips.

Her face no longer burned with fever, and her pulse was slower now. A profuse and saving perspiration told him the crisis had been passed.

"Thank God! Thank God!" he breathed from his inmost soul. In his arms he caught her. He drew her to his breast.

And even in that hour of confusion and distress he knew the greatest joy of life was his.

CHAPTER XXIX

ALLAN'S NARRATIVE

THE week that followed was one of terrible labor, vigil and responsibility for Stern. Not yet recovered from his wounds nor fully rested from his flight before the Horde—now forever happily wiped out—the man nevertheless plunged with untiring energy into the stupendous tasks before him.

He was at once the life, the brain, the inspiration of the colony. Without him all must have perished. In the hollow of his hand he held them, every one; and he alone it was who wrought some measure of reconstruction in the smitten settlement.

Once Beatrice was out of danger, he turned his attention to the others. He administered his treatment and regimen with a strong hand, and allowed no opposition. Under his direction a little cemetery grew in the palisade—a mournful sight for this early stage in the reconstruction of the world.

Here the Folk, according to their own custom, marked the graves with totem emblems as down in the Abyss, and at night they wailed and chanted there under the bright or misty moon; and day by day the number of graves increased till more than twenty crowned the cliff.

The two Anthropoids were not buried, however, but were thrown into the river from the place where they had been shot down while rolling rocks over the edge. They vanished in a tumbling, eddying swirl, misshapen and hideous to the last.

With his accustomed energy he set his men to work repairing the damage as well as possible, rearranging the living quarters, and bringing order out of chaos. Beta was now able to sit up a little. Allan decided she must have had a touch of brain-fever.

But in his thankfulness at her recovery he took no great thought as to the nature of the disease.

"Thank God, you're on the road to full recovery now, dear!" he said to her on the tenth day as they sat together in the sun before the home cave. "A mighty close call for you—and for the boy, too! Without that good old goat what mightn't have happened? She'll be a privileged character for life in these diggings."

Beta laughed, and with a thin hand stroked his hair as he bent over her.

"Do you remember those funny goat-pictures Powers used to draw, a thousand years ago?" she asked. "Well, he ought to be here now to make a sketch of you handing one to our kiddums? But—it was no joke, after all, was it? It was life and death for him!"

He kissed her tenderly, and for a while they said nothing. Then he asked:

"You're really feeling much—much better to-day?

"Awfully much! Why, I'm nearly well again! In a day or two I'll be at work, just as though nothing had happened at all."

"No, no; you must rest a while. Just so you're better, that's enough for me."

Beatrice was really gaining fast. The fever had at least left her with an insatiable appetite.

Allan decided she was now well enough again to nurse the baby. So he and the famous goat were mutually spared many a *mauvais quart d'heure.*

Tallying up matters and things on the evening of the twelfth day, as they sat once more on the terrace in front of Cliff Villa, he inventoried the situation thus:

1—Twenty-six of the Folk are dead.

2—H'yemba is disposed of—praise be!

3—Forty still survive—twenty-eight men, nine women, three children. Of these forty, thirty-three are sound.

4—The Pauillac is lost.

5—The bridge is destroyed, and eight of the caves are gone.

6—The entire forest area to the northward, as far as the eye can reach, is totally devastated.

7—The Horde is wiped out.

"Some good items and some bad, you see, in this trial balance," he commented as he checked up the items. "It means a fresh start in some ways, and no end of work. But, after all, the damage isn't fatal, as it might easily have been. We're about a thousand times better off than there was any hope for."

"You haven't counted in your own wounds just healing, or the terrific time you had with the Horde," suggested Beatrice. "How in this world you ever got through I don't see."

"I don't either. It was a miracle, that's all. From the place where I descended for a little repair work, and where they suddenly attacked us, to the colony, can't be less than one hundred and fifty miles. And such hills, valleys, jungles! Perfectly unimaginable difficulties, Beta! Now that I look back on it myself, I don't see how I ever got here."

"They killed both the men you had with you?"

"Yes; but one of them not till the second day. You see, the carbureter got clogged and wouldn't spray properly. I realized I could never reach Settlement Cliffs without overhauling it. So I scouted for a likely place to land, far from any sign of the cursed signal-fires.

"Well, we hadn't been on the ground fifteen minutes before I'm blest if one of my men didn't hear the brushwood crackling to eastward.

"'O Kromno, master!' said he, clutching my arm, 'there come creatures—many creatures—through the forest! Let us go!'

"I listened and heard it, too; and somehow—subconsciously, I guess—I knew an advance-guard of the Horde was on us!

"It was night, of course. My search-light was still burning, throwing a powerful white glare into the thicket about a quarter-mile away, beyond the sand-barren where I had taken earth. I turned it off, for I remembered how much better the Folk could see without artificial light in our night atmosphere.

"'Tell me, do you see anything?' I whispered.

"The other fellow pointed.

"'There, there!' he exclaimed. 'Little people! Many little people coming through the trees!'

"For a moment I was paralyzed. What to do? There was no time now for a getaway, even if the machine hadn't been out of order. My mind was in a whirl, a rout, an utter panic. I confess, Beatrice, for once I was scared absolutely blue—"

"No wonder! Who could have helped being?"

"Because you see, there was no way out. Lord knew how many of the little fiends were closing in on us; they might be on all sides. The country was much broken and absolutely new to me. I had no defenses to fight from, and it was night. Could anything have been worse?"

"Go on, dear! What next?"

"Well, the Horde was coming on fast, and the darts beginning to patter in, so I saw we couldn't stay there. I had some vague idea of stratagem, I remember—some notion of leading the devils away on a long chase, outdistancing them and then swinging round to the machine again by daylight, and possibly fixing it up in time to skip out for home. But—"

"But it didn't work out that way?"

"Hardly! I emptied my automatics into the brown of the advancing pack, and then retreated, flanked by my two men. They were keen to fight, the Merucaans were—always ready for a mix—but I knew too much about the poisoned arrows to let 'em. We stumbled off through the woods at a good gait, crashing away like elephants, while always, apelike, creeping and hideous, the little hairy beast-people stole and slithered among the palms."

Beatrice shuddered.

"Heavens!" she exclaimed. "I—I'd have died of sheer fright!"

"I didn't feel like dying of fright, but I infernally near died of rage when in about five minutes I saw a flicker of flame through the jungle, and then a brighter glare."

"They burned the Pauillac?"

"I guess so. I never went back to see. They probably burned the planes, and tried to batter up the rest of it with rocks and things. They wrecked it all right enough, I guess. *That* was for the attack we made on 'em from its safe elevation at the bungalow. Well—"

"What then?"

"I can hardly remember. We trekked south, as near as I could reckon it, or south by east, with New Hope River as our objective-joint. Oh, what's the use trying to tell it all? You know the jungle at night?"

"Wild beasts, you mean?"

"And snakes, Beta! *Some* sensation to step on a copperhead and then leap off just in time to miss the snap of the fangs, eh?"

"Oh, don't Allan! Don't!"

"All right; I'll skip that part. Anyhow, we hiked till daybreak, when my men began to complain of severe pain in the eyes. I had to stop and rig up some shields for them, and smear their hands and faces with mud to keep off the sun. Well, we managed to eat a little fruit and get a drink of water; but as for rest, there was none. For inside an hour, hanged if the darts didn't begin dropping again!"

"They'd come up with you!"

"Maybe. Or else it was another group of 'em. No telling. The whole country seemed to swarm with the devils. Anyhow, we had to mosey again. But—well—one of the darts got home on my best fighter. And—h-m!— he didn't last five minutes. He turned a kind of bluish-green, too. And swelled a good bit. I'll spare you the details, Beta. At any rate, we had to leave him. So there were only two of us now, and God knew where home was, or how many thousand of the hairy devils were lying in ambush on the way. So then—"

"What did you do?" she asked, shuddering.

"We hiked, and kept on hiking! All day we beat and trampled through the forest, and toward night there was no more go in us. So we decided to make a stand. Pretty objects we were, too, torn and bruised, mired from swamps clear to our waists, and a mass of scratches and bruises! Well, we hadn't long to wait when the attack was on again.

"I gave my one remaining man the spare automatic, and showed him how to handle it; and for about an hour we stood off the devils. But they flanked us, and all at once my man grunted and pitched forward. I'm damned if they hadn't driven a spear clean through his lungs!

"After that, good God! it was just a man-hunt, endless and horrible, through trackless wilds, over hills and mountains, through valleys, across rivers, Heaven knows where! But I always tried to keep my wits and beat to southward, hoping, ever hoping I might reach the New Hope. Well—now and then I could get far enough ahead to snatch a bite or a drink. Twice I slept—twice, in about a week; think of that, will you? Once in a hollow tree, and once under a rock-ledge. Only a few hours in all. But it helped. Without that I couldn't have got through."

She took his hand, and kissed and caressed it.

"My Allan!" she whispered, while in her eyes the tears started hot. "You suffered all that just to come home again?"

"What else was there to do? The last few days I hardly knew anything at all. It was a daze, a dream, a nightmare. There was so much pain in every part that no one part could hurt very much. The bushes pretty nearly stripped every rag of clothes off me—and the skin, as well. My sandals went all to pieces. I lost my sense of direction a hundred times, and must have often doubled on my tracks. I ate and drank what I could get, like an animal. Once, in a period of lucidity, I remember finding a nest of fledgling birds. I crunched them down alive, pin-feathers and all! Well—"

"My boy! My poor, lost, tortured boy!"

"When they wounded me I never even knew. All I know is that the spear wasn't one of the poisoned ones. Otherwise—"

"There, there! Don't think about it any more, darling! Don't tell me any more. I know enough. It's too awful! Let's both try to forget!"

"I guess that's the best way, after all," he answered. "I found the river somehow, after a thousand or two eternities. Instinct must have guided me, for I turned upstream in the right direction. And after that, all I remember is seeing the bridge across to Settlement Cliffs."

"And so you came home to us again, darling?"

"So I came home. Love led me, Beatrice. It was my chart and compass through the wilderness. Not even pain and hunger could confuse them. Nothing but death could ever blot them out!"

"And after all you'd been through, dear, you did what you did for us? Without resting? Without delay or respite?"

"That's life," he answered simply. "That's the price of the new world. He who would build must suffer!"

Her arms embraced him, her breath was warm upon his face, and in the kiss that burned itself upon his eager lips he knew some measure of the sweetness of reward.

CHAPTER XXX

INTO THE FIRE-SWEPT WILDERNESS

LESS than three weeks after the extermination of the Horde, Stern had already completed important measures looking toward the rehabilitation of the colony.

The damage had been largely repaired. Now only some half-dozen convalescent cases still remained on the sick-list. What the colony had lost in numbers it had gained in solidarity and a truer loyalty than ever before felt there.

All the survivors, now vastly more faithful to the common cause than in the beginning, showed an eager longing to lay hold of the impending problems with Stern, and to labor faithfully for the future of the great undertaking.

The fishing, hunting and domestication of wild animals all were resumed, and again the sound of hammers and anvils clanked through the caves.

Under Stern's direction, half a dozen men crossed the pools in boats, descended the north bank of the river, and got hold of the cut bridge cables.

Stern shot a thin line over to them by means of a bow and arrow. With this they pulled a stouter cord across, and finally a strong cable. All hands together soon brought the bridge once more up the cliff, where it was lashed to its old moorings.

Barring a few broken floor-planks, easily replaced, only slight damage had been done. One day's labor sufficed to put it in repair again.

The parapet was rebuilt and a wall constructed across the end of the broken terrace. Work was begun on new cave dwellings, with great care not to weaken the strata and so invite another disaster.

Stern, very wise by now in gauging the barbarian mentality, undertook no direct punishment of such as had been led away by H'yemba. But he gathered all the Folk together in the palisade, and there—close to the mutely eloquent object-lesson of the little cemetery—he made them a *charweg,* a talk in their own speech.

"My people!" cried he, erect and strong before them all, "listen now, for this thing ye must know!

"The evil of your hearts, thinking to prevail against me and the Law, hath brought ye misery and death! Ye have rebelled against the Law, and behold, many are now dead—innocent as well as guilty. The landslide smote ye, and enemies came—enemies far more terrible than the dreaded Lanskaarn ye fought in the Abyss! But a little more and ye had all died with battle and disaster. Only my hand alone saved ye—all who still live to breathe this upper air.

"Men! Ye beheld my doing with the earthquake and the Horde! Ye beheld, too, my answer to H'yemba, the evil man, the rebel and traitor. Him ye saw hurled, bleeding, from the parapet! That was my answer to his insolence! And if not he, then who can ever stand against me?"

He paused, and swept them with his glance, letting the lesson sink deep home. Before him their eyes were lowered; their heads bowed; and through them all ran murmurs of fear and supplication.

"My Folk! Rightly might I be angered with you, and require sacrifice and still more blood; but I am merciful. I shall not punish; I shall only teach, and guide, and help! For my heart is your heart, and ye are precious in my eyes.

"But, hark ye now, and think, and judge for yourselves! If any ever speak again of rebellion, or of treason, and seek to break the Law, on his head shall be the blood of all. For surely woe shall come again on us. In your own behalf I warn you, and ye shall be the judges. Now answer me, O my Folk, what shall be done unto any who rebels?"

"He shall die!" boomed the voice of Zangamon. The loyal fighter, now lean and gaunt with great labors, but still powerful, raised his corded hand on high. "Of a truth, that man shall die!"

"What death?" cried Stern.

"Even the death of H'yemba! Let him be cast from the parapet to death in the white rushing river far below!"

All echoed the cry: *"Death to all traitors, from the rock!"*

"So be it, then," Stern concluded. "Ye have spoken, and it shall be written as a Law. From Execution Rock shall all conspirators be cast. Now go!"

He dismissed them. While they departed and filed down the terraces to their own homes, he stood there with folded arms, watching them very gravely. The last one vanished. He nodded.

"They'll do now!" said he to himself. "No more trouble from *that* source! Another milestone passed along the road of self-control, self-government and communal spirit. Ah, but the road's a long one yet—a long and hard and stony road to follow!"

Next day Stern began making his plans for the recovery of the lost aeroplane.

"This is by far the most important matter now before the colony," he told Beatrice, watching her nurse the boy as they sat by the fire, while outside the rain drummed over cliff and cañon, hill and plain. "Our very life depends on keeping a free means of communication open with the mother-country of the Folk, so to call it, and with the city-ruins that supply us with so many necessary articles. No other form of transportation will do. At all hazards we *must* have an aeroplane—one at least, more later, if possible."

"Of course," she answered; "but why not make one here? Down there in your workshop—"

"I haven't the equipment yet," he interrupted; "nor yet the necessary metal, the wire, a hundred things. All that will come in time when we get some mines to work and start a few blast-furnaces. But for the present, the best and quickest thing to do will be to look up the old machine again."

"But," she objected, terrified at thought of losing him again; "but I thought you said the Horde wrecked it!"

"So they did; but beasts like that probably couldn't destroy the vital mechanism beyond possibility of repair. That is, not unless they heaped a lot of wood all over it, and heated it white-hot, which I don't think they had intelligence enough to do. In any event, what's left will serve me as a model, for another machine. I really think I'll have to have a try for it."

"Oh, Allan! You aren't going to venture out into the wilderness again?"

"Why not, dearest? You must remember the forest is all burned now; perhaps for hundreds of miles. And the Horde, the one greatest peril that has dogged us ever since those days in the tower, has been swept out with the besom of flame!"

"Which has also surely destroyed the machine, even if *they* haven't!" she exclaimed, using every possible argument to discourage him.

"I hardly think so," he judged. "You see, I left it in a wide sand-barren. I think, on the whole, it will pay me to make the expedition. Of course I shan't take less than a dozen men to help me bring it back—what's left of it."

"But Allan, can you find your way?"

"I've got to! That machine must positively be recovered! Otherwise we're totally cut off from the Abyss. Colonizing stops, and all kinds of hell may break loose below ground before I can build another machine entire. There are no railroads running now to the brink," he added smiling; "and no elevators to the basement of the world. It's the old Pauillac again or nothing!"

The girl exhausted all her arguments and entreaties in vain. Once Allan's mind was definitely made up along the line of duty, he went straight forward, though the heavens fell.

Four days later the expedition set out.

Allan had made adequate preparations in every way. He left a strong and well-armed guard to protect Settlement Cliffs. By careful thought and chart-drawing he was able to approximate the probable position of the machine. With him he took fifteen men, headed by Zangamon, who now insisted he was well enough to go, and ably seconded by Frumuos.

Each man carried an automatic, and six had rifles. They bore an average of one hundred cartridges apiece, and in knapsacks of goat-leather, dried rations for a week. Each also carried fish hooks and a stout fiber line.

The party counted on being able to supplement their supplies with trout, bass and pickerel from countless untouched streams. They might, too, come into wooded country, if the fire had left any to northward, and here they knew game would be plentiful.

One thing seemed positive in that new world: starvation could not threaten.

Cloudy and dull the morning was—yet well-suited to the needs of the Folk—when the expedition left Settlement Cliffs. The convoy, each man provided with eye-guards and his hands and face well painted with protecting pigment, waited impatiently in the palisade, while Allan said farewell to Beta and the little chap.

For a long moment he strained them both to his breast, then, the woman's kiss still hot upon his lips, ran quickly up the path and joined his picked troop of scouts.

"Forward, men!" cried he, taking the lead with Zangamon.

Some minutes later Beatrice saw them defiling over the long, shaking bridge.

Through her tears she watched them, waving her hand to Allan—even making the baby shake its little hand as well—and throwing kisses to him, who returned them gaily.

On the far bank the party halted a minute to shout a few last words to the assembled colonists that lined the parapet of the terrace.

Then they turned, and, striking northwest, plunged boldly into the burned and blackened waste.

Long after the marching column had disappeared over the crest of the second hill Beatrice still watched. Up on the cliff-top, with the powerful telescope at her eye, she followed the faint, drifting line of dust and ash that marked the line of march.

Only when this, too, had disappeared, merged in the somber gray of the horizon, did she sadly and very slowly descend the path once more, back to the loneliness of a home where now no husband's presence greeted her.

Though she tried to smile—tried to believe all would yet be well, old Gesafam, glancing up from her labors at the cooking-hearth, saw tears were shining in her beautiful gray eyes.

Barbarian though the ancient beldame was, she knew, she understood that after all, now as for all time, in every venture and in every task, the woman's portion was the harder one.

CHAPTER XXXI

A STRANGE APPARITION

AT a good round pace, where open going permitted, the party made way, striking boldly across country in the probable direction of the lost aeroplane.

Some marched in silence, thoughtfully; others sang, as though setting out upon the Great Sunken Sea in fishing-boats. But one common purpose and ambition thrilled them all.

A man less boldly resourceful that Allan Stern must have thought long, and long hesitated, before thus plunging into a desolated and unknown territory on such a hunt.

For, to speak truth, the finding of the needle in the haystack would have been as easy as any hope of ever locating the machine in all those thousands of square miles of devastation.

But Stern felt no fear. The great need of the colony made the expedition imperative; his supreme self-trust rendered it possible.

From the very beginning of things, back there in the tower overlooking Madison Forest, he had never even admitted the possibility of failure in any undertaking. Defeat lay wholly outside his scheme of things. That it could ever be his portion simply never had occurred to him.

As they progressed he carefully reviewed everything in his mind. Plans and equipment seemed perfectly adequate. In addition to the impedimenta already mentioned, a few necessary tools, a supply of cordage for transporting the machine, and three bottles of brandy for emergencies had been judiciously added to the men's burdens.

Each, in addition, carried a small flat water-jug, tightly stopped, slung over his shoulder. Allan counted on streams being plentiful; but he meant to look out even for the unexpected, too.

He had wisely taken means to protect their feet for the long tramp. In spite of all their opposition he had made them prepare and bind on sandals of goat's leather. Hitherto they had gone barefooted at Settlement Cliffs; but now that was no longer permissible.

The total equipment of each man weighed not less than one hundred pounds, including tools and all. No weaklings, like the men of the twentieth century, could have stood the gaff marching under such a load; but these huge fellows, muscular and lithe, walked off with it as though it had been a mere nothing.

Allan himself bore an equal burden. In addition to arms and provisions he carried a powerful binocular, the spoil of a wrecked optician's shop in Cincinnati.

Underfoot, as the column advanced in a long line, loose dust and wood-ashes rose in clouds. The air grew thick and irritating to the lungs.

Now and then they had to make a détour round a charred and fallen trunk, or cut their way and clamber through a calcined barricade of twisted limbs and branches. Not infrequently they saw burned bones of animals or of Anthropoids.

Here and there they even stumbled on a distorted, half-consumed body—a hideous reminder of the vanquished enemy—the half-man that had tried to pit itself against the whole-man, with inevitable annihilation as the only possible result.

The distorted attitudes of some of these ghastly, incredibly ugly carcasses told with eloquence the terrified, vain flight of the Horde before the all-consuming storm of fire, the panic and the anguish of their extinction.

But Allan only grunted or smiled grimly at sight of the horrible little bodies. Pity he felt no more than for a crushed and hideous copperhead.

The country had been swept clean by the fire-broom. Not a living creature remained visible. Moles there still might be, and perhaps hares and foxes, woodchucks, groundhogs and a few such animals that by chance had taken earth; but even of these there was no trace. Certainly all larger breeds had been destroyed.

Where paradise-birds, macaws and paroquets had screamed and flitted, humming-birds darted with a whir of gauzy wings, serpents writhed, deer browsed, monkeys and apes swung chattering from the liana-festooned fern-trees, now all was silence, charred ashes, dust—the universal, blank awfulness of death.

Naked and ugly the country stretched away, away to its black horizon, ridge after ridge of rolling land stubbled with sparse, limbless trunks and carpeted with cinders.

A dead world truly, it seemed—how infinitely different from the lush, green beauty of the territory south of the New Hope, a region Stern still could make out as a bluish blur, far to southward, through his binoculars.

By night, after having eaten dinner beside a turbid, brackish pool, they had made more than twenty miles to northwestward. Stern thought scornfully of the distance. In his Pauillac he would have covered it easily in as many minutes.

But now all was different. Nothing remained save slow, laborious plodding, foot by foot, through the choking desolation of the burned world.

They camped near a small stream for the night, and cast their lines, but took nothing. Stern gave this matter no great weight. He thought, perhaps, it might be a mere accident, and still felt confident of finding fish elsewhere.

Even the discovery of three or four dead perch, floating belly up, round and round in an eddy, gave him no clue to the total destruction of all life. He did not understand even yet that the terrific conflagration, far more stupendous than any ever known in the old days, had even heated the streams and killed there the very fish themselves.

Yet already a vague, half-sensed uneasiness had begun to creep over him—not yet a definite presentiment of disaster, but rather a subconscious feeling that the odds against him were too great.

And once a thought of Napoleon crossed his mind as he sat there silently, camped with his men; and he remembered Moscow, with a strange, new apprehension.

Next morning, having refilled their canteens, they set out again, still in the same direction. Stern often consulted his chart, to be sure they were proceeding in what he took to be the proper course.

The distance between Settlement Cliffs and the machine was wholly problematical; yet, once he should come within striking distance of the scene of his disaster, he felt positive of being able to recognize it.

Not far to the south of the spot, he remembered, a very steep and noisy stream flowed toward the east, and, off to northwest of it rose a peculiarly formed, double-peaked mountain, easily recognizable.

The sand-barren itself, where he had been obliged to abandon the machine, lay in a kind of broad valley, flanked on one hand by cliffs, while the other sloped gradually upward to the foot-hills of the double mountain in question.

"Once I get anywhere within twenty miles of it I'm all right," thought Allan, anxiously sweeping the horizon with his binoculars as the party paused on a high ridge to rest. "The great problem is to locate that mountain. After that the rest will be easy."

At noon they camped again, ate sparingly, and rested an hour. Here Allan brought his second map up to date. This map, a large sheet of parchment, served as a record of distances and directions traveled.

Starting at Settlement Cliffs he had painstakingly entered on it every stage of the journey, every ridge and valley, watercourse, camp and landmark. Once the goal reached, this record would prove invaluable in retracing their way.

"If the rest of the trip were only indicated as well as what's past!" he muttered, working out his position. "One of these days, when other things are attended to, we must have a geodetic survey, complete maps and plans, and accurate information about the whole topography of this altered continent. Some time—along with a few million other necessary things!"

The third day brought them nowhere. Still the *brûlé* stretched on and on before them, though now, far to right, Allan occasionally could glimpse a wooded mountain-spur through the binoculars, as though the limits of the vast conflagration were in sight at least in one direction.

But to left and ahead nothing still showed but devastated land.

The character of the country, however, had begun to change. The valleys had grown deeper and the ridges higher. Allan felt that they were now coming into a more mountainous region.

"Well, that's encouraging, anyhow," he reflected. "Any time, now, I may sight the double-peaked mountain. It can't heave in sight any too soon to suit *me!*"

There was need of sighting it, indeed, for already the party had begun to suffer not a little. The perpetual tramping through ashes had started cracks and sores forming on the men's feet. Most of them were coughing and sneezing much of the time, with a kind of influenza caused by the acrid and biting dust.

The dried food, too, had started an intolerable thirst, and water was terribly scarce. The canteens were now almost always empty; and more than one brook or pool, to which the men eagerly hastened, turned out to be saline or hopelessly fouled by fallen forest wreckage, festering and green-slimed in the cooking sun.

In spite of the eye-shields and pigments, some of the men were already suffering from sunburn and ophthalmia, which greatly impaired their efficiency. Their failure to take fish was also beginning to dishearten them.

Allan pondered the advisability of suspending day travel and trekking only by night, but had to give over this plan, for it would obviate all possibility of his sighting the landmark, the cleft mountain. Though he said nothing, the pangs of apprehension were biting deep into his soul.

For the first time that night the idea was strongly borne in upon him that, after all, this might be little better than a wild-goose chase, and that—despite his desperate need of the Pauillac engine—perhaps the better part of valor might be discretion, retreat, return to Settlement Cliffs while there might still be time.

Yet even the few hours of troubled sleep he got that night, camped in a blackened ravine, served to strengthen his determination to push on again at all hazards.

"It can't be far now!" thought he. "The place simply can't be very far! We must have made the best part of the distance already. What madness to turn back now and lose all we've struggled so hard to gain! No, no—on we go again! Forward to success!"

Next morning, therefore—the fourth since having left New Hope River—the party pushed forward again. It was now a strange procession, limping and slow, the men blinking through their shields, their hands and faces smeared with mud and ashes.

Painfully, yet without a word of complaint or rebellion, they once more trailed over the fire-blasted hills on the quest of the wrecked Pauillac.

Hour by hour they were now forced to pause for rest. Some of the impedimenta had to be discarded. During the forenoon Allan commanded that most of the fishing-gear and part of the cordage should be thrown away.

Toward mid-afternoon he sorted out the tools, and kept only an essential minimum. Now that they had seen no possible need for ammunition, he decided to leave half of that also.

The tools and ammunition he carefully cached under a rock-cairn and set a tall, burned pole up over it, with a cross-piece lashed near the top. The position of this cairn he minutely noted on his map. Some day he would return and get the valuables again.

Nothing could be spared from the provision packets, but these were much lighter, anyhow. This helped a little. But Allan could see that the strength of his men, and his own force as well, was diminishing faster than the burden.

So, with a heavy heart, now half inclined to abandon the task and turn back, he surveyed the horizon for the last time that night in vain search for the landmark mountain of his hopes.

Morning dawned again pitilessly hot and sun-parched. By five o'clock the party was under way, to make at least a few miles before the greatest heat should set in.

Allan realized that this must be the crucial day. Either by nightfall he must sight the mountain or he must turn back. And with fever-burning eagerness he urged his limping men to greater speed, chafed at every delay, constantly examined the horizon, and with consuming wrath cursed the Horde which in its venomous hate had brought this anguish and disaster on his people.

Just a little past eight o'clock a cry suddenly burst from Zangamon, who had left the line during a pause to look for water in a near-by hollow.

Stern heard the man's hoarse voice unmistakably resonant with terror. To him he ran.

"What is it, Zangamon?" he cried thickly, for his tongue was parched and swollen. "What have you found? Quick, tell me!"

"See, O Kromno! Behold!" exclaimed the man, pointing.

Stern looked—and saw a human body, charred and distorted, face downward on the blackened earth. Up through the back something projected—something hard and sharp.

He stooped, wide-eyed, staring at the thing.

"A spear-head, so help me!"

Then he realized the truth. They had found one of his slaughtered companions of the terrible flight from the Horde!

Stern recoiled. Shocked though he was, yet a certain joy possessed him. For now he knew he could not be far from the path of success. The wrecked machine, he knew, could not lie more than one or two days' march ahead. If the party could only last that long—

The others came hobbling. When they, too, saw the mournful object and knew and understood, a deep silence fell upon them. In a circle they surrounded the corpse of their murdered comrade, and for a while they looked on it with woe.

Allan realized that he must not let inaction, thought and fear prey on them, so he commanded immediate burial of the body.

They therefore dug a shallow grave in the baked soil, and, taking good care not to touch the poisoned spear-head, carefully laid their companion to rest. Over the filled-in grave they heaved rocks.

"Does anybody know his name?" asked Allan.

"He was called Relzang," answered Frumuos. "I knew him well—a metal-worker, of the best."

"That's so—now I remember," assented Stern. "What was his totem?"

"A circle, with a bird's head within."

"Let it be placed here, then."

Their best stone-cutter roughly hewed the mark in a great boulder, which was set on top of the pile. Then, nothing more remaining to do, the exploring party once more pushed forward.

But Allan could sense that now even its diminished strength had greatly lessened. Discouragement and forebodings of certain death were working among the men.

He knew he could not hold them more than a few hours longer at the outside.

During the noonday halt and rest, under a low cliff, he made a *charweg*, saying:

"O my people, barring the matter of the patriarch's death, I have always spoken truth to you. Now I speak truth. This shall be the last day. Ye have been brave and strong, uncomplaining in great trials, and obedient. I shall reward ye greatly. But I am wise. I will not drive ye too far. The end is at hand.

"Either I see the cleft mountain by to-morrow night or we return. I shall push no farther forward than the march of one day and a half. After that I shall either have the flying boat or we shall go quickly to our safe home at Settlement Cliffs.

"Be of good heart, therefore. The return will be much easier and shorter. We can follow the picture of the way that I have made. Despair not. All shall be well. I have spoken."

They greeted his promise with murmurs of approbation, but made no answer, for body and soul were grievously tried. When he gave the order to advance again, however, they buckled into the toil with a good heart. Their *morale*, he plainly saw, had been markedly improved by his few words.

And, now filled with hot, new hope, once more he led the painful march, his binoculars every few minutes swinging round the far horizon in a vain attempt to sight the longed-for height.

But other events were destined and were written on the book of fate. For, as they topped a high ridge about five o'clock that afternoon—dragging themselves along, parched and spent, rather than marching—Allan made a halt for careful observations from this vantage-post.

The men sank down, eager to lie prone even for a few minutes on the ash-covered soil, to hide their eyes and pant like hard-run hunting dogs.

Allan himself felt hardly the strength to remain upright; but he forced himself to stand there, and with a tremendous effort held the glass true as it slowly scoured the sky-line to north and west.

All at once he uttered a choking cry. The glass shook in his wasted hands. His eyes, staring, refused their office, and a strange purple blur seemed to blot the horizon from his sight.

With the binoculars he stared at a point N. N. W., where he had thought to see the incredible apparition; but now nothing appeared.

"Hallucinations, so soon?" he muttered, rubbing his eyes "Come, come, buck up! This won't do at all!"

And again he searched the place with his powerful lenses.

"My God! but I *do* see them—and they're real—they're moving, too!" he exclaimed. "No hallucination, no mirage! They're *there!* But—but what— *What can this mean? Who can they be?*"

Tiny and clear against the dazzling background of the afternoon sky he had perceived a long line of human figures trekking to southeast over the distant hill-top, almost directly toward the point where his exhausted troop now lay inert and panting.

CHAPTER XXXII

THE MEETING OF THE BANDS

CONVINCED though Stern now was of the reality of the amazing sight he had just witnessed through his binoculars, yet for a long moment he remained silent and staring, utterly at a loss for any rational explanation of the re-markable apparition.

Exhausted in body and confused in mind, he could hit upon no answer to the riddle.

Might these be some detached and belated members of the Horde? No; for their figures and their gait, as he now for the third time studied them through the glass, were unmistakably human.

But if not Anthropoids, then what? Enemies? Potential friends? Some new and strange race, until now undiscovered?

A score of possible explanations struggled in his mind, only to be rejected. But this was now no time for questions, analysis, or thought. For, even as he looked, the end of the line came to view, then vanished down the blackened hillside.

Invisible, now that they no longer stood silhouetted against the sky-line, the strange company had disappeared as though swallowed up by the earth. Yet Stern well knew that they were coming almost directly down upon him and his little party. Already there was pressing need for swift decision.

What should he do? Advance to meet these strangers? Risk all on a mere chance? Or turn, retreat and hide? Or ambush them, and kill?

He found himself, for the moment, unable to make up his mind. Yet, should a pinch arise and the last contingency become necessary, he felt a powerful advantage. He was positive his little band, armed as they were, could easily wipe out this column. But, after all, must he fight?

His questions all unsettled and his mind confused from the terrible exhaustions of the march, he waited. He surveyed the neighborhood, with a view to possible battle.

On his left rose a ridge that swung to northward between the advancing column and his own position. On his right an arroyo or gully, choked with fallen tree-trunks and burned forest wreckage, descended in an easterly direction toward a rather deep valley. In this gully he saw was ample hiding-place for his whole force.

"Men!" he addressed them; "it is strange to tell, but there be others who come against us there!" He pointed at the far crest of the sawlike highlands, where now he thought to see a hazy, floating pall of dust.

"Until we know their purpose and their temper we must have care. We must hide ourselves and wait. Come, then, quickly! And prepare your guns against the need of battle!"

His words aroused and heartened his exhausted men. The prospect even of war was welcome—anything in place of this unending trek through the burned wilderness.

Zangamon cried: "Where be those that come, O Kromno? And what manner of men?"

"Yonder," indicated Stern. "I know not who, save that they be men. Wait but a little and you shall know. Now to the ravine!"

All got up, and with more energy than they had shown for some time, they trailed to the gully. Here they were soon well entrenched, with weapons ready. Stern now felt confident of the situation, however it might turn.

They waited. Some little talk trickled up and down the line, but for the most part the men kept quiet, watching eagerly.

Now already the dust of the advancing column had grown unmistakably visible, drifting downwind in a thin haze that ever advanced more and more to the southeast, came nearer always, and rose higher in their view.

"Be ready, men," cautioned Stern. "In a few minutes, now, the foremost will pass over that blackened hilltop there ahead of us!"

Higher and thicker grew the dust. A far, shrill cry sounded; and some minutes later the breaking of wood became audible as the column cut through a charred barrier.

Stern was half standing, half lying in the arroyo, only his head projecting over a charcoal mass that once had been a date-palm.

His weapon hung, well balanced, in his hand. All along the edge of the gully other pistol and rifle barrels were poked through débris. Forgotten now were sore and wounded feet, thirst, hunger, ophthalmia, discouragement,—everything. This new excitement had wiped all pain away.

Suddenly Allan started, and a little nervous thrill ran down his spine. Over the top of the hill they all were watching a moving object had suddenly become visible—a head!

Another followed, and then a third, and many more; and now the shoulders and the bodies had begun to show; and now the whole advance guard of the mysterious marching column was plainly to be seen, not more than a quarter-mile away.

Allan jerked the binoculars to his eyes, and for a long moment peered through them.

His eyes widened. An expression of blank amazement, supreme wonder and vast incredulity overspread his face.

"*What?*" he exclaimed. "But—it's impossible! I—it *can't* be—"

Again he looked, and this time was forced to believe what seemed to him beyond all bounds of possibility.

"*Our own people! The Folk!*" he cried in a loud voice. And before his men could sense it he was out of the ravine.

His first thought was a relief expedition from Settlement Cliffs; but how could there be so many? Those who had remained at the colony were only twenty-five, all told, and in this long line that still at a good pace was defiling down the hillside already more than fifty had come to view, with more and ever more still topping the rise.

Utterly at a loss though he was, incapable of seeing any clue to the tremendous riddle, he still retained enough wit to hail the column, now passing down the slope some three or four hundred yards to westward.

"*Ohé, Merucaan v'yolku!*" he shouted between hollowed palms. "*Yomnu! Troin iska ieri!*"

Already his men had scrambled from concealment, and were waving hands and weapons, cloaks, burned brushwood, anything they could lay hands on, to attract attention. Their shouts and hails drowned out the master's.

But the meaning of the words mattered little. For the column on the hillside, understanding, had stopped short in its tracks.

Then suddenly, with yells, it dissolved into confusion of its component parts; and at a run the People of the Abyss swarmed to the greeting of their kinsmen and their own, the colonists.

Barbarians as the folk still were, they met with a vociferous affection. A regular *tangi,* or joy-wailing, followed, and all crowded vociferously about Stern, with hails of "*Kromno!* Long live our *Kromno,* our great chief!" in their own speech.

But Allan, dumfounded by this incredible happening, broke the ceremony as short as possible. The sight of these unexpected reenforcements dazed him. He managed to keep some coherence of thought, however, and flung rapid questions, to which he got scant answers.

Amazed, he stared at the newcomers, now shouting with their relatives from the colony in wild abandon. To his vast astonishment he saw that they had contrived eye-shields similar to those of his own party, and that they had likewise painted their faces.

They had supplies as well—dried fish, seaweed, crated waterfowl, and even fresh game. Allan's astonishment knew no bounds.

He laid a compelling hand on the shoulder of one, Rigvin, whom he remembered as a mighty caster of the nets on the Great Sunken Sea.

"Oh, Rigvin!" he commanded. "Come aside with me. I must have speech at once!"

"I come, O Kromno. Speak, and I make answer!"

"How came ye here without the flying boat? How did ye escape from the Abyss? Whither went ye? Tell me all!"

"We waited, Kromno, but you came not. Did you forget your people in the darkness?"

"No, Rigvin. There has been great distress in Settlement Cliffs. The flying boat is lost. Even now we seek it. Enemies attacked. We destroyed them, but had to sweep the world with fire, as ye see. Many things have happened to keep me from my people. But how came ye here? How have ye done this strange thing, always deemed impossible?"

"Harken, master, that I may tell it in few words! Later, when we reach the colony whereof you have spoken, we can make all things clear; but now is no time for a great talking."

"Go on quickly!"

"Yea, I speak. We waited for you many days, O Kromno; but you came not again. Days on days we waited, as you measure time. Sleepings and wakings we waited eagerly, but no sign of you was seen. Then uneasiness and fear and sorrow fell upon us all."

"What then?"

"We held a great *charweg* there at the Place of Bones, near the Blazing Well, to take thought what was best to do. For you were our chief; and our very ancient law commands that if any chief be in distress, or deemed lost, the Folk must risk all, even life, to save and bring him once more to his own.

"For many hours our wisest men spoke. Some declared you had deserted us, but them the Folk cried down; and barely they escaped the boiling vat. We agreed some calamity had befallen. Then we swore to go to rescue you!"

"Ye did?" exclaimed Stern, much moved. "Gods, what devotion! But—how did ye ever get out of the Abyss? How find your way so straight toward Settlement Cliffs?"

"That is a strange story, and very long, O Kromno! All our elders took thought of what ye had told us so often, and they made a picture of the way. We fashioned protections for the eyes and skin, as ye had said.

"Then the wise men recalled all the ancient traditions, which we had long deemed myths. They looked, also, upon certain records graven in the rock beyond the walls, past the place of burial. They decided the way might still be open past the Great Vortex and through the long cleft, whereby our distant fathers came.

"But they said it might mean death to try to pass the Vortex. They forced none to go. Only such as would need try."

"A volunteer expedition, eh?" thought Allan. "And look at the size of it, will you? These people are without even the slightest understanding of fear!"

"Thus it was arranged, master," continued Rigvin. "Eight score and more of us offered to go. All things were quickly made ready, and much food was packed, and many weapons. In fifteen long canoes we started, after a great singing. Men went in each canoe to bring back the boats—"

"They didn't even wait for you? But if ye had been lost, and sought to return, what then?"

"There was to be no return, master. All swore either to find you or die!"

"Go on!" exclaimed Allan, deeply moved.

"We sailed across the Sunken Sea, O Kromno, and reached the islands of the Lanskaarn. There we had to fight and thirty were killed. But we kept on, and in two days, watching for the quiet time between the great tempests, entered the Vortex."

"You all got through?"

"No master. There was not time. Many were lost; but still we kept on. Then on the fourth day we reached the great cleft, even as our traditions said. And here we camped, and sang again, and once more swore to find you. Then the boats all returned, and we pushed forward, upward, through the cleft."

"And then?"

Rigvin shook his head and sighed.

"O Kromno," he answered, "the story is too long! We be weary, and would reach the place whereof ye have told us. Later there will be time for talk. But now we cannot tell it all!"

"Ye speak truth, Rigvin!" he exclaimed. "I, too, have many things to tell. It cannot be this day. We will lead ye to the colony. We, too, need rest. My men are in sore straits, as ye see!"

He gestured at the groups gathered along the edge of the ravine. A great noise of talking rose against the heated air; and food and water, too, were being given to the Settlement men by the newcomers.

Stern knew the day was saved. Deep gratitude upwelled in his heart.

"Nothing that I can ever do will repay men like these!" thought he. Then, all at once, a sudden hope thrilled him, and he cried:

"Oh, Rigvin, one thing more! Tell me, in your long journey from the brink, have ye chanced to see a cleft mountain with two peaks on either hand?"

"You mean, master—"

"A mountain; a high jut of land, with two tops, side by side—like two grave-mounds?"

Rigvin stood a moment in thought, his soot-smeared brows wrinkled with the effort of trying to remember. Then all at once he looked up quickly with a smile.

"Yea, master!" he cried. "We saw such!"

"Where, where? For God's sake, where was it?" ejaculated Stern, gripping him by the arm with a hand that shook with sudden keen emotion.

"Where was it, master? Thus one day's marching."

Rigvin wheeled and pointed to northwestward.

"And ye can find it again?"

"Truly, yes. Why, master?"

"There, near that mountain, lies the wreck of the *vlyn b'hotu*, the flying boat, Rigvin! Lead us thither! We must find it. And then Settlement Cliffs!"

Through all his exhaustion and his pain he knew that now the goal was close at hand. And beyond toil, suffering and hardship once more beckoned prosperity and peace and love.

CHAPTER XXXIII

FIVE YEARS LATER

LONG before daybreak that morning, the thriving village of Settlement Cliffs, capital and market-town of the New Hope Colony, was awake and astir.

For the great festival day was at hand, the fifth anniversary of the founding of the colony, to be celebrated by the arrival of the last Merucaans from the depths of the Abyss.

The old caves, now abandoned save for grain, fruit and fish storehouses were closed and silent. No labor was going forward there. The nets hung dry. From the forges, smithies and work-shops along the river-bank at the rapids arose no sounds of the accustomed industry.

The road and bridge-builders were idle; and from the farms now dotting the rich *brûlé* across the river—each snug stone house, tiled with red or green, standing among its crops and growing orchards—the Folk were coming in to town for the feast-day.

The broad wooden trestle-bridge across the New Hope echoed with hollow verberations beneath the measured tread of two and four-ox teams hauling creaking wains heaped high with meats, fruits, casks of cider, generous wines, and all the richness of that virgin soil.

On the summer morning air rose laughter from the youths and maidens coming in afoot. Sounded the cries of the teamsters, the barking of dogs, the mingled murmur of speech—English speech again; and the fresh wind, bearing away a fine, golden dust from the long roads, swayed the palm-tops and the fern-trees with a gentle and caressing touch.

All up and down the broad, well-paved street of the village—a street lined with stone cottages, bordered with luxuriant tropic gardens, and branching into a dozen smaller thoroughfares—a happy throng was idling.

Well clad in plain yet substantial weaves from the vine-festooned workshops below the cliff, abundantly fed, vigorous and strong, not one showed sickness or deformity, such as had scourged the human race in the old, evil days of long ago.

Loose-belted garb, sandals and a complete absence of hats all had their part in this abounding health. Open-air life and rational food completed the work.

No drugs, save three or four essential ones, and no poisons, ever had crept in to menace life. Wine there was, rich and unfermented; but the curse of alcohol existed not. And in the Law it was forever banned.

On the broad porch of their home, a boulder-built cottage facing the broad plaza where palms shaded the graveled paths, and purple, yellow and scarlet blooms lured humming-birds and butterflies, stood Beatrice and Allan.

Both were smiling in the clear June sunlight of that early morning. A cradle rocked by Gesafam—a little older and more bent, yet still hardy—gave glimpses of another olive-branch, this one a girl.

The piazza was littered at its farthest end with serviceable, home-made playthings; but Allan, Junior, had no use for them to-day. Out there on the lawn of the plaza he was rolling and running with a troop of other children—many, many children, indeed.

As Beatrice and Allan watched the play they smiled; and through the man's arm crept the woman's hand, and with the confidence of perfect trust she leaned her head against his shoulder.

"Whoever could have thought," said he at last, "that all this really could come true? In those dark hours when the Horde had all but swallowed us, when we fell into the Abyss, when those terrible adventures racked our souls down beside the Sunken Sea, and later, here, when everything seemed lost—who could have foreseen *this?*"

"You could and did!" she answered. "From the beginning you planned everything, Allan. It was all foreseen and nothing ever stopped you, just as the future beyond this time is all foreseen by you and must and shall be as you plan it!"

"Shall be, with your help!" he murmured, and silence came again. Together they watched the holiday crowd gradually congregating in the vast plaza where once the palisade had been. Now the old wooden stockade had long vanished. Cleared land and farms extended far beyond even Newport Heights, where the Pauillac had first come to earth at New Hope.

Well-kept roads connected them all with the settlement. And for some miles to southward the primeval forests had been vanquished by the ever-extending hand of this new, swiftly growing race.

"With my help and theirs!" she rejoined presently. "Never forget, dear, how wonderfully they've taken hold, how they've labored, developed and grown in every way. You'd be surprised—really you would—if you came in contact with them as I do in the schools, to see the marvelous way they learn—old and young alike. It's a miracle, that's all!"

"No, not exactly," he explained. "It's atavism. These people of ours were really civilized in essence, despite all the overlying ages of barbarism. Civilization was latent in them, that's all. Just as all the children born here under normal conditions have reverted to pigmented skin and hair and eyes, so even the grown-ups have thrown back to civilization. Two or three years at the outside have put back the coloring matter in every newcomer's iris and epidermis. Just so—"

A sudden and quickly-growing tumult in the plaza and down the long, broad street interrupted him. He saw a waving of hands, a general craning of necks, a drift toward the north side of the square, the river side.

The shouts and cheers increased and cries of *"They come! They come!"* rose on the morning air.

"Already?" exclaimed Allan in surprise. "These new machines certainly do surprise me with their speed and power. In the old days the Pauillac wouldn't have been here before noon from the Abyss!"

Together, Beatrice and he walked round the wide piazza to the rear of the bungalow. The home estate sloped gently down toward the cement and boulder wall edging the cliff. In its broad garden stood the stable, where half a dozen horses—caught on the northern savannas and carefully tamed—disputed their master's favor with the touring car he had built up from half a dozen partly ruined machines in Atlanta and other cities.

Up the cliff still roared the thunder of the rapids, to-day untamed by the many turbines and power-plants along the shore. But louder than the river rose the tumult of the rejoicing throng: "They come! They come!"

"Where?" questioned Beta. "See them, boy?"

"There! Look! How swift! My trained men can outfly *me* now—more luck to them!"

He pointed far to northwestward, over the wide and rolling sea of green, farm-dotted, that had sprung up with marvelous fecundity in the wake of the great fire.

Looking now out over the very same country where, five years and a month before, she had strained her tear-blinded eyes for some sign of Allan's return, Beatrice suddenly beheld three high, swift little specks skimming up the heavens with incredible velocity.

"Hurrah!" shouted Allan boyishly. "Here they come—the last of my Folk!"

He ran to the corner of the piazza and on the tall staff that dominated the cañon and the river-valley dipped the stars and stripes three times in signal of welcome.

And already, ere the salute was done, the rushing planes had slipped full half the distance from the place where they had first been sighted.

A messenger ran down the gravel driveway and saluted.

"O Kromno!" he began. "Master—"

"Master no longer!" Allan interrupted. "Brother now, only!"

The lad stared, amazed.

"Well, what is it?" smiled Allan.

"The Council of the Elders prays you to come to help greet the last-comers. And after that the feast!"

"I come!" he answered. The lad bowed and vanished.

"They aren't going to let me out of it, after all," he sighed. "I'd so much rather let them run their own festival to-day. But no—they've got to ring me in, as usual! You'll come, too, of course?"

She nodded, and a moment later they were walking over the fine lawn toward the plaza.

On the far side, in a wide, open stretch that served the children sometimes as a playground, stood the great hangars of the community's air-fleet. Beyond them rose workshops, their machinery driven by electric power from the turbines at the rapids.

Even as Allan and Beatrice passed through the cheering crowd, now drifting toward the hangars, a sound of music wafted down-wind—a little harsh at times, but still with promise of far better things to be.

Many flags fluttered in the air, and even the rollicking children on the lawns paused to wonder as swift shadows cut across the park.

On high was heard the droning hum of the propellers. It ceased, and in wide, sure, evenly balanced spirals the great planes one by one slid down and took the earth as easily as a gull sinks to rest upon the bosom of a quiet sea.

"They *do* work well, my equilibrators!" murmured Allan, unable to suppress a thrill of pride. "Simple, too; but, after all, how wonderfully effective!"

The crowd parted to let him through with Beatrice. Two minutes later he was clasping the hands of the last Folk ever to be brought from the strange, buried village under the cliff beside the Sunless Sea.

He summoned Zangamon and Frumuos, together with Sivad and the three aviators.

"Well done!" said he; and that was all—all, yet enough. Then, while the people cheered again and, crowding round, greeted their kinsfolk, he gave orders for the housing and the care of the travel-wearied newcomers.

Through the summer air drifted slow smoke. Off on the edge of the grove that flanked the plaza to southward the crackling of new-built fires was heard.

Allan turned to Beta with a smile.

"Getting ready for the barbecue already!" said he, "With that and the games and all, they ought to have enough to keep them busy for one day. Don't you think they'll have to let us go a while? There are still a few finishing touches to put to the new laws I'm going to hand the Council this afternoon for the Folk to hear. Yes, by all means, they'll have to let us go."

Together they walked back to their bungalow amid its gardens of palm-growths, ferns and flowers. Here they stopped a moment to chat with some good friend, there to watch the children and—parentlike—make sure young Allan was safe and only normally dirty and grass-stained.

They gained their broad piazza at length, turned, and for a while watched the busy, happy scene in the shaded street, the plaza and the playground.

Then Beta sat down by the cradle—still in that same low chair Allan had built for her five years ago, a chair she had steadily refused to barter for a finer one.

He drew up another beside her. From his pocket he drew a paper—the new laws—and for a minute studied it with bent brows.

The soft wind stirred the woman's hair as she sat there half dreaming, her blue-gray eyes, a little moist, seeing far more than just what lay before them. On his head a shaft of sunlight fell, and had you looked you might have seen the crisp, black hair none too sparingly lined with gray.

But his gaze was strong and level and his smile the same as in bygone years, as with his left hand he pressed hers and, with a look eloquent of many things, said:

"Now, sweetheart, if you're quite ready—?"

CHAPTER XXXIV

History and Roses

Allan sat writing in his library. Ten years had now slipped past since the last of the Folk had been brought to the surface and the ancient settlement in the bowels of the earth forever abandoned. Heavily sprinkled with gray, the man's hair showed the stress of time and labors incredible.

Lines marked his face with the record of their character-building, even as his rapid pen traced on white paper the all but completing history of the new world whereat he had been laboring so long.

Through the open window, where the midsummer breeze swayed the silken curtains, drifted a hum from the long file of bee-hives in the garden. Farther away sounded the comfortable gossip of hens as they breasted their soft feathers into the dust-baths behind the stables. A dog barked.

Came voices from without. Along the street growled a motor. Laughter of children echoed from the playground. Allan ceased writing a moment, with a smile, and gazed about him as though waking from a dream.

"Can this be true?" he murmured. "After having worked over the records of the earlier time *they* still seem the reality and this the dream!"

On the garden-path sounded footfalls. Then the voice of Beatrice calling:

"Come out, boy! See my new roses—just opened this morning!"

He got up and went to the window. She—matronly now and of ampler bosom, yet still very beautiful to look upon—was standing there by the rose-tree, scissors in hand.

Allan, Junior, now a rugged, hardy-looking chap of nearly sixteen—tall, well built and with his father's peculiar alertness of bearing—was bending down a high branch for his mother.

Beyond, on the lawn, the ten-year-old daughter, Frances, had young Harold in charge, swinging him high in a stout hammock under the apple-trees.

"Can't you come out a minute, dear?" asked Beatrice imploringly. "Let your work go for once! Surely these new roses are worth more than a hundred pages of dry statistics that nobody'll ever read, anyhow!"

He laughed merrily, threw her a kiss, and answered:

"Still a girl, I see! Ah, well, don't tempt me, Beta. It's hard enough to work on such a day, anyhow, without your trying to entice me out!"

"*Won't* you come, Allan?"

"Just give me half an hour more and I'll call it off for to-day!"

"All right; but make it a short half-hour, boy!"

He returned to his desk. The library, like the whole house now, was fully and beautifully furnished. The spoils of twenty cities had contributed to the adornment of "The Nest," as they had christened their home.

In time Allan planned even to bring art-works from Europe to grace it still further. As yet he had not attempted to cross the Atlantic, but in his seaport near the ruins of Mobile a powerful one hundred and fifty-foot motor-yacht was building.

In less than six months he counted on making the first voyage of discovery to the Old World.

Contentedly he glanced around the familiar room. Upon the mantel over the capacious fireplace stood rare and beautiful bronzes. Priceless rugs adorned the polished floor.

The broad windows admitted floods of sunlight that fell across the great jars of flowers Beta always kept there for him and lighted up the heavy tiers of books in their mahogany cases. Books everywhere—under the window-seats, up the walls, even lining a deep alcove in the far corner. Books, hundreds upon hundreds, precious and cherished above all else.

"Who ever would have thought, after all," murmured he, "that we'd find books intact as we did? A miracle—nothing less! With our printing-plant already at work under the cliff, all the art, science and literature of the ages—all that's worth preserving—can be still kept for mankind. But if I hadn't happened to find a library of books in a New York bonded warehouse all cased up for transportation, the work of preservation would have been forever impossible!"

He turned back to his history, and before writing again idly thumbed over a few pages of his voluminous manuscript. He read:

"March 1, A. D. 2930. The astronomical observatory on Round Top Hill, one mile south of Newport Heights, was finished to-day and the last of the apparatus from Cambridge, Lick, and other ruins was installed. I find my data for reckoning time are unreliable, and have therefore assumed this date arbitrarily and readjusted the calendar accordingly.

"Our *Daily Messenger,* circulating through the entire community and educating the people both in English and in scientific thought, will soon popularize the new date.

"Just as I have substituted the metric system for the old-time chaotic hodge-podge we once used, so I shall substitute English for Merucaan definitely inside of a few years. Already the younger generation hardly understands the native Merucaan speech. It will eventually become a dead, historically interesting language, like all other former tongues. The catastrophe has rendered possible, as nothing else could have done, the realization of universal speech, labor-unit exchange values in place of money, and a political and economic democracy unhampered by ideas of selfish, personal gain."

He turned a few pages, his face glowing with enthusiasm.

"April 15—The first ten-yearly census was completed to-day. Even with the aid of Frumuos and Zangamon, I have been at work on this nearly two months, for now our outlying farms, villages and settlements have pushed away fifteen or twenty miles from the orignal focus at the Cliffs, or 'Cliffton,' as the capital is becoming generally known.

"Population, 5,072, indicating a high birth-rate and an exceptionally low mortality. Our one greatest need is large families. With the whole world to reconquer, we must have men.

"Area now under cultivation, under grazing and under forests being actively exploited, 42,076 acres. Domestic animals, 26,011. Horses are already being replaced by motors, save for pleasure-riding. Power-plants and manufacturing establishments, 32. Aerial fleet, 17 of the large biplanes, 8 of the swifter monoplanes for scout work. One shipyard at Mobile.

"Total roads, macadamized and other, 832 miles. Air-motors and sun-motors in use or under construction, 41; mines being worked, 13; schools, 27, including the technical school at Intervale, under my personal instruction. Military force, zero—praise be! Likewise jails, saloons, penitentiaries, gallows, hospitals, vagrants, prostitutes, politicians, diseases, beggars, charities—all zero, now and forever!"

Allan turned to the unfinished end of the manuscript, poised his pen a moment, and then began writing once more where he had left off when called by Beatrice:

"The great monument in memory of the patriarch, first of all our people to perish in the upper world, was finished on June 18. Memorial exercises will be held next month.

"On June 22 the new satellite, which passes darkly among the stars every forty-eight hours, was named *Discus*. Its distance is 3,246 miles; dimensions, 720 miles by 432; weight, six and three-quarter billion tons.

"On July 2, I discovered unmistakable traces either of habitations or of their ruins on the new and till now unobserved face of the moon, hidden in the old days. This problem still remains for further investigation.

"July 4, our national holiday, a *viva-voce* election and Council of the Elders was held. They still insist on choosing me as Kromno. I weary of the task, and would gladly give it over to some younger man.

"At this Council, held on the great meeting-ground beyond the hangars, I again and for the third time submitted the question of trying to colonize from the races still in the Abyss. If feasible, this would rapidly add to our population. The Folk are now civilized to a point where they could rapidly assimilate outside stock.

"In addition to the Lanskaarn, a strong and active race known to exist on the Central Island in the Sunken Sea, there remain persistent traditions of a strange, yellow-haired race somewhere on the western coasts of that sea, beyond the Great Vortex. Two parties exist among us.

"The minority is anxious for exploration and conquest. The majority votes for peace and quiet growth. It may well be that the Lanskaarn and the other people never will be rescued. I, for one, cannot attempt it. I grow a little weary. But if the younger generation so decides, that must be their problem and their labor, like the rebuilding of the great cities and the reconquest of the entire continent from sea to sea.

"In the mean time—"

At the window appeared Beatrice. Smiling, she flung a yellow rose. It landed on Allan's desk, spilling its petals all across his manuscript.

He looked up, startled. His frown became a smile.

"My time's up?" he queried. "Why, I didn't know I'd been working five minutes!"

"Up? Long ago! Now. Allan, you just simply *must* leave that history and come out and see my roses, or—or—"

"No threats!" he implored with mock earnestness. "I'm coming, dearest. Just give me time—"

"Not another minute, do you hear?"

"—to put my work away, and I'm with you!"

He carefully arranged the pages of his manuscript in order, while she stood waiting at the window, daring not leave lest he plunge back again into his absorbing toil.

Into his desk-drawer he slid the precious record of the community's labor, growth, achievement, triumph. Then, with a boyish twinkle in his eyes, he left the library.

She turned, expecting him to meet her by the broad piazza; but all at once he stole quietly round the other corner of the bungalow, his footsteps noiseless in the thick grass.

Suddenly he seized her, unsuspecting, in his arms.

"My prisoner!" he laughed. "Roses? Here's the most beautiful one in our whole garden!"

"Where?" she asked, not understanding.

"This red one, here!"

And full upon the mouth he kissed her in the leaf-shaded sunshine of that wondrous summer day.

CHAPTER XXXV

THE AFTERGLOW

EVENING!

Far in the west, beyond the cañon of the New Hope River—now a beautifully terraced park and pleasure-ground—the rolling hills, fertile and farm-covered, lay resting as the sun died in a glory of crimson, gold and green.

The reflections of the passing day spread a purple haze through the palm and fern-tree aisles of the woodland. Only a slight breeze swayed the branches. Infinite in its serenity brooded a vast peace from the glowing sky.

A few questing swallows shot here and there like arrows, blackly outlined with swift and crooked wing against the vermilion of the west.

Over the countryside, the distant farms and hills, a thin and rosy vapor hovered, fading slowly as the sun sank lower still.

Scarcely moved by the summer breeze, a few slow clouds drifted away— away to westward—gently and calmly as the first promises of night stole up the world.

An arbor, bowered with wistarias and the waxen spikes of the new *fleur de vie,* stood near the woodbine-covered wall edging the cliff. Among its leaves the soft air rustled very lovingly. A scent of many blossoms hung over the perfumed evening.

Upon the lawn one last, belated robin still lingered. Its mate called from a sycamore beyond the hedge, and with an answering note it rose and winged away; it vanished from the sight.

Allan and Beatrice, watching it from the arbor, smiled; and through the smile it seemed there might be still a trace of deeper thought.

"How quickly it obeyed the call of love!" said Allan musingly. "When *that* comes what matters else?"

She nodded.

"Yes," she answered presently. "That call is still supreme. Our Frances—"

She paused, but her eyes sought the half-glimpsed outlines of another cottage there beyond the hedge.

"We never realized, did we?" said Allan, voicing her thought. "It came so suddenly. But we haven't lost her, after all. And there are still the others, too. And when grandchildren come—"

"That means a kind of youth all over again, doesn't it? Well—"

Her hand stole into his, and for a while they sat in silence, thinking the thoughts that "do sometime lie too deep for tears."

The flaming red in the west had faded now to orange and dull umber. Higher in the sky yellows and greens gave place to blue as deep as that in the Ægean grottos. The zenith, a dark purple, began to show a silver twinkle here and there of stars.

A whirring, roaring sound grew audible to eastward. It strengthened quickly. And all at once, far above the river, a long, swift train, its windows already lighted, sped with a smooth, rapid flight.

Allan watched the monorail vanish beyond the huge north tower of the cable bridge, sink through the trees, and finally fade into the gathering gloom.

"The Great Lakes Express," said he. "In the old days we thought seventy miles an hour something stupendous. Now two hundred is mere ordinary schedule-time. Yes—something has been accomplished even now. The greater time still to be—we can't hope to see it.

"But we can catch a glimpse of what it shall be, here and there. We must be content to have built foundations. On them those who shall come in the future shall raise a fairer and a mightier world than any we have ever dreamed."

Again he relapsed into silence; but his arm drew round Beatrice, and together they sat watching the age-old yet ever-new drama of the birth of night.

Half heard, mingled with the eternal turmoil of the rapids, rose the far purring of the giant dynamos in the power-houses below the cliff. Here, there, lights began to gleam in the city; and on the rolling farmlands to northward, too, little winking eyes of light opened one by one, each one a home.

Suddenly the man spoke again.

"More than a hundred thousand of us already!" he exulted. "Over a tenth of a million—and every year the growth is faster, ever faster, in swift progressions. A hundred thousand English-speaking people, Beta; a civilization already, even in a material sense, superior to the old one that was swept away; in a spiritual, moral sense, how vastly far ahead!

"A hundred thousand! Some time, before long, it will be a million; then two, five, twenty, a hundred, with no racial discords, no mutual antipathies, no barriers of name or blood; but for the first time a universal race, all sound and pure, starting right, living right, striving toward a goal which even we cannot foresee!

"Not only shall this land be filled, but Europe, Asia, Africa and all the islands of the Seven Seas shall know the hand of man again, and own his sovereignty, from pole to pole!"

His clasp about Beatrice tightened; she felt his heart beat strong with deep emotion as he spoke again:

"Already the cities are beginning to arise from their ashes of a thousand oblivious years. Already a score of thriving colonies have scattered from the capital, all yet bound to it with monorail cables, with electric wires and with the ether-borne magic of the wireless.

"Already our boy, our son—can you imagine him really a man of thirty, darling?—elected President on our last Council Day, guides a free people—a people self-reliant and strong, energetic, capable, dominant.

"Already the inconceivable fertility of the earth is yielding its bounties a hundred fold; and trade-routes circle the ends of the great Abyss; and all the vast territory once the United States has begun to open again before the magic touch of man!

"Of man—now free at last! No more slavery! No more the lash of hunger driving men to their tasks. No more greed and grasping; no lust of gold, no bitter cry of crushed and hopeless serfdom! No buying and selling for the lure of profit; no speculating in the people's means of life; no squeezing of their blood for wealth! But free, strong labor, gladly done. The making of useful and beautiful things, Beatrice, and their exchange for human need and service—this, and the old dream of joy in righteous toil, this is the blessing of our world to-day!"

He paused. A little, swift-moving light upon the far horizon drew his eye. It seemed a star, traveling among its sister stars that now already had begun to twinkle palely in the darkening sky. But Allan knew its meaning.

"Look!" cried he and pointed. "Look, Beatrice! The West Coast Mail— the plane from southern California. The wireless told us it had started only three hours ago—and here it is already!"

"And but for you," she murmured, "none of all this could ever possibly have been. Oh, Allan, remember that song—our song? In the days of our first love, there on the Hudson, remember how I sang to you:

> "*Stark wie der Fels,*
> *Tief wie das Meer,*
> *Muss deine Liebe,*
> *Muss deine Liebe sein?*"

"I remember! And it has been so?"

Her answer was to draw his hand up to her lips and print a kiss there, and as she laid her cheek upon it he felt it wet with tears.

And night came; and now the wind lay dead; and upon the brooding earth, spangled with home-lights over hill and vale, the stars gazed calmly down.

The steady, powerful droning of the power-plant rose, blent with the soothing murmur of the rapids and the river.

"Seems like a lullaby—doesn't it, dearest?" murmured Allan. "You know—it won't be long now before it's good-by and—good night."

"I know," she answered. "We've *lived,* haven't we? Oh, Allan, no one ever lived, ever in all this world—lived as much as you and I have lived! Think of it all from the beginning till now. No one ever so much, so richly, so happily, so well!"

"No one, darling!"

"But, after toil, rest—rest is sweet, too. I shall be ready for it when it summons me. I shall go to it, content and brave and smiling. Only—"

"Yes?"

"Only this I pray, just this and nothing more—that I mayn't have to stay awake, alone, after—after *you're* sleeping, Allan!"

A long time they sat together, silent, in the sweet-scented gloom within the flower-girt arbor.

At last he spoke.

"The wonder and the glory of it all!" he whispered. "Oh, the wonder of a dream, a vision come to pass, before our eyes!

"For, see! Has not the prophecy come true? What was then only a yearning and a hope, is it not now reality? Is it not now all even as we dreamed so very, very long ago, there in our little bungalow beside the broad, slow-moving Hudson?

"Is *this* not true?"

I see a world where thrones have crumbled and where kings are dust. The aristocracy of idleness has perished from the earth.

I see a world without a slave. Man at last is free. Nature's forces have by science been enslaved. Lightning and light, wind and wave, frost and flame, and all the secret, subtle powers of earth and air are the tireless toilers for the human race.

I see a world at peace, adorned with every form of art, with music's myriad voices thrilled, while lips are rich with words of love and truth—a world in which no exile sighs, no prisoner mourns; a world on which the gibbet's shadow does not fall; a world where labor reaps its full reward—where work and worth go hand in hand!

I see a world without the beggar's outstretched palm, the miser's heartless, stony stare, the piteous wail of want, the livid lips of lies, the cruel eyes of scorn.

I see a race without disease of flesh or brain, shapely and fair, the married harmony of form and function; and, as I look, life lengthens, joy deepens, love canopies the earth—and over all, in the great dome, shines the eternal star of human hope!

THE END